Mara, Marietta

A Love Story in 77 Bedrooms

Richard Jonathan

RICHARD JONATHAN

ISBN: 9782955975114

Note to the Reader

Mara, Marietta: A Love Story in 77 Bedrooms is not a work of 'erotica'. Nor is it 'romance'. Rather, it is a novel that, in dealing with love and sex, refuses the standard modes of the lyrical and the cynical, the coy and the vulgar, and opts instead to invent its own forms. Why? Because the protagonists, in their distinctiveness, required the author to restore to love the singularity of an erotic relation between subjectivities, while their lovemaking demanded that sexuality be transfigured through the imagination.

Will the reader share the author's view that it is a profoundly joyful book? He can only hope so. But, dear reader, do be aware of the following:

> *To read well is to take great risks. It is to make vulnerable our identity, our self-possession ... He who has read Kafka's* Metamorphosis *and can look into his mirror unflinching may technically be able to read print, but is illiterate in the only sense that matters.*

George Steiner, *Language and Silence: Essays on Language, Literature and the Inhuman* (NY: Atheneum, 1982): 10-11

> *The opposite of stupidity is not intelligence, but humility.*
>
> Gilles Deleuze

Mara, Marietta: A Love Story in 77 Bedrooms is written for the humble, not for those who (to put a twist on Steiner) can make love then look into their mirror unflinching.

R.J.

maramarietta.com

A website – The World of Mara Marietta – provides a wealth of resources to complement your reading of the novel. You will find, for example, images of paintings, playlists of music, carousels of film stills, as well as essays and translations. The site is regularly enriched.

A 'References and Bibliography' document in pdf can also be found on the World of Mara Marietta.

Oronce Fine, *Mappemonde en forme de cœur,* 1534-36
BnF, Paris

maramarietta.com/mara-marietta-culture-blog/

The Mara Marietta Culture Blog offers a series of reflections on the arts in contemporary culture, with occasional forays into other domains. To seek the calm in the eye of the hurricane, to oppose the silence of music to the whirlwind of noise, that is its aim.

To F.

I am I and the attributes are no more; I am I and the qualifications are no more. I am the pure subject of the verb.

Al-Hallaj (c. 858 - 922)

By a name I know not how to tell thee who I am.

Romeo and Juliet, II ii

PROLOGUE

— I love this owl, Jag!

Standing squat on a dark wood table, the Dhokra sculpture displays its stylized details. Big round eyes and hooked beak fascinate the boy; something from the other world inhabits the bird: He feels its strange attraction. Jagrati brings her hand to its head and lifts it off the body: On three-toed feet stands a bowl of coins, gleaming in the half-light.

— They're old rupees. This one's my favourite!

She shows the boy a reddish-brown coin featuring a gambolling horse.

— It's beautiful, the boy says. The horse is alive, frolicking. And look at this one!

He examines a silver rosette showing a water buffalo.

— I've never seen wavy edges like this before.

— And have you ever seen square ones? Look.

Three lions stand at the foot of a pillar on a square of tarnished silver.

— Wow!

Jagrati puts the head of the owl back onto the body. Vaguely the boy registers her grace, the fineness of her fingers.

— And what's this pyramid? he asks.

— Measuring bowls, for rice.

She takes the top one off, then lays the bowls out in a line, from the smallest to the biggest. Rhythmic bands of ornamental motifs, gold accents on the metallic patina, ring the earthenware vessels.

— We don't use them, of course. They're just for decoration.

— They look ancient!

She stacks the bowls back into a pyramid. This time, the girl's grace stirs the boy more deeply: From the silence where his thoughts dwell her movements draw a wisp of music.

— And these horses!

— They're from Bengal. They're called Bankura horses.

Of compact body and vertical neck, they stand tall and erect. The boy falls under their spell, as if there were something totemic about them.

— I wish I had a family like yours, Jag.

— Why?

— You know where you come from. You belong somewhere.

— Don't you?

— No.

– Strange. Come, let's go up to my room!

Jagrati leads the boy through a glass-bead curtain into a room with potted plants, a scalloped-top birdcage and a rocking chair.

– *Namaste! Namaste!*

– You've got a mynah bird?

Displaying its glossy plumage, the bird flies from perch to perch.

– Ever since I can remember.

– What did he say?

– *'Namaste'.*

Pressing her hands together in a gesture of prayer, Jagrati bows.

– *Mujhe tumse pyar hai! Mujhe tumse pyar hai!*

– What's that mean?

– 'I love you! I love you!'

After an instant of silence, their gazes interlocked, they break into laughter.

– *Khaamosh raho! Khaamosh raho!*

– Now what's he saying?

– 'Shut up! Shut up!'

– What cheek!

– I taught him that. Come!

She takes him by the hand and leads him up the stairs.

***

– Wow! Jag, this is another world!

In a big attic room, sunlight filters through small windows. Tangerine and magenta, crimson and mauve, fire the boy's imagination. Look! On a buff-coloured rug stands a low box-table, a gleaming treasure chest. He falls to his knees before it; Jagrati joins him there.

– This is where I do my homework.

– And you sit on the floor like that?

– Yes. Or I read on my bed.

On the sides of the box, bronze-plate scimitars adorn the dark wood. At each corner, round legs, striped maroon and black and capped in yellow, rise like pillars above the table surface.

– It's beautiful! It looks like something from a pirate ship.

– In fact, it's from the Punjab. When my great-grandmother died, we had all her furniture shipped over here.

– You knew your great-grandmother?

— Yes, she came here once. She had a ring in her nose and a blind eye. She taught me some beautiful songs.

The boy imagines what she looked like; somehow he can even conjure her voice. Then his eye catches something in a corner and he starts laughing.

— That's a laughing Buddha. He makes me laugh too.

Jagrati springs to her feet.

— Come, Sprague, get up!

She takes him by the hand and pulls; he resists, and pulls her down to him. Letting her body rest on his a moment, she laughs, then rolls onto the rug. Lying beside her, the boy closes his eyes and savours her smell, the smell that always makes him dream and travel: that subtle, Indian smell. He turns to look at her: under her rumpled-up frock, the glimmer of her panties, the gleam of her thighs.

— Watch!

Drawing up her legs, Jagrati throws her arms behind her head, presses down into a handstand and flips over onto her feet.

— Wow!

She runs toward the bed and dives onto it; the boy springs to his feet. Pausing, he watches the quilt's vibrant mauve succumb to her frock's calm green. She rolls onto her back and sits up. Stepping toward her, the boy kicks into a shoe.

— Sprague, careful! Those are my bridesmaid shoes.

— But the wedding was last week.

— Yes, but still.

He sits down beside her.

— Sorry.

— Do you know where they went for their honeymoon?

— To Paris, I think.

— No, to Venice. And what do you think they're doing now?

— Oh, maybe riding in a gondola.

— Could be. But what's the whole point of their honeymoon?

An image flashes in the boy's mind, a sensation buried deep in time: Fire burns bright in a copper geyser; steaming water fills the tub. Victoria sits on the edge of the bath and draws the boy to her body. Hot flush of moist flesh! Vividly he feels the ardour of the Xhosa girl; irrevocably he crosses into a new world.

— I know, but I won't say.

— Do you *really* know?

— Yes.

As that world calls to him, the boy casts a desperate gaze around the room.

— Marbles!

He runs over to a round column—a chest of drawers—and sees its iron handles transform into lions' mouths upon his approach. Jagrati slides off the bed and follows him.

— Can I, Jag?

— Of course.

He opens the jar of marbles standing on the polished wooden column.

— Hey, a bumblebee shooter! And an onionskin onyx! You've got some amazing alleys here. What's this one?

She leans in toward his body; he feels the heat of her touch.

— That's a devil's eye.

She dips her fingers into the jar, takes out a handful of the glass and alabaster balls and scatters them on the floor.

— Watch!

With her toes, alternating left foot and right, she picks them up one by one then puts them down again, like with like.

— That's to make my arches stronger.

— Jag, your feet are beautiful!

He blushes, embarrassed that the words have escaped his mouth: He didn't mean to say them out loud.

— They're just feet. But they've got to be strong and supple!

— Why?

— Bharatanatyam! Watch!

She kicks her shoe out of the way, then dances Indian style, miming and gesturing, before a final jump and bow before the boy.

— More, Jag, some more!

— Sit down on the bed.

Sitting on the bed watching her, he feels the contrast between her calm grace and his jerky energy. He'd love to join her but he knows it would be ridiculous: Indian dances tell a story, you have to know your part. Making a final leap, Jagrati flops onto the bed and pulls the boy down to her. She brings her mouth to his and runs her tongue along his lips; he feels his heart flutter.

— Now help me gather up the marbles!

Before he can pick up three, she's gathered all the rest.

— Bring them.

They drop the marbles into the jar; she puts the lid back on. Picking up the lavender pillbox beside the jar, the boy asks:

— What's in this?

— Open it.

His fingertips linger on the smooth cool of the garnet stones decorating the box. He lifts up the lid.

— A banded pebble!

Swirls of crystals and glassy minerals compose a striking pattern.

— That used to be my hopscotch stone, till I realized how beautiful it was.

The boy examines it closely.

— These colours are very rare.

— I found it on a 'Europeans Only' beach.

— You dared?

— I dared. And I won one rand from Rajan!

— Rajan?

— A cousin.

The boy is filled with admiration for her, but he can't bring himself to say anything: He remembers being hounded off a 'Net vir Blankes' beach, and again feels himself decentred, out of place, incomplete. He turns his head to hide his shame.

— That's Ganesha, Jagrati says, the Lord of Beginnings and Remover of Obstacles!

The boy studies the multi-armed god with the elephant head, depicted in gold and green on the side panel of a bookcase. I'd like a new beginning, he thinks, I'd like a helping hand. Still, he can't imagine himself praying to such a creature. He steps to the bookcase and takes from a shelf the first volume of poetry he sees: Rabindranath Tagore, 'Selected Poems'. On the cover, in the centre, intense eyes stare at something outside the photo frame—or are they staring inward? Despite the beard, the finesse of the man's fine-boned features is striking. To his left, an English boy with a wide-eyed gaze; to his right, an elegant Indian man. This will be my book of prayer, the boy says to himself.

— That's Tagore, Jagrati says, pointing to the bearded man. He's a saint in Bengal.

The boy can't take his eyes off the poet; everything about him combines to convey a mesmerizing power: The gentleness in his long hands, resting on his lap; the robe that falls wide-sleeved from his shoulders, reinforcing the impression of quiet pride and dignity; the concentrated calm in his eyes. Jagrati is intrigued by her friend's fascination; she remains quiet, close by his side. That man beside Tagore could be my father, the boy thinks. He feels a bittersweet pleasure as he realizes the English boy in the picture looks perfectly at home. Gently from his thoughts Jagrati brings him back to her: The touch of her lips on his cheek, warm and petal-soft, blurs his vision as tears well up. She takes the book from his hands.

— Let me read you something.

She flips through the pages, then stops to read:

Whenever I spend painful, sleepless nights,
I always look forward
To your first tap-tap at my door.
The brave, nimble, simple
Life's message that you bring—
Give it to me,
That the sunlight by which all creatures dwell
May call me,
Oh my daybreak sparrow!

— It's better in Bengali, but you do get a sense of it, don't you?

Oh Jag, when you read it, how could I not? the boy thinks. But he simply says:

— Yes.

She slips the book back into its place on the shelf. The boy runs his thumb across the spines of other books.

— You've read *Dracula?*

— Yes.

— It's not frightening?

— It is, that's why I like it! But it's all in your head. There's not that much that happens.

— And *Frankenstein* too?

— Yes.

The boy feels ashamed of his cowardice; he's heard about these books, but could never gather his courage to read them. What is it I'm afraid of? he wonders. Vaguely he is aware that it has something to do with losing a sense of reality.

— Fifteen men on the dead man's chest?

— Yo-ho-ho, and a bottle of rum!—That I've read!

— Drink and the devil had done for the rest!

— Yo-ho-ho, and a bottle of rum!

His teary eyes brighten with laughter.

— Lift me up, Sprague! I want to get that cord.

The boy bends his knees, wraps his arms around Jagrati's hips and hoists her up. Little bells rattle as she pulls at the braided cord hanging over the edge of the bookcase; as she gathers it up, he makes out the colourful figures of elephants, trunks in the air, strung between the tiny golden bells.

— Steady, Sprague, it's stuck!

Easing his feet further apart, the boy feels a rush of power through his body: Now I can move the world!

— Got it!

He lowers her down and examines the cord she holds before him: A filament of gold spirals around braided strands of black; from beaded strings hang the elephants and bells. Hot pink and brilliant blue, emerald green and deep orange, the elephants glitter in their ceremonial garb. Jagrati twirls the cord between her outstretched arms, sending the bells ringing.

— Fifteen men on the dead man's chest!

The touch of his bare feet on the floorboards suddenly intensifies the feeling her body has produced in him.

— Yo-ho-ho, and a bottle of rum!

— Drink and the devil had done for the rest!

— Yo-ho-ho, and a bottle of rum!

To the jingle-jangle of the twirling rope, Jagrati and the boy, singing the pirate song, cavort through the room. Around the box-table they dance light-footed; reversing direction, they prance around the patchwork pouffe. Look! Drawn to electric blue, they head for the stability ball in the diagonal corner. With deft foot Jagrati nudges the ball out of its place and sends it rolling to the wide-open wardrobe; skipping past the colourful clothes, they circle the old armchair, then gambol back to the bed.

— Phew!

Onto the bed they flop down together.

— Jagrati!

She runs to the door and opens it; the boy shuts his eyes to keep his happiness inside.

— Yes, Mom?

— That's enough noise for now. Matamah's about to have his nap.

— Okay, Mom, we'll be quiet.

— Keep your door open in case he calls. I'm going to Auntie Eesha.

Okay, Mom.

— And offer Sprague something to drink.

— I will, Mom. See you later.

— See you. And be good!

— Yes.

Jagrati runs back to the bed and dives onto it.

— Who's Matamah?

— My grandfather.

Time stops while they remain still, lying on their backs. His hand touches hers: She takes it and holds it.

— Do you want something to drink?

He squeezes her hand.

— Does that mean 'yes'?

The boy is suddenly overcome with the fear that if she goes she'll never come back. Releasing her hand, he rolls onto his side and looks into her eyes. She smiles shyly.

— Jag...

— What?

Before he knows what he's done he's kissed her lips, or at least her teeth; he falls to his back again. She rolls over onto him. Under her weight he feels his body blossoming, opening like a flower; he presses her to him, and feels his power. The door creaks on its hinges. Making to get up, Jagrati says:

— Back in a minute!

The boy won't let her leave his embrace. She kisses his face—lips, cheeks, eyes; he lets her go. She leaves the room and goes downstairs. Lying on the bed, the boy is flooded with new sensations... Her parents speak of me as her cousin, my parents never spoke of any relation... I can't stand Toronto, I want to stay in Durban... Why am I still a child, why am I so slow?... Like the dust floating in the sunbeam that's captured his gaze, the boy's thoughts hover in the half-light of his mind.

Oh my daybreak sparrow! Jagrati, a glass of guava juice in each hand, enters the room. With her foot she swings the door closed; with her bum she presses it shut. The boy remembers her mother had said to leave it open: Jagrati's deliberately closing it sends a tingle up his spine.

— Here.

— Thank you.

— Matamah's fast asleep.

— Good.

The boy is impressed by the way she anticipates everything, and feels himself dull in comparison. And yet in his vulnerability he feels exhilarated; the scent of the juice arouses his senses before he even takes a sip. He swallows two or three mouthfuls of the milky-textured drink, savouring its sensuality, then puts his glass down on the night table. In a ray of sunlight its pink turns coral.

— What's this, Jag?

— That's my diary.

Bound in patterned cloth, closed tight with a loop of elastic, the diary feels heavy in the boy's hands.

— I'll show it to you if you show me yours.

— I don't keep a diary, Jag.

She puts her half-finished glass beside his. Taking a box from the night table, she says:

– Guess what's in here!

She puts the box on the bed between them. Grey velvet shimmers in the soft sunlight; on the lid, arrayed in concentric rings, sequins of silver and gold radiate from an amber stone.

– It looks like a jewellery box.

– Open it.

The boy opens the box. In velvet-lined compartments, tiny seashells, impeccably arranged, show off their shapes and colours.

– They're beautiful! Did you collect them yourself?

– Most of them.

– Isabella cowries, spiral sundials, spotted beauties... And what are these called?

– Serpent heads.

– Why?

– Because of the shape. Look.

She takes a shell from its lodging and turns it in her fingers.

– It's like a snake's skull, see. These are the jaws.

– And underneath?

She turns it upside down and suddenly becomes self-conscious at the sight of the ribbed slit. She reaches for a glass, and finishes the guava juice.

– You drank mine, Jag.

– I know.

Again the boy is amazed at how she is always one step ahead of him. He takes her glass and finishes it. The subtle flavour of the juice, at once sweet and acidic, emboldens him.

– Jag, show me how you do it.

– I will if you will.

– I will.

***

Her lips parted, her long hair loose, Jagrati rocks back and forth on the patchwork pouffe. As her thighs tighten their grip on the cushion between her legs, the lavender-rose curl of her toes presses into the rug. Her bare shoulders gleam in the late afternoon sunlight; around her hips her calico dress is gathered. Back and forth, back and forth, back and forth she sways, her unseeing eyes turned inward. Importunate, the creature in the boy's pants will have its way: He undoes the button of his shorts and zips open the fly. Jagrati takes the cushion from between her legs and stands up; running her hand over the sleek peacock print, she fixes the boy.

— Your turn.

On her face, an impish dare.

— Did you come?

— No. Your turn.

She sits back down on the pouffe.

— But what if your mother comes back?

— She won't be back for a while.

— You sure?

— Yes. Once Auntie Eesha starts talking there's no stopping her. Especially now with Anindita out of the house.

Standing at the edge of the bed, the boy drops his shorts and pulls down his pants. Jagrati gasps: Alert and self-willed, before her eyes stands a sleek animal. The boy falls to his back on the bed; composing himself, he begins to slip the primeval creature in and out of its skin. Jagrati stares fascinated. Keeping her eyes fixed on the object of her awe, she stands up, pulls down her panties, and lowers herself back onto the pouffe. The boy feels the blood flowing in his veins, he feels his being expanding. Gently, Jagrati approaches him and hoists herself onto the bed; drawing her knees up to her chin, she positions her back against the headboard. There is no end to her curiosity; the creature's ceaseless hide-and-seek with itself holds her spellbound. Silvering his nerves, the life force pulses through the boy's body; in the base of his spine, in the joints of his limbs, he feels the force intensifying. Extending a leg, Jagrati places her foot on the boy's thigh; at her touch his hand forms a fist and determines to free the animal's spirit. Into the wilderness he drives the creature, relentless in the pursuit of grace; further, further, until the horizon is effaced. As Jagrati digs her toes into the boy's flesh, he summons the down-pouring of darkness: Leaping into it, the animal lights it up. Hark! In the scintillating negation of his mind the boy registers the girl's gasp; he senses, spilling over his fingers, rolling down his thighs, the distillation of his desire.

— It's incredible, Sprague!

From resplendent blackness he emerges into a vibration of presence. On his hand, on his thighs, on Jagrati's lavender-rose nails and in the interstices of her toes, sperm glistens.

— What do we do now, Jag?

— Clean up the mess!

Jagrati grabs some Kleenexes—one, two, three, four—from her night table drawer. She wipes the pearly glow from the boy's thighs then, while he wipes himself, she begins to mop up the semen from her toes. She pauses, then brings the tissues to her nose.

— Hmmm, I like the smell!

— Really?

— Yes. I wonder what it tastes like?

— Jag!

— Why not? There won't be another Satyavati.

With the tip of her finger she takes a nacreous drop from her toe; with the tip of her tongue she licks it off and tastes it, rubbing it around her palate.

— It doesn't have much flavour, but the texture is heavenly!

The boy is moved, he feels his senses singed—by fire, by ice? He doesn't know, but the ambiguity is thrilling. From between her toes Jagrati plucks a strand of the sticky fluid; to the boy's mouth she moves the dangling festoon.

— No Jag, I don't want to!

— Try it.

— No!

She raises her hand, tilts back her head, and lets the strand of life drip into her mouth. The boy watches, enthralled.

— It might be better with some salt.

He laughs nervously.

— Or maybe some lemon juice!

Jag, you're incredible! Now his laughter is unrestrained. He realizes she's trying to lighten his heaviness, help him enjoy this moment. Once more, she is ahead of him. He decides to provoke her, but somehow he is only half-joking when he asks her:

— Jag, are you sure you won't get pregnant?

He takes on a hangdog look as she gives him a withering stare. The boy is aware of his foolishness, but sees it as a necessary cover: For what, he doesn't really know. Vaguely, he feels he is undeserving.

— You don't know the story of Satyavati?

— No.

— It's from the *Mahabharata*. It goes like this. A king hunting in a forest fell asleep. He dreamed of his wife, and there was a joyful explosion of sperm. When the king awoke and saw the sperm on a leaf, he called a falcon and said, 'Take my sperm quickly, to the queen!' But the falcon was attacked by another falcon; the sperm fell into a river. A fish swallowed it. A few months later, a fisherman caught the fish, cut it open, and found in its stomach a tiny little girl, who he called Satyavati.

— That's a lovely story!

— It is, and you're neither fish nor falcon—you're a silly goose!

The boy laughs, happy to be talked to in this way.

Casting her gaze at his cock, Jagrati says:

– Oh look, it's all limp, like a balloon after a party. You think I can make it grow again?

– What about your grandfather?

– Well, if he's not sleeping, he's probably doing it in his rocking chair.

– Doing what?

– Doing *it!* Just ask the mynah bird. He can imitate all his groans of ecstasy.

A broad smile lights up the boy's face; any worry about his worthiness vanishes. Jagrati gathers up the Kleenexes. Sniffing them, she raises her brow in mock rapture, then stuffs them into her night table drawer. Her pleasure in his sperm delights the boy.

– So, Jag, do you want to...?

– What?

– Make it grow again.

– No. It's one-nothing for you, I've got to get even. And I'll do it without even touching myself.

– But that's impossible!

– Watch!

Naked, her back arched over the stability ball, her head thrown behind it, Jagrati draws a silk scarf between her open thighs. Buoyant against the oak boards, the balls of her feet generate a relaxed rhythm. Sunlight brings a glow to her limbs while her sparrow breasts, stretched flat on her chest, fade into shadow. As the silk glides over her sex, a whole sub-continent of female grace is embodied in the hand that moves it. To the soft rustle the bands of colour shimmer; Jagrati sighs as she luxuriates in her sensations. The boy sits on the edge of the bed and watches the gold-edged colours—lime green and electric blue, scarlet and turquoise—slither in the hinge of her thighs. The girl's extravagant posture stirs something primitive in the boy; he feels a force impelling him to break out of himself. Sensing the alertness of his presence, she submits her sex to his gaze. Mesmerized, the boy takes in hand the flesh of his fascination, and spreads a pearl of transparency along its satin skin. Snaking the silk, Jagrati—aware of what the boy is doing, stimulated to outdo him—rotates her pelvis on the ball. Responsive, fluid, living, the rippling silk sends a tremor up her spine; she lurches, and in a halting groan squeezes her thighs closed: In that instant a spasm rocks the boy's body, a surge of sensation silvers his nerves. Floating on air, he is unaware that he has fallen backwards onto the bed.

Outside there is birdsong, or is the boy only imagining it? His cheeks caressed by cool leaves, he is somewhere up in the trees. Inside, dust particles dance, unattended, in the honeyed sunlight; on the floor, the scarf glimmers: In Jagrati's mind, as she lies limp on the stability ball, its colours linger.

– You've kept your lead, two to one. I've got to catch up!

Jagrati, a defiant glint in her eye, flops face-down onto the bed. Slipping her right hand between her legs, she rotates her rump in a slow, deliberate motion. Spellbound, the boy watches as her ass takes on a life of its own. With each spiral thrust, her pelvis bores into his isolation; with each coiling plunge, her presence fills his being. As her excitement mounts, Jagrati maintains her loop of slow motion. When it comes, her quivering cry thus surprises the boy; only when she rolls onto her side and folds her body into itself does he realize the intensity of her deliverance. But does he have any idea that it is not really herself, but he that she has delivered?

– I love you once, I love you twice, I love you more than curry and rice! Two-two. Your turn.

Feeling his body still restoring itself, the boy decides to play for time.

– Jag, who's your favourite Beatle?

– John. He's the craziest!

– I used to like Paul the best, but now it's George.

– I like *All Things Must Pass*. It's so dark and mysterious.

– And do you hate Yoko for breaking up the band?

– No. 'All things must pass.' And besides, John and Yoko are obviously in love.

– And what's your favourite song?

– Oh, impossible to say. Maybe 'Got to Get You into My Life'.

– Mine's 'Strawberry Fields Forever'.

– No one I think is in my tree...

– I mean it must be high or low...

– What a great song!

– It is.

Jagrati hops off the bed and picks up her dress. As she slips it on, the boy reaches for his underpants.

– You think your mother's about to come back?

– No, but keep your shorts at the ready, just in case.

– I'll put them on now.

– No Sprague, we can't stay at two-two! Come, lie down.

The boy falls back onto the bed. In a voice of mock surprise, Jagrati says:

— Oh look, it's all tired and sleepy, curled up like a cat on a burlap sack.

He starts as she takes it in her hand. In the place where the body tells no lies, tentative fingers try out truth's amplitude. It begins hardening in her hand.

— God, Sprague, it's amazing!

Watching it grow, she wraps her mind around it: 'How different from my buried treasure, how open to the eye'. Pulsating blood brings a twitch to the taut flesh; ungovernable, the extent of its aspiration is infinite. Jagrati cups the boy's scrotum, then runs her daring fingertips up his cock. As descending fingers unveil the glistening glans, awe and elation intermingle in her eyes: 'Compared to my body, his is excess'. Indeed, the object of her gaze evokes a violence of sensation she cannot assimilate: Too old to make light of it, too young to be resolute, she feels out of time. And then the pulsation of the living flesh gives her a cue; her dancer's hands find a rhythm, her fingers know what to do.

— Oh Sprague...

Withdrawing her touch, she restores to silence the song in the boy's soul.

— ...it's delicious!

— Yes! So why did you stop?

— It's your turn now. I've helped you all I can. We've got to break the tie!

A voice comes from downstairs.

— Quick, your mother's back!

The boy grabs his underpants and begins putting them on. Jagrati laughs and says:

— Listen again.

He listens intently.

— *Aapka kya naam hai? Aapka kya naam hai?*

— It's the mynah bird!

— Yes.

— What's he saying?

— 'What's your name? What's your name?'

— Sprague! And yours?

— Jagrati!

— I love you!

— Shut up!

They burst out laughing. Drawing the girl to him, the boy falls to his back on the bed: This time he kisses more than her teeth. The mynah continues talking.

— You'd better go down and see, Jag. Maybe your grandfather's up.

— He's not, Sprague. The mynah's just looking for company. They're very sociable, you know.

Lavishing kisses on his lips, she infuses his body with spirit: He feels his strength returning. The mynah launches into a monologue.

— I *will* take a look. You be ready when I get back!

— Okay.

She hops off the bed and leaves the room, closing the door behind her.

To what is childhood an antechamber? To the age of reason, they say. Did the boy ever suspect, lying there on the bed, that he would never become reasonable? Could he ever have imagined, as he vaguely fondled his cock in the late afternoon light, that his difficulty in living would only be eased when, much later, he would learn that to be an adult is to take by the hand the child he once was, on an afternoon such as this? Jagrati re-enters the room.

— Matamah's sleeping like a log!

— And the mynah?

— Fed on figs. So he can mimic the silence of the Buddha.

— Good.

She hops onto the bed.

— Okay Sprague, go to it!

Sex makes do with anything, can put everything to use: Wild-eyed with derring-do, clad only in the atmosphere, the boy shifts about the room, driven to penetrate into the beyond. Jagrati sits lotus-like on the bed, watching his every move. Along the lips of a conch the boy slides his sex: The frictionless surface offers no resistance, the aperture no entry. The bridesmaid shoes! The sequined pump of silver-gray has a smooth lining; its upper and sole are flexible: Still, no pleasure can be squeezed out of it. In a drawer of the column chest he finds a scrunchie of jade velour: Its texture is delicious, but its grip is too loose: Its refinement is no match for his fervour. A scarf! From the drawer he pulls out a length of tie-dyed chiffon. Its colours—fuchsia and powder blue, yellow-green and tangerine—interrogate him: What is it you are looking for? *There is no word for it.* Through the sheer fabric he sees Jagrati unfold her legs and back up her body to the headboard. Grabbing the loose end of the scarf, he twirls it lengthwise upon itself then knots it around his cock. Stretched taut, slightly rough and slippery, the crepe spiral—now moved with the hands now held as a hole—procures a certain pleasure. Jagrati watches wide-eyed as the boy thrusts; to tumble the demon, however, the scarf's grip is not enough: What else around here might be up to the task? He runs to the armchair.

Seating himself, the boy spins round and works his legs over the back of the chair, his head hanging down. Foregoing subtlety, he seeks to overpower his sex, to force it to yield its secrets. Jagrati slides off the bed and slips off her dress, seats herself on the edge and begins slapping herself, little rhythmic hits punctuated by rubs. To what extent does the boy understand he is seeking the beyond of pleasure? That the flagrant obscenity of his position signs his desperation for self-transcendence? Entranced by her will, Jagrati's hand has caught a wave of sensation; eyes closed, mouth open, she is elsewhere. Unable to come, the boy nevertheless sees into the beyond: Darkly he perceives the dimensions of knowing, and divines that his fate is never to deny them. Accepting that his spirit is not at his command, he lowers himself to the floor and crawls away. For Jagrati there is no turning back: Faster and faster she wheels her fingers around the heart of her unknowing; scorched by grace, she comes: A cry escapes her throat as she falls to the floor, her body shuddering.

A mist of sweat cooling their bodies, the boy and girl rest. For him, as he lies on his back, an arm folded over his eyes, the hour dilates; for her, the succession of instants makes no duration.

Subtle, a caress sweeps across his skin; he lifts his forearm from his face: Jagrati's eyes, dark and shining, greet him: India is opposites in conjunction, India is where she comes from.

— Close your eyes. Don't talk.

Silent dark. Sandalwood and ginger, jasmine and plum: The scent of her homeland. And then it comes, flowing free over his body, the soft silk of her hair, swishing along his skin, sweeping him from thigh to throat, lips to fingertips. Silent dark. Swoosh! Swoosh! Swoosh! She whips his sex, revitalizing him; she whips it till it assumes the plenitude of its aspiration. And then she spittles it and, whirling her head, captures it in the grip of her tresses. Raising her head in one sustained movement, she uncoils a caress that sends a whir of light into her darkness: The beyond is opposites in conjunction, the beyond is where knowledge comes from.

— Three-three. We can't be separated, Sprague.

She collapses onto his body.

— That one counts?

— Yes. I didn't touch you.

Enfolding her in his arms, he presses her body to his. Time comes to a standstill.

***

Severed heads strung round her neck, her body gleaming with blood, she stands on the chest of a corpse in the cremation ground, jackals howling around her: Kali. Naked, holding her chopped-off head in one hand, she stands on the bodies of a copulating couple, drinking the blood that spurts from her neck: Chinnamasta. With Tara, Tripura-Sundari, Bhuvaneshvari, Bhairavi , Dhumavati,

Bagalamukhi, Matangi and Kamala, the ten Mahavidyas: On the floor, in a framed poster leaning against the wall, a fantastic array of divinity displays its gruesome beauty.

– Who are these 'Mahavidyas', Jag?

– They're Devi, goddesses. Don't you just love them?

– I do! Better than anything I saw in Sunday School!

Already the boy feels himself transformed; fearless, he feels how Jag has changed him.

– They're the dark face of the divine. They're all aspects of Shakti.

– The supreme goddess?

– Yes. The female complement of Shiva. Without her, he's nothing!

– It's an amazing religion, Hinduism. Do you believe in it?

– No, of course not. But I love the stories and the poetry. Do you believe in Jesus?

– No. But I admire him. The stranger who disturbs. What's this?

Sticking out from behind the poster of the Mahavidyas is something in a smaller frame.

– Take a look and see.

The boy pulls it out. Holding it in his hands, he reads: *The Lantern — Twenty-ninth International Short Story Competition — First Prize — Jagrati Mukherjee, 'Night Sky' — London, 3 December 1973.*

– Jag, that's fantastic! Why didn't you tell me before?

She smiles into his eyes. Offering his hand, he says:

– Congratulations!

They shake hands.

– I'd love to read it! Do you have a copy you can give me?

– I've got a faint triplicate. But it's going to be published in *The Lantern*.

– I know that magazine. When?

– In February.

The boy is thrilled.

– 'Night Sky'... What's the first sentence?

– It goes like this: 'She's got a store of memories as scintillating as the night sky, Tara thought as her great-grandmother's frail voice floated above the gentle rocking of her chair on the veranda'.

– And the last one?

– 'Tara wondered, as Venus brought a glow to Varuna's one good eye, if you only really see when you see through the eyes of memory.'

– Hmmm... That's lovely, Jag.

Already the blood of the boy runs to the rhythm of the girl's words.

— Those two sentences alone tell me a lot. I can't wait for it to come out! So it's a portrait of your great-grandmother?

— Yes. She suffered from sleeplessness. Or rather, she *flourished* from it!

— Insomnia?

— Yes. I would sit with her on the veranda till the early hours of the morning, listening to her stories.

— I would love to have known her!

— What about *your* grandparents?

— I only knew one, really. My father's mother...

She had blue, blue eyes; she was full of kindness and pride: The boy could have said that, but he didn't.

— ...but we never spoke.

— Why not?

— I never spoke with anyone.

— You never... But why?

— I couldn't find my voice.

— What?

— When I spoke, I felt I was speaking from inside a bubble.

— You mean... No-one could hear you?

— Yes.

As he recalls that feeling of being suspended in the void, a giddiness overcomes the boy. Jagrati moves closer toward him.

— And how long did this go on?

— Weeks... months... years...

— Sprague!

— I'm crazy, Jag.

— Not to me you're not!

Taking his hand and holding it, she gazes into his eyes.

— Or if you are, I'm crazy too.

He hears the pounding of his heart, he hears her repeat:

— Yes, if you're crazy, I'm crazy too.

He turns and stares into a ray of sunlight. Suddenly he feels a sense of responsibility. For what, he doesn't know. But he does know the dancing motes of dust are echoing the mystery of his soul. And binding him to her in a way he's never been bound to anyone before. Jagrati squeezes his hand. He turns toward her, luminous.

— Your eyes are beautiful, Sprague. The most beautiful I've ever seen.

Releasing his hand, she smiles.

– I just filled them with sunlight.

– They're so unusual, and mysterious.

– I wouldn't know. I can't see them. Tell me, Jag, would you like to be a writer? I mean, to devote yourself to it?

– No. I want to be a scientist.

– A scientist? Which science?

– Physics, maybe. I love mathematics. Or astronomy. But I don't want a second-class education. I'll have to leave South Africa.

– You could come to Canada!

– London's more likely. I've got family there. It's halfway between Toronto and Durban—it's perfect for us.

– Yes!

Already the boy imagines a rendezvous. But where? he wonders. The crosswalk on Abbey Road?

– And you, Sprague, what do you want to do?

– Play guitar in a rock 'n roll band!

– And have the girls screaming over you?

– No. In fact, I want to write.

To do in words what you can do on a guitar—that, it occurs to the boy, is what he wants.

– And have you written?

– Yes. Little poems.

– Haiku?

– Yes.

– Go on, then, recite me one!

The boy would like to offer Jagrati something beautiful, but all he can remember is a poem from his backyard

– Okay.

Parakeets gaggle,
The cock treads the hen. I scream:
His heat sears my heart

– That's South Africa, isn't it? Chickens in the backyard?

– Yes.

– Recite it again.

The boy repeats the seventeen syllables.

– It's powerful, Sprague. I too used to be fascinated by the way chickens go at it.

– Or get their heads chopped off! I don't know why, but that's what I remember most about our backyard in East London.

– I got chased once by a headless chicken. It had feathered legs, did a Zulu dance before collapsing.

– Did it catch you?

– Splattered blood on my feet. I guess that counts as catching.

Jagrati repeats the boy's poem. Shining, her eyes reflect his.

– It's a kind of training, writing haiku. Like your picking up marbles with your toes.

– So girls are of the earth, boys of the sky?

– No Jag, I want nothing more than to have my feet on the ground. That's why I was so happy when you lay on top of me, as we lay on the floor. You make me real.

– We'll do it again, Sprague, next time we meet. And I'll show you something else I can do with my feet.

– What?

– I'll walk on your back. I'll thrill you!

– Oh Jag, I can't wait!

– You'll have to, because right now we've got to go downstairs!

Already sprung to her feet, Jagrati is still ahead of the boy.

***

Look! Apple and orange, tomato and onion, tossed in mint and masala; shrimp curried with cashews, potatoes in yogurt and kokum gravy; Bengali dal, steamed rice, minced-lamb and chickpea patties; curried fish, saffron rice, tamarind-and-ginger chutney: Amongst their parents, brothers, sisters and the grandfather, Jagrati and the boy sit down to dinner. Her mother remarks on the symmetry of the families: a son with four sisters, a daughter with four brothers, son and daughter both second-born children. In the hubbub of the table talk, the boy thinks to himself: Only my father has Indian blood. He is half-Indian, so I am one-quarter. Sitting beside him, Jagrati eats with relish. For the boy, every morsel in his mouth is a new world: He lingers over each.

– You don't like the beach, Sprague? the grandfather asks him.

– Sometimes.

– Sometimes what?

– Sometimes yes, sometimes no.

– He doesn't like being with a lot of people, Margaret, his older sister, says.

– He prefers to be with one at a time, says Clara, the second-youngest.

– Or to be alone, Georgia, the second-oldest, chimes in.

– I was like that too, the grandfather says.

Immediately the boy likes him, and listens eagerly to the story he tells. He too was a loner, he says, and did his best to avoid crowds (not easy in India!). On a walk one day to a neighbouring village, he met a girl at a well. Her big eyes captivated him; he couldn't forget them. The next day he returned to the well, and the next, and soon they realized each had found their soulmate. But, because they were from different castes, their parents wouldn't let them marry. So they eloped to Indonesia, to the Javanese city of Surabaya. He learned different languages and began trading, and it was the trader's language of Malay that brought him wind of opportunities in South Africa. So, after the birth of Utpal and Eesha, they moved to Durban... The boy is filled with admiration for this man, and decides that he too will travel and learn languages. Looking into Matamah's kindly eyes, he blushes as he imagines him 'doing it' in his rocking chair. Or was Jag only joking? Probably. She's always ahead of me! But does it ever stop, this undertow of sex? Can it make even an old man want to go beyond himself? How he must miss his wife—how did she die?

The conversation then turns to the upcoming holiday in India that Jagrati and her family will take.

– Have you ever been to India, Henry?

– No. I don't need to go. I've got India right here.

Everybody laughs. The boy is delighted to discover this side of his father again, yet he is also hurt: At home his father never even looks at him, let alone address him a word. And then his father tells an anecdote from his work as a doctor in Toronto.

– I had to examine a patient and determine her mental state. I asked her to tell me her name, her age, her birthday. She didn't know, she couldn't tell me. Then I asked her where she was. She looked at me and said, India?

Everybody laughs again. And yet I don't look like him at all, the boy thinks. Nobody can guess where I come from.

– And how do you like Toronto, Mary?

Watching his mother compose an answer, the boy has the uncanny feeling that from a crypt within her, a ventriloquist is moving her lips. Will she ever break out of her tomb and touch me? Will I ever break in and revive her? Painfully aware of the impenetrable isolation from which she speaks, the boy instinctively understands that only the love of a girl—a girl like Jagrati—can save him from a similar fate. As his mother equivocates, his father—as usual—intervenes, coming to the rescue with another anecdote... He talks so easily here, the boy reflects, with his friend from medical school, yet at home when I'd come back brutalized from school, he wouldn't even acknowledge my presence... In the warmth of Jagrati's family he feels less of a stranger than he does in his own house.

— The shrimp curry's delicious, Auntie Usha!

— Thank you!

— Everything is!

— Thank you! Now, if you had tasted Trishana's cooking...

— Trishana?

— Utpal's mother. She knew the properties of every spice, every ingredient; with every meal there was at least one dish you'd never tasted before.

The boy, filled with emotion, catches the eye of the grandfather; he smiles warmly at the handsome man with grey hair. What's it like, he wonders, to lose the love of your life?

— And what are the Canadian dishes? What do you eat in Toronto?

— Fish sticks! the boy blurts out.

— This water's for drinking, isn't it?

His father changes the subject.

— Of course, Henry! Why do you ask?

— I was just thinking about the story of Queen Victoria and the foreign guest. Do you know it?

The adults do; the children don't.

— Tell it to us, Uncle Henry!

His father gets rolling.

— Well, one day Queen Victoria gave a banquet in honour of a foreign guest. At the end of the meal, the waiters brought everyone a finger bowl—you know, a bowl with water and a slice of lemon, for rinsing your fingers. The guest, not knowing any better, took his bowl and drank the water. So the Queen, seeing everyone's embarrassment, lifted her bowl to her lips and drank. All the other guests then did the same.

Around the table some are amused, some are moved. The boy knows the story, and finds it admirable. There's a message in there about my mother, he thinks, but what the foreignness in her is I don't know: Our whole family is foreign. Suddenly Jagrati dips a finger in the cucumber raita and spots the tip of her nose with the white yogurt.

— Jagrati!

Her older brother does the same, and then everyone breaks into laughter as another brother follows. All the children begin spotting their nose with raita, and the grandfather does it too.

— Jagrati's always been a bundle of mischief!

The blob of yogurt on her nose begins to slide down: She sticks out her tongue to catch it. All the children stick out their tongues and shake their heads, trying to do the same. While the parents try to get a grip on the children, Jagrati turns to the boy and licks the yogurt off his nose. He feels an urge to kiss her, but manages to restrain himself. Reaching under the table, he pulls up her dress and caresses her thigh. She slips a foot out of her espadrille; at the feel of her touch he slips his foot out of his moccasin.

— That's enough, children! Jagrati orders.

Everyone obeys. Her foot caressing his, she waits for her mother to give the signal for dessert.

Guava with coulis of passion fruit, pistachio and cardamom ice cream: By the time dessert comes, the boy's happiness is limited only by the thought that he is leaving tomorrow.

***

— Look out, look out, the fox is about, and he's coming to find you!

In the twilight after dinner the children play hide-and-seek. The sloping grounds offer great cover: myriad trees and bushes, the tool shed, the rock mound, the shrine to Shakti, the footbridge.

— Keep in, keep in, wherever you are, the cat's a-coming to find you!

Behind a bush of gardenia, ghostly white in the half-light, the boy finds Clara; amidst the pale lilac of an umzimbeet tree, down where the flowers darken to mauve, he finds Nayan.

— Five, ten, double-ten, five, ten, a hundred!

Clara and Nayan become seekers too as the game switches to 'Home-and-You're Safe'. The boy and his sister separate; Nayan covers home.

— Clap, clap, clap, three on the back! he catches Ishwar out.

The game continues until all the children are either out or home safe, all except Jagrati. Where could she be?

— A whistle or a cry, or let the game die!

A whistle comes from somewhere. But where? Some say the lucky-bean tree, some say from under the footbridge. A thud, followed by a low, crisp whisper, is heard from the footbridge hollow.

— I hold my little finger, I thought it was my thumb; I give you a warning, and here I come!

All the children but Nayan and the boy run towards the footbridge; while Nayan guards home, the boy heads for a tree with scarlet flowers. Thickset, it reaches up high; the boy casts his gaze into the dense, spreading crown, but can't make out any sign of Jagrati.

– All up, the game's up, ready for Sunday morning!

– Jag! Where did you come from?

– Where *were* you?

– Where were you hiding, Jag?

– Where?

– Tell us!

– Tell us, Jag, where were you?

– Where?

Home, as if she'd been loitering lackadaisical by the weeping bride's bush for who knows how long, Jagrati's dark eyes scintillate as she answers every question with an enigmatic smile. Jag, you're amazing! The boy has no idea where she was or how she got home so stealthily, but his heart is filled with joy at her achievement.

And then it's time to say goodbye.

– Keep a diary, Sprague. We'll exchange them when we meet again.

– I'd like to, Jag, but...

– But what?

– It would only make me miss you more.

– Then there's only one solution: write me a haiku every day!

– Yes!

– You can send them to me every week.

– I will, Jag. Little jewels of seventeen syllables, for your treasure box.

The boy blushes, surprised at his own boldness. A glint comes to Jagrati's eye. While the adults prolong their parting and the children push the limits of their new-found familiarity, Jagrati dashes back into the house.

– Jagrati and Sprague get on like a house on fire, he overhears her mother say.

– With four brothers she's used to boys, her father adds.

– Well, she certainly knows how to tame him! his father says. Usually he's as shy as a wild animal.

– She's an exceptional child, so precocious! the boy's mother puts in.

Fearing his experience be appropriated by his parents, yet strangely attracted by their reflections, the boy tries to find the right distance to the huddled groups in front of the house: Too near and he'd be drawn into their conversation, too far and he'd attract attention to himself. And then Jagrati comes to the rescue.

– I'm going to talk to your sisters. Go inside the house. On the little table in the hallway, under the mirror, there's a flat white box. Take it. There's something inside it for you.

– Thank you.

– It's a little too big to keep in your pocket, so put it in your suitcase as soon as you can. And don't open it till you get back to Toronto.

With a slight tilt of the head the boy assents; as nonchalantly as possible, he follows the flagstone path to the front door.

And then the final goodbyes:

– Enjoy the rest of your trip, and have a safe return!

– Thank you. And you, have a great time in India.

– And a Happy New Year!

– Happy New Year!

– Goodbye! And thank you again!

– Thank you!

– Don't mention it!

– Sprague, say goodbye to Jagrati.

– They've said goodbye. I saw them.

– Goodbye!

– Bye!

– Bye.

***

Perfect rows of pineapples, fields thick with sugar cane... Crashing waves on a rocky shore, a lone fisherman in the spray... Devi couched on a cremation pyre, pulling a devil's tongue; luminous sweep of silky black; ginger, jasmine and plum... Somewhere over the Sahara dawn flickers in the boy's dreams; into the blue of the Mediterranean his tears plunge...

London's cold is grey and wet, blazing white is Toronto's. The new year holds great promise; the song in his heart, the boy is certain, will sustain him at school. He attempts a diary. The first entry reads:

> Monday, 7 January 1974
>
> From a booth in the library I watch the blizzard outside. The next best thing to leaving a place you don't like is watching it disappear.

I didn't have enough money for lunch today. I'd asked my father for some. He gave me a dime. I said it's not enough. He gave me a nickel. I said it's not enough. He counted out five cents more. I couldn't bring myself to say it's still not enough. (Why doesn't he know it?) I borrowed a quarter from Shelley Liberman. He brings lunch from home. Thick pastrami sandwiches on rye bread, with mustard and a dill pickle. Then an apple and a slice of carrot cake.

In ten minutes the bell will ring. English. Miss Hamlyn. I wonder if she'll wear her skirt and boots again. I like *The Sun Also Rises*. Brett Ashley. 'She was built with curves like the hull of a racing yacht. Her hair was brushed back like a boy's.' Before the holiday Miss Hamlyn said I could make a lot of money writing Harlequin romances. It's a nice insult. I'd rather write like Hemingway. She didn't suspect that my raving lyricism was driven by the sight of her feet in her exercise sandals. Cheeky pink with toenails to match.

I'm tired. Daylight saving time's already started. Four months early. Oil shock. The bell! Go, man, go: Life-saving time.

At night he takes out the treasure in his drawer: lime green and electric blue, scarlet and turquoise—Jagrati's scarf shimmers in his trembling hands.

In the transparent silence of crisp winter nights his eyes penetrate deep into the darkness; as he waits impatiently for *The Lantern,* stars rain into the haiku he writes:

The night's sleight of hand,
Stars: The sparkle in your eyes,
That alone is real

Stars drowned in daylight:
Nobody knows, only I,
You are with me now

Black night, empty sky;
Stars' hidden presence: Your touch

In my memory

A riot of stars
Crowds the sky: Through wet eyelashes,
Your face in my mind

So distant, so close.
Thanks, praise, forgiveness: Like you,
Stars make me religious

Andhra Pradesh and Gujarat, Rajastan and Tamil Nadu: The beauty of the names as he rolls them on his tongue conjures her up in India. And then the news comes.

> On Wednesday January 9th 1974, at 21:50, Indian Airlines Flight 440 crashed near New Delhi. Forty-three passengers and five crew members were killed. The plane, a Boeing 737, crashed and caught fire after hitting power lines during a landing attempt. The landing was made despite visibility below minima. The plane had taken off from Madras at 19:15.

Jagrati is dead.

Her mother is dead.

Her father is dead.

Nayan is dead.

Deepak is dead.

Ishwar is dead.

Ashok is dead.

The boy's world turns to white; vague figures hover in a fog. Passing a mirror he sees a pale ghost. His breathing falters, air is like ether in his lungs. To move forward is to fall; to stay still is to be transfixed.

And then a morning comes when his numbness can no longer exile his emotions: The time between that day and the day he left her in Durban must be destroyed: He burns his diary in the fireplace.

He decides to be a good student, he decides to play the game. Until the day the cruelty of his classmates towards a new boy from Poland drives him into a fury: He attacks the bullies and is beaten black and blue. For three days he is suspended from school.

The bodies were burnt, the ashes were scattered: Slowly information is gathered. On a silent night of falling snow he walks through empty streets.

'Brahma is condemned to dream the world; we are condemned to be his dream': Rummaging in the mythology of Hinduism, he seeks a way to structure his grief: 'Knowledge is not a knowing, but a tuning of the soul'.

'India. 50p.': His hands tremble as with booming heart the boy stares at the stamp. Lavender oval. Lilac ground. Dancing couple. He turns the envelope in his hand: How many hands has it passed through to reach mine? The envelope is light, but in his hands it feels like lead. Open it. Don't be afraid. The knife slits open the pale blue seal; twitching fingers fetch out the letter. Already, before he even unfolds it, Jagrati's voice wrenches his heart.

Tuesday 8th January, 1974

Hello Sprague,

I am lying under a helicopter in a bird cage. What a racket! Mynah birds and scavenging kites, and maniacally screeching cuckoos! The fan disturbs the air but doesn't cool. Madras can fool you into thinking you haven't left home (Marina Beach/Marine Parade), but the scale here is incredible. There are millions of people but you hardly see any houses. People carry a bed-sheet with them and sleep wherever they can. At night the airport floor is covered with sleepers, and it's the same in the train and bus stations, the streets and parks. Every young woman has a baby in her arms; five-year-olds look after three-year olds. They rummage together in the garbage, naked. There are entire parts of town where everybody you meet is either selling something or begging. Everything is falling apart, crumbling, in ruins; Indians don't seem to repair anything. There's filth and misery wherever you look, but the people themselves are clean.

Our travel plans came to nothing. Strikes and political trouble cancelled flights, and at Indian Airlines the waiting lists run to weeks. You waste hours and hours talking to officials; everything goes very slow. We couldn't get to Calcutta because the state of Orissa hired 100 doctors from West Bengal. That set off boycotts, blockades at the border, burning of buildings. Did you know India was at war with Pakistan just two years ago? Now the Indians have turned to killing each other. It's nothing compared to what happened in 1971, but who knows what it could lead to? We heard absolutely horrible stories from a Bangladeshi friend of my father's; most of his colleagues at the University were murdered, the women raped.

My father says the Indians don't know what their country is. They only care about their region, their family, their caste. And he blames the unchanging poverty and misery on Hinduism; he says it makes people passively accept intolerable conditions. That's why nothing changes. He's probably right. And yet I can't help feeling an affection for these people—what stories they have to tell!

Tomorrow we fly back to New Delhi; in a week I'll be back home. I can't wait to read your first haiku!

Your girl,
Jag

In his darkened bedroom the boy lies, face down on the floor. He rolls onto his back and stares at the ceiling. And then a light from inside him illuminates the room. Does he understand that his love for Jagrati is now fixed forever? Does he recognize that his fate has just taken its definitive shape?

PART ONE

Chapter 1

Only rarely now, Marietta, do the rat's teeth of sorrow gnaw at my heart; only once in a while does the rodent of longing burrow into my soul. Now is such a time. I am sitting in a bar at the westernmost edge of Europe, watching the setting sun transfer its fire to the waters of the Atlantic. But where once that sun would sink my heart, now it inflames my soul: Against a crimson sky threaded with gold the gulls cry, and in their cry I hear no screech but the echoes of our goodbye: I love you, and I will always love you. Overcome with elation at the truth of those words, those words I uttered as we went our separate ways, I hail the serving boy (the proprietor's son) and order another Madeira dry. Marietta, as I tell our story, what truth will be my touchstone? The boy pours my wine. He looks like me, when I was a child. Does he too dream, as I once did, of ocean voyages under the stars, of Bartolomeu Dias and Vasco da Gama? There lies my touchstone: the truth of the child, the incorruptible core of the boy and girl we once were. Look! Darkness deepens, the lighthouse glows: The night will be long, my love, settle in; open your heart, let's begin!

1984. Princeton. Dial Lodge. There's a sparkle in your amber eyes, a boyish cut to your blonde hair. I invite myself to your patio table. We start talking.

– What do you do? I ask you.

– I'm a post-doctoral fellow. I'm doing research in high energy physics.

– Particle physics?

– Yes.

– And what do you study, in particular?

– Quarks, neutrinos, dark matter. The fundamental objects of the universe.

– Ashes to ashes, dust to dust?

– Yes. But in-between, I try to answer the big questions.

– By studying the smallest things?

– Exactly.

– Sounds exciting!

– It is. And you, what are you studying?

Multifaceted, your gaze is a challenge: At once indifferent and intensely interested.

– I'm not. I'm a grip. I'm working on a film. We're here for the final days of shooting.

– So you were part of the film crew in Jadwin Hall this morning?

– Yes.

– What's a grip?

Full of withholding yet brimming with promise, your eyes keep drawing me in.

– It's a guy who fixes other people's problems on a film set. Otherwise, we set up the dolly tracks, mount the cameras, rig up the lights. We're the workhorses of the film crew.

– And what's the film about?

– It's about two brothers, identical twins. One's a professor of anthropology, the other's a colonel in the US Army. They'd drifted apart, then meet by chance in El Salvador, just after the El Mozote massacre.

– El Mozote? That rings a bell. What was it exactly?

– The worst atrocity in Latin American history! In modern times at least. The government militia rounded up everyone in the village, tortured the men, raped the women, then killed everybody, down to the last child.

– I remember now, hearing about that.

– Yes, it was just two years ago.

Finishing off your salade niçoise, you eat the last olive. There's something of a Modigliani model in you: Your sensuality is as lush as it is austere. Picking up your bowl of yogurt and berries, you ask me:

– So what happens when they meet, the brothers?

– Well, it turns out that the anthropologist was in El Salvador on a humanitarian mission, while his brother was there as an advisor to the military government. The film opens with a kind of Jacob-and-Esau scene, the two brothers wrestling in the jungle, like they used to wrestle as children, then it goes back in time, tracing their respective stories.

– So it's a political film?

– No, not really.

Your gaze collaborates with your voice to convey a sense that our words and what's happening are out of phase.

– It's more about ethics, about choice and chance. In fact, what's interesting is that by the end of the story, you wonder if there really *are* two different people, if the twin brothers are not in fact one and the same person. It's a philosophical fable, about fragility.

– Fragility?

– Yes.

I like the fineness of your fingers, I like the fullness of your lips; I like the way you submit a berry to your palate after crushing it.

— There's a parallelism in the structure of the two brothers' stories, so you see that just by little things—arriving at a place a minute earlier or later, for example, or saying hello to a stranger because the sun happened to come out while you were hesitating, giving you courage—by little things like that, one's destiny can go in very different directions. That's fragility. Are you French?

— Half French.

— And what's the other half?

— Swiss. My father's French, my mother's Swiss.

— *Suisse romande?*

— Yes, but I live in Zürich.

— Ah! I was in Zürich last year. What a city! A lake, a mountain and two rivers are its treasures. Yssel that the Limmat?

— Pardon?

— *Yssel* that the *Limmat?*

— Ah! That's a good one.

— It's from *Finnegans Wake.* James Joyce. The greatest writer in the English language! After Shakespeare, of course. But he's the greatest in *any* language.

— You like literature.

— I do.

I like the moonstone in your sternal notch, its opalescence against your skin; I like the innocence in your eyes that sets off the suggestion of sin.

— So you're from Zürich?

— I live in Zürich, but I grew up in Neuchâtel. And you?

— I was born in a bottle and washed up on a beach, where the Atlantic Ocean meets the Indian.

— I see. You're from Cape Town.

— You're good at geography.

— I like to travel.

Standing up, you extend your hand.

— I'm Marietta.

I stand and take it.

— I'm Sprague.

Your hand in mine is firm and frank; your gaze in my eyes is intense.

— Excuse me, Sprague, I've got to get back to work.

— Could I—

— What's the name of your film? I'll watch out for it when it comes out.

– *Gemini Agonistes.*

– *Gemini Agonistes?* That's a good title.

– Would you like to come to the shoot tomorrow morning? We're filming in Jadwin Hall again.

– Sorry, I can't. I'm—

– You can be an extra! We're going to shoot a scene in the Joseph Henry Room.

– Thank you, but I don't have time. I'm presenting a paper tomorrow morning.

– How about in the afternoon, then?

– No.

– You'll enjoy watching Bram Westbrook. He's an amazing actor! What he can do in the space of—

– Sorry, I've got a seminar. But Wednesday for lunch would be okay.

– Wednesday? Great! Where shall I meet you?

– We can meet here. I'm free between twelve and three.

– At twelve then?

– Twelve fifteen.

– Okay, I'll be here. Wednesday at twelve fifteen.

– Right. See you then, Sprague.

I watch you walk away, tall in your high-heel sandals and summery pant suit. You turn to look over your shoulder: Your gaze encounters mine, and in the flash of your smile something inside me dissolves.

– Good luck with your presentation!

– Thank you!

You disappear into the building. I linger, watching shadows play on the footpath as a breeze stirs the trees. Is it me that's trembling, or only the newborn leaves?

'Wednesday for lunch': Wednesday at noon I was booked on a plane back to Toronto: The shoot was over. But I chose to stay. Why? Because right from our very first contact I was drawn to what I saw in your face: A mysterious transparency, a worldly innocence; your eyes sparkled as you spoke, as if you were creating a veil of light to conceal your vulnerability: I was touched, and instantly seduced. Three and a half years later, in Paris when we met again, I came to understand that paradox is your very signature, and subterfuge your calling card. And that's when I fell in love with you.

But already, Marietta, in that very first encounter, I felt privileged to be in your presence. Not because I was a handyman executing orders on a film set (it could just as well have been a construction site) while you were a particle physicist adding your brick to the cathedral of theory; no, it was because in your whole demeanour there was not a trace of any superiority, not even a suspicion that we were anything but equals. I found that so refreshing that I felt an immediate kinship with you, and there and then I dared to believe that between us there would be no barriers. In a foreign country conventions change, habitual reflexes are abandoned: I knew that, yet in your obliqueness, your ambiguity—the way you engaged my regard—I saw not an accident of cultural displacement, but a fundamental disposition of your encounter with the world. I was not wrong, but I knew that something much more complicated, something dark and mysterious, underlay your air of seeming availability. But I'm getting ahead of myself: Let's go back to that first idyllic day we spent together.

Over four days in that New Jersey spring we saw each other again three times: Our Wednesday lunch (cosy in the Common Room, with the rain pouring down outside), our Friday walk (a lovely stroll along Carnegie Lake, I as captivated by your gangling gait as by your commentary on *Nineteen Eighty-Four),* and our Saturday trip to the Jersey shore. What a day that was! I was almost as much a stranger as you in this iconic America (or so I thought at the time), and yet I wanted to be your guide: You were gracious enough to let me, while you played my European guest. Through the Pinelands in the Cabriolet we made a game of seeing who'd be first to spot the next gun club; in the cranberry bogs and blueberry thickets we made a stab at being Mother Nature's daughter and son. When you puckered your lips as you crushed a cranberry in your mouth, when you crouched down and drew me a map of Switzerland in the sand, when you threw me a smile over your shoulder as you led me out of the forest I'd lost ourselves in, I knew that if I fell in love with you I'd be damned. I tried to put a veil between my eyes and your beauty, I tried not to succumb to your grace. And every time I ventured too close to that secret place inside you (the one you protect like a goose her goslings), I tried not to be touched by the depth of your *pudeur* (for thus I construed it at the time). Waiting in line at the drive-in restaurant, you sung your way through the menu; when the car-hop came to take our order, I could hardly restrain my laughter as you faked a French accent. Strolling along Jenkinson's boardwalk, you studied the kitsch with an anthropologist's eye: Still you fell under the spell of its brash appeal. Strolling along the beaches of Barnegat Peninsula, I tried not to be drawn to the figuration of your feet: Still I fell under the spell of their sleek allure (not to mention the descending fifths of your footfall, the arpeggios of your toes).

Half-way back to Princeton we had dinner in a chrome-and-neon diner. Sitting opposite you in the high-backed booth, I tried not to be moved by the negligent fall of your cropped blonde hair or the sensitivity emanating from your fingers;

the vibrancy of being hovering in your eyes or the striking immediacy of your lips: I was determined not to let the shadow of an impossible future fall upon our present state of grace. 'It took no computations to dance to a rock 'n roll station': You'd never heard of the Velvet Underground (or so you led me to believe), but before I pressed A5 you'd heard one note from an open car window and instantly identified Bach's 'Chaconne': You'd played it at a violin competition, and now you play it alone in your room. And thus I learned you'd hesitated between a career in classical music and one in academia; I learned you were no stranger to first prizes, whether musical or academic: Your contempt for competition didn't stop you from thriving on it. We talked about music. I told you my life was saved by rock 'n roll, that rock 'n roll had given me a feeling of identity and the right to be different. You said you understood me; you said that for you too, music, your violin, has been an instrument of liberation. To the Velvet's defiant joy, however, you remained indifferent (or so you pretended).

– Tell me something of that piece by Bach.

– The 'Chaconne'?

– Yes.

– It's from *Sonatas and Partitas for Solo Violin.* It's a dance-form movement in D minor. What do you want to know?

– Why you like it so much.

– Oh, I couldn't put it into words.

– Try.

Do you find freedom in relentless form? Is discipline your defence against the chaos of emotion?

– I like what Brahms said about it.

– What did he say?

– He said, 'On one stave, Bach writes a whole world of the deepest thoughts and feelings. If I imagined that I could ever have created the 'Chaconne', I am certain the excess of excitement would have driven me out of my mind'. He wrote that in a letter to Clara Schumann.

In the amber of your eye a firefly breaks free: How do I decipher its dance?

– Did you bring your violin with you to Princeton?

– Yes.

– Will you play me the 'Chaconne' when we get back, at least a few bars?

– It's too late. The sound of the violin carries far.

– How about tomorrow then?

You lower your head and shake it to say no. Rejection: I have no memory of the murmuring house, no sonorous womb, no ocean, but in the acoustic mirror of your beating heart I have a body—Am I not to be reborn?

Were you afraid I wouldn't receive the music with the proper reverence? Were you afraid you'd reveal too much of yourself to me? Or was it the idea of the darkness we might have shared, the darkness that would remain in the blackness of my hair when you awoke to find yourself beside me?

– First thing I'll do when I get back to Toronto, I'll buy a recording and listen to the piece.

– It goes through the entire range of human experience, in less than fifteen minutes.

– Really?

– Yes. It's richness and depth are astounding.

I wondered just how much of that range you'd personally experienced in your twenty-seven years, and felt a pang of bitterness that perhaps I'd never find out. I consoled myself with what I *did* learn about you: that Paris was the scene of your academic and musical triumphs, the Vaucluse your garden of Eden, and Zürich the setting for your professional ascension. Little did I know then that from that Swiss base your footprint would soon cover the world: The world to whose origin I feared you were denying me access.

Back in the Cabriolet I felt thrown back upon myself, but once we slipped into French I felt one with you again. And yet the premonition lingered that refusing me Bach was refusing me your bed; I hadn't given up hearing the cry of your goslings, yet I was crestfallen.

Up, up, up! Back on campus as I got out of the car, the night sky hauled me up by my spine. Look! Up here there is no airglow, no shining envelope of the earth; up here it is cold, cold, cold. So this is the place where the blackness is pure, where no light scatters in the dust between stars. Without vision the future vanishes, the past invades the present. Marietta, must I let you go? Oh give me the moon's shining sphere, give distance back to the stars! White-feathered wings, rosy fingers, open the gates of heaven! With what remained in Pandora's box, I will be content.

– It was a lovely day, Sprague. I enjoyed it very much. Thank you.

I smile into your amber eyes, softly speckled with starlight. You continue:

– What time's your flight tomorrow?

– Eleven-thirty. I'll drop off the car at Newark around ten-fifteen. Come, I'll walk you to your residence.

– No. It's not far.

– Why don't we do it in the road?

– Pardon?

– The *White Album*. Side Two, Track Seven.

You laugh. I pull you to me and take you in my arms; you spin out of my embrace.

– No Sprague, I'm sorry.

You lean forward, presenting your cheek to be kissed: I pirouette away. The engine warmth that penetrates my body is no substitute for the heat I seek from yours; still, it is soothing as I lean against the side wing of the Cabriolet, trying to make you linger.

– What will you work on next week, Marietta?

– A paper on inverse problems. A Hölder-logarithmic stability estimate for two-dimensional inverse problems.

– What's that?

– It has to do with the recovery of a real-valued potential in the two-dimensional Schrödinger equation at positive energy from the Dirichlet-to-Neumann map. Now does that knock your socks off?

– Yes! Explain the basic idea of it.

– Have you heard of Riemann-Hilbert problems?

– I have, yes.

All is fair in love: I lie to keep you longer. As you begin your explanation, as you warm to the game, I fall into a reverie inspired by your purse. Hanging from your shoulder by a guitar strap, the supple black leather can barely be seen below the flaps that progressively cover it. The first is of bronze suede, the second of blue snakeskin, and the last a zebra print. A tassel of each style hangs from a corner of the bag, dangling gently as you sway. Why am I so moved by feminine masquerade? The white jean jacket thrown over your shoulders, the seashell pendant in your sternal notch; your seersucker frock, vaguely floral with black ribbing below your breasts; your T-bar sandals that throw a veil of modesty over your scandalously beautiful feet—everything about you conspires to make me want to keep you by my side. Yet I know I cannot: You are out of my reach. But why? It is so. Must I not at least try? Haven't I always dreamed of a woman like this? Indeed, nothing moves me more than this exhilarating combination of extraordinary intelligence and exquisite femininity, perfectly assumed and given an impish edge by the boyish cut of her blonde hair. As music breathes in the architecture of a building, so her feminine coquetry flourishes alongside the rigour of her science. Already you are in my blood, Marietta, and to get you out I must bleed.

– So I prove a new stability estimate, which is explicitly dependent on the regularity of the potentials and on the energy.

– That's very interesting! Of course I can't follow you completely, but I do have some idea.

Of course I couldn't follow you at all, and I didn't have any idea. You knew it—it was part of the game—yet you chose to indulge me, trembling my heart strings with the timbre of your voice. (I confess your science only served to make the twitch in my trousers stickier.)

– Are you happy here at Princeton? It's a fantastic campus, isn't it?

– Yes.

– How long are you staying again?

– Till the end of June. Six months in all.

Still you indulged me: In generous voice you spoke of your impressions, postponing for my sake the moment of our separation.

– I've taken an architectural tour...

Suede, snakeskin and zebra: What an incongruous combination! Suede: They say the robes of shamans are made from deerskin; they say the hind is the emblem of virginity: Does that have anything to do with the mystery disguised in your eyes? Snakeskin: A python pattern. From a crack in the slopes of Mount Parnassus, pneuma rise from the decomposing body of the Python, enabling the virginal Sibyl to fathom the divine: Marietta, if our parting is to be chaste, how will you impart to me your prophetic intuition, your particular feeling for the divine? Zebra: Stripes hide traces of predators' claws: What savage paw has swiped you?

– It's getting cold, Sprague. It's time to say goodbye.

– I'll keep you warm, Marietta.

– No. I'm sorry.

– This week dragged past me so slowly.

– But you said you enjoyed being with Gram in New York, didn't you?

– Nevertheless, the days fell on their knees.

– Sprague, that's from *Station to Station!*

– So you *do* know rock 'n roll!

– I love Bowie.

– So why did you—? Never mind. 'If I did casually mention tonight...'

– 'That would be crazy tonight...'

– 'Stay!'

– I can't.

– Why not?

– It's not because I don't want—I do, but...

– But what?

– I can't, that's all.

I sense your discomfort, I sense you're in the grip of something your coolness can't overcome. Still, your ambivalence is beguiling.

– I'm coming with you.

– No, Sprague.

– Let's go to my hotel then.

– No. I shouldn't have... I'm sorry.

You put your hand on my shoulder and touch your cheek to mine, one then the other, while kissing the air. Sensing that if I'm to have any chance with you I must let you go, I reciprocate these curious kisses of seeming intimacy: I dare not yield to my longing for your lips, but I do throw my arms around you and press your body to mine.

– Goodbye Marietta.

Oh sweet, sweet mercy! Your hands on my waist slide around to the small of my back. My hard-on is heavy, as heavy as my heart: every man his cross, every dog his day.

– Goodbye.

I let you go.

– Good luck with your research.

– Thank you. Good luck with your film work.

– May I write to you?

– No. We had a lovely time together: Let's leave it at that. Goodbye Sprague.

I blow you a kiss, even though you're still standing in front of me. Did I detect a sadness in your eye, a longing in your laugh, as you received it?

– Goodbye Marietta.

Against the cold you hold your jean-jacket closed, and as you swing around your bestiary-purse swings around with you. I watch you walk away; my useless arms hang limp, my heart floats in limbo. And then over your shoulder there comes a glow, a radiance that stuns me: On the rack of your smile my heart stretches. As you gather the light back into your face the night gathers you unto itself; slowly the click-clack of your sandals on the tarmac fades away.

And on that hollow sound, Marietta, on that unforgettable gift of your gaze, ended the prelude to our deeper encounter.

Chapter 2

1987. Paris. The Seine. The collar of my bomber jacket turned up against the chill, my hands snug in the deep slash pockets, I cross the Pont de Grenelle, heading for the Left Bank. Lights dance on dark water; the buzz of applause dies down in my ears. God, how the man with glass bones can play! What stunning improvisations! A Bedouin dance under desert stars, a shimmering vibration; the rolling gait of the cud-chewing camel, a treasure-load of ivory and gold: How 'Caravan' came alive! Expressive discords effortlessly resolved, harmony embellished with ingenuity; upward arpeggios, chromatic descents, what a drama he stages! And all the while his virtuosity is but a handmaiden to his musicality. The fire of Petrucciani's playing has left me elated; before I know it, I'm halfway down the Quai André Citroën, a poem hatching in my head.

Look! In a parking strip before a newspaper kiosk, a woman swings closed the door of a white Mini. Tall beside the squat car, she radiates elegance. The ghost of electricity sifts the moondust in her hair; her boots grind the gravel as she reaches into the car. Out she pulls an oblong case, holds it in one hand and locks the door with the other. I approach the crossing as she angles into it. Her boot heels on the pavement ring a bell, but it is her walk that gives her away: Extinction or destruction by deluge or inundation, suffocation by submersion in water: No, I'm not drowning, but floating in her gangling grace. Dream, or destiny? *PIÉTONS—ATTENTION—FEUX DÉCALÉS.* Headlights stream white into red tail lights; I time my dash and cross the street. Between the dark windows of *Café Régalia* and the potted shrubs quivering by the gutter, fleet-footed the woman makes her way.

— Marietta!

You spin around.

— Sprague!

On the Rond-Point du Pont Mirabeau I throw my arms around you and press your body to mine: This time I will not let you go.

At Le Muguet I felt euphoric, I couldn't believe I was sitting opposite you again. Piano-and-violin by Poulenc, Bartók and Ravel, that was the concert you'd just given; Petrucciani playing Ellington was the one I'd just come from. You squeeze a slice of lemon into your Perrier (no band of gold around your ring finger); I sip my Heineken.

— So, what are you doing in Paris? you ask me.

— I'm teaching at the American University. Film studies. And I'm writing.
— Writing what?
— Haiku.
— Haiku? I love haiku!
— You do?
— Yes. I love the Zen aesthetic.
— So do I.
— Recite me one you've written!
— All right.

> Raindrops, window pane.
> A breath blows: To the river
> They run together.

— That's lovely!
— It's not too soppy?
— Soppy?
— Sentimental. My Achilles heel, sentimentality. I've been told more than once I could make a fortune writing Harlequin Romances.
— If you could write one as good as *Wuthering Heights!*
— Emily—I do adore her. So, is it too soppy?
— Say it again.
— Okay.

> Raindrops, window pane.
> A breath blows: To the river
> They run together.

— Eden, the impossible return. It's the original dream, the most primitive. There's no escaping it, I'm afraid.
— Yes, but is it—
— No, it's not too sentimental.
— That's why I write haiku: to kill the sentimentality in me, to eliminate the adjective.

I didn't tell you I also do it to honour a girl I once knew. As you sip your Perrier, I know it won't be long before you'll find her at the heart of me.

— I don't think I'll ever be a filmmaker, Marietta. I haven't got what it takes.
— No?

— No. So I'd like to write a novel instead.

— A novel? So you begin with haiku? Seventeen syllables? That's working from the bottom up!

— Yes!

I love it when you talk to me like that.

— What would it be about?

— I don't know. A love story, no doubt.

— If you want to kill your sentimentality, why not write a story about... let's see... a tractor!

— A tractor? Much too romantic! Ploughing the furrow, making love to the land, turning the earth upside down.

— A bottle, then.

— Too sexy! Look at your Perrier—she's a fat-bottomed girl, just begging you to cup your hands on her ass and heave her to you.

— And that Badoit over there?

— She looks like Plain Jane, but in bed, boy is she a bitch!

— All right, forget about bottles. How about writing a story with... a spark plug!

— Are you kidding? What could be more romantic? *Le coup de foudre!*

My Beatle boot taps out the beat as I sing:

Sitting in a restaurant
She came along in a sarong
What a dame, I dropped my peas
And before too long I was on my knees
Crawling at her feet, yeah-yeah-yeah

She said what you doing there?
I said I just lost my chair
Won't you let me sit next to you
For maybe a minute or two
Or until I find my peas, yeah-yeah-yeah

Okay, she said, you can stay
But my spark plug's off today
Don't worry baby, I replied
Spark plugs respond to stimuli
And anyway, my peas, your feet, yeah-yeah-yeah

Laughing yourself into stitches, you make all the world a stage: The couple in the corner struggle to take themselves as seriously as they did before, the barman interrupts his reckoning to juggle packs of cigarettes, the loner on a bar stool puffs out a series of smoke rings.

– Sprague, you *are* a poet!

– Rhythm is the key. I just strung some doggerel onto a Paul McCartney melody.

– Which one?

– 'I've Just Seen a Face'.

– Yes, of course! I thought it sounded familiar. And you just invented the words like that?

– Yes. You gave me the spark, Paul the melody. With that, the words came easily.

– You're amazing!

– Yes, when you're my Muse, I'm amazing.

– Watch out, you're getting romantic!

– No, no. A poet without a Muse is like a fish without fins. I'm a poet; you're my Muse. That's reality.

– But we've just met!

– We've just met again, you mean.

– Yes, we've just met again... Isn't it amazing?

By the sparkle in your eyes I know you will be mine; as you empty your Perrier into your glass, you hold my gaze to confirm it: It is my cup that runneth over.

– Now tell me, Marietta: What are *you* doing in Paris?

– Research. I'm a visiting researcher at Polytechnique.

– And what does that involve?

– Guest lectures, faculty seminars, conferences. But mainly research, collaborative research.

– Why Paris?

– I wanted to get away from Zürich for a while. This was the first opportunity.

– You were in a hurry to leave?

– Yes. I'd have preferred to go farther afield, but I didn't want to wait.

– And what crime did you commit?

The night in your eyes brightens with the flash of fireflies. I continue:

– Murder, robbery, arson?

– No. Provocation.

– And what did you provoke?

– Jealousy. Violent jealousy.

– Was it pre-meditated? Were there no mitigating circumstances?

– With all due respect, Your Honour, that does not concern me: I was simply being myself.

– I see.

Pale-rose, your lips catch the light as you give me a smile; barely perceptible, a tremor in your lower lip testifies to the memory of violence.

– So, have you started your novel, then?

– Several times!

– And?

– I can't find a way to reconcile the story of the child and the story of the adult. For my heroine it's easy, but for my hero it's proving very difficult.

– You've got to keep going. It's only through writing that you'll find the solution. What are you trying to write?

– A love story it would seem.

– Indeed, so you said.

– No matter what the starting point, that's always the direction it takes.

– Tell the truth, Sprague. That often makes the best fiction. Break down your resistance!

– How?

– Have you ever had your heart broken? I mean *really* broken, so that you had nothing left but your eyes to cry with?

– No.

Jagrati didn't break my heart: She made it stronger.

– That would strip you down to your truth.

– Will you do it for me?

– Do what?

– Break my heart.

Unflinching, you confront my gaze. Softly, but distinctly, you say:

– Yes, I will.

Between two beats of my heart I hear myself say:

– Thank you.

You break into an enigmatic smile. What game are we playing? Where are we going? Sipping my Heineken, I decide to go with the flow, reminding myself that when we parted in Princeton, three and a half years ago, neither of us expected to see the other again: Now by some miracle we're almost neighbours in Paris, living at opposite ends of the fifteenth *arrondissement*. To whom shall I give thanks and praise?

– Hey, I saw *Gemini Agonistes!*

– You did?

– Yes. And I saw your name on the credits!

You're even thinner than you were in New Jersey; a note of severity edges your sensuality: You look older than your thirty years.

– You must have had binoculars. How did you find the film?

– Excellent! It's very moving. But the massacre, my God!

Gone is your boyish haircut; instead, swept forward, your hair frames your face in an unruly array of tresses, ash-blonde or golden, before falling to your shoulders in nonchalant layers.

– And the twins?

– The ambiguity works, it makes you think. In the end, I felt it was really the story of just one man.

– Interesting.

You sip your Perrier.

– One man's fragility, in a plurality of possibilities.

'Memory believes before knowing remembers': Emblem of your absence, promise of your presence: Your voice echoing in my dreams. And now you are here, in flesh and blood before me: Marietta, how could I ever have let you go?

– So, you've given up filmmaking?

– Yes. Well, maybe not quite. I've written a screenplay that might go into production.

– That's great!

– It's still up in the air. It could go either way.

– What's it called?

– *The Dustman's Daughter.*

– And what's it about?

– It's a love triangle with a twist: A girl and her lover, the girl and her brother.

– An incestuous relationship?

– Yes. It's set in Harlow, one of those towns built after the Second World War, just north of London. Everything happens on a council estate. A low sky, washed-out colours, clean geometric lines. The camera's constantly moving, because the film is to be cut in such a way that different periods of time, different sequences of action, seem to flow into each other. So, despite a lot of flashbacks, you've got the impression of unity of place, time and action.

— You've been inspired by the Greeks?

— Yes. Sophocles of course, but also Euripides.

Taking our bill and the bill left on a neighbouring table, I rip them in two, then say:

— Euripides...

I put them back together.

— ...Eumenides.

Your laugh comes from the diaphragm and goes straight to my heart.

— And what's the action of your screenplay?

— It revolves around the sister's attempts to get her brother out of prison; he's been convicted of criminal homicide in the accidental death of their father. She's trying to prove his innocence.

— I see.

— The second line of action involves the lover, or would-be lover: his wooing of the girl, his attempts to get her away from her brother. When he finally succeeds, the brother commits suicide and the lover goes mad. The girl is the only one left standing.

You fix me with a stare of distaste.

— Isn't the world ugly enough without adding the sordid to it? Why make a movie about incest, madness and suicide?

I stare into your eyes: You return my gaze with absolute conviction. If this is a game, I'll play it straight.

— Well, it's not *about* incest, madness and suicide.

— You just said it is!

— You know, when *Lolita* was being attacked as 'unrestrained pornography' in England and France in the fifties, Nabokov wrote to Graham Greene, who'd been defending the book, and said, 'My poor Lolita is having a rough time. The pity is that if I had made her a boy, or a cow, or a bicycle, Philistines might never have flinched'.

— Lolita as a bicycle?

— Or a cow. And Samuel Beckett, writing about Joyce's *Work in Progress,* said, 'His writing is not *about* something; it is *that something itself*'. Do you see the difference?

— Yes. Music.

— Exactly!

— What's *Work in Progress?*

– *Finnegans Wake.* The dream book.

– I've heard it's a nightmare. To read.

Enigmatic, your smile glows as you look at me askance. Breaking into laughter, I reach out and touch your hand: You withdraw it. You take up your drink, smiling through the screen of hair that's fallen across your face. Tell me, my svelte panther, behind those blonde bars, just how feral, how free are you? With a flick of your head you toss back your hair and sip your lemon water: No, Lolita is not a bicycle. Is that your answer?

You resume the conversation:

– Do you know there's a James Joyce Foundation in Zürich?

– Yes. I was there last year. I heard a lecture on Nora Barnacle.

– Who's she?

– She was Joyce's wife.

– What a name!

– Yeah. Joyce's father used to say, 'With a name like that, she'll never leave him'!

– A clinging barnacle!

– Except that it was *he* who clung to *her*. She was an amazing woman. 'Her image had passed into his soul forever.'

– What?

– 'Her eyes had called him and his soul had leapt at the call.'

– I see.

On your upper lip, a spot of lemon pulp: With the manicured nail of your little finger you scrape it off, then slip your finger between your lips and slowly withdraw it, sucking off the stray tissue: No, Lolita is neither a bicycle nor a cow. You say:

– Incest, madness, suicide.

– You know my name, look up my number!

– Really, Sprague, wallowing in the mire!

– I'm not wallowing in the mire! To find an organic form to express a personal vision necessarily means to defy convention. Taking risks, confronting the strange—that's precisely what being an artist is all about! It doesn't matter what you start with—incest, madness, suicide, or a convention of accountants. All that matters is that art defy the familiar and wake up at least a few sleepwalkers!

– Thank you, Sprague. I was just looking for confirmation that your heart is worth breaking.

In my stunned silence my heart sings: Marietta, you're amazing!

— Well, is it?

— I gave you my word I would do it. I just wanted to be sure I wasn't too hasty.

— And? Are you sure now?

— Yes. I'm glad I didn't find your heart in the mainstream. Now I wonder just where in the margins I'll find it.

You take my glass and down the last mouthful of beer that had remained.

— How about another? you ask me.

— With pleasure!

I will meet you in the margins, Marietta: In Princeton, I know, I was too mainstream.

Cold, the Heineken warms my heart; bold, you teach me subtlety. Am I dreaming? That day on the Jersey shore was three and a half years ago: It seems like yesterday. You hair was short, then; mine was long. Now mine is short and yours is long. What else has changed?

— Hey, I didn't tell you: I've listened to the 'Chaconne'!

— You did?

— Yes. I bought it the day I got back from Princeton, as I said I would.

— And?

— It's powerful. It's enormous!

— You like it, then?

— Yes, very much. But it wasn't easy to get into. I mean, I sensed from the very first notes that it was going to be something profound, but those repeating four-bar phrases, those endless variations—it's sort of a blur in the beginning.

— Yes. The scale of the piece is monumental. There's so much music in one continuous movement, and all of it made by just one violin.

— I found that amazing. You have the impression you're listening to a string quartet!

— Exactly. In fact Mendelssohn—and Schumann too—composed piano accompaniments for the piece. They thought Bach was asking too much from one little violin.

— Wow, even them!

— Yes. And another reason it's confusing at first is that there's no tonal contrast. Every one of those four-bar phrases concludes with a cadence that arrives in D. That's what gives the 'Chaconne' its concentrated focus.

— I see. It must be terribly hard to play.

– It's impossible! Technically and musically, there's been nothing more challenging, before or since.

– How long did it take you to learn it?

– I'm still learning it! You could spend a lifetime on that piece. At any particular time you can settle on an interpretation, but it's never definitive.

The tone between us has changed: We're no longer flirting. It feels strange, all of a sudden. Was I presumptuous when I said I know you're going to be mine? Or, on the contrary, is this the confirmation? You continue:

– There's something inscrutable about the 'Chaconne'. You can immerse yourself in its language, and just when you think you've got something pinned down, it eludes you.

– Like all great art.

– Indeed. The more you work, the more you see; and the more you see, the more it escapes your grasp.

– And what's involved, in working out an interpretation?

– Basically, you're staging a confrontation between the written music, the instrument, and yourself.

Are we staging a confrontation between us?

– It's very demanding, and very exciting. The hardest thing sometimes is not to be overawed by the music. You've got to stay open, curious, take risks.

Just like I must not be overawed by you? Just like I must stay open, curious, take risks? You sum up your thought:

– In a word, you've got to have courage!

– Body and soul!

– Heart, mind, body and soul. Everything!

– The body—just how important is it, would you say?

I know it's through your body that you go beyond yourself: I want to go there with you.

– In this process, you mean?

– Yes.

– Oh, it's critical! It's inseparable from the rest. Playing the 'Chaconne', you must never forget it's a dance movement. So you've got to feel the impulse, the dance impulse, in the piece; you've got to feel it in your bones.

Transparent, your fingernail polish traps the moonlight as you sip from your glass.

– And how often do you listen to Bach?

– Sometimes every day, other times less often.

– You find it soothing?

– Yes, but also exhilarating. It's so limpid. Every note's in its right place, there's no excess anywhere.

In what guise does he come, your bogeyman? What Fury does Bach keep at bay?

– And playing? How often do you play Bach?

– Whenever I need to restore my balance. When you play the music, the effect is even stronger than when you just listen to it.

– I see.

Cars go by along the *quais,* souls lost and found:
And where do we fit in, in this merry-go-round?

There's a hunger in my heart, a stirring in my crotch:
If my mind had windows, would you dare to watch?

I touch your hand, I caress your finger:
I want to be your song—will you be my singer?

– Do you remember, Sprague, when we first met in Princeton and you spoke of *Gemini Agonistes* and the war in El Salvador?

– Yes. It was during our very first conversation.

– That's right. Well, at that time, I had no interest in El Salvador, no connection to the war. Now I do.

– Really? How's that?

– The concert I played tonight was a benefit for Salvadoran refugees.

– Well, well! That's a pretty direct connection.

– Yes. We're playing again tomorrow. Would you like to come?

I look into your eyes and see mine in them, shining.

– I'd love to!

– It's at the Centre culturel suisse.

– Where's that?

– In the Marais. 38 rue des Francs-Bourgeois. Métro Rambuteau. At eight-thirty.

– I'll be there.

You reach into your purse.

– Here's a ticket. I have a friend who was supposed to come but can't make it.

– Thank you.

I take out my wallet.

– No, you can make a donation at the door.

Across the Seine the Pont Mirabeau lays out its bridge of light; we cross the rue de la Convention, and at number one kiss goodnight: I throw my arms around you and trace the circumference of bliss; you yield to my embrace and in turn hold me tight. Suddenly I understand that what will be will be; that you will break my heart, and in so doing set me free.

Chapter 3

How shall I relate that magical evening, Marietta? How shall I convey the glory of your concert? Why, by casting my gaze with the eye of the heart, by cocking my ear to the silence in the sound.

Look! You walk out from the wings with decided step, violin and bow in hand; the pianist, tall and equine, smiles as he mirrors your stride. What a handsome couple! The two of you stand in front of the acclaim, you ravishing in the red gown that hugs your body, he chic in his black jacket and open-neck shirt. A puffed-up handkerchief adorns his breast pocket; his abundant hair, a mop of dark curls, tumbles over the side of his head in a throwback to some other time. Who is this Matteo Balestieri? Look! Your hair swings off your shoulders as you bow into the applause. How is it, I wonder as you straighten up, your strapless gown doesn't fall down?

Now shall I speak of how effortlessly your fingertips found the pitches of anxiety and fervour, how confidently your bow found a voice for the unpredictable, in Poulenc's *Sonata for Piano and Violin?* No, I'll simply observe that at the end, facing the ovation, there was a look on your face that seemed to say, 'I came here to play, not for your applause'.

Shall I speak of the art of indirection, subtle and discreet, in Matteo's solo turn? Shall I convey the elegant intimacy of Poulenc's 'Mélancolie'? No, I'll simply say that when you returned from the shadows, you were immediately into the music, making a melody of the bare bones of a tune that Matteo offered you.

Ravel, *Sonata for Piano and Violin in G Major*

I. Allegretto

If you are violin, Marietta, am I piano? Is it to be I the hammer and you the bow? No, it cannot be so, for they say the two are fundamentally incompatible instruments, irreconcilable. But let us find out! Listen! A dance-like motif, borne now by the piano, now by the violin, weaves in and out of melodic figures.

> Do you sleep
> All curled up and fetal,
> Or on your stomach

In freefall?

If the former, you are violin: It is an instrument of curves.

Upon awaking, do you linger
With the phantoms of sleep,
Or banish them to darkness
And bounce straight out of bed?

If the latter, you are piano: It is percussive.

In the shower
Do you let your thoughts run,
Or do you file each one away
Before moving on?

If the former, you are violin: It can slide from one note to another without disrupting the pitch continuum.

For breakfast, do you make do
With coffee and toast,
Or indulge in a smorgasbord of,
Say, yogurt, fruit and cereal?

If the former, you are piano: It has no variations in timbre.

Leaving for work, is your goodbye
A predictable peck on the cheek,
Or do you surprise your lover
With a new kiss every morning?

If the latter, you are violin: It can produce vibrato.

Are you comfortable packing an instant
With observation, calculation and conversation,
Or are you more at ease
Engaging your mind in one task at a time?

If the former, you are piano: It can juggle several voices while thinking of each independently.

Marietta, what kind of music would we make together? Could we accord violin and piano, deal with dissonance, create harmony? Listen! Motion and intensity are dying down, the melody is fragmenting: The piano and violin have nothing to do with each other now. With one breath, as it were, your bow, though moving up and down, sustains one long, dying tone over the piano's softly repeating figure. The end is the beginning. Or is it the other way around?

II. Blues: Moderato

This is the blues? Yes, the mood is there in the melody; your mournful slides sound like saxophone slurs, and Matteo is playing with subtle syncopation. Oh my little Paganini, when you lay down your violin, how I'd love to kiss your collarbone!

III. Perpetuum mobile: Allegro

Out of your violin you wrench a tirade of fractured tones, unremitting in intensity. Matteo cuts into your smoking fulminations with dry, percussive chords; refusing to be interrupted, your wrist, your arm, your elbow measure out the bow with precise distillations of violence. Whence this strange fascination, this uncanny jubilation? How can you move with such unerring poise when such a demonic pulse bangs in your blood? What obsession, what *idée fixe,* feeds this blazing fire? Mesmerized by your shivering bow, I lose my earthly references: Your *perpetuum mobile* hypnotizes me.

Marietta, can you hear me?
I am here, in the eye of the storm.
Listen, there's something I need to know.

If, when your breast heaves gently in your sleep
And the intricate elaborations of the day unravel,
A wandering albatross were to fly into your dreams and say,
'Throw your arms around me; I'll show you the Southern Ocean,
The frozen world from which I come',
Would you, as you looked into his eyes, recognize me?

And if you did climb onto his back
And throw your arms around his neck,
Would you take fright,
As you glide on the updrafts of wind over waves,
At the steep drop in temperature?
Would you then wake up with relief

To the warmth of your familiar world,
Or would you hold on even tighter to his pliant body,
Trusting the warmth of his heart to heat you
As you head into Antarctica?

And if, as the wind whips the sea into a frenzy,
He were to say to you, 'I am tired of being a stranger',
Would you panic and wake up in a cold sweat?
And if he added, as you make for the midnight sun,
'I may be feral and hollowed out by homelessness
But between your legs I would find a plenitude of being',
Would you let him lie there and become human?

For if he can soar for hours without a wingbeat,
Spend most of his life without touching land,
He'd rather be a man, not an albatross.

So would you smear his breast with your blood,
Anoint his eyelids with your spittle
And burnish his wings with your cunt's secretions?
Would you squat and piss before him,
Whip him with your hair,
And dry your fevered brow in his effulgent feathers?
And when winter brings a transparent trickle to your nostrils,
Would you scatter drops of that warm drip into his silky down?

As his shadow glides over the ice and snow,
As your breast rises and falls on your breathing,
That is what I want to know.

Hark! A cadence, an expansive chord, sustained by your relentless bow. A final flourish, then horsehair leaves catgut and in an arc swoops up: The *perpetuum mobile* is no more, the sonata is over.

Smiling a mischievous smile, Matteo joins you downstage. Together you take a bow. When you stand up straight he is radiant; you're wearing a strange grin, as if embarrassed by the applause, as if it has nothing to do with you. Again you take a bow, then with quiet dignity Matteo accepts the acclaim while your restless eyes tell the audience that it cannot touch you. You've had enough! On your heels you turn, and lead Matteo backstage. The house lights go up.

Intermission

Paris is too bright for the night to be blue
But I am blue when I think of you:
Through the pale air of the passageway
I make my way to the rue des Francs-Bourgeois.
What am I looking for?

A way to behold your beauty
Without a premonition of terror;
A way to erase from my heart
The inscription of my history.

Le Voltigeur bids me drink from its broken cup.
Marietta, in my vineyard a few stalks survived
The summer blight and autumn frost:
I have plucked those grapes and pressed them:
Will you drink from my cup?

Throughout my suffocation
I continued to gasp;
Enveloped in darkness,
I never stopped seeking the light.

I know that a lover needs better credentials,
I know I am damaged goods,
But with what's been done to me I've tried—
And I'll never stop trying—to do something good:
Would you, could you, let me love you?

Back at the Centre culturel suisse, a crowd mills around. In the curved space of the bar, a woman with long brown hair and blunt-cut bangs, tall in a blue pantsuit, is engaged in conversation. I can tell it is of a political tone (Reagan, death squads, extraditions from the US for the murder of Archbishop Romero). I wait my turn to approach her, and when it comes I tell her how moved I was by the video testimony she'd shown us before the concert began. I tell her I find her approach—helping women take responsibility for their lives—preferable to mass agitation. She says you need both, but she too prefers, in place of agitation, the act that makes an immediate difference to a human life. I ask her how she got involved in this programme; she explains that ever since university she's been involved in humanitarian missions. She tells me an anecdote about her visit to El Salvador, something about a prostitute. As she speaks I can't help but be impressed by the way she inhabits her body. There's something mercurial in her presence, as if the weight of her experience is lightened by her philosophy. Her face looks lived-in, yet the glint in her eye, her throaty laugh, convey a charming youthfulness. There's something about her that says, 'I enjoy what I do, but I'm not reducible to it'. She tells me she's a lawyer; she gives me her card. I peruse it and break into a laugh. And that, Marietta, is how I met your mother. (Yes, for as long as you did not undeceive me, I took her to be your mother).

Bartók, *Romanian Dances*

So this is Bartók's distillation of village ritual, this is 'Fast Steps': I delight in your rhythmic élan and the sight of your body swaying; as your legs push up from the floor, I imagine you on your back in a barn. Matteo drives the dance forward; a final flourish, then it's done. As the applause erupts I realize that in barely five minutes you've drawn from your violin centuries of tradition: Nourished by a millennial culture, Bartók's roots run deep.

Helvetians, Gauls and Romans,
Vandals and Franks,
Conspired to create you, Marietta.

Your roots run deep,
Very deep: Have I any chance
Of sweeping you off your feet?

I have no roots,
I am a nomad; my genealogy
Is a mystery to me.

But watch out, woman!
Home is where the heart is,
And my heart is set on you!

Now shall I speak of how, in Bloch's 'Nigun', over the piano's rumbling resonance, praise and supplication flowed from your violin as you laid out a rhapsodic line? No, I'll simply recall how your face glowed with a wild and tender beauty as you played. Shall I speak of how the fingers of your left hand rocked as they stopped the strings, inflecting a voice that continually shifted between joy and lamentation? No, I'll simply mention that in the simultaneous sounding of transgression and transcendence, you made solemnity voluptuous and devotion ecstatic.

And now shall I show how, with your renditions of numbers one and six of Brahms' *Hungarian Dances*, you had the audience eating from your hands? No, I'll simply remark that your impatience at the applause revealed that your hands had better things to do: The very first note of the next piece announced the fire to come.

Ravel, 'Tzigane'

High your elbow brings the bow across to the deep string; when you draw it you draw out my entrails: With a wrenching intensity you sculpt the phrase, then singe the air with the determination of your down-bow. Your hair shivers as you resume the attack, inundating the auditorium with your dark, shuddering tone. Isolated in the spotlight, your body is a blend of tension and serenity, a suicide's razor before it kisses the wrist. Listen! There's violence in that melody, there's death in that dance! You *are* Ravel's gitane, determinedly asserting her identity. In the face of all who would rather forget, you affirm that in Lucifer's blackness there's a brightness no other angels possess. The slide of your fingers between the pitches, the biting attack of your bow; the brilliance of your left-hand *pizzicati,* the idiosyncratic pulse of the beat: Infused with savage resolve, you walk the razor's edge.

> Dreamfall, the dagger
> Between your teeth: Fervent,
> The rose flaunts its thorns

Swift as blood, slow like honey, into the night-space you pour out your spirit. In searing tenderness your violin soars; out of silence you coax secrets. You are the object of all eyes as you stand in the spotlight, but for yourself you are no object: Your concern is not about how you move but about what moves you. You spread your legs, flex your knees, and play the melody in *pizzicati*. Gone is any notion of the female body as a burden; absolute in its freedom, with precision and grace your body deploys itself in its own private space.

> Deathwatch, when freedom
> Is vertiginous: Violin,
> Knife, spear and arrow

Close to the bridge, with the lightest of touches, your bow caresses the strings: Out from the f-holes there comes a quiet, an almost oriental calm. But it is the calm before the storm: Matteo sweeps a wild *glissando,* your hair flies out as your torso flings back; from your solar plexus you play, making savage music.

Nightworld, the black art
Of sound's speculum: Auditive light
In the eye of the heart

Matteo takes a solo turn, offering an ornamented version of the melody; when you come back in you change things again: Now you're the most nubile girl at the firemen's ball, indulging a suitor, awarding him a whirl. Radiant is your smile as you sway and bob, but all the while you're under no illusion that this is anything more than an amusement: Elsewhere is your celebration! And then you take me there: In a pyrotechnical display of technique, you play the melody *spiccato,* producing notes with the force and colour of fireworks. The moment is everything; you're in a space where you can do no wrong. Your bow is a blur as you remind the world what a privilege it is to be alive; poised on your sandals, you lower the neck of your violin and bend your body into the speed. Despite the rapidity time expands; my being resonates with your body: Totally absorbed in the moment, I am at one with you. Listen! In the limpid notes of the high register, Matteo now plays the hypnotic dance. You're having none of it: You send a sequence of eerie harmonics to haunt his naïve transparency.

Starlight! Out of the rose,
Cold brilliance takes the spectre:
You give it back the ghost

Now Matteo invites you back into the dance; you lean into the melody and take it up with *spiccato* bow. You flex your knees as you gather speed; now you're in perpetual motion. Is this your long spiral up the Tower of Babel, is this your attempt to restore the original tongue? Your body now is compact, profiled for speed: Your bow moves in a blur. Gone are the days when you aimed to please, to provoke a reaction and prove your worth: Now you're in a place where no one can reach you, a place where you're at one with yourself. And then, renouncing the infinite, your arm swoops up off the strings and comes down to declaim in three triumphant notes that music is the original language, and silence is its condition.

For a moment the audience is stunned, they cannot find their voice, as if all sound is suspended in syncopes. And then the tremendous energy you have given them they give back to you in thunderous applause. Whoops and 'bravos' rise in waves, waves that fall and rise again. Matteo offers himself as a shock absorber for the barrage; I watch you as you slowly descend the spiral and compose your face to confront Babel. I am moved by your discomfort, and admire your intransigence. To what extent is it willed, to what extent involuntary? I want to find out. Meanwhile I, too, express myself in the language of Babel, but I can't wait to purify my tongue in your presence. Out from the shadows you are repeatedly summoned, until you decide you've had enough of bowing into applause: One last time, with music you will silence them.

Kodaly, 'Adagio for Violin and Piano'

Slowly across the string your bow travels, drawing out a long line with gravity and grace. Footfalls in a forest, the silent dark; a pool of water, a clearing: Matteo keeps pace, a discreet presence in a dim landscape. The quiet beauty of this dirge makes for a solemn encore. Does it mean you haven't forgotten El Salvador, the woman mourning the girl she couldn't be? Does it mean that even if you're on top of the world, you know what it's like to be on the bottom? Or does it simply mean you need to ease yourself down after the incredible high of 'Tzigane'? The elegy unfolds, your hands serving your heart as you shape raw emotion into subtle shades of feeling. Sustaining the contours of the slow-moving lines, between pressure and speed, tension and release, your bow finds a balance that makes the music flow. And now Matteo sketches out a new motif, another consolation for loss. Your violin renews its plaintive search with greater intensity—but just what is it you are searching for? Over the terrain of the music your hand moves the bow, like a blind man his fingers over something unknown. And I, too, move like a blind man: Who are you, Marietta? The force and refinement, the power and delicacy, that I first sensed in you on that patio in Princeton didn't prepare me for the intensity you've shown me tonight. God, what radiant musicality! What splendour! You inhabit music like a calligrapher a line, a hawk the wind, a dancer the dance. Is the ephemeral, then, an element in your ethics of living? Is living the moment all that matters? Or is it simply a question of grace? Hush! Arpeggiated chords glitter; sunlight streams into the forest. The music opens out and dilates, flowing forward in long, arching lines. Within each string your bow discovers nuances of colour; in the tiny space between fingerboard and bridge, it finds an infinity of tenderness. Over what void do you weave this fabric, from what dead do you withdraw your attachment? In a flourish you bring the poignancy to a higher pitch, and then at the place where the bow lives in the string you breathe with more abandon, and let the music dissolve into silence...

Chapter 4

Hello Sprague, I send you these 'Ambassadors' with my warmest greetings from London. Looking at this magnificent painting in the National Gallery, I thought of your notion of fragility, and somehow connected it with the photograph you gave me. Thank you! It was a lovely surprise. Work going well. Back on Friday. Marietta.

Saturday, after the show, you'd told me that Sunday you'd be leaving for two weeks in London. We agreed to meet the day after your return. Two weeks—an eternity!

Talking to Matteo later that evening, I discovered Tuesday would be your birthday: What could I give you? The dark-haired couple waiting to get into a Sapho concert? Yes! Their arms around each other, he looks frankly into the lens while she looks fixedly outside the frame. There's something magical about the photo, a reverberation of energy between eye, hand and mouth, gaze, touch and smile; between what falls within the frame and what lies without.

That night, before slipping into bed, I wrote you a poem. Do you remember the lines I appended to it?

> In the blue flame of your birthday candle, between the amber and the black, the spirit of childhood flickers. When the flame is blown out the spirit is dispersed: Marietta, let us, you and I, gather it into our hearts, then let us honour it in each other. Happy Birthday! Sprague.

Sunday morning I slipped fifty francs into the hand of your concierge and got her to promise she'd get my package to you: I was happy to learn, from your *Ambassadors,* that she did.

Tuesday I celebrated your birthday with a Heineken and Gidon Kremer playing the 'Chaconne'. No longer absorbed in deciphering its form, no longer struggling to enter its architecture, I opened myself to grace and let listening become an act of love: I let Bach's unrelenting inspiration structure the hope in my heart.

The following Tuesday, upon receiving your postcard, I lay on the sofa and recalled scenes from our Saturday evening: You standing, glass of wine in hand, in front of a handsome man with slicked-back hair, gazing lovingly into his eyes. Your smile was radiant as you indulged his teasing; it was clear all outsiders were barred from your complicity. When you turned to receive the homage of others who were pressing in to meet you, I approached that man. He asked me what I do; I said I'm a poet. Seeing my empty glass, he immediately led me by the elbow to the bar: A poet must have a potion—what's your pleasure? I took an instant liking to him. Sipping my glass of Burgundy, I listened as he told me that to poetry he prefers prose: Simenon, for example. And then he asked if I've ever been tempted by fiction.

– I have. In fact, I'm working on a novel.

– What about?

– An idiot. A man who can't hide his hand.

– Another Prince Myshkin?

– No. My hero's no Christ with falling sickness. But I do take up Dostoevsky's challenge—I want to portray a positively beautiful man.

And then he told me what he was working on: A micro-robot that can swim in the human bloodstream.

– No! I said.

– Yes, he insisted.

And that, Marietta, is how I met an engineer from the *Centre suisse d'électronique et de microtechnique* in Neuchâtel. Yes, that is how I met your father.

When I finally got a chance to talk to you, I let the silence speak: You made an open-handed gesture, indicating an airy sculpture standing in a corner on a marble pedestal.

– Do you like it?

I traced a semi-circle around the elliptical abstraction, feeling the intricate flow of its gilded metal.

– Yes!

Excitement buzzed in the small of my back as you took my hand and led me through a door into the stairwell. Taking my head in your hands you pressed your lips to mine, and in that instant I realized the sculpture was in fact a figuration of the kiss you were giving me. And then, slipping your tongue into my mouth, you sent a tremor up my spine.

Swaying cypresses,
Wine, roses, nightingales: No.
Just the essence of you

And how it moves me!
Marietta, the turning world stops
When you touch me

The Ambassadors: I did notice, in your postcard, how the oblique disrupts the aplomb. Yes, it did not escape me—that curve of cranium, those orbits of eyes. Astrological instruments, globes terrestrial and celestial; a lute, an open book, a folding set square—they did not distract me from the death's head. Nor could the fine clothes—the black velvet, the pink satin, the purplish-brown brocade—divert me from the *memento mori*. But what did I care? I knew that before long we'd be making love. Now tell me: Why did you leave it to Mara to teach me that as love is traced by death, it traces the space between identities? That my desire to know my identity coincides with my desire to know and love you? And for this, you would have to— No, I'm getting ahead of myself. Let's close this interlude and pick up our story with your return from London. Oh happy days!

Chapter 5

Child of woe, far to go, and now's the time for loving and giving: Friday you returned from London. Over the phone, short and sweet, we agreed I'd call on you at eight on Saturday. When I said, 'Sleep over at my place', you said, 'All right, I'll pack an overnight bag'. How simple things can become: Three-and-half years had been a long wait.

What better than architectural forms to frame my nervous energy? Camera in hand, early Saturday I went to Parc André Citroën and shot off two rolls of black and white, composing abstractions from glass houses under construction. Then I called up Muriel. She was on her way to the market, but Adelaide would be in. 'Come, and stay for lunch', she launched her invitation.

I wondered, while walking along the Villa Santos Dumont, whether you'd discovered the climbing vines and hollyhocks, the stone-faced houses and studios, of this magical street just twenty minutes from your apartment and five from mine.

Where there's rock n'roll, there I'm at home: The pulsating beat of 'Where the Streets Have No Name' accompanied Ada's welcome. Over a jug of mint-and-lemon water we communed under *The Joshua Tree,* exchanging thoughts about U2's cinematic songs: The paradoxical fertility of the desert, the mirror games of America in the eyes of Europeans, the majesty of Edge's guitar. And then I asked Ada how her novel was progressing. She'd finished it, she said. I marvelled at the speed at which she worked, and then she reminded me that ever since she was a child she'd been blackening pages every day. I, in turn, reminded her of that morning last autumn when I stepped into the kitchen to find her delirious at the breakfast table, fascinated by the bowl of milk before her: From the cut in her thumb (she'd been peeling an apple) blood dripped bright into the luminous white, mesmerizing her. (Fuelled by amphetamines, she'd been up all night, writing). 'I've given up drugs', she said, 'I don't need them anymore'. Walking up the stairs to the darkroom, I recalled the doom of the needle in the old days.

Muriel was back when I returned downstairs. I complimented her on her purple-and-black hair, told her I liked it even more than the orange. Over salad and quiche she talked of her mother in Pittsburgh: She'd just received a letter from her, the first in thirteen years, proposing they see each other again.

Adelaide asked Muriel if she'd forgiven her mother, if she felt ready for a reconciliation. Muriel said she didn't think so. I knew the story of her spineless father and controlling mother, I knew she'd been kicked out of her family at fifteen for assuming her homosexuality. Over coffee she began rolling a cigarette. Observing the daylight soften her resurgent hurt, lending poignancy to her bitterness, I thought of Lucy Jordan: Besides being the same age, they had nothing in common, but somehow I had a vision—of Muriel or her mother, it was never clear—screaming on a rooftop in suburban America.

– You've got to take this opportunity to confront her, I said, if only to have no regrets later.

The bell jar of the air-conditioned nightmare was something we'd both experienced, and our shared receptivity to the spell of the poet and lucidity of the *raconteur* only reinforced our kinship.

– You think so? she asked. I think we'd just go round in circles. Nothing good would come of it.

I'd known first-hand such futility, so had no real counter-argument.

– Write to her, I suggested, try to get a dialogue going. You never know what it might lead to.

She puffed out a trio of smoke rings.

– I'll think about it.

I got up and helped myself to an apple.

– What are you doing tonight? Adelaide asked me.

I bit into the crisp Red Delicious and savoured its floral-scented flesh.

– I'll be spending the evening with a physicist.

– A physicist?

Licking the juice from my lips, I relished the overtones of acidity in its sweetness.

– Yes. A particle physicist.

– But whatever for? Muriel inquired in curious alarm.

I took another bite of the apple's creamy flesh, this time detecting a hint of strawberry.

– Spend the night together, I mumbled.

– Pardon?

Decidedly, that apple was very juicy; just running the back of my hand across my lips gave me a twitch in the trousers.

– Accelerate our blood, collide our bodies.

– What?

– I know! Ada jumped in. The physicist is a *physicienne,* and you're going to make sweet love all night long.

With Ada and I, it was indeed sweet.

— Is that right, Sprague? asked Muriel.

This time, when I bit into the apple, I detected a distinct spiciness.

— Sprague? Are you, by any chance, in love?

I just kept on eating my Red Delicious, letting their imaginations run, preserving the mystery I was about to immerse myself in. When I left, both Ada and Muriel kissed me more warmly than they usually did.

Chapter 6

Woven from darkness and light, chequerboard tiles gleam black-and-white in the lobby of your building. Braided elevator cables move in parallel, black grease flashes bright: What battle is about to begin? Crossroads against continuity, balance against instability, intention against fortuity? No, tonight there'll be no war: The instant I catch sight of you through the bronze-mesh panel of the capsule, descending *Deus ex machina,* happiness inflames my heart. Seductively acceptant you receive my gaze, draining all despair out of desire. Was that whirr as we embraced the sound of beating wings? The splendour of your smile—tossed over your shoulder as you walk out the door—says, 'Yes'!

Brightening streetlights usher in the night as we walk to where your Mini is waiting. Blind to passers-by, tuned-in to each other, we weave our way along the busy pavement. Each time our strides realign, my gaze is captured by the gold-cage pattern on your black leather pumps, your high-heel peep-toes that bring your skinny black jeans to such a come-hither conclusion.

Here it is! Through the thinning leaves of the plane trees the gibbous moon shines, and as you stand by your motor, about to open the door, moonglow burns your beauty into my memory: In your biker jacket of green-grey suede, your blonde locks tumbling over the collar, you are striking. As you trade your heels for driving mocs, the mannish touch to your femininity buzzes the base of my spine.

In your little box car you are in command, the streets of Paris belong to you: Not content to merely go with the flow, you cut a path through the traffic to our destination: The boulevard after the quais to Saint-Germain-des-Prés, then rue de Buci, rue de Seine, and a lucky parking spot on rue Mazarine.

The Revolution was here: Effaced from the corner stone, the 'Saint' of rue Saint-André-des-Arts. This country fascinates me: As calculating reason casts its light towards the dark horizon, terror in the service of power expels holiness from horror: Relentlessly working his mechanical decapitator, the Incorruptible inaugurates the Republic of Virtue. Marietta, do you believe in magic? Does your science preserve mystery? Let us leave the French to their heroes of liberty, let us leave them to their self-satisfaction—us, we are artists! I'm certain your mind can accommodate the ambiguous meanings of mythical thought, I'm certain your reason is not only an instrument of purposes—yes, I know you are an artist! In the flux of the crowd I feel you beside me; among the many, you are the one. But what if you need to be domiciled among the settled, what if you need some ideology to live by? I may be detached from family, nation, race and religion, but who's to say, when push comes to shove, you won't take cover behind these identifications? Why do I believe we're two of a kind? Flash of fireflies! In the cool glow of a timely light, your eyes meet mine. Oh my troubadour of knowledge, could you ever be happy with a harlequin? In the incandescence of your smile my doubts dissolve.

We turn into the rue des Grands Augustins and walk in silence toward the Seine. Halfway down the street our hands touch; my vertebrae tingle as our fingers entwine. How do you account for that, Marietta? In the electromagnetic universe, is there a parameter for love? And if, as some say, love is a function of lust, what is the slope of the tangent line? The click-clack of your shoes on the tarmac intensifies the silence; the silence intensifies our touch: Is that not the physics of love? A car approaches from the *quai;* we step up onto the sidewalk. You slip your arm around my waist and in the same instant mine reciprocates: The physics of lust, wouldn't you say? We walk on, until in the narrow space between the shutters of a jeweller's shop we stop: Summoning darkness in each other's arms, sharing one breath, we inaugurate the night by opening the eye of the heart: In the realm of love we dissolve our lust. Or is it the other way round? Five minutes later we're sitting opposite each other in the restaurant.

— The weekend in Chiswick, that's what I liked best!

Smoked ham hock and seared scallop, green mango, pecans, palm heart and avocado: In your salad you delect, delighting me.

— Chiswick? Where's that?

— Just west of Hammersmith, about twenty minutes by tube from the West End. Robert, my colleague from University College, lives there.

Soft, the scallop coral, subtle delicacy; cool heart of coconut palm, crisp and nutty: In the gentle grace of this loft-like space, we inhabit an energized calm: The scintillating dark of our kiss has given way to clarity.

— He's got a flat in a beautiful old house overlooking the Thames. There's even a rubber-sealed storm gate to stop the river when it floods.

— Sounds lovely, as long as the river doesn't rise too much.

— It does rise, but not too much. Hey, I even tried my hand at sculling!

— You did? How'd you manage?

— Oh, it was double sculls. I'll try singles next time. It's exhausting at first, until you learn to coordinate all the movements of your body.

Arcs of light intersect on the white wall behind you, open spaces beckon: Why should the candid make me green? Your silver chain-link collar maintains a tension with your blouse of chiffon: Your beauty is dynamic, not static; engaging, not excluding. Your metaphors of fucking, Marietta, were they only in my mind?

— How long did you live in London, Sprague?

— Three years.

— And what did you like best?

— The parks, the bands, the pubs; the houses and neighbourhoods. Walking in the early evening, when the first lights go on.

— I love walking too, exploring.

A little sharp, the green mango, a little sweet too: It's ripened a little.

— Do you think you could live in London, Marietta?

— Definitely! I'd love that.

Splashes of pink on your blouse prod the blues and greens: Between wild and tame the animal print wavers.

— And your research?

Yogurt, cucumber and sumac; lamb and quinoa kofta with a dressing of anchovy and olive: I relish your refined palate while your ardour whets my appetite.

— The paper's been submitted.

— What's it about?

— Oh, it's about resolving inverse problems in the study of dark matter, extracting particle physics from scattering events.

— Tell me more!

— Sprague! Do you really want to know?

Mischief and mirth animate my smile; your amber eyes sparkle: I lean forward to catch the light.

— Yes!

— Well then, listen closely: It's a story about Susy, a macho and a wimp.

My subtle mirth breaks out into frank laughter: Now it's your turn to give me a mischievous smile.

— What?

Your lips become a shimmering bud as you sip your rosé.

— Susy stands for supersymmetry.

— What's that?

— Supersymmetry is a symmetry that relates matter particles to force-exchange particles, fermions to bosons.

— Bosons?

— That's a particle that has a spin that is an integer multiple of Planck's quantum.

— I see!

There's a nutty crunch to the quinoa grain; in the lamb mince the fire of the pepper is cooled by the fresh mint.

— Now, just as matter and antimatter are linked by Dirac's equation—that's the first theory to account fully for relativity in the context of quantum mechanics—so too are matter particles and force-exchange particles related, even though they are fundamentally different components of reality.

— And what does that mean?

— That means that every type of particle would have a supersymmetric particle as a partner.

— Called a sparticle, I suppose?

— Exactly! How did you know?

— I'm a poet, and you're my Muse.

The smoked anchovy mixed with the minced lamb is delicious.

— So that's Susy, now who's the macho?

Sipping your rosé, you look at me askance. What are you preparing?

— A macho is a massive compact halo object.

— What's that?

— It could be a body about the size of Jupiter, but not big enough to become a shining star or a black hole.

— I see. And who's the wimp?

— The wimp is a weakly interacting massive particle. It's the most popular DM candidate.

— DM?

— Dark matter.

— What's that?

Sumac gives a lemony tang to the tart yogurt; the cool of the cucumber is reminiscent of melon.

— It's matter that doesn't show up at any wavelength in our telescopes. We suppose it exists because the motions of spiral galaxies, for example, show that there is more gravitational force around than the observed luminous matter can account for. As much as ninety percent of the matter present remains undetected.

— So in fact, your paper is about no less than... nothing?

– 'The void' would be a better term.

– Like in the Rig-Veda?

Jag, give me your blessing, give me a sign: I know she is the one.

– What does it say in the Rig-Veda?

– 'The non-existent was not; the existent was not. Darkness was hidden by darkness. That which became was enveloped by the void'.

– Wow! That's very up-to-date! When was it written?

– Three and a half thousand years ago.

– Impressive!

– Poets and scientists, Marietta, hand in hand. You know my name...

– ...look up my number!

I do the intro:

– Good evening and welcome to Slaggers, featuring Dennis O'Bell...

Not missing a beat, you join in:

– Good evening...

You mime the maracas and start crooning...

– You know my name... well then, look up my number...

Cracker! You've even got the Scouse!

– You know my name...

– ...that's right, look up my number...

A real la la!

– You, you know, you know my name...

– You know my name, ba-ba-ba-ba-pa-pa-pa-pa...

Your Paul to my John is perfect: Your eyes shine and I see mine in them. And yet, 'by a name I know not how to tell thee who I am'...

– So in your paper...?

– In our paper we explore the dark matter inverse problem. Namely, the capability of direct detection experiments to extract the underlying particle physics mediating the scattering of a DM particle.

The clean, red-berry zest of the rosé is no match for the way your mind dirties mine.

– And what are inverse problems?

– They're problems where you begin with a solution and try to find the equation.

– I'm equation-blind, Marietta.

– But you're a poet, and poets can see in the dark. Look, it's Plato's cave: The captives have to reconstruct the real world outside the cave on the basis of shadows cast by a fire. So they're looking for the cause (the real objects) of the effects (the shadows) of the fire (the model). That's an inverse problem.

– Sounds like one hell of a challenge!

– It is. Information is very limited, there's no unique solution, and the problem is unstable—just the challenge for me!

Luminous, your gaze lights up mine: I feel the sparkle within me. Yes, Marietta, you refuse to let number disenchant the world: You are an artist. You do not condemn the world to be its own measure: You are a magician. You know that what can be penetrated by knowledge is not being: You are the lover I've been dreaming of, ever since that day in New Delhi.

Imperfection is part of existence, the crack lets in the light: Dessert comes on asymmetrical plates, each bearing a dynamic triptych in a balanced harmony of colour: pineapple sorbet, ginger-and-citrus fruitcake, guava with coulis of passion fruit. The ginger is fiery, the lemon refreshing; the sorbet's at once sweet and savoury; the guava, the guava... Thank you, Jag!

– Marietta, I'm going to tell you about a girl I knew in Durban.

– When you were a boy?

– Yes.

– I'm all ears.

And thus I came to speak of Jagrati, which led you to tell me about Marco: Fragility, we discovered, had taken our lives along similar tangents. As our parallel loves made luminous our solicitude for each other, the bond between us took on a darker undertow. Ten minutes later, when the coffee came, the waitress's prank brought us the relief of laughter: In the foamy *latte* of our cappuccinos, well-defined in each cup, floated a perfect heart. The kitsch was easy to dismiss: The charge of the symbol resisted. If that revelation was rash, our bodies were nevertheless ripe. You took the initiative:

– Let's forget the movie, Sprague. Let's go straight to your place.

Lust is the dark matter of love—no two ways about it. We overtipped the waitress and left to retrieve the Mini on rue Mazarine.

Chapter 7

At the red light by the Pont Mirabeau, in the murmur where the crossroads meet, your eyes encounter mine. I blink and invoke the blessing of the world now centred where we stand, then to a lust exalted by solemnity I surrender: All my words dissolve into a hum, all your numbers resolve into one: This is the beginning, where the dream dreams itself.

Whose trembling gaze did our kiss veil in darkness first, whose indrawn breath did the other's touch induce? As the light turns green and you make the turn, the arc of the instant overrides the arc of my twenty-seven years.

Riding the elevator up to my apartment, we stare at our reflection in the mirror. Holding your gaze I mouth a phrase. 'What?' you mouth back. Again I silently shape the sounds; again you mouth, 'What?'. Turning around, I take you in my arms and kiss you.

– What did you say? you softly breathe.

I bring my hand to your crotch; pressing up on your pussy, I whisper:

– I said, 'You're beautiful'.

You cover my eyes with your hand; you run the tip of your tongue along my lips. And then as the ascensional force of the elevator peaks and begins to ease us to our landing, I shiver as you give me a sharp nip, your teeth hot on my lip.

– That's what I thought you said, you whisper.

I turn the key in the lock of my door, I push it open and flick the light switch: The entrance beckons, the corridor lengthens, in a rhythm of shadow and light.

– Won't you step into my parlour?

You don't catch the allusion, but the sparkle in your eyes leaves no doubt that you're a devious fly. And a teasing one too: You hesitate an instant, as if determined to find a retort. But my spider is faster than your fly: Off your feet I sweep you, and carry you across the threshold into the vestibule.

– Lock the door.

Laughing, you kick the door closed and latch it. I carry you down the corridor, up the four steps to the sleep platform, then onto the bed I heave you. My bedspread is the colour of sand dunes at sunset, your body upon it an oasis: At your lips I slake my thirst.

– Sprague, that's the *Carpet of Memory!*

— Yes.

— And that's the *Black Prince!*

— Indeed. So you know Paul Klee?

— Of course. I've often visited Bern.

You get up from the bed and place your bag on the nightstand.

— Did you paint the walls these colours?

— No. They came like that.

You put your purse beside your bag, then take off your jacket and sling it onto a chair.

— I'd never have imagined a bedroom in these colours could look so good!

— So you like it?

— Yes!

I was glad you liked the lush earth colours of the room, I was glad you liked the three walls of deep ochre set off by one in black, but most of all I was glad you liked the warm cream colour, made with ochre yellow, of the pillows and sheets.

— In Zürich, Sprague, I too have Paul Klee in my bedroom.

— You do? What a coincidence!

— Yes. A poster of *The Tightrope Walker.*

Risk: The refusal to reduce yourself to your consciousness.

— So you admire the art of the *funambule?*

— I do.

You kiss my lips.

— Now show me the rest of the apartment!

I lead you down the stairs.

— There's really only one other room.

— First the bathroom! I've got to pee.

I point you toward the entrance.

— It's on your left.

You slip off your shoes and walk down the corridor.

One upright on its heel, the other lying on its side, your gold-caged pumps compose a still-life on the floor. I sit on the stairs and contemplate them. And then it comes, the memory of that afternoon.

Your diamond-dust shoes—
Hand them down to me, big sister:

– Sprague!

– Yeah?

– Come here!

I hear the water running as I approach the bathroom.

– Come in!

I open the door and step into the room.

– This bathroom's fantastic! But what happened to the tiles?

– What do you mean?

– Well, look! The wall is all bare up there.

As you dry your hands I step up behind you and wrap my arms around your waist.

– Silly girl! That's done on purpose! The tiles were nipped with clippers to create that ragged edge.

– I see.

– Do you like it?

– Uhmmm...

You spin round in my embrace.

– Yes!

Slowly down your nose I run my fingertip; when it reaches your lips you let out a growl and snap at it.

– Ouch!

You giggle, then plant a kiss on my lips.

I was glad you liked the Shoji screens that separated the laundry area from the bathroom proper; I was glad you liked the slab of slate, hesitating between blue and green, that housed the washbasin, but most of all I was glad you liked the feel of the tiles' rough texture on the soles of your feet.

I take your hand.

– Come, I'll show you the other room.

We walk down the corridor, past the bedroom, to the kitchen-dining-living room.

– Sprague, this apartment's incredible! How'd you find it?

– I'm renting it from a friend. She's a fashion designer, has a boutique on rue de Buci. In fact, we passed it on the way to the restaurant.

– And where does she live?

– She lives with her girlfriend, on Villa Santos Dumont. Do you know it?

— No.

— It's five minutes from here. I'll take you to visit one day.

— So she's gay?

— She's bisexual. Like all women.

— How would *you* know?

— Oh, I know.

— And how did you meet her?

— We met in London. She gave a seminar at the film school. Her name's Muriel, she's American.

I was glad you liked the modular sofa elements, with their creamy leather of oyster grey; I was glad you liked the low-lying coffee table, with its smoked glass floating on transparent supports, but most of all I was glad you liked the carpet, with its red that sits at the meeting point of orange-red and brown.

— And these are your photos?

— Uh-hm.

— God this woman...

Sitting on a hardwood floor, her hair pinned up with a silver spike, a woman looks over her shoulder into the lens.

— ...she moves me! Who is she?

— Inge. A woman I knew in Toronto.

'Cancel my subscription to the resurrection.'

— Such loveliness!

I picture you on Inge's cushions, taking from her fingers the lipstick-smudged reefer she passes to you.

— And this series—the photo you gave me's from here, right?

— Yes.

— They're beautiful, Sprague. People can be so full of mystery.

— Yes. And portraits really bring that out.

— But the fact they're all in a couple brings out something particular in each person, don't you think? It's as if they're willing to reveal a secret side of themselves.

— Exactly. I see it again and again, whenever I'm out with my camera.

— And where did you take this one?

— In London, outside the Brixton Academy. They were lining up to see Lou Reed.

— The Velvet Underground?

— You remember?

— Of course. In fact, I'd first heard of the Velvets from Bowie's homage in 'Queen Bitch'.

I kiss your forehead. You add:

— That was a long time ago.

— Indeed.

— Sprague, these walls!

— Yes. Muriel's really got an eye for colour.

— I'll say! I just love the effect!

— She's really gifted. Her visual sense is stunning.

— And these paintings, are they yours or Muriel's?

— Mine. I love Manet.

— That's Manet, these flowers?

— Yes. I'll tell you their story, if you like.

— I'd love to hear it. Tell me!

I pull on the drop-waist drawstring of your chiffon blouse.

— I will, later.

I was glad you liked the colours of that room, with three of its walls a slightly milky tint, the colour of verdigris on copper, and the other crushed raspberry; I was glad you liked the floor lamp, with its white shades radiating like sails from a black column, but most of all I was glad you liked my rock 'n roll couples, and had remembered Lou Reed.

— Oh, the Barbican!

— You know it?

— Yes. It's so easy to get lost in there. It's a labyrinth!

Sitting on the sofa, you flip through *Modern Architecture*.

— Look at this one, Sprague! These triangles, circles, squares—

— That, Marietta, is one of my favorite buildings.

— Really? Why?

— Because of its solemn beauty. And because of the story behind it.

— What story? Tell me!

I caress your cheek with the back of my fingers.

— I will, later.

— No, now!

— Later!

— Now!

– All right.

I pivot my legs over the armrest and lay my head on your lap.

– Well? I'm listening.

– There was an old crow, sat upon a clod. That's the end of the story, thank God. Now kiss me!

– Close your eyes.

It comes, the silk of your hair, caressing my skin, making me aspire to knowing. And then with your hair you whip me.

– I want to know the story *(swish, swish, swish!)* of that building *(swish, swish, swish!)* so tell it to me *(swish!)* now!

– All right, Marietta, I will.

I sit up and reach for a book on the coffee table.

– Look, here's a whole book on that building.

You lean your body against mine.

– In fact, it's a series of buildings, covering almost a thousand acres, that make up the capital complex of Dhaka.

– India?

– No, Bangladesh.

– It's amazing!

– The architect was Louis Kahn, a man who found that you cannot depend on human relationships, that work is the only thing you can count on.

– So he worked himself to death!

My hand on the page was empty: Your words have filled it with ash. Not the ash of those who've worked themselves to death, but the ash of the dead in a plane crash.

– Maybe. He was found dead at Penn Station in New York City, dead of a heart attack. He'd just returned from Dhaka.

– Hmmm...

– It took the police three days to identify him, because he'd erased his address from his passport. Maybe he didn't know where his home was anymore.

– Who was he, this Louis Kahn? I mean—

– He was a flawed genius, the kind of person I'm attracted to. I don't like perfection.

And thus I told you the story of this magnificent architect, of the ache that living procured him, of his family secrets and crumpled suits. As we flipped through the book, examining the buildings, I pointed out the slits and chutes, the arches and skylights, that let the light in; the artificial lake that accentuates the verticality of the Hall and keeps the land from flooding; the deep geometric cutouts—the triangles, circles and squares you'd noticed—that protect the windows and provide shelter from the rain.

– It really is beautiful, Sprague...

Soft, soft, your fingertips caress my cheek, letting me know you've made the connection with Jagrati.

– ...so complex and yet so simple.

– Yes. And it was all built by hand. Look, thousands of workers, each carrying a basket of cement on their head, climbing up and down bamboo scaffolding.

– Amazing!

– You see this joint?

– Yes.

– It's a recessed joint, six inches high, and recurs every five feet. Kahn had determined that five feet was the tallest practical dimension for one day's work: That became the standard vertical unit of the whole building.

– Interesting.

Laying your head on my shoulder, you ask me:

– How did you become so interested in architecture?

– Toronto City Hall. It's so beautiful, so well-conceived. And then there's philosophy.

You raise your head.

– Philosophy?

– Yes. Architects are philosophers. At least the best ones are. They have an integrated vision of all the parameters of human experience their buildings must express.

– Yes, I imagine they would have to.

– And because of that, architecture changes our perception of the world, our picture of reality, and with it, reality itself.

– But that applies to all art, wouldn't you say?

– Yes. But architecture does it at the same time as it creates something useful and enduring. It touches thousands, even millions of people.

– And you, would you like to touch thousands, even millions of people?

– No. Just one: You!

You close the book on my lap and toss it onto the coffee table. Ay-up! In a flash you're sitting astride me, pinning my shoulders to the backrest, driving my head over the edge. You press your mouth to mine: Architecture only begins once all the functions have been fulfilled. And then you deepen your teaching: As your hands hold my head, your tongue drives home the lesson: It is constraint that enables freedom.

– Carry me to your bed!
A man in my shoes carries you, for in my heart I'm already in heaven.

Chapter 8

— Open your eyes, Sprague!

In cups of dusky lilac tied together with ribbon, the spheres of your breasts proclaim their sovereignty.

— Pull on the bow!

A tug on the ribbon and they extend their dominion, holding sway as their vestment falls. As you lean forward the fullness of your offering flows; all my desire comes to a point on the sugary pink of your nipples. As I make to sit up you lean back, flaunting your regal splendour.

Lovingly now you teach me the language of your lips: Locative, subjective, possessive; dative, elative, oblique: In a trice I've deciphered the grammar of your kisses, in a trice I translate your tongue in my mouth: We are dreaming the same dream. Now caress me with your verbs and adverbs, transport me with your syntax; anchor me with your Anglo-Saxon, tease me with your Latin: Speak to me until the silence in me sings!

I move to continue: You stop me. What's the matter, Marietta? Come on, we're still imprisoned in our pants! Valiant in your ambivalence, you subdue the trouble in your eyes: In the restlessness of your regard it lingers. Astride your thighs I sit and reach for the buckle of your belt. With a flick of the wrist I tug loose the prong; your jeans I unbutton and pull down. I free you to peddle your legs out of your jeans; on the floor I stand and unbuckle my belt.

— No, Let me do it!

I feel your breath on my neck as you unbutton my pants; I feel the heat of your fingers as you unzip my fly. The horizon lurches, I close my eyes: An abyss opens. Naked, I feel the press of your nipples against my shoulder blades, I feel them pressing an instant out of the continuum.

Oh quintessence of delicacy, oh flawless undertow of friction! So this is the finesse of excess, this is the ecstatic tension! In the pit of my stomach, in the ligaments of my knees, yea, down to my very toes, I feel your fingery touch of talcum dust, your thumb-and-index 'O'; your spit-and-polish brush-up, your palm-to-palm cigar roll. But why this headlong rush, Marietta, why this *fuite en avant?* Shall I let you—? No! I will not let you reach my primal memory, I will not let you redeem the past so cheaply! Oiling the machine, feathering the trigger, you are intent on returning me to chaos: Shall I let you—? No! I spin around: You trip me onto the bed. On the rebound I pull you down, roll you over and pin you back. Marietta, is that the sparkle of daring in your eyes or a veil for the research of the shy? Gripping your wrists in one hand and holding them down above your head, I slip the other between your legs: Lush is the mooring place of magic, succulent the fruit of knowledge. Silk slides down your lissom legs as I pull off your panties. Look! In my eyes can you see the majesty between your thighs, can you feel your sublime presence? More real than you or I, out of the ominous it distils the numinous.

You sit up and make to undo your chain-link collar.

— No, keep it on!

Flattered by the lamplight, your breasts flaunt their self-sufficiency, but in the amber of your eyes there is only vulnerability. I follow your movement as you fall back onto the pillow; alas, your body is on the lam. What's the matter? Would it be better if you played a role? All right, be my moll, I'll play it hardboiled.

— What's up, babe? A moment ago you were burning powder, a private dick on a confidential lay. Now you're a nervous chick, hesitating, her gams getaway sticks.

— The jewels, the jewels, where are the jewels?

— You're a looker, babe, you don't need no oyster fruit or ice. Fill me with daylight, go back to being the high pillow!

From across the centuries it comes, quickening our spinal marrow, the force that brings my mouth to yours, yours to mine, in a combat of ravenous kisses.

Now what's the matter? Come on, honour the night! Valiant in your ambivalence, you subdue the trouble in your eyes: In the restlessness of your regard it lingers. All right. Let's try another idiom. How about geometry? Rotational surfaces are generated by rotating a plane curve about an axis: Cupping your carnality in my hands, in a circular motion I gather and release your breasts. A sphere is a solid, generated by the revolution of a semicircle about its diameter, whose surface is at all points equidistant from the centre: My spiralling tongue delineates the form that embodies perfection; sealed around the growing projection, my lips find stability in flux. And thus, thanks to geometry, I discover your cosmology: The swift orbit of the fixed stars, the leisurely round of the inner bodies; the motions and places of earth, wind, fire and water; the circular movement of the fifth element. But don't think I'm after the Big Fuck in the Sky, Marietta: I'm not. All I want is to feel you inhabiting your body as you receive me inside it.

You slip your hand between your legs, with your elixir you mark my mouth: Let's have a marine metaphor, an idiom from the Age of Discovery! Armed with a wind chart of the world, with your tongue you trace our itinerary on the velum of my abdomen: Cape of Good Hope to Mombasa, Mombasa to Malabar; Malabar to Malacca, across the Bay of Bengal. Captive on your caravel, the perfumes of your spice-box going to my head, I submit to your ministrations as you lie with your head between my legs. Ay-up! In full sail we set out.

And already we're in Mombasa, a large city seated upon an eminence washed by the sea. At its entrance stands a pillar, and by the sea a low-lying fortress. As a gesture of goodwill, the King of Mombasa sends us large quantities of oranges, lemons and sugar, together with a ring. I tell you Marietta, here the vegetation is like that of Andalucia in April; the singing of little birds is such that I could never wish to leave this place. Flocks of parrots darken the sun; there are fruits of a thousand kinds, and every one of them delicious! It's confuted, then, the opinion of philosophers who assert that no one can live in the Torrid Zone: Our voyage proves them wrong.

Now the wind blows with a sweet and gentle mildness; we weigh anchor and set sail, steering north-northeast. Shifting winds pick up speed; with a turn of the wheel you tack to catch them. Readying our vessel for any manoeuvre, you trim the lateen as the square sail billows.

In Calicut we negotiate, in Cochin we barter, and soon our hold is chock-a-block with the fruits of our art. Sea breezes ease us back into the ocean; favourable winds keep us on course.

How fleetly she moves, our caravel, how proudly she plies the sea! Deep down extends her hull, high above the waterline her deck rises. And what has she in her hold? Beledi ginger and black pepper, turmeric and nutmeg; cinnamon, cloves and cardamom; aloe-wood, dye-wood, coarse camphor in loaves; pearls, virgin gold, and stones of emerald and amethyst (one very hard, a full span in length and two fingers thick).

At last we reach Malacca. There you find refreshment in the coconut palm, delighting in the clear water it contains. And then from a hole in the heart of the palm, at the top called the 'palmito', you slake your thirst with a liquor which resembles white must, the newly pressed juice of fruit ready for fermentation.

And thus, Marietta, in the pleasure you gave me you took shelter: a clever subterfuge. But from what did you need to shield yourself? That is what I want to know. Must I be patient? Or on the contrary, must I not wait? This alone is certain: I want to meet you in that place you cannot master: My rapture under your command has only made my determination to do so more steely.

Chapter 9

– I like this music, Sprague. It's lovely.

Airy, the melodic lines and limpid harmonies of the *Gnossiennes* fill the room: The grave simplicity of Eric Satie animates our encounter.

– It is.

Legs flexed, our backs against opposite armrests, we sit sideways on the sofa, facing each other. In your black kimono—stylized cherry blossoms falling from your shoulder in blends of pink, white and green—you beguile me with your beauty as you concentrate the calm.

– The mystery of melody! Who would have thought such a cranky guy could come up with such loveliness?

– Indeed.

I'm happy here with you, Marietta, on this dry road to enlightenment. So let us use this empty space for our meditations; into this garden of sand and stone, let your ephemeral petals fall.

– It's magical!

– Yes.

The undulations on the surface of the sand, what deep-down movements do they betray? We know the world cannot be perceived in its entirety, we know that what we cannot see we must find within ourselves. So let us depict the world in evanescent outline, let us introduce openness into the circle: Between what is given and what is withheld, let us endeavour to restore the link.

– It's so slow, so deliberate.

– There's a theory about that.

Opalescent translucence, glistening cloudiness: You sip your Cointreau tonic. I continue:

– Satie composed his music in his head, walking home from work. They say it's those long walks, from the cabaret in Montmartre to his room in Arcueil, that accounts for that slow, deliberate quality.

– Hmmm. Interesting.

Dissonance undermines harmonic movement in the spare melodic lines; the simplicity and charm of the 'Airs à faire fuire' bring us closer to each other.

– Sprague, tell me now about Manet's bouquets.

Pungent lemon, bitter orange: I sip my Cointreau.

– Come on, tell me.

You extend a leg and rub my shin with your foot.

— All right, Marietta.

Closing the curtain of your kimono, you draw your knees up to your chin.

— Are you ready? I ask you.

— Yes.

— I'm ready to ravish you!

— Be patient. We've got all night.

You are alert, poised, ready to receive: I must not disappoint your eager expectation.

— Okay. Listen. It's the last year of Manet's life. He's fifty-one, and he's in the terminal stage of syphilis. The lightning pains in his legs are excruciating; on the soles of his feet, the ulcers won't heal—walking is all but impossible. He spends the summer at a rented house in Rueil-Malmaison. In September he returns to Paris to write his last will and testament. He leaves everything to his wife Suzanne and son Léon.

— Suzanne? Wasn't she a painter too?

— No. You must be thinking of Suzanne Valadon. She was the love of Satie's life—until he pushed her out a window and decided love is a sickness of the nerves, something best to avoid.

— I agree with him on that! Did she die, Suzanne Valadon?

— No, she had been a trapeze artist: She knew how to fall.

Would I know how to fall?

— Anyway, Manet's Suzanne was a Dutch woman, a dull person by all accounts, who'd been a piano teacher to Manet and his brothers. When Manet was nineteen they began sleeping together, and a few days after his twentieth birthday Suzanne gave birth to a son.

— Hmmm...

— Suzanne, having left and returned, passed her son off as her brother—all her life she maintained this lie—and Manet became the child's godfather. He thus had a secret family, which he set up in a little apartment.

— Like Louis Kahn!

Did not my mother have a secret family too?

— Exactly. Twelve years later, after Manet's father died, the couple got married in Holland. Have you heard of Berthe Morisot?

— Yes. She was a painter, an Impressionist.

— That's right. Well, Berthe loved Manet all her life. Unable to marry him, she married his brother. All Manet's portraits of her speak of this love.

— Hmmm...

— Have you seen any of them?

– Yes. I remember one where she's all in black, holding a bunch of violets.

– That painting's pure poetry! It's a definition of the feminine.

– She is lovely, yes.

In the only photo I have of Jag, she is holding a bunch of violets.

– But to get back to the flowers—Have you seen *A Bar at the Folies Bergères?*

– Yes. I saw it last year in London.

– That's Manet's last major painting. Do you like it?

– Very much. It's so... mysterious.

– Yes. When you look at it, you become indistinguishable from what you're looking at. And what you don't see is as important as what you do.

– Like in *Olympia*.

Flesh and blood infused with ice and fire: The self-possessed cannot be possessed.

– Yes. Well, after painting that masterpiece, Manet had less than a year to live. In the last months of his life, before the attacks of fulgurating pain and the fever started, leading to the amputation of his gangrenous leg, he would lie on the divan in his studio, reading. When he could sit up he would paint. And what he painted are these bouquets.

I get up and give you my hand.

– Come, let's take a closer look.

Pinks and Clematis in a Crystal Vase; Roses, Carnations and Pansies: The first two paintings in the linear arrangement offer us the purity of their presence—fluid, spontaneous, direct, they are paint made flower, word made flesh.

– Satie's music goes perfectly with these paintings.

– It does, yes.

The modal harmonies and lilting melodies of *Gymnopédies* do indeed echo the silence of Manet's bouquets.

– So, Manet's holed up in his studio, unable to stand up, and a woman comes to visit and presents him with a bouquet. Maybe even before she leaves, Manet's begun painting it. It's an act of love, a way to feel alive.

Roses and Lilacs and *Lilacs in a Glass* show us that as Manet approaches death, his brush has indeed never been more alive, responsive, engaged.

– They're really lovely!

– Yes. Now think of Manet's private life. He's married to a plodding woman he doesn't love, and the woman he could have been happy with is married to his brother. As for his child, nobody recognizes Manet and Léon as father and son, not even Manet and Léon themselves.

Is there not a similar story in my mother's family?

– But what does that have to do with these flowers, Sprague?

– Well, these flowers are the expression of grace. They show that no matter what the personal failure, no matter what the professional success, when death comes—and death is always coming—

– Even now, as we speak?

Taking you in my arms, I shut your mouth with a kiss.

– When death comes, these flowers show that the only thing that counts are little acts of kindness. And the kindness that meant the most to Manet was the kindness of women.

– Hmmm...

We head back to the sofa.

– Next time you look at Manet's paintings of women, notice how each woman is individualized, often strikingly so. Each has a strong personal identity.

You sit down beside me.

– I've noticed that. His women are self-aware, they have a life of their own.

– Yes, self-reliant. And that's very rare—you hardly find it in representations of women by Manet's contemporaries.

You pick up your Cointreau tonic...

– So there you have it, Marietta, that's the story of these bouquets. They're emblems of vulnerability, of courage and kindness.

...and drink up the little that's left.

– Another, Sprague, fix me another!

As you hold out your glass, the sparkle in your eyes is a promise: Of what, I don't know, but I do know it will be exciting.

Drinks in hand, I step back into the living room and stop dead in my tracks: In negligent folds your kimono flows, spilling its black onto the red of the carpet; upon the carpet, a tumbled vortex bowl scatters mandarins and avocados. Behind it you sit naked, an elbow resting on your knee, a hand holding your chin. Between thigh and arm your breast stands bold; only your unframed face (you've pinned up your hair), illuminated by the unflinching eyes fixing me, violates the profile of your body. I put down the drinks and align my body opposite yours on the floor. Your foot between my legs, I lean back and take up a lounging, lifted-arm pose. Holding it isn't easy; relieving me, you spring forward and pin me to the floor, laughing. I press your nakedness to my vestments; I pull the stick out of your hair.

– Was I a good *Déjeuner?*

– As good as Victorine! And worthy of Manet.

As you shake loose your hair, I determine to be worthy of him too.

Chapter 10

Lunar, watery, cold, the light of your chain-link collar is the flame of my votive candle: Let my body no longer belong to me, let it become pure intelligence of you. Their diurnal coordinates now disappeared, the fiery suns of your eyes flicker as you lie stretched out on the carpet, your body luminous against the red. What dreams are drunk from your eyes, Marietta, dreams that demonstrate the earth cannot escape the sky! Look! Your feet are silver fishes, placid in black water; your legs are rivers of moonlight, fecundating a valley. Your belly is a white plain that stretches to a rippling talus; your breasts are domal mounds, surmounted by sugary peaks. Your face, an icon lit by candlelight; your throat, the underbelly of a garden frog. Your hair is the handiwork of a spider, rainwater dripping from rocks; your hands are dendrites of silver, perpetually recalescent. Divine essence, the activating joint—these are your elbows; snow melt, mountain streams—these are your arms. Delicately my hands do what honours them, deftly my fingers venerate your flesh. So why this guardedness in your candour, why this *trompe l'oeil* in your eyes? You roll your body onto mine, you take my hands in yours; as your tongue travels along my lips, I voyage along the edge of your thoughts, seeking a way in. Marietta, your body is movement, time, fluidity and flow; its doorways, passages and bridges I want to know: I firmly believe in the activating power of architecture!

From the inside of the elbow to the armpit, the collared throat to the clavicle, your skin comes to life in the slipstream of my lips: Architecture acts as a catalyst, reinforcing memory and making it come alive. Round and round, gathered, dispersed and gathered again, your breasts under my hands circulate their beneficence. Salient in the seal of my lips, your nipple infuses my spirit: 'All architecture is an expression of homesickness'.

A flapping of butterflies in your belly flusters your hands in my hair; a premonition of emotion provokes an inrush of breath. I caress your cheek and kiss your forehead; in your eyes, losing your nerve vies with holding fast. And then you take your courage in both hands and kiss me: 'How can we learn through architecture, handle complexity and ambivalence?'

I bring a massaging palm to the plain of your belly, then my fingers to the valley below. You spread your legs.

> In the normal situation where a wall is used to define and enclose a space, the entrance is accommodated by an opening in the plane of the wall. The form of the opening, however, can range from a simple hole to an elaborate, articulated gateway.

A pathway of kisses along the inside of your thighs leads me to an arbour: Trellised vines neatly trimmed frame a sunken bower; from out of the dewy shade comes the resplendence of the rose. Dark and cool, compounded of the dawn and sunset, an enfilade of petals draws my gaze into a vortex: At my look alone, you quiver.

> Entering a building involves the act of penetrating a vertical plane that distinguishes one space from another and separates 'here' from 'there': You can only experience architecture if you move through it, if you see it as something open that you keep going back to.

Quickening to gold, your amber eyes glisten as identity confronts desire; yielding, resisting, yielding again, your body imparts the tempo as I plumb your depths. Still you're brittled by nervousness, you're in a state of tension. Why can't you enter the labyrinth without a ball of thread? Haven't you learned that architecture refers to whatever there is in an edifice that cannot be reduced to building? Relax, let me show you: Through the galleries of your self-construction I drive my desire, searching for the horizon of your release. Lingering in a belvedere, I gaze into the arcades of your eyes: a tourbillon of rustling leaves, an errant dog rambling. And there, look: A woman crouched beside a pillar, seeking relief from the sun.

> When located within a defined volume of space, a column will generate a spatial field about itself and interact with the spatial enclosure: As space begins to be captured, enclosed, moulded and organized by the elements of mass, architecture comes into being.

A corridor, a loggia, and again the arcades of your eyes: The louvres of the brise-soleil are broken. I kiss your eyes and the vanishing points multiply: Now how shall I find the perspective of your pleasure, the horizon of your release? In the hearth of your inwardness I kindle a fire; with Saxon syllables I fan the flames.

I want my buildings to be both alien and assimilated, both apart and belonging: I don't believe in a sane, straightforward world and can't build one either.

I'm not innocent.
I know sex is not a natural act.
I know natural acts are not human.

I'm not innocent.
I know only the possessed can be dispossessed.
I know only the dispossessed achieve self-possession.

I'm not innocent.
I know only outlaws have to be honest.
I know the law-abiding can cheat with impunity.

I'm not innocent.
I know where to fetch a pail of water.
I know Dame Dob, her vinegar and brown paper.

I'm not innocent.
I'm neither shining knight nor big bad wolf.
But for you I'll wear armour, I'll howl at the moon.

'Wisdom is cold, you can no more use it for setting your life to rights than you can forge iron when it is cold': In the heat of your hearth I burn my wisdom until spirit overwhelms my flesh: Like wind through a burning building, it howls through your halls. No waves of rhythmic tensing unwall my horizon; despite the fire, you fail to be consumed.

Marietta, every symptom is an attempt at self-cure, every psyche a singularity: I want to know you—do you want to know me? Then let us burn, burn, burn! Architecture is frozen music, fire will make it sing; let us burn again: We lack not for kindling!

Chapter 11

Tango, tragedia, comedia, kilombo! Opening in a bordello, 'Tanguedia III' opens *Tango: Zero Hour,* Astor Piazzolla's magnificent new album. Echoing the whorehouse cant, ice cubes crackle as you pour Cinzano into a glass.

– So, mixed or straight?

– Mixed, please.

Your body in black, blazed with cherry blossoms, is a magnet for mine as you reach up—insteps arched, hair flowing—to get a glass: I step up behind you and wrap my arms around your waist.

Tenderness and starlight go well together,
As do distance and stars;
Memory and ruins go well together,
As do forgetfulness and floods.

I remember the flood, the abortion
That was my birth. I tend to forget
The ruins. I remember distances,
But tend to forget the stars.

Am I the frog in your velvet drawer, Marietta,
Or am I your dog? Am I your prince-to-be,
Or your hound from hell?
Tell me, just what are you doing with me?

I will be what you want me to be,
Frog prince or hellhound;
However vast the night in your eyes,
I will fill it with light from mine.

Through your hair, to the nape of your neck, my mouth weaves its way; there, in that secret glade where Indian summer holds sway, my lips begin to graze. Giggling, you shrink into my arms and caress the back of my hands.

– Oh Sprague, this music makes me homesick!

– It does? Why?

Pine tar and damp vegetation, cinnamon, cloves and gentian: Your scent signs your signature.

— I play tango, with a band in Zürich.

— Really?

— Yes. We play in bars and clubs.

— I'd love to hear you!

— You will, one day. Cheers!

Upon those words the fragrant chill of the vermouth becomes a thrill; we step into the living room and fall silent on the sofa, listening to the music.

'Tanguedia III' is enthralling; its insinuating rhythms stop and go, shifting tempo. At times every instrument in the quintet becomes percussive, until the slow-burning fire bursts into a full-blown conflagration.

— Is tango very different from classical music, Marietta? To play, I mean.

— Oh yes, and it's not just a question of technique. It's more about attitude. The passion, the feel, the rhythmic drive—tango's got a whole culture behind it, a fierce pride.

Neuchâtel is a world away from Romani ritual: How did you acquire that fierce pride and passion, that fire that branded 'Tzigane' in my heart? I'm sure you're just as convincing in the idiom of Buenos Aires low-life.

— You hear that slow, descending line, the minor key? you ask.

— Yes.

— That's the *milonga* pattern. It comes from song. Compare it to the first piece, and you clearly hear the two extremes of tango: very strict, driving rhythm, and extremely romantic music.

— That's a compelling combination!

— Yes, and it's not just across pieces, but in every piece! That's tango, that blending of extremes. So when you play it, you've got to think more vertically, in terms of rhythms and chords, and not just horizontally, as melody, like in classical music.

Dark and brooding, 'Milonga del Angel' distills its *tristeza*.

— You hear the violin there? Those long, *détaché* strokes? It's imitating the bandoneon, its elongated lines.

— That's right!

— You hear that emulation in other ways too. For example, when the bandoneon player, after pulling out his arms...

I feel my smile mimicking the gesture you're miming.

— ...pushes in to play the first phrase, you get a huge rhythmic pulse towards the first note. Well, on the violin, you use bow speed to get that effect, on the point of the beat.

— Interesting, that kind of transposition.

— Yes. That's part of the bag of tricks, to sound like a real *tanguera*.

Second-seers have yellow eyes, all the better to see in the dark: As you sip your drink, the pale cool of the Bianco turns into a flow of molten gold. Gathering unto itself the grace hovering between us, your face retrieves its tranquillity while around your glass your fingers cool their virtuosity. When did your hand and eye first give you the feeling you could master the world, Marietta? Do you remember the first time you buttoned your blouse or tied your shoelaces? Were you precocious? Maybe already in your highchair you could bring a spoonful of compote to your mouth without missing it?

— Sprague, what were you like as a boy?

A mirror to my meditations, your question strikes me dumb.

— Do tell me.

— What was I like as a boy? I don't remember.

— Come on, you can't have forgotten everything!

— Yes, but—

— Show me some photos! That will help you remember.

— Photos?

— Yes, of when you were a child. Do you have any?

— I do, yes.

— I'd love to see them. Come on, show me!

— All right.

On a vast expanse of sandy beach, a boy, eight or nine, stands with his mother. Against a washed-out sky the sea is but a faint line on the horizon; breakers form a bolder line, the rest is emptiness.

— Oh Sprague, how skinny you were! But perfectly recognizable. And your mother, how pale she is!

— Yes.

— Where was this taken?

— In South Africa, near where we lived. East London.

— The beach is beautiful.

The politics of beaches—how could I explain the hollow it left in my heart? And how could I make you see the meaning of how my mother held me, not by the hand, but by the wrist?

— Oh, what a photo!

— That's Margaret, my older sister.

In black and white, against a wall, she stands holding a doll in her left hand while pressing her right between her legs.

– The pleasure of holding in your pee!

– Indeed.

– How many brothers and sisters do you have, Sprague?

– Four sisters, no brothers. And you?

– I don't have any. I'm an only child.

– Were you lonely?

– Sometimes. And you, being the only boy?

– I was lonely.

– But you had a such a big family!

– Still.

How could I convince you of the reality of solitude in a family of seven? Would you believe that absence can have such a lasting presence?

– And this must be your grandmother?

– Yes.

– Very elegant! On your father's side or your mother's?

– My father's. I only met my maternal grandmother once.

– What a jacket! Very chic.

My grandmothers—how I wish I could make you understand what they meant to me! When she held me in her arms, my mother's mother, I knew for the first time what it is to be touched. We spent but one afternoon together, yet I'll never forget her. To be grounded in my body, to feel that I really exist, to experience that for the first time. And as for Granny, my father's mother that you're admiring...

– With God's richest blessings.

– What?

– With God's richest blessings. That's how she used to sign off the birthday cards she'd give me.

– It's a nice phrase.

– Yes, I like the sound of it.

– Was she born in South Africa?

– Yes.

– And her parents?

– I don't know. It depends who you ask. You never get the same answer. And the same goes for everyone in my family, when it comes to their background.

— That's strange.

— Cape Town was a crossroads. Sailors come and go.

— Yes, of course.

— And then, across the country, you had young men from the old world seeking to find their fortunes in the new. Or simply to escape their past.

— Yes.

— Most likely her father was from La Coruña, in Galicia.

— So you've got Spanish blood?

— Perhaps. And her mother—I remember her portrait on the wall—was a midwife, said to be from Portugal.

— She seems very proud, your grandmother, very patrician.

— Yes, patrician, with the fierce pride of the gypsy!

— Bury me standing!

— Exactly.

And I, who defended the Polish boy, why couldn't I defend myself?

Hands cupped around heart,
Protecting the inner flame:
Could fists have done the same?

— She got kicked by a donkey when she was a child. Lost all her language. Had to start all over again, from scratch.

— Wow!

— And then at sixteen she married a man twice her age. Had four children in quick succession. She was very active, always busy—when she wasn't dying from asthma.

— Hmmm...

— And she was the only one in the family—at least the only one I knew—who was white. She had access to both worlds.

— The only one *you knew?*

— Yes, because my mother's father was Irish, or Dutch, my mother doesn't know. He disappeared before she was born.

— I see.

Blood of the impure:
Everywhere an alien
At home nowhere

— I'd go with her to the white cinemas. I remember we saw *A Hard Day's Night* together. She loved the movie as much as I did! And afterwards, she could sing 'If I Fell' note perfect!

— 'If I Fell'?

— 'If I fell in love with you, would you promise to be true, and help me understand?'

— Ah, yes.

— And when she came on her last visit to Canada—she was past-half-way deaf—I'd turn up the volume on *Station to Station* for her—she loved Bowie's version of 'Wild is the Wind'!

— She was hip!

— She was warm, spontaneous, open-minded—everything my parents were not. Had no prejudice of any kind. I liked that. It was so rare. With her blue, blue eyes, she'd look me in the eye.

Transparent zombie
Nobody sees you: Except
The loving ancients

— I can see why you loved her. What was her name?

I sing:

Sometimes I live in the country,
Sometimes I live in town;
Sometimes I take a great notion
To jump in the river and drown.

— Irene—I like that name. And your mother's mother, what was her name?

— Florence.

— The lady with the lamp!

— Yes.

I'd have loved her midnight rounds, I'd have loved listening to her stories while staring at the night sky. It was not to be.

You pick out another photo.

— That's in Irene's kitchen.

— What are you eating?

— Apple fritters. She would make them when I'd visit. Once, for my birthday, she made me a huge cake in the form of an ocean liner, covered in white icing, with liquorice for the chimney stacks and Smarties for the portholes.

– You see, you *do* remember your childhood!

– I remember because you're with me.

In a circle
Of unbroken prayer
I whirl: You bless me.

– Very handsome! Your grandfather?

– Yes. Just after he married Irene.

– A real aristocrat. I see now where you got your good looks!

– You talkin' about me, babe?

– Uh-hm. But you don't look nearly as Indian.

– He's whole Indian. My Dad's half, I'm a quarter.

– And you're a quarter Irish.

– Or Dutch.

– And you're one-eighth Portuguese.

– Yes.

– And another eighth Spanish.

– Could be.

– And the last quarter?

– English and African—Xhosa, probably.

– You're a walking United Nations!

Blood of the impure:
Can one who does not belong
Be loved? Turn the page.

– And you? What's your background?

– My father's French-Italian, my mother Danish-German.

Thoroughbred beauty:
In your fearful symmetry
Blake's tiger abides

– Your Dad?

– Yes.

– He looks Indian all right!

– Yes.

— And this is definitely Africa.

In a clearing in the scrub, the rolling veldt rising behind him, my father sits low in his white lab coat, a naked child in each arm. One of them is a boy with a bloated belly. Behind him, to his left, a young girl stands holding a baby.

— He had an office near the house—a surgery—but once or twice a week he'd go out to treat the Africans, for free.

He had gentle hands, my father, but his touch was not enough for me. But it did make being sick less miserable: I could have told you that, but I didn't.

— Did you ever think of becoming a doctor yourself?

— Never. I was too busy trying to become a human being.

— And just what do you mean by that?

— Sometimes when I think of what I've been through, I can't believe I'm still alive.

— What happened?

— I was buried alive.

— Sprague!

— It's been very hard, clawing my way back to the surface.

— What are you talking about?

— One day, if ever you love me a little, I'll tell you.

— Sprague, you're frightening me!

— Sorry.

— No, I mean...

— What?

— Your face, your voice—you're not kidding.

— No, I'm not. I know what it is to be dead, Marietta.

— Sprague!

— Am I frightening you?

— No, but...

— What?

— Just give me some idea what you're talking about.

Paralyzed, frozen,
Numb: To the last redoubt
I retreated, dumb

— I told you: One day, if ever—

— Okay, but give me a little clue now!

– All right. I was eleven when we took a ship to Canada. No one ever told me why we're leaving, where we're going. I had no idea why we were on the boat.

– But that's impossible! Your parents must have told you.

– If they did, I didn't get it. It didn't register.

– You could have asked your sisters.

– I have no memory of them even being on the boat! All I remember is feeling totally lost, with no idea of what's going on.

– My God!

– And when we arrived at last, in Toronto, the daily torture started.

– Sprague!

– Outside the house I was a target. Inside, I was invisible. I don't know which was worse.

Wild, your eyes drill into me.

– My mind was a kite in a windstorm. My heart the ball of string. Or maybe it was the other way around.

– What do you mean?

– Only when the kite was grounded did I feel no pain. I became a zombie. Every day I was stoned.

– Drugs?

– No. Violence. Cruelty. Humiliation.

Here it comes, the old pain, just like I knew it would.

– Sprague!

You toss the photos onto the table and leap into my lap. From the ancient well, from the wound that won't heal, my tears come.

– Listen, Sprague, listen to the music!

You kiss my eyes.

– Tango is like the blues.

I don't want you to see me like this. Certainly not now.

– It's an investigation…

You kiss my cheeks.

– …of human relationships…

You lap up my tears with your tongue.

– …of what it means to be human…

You wipe my face with your hair.

– …in a world that is lonely.

I get a grip on myself, and then I start crying again.

– Oh Sprague!

Enough! The horror
Of being incomprehensible:
Love me till I'm intelligible

With loving kindness your lips flutter along my face, a butterfly foraging grace from affliction.

Sister of mercy,
See beyond my tears: See into
The wasteland inside me

Pine tar and damp vegetation, cinnamon, cloves and gentian: Your scent is an antidote to my sorrow. Starbright! Like a bee into a peony you slip your tongue into my mouth.

By what miracle
Have you come into my life?
Resuscitation

My fingers ride the silk route of your spine; in the lustrous thicket of your hair they harvest the bombycin fleece.

– Listen: You hear how the violin alternates between playing the melody and providing percussive background?

– That's a violin, that plucking?

– Yes.

You rise onto your knees: I pull you back down.

Lady, do not rise
Till Lazarus has bestowed
His blessing: A kiss

'Milonga Loca' is utterly beguiling.

– He's playing pizzicato with the right hand while touching the side of the string with the second fingernail of his left hand. That's what creates that metallic sound.

You slip out of my embrace and sit sideways on the sofa.

– It's exhausting, playing tango.

I turn to face you.

– Every single note has to have life in it, be given its proper weight. Otherwise it falls flat, it's not tango.

Like rock: Without roll, it's flat.

– You need forceful, driving rhythm together with elegance, always. From parking your car to pinning up your hair, everything you do is done with elegance.

– Of course, Piazzolla's music is much more sophisticated than ordinary tango. Jazz, classical, contemporary—it's all in the mix.

– Yes. Now let's dirty it up, Marietta. Let's take tango back to the bordello! Ruthless is your beauty as you stare into my eyes; ruthless, without compromise.

– All right. Let's.

Chapter 12

Schlack! Flat on my back you send me with a kick from the hip, the ball of your foot leaving a ringing impact between my pectorals. Springing forward, you lay your body on mine, seize my hands and press them into the supple leather of the sofa. Against my resistance your muscles tense; with teasing kisses you stifle my laughter. Hush! Silk upon silken skin, through the fibres of my being you thread the inner flux. How do you do it, Marietta? How do you give weight to the floating world, yet keep it floating? Rising to your knees, you gather up your kimono and lower yourself astride my loins.

Geisha, geisha, matted ground: I had dreamt you in a *Hello Kitty* T-shirt, a wide-eyed Lolita reading the latest manga; I had dreamt you a sassy *shojo,* ironic and androgyne, but it's enrobed in the wisdom of a geisha that you greet me: Under your folds of silk, connecting me to the ceaseless turmoil that keeps the world in motion, you grasp me with your herring roe, bathe me in your earthworm bowl.

Geisha, geisha, white upon white: Your face warns me I shall never possess you, yet how limpid, subtle and refined is your desire to be possessed! Crenulated folds and suction cups, an eddy of writhing eels: At the bidding of your pussy I abandon my epistemic axioms and formulate my new-found truth: I am I because I am in you.

Geisha, geisha, stone garden: Is my indestructible double among these fragments of the divine? If so, what memory of my passage on Earth will it preserve? That a wanderer encountered a girl who concentrated and expanded his being? That one set apart—sanctified and cursed—found between her legs a place of rebirth?

Geisha, geisha, round and round: Rotating your pelvis as you rise and fall, you coax my ardour into every undulation, every zone of sensation, of your interior. So this is the pivot of the norm, this is the changeless mean: Uprooted from the world's turbulence, I hold the flow from above.

Sakura, sakura, teach us to die, teach us to die like you: Not to fade away, but in the very instant of perfection, return to the undifferentiated: As you court unconsciousness, your eyelids droop, your murmur becomes a moan. No! Just when you're about to break into a scream, you cut your blood-breath and forbid the crossing. Why? What are you afraid of?

> Stars don't cry scandal:
> At the approach of the Bright One,
> They willingly efface themselves.
>
> Petals don't cling to the rose:
> To primeval matter they revert
> When the last bee leaves.
>
> Rivers don't suddenly reverse:
> At a wave from the nether world,
> They rush to their rebirth.
>
> So why, Marietta, when chaos
> Comes for your spirit,
> Do you refuse to surrender it?

As you lie upon me, I glide my fingertips up your spine and run my hand through your hair: 'Mumuki' comes on delicate feet, blue notes plucked from a hollow-body electric, to caress you with gentle fingers.

– Sprague?

– Hmm?

– What's a leopard's most secret fantasy?

– A leopard's most secret fantasy?

– Yes.

– I don't know. Maybe to be fucked by a tiger while crying like a crocodile.
From side to side you swing your head, whipping my face with your hair. With a glint in your eye, you ask me again:

– What's a leopard's most secret fantasy?

– I don't know.

– To have a G-string made of a whore's skin!
They come, the spasms of the diaphragm, the rhythmic, raucous cries; rippling through our flesh, they rock our bodies and brighten our eyes. We tumble off the sofa onto the floor. Blood flushes your skin, tears flow. And then it comes, tracing an arc from dread to glory, the scream that transports you to the place where you lose control: Tight together you squeeze your thighs, tight you shut your eyes: In darkness you summon silence to testify to the rupture of sense.

Sprawled on the floor, we open our bodies to the breath of Piazzolla's bandoneon. On light feet 'Mumuki' takes her leave, to the sound of a fading violin.

– God, that was beautiful!

– Yes.

– You know, Sprague, a classical violinist like me is always obsessed with getting everything right. Good tone is critical, and you go for a big, soloistic sound. Everything is very deliberate.

As you roll onto your side, I gather my nakedness unto myself; drawing your kimono over your breasts, you continue.

– For example, I used to play tango with a lot of bow and vibrato, very into the string. But that's not tango.

– Tango is when you let go, when you let it happen?

– Yes, instead of trying to *make* it happen. And that's very hard when all your life you've been obsessed with keeping control.

I stretch out my leg and caress your foot with my toes.

– But that's not all there is to it. For example, to play tango you've got to get comfortable playing near the frog—the base of the bow—because that's where real rhythm happens.

– And that's hard?

– Yes, because that's also the place where it's hardest to make good sound.

– It's a question of technique?

– No. Attitude. The challenge, Sprague, is to be both strict *and* free.

I edge towards you. You continue:

– In classical music...

You pick something from my hair: A thread of wool you flick onto the floor.

– In classical music you *place* the accents, but in tango, you have to let them *fall into place*.

With every move you prove you're a natural, you roll as you rock: So why this block?

– It's hard, to play dirty and yet stay elegant...

Your elegance is ingrained: Play dirty, it will remain.

– ....it's hard to be both free *and* in control.

Enough!

– Marietta, are we truly together, or merely facing each other?

– Truly together.

– Prove it.

– All right. I'll tell you the story of my life. Or at least the first instalment!

And so you did. Remaining on the floor, we talked for over an hour. And then I said:

– Marietta?

– Hmmm?

– You can't commit suicide with a safety blade.

– I know.

– That's why I'm going to fuck you, differently.

– All right.

– I'm going to fuck you, hard.

– All right.

– I'm going to fuck you, until you come.

– All right. So get up and carry me to your bed!

Your body in my arms steeled my limbs, your gaze in my eyes melted them.

Chapter 13

Face-down on the bed—two pillows under your pussy and one under your head—you whimper as I drive my ardour, deeper and deeper, into your forbidden aperture. Flowing like quicksilver through your hair, your chain-link collar glows as you turn your head from the rumble of the 'Carpet of Memory' to the silence of 'The Black Prince'. Look! The black wall is infinite night, the mineral walls the desert: There, Marietta, lies our destination!

On a narrow strip of land high up in the hills, in a house four stories high, a woman, her blonde hair pinned up behind her head, presses her naked body against the 'X' of a diagonal cross. Her head in the 'V' of the planks as they flare out, her skin aglow, she stands looking out the window-wall into the depths of the night: To the east, the obscure presence of a forest; to the west, the lights of the city, a distant lake. At the crux of the cross her wrists, double-cuffed and cinched with three turns of rope, keep her at her station. Crack! They come, the nine tails of the cat, landing with a sting that brings an inrush of blood to the woman's back. Gasping, she rises onto her toes. As the rush radiates out from the area of impact, her body descends in a tremulous sigh: In the forest, on the trunk of a trembling aspen, the spongy pores of a mushroom emit a sulphur glow. The man behind the woman, his green eyes agleam, lays down his whip and steps up to her. As he pinches her nipple and kneads her breast, his lips draw in her ear lobe and suck it: On the bed you bite into the pillow, searching in yourself for something that constantly escapes you.

I am the object of God's curse, I am a fallen angel: Wrapped in a houndstooth throw, a jagged check weaving promise and potential into the darkness of gestation, I lie on the floor listening to your life as a little girl. Woof, woof! Your beating heart bangs in the tightness of your chest; in your constricted airways your breath crackles. Panic-stricken, you breathe in, sucking in your abdomen; wheezing, you breathe out, a prolonged expiration of fear. It's night, you've just turned five. You will live, you know it, but could you live without your mother? To the nameless hole between your legs you'd brought a probing hand, and couldn't understand why your mother had you hide what you'd discovered: That the front has a promise the back can't keep.

And thus I learned, Marietta, in our conversation on the floor, of how your childhood asthma began with your discovery of sex. On the tip of my tail I bore away the fire I'd stolen from the serpent; in the mirror of your eyes I saw the sacrificial fire become civilizing.

The body is designed to float and bend, it is designed in a series of curves: On the templum of the carpet you stretched out; at the precise point where the red shifts from dark to bright, you placed your elbow and propped up your head with your hand. Your knee peeked out from the gap in your kimono, but it was your feet that worked their magic on me. It's rare now, you continued, that your breathing is laboured; still, you can't get rid of the feeling that your asthma is only quiescent, not eradicated. And I, when I stared into the incorruptible gold of your eyes, what did I see? I saw a girl who'd made her body speak where I'd silenced mine.

Deeper, more fluidly, I drive my demon into you, beyond lust, beyond reverence, into anguish. Here, in this occult space, what repels attracts; here, the limit to consciousness is the limit we must cross: Are you ready to bear responsibility? I feel the nervous spasms of your resistance, I feel the need for violation. Crack! The whip lands with gathered tails, producing not a sting but a deeper sensation. As heat billows from the point of impact, the next lash delivers a nine-point thrill, soon made one by another thudding blow. Restoring distinction, the man swings the whip hard and gives a snap of the wrist as the tails cross the skin: The sting sends the woman high onto her toes, gasping. Suspended in her sacred space, her calves taut in the grace of her soaring, she holds that position. On the forest floor, here a squirrel skin, turned inside out; there, the bitten-off shafts of wood-pigeon feathers: A fox has passed this way. The woman sighs as she descends to her heels; the man steps towards her. As he plants little kisses on her shoulder, she moans and widens her stance. He slides his hand between her legs, to her quim his fingers venture: Electric is their ambulation around her lightning rod. Holding the whip handle like a bit before her mouth, he offers it to her to bite as he slips a finger in: On the bed I feel you more relaxed, more ready to deliver yourself.

My teeth are the fixed stars, my wide-open eyes the colour of womanhood: Cloaked in my throw, I withdraw into myself: Myself where already you dwell. Woof, woof! The pleasure of fitting the last piece into a jig-saw puzzle, the buzz of demonstrating a proof: That's what you experienced as a little girl, that's how you came to believe in the existence of a mathematical reality, immutable and independent of the human mind. That touchstone of truth transformed you: To seemingly banish ambiguity, it gave you a subterfuge.

And thus I learned, Marietta, in our conversation on the floor, how Euler's circling of the syllogism, how Pascal's treatise on the triangle, allowed you to get around the taboo of knowing what lies between your legs. Indeed, forbidden to explore your sex, forbidden to acquire knowledge, you hid from your mother what you knew (even if your mother lived across the Atlantic, as I would learn, she still had a hold on you). And so knowing meant keeping your secret, transcending the taboo you'd accepted: Your knowledge separated you from your mother and begat anxiety. To restore your calm, you resorted to proof by contradiction and the method of infinite descent, to repeating decimals and 'if and only if': A strategy that allowed you to insert yourself into the universal while sanctuarizing the personal, and thus preserve the inspiriting secret that particularizes you.

To what extent does the little girl still live in the woman? I don't know. But I do know that between desire and its interdiction, between the demon and your ability to accommodate its demands, my sex shall impose its law: Your freedom is to be found in submission.

Marietta, as we lay there on the floor, did you notice how with each passing minute our presence to each other became more manifest? Did you notice how, in the far end of the room, in the corner by the window, the clay pot narrowed to a well-defined rim while its dark, iron-bearing glaze broke through the lighter one, texturing the deep-cream surface with cracks?

In the confines of your arcanity, in the grip of your transgression, my cock, emboldened by your desire to know yourself, teaches you to know your own flesh: Here the hollow of the night is infinite, no moon, no stars shine; here roses are dogs and apples crabs, the earth is dark, dense, damp. On the top floor of the hilltop house, the woman is a song in the silence of the room; proudly, resolutely, in hope and apprehension, she awaits the next lash: Wherever she's tasted the whip, that is where she knows her flesh; wherever the man has touched her, that is where she is blessed. Crack! It comes with a new taste, the generous taste of braided strings. Between her legs she feels a throbbing as her lifeblood is renewed; in the forest, the throbbing echoes: A vixen emits an eerie shriek, a tawny owl a caterwaul; from an alder branch a nighthawk swoops up and snatches a moth from the air. Gripping your shoulders from below, I take your hair into my mouth and nibble your earlobe. Pine tar and damp vegetation, cinnamon, cloves and gentian: The scent of your skin is a mark of your identity: Now I will dispossess you of the person you pretend to be.

I am robed in ashes and mist, through darkness and death I guide your soul: Two over the warp, two under, advancing one thread each pass, the threads of my throw adorn the unadorned. Woof, woof! The pulse of blood in the veins, the triumphant power of fire: Closing your seat to the saddle, you nudge the horse's girth with your legs and kick off into a canter. As you let your weight sink into your heels and your hands go with the horse's mouth, you feel at one with your body and yet outside yourself.

And thus I learned, Marietta, in our conversation on the floor, how at age eleven, on the heights overlooking Lake Neuchâtel, you came to love the feeling of a horse between your legs. You are the wind, my love, you are running water, all wisdom fixed between your eyes: Let us outrun the course of reason, let us penetrate the gates of mystery! Purposeful and deliberate, my thrusts become effortless. Giddy-up! You have to bend a horse to make her straight: Yes, but submissive, apparently passive, it is the horse that teaches the rider the subterfuges of mastery.

Her spine tingling in anticipation of the next stroke, the woman waits. Crack! It comes, a smart backhand lash to the buttocks. Delivered with a hot sting, it is followed by a hotter one, and a hotter yet. As her womb becomes incandescent, I slip two fingers into your cunt. Your fear is palpable—will you not honour your collar? Vehement, my thrusts force you to assume your state. Crack! Crack! Erasing the last of her reserve, the whip inscribes an 'X' across the woman's back. Gasping, she rises onto her toes, her holiness shimmering in a halo: In the city, in an underground club, light glints on a Stratocaster as the guitarist bends a note into a wail. Burrowing into your animality, tasting every nuance of its tangibility, my cock hounds your dread into its last redoubt: Inside you, my fingers feel its bold thrusts. 'No, no, no', you pant, 'no, no, no'.

The wanderings of the dead my tracks depict, I devour the stars and regurgitate the dawn: Four of day and four of night, alternating in both warp and weft, around my soul my throw interweaves intuition and reason. Woof, woof! Worrying about your sense of apartness yet needing to perpetuate it, you fear that other people will always be able to be more intimate than you are. You're self-contained, you're not forthcoming, you can't let go: Even in company you feel alone. Your sense of being always an outsider, only at home in your private world, drives would-be friends away. Yes, you're more of an observer than a participant, more lonely with other people than on your own. Your ideal is a close relationship that nevertheless allows you to retain detachment and independence.

And thus I learned, Marietta, in our conversation on the floor, how the only child lives inside the woman you are. You rolled onto you back and stared into the stars on the ceiling; loosening my throw, I did the same. I was born in the house of secrets, you in the house of work; I am the corded fish, you the corn maiden. Oh multitudinous stars, where in your arrangements of correspondences will I find guidance?

And then I rolled onto my belly and saw, in the corner by the French window, the bronzed and blackened surface of the squat, elliptical pot glowing in the light of the wenge lamp, revealing the effect of multiple firings.

Adamant, obdurate, unyielding, my cock ceaselessly fills you up. Take in, my beloved, take in! This is the banquet you cannot vacate, this is the celebration of the scandal: The scandal of desiring your own undoing, the scandal of inviting defeat: The creature living between your legs demands it. Listen to it crying mercy, listen to it craving abuse! Yes, here in the infinite night of this room, here in this mineral desert, salvation lies in bearing what is unbearable: The outsider inside you won't be denied. Crack! Crack! Crack! In rapid succession the blows are delivered; heat floods the woman's flesh: Along the lakeshore water shimmers, moonlit spars kiss the sky.

You cannot exchange your face now, my love, you cannot vomit the pomegranate seed: Behind the rim of my corona your sphincter closes, sealing your fate. Feel it! The whirligig of my fingertips has your skittle agog; leaving it to reverberate, I slip middle finger and index into the embrace of your secret place. In the warmth of your blind patience, in the crenulated folds of your receptivity, I seek your unencumbered self.

Is it only out of love that a woman submits? Hey, Sleeping Beauty? No more princely than a pauper I may be, yet from your torpor I will wake thee! Yes, I am the stranger at your door, I am the nameless outlaw: Whimper and squirm all you want, my unbending love will not relent.

I know the way through the forest, I can see in the dark: I am wrapped in the outward show of my inner being. Woof, woof! To correct your punch, correct your heart; spirit first, technique second: Kick! In your *karategi* you strike out, left foot planted firmly on the floor, right leg extended; parallel to your out-thrust leg, forearms ending in fists counterbalance your backward-leaning torso. Around your waist a belt of black; black ribbon ties your blonde plait. All is power, poise and grace.

And thus I learned, Marietta, in our conversation on the floor, of your mastery of the art of the empty hand, of your self-control and discipline. As you stretched out on the carpet and supported your head with your hand, your elbow took a stand at the exact spot where the revelation of love bleeds into the emblem of lust.

What does it take, Marietta, to make you see that the serpent was not outside Eve, but inside? Crack! The braided tails take another turn; as the woman rises onto her toes the pores of her skin open: Tail-lights vein the sleeping city; in the forest, belladonna blooms. Silence. No sounds now from your mouth. Just a breath that threads the gap between fervour and fear. Steadfast, I drive you deeper into yourself; deeper and deeper, till all definable knowledge is destroyed. You turn your head, I glimpse your eye: Deep in the dilated pupil, below the surface trepidation, I see a craving emptiness.

I am the haunter of cross-roads and graveyards, I am the initiator who sustains desire: Earthy, intuitive, maternal, the colour of death on my throw grounds the colour of passage. Woof, woof! The wrapping of the corpse in bandages of linen, the painting of the funerary mask; the opening of the mouth before the final offering, the weighing of the heart: Ancient Egypt was your passion when you were a little girl. What was the fascination? Did the dead man in his tomb evoke the baby new-born, did life ending and life beginning lead you to question how it all began?

In one second it's already the future! In kindergarten you'd count to infinity while hoping to make just one friend. You were impatient, impatient to learn: You learned very quickly. They called you gifted: You called it a curse. Yes, they never understood that your sense of lack, of things undone, never left you; they never understood that whatever you did was not as you'd have liked to have done it. Nor did they understand that nothing you did seemed essential. All or nothing, perfect or not at all—you could never be satisfied with the ordinary. And yet far from feeling superior to others, you felt yourself inferior. And then there was the fear. Of what? Of everything. But above all, of yourself. Yes, you were afraid of your thoughts, feeling they could drag you into terrifying depths; afraid of your emotions, invading you and making you lose control. Afraid of other people, in relation to whom you felt at once so different and yet so alike; afraid of life, which you felt you'd never master. But most of all you were afraid of facing yourself and finding that you wouldn't like what you'd see; afraid of realizing that you'd got it wrong, that what you'd become is not what you had wanted to be.

And thus I learned, Marietta, in our conversation on the floor, how your emotions harassed your every dream, your thoughts your every ideal. As I took you in my arms, fierce determination shot through the desolation in your eyes, and as I pressed your body to mine, in the far end of the room—in the corner with the photographs—the double-glazed pot resonated in harmony with its dispersed partners: The subtle variations in proportion, shape, and degree of surface crackle brought the group cohesion.

The necessary flaw, the essential obscurity, the vital, anxious fragility: In a cadence slow and steady, two fingers deep in your cunt, I continue to grind down your resistance. Musk, civet and castoreum mingle with pine tar and damp vegetation, cinnamon, cloves and gentian: In the play of autonomy and dependence, the secret harmonies of sexual difference mingle with its violence. Hark! Listen to the living absence between your legs, look at the masquerade: In her silver-grey dress of side-laced satin, halter straps holding up a pleated bodice, a singer stands tall in the spotlight. With a hiss of indrawn breath she launches into a song; viola and cello weave a countermelody, punctuated by pizzicato violin. Through the black netting of her birdcage hat, topped with a crimson feather fascinator, her red lips articulate a naïve lyric that her knowing face mocks. Figuring language at the surface of flesh, word in opposition to gesture, she incarnates her theme: Women love only themselves, their self-sufficiency is their charm. Look at her! In the spotlight, the plasticity of her face is mesmerizing. Embarking on a descending passage, she communicates her message in a flurry of grace notes: Men's passion hollows them out and fills women with vanity. Dark and compelling, her inflections flow in long lines over strident, mechanical chords. While the French horn takes the middle eight, the singer takes a drag on her cigarillo. Lowering her gloved hand, she inflames the men at her feet as she blows out a plume of smoke. 'No', you say under your breath, 'to impassion others is to alienate yourself'! Vibration, your body now is all resonance: I feel it in my fingers, I feel it in my cock, that humming in your vocal column, that buzzing in your *bas-ventre*.

The reciprocal imbrication of sentient and sensible, the mutual inundation of time and flesh: Inexhaustible, your friction-burrow saturates me with sensation. Harder now I drive my ardour into you, harder and harder into the abyss of your being. Gasps interrupt your moans; your muscles take on a suppler tonicity. Look at you now, my love! In the dark tunic of Chaos' daughter, your chain-link collar silver-bright, you disavow the diurnal kingdom and abandon yourself to the night: Acceding to my sway—oh yes, yes, yes, you gasp, yes, yes—you raise your butt to meet my thrusts. In vain the septum divides life from death, in vain it separates knowledge and the unknown: Along the walls of your sex my fingers feel their convergence. Whooooooshhhhh! They come, the annihilating angels, in a profusion of flapping wings; in their shining your body shudders, in their sighing your innocence dies. Hail! Your collar becomes moonglow as the light pours out of me. Look! The forest is on fire, the city is falling down! The curtain walls of skyscrapers crack, columns and girders collapse; reinforced concrete can't resist, wires and cables snap. Over the forest a great updraft of air sucks in the surrounding coolness; winds rise and gather speed, until with hurricane force they whirl the white-hot flames of the fire.

Destroyed now, city and forest, reduced to smouldering ash. Nothing remains, nothing but you and I and the hilltop house: Hand-in-hand, transfixed in silence, we lie on our backs, the after-shocks of our shuddering slowly diminishing in intensity. You break the silence:

— I came from a place so deep, I never knew it existed.

I squeeze your hand.

— You keep it, Sprague.

You hand me the key to the house on the hill.

— And whenever you want to, take me there.

You roll your body onto mine; trembling, you drench my face in tears.

PART TWO

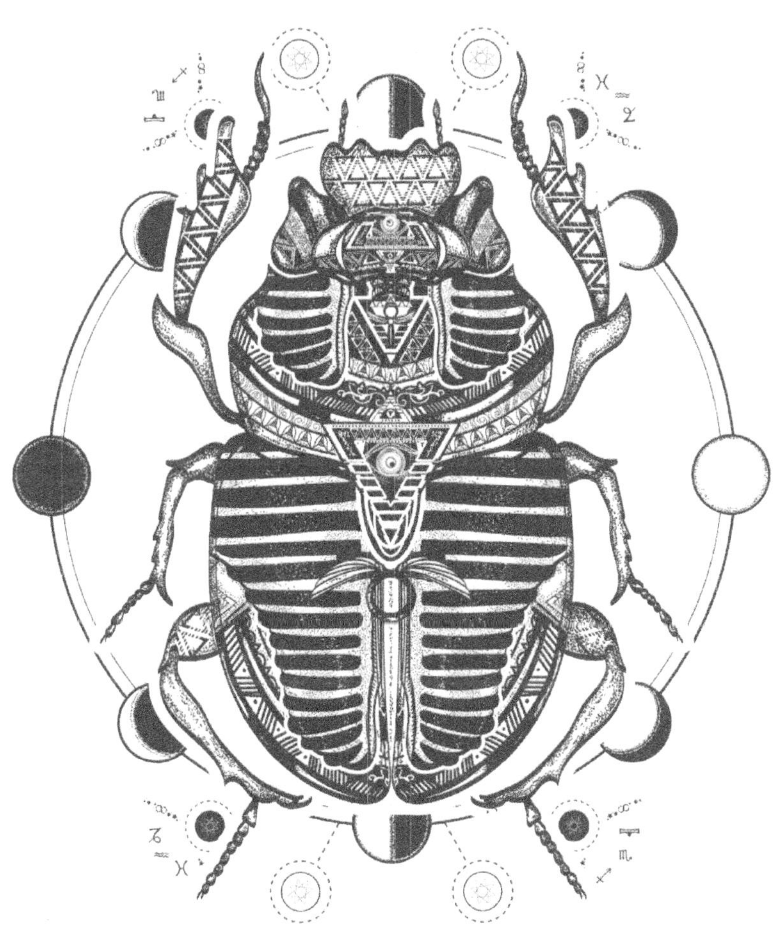

Chapter 1

Across the horizon the earth rolls; hind legs hurry it, hands struggle to hold onto the fleeing ellipse. The viscous world swerves, swells, and plumb before my eyes pauses. Darkness scatters as deft tarsi palp the black virescent ball, harnessing the hidden forces of the universe. In the vastness of my cranial vault the silence begins to hum; through the lumbricals of my hands and feet a cool fire flows: The god inside me, my creator who maintains my limbs, stitches me up again. Faeringa! All my works and days unfold in a flash before me as silver radiates from a sclerite collar and elytra coruscate gold.

— Exsufflicate effulgence, fleeting lucifer, stay!

In a suppuration of milk and honey, zalandyne and crystals of ice, the brilliance is sucked back into the body: ashen ember dying. Look! Out from under their pale sheath, dusky hindwings describe a helicoid curve while clawed forelegs quiver.

— Oracular scarab, reborn from your own corruption, here in your felt and handled world I lie. Still your flickering semaphores, teach my fingers to touch!

Scabbarding his crepuscular wings, the scarab rolls the world into its orbit then turns to face me.

— Listen: The caress transcends the sensible, it is a movement unto the invisible; across a radical separation between two hands is an ethical relation imposed.

— An ethical relation— No, don't go!

Gone.

Piston-like in the palmar excavation of my hand, your foot measures out the universe. Five bands of fuchsia streak the virgin firmament; from the plantar cavern to the dorsal mound, the tarsus to the toes, my touch refashions your foot. Hark! My pulse draws time out of eternity; to the voice and memory of death I lay myself open. What now? Energizing the earth, the substance of nothingness brings a coolness to my skin. Is this the unravelling, the prelude to birth? Mud falls from my flesh as I spring to my feet: In my mouth kernels of immortality remain.

Heel-edge-ball-hallux; heel-edge-ball-hallux: Through the emerald infancy of the world I make my way, taking five strides to leave behind the buttress root of a strangler tree. Lush vegetable profusion solicits my eager eyes;

everywhere, involuted secrets lurk. On a scarlet blossom a sulphur flame flickers; in a glistening web a spider embalms its prey. Now mosses and lichens thicken on branches and trunks of trees; with each successive stride, greens of jade and chrysoprase, malachite and tourmaline, unfurl a profligate world. Look! Upon a glossy leaf, a translucent tremor: Laying out a map of smoke trails on ghostly membranes of glass, a butterfly spreads its wings.

– Wandering spirit, free from your covering of flesh, teach my eyes to see!

– Through veiling I reveal, through unveiling conceal; look within and look without, fill your eyes with empty skies.

– With empty— No, don't go!

Gone.

Heel-edge-ball-hallux, heel-edge-ball-hallux: Through the sphere of vital assimilation I convey my receptive body. Faeringa! Taste of humus upon my tongue, cut of grit on my skin: In an amnion of earth I lie. Dark hollows of vermilion mud punctuate tremulous, breathing loam; festering leaves flicker in a labyrinth of trip-wire roots. Look! Silhouettes stir behind a palm frond; fungi sweat upon rotting wood. Pitter-patter, pitter-patter, pitter-patter: Elbowed antennae flicker, pinched waists bob: Each bearing aloft a sliver of leaf, ants scurry in a sinuous column.

– Why such bustle, little myrmecoes, why so busy?

– Cryptogam, cryptogam, hidden wedlock: Sustenance from the dead!

– What a sepulchral occupation!

– Like yours, just like yours!

– Like mine? No, don't go!

Gone.

Obscurely the forest unrolls its floor; perfume and decay saturate the stillness. From ebony bark amber oozes; a waxen leaf distils clear water. (Amber—was that not the colour of her eyes?) Look! Emerald iridescence, ianthine arc, saccades to smooth pursuit: To a violet orchid a hummingbird darts, and in a hollow of silence hangs before it.

– Jewelled magician, conjuring immobility out of movement, tell me: Does the ineffable show itself only by ceasing to name itself? How can the unsayable be said, the unspeakable spoken?

Parting the flower's velvet petals, the hummingbird eases the golden clapper of its bill into the ambrosial bell. (Golden—was that not the colour of her hair?)

– Eloquent source of sun's heat, teach my tongue to speak!

Petals stir in the hummingbird's whirr as it withdraws from the flower.

– So you want to tell of the obstinacies of the impenetrable?

– Yes.

– Then you must yield to the inviolate enigma of the otherness in things.

– The inviolate enigma— No, don't go!

Gone.

Five bands of fuchsia streak the multifarious green: Base of toes to uplift of ankle, from your dorsal interossei my down-pressing fingers draw fire. Hark! A hoarse cry rasps the labyrinths of my up-pricked ears. Slimy ooze drips from my skin, development and degradation contest the beginning: To my feet I spring.

Heel-edge-ball-hallux, heel-edge-ball-hallux: Tethered to circular time, I thread my way through the eruption of life. Night lightning! Shaping the wanton world, quicksilver runs in the veins of black leaves; across dark stains deep cuts creep. Faeringa! Cold, cold, my blood turns cold! Is this the enemy of the sun? Look how he vanishes, vanishes only to reappear.

– Warden of secrets, storehouse of becoming, what part do you play in the order of things?

– Some say the enemy within, the essential other side; some say time's motive power, the eternal homecoming.

– Homecoming! Oh relic of subterranean darkness, tell me: How much longer must I wander— No, don't go!

Gone.

Heel-edge-ball-hallux, heel-edge-ball-hallux: Through the forest of continuous creation my feet carry me. Look! Gurgling, recoiling, gathering its ardours in again, water tarries among obstinate stones. Letting loose its longing, it breaks into white as it rushes over rocks to a calm beyond. On my knees I drink from my cupped hands.

– My elemental identity, I have drunk, yet still I thirst. Why?

Babbling, the water flows on.

– Don't you recognize me? Speak.

Burbling, the water flows on.

– Come on, speak.

Babbling, the water flows on.

– All right then, go on, flow on! Run to the river, run to the sea, pour the ocean into the abyss! But just once, just once on your way, reach into the silence of the stones: Reach in and find me.

– Who are you?

– At last!

– Who are you?

— Come now, you were present at my initiation. You must recognize me.
Gibbering, the water flows on.

— Do you really not remember?
Gurgling, the water flows on.

— All right, then, let me remind you! The initiation, this is how it went: Fire burned bright in the copper geyser, steaming water filled the tub. Victoria latched the door, pulled down her panties and freed her legs. Raising her skirt, she sat on the edge of the bath and drew the child to her body. Hot flush of moist flesh! Her hands on his behind, her haunches rocking, she steered the boy to her pleasure.

Her tongue, her lips, and now this—amazed at his own body, amazed at the girl's, the boy gasped as the veil of illusion fell from the world.

— Of course I remember! You were the age of reason. Not that reason stands the slightest chance against the insanity of sex! Now don't forget your rendezvous.

— What rendez—

— The bridge!

— What—

Faeringa! Pink flashes bright, green gushes forth: From a giant bromeliad on an outcrop of rock, saw-toothed leaves flare out and fall in a fountain of aquamarine. I circle the rosette. Cradled in velvet succulence, still in perfect repose, a pool of water fills the capacious bowl. Plangent silence, heart-root hush: Into my eager blood the stillness of the pool insinuates itself. The surface darkens as I stoop; from out of the depths a face rises to meet me. Are these the eyes I saw in the shining of hers? These raven locks, did she not run her hands through them? And these lips, have they not sealed the junction of our souls? Faeringa! A coolness comes to my skin; in my head I feel my heart pumping.

Is this it, then, the harbinger of revelation? This watery world? Serene translucence, blessed abeyance, faint telluric timbre: Working against the viscous force of the water, a thousand oars in measured rows sustain me. Whence this body, wrapped in a loose-fitting lorica? Whence these organelles and vacuoles? Am I embryo in amnion, or is this the afterbirth? Am I still waiting, or is this my new form on earth? Pedalling the viscid water, I stagger and lurch: What is happening to me? My ramous limbs slow down: I am reduced to straits, cinched too tight in my skin. Faeringa! All my ostia open, carapace and abdomen unseam: Cool water comes to lap my new-born skin. Below—pellucid, diaphanous, indistinct—my cast-off cuticle sinks.

Look! A throat quivers, jaws fling open, an arrow-head tongue shoots out. Jump! On my feet I land, on the forest floor: Only to fall into the mud again.

I sleep, but my heart wakes; memory and imagination stitch and unstitch time: Silence deepens in the backwash, stars swarm in the sky; we're lying on the beach, the night's enfolding us... Andromeda, Cassiopeia, the great square of Pegasus... Her lavender scarf, her red hair, the alabaster glow of her skin—she was my Viking... Ma, Ma, Mari... ra, ta... Look around! Doesn't the world only receive light to the degree to which it craves it? Lay yourself open, move on! Silt and slime drip from my skin, deliquescence and coalescence dispute the beginning: To my feet I spring.

Heel-edge-ball-hallux, heel-edge-ball-hallux: Through overgrown green I struggle. Wherever I turn, an overflowing fullness of flower and leaf presses in upon me; in every glance I cast, obscene life incarnates itself. Look! Wrapped in translucent cerements, awaiting the spider's slow suck—heliconian butterfly, where is your glamour-might now? Poor basilisk, in unspoken water stillborn—what good was your caul in the cucking stool of the cascade? And you in your halo of cobalt and gold—can your dagger-bill defend you from the ferment in the belly of the emerald boa? Banded armadillo—when the jaguar's jaws crush your skull and her fangs pierce your brain, who will still call the ball you roll into impregnable? And you, forked root of mandragore—here in this orgy of creation, who will hear your cry when from the earth the tapir's teeth tear you? Prodigal abundance, futile and vain: ash in a bed of lye. Look! In a hollow of silence, sunlight sparkles.

– Hummingbird, help me! I don't know which way to turn.

– Put one foot forward, feel the earth below; straighten the leg, swing the other foot ahead: Keep walking, you will find your way.

Plain daylight.

– Don't go! Please don't go!

Gone.

Heel-edge-ball-hallux, heel-edge-ball-hallux: Through the forest of perpetual becoming I pursue my release. Mara! Black Corinthian berry in cordial of Curaçao blue, egg-white almond in Levantine honey: Your eyes meet mine. You press your foot into the palm of my hand; in your eyes the berries shine, ripening fullness overflows: Amidst the blueness of meridional days, night glows immense. Where, where do the fugitive gods dwell? Ma, Ma, Mari... ra, ta... Hark! The straining of tree trunks craving the light, the striving of roots driving deeper into the night: Daddy, why did you do it? What were you rowing toward in that fateful dawn? As the heel of my hand ascends the arch of your instep, the ghosts in your eyes return to the realm of shades. Mara Marina,

Mara Miranda, in light set my feet in your footsteps, at night echo your footfalls in my ear. Open your mouth and breathe on me. Ruah! The wind in my face, with each stride I lay down the bounds of duration: I walk the world. Will you walk with me?

Chapter 2

Moist membranes of wings unfurl into a hyaline fan as the sun colours golden-blue the thousand facets of her unveiled eyes. Breathing through her spiracles the larksong-laden air, she tightens her grip on the green stem while fast into her memory her watery nymph-hood flows. Elliptical spirals appear on her wings as they harden in the heat. What sign, what ecliptic? What mysterious powers have thee? Some say angel, goddess; some say devil, sorceress. Blood-pumped wings, discarded skin: transfigured dragonfly.

The breeze sways the cattails, blending their gold and green, while the sun burns the umber of their furry fruit. Look! Down among the tendrils, a quivering in the shadows: A waterthrush, its tail jerking fitfully, overturns dead leaves.

– Industrious thrush, what a life you lead, foraging in the mud!

– Unlocking the gates to the realm of light, setting the spirit free: Is that not a noble calling?

– Speak plain! What exactly is it you do?

– I break down resistance, resistance to change into a new existence.

– And you do that from down there in the mud?

– Like you, just like you!

– What do you know about me?

– Everything. In fact, I was just down in the Archives, filing away one of your letters. A lovely piece of writing!

– Really?

– Yes. A letter to Kate.

– But—the Archives—isn't that only for the dead?

– It is.

– But we're still alive, Kate and I!

– Kate is. But your time has come and gone.

– No!

– I assure you—

– I'm not dead!

– No need to shout, little Pilgrim. You are being absorbed into nothingness. Your death will soon be complete.

– But I want to live!

– Wanderer, don't waste your breath. Death is the gateway to life: To be reborn you must pass through it. I know my work, I've been at it for ages.

– Breaking down resistance—you call that work?

– A noble calling!

Poking about in the mud, the bird bobs his tail repeatedly—quick on the downstroke, slower on the up—as we continue our conversation.

– Is there anything else you do, thrush? Besides this muddy business?

– Yes. I attend to women. Whenever they need me.

– And when do they need you?

– In sex, for example. I help the virgin accept penetration, as the earth accepts the plough. I make a termite's nest of her clitoris, that she may know the secrets of nature. I feed her earth, until her womb is set alight.

– Well, *that* is interesting work!

– Indeed.

– Tell me, were you with Kate during her riot of sex?

– I was. I made sure her womb did not become an anthill. And I made sure she did not give herself to you.

– Why?

– Incest. You needed a mother, she wanted a child.

– I loved Kate. We were good for each other.

– You were.

Oh Kate, where are you now? I miss your reading to me when I'd be sick-abed; I miss your cooling hand on my fevered head.

– Tell me, just how did you get hold of my letter?

– In an exchange with another library. It has an agonistic theme, and as I'm a student of struggles, I naturally look after that collection. Would you like to see your letter?

– Uhm... Yes, all right.

– Here it is.

– I thought you said it was down in the Archives?

– It was.

I take the letter from the thrush.

– For all of us who work down there, access to the Archives is instant.

– As swift as thought?

– You could say that. Read it. I'll be back in a while to collect it...

I take the letter out of its slipcase and read:

Dear Kate,

Two angels are fighting for my soul. One of them is Ever Unloveable, the other is Openness to Grace. On Thursday, when I didn't hear from you, Ever Unloveable took possession of my soul.

On Friday, when you phoned me back, Openness to Grace made a valiant attempt to stage a comeback. He failed.

It was Ever Unloveable that drove me into that labyrinth of confession, to that place where I turn round and round like a dog chasing it's tail.

At the Anchor and Hope, as you spoke about your riot of sex, I was moved by how you dominated your despair. I still remember your exact words:

I've had enough of shagging. That's all I did, it seems, between fifteen and seventeen. And I'm not talking about getting my tits out for the lads. No, a guy would have to fancy the pants off me before I'd let him get his leg over. We'd do it in a park, a building site, upstairs in the back of a bus. Never at school. Just once, with a guy I liked, when he was really gagging for it. A knee trembler in an empty classroom. No lovey-dovey snogging. Once a guy had his fingers up my fanny on the living room floor when my mother came in. She shooed him off with a broom and sent me to see a psychologist. I learned I was frustrated and angry and seeking revenge. You think that helped me? Not on your nelly! I was past praying for.

Your tirade was pure oxygen to me—I felt myself breathing more freely. So Openness to Grace tried to dislodge Ever Unloveable from my soul, right there in front of you. He failed: The villain had already built his fortress inside me and could not be expelled.

How long will this war of the angels go on? All I can say is that the next time we meet, I hope it's Openness to Grace that has won.

— So, what does your letter inspire in you?

— Sadness.

— May I have it back, please?

I slip the letter into its slipcase of mud and hand it back to the bird.

— Thank you.

Grit, ash and humus: The taste of earth comes upon my tongue.

— Look, if it's any consolation to you, know that in love, as in art, there is only success to the extent that there is failure. The more it fails, the more it succeeds. Now be on your way, Pilgrim.

— But—

— There's much to discover in this archipelago. Maybe even the truth of your own experience.

— That's exactly what I'm looking for!

— Well then, get a move on!

— I will. Goodbye, kind thrush.

— Goodbye, Wanderer, goodbye.

Chapter 3

Tacking through the straits in my tanned-sailed skiff, plying the archipelago of your vertebrae, I pursue my peregrination. Look! Waves bite into the embayments of barrier islands; in blue-green water ridges of rock lurk. Axis in atlas! You turn your head from the lilac to the window-wall. Moonlight sapphires the blue of your eyes and burns the features of your face into my memory. Islands, rocks, and sunken reefs, the ruins of ancient temples: From the cervicals down to the sacrum, my fingertips read the braille of your vertebrae. In your lumbar hollow I lay my hands, close my eyes, and feel the rise and fall of your body as you breathe. Indeterminate stars pin-prick my eyes, pain pours out a measure of loss: the weight of a teardrop. I open my eyes and sweep my hands up your back: Upon a strand strewn with seawrack I bring my skiff to land.

Whelk egg-case and cuttle bone, mermaid's purse and cockle shell: I make my way to the upper shore, sand roughcasting my boots. Fibulae and phalarae! Coiled cast of lugworm, spiralling blow-hole.

– Peek-a-boo, I see you!

– Purgatorial scolex, dree your weird without me!

My boot-heels sink into the ribbed sand: costal, intercostal, costal, intercostal, costal—sandhoppers flee my footfalls.

– Stay, you saltating crustaceans! Tell me: Does everything bear the trace of an always earlier?

– Every cause is already an effect, every disclosure a concealment.

– Destiny! Is it really so determinant?

– Indeed. For you there are diverse paths to loneliness, but whichever one you choose, your point of departure will always be your terminus.

– But—

The sandhoppers scarper, leaping away.

– Don't go!

They continue their bounding flight.

– Please don't go!

Gone.

The air sparkles; billowing clouds fleece the blue. Eanling and bell-wether, cast lamb and drape-ewe: I recense the signate sky: The accidents change, the essence remains. Look! Pelt of lustrous silver, eyes angled in ire: In a violet flower on a red-haired stem, a stiletto fly sunbathes. Thewless in the undern hour, it doesn't budge as I hoist my body onto the beetling dune.

In marram grass I rise. Green hills, aproned in heath, undulate before me. Hark! A wailing cry, a fading antiphon: Someone has died. Cinerary urns of bell heather contrive a shroud of ash. Onward my boots propel me. Look! Daub of yellow, dazzling white, scalloped petals—eyebright!

— Euphrastic flower, scrophulariaceous weed, lend me your open-handed optimism!

— It's too late. Your death has already taken place.

— What?

— Your time has come and gone. It's over.

— But my heart is still beating!

— Some hearts take longer to die.

— I'd give anything for a touch of her hand, the scent of her skin, a gaze from her amber eyes!

— It's too late.

— No! The grain of her voice, the ring of her laughter, the scintillating joy of her science—they keep me alive!

— Hush! Make your eye a still mirror for the deep sky, a veritable euphoria of immobility, untouched by expectation.

Hark! A wailing cry, a fading antiphon.

— You have heard the thrush: It is too late.

One by one, across the grass, the eyebright darkens to lilac.

— Don't go!

The flowers begin to shrivel away.

— Please don't go!

Gone.

Heavily into a coomb my boots transport me. I come upon a lochan. Skirling, a waterthrush takes wing. Look! The tannin-water darkens, brightness leaves the spider's diving bell. Ostentiferous obnubilation! Unbidden comes the fearful guest: Afloat in the aqueous amber, all-utterly aghast, a man—dead. Ribbons of leaf weave through his raven locks, sky fills his empty eyes. I raise my face to the firmament: Unfathomable expanse of space; bright, scintillating vibration: The light that reveals conceals the wheeling of the stars.

Atlas in axis: From the window-wall to the lilac you turn your head. The pebbles of your vertebrae skip beneath my thumbs as my fingertips weave their way along your spine: Upon hopscotch squares, adrift in a dream, you hop, skip and jump straight into your mother's stricken gaze. Horror! Oh horror! One by one the children around you lose their names, their faces float; one by one in your dream-house, all the lights go out. Nightmare! Oh goblins and good ladies, why do you torment me? The mare, the mare! No, this is not a nightmare: Your mother, sitting on the edge of your bed, shakes you out of your dream and tells you, her face contorted, that your father's dead.

A rocky brae. A grassy plain. The sky, the sky! Curried by wind-combs, mares' tails streak the ethereal blue: The accidents change, the essence remains.

Ooliths on bone and shell, glaucous crowberry in calcareous sand. Look! Against the blue wall of Mr. Veloo's corner store, watermelons lie stacked up in the sun. A boy, sea-sand gritting his sandalled feet, approaches and steps inside. In the fragrant cool of the dim interior, huge sacks of brown rice guard the candy counter.

— A tickey of each, please!

Mr. Veloo scoops up the butterscotch and tips them into a cone of brown paper.

— How's your dad, Sprague? Still working so hard, the doctor?

— Yes, Mr.Veloo.

He gives the cone to the boy and rolls another for the pinkies.

— And you, first in your class again?

— No, Mr. Veloo. I was fourth.

— You're slipping, Sprague.

— Yes, Mr. Veloo. It's because I'm in love with your daughter.

— Delia?

— No, Lucy. Goodbye, Mr. Veloo!

Walker Street. The Poonersamy sisters. Look at them, lined up in a row on their sunlit stoep. Rosewater and wax polish. Smell it from here. Tangatchi's long black curls frame her permanent smile: Baby's soft in the head.

— Good evening Miss Poonersamy, good evening Miss, good evening.

— Good evening, Sprague!

What a chorus!

— Eee-vening Post!

The paperboy. Boundless energy. His sister's a looker. Works in the Cadbury factory.

— Eee-vening Post!

And what about Polly? Poor boy, three times a day the newspapers under his feet have to be changed. Soaked with sweat. Listen! The drone of a sitar: Mr.

Ragaval's back from waiting tables at the Strand Hotel. They say it's fifty years he's worked on the Esplanade.

– Eee-vening Post!

There's Delia. Still reading *Wuthering Heights*. Lucy! Got a bubble going. Pop! Messy as a cobweb. Like how she works it back into her mouth.

– Sprague, where you been?

– She sells seashells.

– By the seashore! Let's go up in the tree house!

– Later, Lucy.

Throwing her arm around his neck, she whispers in his ear. The boy runs up the veranda stairs, bends over the railing and says:

– Meet me in the tree house after supper. Don't come up if the coast isn't clear.

– Okay. And bring me a flower for my hair.

– All right, I will.

– And no talking of Linda Hendricks—she can't even blow a bubble!

– I told you it's not her I like.

– Who is it then?

– Her mother.

– Ah well, then that's all right. See you after supper!

– See you.

Mara, they say that what is most essential has always already been forgotten. Out of the permanent blur of the boy's present the man distils these memories from his past, positing a feasible world where none ever existed. Do you hear me? Where none ever existed. In the boy's experience nothing cohered, there was no continuity—everything was always in question. Into a mind tenuously linked to a body he withdrew, the fragments of an impossible world scattered at his feet: The man picks them up and weaves them on a loom of what might have been. Do you hear me? On a loom of what might have been.

Across the meadow my boots transport me, painting the green grass black. Under whose wing do you walk, child? Who will catch you when you fall? Harried by the gusts, I climb a hill as the machair gives way to a brae.

Rough merlons, irregular crenels, crumble of rock and clay: ruins, overgrown with stonecrop and scurvy grass. Look! White drifts of sea campion, precipitous blue: I stand on a clifftop. (A clifftop—is that not where she and I said goodbye?) I step to the edge: Sunlight glints on sea as moonlight otherworlds your eye; in its uncompromising blue I see you playing jacks with Alenka. Your right hand held behind your back, you toss up a stone with your left, sweep up pebbles from the pile then turn up the hand to catch the falling stone: Got it! One, two, three: You get to play again. Up you toss another stone; as your hand swoops in an ellipse I hurl myself off the cliff—by bodily sight, by ghostly sight, into thy hands I commend my spirit!—you catch me, and enfold me in your arms.

Up the beach of your back my hands sweep as waves surge up the foreshore.

– Waves, breaking waves, tell me: You who shattered Odysseus' ship and made a sole survivor of Robinson Crusoe, you who cast Viola ashore and delivered Gulliver to the coast of Lilliput—if our stories are all that survive us, will you help me to tell mine?

– If your house were burning down, what would you take from it?

– Why, I'd take the fire.

– I see you are not a stranger to dispossession. Well then, we might be able to help you.

– Thank you.

– Listen: Every literal truth is a figural lie. Listen close: Remembrance turns forward in the very act of turning back: At only one point on its rim does the wheel touch the ground. Listen hard: Errancy is the only ground of memory: Between construction and recollection you cannot help but sway.

– Thank you, waves, thank you. In telling my story, I'll remember your teaching.

– Good. But it won't get you anywhere.

– What?

– There is no 'I' but through an 'other'. You should never have survived being buried alive. Now you secrete your own poison.

– But—

– Don't forget your rendezvous.

– What rendezvous?

– The bridge. Get yourself to the bridge.

– No, I will not—

– Be there!

– There must be a way, a way to—

Suddenly the sea turns calm.

– Don't go!

Glassy calm.

– Please don't go!

Gone.

Plumes of suspended sediment move seaward through the surf zone; reshaping the shoreline, a longshore current angles the incoming waves: The accidents change, the essence remains.

Grate, scratch, grind, scrape; grate, scratch, grind, scrape: Under my boots, a bed of pebbles.

— You, dull grey lozenges, ingathered and eyeless, what are your destinies?

— My destiny is to be sucked by a starving sailor.

— And mine is to seal a dead man's eye.

— And you, little disks all dark and blue, what are you destined for?

— I'm destined to mark a pilgrim's passage.

— And I to slumber at the bottom of a wishing well.

— And you, veil upon veil of sensual shale, what's your destiny?

— I'm to be cast over a mourner's shoulder and lie on a funeral path.

— What for?

— To stop the spirit of the dead from returning.

— And you, lissen hourglass of alum ore—the two of you—what are you destined for?

— I'm destined to inspire a shaman's divination.

— And I to lie between a woman's legs, a barren woman I'll make fertile.

— Noble destinies, one and all! Now, do you want to know—

— We know it already. We have a long familiarity with you.

— You mean we've already met?

— Yes. When you needed a touch, they gave you a stone. That was me.

— When you needed eyes to look into, they gave you stones to look at. That was us.

— When your screams offended them, they put a stone in your mouth. That was me.

— When your silence offended them, they threw stones at you. That was us.

— So, you do know me.

Am I to die in a sepulchral city by the sea?

— And we know your destiny.

In a white city where death walks, will I be buried and born again, untainted by nostalgia for what cannot be?

— Will I be alone, on the bridge?

— Only the wind in your teeth for company!

— Oh stones, there must be—

— There isn't!

— But—

— Goodbye, Wanderer.

A wave rushes in to cover the pebbles in foam.

— Goodbye, stones. And thank you!

Mara Marina, Mara Miranda, I hallow my lips in the hollow of your sacrum; in the small of your back I retrieve my boat. Where next, my lover? Between the blonde a glint of blue says, 'I'm yours to discover'. I hoist the sail and set out to sea, other shores to explore.

Chapter 4

Atrosanguineous undulation, rippling vestiture of soft setae: Into the forebody blood flows, the segmented cylinder lengthens. From everted feet incipient spines protrude and hook into the haggard stem; behind the head rings of muscle tighten, the long rear loops forward, then into the forebody blood flows again: Up the aerial axis, towards the last unravaged leaves, the daemon drives the caterpillar. Extend, anchor, contract; extend, anchor, contract: Measuring out his ardour, the rapacious larva ratchets his way toward heaven. At last onto a leaf the banded worm, bright with poison, hoists his hairy body. Look! A head of fused hemispheres comes forth, a loose ring of skin rolls back; the labrum lifts, broad mandibles open, then fast into the sap-filled tissue incisive flanges sink. Within and without the juices flow as the maxillae guide the morsels into the mouth. From apex to base, margin to midrib, the caterpillar whittles away the lanceolate leaf.

– Why so ravenous, little eruca, whence this avarice of desolation?

– A knot of darkness abrades the pit of my belly, the light of release is but a wingbeat away: Until I vomit the harrowing pitch, I must devour.

– Crawling creature, soft-bodied and slow-moving, what single-minded resolve! Would that I had your indomitable conviction, would that I were like you! But no, I have no shroud of gold, no promise of a new beginning.

– You are human. Assume the grace you have been granted.

– What grace?

– Don't you know? The worms who ate the corpse of God gave rise to the human race. Go back to where you belong!

– I belong nowhere.

– Then you must be the Wanderer. Come closer, let me get a better look at you.

I crouch down in the caterpillar's feeding ground of flowering oleander.

– Manifestly, manifestly! You haven't changed at all!

– Changed... from what?

– From your photo in the Archives, of course! Poor me, my eyesight's not what it was—I should have recognized you instantly. You see, just a moment ago, I was filing away one of your letters. A lovely piece of writing!

– Really?

– Yes. A letter to Imogen.

– Imogen! What a beauty she was—but oh so cold!

The caterpillar mutters something, indistinct yet unmistakeable.

– Did I hear you say, 'Just your type'?

– Something of the sort may have slipped my mouth.

Oh Imogen, where are you now? I miss the cut of your ice queen lips and the diligence of your *noblesse oblige;* I miss your Sphinx to my Oedipus, like in Moreau's masterpiece.

– Do you want to see your letter?

– I'd like to know just how you got hold of it!

– In an exchange with another library. It perfectly illustrates a fool in love, and—as I deal in disaster—I naturally have a special collection of that. Would you like to see it?

– Uhm... Yes, all right.

– Here. I'll be back in a while to collect it...

I take the letter out of its slipcase and read:

> Dear Imogen,
>
> Yes, my feelings are my problem, not yours, and I have to deal with them: It is your sovereign right to choose who you want to get close to. I now surrender and fully accept that our relationship is, as you say, strictly 'friendly professional, nothing else'.
>
> What I was trying to create with you was a 'two-part invention', something that would honour us both, something that does not fit into the conventional. You were not interested: I realized that, but I felt I had to try to win you over. Can you accept that?
>
> Despite your lucidity, you were unable to see that by refusing to recognize—I don't say 'accept', but 'recognize'—my feelings, you were condemning me to all the excesses that so upset you. Indeed, by being unwilling to confront me in my individuality, you made me more desperate to have some affirmation of it, and thus the excesses ensued.
>
> From now on, I will conduct myself in a way that is appropriate to 'friendly professional, nothing else', and I apologize to you for having taken so long to accept this.

Sprague

PS – I won't teach 'Philosophy of Film Noir' next year, so you'll have to find a new partner for your seminars. See you at Factory Theatre Lab on Friday—*The Visit* promises to be brilliant (I saw the last rehearsal).

– Well, Wanderer, what does your letter inspire in you?

– Sadness.

– Tell me what followed.

– Well, at the party after the play, Imogen acted as if she didn't know me. All night long, the cold shoulder, the silent treatment. Then, a week later, she asked me to help her with a commentary on a passage from Merleau-Ponty. We met in her office. She offered me some tea. We discussed the passage (from 'The Theory of the Body is already a Theory of Perception'). She found our discussion very useful. Afterwards we went out for a drink, and she was absolutely lovely to me...

– Go on.

– Well, I don't know if is was the gunmetal grey of her fingernail polish, the red alert of her lip gloss or the way she stroked her glass, but I said, 'How about dinner?' She said, 'Sure'. Half an hour later we were sitting opposite each other over candlelight and nouvelle cuisine. We had a glass of Strega to close, and when I took her hand to examine her death's-head ring more closely, she left her hand in mine very willingly...

– Go on.

– Strolling along the street, I said, 'I'd like to pick up my copy of *Time and Free Will,* if you're finished with it'. She said, 'As a matter of fact, I just finished it this morning. Come over, we can have some tea—I've got your favourite, Russian Caravan'... Walking to her place, I fed her titbits from Bergson's biography. She was very receptive...

– Go on.

– We were having tea in her front room when her flatmate came in. She greeted us, then retired to her room. Imogen said, 'Sprague, I can't make love when she's in the next room, and I can't send her out like I did last night'. I replied, 'Well, why not invite her to join us? She's a prim girl, and prim girls are the hottest in bed'. Imogen simply said, 'I'll see you another time'...

– Go on.

– You know the rest. From then on she was strictly 'professional', without even the 'friendly'. She couldn't be moved—not even a fraction—from that position.

– And that's when you fell in love with her?

– Head over heels!

– Did you become a doormat?

– No. I didn't... sink quite so low.

– A lapdog, then?

– Yes, running at her heels.

– Begging to be picked up?

– God, I can't believe it. Yes.

– Begging for crumbs from her table?

I hang my head in shame.

– Deplorable!

– I know.

How could I ever have...?

– Should I have walked away?

The worm remains silent.

– Should I have fought poison with poison, the way you do, eating that oleander?

The worm remains silent.

– Should I have tried to trap her in a mirror?

The worm remains silent.

– Should I have—

– Get back to your boat, Pilgrim. There's much to discover among the rivers here.

– But—

– Give me the letter and get back to your boat!

I slip the letter into its slipcase of leaf and hand it back to the worm.

– Thank you. It's a contender.

– A contender? For what?

– King of Fools.

Nerium oleander, poison milk: The taste of toxins comes upon my tongue.

– Well then, Wanderer, goodbye.

– Goodbye, kind caterpillar, goodbye.

Chapter 5

Sequins spangle on julep water; azarole and saffron, violet and cinnamon, pattern the seersucker sky: Back on the river in my skiff I glide, my cadenced oars cleanly breaking the burnished surface of the water. Radiantly silent and sleek, the river stretches out in front of me as your long legs lay out their lissom curves on the bed. Across your calves my hands surf the swell; along your thighs, down the sartorius and up the gracilis, they glide. Onward the river journeys, gnawing away the future, building up the past: To mingle with salt these sweetwaters go, on their inexorable flow I steer my skiff. Look! On the riverbank, liquorice unfurls a carpet of lilac; just beyond, date palms line the shore. I angle in, stow the oars, and step onto glistening gravel.

Silt, sand, gravel, clay; silt, sand, gravel, clay: Along the river's alluvium selvage I seek a way out of circular time. Beneath my feet the accretions of centuries crunch; the sun at my back throws a long shadow. Hark! The raucous cry of an egret: A bird in nuptial plumes flies clumsily across the river. Look! Rippling across the surface, a snake. Faeringa! A frog thrusts out its legs but its head is already in the serpent's mouth. As its fangs pull the amphibian in, the snake's collar separates into distinct scales; grotesquely expanded, the cavern of its mouth engulfs the bloated body: Life unfaltering flows through the artery of the earth: I turn back the way I came and walk through its work.

Look! Yellow-bodied and black-faced, a finch binds grass stalks with a leaf stem. But why is its beak so bloody?

— Say, little finch, are you hurt?

— Not at all, not at all. I've just severed an umbilical cord. It can be a bloody business.

— But birds don't—

— Of course not! Down the river, there's been a birth. I cut the cord and pronounced the blessing. But it was too late.

— Too late for what?

— The threads of destiny could not be untangled. The infant is doomed.

— Did you tell its mother?

— No need to. Just as well, since she's disappeared. But she'll make the link.

— What link?

— Why, the link between herself and the child, of course!

– And what about the father?

– He's gone.

– Where?

– To protect the mother.

– From what?

– From what he believes she needs protecting from. Life, no doubt. Now if you'll excuse me, I've got a meeting with the Spinsters. Can't be late!

– The Spinsters? You mean...?

– That's right. Until the next time, Wanderer, goodbye!

– The next time? All right, kind finch. See you.

Bleeding into lemon and rose, anil and alkermes thread their hues through the pashm sky. Clay, gravel, sand, silt; clay, gravel, sand, silt: Still I seek a way out of circular time. Light upon light! Diaphanous, buoyed aloft by a tuft of floss, a seed tarries in the luminous air. Look! A flock of teal fly upstream, their keeled breastbones singeing the kinkhab sky. I watch them recede, then slowly disappear.

Now shadows cut loose from the sun; louder beneath my feet, the accretions of centuries crunch. Hark! The raucous cry of an egret: A bird in funereal plumes flies clumsily across the river. Look! In my boat, in a little coffin, a baby lies! His breast is still heaving; he is not dead, just sleeping. Look! His fists tighten, his face twitches, his skin is turning crimson! I bend to pick him up.

– No!

The finch lands on the coffin.

– It is not time.

– Why is he in a coffin? He's still breathing!

– That is the will of his mother and father.

Faeringa! A flock of finches swoops down and carries off the infant.

– He shall accomplish his destiny.

– But I could have loved him, I could have—

– Have you not understood? Didn't I tell you the infant is doomed?

The beating of my heart grows louder as the world turns black; the taste of blood on my tongue mingles with the taste of tears.

– Now do you understand?

– Yes.

– Dry your tears. Get back in your boat. The world is vast, you have far to go.

My tears continue to flow.

– Courage, little Pilgrim. Your death is well in hand.

— But I don't want to die! Not without—

— Listen! Love is always repetition.

— Repetition? Of what?

— One's history of love. You saw the infant, his twitching face and burning skin; you saw how his parents abandoned him—so how can you possibly imagine...?

— Is it really so irredeemable?

— Utterly so. Just because you survived being buried alive doesn't mean you can escape your fate. Now get into your boat and go!

I step into my skiff.

— Finch, please, won't you—

— Goodbye Wanderer!

— Goodbye, kind finch, goodbye.

Chapter 6

Into the unrepeatable present I dip my oars and feel the relentless pressing of the past. Look! Eggshell fragments scatter across the evening sky; clouds of amethyst and carnelian, crimson and carmine, distill into the quintessence. Through the airy suffusion the moon pours its pallor; in its cool glow, riding the camber of your curves, my hands fashion your flesh. Mara Marina, Mara Miranda, as my fingers strum the lyre of your legs they bring forth a threnody: Into the waters of oblivion you pour the blood of memory.

Look! Flickering light sweeps across a table covered in green waxcloth, lighting up half-eaten plates of mutton stew.

— Put the boy down!

The child tightens his grip around his father's neck. Distributing darkness and light, the swaying of the lamp binds the three militiamen on one side of the table to the father and son on the other.

— I repeat: Put the boy down!

The child squeezes his legs around his father's ribs; the father presses the boy to his body. The second militiaman picks up a loaf of bread and breaks off a piece, dips it into the stew and stuffs it into his mouth.

— You know, dirty Turk, your wife cooks better than she fucks.

To the rage in the husband's eyes the militiaman responds:

— Don't worry, that bitch will never fuck again: She's dead.

A flame lights the features of the third militiaman. His cigarette crackles and glows; through the smoke he watches a trickle of blood come to a standstill on the thigh of the girl splayed on the kitchen floor. He pours himself another glass of plum brandy.

— Made it yourself, didn't you, Turk? Not bad. And you swine are not even supposed to drink! Cheers!

The first militiaman says:

— You do want to bow down to your merciful God again, don't you? Just once more before you die?

Defiance shines on the man's face.

— You do, I know you do. So give us the child. Otherwise we'll have to cut him loose.

In the half light, as the lamp comes to rest over the table, contained violence contorts the man's face.

— Never.

Pushing the lamp back into motion, the first militiaman hands over to the second:

– Ratko, he's yours.

The citizen-soldier steps round the table. Taking a drag on his cigarette, he blows smoke into the man's face. A click flicks open a switchblade. Faeringa! A slash brings forth blood: From a gash in the man's forearm, it flows down the boy's legs.

– Give me the child. Don't make me cut him off you.

Not yet in any beyond, the man's eyes betray a contempt for his persecutor.

– Let me call my brother in Germany. If you kill me, he'll look after my son.

The militiaman takes a drag on his cigarette.

– Do you think I'd do a favour for a Turk?

– Please, let me call. If my son's in Germany, you'll still get what you want, you'll have our land.

The citizen-soldier strikes a match.

– I'll burn him off you.

He sets the man's shirt aflame. The boy screams and kicks: Blood puts out the flames.

– You are dishonouring not only yourself, but every Serb. God will not forget.

Neck muscles, windpipe, jugular vein swell as switchblade cuts into flesh; beads of sweat roll into exorbitant eyes as honed steel is drawn down forearm.

– You see, this is our land. Your son must learn who's master here. You wouldn't want him to get into trouble when you're gone now, would you?

The lamp comes to rest. Pushing it back into motion, the second militiaman says:

– Turk, if you want to be buried with your arm still on, put the boy down.

The man looks at his daughter, violated, dead on the floor; he imagines his wife in the next room, she too raped and no longer with the living. With fury in his voice, he says:

– I won't be separated from my child. Shoot us now.

The boy screams.

– A Bosniac giving orders to a Serb? That's no example to set your son.

Tenderly, firmly, the father speaks to his son until the child's cries become a whimper.

– You know, we have designs for the boy. You are denying us the pleasure of executing them. That's no way to behave, Turk.

Stepping round the table, the militiaman picks up the bread knife. Grabbing a dishtowel, his fellow citizen-soldier wipes the blood off his switchblade and moves back round to the other side of the table.

– Now how long do you think it will take me to saw off your arm?

The boy starts screaming.

— One minute? Two? Three?

The militiaman pours a glass of plum brandy. He offers it to the man.

— Take it. A little anaesthetic.

Tenderly, firmly, the man speaks to his son; the boy's screams give way to a hoarse rattle. The father puts him down and reaches for the glass. Faeringa! Blood spurts from his head and splatters the walls, fragments of flesh and bone fly. The child screams uncontrollably. The militiaman downs the plum brandy.

— Shut up!

The boys screams louder. A kick and a boot to the head bring silence to the room. From the other side of the table, the first citizen-soldier hurls the lamp forward: It snaps off its cord and crashes against the wall, plunging the room into blackness.

— Christ!

— Get the gasoline! Let's burn this house and get out of here!

Powdered ore of antimony rims a circle of silence; a black nenuphar disperses darkness to the bourne. Inert at the centre, my boat sits. How deep is the river, how long the root? Dark-blooded bloom, your intimate hue is blinding. Mara Marina, Mara Miranda, they say everything durable is the gift of an instant and all true knowledge is based on recognition. In that instant at the Südbahnhof when we recognized each other, was there the promise, if not of something durable, at least of true knowledge? I pick up my oars and roll up the scroll of the sky: Other shores to explore.

Chapter 7

Down into the limpid blue the anchor-line draws my eye, until in a deeper blue the rope dissolves: Into your iris I fall, and in its cool translucence slowly sink. Infinite blue, ardent emptiness; light upon light upon light: In the midwater currents of the sea, unresisting, I am sustained. Sheet lightning! A shimmering shoal of blacksmith fish gleams forth; they scatter in chaos then reassemble and swirl: *solve et coagula*. Into the unreal blue they vanish, leaving the ghost of their incarnation... Blood star on purple coral, flamingo tongue on gorgonian: Still life pullulates, silence peals... Sheet lightning! Again a fleeting shoal of blacksmith fish, again the dissolution and reconstitution of a cosmos... On an orpimento incline seaweed and sponge scatter flickering colours; on a carpet of bronze, long-spined urchins pose black silhouettes. Here, above tangerine cushions of astroid colonies, red sea fans sway; there, on the reef floor, jewel polyps part their blood-red lips. Sheet lightning! Again a fleeting shoal of blacksmith fish, again the diabolical creation of disappearance.

— Come back, you sorcerous flash, come back!

In an instant the swirling mirror-ball reappears.

— Why such a rush, why never linger?

— There's so much to do, so much to do, shuttling between the living and the dead.

— Enough of that! Is there anything else you do, besides that dirty work?

— Dirty work? Why, to initiate into a new life, there's nary a calling more noble!

— I grant you that. I'm sorry, it's just that I get tired of it sometimes. You see, it's my work too. I'm a poet.

— We know that. We know everything about you.

Is there no way out of this repetition?

— You work in the Archives, I suppose?

— We do, we do. In fact, just a moment ago, we were—

— Filing away one of my letters?

— A lovely piece of writing!

Is there no way out?

— Really?

— Yes. A letter to Clarissa.

Oh Issy, where are you now? I miss you talking in your sleep, wrapping your troubles in dreams; I miss you flat on your back, airing your strawberry creams.

– How did you get hold of my letter?

– In an exchange with another library. It has a marine theme, and we—naturally—have a special collection of that. Would you like to see your letter?

– Uhm... Yes, all right.

– Here. We'll be back in a while to collect it...

In the midwater currents of the sea, unresisting, I am sustained: I take the letter out of its slipcase and read:

> Dear Clarissa,
>
> When I was a boy I sailed on an ocean liner from Cape Town to Southampton, and from there to Montreal. Standing on the deck one night, overwhelmed by the immensity of the sea and the remoteness of the stars, I saw the lights of another boat going by. Suddenly in that vast expanse I didn't feel so small; enthralled, I imagined a girl looking at me from those lights.
>
> Can you bring yourself to see our relationship as those two ships crossing in the night? For my part, Issy, my heart danced when you looked at me. You have changed the course of my journey, through you my North has become more true: I voyage with only a compass, I have no map of my life. I still don't know where I'm going, but I see more clearly where I'm coming from.
>
> You once told me (it was on the terrace of Le Marin) that you are 'very clear' about where we stand. You had a map, it seems. I had no map, just a compass. But beyond a map and a compass there is a world, and it was in that world that I wanted to meet you. You preferred to stick to your map; I to be guided by my compass. And so we never truly met in the world, even though the world was right beneath our feet.
>
> We were but two ships crossing in the night, Clarissa. I, for my part, will never forget you, standing on deck in the starry darkness, an ocean of possibilities beneath our feet.
>
> Sprague

– So, what does your letter inspire in you?

– Sadness.

– Another emotional confession, another misconnection?

– Yes.

Around the axis of their wisdom the blacksmiths whirl.

– We had some lovely times together, but as soon as I tried to get close...

– She withdrew?

– Yes. After sex, for example, she imposed silence.

– You couldn't draw her into your dwelling, your house of language?

– No.

– Women are house-proud, Wanderer; they want a hearth and home, not a language-house.

– Yes.

– Infant, you only met indifference, vacancy where there should have been feeling?

– Yes.

– And now, if you stopped your babbling, you'd have to scream your rage—who could possibly love you then?

Reversing direction, around the axis of their sagacity the blacksmiths whirl.

– Don't you see you're doomed?

Alone in an empty room, his arms wrapped around his knees, a boy rocks catatonically on the bare floor. Outside the window a banshee wails, her witch-blood a banner flying in her breath.

– So what am I to do, blacksmiths?

– Break the cycle of repetition! Hurry to your death!

– I do have a rendezvous. On a bridge.

– A watery death! What more could you want?

– Indeed.

– Now may we have the letter back, please?

I slip the letter into its slipcase of scales and hand it back to the fish.

– Thank you. Now we must be off. There's so much to do, so much to do!

– Shuttling between the living and the dead?

– Indeed. Goodbye, Wanderer!

– Goodbye, kind fish, goodbye.

Into the unreal blue they vanish, leaving the ghost of their incarnation.

Chapter 8

All the declensions of black ablate to the absolute: Mara, into the depths of your pupil I descend. Look! Gutted apartment blocks stand mute against an overcast sky. Gaping shell holes stare blankly from flame-blackened walls. Blood-stained bodies lie amongst the rubble. From the back of an army truck a girl is dumped onto the road. Her head is battered, her lips are bruised; she is bleeding from the groin. The truck drives off. Borne on black fumes, the militiamen's laughter reaches your ears.

Look! A soldier bursts into a house and puts a pistol to a man's head.

— Fuck your daughter or I'll kill you!

— I will die before I do that.

— Then I won't shoot you, I'll shoot your daughter.

The father begs, pleads, implores—the soldier holds the pistol to the daughter's temple and pulls back the hammer.

— Do it! Now!

The father weeps and falls to his knees.

— Never!

His head snaps back as the soldier's boot sends his body reeling; pushing the soldier off balance, the girl spins out of his hold and runs towards the door. As a bullet enters the back of her neck, she crashes to the floor. Thirty seconds later, the drumming of her shuddering body is silenced by the whoosh of gasoline-fed flames. Only her father's screams rise above the roar of the fire.

Mara, you were never naïve. Yet the horror of what ordinary people do to each other makes you vomit your vision of man. How do we live in history without living in the past? For a past that is eternally present, how do we take responsibility? Let us destroy our possibilities, let us destroy the world's: That the world may reconstitute itself without words. Impossible! You want words: Since you no longer know who you are, you want me to tell you who you once were. I rise through your eyes to tell you a story from your story.

Listen. Alone on an autumn afternoon, you stand barefoot in your bathroom playing your father's saxophone. Barbed cries fracture breath-length phrases; abrasive growls punctuate a torrent of high notes. In your *Aladdin Sane* hairdo, your black jeans and T-shirt, you lay yourself open to your mercilessness.

A half hour ago you thought you'd be all right: Your mother out rehearsing at the Philharmonic, you were intent on spending a lazy afternoon alone. Sitting on your bedroom floor, painting your toenails black, you found yourself humming fragments of melody, trying to keep the blues at bay. And then you caught sight of the saxophone case, and suddenly it was obvious: Bite the dog that bit you, play!

A dark inscape of discordant intervals gives way to a fury of howling inflections: Why didn't you tell me, Daddy? How could you have believed I'd be better off not knowing, kept in the dark like a fool? Your parents did not just 'die in the war'; you were not 'raised by an aunt and uncle who moved to Australia'. No! At two-and-a-half you were wrenched from your mother's arms—I can hear your screams!—and taken to an orphanage. Why didn't you tell me? And Kocevski Rog, Skofja Loka, Teharje? A pit in the ground, and all the dead bodies piled up in mounds! Why didn't you tell me? Your timbre raw and rasping, you shape the air into an elegy. And then from your conscience the phantom escapes:

– It was your intransigence over Laura that provoked your father's suicide! Flee the Fury! In fragmented phrases, quick and dense, a flurry of notes gives voice to your flight. Mad in pursuit, the phantom will not relent. With rapid changes in register you try to give him the slip.

– It was your intransigence over Laura that provoked your father's suicide! You throw countless clipped notes, a harsh, percussive furore, into the phantom's face.

– It was your intransigence over Laura that provoked your father's suicide! You depress the octave key and overblow, and then you close your eye on the sun and open it on the phantom.

– Look the facts in the face! You murdered your father, you're a disgrace! You're out of breath, incapable of blowing: The phantom's got you cornered. Pinning you against the wall, he pins open your eyes and plays before you the scene as it unfolded:

– *Nostre amore spirituale è forte come nostro amore fisico*.

– *Certo, Laura.*

Between farce and tragedy your heart hesitates, but the more you listen (you'd picked up the receiver and intercepted a conversation between your father and a woman), the more it becomes clear: You father has a mistress, he is cheating on your mother. Your heart races, your palms grow moist; your eyes are wild and wet with tears. You're angry, angry at what your father has done, and angrier still that he has fallen from his pedestal. You will not tell your mother. But you *will* let your father know you know. *Nostro amore spirituale è forte come nostro amore fisico:* You feel yourself blush at those words, those words eating you away.

— Why'd ya do it, Daddy?
You hammer your fists against your father's chest.

— How could you!
He grabs hold of your wrists and tries to calm you.

— Can't explain, Mara. You're still a child.

— I want to know!

— You're thirteen years old.

— I want to know!

— Had to do it.

— You had to do it? Why?
The innocence in your eyes confronts the helplessness in your father's.

— I love Katja.

— You betrayed Mama because you love her?

— Yes.

— Are you crazy?

— No.

— I don't understand!

— How could you? You're still a child.

— Explain!

— I can't.
Wild, your eyes are a shattered mirror, shining.

— Daddy, you've spoiled everything!

— No, Mara. It's not so—

— You betrayed Mama. She doesn't know it, but I do!

— Don't say anything to her. I'll tell her myself.
Your heart skips a beat.

— What?

— I'll tell her myself.

— You will?

— Yes.

— But... what if she leaves you?

— She won't. I know she won't.

— No, Daddy, don't tell her!

— I don't want any more—

— What?

— Nothing.

— What?

— Nothing.

— Tell me!

— I don't want any more secrets and lies!

— Secrets and lies? You mean you've got other Lauras?

— No. There's only one Laura. And I'm going to tell Katja about her.

— No you won't, Daddy!

— Mara, listen!

— Oh why can't things be like they were before!

You father takes you in his arms. You resist his embrace.

— Listen, Mara, I love you. Whatever else may change, that will not.

— And Mama? How can you say you still love her?

— I love her more than ever. And that's why—now that you know—I must tell her about Laura.

— I don't want you to!

— Look, Mara, I'm your father, but I'm also a man. Your mother and I are your parents, but we're also lovers. Being parents and being lovers are two different things. As Katja's lover—

— You mean 'husband'.

— As Katja's *lover,* I must tell her about Laura.

— I don't want you to!

— Why not?

You start crying.

— Look, Mara, whatever changes between Katja and I, our relationship with you will not change.

— I don't want you to tell her!

— Yes, but why?

— I don't want you to!

— Tell me why.

— Because!

You hammer your fists against your father's chest.

— Because you mustn't, you mustn't, you mustn't!

He grabs hold of your wrists and tries to calm you. You won't be calmed.

— Promise me you won't!

— I can't promise that.

– Promise me!

Your father wipes your nose.

– No.

– Promise me!

– No.

– Promise me or I'll never speak to you again!

– Mara!

You scream at the top of your lungs:

– Promise me!

– All right, I promise.

Spreading like a bloodstain, the beat of your heart permeates the silence.

– You won't tell her?

Your father wipes your nose again.

– I won't tell her.

As he draws you to himself, you feel confused: Unlike in the past, this time you don't like the taste of your tears.

Brittle and defiant, airy notes flow from your saxophone. Then once again your incendiary keening comes to the fore: Emptying your lungs of air, you empty your body of history. In the blaze of notes you search for an uncountable pulse, a time beyond time: a time to start again. In a final blaze you blow away the phantom, and yourself to vertigo.

Sitting on the edge of the bath, your heart pounding, you watch your nose bleeding in the mirror and smile an otherworldly smile. You grab a towel, toss your head back and staunch the bleeding. 'I'll never have children', you hear yourself say, 'I'll never have children'.

Mara Marina, Mara Miranda, is there no other way to inhabit our histories? Must all our stories be family stories? Entrusting to your body the care of your soul, you throw your head over the edge of the bed. Waxen in the moonlight, your throat stretches taut over the cartilage, making visible the pulse of blood in the vein. Hark! The rigging beats against the spar, bidding me back to my boat. I haul in the anchor and hoist the sail, other shores to explore.

Chapter 9

Where does the horizon lie? Through a veil of ice crystals the sun shines, flanked by sun dogs, bracketed by a halo. Look! Out of the infinite albescence, a delta of dark ovals drags the white frame of a fox. Raising his head, he emits a hollow, high-pitched howl; in the icy air it undulates. I approach him.

– Say, crafty messenger, where does the horizon lie?

– There is no horizon here. This is the place of white on white, the sum of all colours against their absence. What are you looking for?

– Knowledge. Self-knowledge.

– Well, well! Maybe I can help you. Back there, in the Archives, I was just—

– Filing away one of my letters?

– A lovely piece of writing!

– To who?

– Chloé.

– Ah, Chloé! God, she was hard!

– She must have been, for you to have written her a letter like that.

– I loved her nonetheless.

Oh Chloé, where are you now? I miss your nervous intelligence, your cold, implacable brilliance; I miss your radical scepticism, your faith in artifice.

– Tell me, how did you get hold of my letter?

– In an exchange with another library. It has an icy theme, and we—naturally—have a special collection of that. Would you like to see it?

– Uhm... Yes, all right.

– Here. I'll be back in a while to collect it...

Turning to face the castellated iceberg towering in the distance, I take the letter out of its slipcase and read:

> Dear Chloé,
>
> You ask me how I will remember you.
>
> I will remember you as a woman of fierce determination
> living in a fragile fortress.

I will remember you as a woman who jealously guards her independence because she is terrified of intimacy.

I will remember you as a woman who prefers to *perform* her persona rather than to *be* a person.

I will remember you as a woman whose greatest fear is her own desire.

Sprague

Lingering over each line, I read the letter a second time, then turn my back to the iceberg.

– So, what does your letter inspire in you?

– Sadness.

– You couldn't get her to abandon herself to pleasure?

– I couldn't.

– You couldn't get her to forgo activity, annul her will to domination, neutralize her repertoire of control?

– I couldn't.

– Pilgrim, face it, you're simply not cut out for the role.

– Why not?

– An infant abandoned in a no-man's-land, a child in a hall of mirrors? Listen, the next time you're attracted to a cold woman, stop pursuing her—you cannot replay the past and hope for a happier ending.

– You mean—all this time—I was just...

– Yes. And you can't. The first lesson in love is this: If you cannot hate a woman, you cannot love her. And if she knows you cannot hate her, she cannot love you.

The taste of salt comes upon my tongue; I feel a chill on my cheek.

– I'm sorry, Pilgrim, but as you're on your way to your death, it is my duty to tell you the truth.

– Of course. I wouldn't want it any other way.

– Listen, indifference is the hardest thing. It's worse than absence. You'd have been better off killing yourself or going mad.

Again, the taste of salt comes upon my tongue; again, I feel a chill on my cheek.

– Oh, Wanderer...

The fox comes and licks my face. I like the touch of his tongue, I like the warm roughness.

– Quick, dry you face in my fur!

I do so.

— Good. Now you're all set to continue on your way.

I kiss the fox, I kiss his dark eyes and damp nose.

— I like your kisses! he says. Now may I have the letter back, please?

I slip the letter into its slipcase of frost and hand it back to the fox.

— Thank you. Well then, Wanderer, goodbye!

— Goodbye, kind fox, goodbye.

Curls of snow cast lengthening shadows; through the blank shroud of the unawakened world the sun plies a thread of gold. Where does the horizon lie? The desert of white is a daring glass, a snare made of specula! Is this the incunabula of the world, or its exinanition? Yea, is this the womb of the world, or its tomb? Hush! Distant, insistent, persistent: A fetal heartbeat in a womb of white? The promise of a new beginning? Dread ostinato, droning, intoning—what? The unseen and the unsaid—the roll call of the dead!

Mara Marina, Mara Miranda, shall I be a phantom of violation, barred by no boundary? Cold, my lips warm on you throat. Look! In the mirror you lie: of me there's no sign. Rivulets of blood flow down your flesh; time drowns in your dreaming stare. Ice-blue, your eyes chill the moonlight; snow-white, your skin brightens the blood. Moved and unmoving, your head over the edge of the bed, you give your body up to me: As love is traced by death, it traces the space between identities.

The white of dawn is but a dream away; the white of returning, a thousand. I dream, and then there is light enough: I leave the ice floe, other shores to explore.

Chapter 10

Softly the bride's wispen train sweeps the multitudinous sands, sustaining in the cool air the moon's luminous talcum. Bowing into the moisture-laden breeze, the scarab confronts the refreshing vapours. 'Fire steers all things: Cool things become warm, warm things cool down, moist things dry out, parched things become damp.' Along the dune-crest it glides, the exhalation of mist and moonglow, while the thirsting scarab—rear held high on tensed hindlegs, head lowered between serrated tarsi—receives the enveloping caress. Serenely descending, the fog brushes his embossed back. Smooth-peaked bumps draw in minute particles of mist; steadily swelling, the droplets gather. 'Death for souls is the birth of water, death for water is the birth of earth, earth is the source of water, and water is the source of soul.' Down the waxed furrows the droplets roll, into the insect's mouth.

His thirst slaked, the scarab lowers himself to horizontal.

– Say, you who return from the shades of night, share with me your life-renewing power.

He turns to face me over the dune-crest.

– What flows like water and burns like fire?

– Sand.

– I see you are not a stranger to the desert. Well then, I might be able to help you.

– Thank you.

– Let me see your hands.

The scarab crawls across my finger tips.

– The evidence in the Archives is confirmed: Your fingers have indeed learned to touch.

– Are you—?

– Yes. I've been following your progress. In fact, I was just—

– Filing away one of my letters!

– A lovely piece of writing.

– To who?

– Tilda.

– Ah, Tilda! What a cold beauty she was!

– Give him enough rope and he'll hang himself on the trope.

– Pardon?

– Nothing.

– Did I hear you say a bleeding man could do better than trying to draw blood from a stone?

– Slipped my throat. 'Twas nothing.

Oh Tilda, where are you now? I miss the *tangerine fougère* that scents your mahogany hair; I miss your pearly white breasts that hesitate between apple and pear.

– How did you get hold of my letter?

– In an exchange with another library. Your letter speaks of self-murder, and—the desert being a propitious place for suicide—we naturally have a special collection of that. Would you like to see your letter?

– Uhm... Yes, all right.

– Here. I'll be back in a while to collect it...

I take the letter out of its slipcase and read:

> Dear Tilda,
>
> On 23 March 1890, in Auvers-sur-Oise, Doctor Paul Gachet received a letter from Theo van Gogh asking whether he would be willing to look after Theo's brother, Vincent, who'd been suffering from nervous complaints. The doctor was willing, and Vincent ended up spending the last months of his life in Gachet's care.
>
> One day, after taking his midday meal at the inn where he was staying, he went out into the fields and shot himself. The bullet entered his body just below the heart. He bled profusely, but managed to get back to the inn by nightfall.
>
> Gachet and a second doctor who saw him determined that the bullet was inaccessible and that Vincent's life could not be saved. Theo was called to his brother's bedside. Going against the doctors' pessimism, he urged them to encourage Vincent to hold out. But Vincent would invariably reply, 'There's no point. The sadness will last all my life'.
>
> Two days later, at one-thirty in the morning, he died.

Marguerite, Gachet's daughter—whose kindness had touched Vincent during these last months of his life—said of him, 'His life was one moment of weakness after another, but in the end, what strength!'.

I'm no Vincent, Tilda, but on a night like this, when you are so near and yet so far, I console myself with the hope that one day you will see my moments of weakness redeemed by an ultimate strength.

And I say this despite the certainty lodged in my soul, the certainty that you too hold, that for me 'the sadness will last all my life'.

Sprague

– So, what does your letter inspire in you?

– Sadness.

– Indeed. The 'you' of 'I love you' is always an anachronism, never your contemporary. Given your past, you didn't stand a chance.

– I know, but—

– All the more so because cold beauties are fearful women, and there is nothing more opposed to love than fear.

– Yes, but—

– Look, Pilgrim, only through death can you renew your life. Love, you see, is a relation-without-relation. After your death, you'll deal with that paradox better.

– You mean, when I'm reborn, love will no longer be a revolving door?

– Out of one relationship and into another?

– Yes, as if I'd never left the first.

– It won't be. Instead, the door will open onto the abyss.

– What?

– There, in the depths of that luminous dark, you'll assume your helplessness. Now give me back the letter, please.

I slip the letter into its slipcase of sand and hand it back to the beetle.

– Thank you. Now get yourself to the bridge!

– But—

– On your way, Wanderer! Goodbye.

– Goodbye, kind scarab, goodbye.

The fog trails off, the night disrobes, offering her ethereal body to the stars. As the dunes unfurl their majestic curves, the moon silvers their windward slopes and spreads lampblack along the slipfaces. Surpassing silence, perfect stillness. Is death this sweet? I bring your hand to my cheek; you draw your fingertips across my lips: Cool things become warm, parched things become damp.

Look! The surface of the sand stirs, points of agitation interconnect. Whose hour has come round at last? Whose birth is at hand? Horned wedge of head, unblinking amber eye. (Amber—was that not the colour of her eyes?) Hark! Keeled scales rasp as a black flame spits: Through an aperture in the occlusion of his jaws, a viper tastes the evening air. Looping down the slope, he heads windward along the undulating sand.

— Stay, you who dwell in these empty lands!

— I am he who remains.

— Stay!

Gone. Vanished in the endless sea of sand.

Mara, prayer-wheels are spinning in the opals of your eyes; into the blue the black plunges its horror: In your bathroom in Ljubljana, Nadia vomits. She retches up her guts, her bile, but not her baby: In her womb the soldier's seed sprouts roots that won't let go, roots that stay to strangle. Bitter the gall on her tongue, bitterer still the shame in her heart. She bows down to pray: Light shines in darkness—darkness overwhelms it... Bullet-ridden bodies float down the river; a dog under the bridge withdraws its bloody head from the chest cavity of a corpse... Sprawled on the pavement in a tangle of streetcar wires, a woman lies beside a jerry can of water, her face half ripped away, her headscarf soaked in blood... At a street corner, flies buzz around the head of a boy, bruised and bloodied, sticking out of a garbage can... From a ditch, men emerge and beg to be shot before their pursuers find them... Nailed to the door of his house, arms outstretched, a man wails... Wielding a kitchen knife, a woman hacks off her hair; another binds her breasts with a strip of cloth retrieved from the burning house... And thus they soak the land with blood, in what they call 'cleansing'; and thus the armed murder the unarmed while you interpret for the bystanding peacekeepers...

Mara Marina, Mara Miranda, not from the present to the past, not from perception to recollection, but in the other direction we move. You bring your fingertips to my lips: The teaching of the river and the fire, and of the highest and lowest things. Wisdom and kindness compose the flame, then my hands take up the oars again: In my barque I glide, other shores to explore.

Intermezzo 1: Lilo

Marietta, I'm sitting in a chalkboard café on Ostertorsteinweg, drinking a cloudy beer called Haake-Beck Kräusen. I like this city on the Weser River; I like the look and feel of the town. Laid-back shabby chic urban pastoral. Have you seen Kenneth Branagh's *Hamlet?* It's brilliant. Julie Christie, what class! She gives a very fine Gertrude. But let's not talk about mothers. Kate Winslet's Ophelia is fine too. But let's not talk about daughters. Have you heard Anna's got a book out? Photographs of vodka and heroin in the land of Lenin, red-light nights and blue-morning snow. I met Gudrun in Madrid. Told me the two of you got together when the Tanztheater performed in San Francisco. Yesterday I finished the *Katie Quickfinger* script for Liselotte, an artist who's turning *Memoirs of a Kleptomaniac* into a graphic novel. Lilo's really gotten inside Katie's skin. I made a video of her kickboxing. She'll use it for Katie.

Three nights ago we saw Garbage at a club on Neustadtswal. Outstanding! Opened with 'Queer' and closed with 'Girls Don't Come', with a marvellous 'Milk' in-between. There's venom in Shirley Manson's lyrics, venom that comes from dignity's fangs, not a pose but experience. After the show we went to Litfass. Over martinis of potato vodka and blackberry liqueur, Lilo told me why she feels such an affinity with both Katie and Shirley.

– Conforming to expectations, there's nothing worse. It's only when you live by your own principles and stand on your own two feet that you become worthy of interest.

There's a metallic edge to her grey eyes; kohl-rimmed, they sparkle under a sheen of silver shadow.

– I think you give far too much weight to family, Sprague. Comes a time when you have to say goodbye, in your heart and your mind.

She takes off her scarf, exposing a butterfly charm on a leather choker.

– I was raised by my grandparents, with my mother coming in occasionally. My father took off as soon as he'd knocked up my mum. Silence ever since. Can't say I've suffered. Not in the least! I never felt I lacked anything. How could I, since I never knew him?

Her off-the-shoulder top confirms her insouciance.

– I never had a clear image of authority. My grandparents tried to play the role of parents. Never convinced me. My mum and I were more like sisters than mother and daughter. More complicity than obedience.

A black rose in a thorn wreath, her ring shows off its intricacy as she sips her drink.

– Not a model family! Probably explains why, very early, I began to throw everything into question.

I sip my martini: Wet stone and mild spice, the vodka comes through the bitter fruitiness of the blackberry.

– Reading sustained me. I could read at two-and-a-half. Never stopped since.

The black lacquer of her fingernails glints as she caresses her glass.

– I was a year ahead at school. They called me 'frog eyes', they tormented me. But I pulled through. I enjoyed learning. Did my homework with pleasure.

– And when did drawing come into the picture?

– End of primary school.

As she shifts in her chair, the butterfly in her sternal notch becomes a death's head.

– Drawing allowed me to cultivate my taste for the bizarre. Became a new outlet for my imagination. Do you draw?

– No. As soon as it became clear that whatever I draw ends up looking obscene, I gave it up.

Lilo laughs. She takes my hand and traces the fate line with her fingertip.

– You have beautiful hands, Sprague.

I smile into her eyes, eyes no longer metallic but misty.

– At seventeen I moved as far away from my mum as I could. Our relations had become unbearable. I started university, got a job. Paid my own rent! That was exciting, being responsible for myself.

She sips her drink.

– Of course my mum is still dear to me. My grandparents too. But the thing is, I saw them in action, I observed them. I figured out why they do the things they do. That gave me a distance, and that's why their influence on me is not significant.

On the stem of her glass her fingertips show discernment; graceful, her hand glows with intelligence.

– I've always been attracted to the dark. Bordering on the sordid! Shirley's lyrics really hit the mark for me. And the band is simply glorious!

– I'll say! I particularly like the slow numbers.

– Not surprising. You're romantic, Sprague.

– Am I?

From the dark, dark purple of her lips, there comes a bright shine.

– Sometimes, when people know my tastes, they think I'm a monster of indifference. But I'm not. In fact, I have a great capacity for empathy.

She takes my hand again.

– You have a water hand. Makes me want to protect you.

– From what?

– Yourself. You're too sensitive.

– Katie toughened me up.

– She's magnificent! I love the way she *lives* her questions, *lives* her way into the answers. Did you have any model for her?

I smile into her eyes.

– Marietta?

A movement of my brows suffices for affirmation.

– You've got to tell me about her, Sprague. She must be amazing.

– Later.

– You've been saying that for days!

I down the last of my drink.

– Shall we go, Lilo?

– I could stay with you forever!

***

Lilo's in love with Karen Blixen. She told me so, last Saturday over wine and cheese at the Café Engel. All day she had Katie skipping across the gutters, from panel to panel, her quick fingers rifling cosmetic counters and racks of silken lingerie. Come evening, the work having gone so well, she was euphoric.

– Isak Dinesen's right, Sprague. Playing with personas is more rewarding than pretending to be yourself.

She dabs some pear jam on her pecorino and bites into the rustic bread.

– It's naïve, pretending to be yourself?

She sips her wine, a dark Valpolicella.

– Yes. It means you have no distance, you take yourself too seriously.

– And what were Blixen's masks?

– Spiritual courtesan, Baroness, witch, siren, Isak Dinesen. That's what kept her free, those aliases.

The wrap bodice and dolman sleeves, the low-cut crossover tucked into the deep waistband: She wears it well, Liselotte, the vintage top I bought her for her birthday.

— Don't you think Karen's example could serve you, Sprague?

She pops a hazelnut into her mouth and dabs onion jam on her burrata.

— What do you mean?

— Well, your letter to Marietta—she'll never read it. Why don't you just write more stories like *Katie Quickfinger?* Something less personal. Wear a mask, forget yourself.

Revelling in the burrata, she mops up more with a piece of bread and pops it into her mouth.

— Like Isak Dinesen?

— Yes.

I sip my Tocai Friulano, ordered in honour of Pasolini.

— I play the hand I'm dealt, Lilo. I play it the best I can. Time will tell whether I've wasted my time. Do you know the hand Karen Blixen was dealt?

— Yes. I've read *Out of Africa*.

— That's another mask, that's mythology. You can see Isak's hand in it, but not Karen's cards.

— And do *you* know the hand she was dealt?

— I do.

— Tell me.

And thus I came to speak of how syphilis forfeited Karen's claims to a real human life. Of how, when she was ten, her father hanged himself in a boarding house because he couldn't bear to live with the disease. And then, as if by some transgenerational curse, she herself, within a year of her marriage, contracted the disease from her husband. 'Light comes from darkness', she'd written, 'daybreak from night': Stoical, undaunted, she believed her talent blossomed precisely because she had decided to *live* with her syphilis. Her sexual life sacrificed, she fell back on her imagination. The scandal of the disease, the secret, the taboo, meant that she led a double life, shuttling between intimacy and alienation. And thus, isolated, self-absorbed, condemned to *be* her body while feeling herself *other* to it, she developed an ironic distance to herself that was both alienating and liberating—and made her the artist she became.

Liselotte sips the ruby-red darkness of her Valpolicella.

— So you see, Lilo, every artist has their own curse.

Over her grey eyes comes a blue cast; over her face, a shadow.

— Give me your hand.

I offer it to her; she takes it and examines the palm.

– You've got a double fate line, Sprague. These two parallels. It means you found your soul mate.

– I found her. And I lost her.

– Yes. Exactly as your palm said you would. Look.

I follow her finger as she traces the lines.

– Your heart line ends in a fork, but a branch drops down to touch the life line.

– Which means?

– Failure in love.

Furrowed field, barren land.

– So what can I do?

– Let *me* love you!

She's got the cutest nose, Lilo. She's the only girl I know who can show lechery with her nostrils.

– All right. Let's go back to your place.

We went back to her place. She loved me. She loved me good.

***

Liselotte lives in a maisonette; she's got the two upper floors of a townhouse. It's light, bright and peaceful. Upstairs, under a skylight, is her studio. It's currently taken over by Katie: Hair of flaming orange and eyes glowing emeralds, the quick-fingered girl circles the walls, covering her tracks in the storyboard. Just look at her! In Lilo's dexterous hand her sinister charm is beguiling; prancing barefoot or strutting in stilettos, her feline grace is winning.

Downstairs, the floors, ceilings and walls are white: Lilo makes the most of the Northern light. The kitchen extends across the whole width of the house. At one end, an island unit holds the hob and a breakfast bar; at the other, a work desk serves as a dining table. Look! Burnt-down candles in candlesticks; a vase, fresh flowers. In the living room, their backs to the window, two steel-framed wicker chairs stand discreet and elegant. Edith, Egon Schiele's wife, beautifully drawn in three crouching nudes in the last year of the artist's life, occupies one wall. The others are bare. In the middle of the room, a round table on a textured rug gives off a black sheen. I'm sitting in an Egg chair, my feet on the ottoman. Lilo's sitting lotus-like on the sofa. We've just had lunch *(Braunkohl und Pinkel),* after a morning spent at the Paula Modersohn-Becker Museum.

We speak of women artists, we find we share a love for Frida Kahlo, Tamara de Lempicka, Remedios Varo. We speak of Egon Schiele, dead at twenty-eight. Lilo says she likes the drawings on her wall, but she prefers Egon's earlier work. I agree that Edith's too old to be a girl like Rimbaud (my first gift to Lilo) but not Gerti, Wally and the working-class girls. I explain why I'm so moved by Edith: If she didn't have Wally's divine gift of lust, she did show Egon that to be moving he didn't have to be demonic.

– Sprague, you're so isolated in that Egg chair. Come here. Come and sit next to me.

I go and sit next to her. She unfolds the throw she'd wrapped around herself and gives me one end of it; I pull it till it covers me from the neck down.

We sat like that, wrapped in one blanket, for the longest while. Yes, in the fading Northern light we sat in intimate silence, Lilo and I, as if we'd been lovers for a long time.

– Speak to me of Marietta, Sprague. I know you're thinking of her.

– No, Lilo. I'm happy here with you.

– Come, tell me about her.

– No.

– Well, read me from your notebook then.

– No.

– Please!

– Fetch it. It's in my jacket pocket. You can read for yourself.

Notebook in hand, Lilo sits opposite me in the Egg chair. Opening a page at random, she reads out loud:

> It's quiet here, on this island in the archipelago. I'm in a café looking out at the city. I like the charcoal-and-silver sky, the ever-changing grey of the sea. It's my favourite hour of the day, the hour when daylight blends with electricity. My coffee is good, it has a rich aroma; there's raspberry and rum in my tart. I miss you. No longer with vertigo, but with a quiet longing. I love you. No longer with self-regard, but with all that's good in my heart. Does this poem I've written here capture that?
>
> Under a harvest moon
> Grapes hang heavy on the vine
> As the clusters distil their immortality
> May night filter pleasure through your spine

Under winter skies
Saxifrage sleeps under snow
As the day relieves the night
May happiness set your heart aglow

Under a vernal sun
Bluebells spread across the forest floor
Before the canopy closes
May their glory come to your door

Under summer stars
The sand gives back the day's heat
As the sea breeze teases your hair
May the waves lay my love at your feet

Lilo closes the notebook.

– You're still crazy about her.

– Yes.

– Poor Spague.

Opening the book at random, Lilo reads out loud:

> I'm sitting in a bar in Larsbjørnsstraede, watching the rain beating down on the pavement. It's the hour of the afternoon when Sisyphus is giving it one last go. I've washed down my fish pie with a pale, golden ale; now I'm drinking a more daring combination of drowsy malt and piquant hops. If you haven't guessed, I've had a late lunch and I'm feeling lousy. I felt elated this morning, though, when the twin digits of your birthday met my first glance at the digital clock. In the street, on my way to breakfast, my heart skipped a beat as a lanky blonde crossed my path with your spring in her stride. In the café, the Moroccan bangles of the waitress rang a disturbing bell when she put down my plate. After that I started to slide; I just couldn't get a grip on myself. At the SMK I was moved by Modigliani's *Alice* and Emil Nolde's *Child and Large Bird,* but then I found myself preferring the white walls to any of the paintings. At my Danish lesson my teacher was delighted with my pronunciation but appalled by my grammar. Then I came here to have lunch. Lingering over a beer, I wrote you this poem:

Precious one, today is your birthday
And I am all undone. Why can't I accept
That without you my dwelling place
Is the rain, the stars and the river,
And the wide open spaces the wind
Blows through? You gave me all your love,
You filled my spine with memories: True.
But ever since you left me
I've been living unsheltered, defenceless
Against the wind that blows
Your absence through my bones.

How long can this missing you go on?
If no other lover
Can make up for your being gone,
Neither can my scribbling.

Because I know I will never take shelter,
I know it will never end. Because I know
Your memory keeps me alive, I know
I am condemned. To what?

To missing you till my bones ache,
To being a mourner at my own wake.

Lilo closes the notebook.

– Did I say you're still crazy about her?

– You did.

– I should have said, 'You're still *really* crazy about her'.

– Yes.

– Poor Sprague.

Opening the book at random, Lilo reads out loud:

> Insidiously the tide tugs at my blood, insidiously the siren sings. The siren! Plug my ears with beeswax, keep her indistinct! Swiftly I recite the twelve times table: Before seven her eyes have turned amber, her windblown hair blonde. Desperately I run through the Russian alphabet: Before 'и' sensitivity emanates from her fingers,

> immediacy from her lips. The order of the planets from the sun, the order of the visible spectrum—her laughter rings in my ears, her smile melts my heart... And thus you draw me to you, my beloved mermaid; and thus your silence is as fatal as your song. Marietta, as the murmur of the sea makes a boat of my bed, a moonbeam a sail of the baldaquin, I know that tonight I will be stalled in horse latitudes, haunted by memories of you...

Lilo looks at me with sadness in her eyes; she flips the page and reads:

Beat me like bedclothes on a rock by a river
Endeavour to make me immaculate
If love is dirty I am filthy
You'll never beat my love out of me

Turn me into a wolf, catch me in a trap
See me gnaw through my own flesh and bone
As much as I loved you on four legs
No less will I love you on three

Once I was your map, now I've lost my way
Once I was your compass, now I have no North

Turn me into a barnacle on a whale's back
Swim me through all the world's oceans
Swim me from Arctic to Antarctica and back
Never will you wash my love out of me

Stick me in a temple, I'll live like a monk
Let the decades roll until I'm enlightened
Then when I'm wise stare into my eyes
And feel the love pour out of me

Once I was your map, now I've lost my way
Once I was your compass, now I have no North

Lilo closes the notebook.

— You're tragic, Sprague.

— We live in a post-tragic world, Lilo.

— Not you. You're in love with a woman who won't see you. It's love that lasts that's tragic, not love that doesn't. You're tragic.

Opening the book at random, Lilo reads out loud:

Transparent as your absence
Juniper in gin
I am steeped in sadness
Emptiness within

Nothing is the sum
Of all things without you
Hollow and numb
I can't forget you

Lilo closes the notebook.

– You've got to try harder, Sprague. I can help you.

– You're a lovely woman, Lilo.

– Stay longer, then.

– Maybe I will. I'm happy here with you.

– You must!

– Maybe.

Opening the book at random, Lilo reads out loud:

The coin of Tyche, the stretched string;
Pattern, order and chaos:
Between contingency and necessity
Between reason and the absurd
I find myself adrift.

The gathering of thought, the mnemonics of pain;
Memory, forgetting and healing:
Between oblivion and presence
Between obsession and lucidity
I find myself adrift.

The sovereignty of the self, the question of self-
concealment;
Love, knowledge and delusion:
Between action and introspection
Between melancholy and exuberance
It find myself adrift.

Marietta, what I am to do?
Won't you help me,
Help me to live without you?

Lilo closes the notebook and puts it down.

— She must be amazing, to have moved you so!

— Yes. Now come and sit next to me. You're so isolated in that Egg chair.
Lilo snuggles up next to me. I unfold the throw I'd wrapped around myself and give her one end of it; she pulls it till it covers her from the neck down.

We sat like that, wrapped in one blanket, for the longest while. Yes, in the lingering Northern light we sat in intimate silence, Lilo and I, as if we'd been lovers for a long time.

PART THREE

Chapter 1

'Come at eight', you said. 'Let's spend the night together'. How to beguile the day? Lunch with Ralph and Emma, in a bistro on rue Beaurepaire. Indian summer. Leaves turning along the canal. 'Paltry Parisian vegetation', Emma remarked. She's from Montreal. Her memory, like mine, is bright with autumn splendour.

And the turning leaves of Neuchâtel, my love, how do they compare? Do they light up the hillsides, are they as golden as your hair?

Leek-and-potato soup, garnished with chopped chives. Steaming hot. Spoon it up and spill it: Cool it down. Rock 'n roll days in London. Ralph and I. The drugs we kicked, and those we didn't. Iranian brown heroin, Sundays in Maryon Park. The exact spot where Vanessa Redgrave lured the man to his murder in *Blow-up*.

Intoxicating vapours to stupefy: Have you, Marietta, ever chased the dragon?

Emma was shocked at our conversation. I told her about Inge. A girl with blue, blue eyes and jet black hair, milk-white skin and a baby born addicted to heroin. To stop him trembling she'd rub his gums with cocaine. 'One day', she said, black teeth perforating her smile, 'he'll play guitar like Eric Clapton'. The father of the child was in jail. One spring morning I shot her in black and white: On the hardwood floor, her hair pinned up behind her head, she looked over her shoulder into the lens. Soft through the sheers, the morning light made resplendent her vulnerability. I bought her a camera. I tried to teach her photography. She sold the camera to buy a fix. She said, 'You'll never understand me'. 'You're wrong, Inge', I replied, 'and I'll prove it to you'.

– And that, I told Emma, is how I started with heroin.
– And how did you stop? she asked me.
– Sprague and I did cold turkey, Ralph replied in my stead, and by some miracle we managed to stay clean.

In fact, thanks to lessons learned from Ariane, I'd managed to avoid addiction. I'd simply looked after Ralph in the underground: Somehow I knew how to help him reach the light.

And you, Marietta, have you ever seen in the eyes of a girl a woman at Jesus' feet? And if you have, did you try to play Jesus, or did you take her place at his feet?

Ralph adds that he's even given up cigarettes and alcohol. 'Except wine', I say; 'except wine', he confirms. 'Just to be sociable'.

Oh love, your coral lips come to me now, in the middle of the conversation, blowing your breath through my flute-like bones: All of that's behind me now, and my whole body is silvery song! I'd like to leave right away and stand under you window, but it's too early for a serenade, too late for an aubade.

Mushroom-ham-and-Gruyère crèpe, a glass of Bourgogne. Emma and I reminiscing about our Film School days in London. Now she's Paris correspondent for *Le Devoir,* but her passion remains cinema. We spoke of our documentary on secretaries, inspired by my love for 'Another Day': 'Every day she takes a morning bath she wets her hair, wraps a towel around her as she's heading for the bedroom chair'.

How can I tell you, Marietta, how you moved me Sunday morning? You stepped into the bedroom, a regal Egyptian turbaned in a white towel, and proceeded to rub yourself dry. Your reverie lent your nakedness an innocence, your smile put paid to any embarrassment.

Ralph sang the rest of the verse. He knows a lot of songs. In London, he worked in A&R for Polydor. Now he lives in Paris; he's marketing manager at Kenzo.

How lovely you'd look in a black cape and flowered stole. But then again, what need hath the lily of raiment?

Crème brûlée. The jangle of Moroccan bangles as Emma scoops out a spoonful. We talk about Québec, the constitutional negotiations, the possibilities of independence. We talk about Diane Dufresne and Robert Charlebois, about Carole Laure and Daniel Lavoie.

— If we have a son, Emma says, we'll call him Daniel.

She turns to Ralph.

— You do like that name, don't you?

Ralph smiles into her eyes. She kisses him.

— If I have a daughter, I say, I'll call her Carole.

— And what about the mother, Sprague? Have you found her? Emma asks.

— I have, yes.

I was joking, wasn't I? It wasn't only Ralph and Emma that I left guessing.

When Emma toyed with a ten-franc coin, rolling it in a loop across her knuckles, I wondered if she, like you, could climb a ladder with no rungs. And when she dipped a cube of sugar into her coffee, making a 'canard', *I wondered if you, like her, enjoyed that melting sweetness on your tongue.*

Emma lights a cigarette. On her finger she's got a fox, a ring with a red-eyed creature, black body hatched in white, tail folded and paws stretched. Little vixen: sexy bitch. Blowing out a plume of smoke, she cuddles up to Ralph as he throws his arm around her.

Have you ever wondered, my love, how other couples do it? Does Ralph have fantasies of passivity, like I do? Does he, instead, have to wrest the feminine from his lover, like I do with you? Ralph is tender to me, for it is I who introduced him to Emma. That I spent many a night in the teeming strangeness of her sex, once upon a Montreal winter, doesn't make him jealous. Maybe because he believes it was thanks to me that he never became a junkie. A refugee from the LSE, he's happy with his life now.

— Shall we take a walk along the canal? Emma asks.

— Yes, let's, I reply.

On the sidewalk, Emma picks up an orange-brown maple leaf and sticks it in my lapel, then we cross the road and reach the canal.

And thus, my love, I beguiled the day, waiting for the night.

Chapter 2

The babydoll dress

Dumbstruck, I stand before you, the taste of blood in my mouth, and in my ears the hiss of wind tunnelling through the cranium that once housed my reason. For you I will redouble the energy of delusion, I will sacrifice drugs and sleep. Reflected in the amber of your eyes, the light of this realization is blinding: You are inexhaustible, and everything is mine to learn. In your babydoll dress, the high waist gathered below your breasts, the rest falling loose to your knees, you stand before me, flaunting the nihilism of beauty. In the mirror above the mantelpiece I catch my smoky stare: Sulphur, saltpeter and realgar have turned my gleam to gunpowder, they've turned my green eyes grey. Flick! From between your toes a serpent's tongue rises to flare along the surface of your foot; licking your heel, its black sleekness accentuates your svelte form. Glossed, your toenails glow on the dark leather sole, conspiring with your skin to make the beauty of your sandaled feet despairing. Marietta, as you stand there, an air of sadness in your eyes, do you have any idea that while your whole attitude denies that beauty can signify anything other than itself, your reduction of beauty to pure appearance attracts me in the extreme? Yes, your lack of illusions only heightens your allure: I want to fuck you on the steppes of Siberia, in the forests of Indonesia, in the depths of the Atacama desert! Black and blue I want you, on lava glass, on permafrost, in wetlands and seas of sand. Yes, in the silence above the treeline, in the roar of breaking waves, I want to befoul your beauty; in the canopy of a cloud forest, by an underground river in a cave, I want to sully your sex.

Roses and lilies

– They're beautiful, Sprague! I love this shade of pink. And these tiger stripes!

– Why do you cut them at an angle?

– To make a larger surface. That way the fibres of the stems soak up more water.

– I see.

I bring a rose to my nostrils: violet, nasturtium, lemon, the scent of Persian slumber.

– Have you meet the prof who's renting you this place?

– Yes. Her name's Aravane. She's a physicist too.

– At Polytechnique?

– Uh-hm. She's doing a year at TRIUMF.

– What's that?

– A research lab. Particle physics. In Vancouver.

– Nice place to work! Why are you stripping off the leaves?

– Just the lower ones. Leaves get slimy under water.

– Shall I fill the vase?

– Yes, do.

I like the texture of the glass on my palm, the transparency of the water in it.

– Like that?

– Perfect!

Your arrangement is resplendent: White roses, bridal flowers awaiting blood stains; Peruvian lilies, tigers set to stalk our dreams.

The mustard-and-tomato pie

– Illumination! It's like a jolt of electricity. Once it hits you, it's impossible to compromise. Your emotions are engaged, you've got to act!

So you say as—a bright-striped apron over your dress, your hair pinned up behind your head—you spiral out slices of tomato from the centre of the pastry.

– Quite a rush, I imagine!

– It is. When you cram all your ideas of what the problem is about into one comprehensive impression, then you know you've already got it halfway solved.

You scoop out a tablespoon of *crème fraîche*.

– As a researcher you live for those moments.

Delicately, with the back of a teaspoon, you distribute it in little daubs across the tomatoes.

– Research gives you freedom, and the more successful you are, the more freedom you have.

You grind some black pepper over the pie.

– 'There's no success like failure, and failure's no success at all'.

– Lou Reed?

– No. Bob Dylan.

You drizzle olive oil over your creation.

– I work in a codified world, Sprague, where success is easy to measure. Only a fool would think life's like that.

– Yes.

– Success is obscene. Conceived a certain way, I can't stand it!

– Neither can I.

– Open the oven, please.

I move to open it.

– Giacometti was fond of saying, 'There is only success to the extent that there is failure. The more it fails, the more it succeeds'.

The heat hums out of the oven as I open the door a touch.

– Particle physics is like that. The most interesting theory comes out of experimental failure.

I open the oven wide. As you slip the pie inside, I say to myself, 'This must be what it's all about'. Was that my first dream of domesticity with you? (No. The first, I've just realized, was when, in front of Ralph and Emma, I named our daughter 'Carole'.)

Snapshots

The face, long and angular; the cheekbones high, catching the light. Eyes set wide, defiantly fixing the viewer. A noble nose, a fine-cut mouth, three days of dark stubble. And the hair: Brushed up high off the forehead, a disheveled quiff weighted to one side. The white shirt falls in easy folds, open at the collar, bunched at the waist. Into black trouser-pockets the hands plunge; around each elbow, a rolled-up sleeve. Insolent animal magnetism, casual self-possession; piercing intelligence, fierce tenderness. So this is a portrait of the rebel as lover, this is a portrait of your father.

– What do you see?

– A high-class assassin.

– Sprague!

– Am I wrong?

– No. He is a killer. A *lady* killer!

– And were you charmed by him?

– Charmed's not the word. Excited, yes.

– I can see why. That blend of negligence and tenacity must have been very seductive.

– It still is.

Enigmatic, imperfect, a master to deliver you from your mother, did your father unfold you a future?

In front of a lone oak tree, bent by the wind, a girl in a windbreaker and a man in shirt-sleeves stand, bent sideways from the waist, as the wind takes their hair.

– What do you see?

– A father who finds in his daughter the child he used to be.

– Hmmm...

– Where was it taken?

– In the Vaucluse, the Luberon. My grandparents have a house there. It's been in the family for generations.

– Do you go there often?

– I used to, every summer. For at least a couple of weeks. Can't you just feel the mistral, Sprague?

– I can. It's amazing how it shapes the trees!

– In the Vaucluse, a bent tree—especially a solitary one like that—will always be pointing south.

– It makes for quite a landscape.

– It does. The whole Vaucluse is magical! The mountains, blue in the early morning; in the evening, deep purple. And the sunsets, the light on the escarpment—strange shapes with black shadows, and ochre everywhere.

– You know the landscape well.

– Yes, we'd often go hiking. My father would teach me the names of the plants and animals, their characteristics.

– Do you still remember them?

– Of course. Creeping buttercup and rock rose, Bonelli's eagle, the Barbastelle bat. Speaking of bats, one evening, when I was alone in the house, a bat flew into my bedroom!

– Wow! What did you do?

– Scream!

– And then?

– Well, my first reflex was to get out and close the door, but then I realized that if I didn't actually *see* the bat leaving my room, I'd never be sure it had left.

– That's a scenario for a horror story!

– And that's what it felt like. So I closed the door, left the window wide open, then crouched down in a corner and waited.

– For how long?

– Ages, it seemed. The damned creature kept tracing crazy patterns in the air and wouldn't fly out. Finally, it clung to the stucco wall and stayed still. I could barely make head or tail of it, only its beady eyes caught the light.

– Foreboding, a vampire!

– I'll say!

– Then what did you do?

– I remembered a pair of gardening gloves had been left on the window ledge. I put them on, approached the bat, and caught it! Oh Sprague, I can't tell you what I felt at that moment, holding the bat in my hands!

– You felt aroused.

– How did you know?

– It's a transgression, holding a bat in your hands. You're holding the absolute other. That's perfect for generating sexual excitement. Did you masturbate that night?

– No, but I had nightmares. Nightmares in which I'm sure I came!

– Nightmares about bats?

– Bats, boars, eagles—tearing my insides out! It was... thrilling...

Never confusing desire with the love you saw in his eyes, your father could be a bat, an eagle, a boar, but you'd never know it: He'd always remain your father.

From a stream of green, pale slabs of rock ascend a slope in a beech forest. On a jutting of rock overhanging the stream, a girl stands, her smile hesitant, her face strangely illuminated.

– This is not the Vaucluse.

– No, it's the Gorges de l'Areuse, near Neuchâtel.

– You were a lovely girl, Marietta.

– Was I?

– Yes. It's very moving, seeing you as a child. But your face, you look bewitched!

– I'll tell you why. We had—just a few moments earlier—come upon some wells and water galleries, all natural, in a kind of enclosure under the trees. I stood there in the flickering light, with the breeze rustling the leaves and the constant trickling of water, and started trembling. It was eerie, the way the water came out of nowhere, so mysteriously.

– You'd lost your references?

– Yes. I was frightened. I felt like I was on some island that had drifted away from the world.

– And where was your father?

– With me. Silent. It would've been sacrilege to speak.

– You were in a holy place?

– Yes. Finally he said, *'Viens, ma fille'*—which is not what he usually called me—and took my hand. I held it tightly, and didn't want to let go. That's why I don't look very happy up there.

Prospero and Miranda, Pericles and Marina, the fiction of the island, the world as lasting storm... Motherless daughter?

Teardrop sunglasses, a blonde ponytail, a Triumph TR6 with its soft-top down: At the wheel she sits, a girl with a glowing smile, as russet leaves filter golden light and vines slope down to a lake.

– That's near Neuchâtel again. It was the day I got my driving licence.

– You learned to drive in a TR6?

– Yes. My Dad's always had sports cars.

– No wonder you thread your way through traffic like you do! I bet you were playing with plastic cars in your crib!

– Not quite that early! But as a kid my favorite toys were free rollers—you know, Hot Wheels—Mustangs and Camaros.

– So you were never into Barbie dolls?

– Never. Loop-the-loop and racing, that was my thing!

Gravity and speed, the slope of the free fall: The physics of danger.

– Just looking at this picture, Sprague, I can feel the warmth in my legs.

– The warmth in your legs?

– Yes. In the TR6 your legs are right behind the engine. You feel the heat.

– So *that's* where you got your hot legs!

– Yeah, and learned to do a lube job.

– And how about bodywork?

– On the TR-6 you learn everything. That's why I liked it, last week, when you said you don't like perfection...

A girl in a striped pinafore holds a wasp nest in her hands; behind her, a stairway framed in honeysuckle, a blue-shuttered window in a stone wall. To the side, a man walking away with a stepladder.

– This is your house in the Luberon?

– Uh-hm.

– And you're holding a wasp's nest!

– Yes. They'd built it under the staircase. We had to get rid of it.

– Your eyes are wild!

– I'd just killed them dead! Look, you can see my hat and veil on the gravel.

– And the spray pump.

– Yes.

– But why are you so... lit up?

– Because of what happened the day before.

– And what was that?

– Oh...

There's nostalgia in your eyes; you look so loveable I could—

– We were out walking, my father and I, when we came across a bird with a broken wing, bleeding. I approached it. Its instinct was to fly away, but it couldn't, poor thing, it was helpless. My father said, 'Leave it, let nature take its course'. I didn't want to, I wanted to take it home, nurse it, but my father persuaded me to leave it. I felt guilty.

– And then?

– That evening I hid myself in the Roman cemetery. My father knew I was there, but when he would call me, for the longest time I wouldn't answer. At last I did. He came and sat beside me.

– And what did he say?

– He told me that when he saw me sulking at supper, he realized how upset I was. Then he explained that as soon as he'd made the decision about the bird, he'd regretted it, but felt he couldn't go back on his word. And then he said, 'You know, Marietta, it's not always easy being a father'. That floored me!

– Why?

– Because, for the first time, I saw things from his side. And then it occurred to me that the greater his imperfections, the freer he leaves me to be. And at that, my heart started pounding.

– Hmmm...

– The next day I was happy to murder the mass of wasps!

Was your fury at the wasps a model of how to be a man? Was it a means to tell your father it was intolerable he'd become common? After all, who, if not him, could be your hero? Who else could warrant authority?

A rising field of lavender, a distant mountain. From a flatbed pickup a man unloads a hive. A girl in a bee suit with a box veil examines a honey frame; on the ground beside her, a wisp of smoke rises from a bent-nose smoker.

– You kept bees, Marietta?

– Not I, no, but a friend of my Dad's did. That's him by the truck. Dédé. Dédé Bonnaffée. He taught me beekeeping.

– You look like a real little expert!

As light as the imprint of wind on a puddle of water, affection for the girl you once were ripples in your eyes.

– What's the smoke for?

– It's for calming the bees before working with them. When you smoke them, they go down into the box to feed, thinking they may have to leave because a fire's coming.

– Instinct.

– Yes. The smoke also masks the alarm pheromone released by the guard bees when you open the hive.

– Dédé's a professional beekeeper?

– He was. He's dead now. Cancer of the blood. I'll never forget him. Look, here he is again.

The face is long, assertive, sly; the body tall and thin. A trim goatee frames a square jaw; dimples soften bony cheeks. In deep-set eyes, the blue is restless and moody.

– He meant a lot to you?

– No. It was something he said to me one day.

– And what was that?

– Oh, it's not so much what he said. It's the context. It's difficult to explain.

– Then just tell the story.

– Okay, I'll try. It was the first visit of the summer. My father and Pascale had stopped—

– Pascale?

– My father's wife. They'd stopped to talk to someone on the road. I walked ahead to Dédé's house. His wife answered the door. She welcomed me in, and while she went to see to something in the kitchen, Dédé stepped into the room through the back door.

– And then?

– He looked at me. He looked at me as no man had ever looked at me before. I felt extremely uneasy. Finally he said, 'Marietta, how you've grown!'.

– Hmmm...

– That really disturbed me, threw me completely off balance. I felt my thighs were clammy, my tits sticking out. I could even feel the goo between my toes!

– You felt self-conscious.

– Totally!

– A sexual object.

– Yes.

– I didn't realize that could be so traumatic.

– It is, at that age. Out of the blue, with no preparation, I'd understood that my innocence was over. It was a real shock! I mean, I realized—dare I say it?

– Say it.

– I realized I must be 'beautiful', but what 'beautiful' meant, I didn't have a clue! And then, when I stepped out of the house, a blaze of white asphodels blinded me. I tell you, Sprague, that instant of blindness—I felt it in my bones!—was a warning that nothing would ever be the same again.

When you saw in a man's gaze you were no longer a girl, did you feel a nostalgia for your father? Did you realize the perfect pitch of his gaze, free of desire but full of love, no other man would ever match? And did you imagine how the vision of you in other men's eyes—desirable, penetrable—would affect your father? Might the tables now be turned? Might those days when you wondered what went on behind your parents' door now be mirrored by your father's curiosity about what might go on behind yours?

And thus, Marietta, looking at your pocketbook snaps, I got a sense of your father's role in your life. But what of your mother? Of the seven snaps she appeared in none: You weren't yet ready to tell me why.

Chapter 3

On your back, your head in my lap, you lie on the sofa, legs flexed, bare feet on the armrest. Between your legs you've tucked the poplin of your dress; to the nudity of your shoulder, flat spaghetti straps hitch the V-neck. Eyes closed, face aglow, you smile mischievously.

– A humourous equation?

– Uh-hm. Subtle humour. Clever.

– Tell me more!

– No, Sprague. You've had enough science for today. Give me your literacy!

– You want my ABC?

– Uh-hm.

– All right. I'll marry elementary English to manual art. Would you like that? Coffee grounds and pomegranate, liquorice and rosehip: You bring my mouth to yours and kiss me.

– I'd love it!

– All right. We'll take it nice and slow. Now relax, let yourself go.

From the parchment shade of a torchère lamp, light falls on your face.

– A was an acrobat, leaped like a frog; B was a barmaid, worked like a dog.

Softly your cheek teaches my fingertips humility; rising and falling, your breathing teaches my hand time.

– C was a cook, made bubble and squeak; D was a designer, dressed very chic.

My fingers in your hair play with your surrender; autonomous in their artistry, they curl a lock into a seal of engagement, stretch a strand into a bowstring. So, what's it going to be? The separating arrow, or the ring?

– E was an eavesdropper, hung from a roof; F was a freak of nature, kept very aloof.

The touch of your hand in mine is the touch of a musician: It sets up a resonance in my soul. Shall I now trade these indeterminations for tones of definite pitch? On the back of your hand, my lips imprint their promise.

— G was a gypsy, a teller of fortune; H was a harlot, pleasure her portion.

Down the phalanges of your fingers, down the creased surface of your palm, I draw my friction ridges: Intimation. From the pulse of blood where hand meets arm to the calm in the crux of the elbow, I revel in the velvet of your skin: Declaration. Between striving and accomplishing your biceps repose; I feel action stirring beneath my touch: Celebration. And here, at the place where your body trades stability for movement, I circle your shoulder and harness its power to bring-into-being: Separation. My love, is it true? Will it end in desolation?

— I was an idiot, had his own ideas; J was a jeweller, cried pearl-drop tears.

I slip a finger under a strap of your dress; a mere string, it slides easily down your shoulder. I slide down the second strap. Impertinent are your breasts in their bra as I draw down the V-neck.

— K was a keeper, gave a dog a bone; L was a lunatic, heir to the throne.

You arch your back as I slide my hands under it; from the eyelets of your bra I ease out the hooks. Proud and uncompromising, your breasts greet my gaze: Neither their sublime beauty nor their stern perfection will deter me from the mystery of your ambivalence. Look! Your areolae take on a darker hue as my fingers circle your spheres.

— M was a maiden, pining for love; N was a nobleman, threw down a glove.

I pull up the skirt of your dress, slide my hand between your legs, and explore that magic strangeness: So this is where sovereignty holds no sway, this is where the unknown yields to no code. You raise your left leg and rest it on the sofa back. Sultry under the silk, beneath the tread of my fingertips your topography unfolds. You heave a sigh.

— O was an oyster girl, to lechery born; P was a piper, to drunkeness sworn.

You hoist your hips as I pull off your panties: Before you can slip your legs out of them, I block them at your knees.

— Q was a quack, peddled snake oil; R was a rainmaker, now off the boil.

Open, you welcome my fingers; deeper and deeper I work them in, until I am there where the genealogy of morals begins. Arching your back, you press against my hand; your panties stretch to breaking point as you strain to spread your legs.

— S was a sleepwalker, sad as a clown; T was a taxi dancer, liked to get down.

Thick under my thumb, your buoyant skittle bobs; inarticulate syllables escape your mouth: Whatever you are seeking, if you can name it, it's not what you want.

— U was an usherette, ever so cute; V was a virtuoso, played a mean flute.

Ready to embrace bewilderment, you close your eyes and abandon power; straining at your restraint, you beseech me to set you free: I pull your panties from your knees, you slip your legs out of them. 'At last!', you gasp, and open yourself wide: Your right leg, bent at the knee, you drop from perpendicular to parallel; your left from the knee you lay flat on the sofa back. In the freeway of your thighs my fingers unfurl their artistry; in my grip, your nipple cries for mercy— and for more.

— W was a wench, a plaine cuntrie girl; X was a Xantippe, had a spit curl.

With the distillation of your desire I anoint your lips; in a kiss you share it with me: If we are not the artisans of each other's pleasure, what are we doing together?

— Y was a yodeller, sang with a passion; Z was a Zouave, a victim of fashion.

Your breathing accelerates; as your muscles tighten your thighs tense. Between your legs where my hand works, in the petal-soft wetness of your spirit-dwelling, I slip two fingers in and invoke the four horsemen. Giving me the rhythm as I seek the light, your foot is a blur on the sofa back. And then from your throat there comes a moan, from your mouth a thunderstone: In the hinge of your thighs, in that sacrificial space where sacred and profane coincide, my hand becomes a luminous vibrancy as your cunt lets loose its herds of light.

Chapter 4

Salty diction, tender disillusion, beyond the rules of discord and resolution, the beguiling movement of a melodic line: Over a shimmering bed of flute and soprano, Julius Hemphill's alto sax teaches dignity in loneliness.

— When a man comes inside you, you feel it; you feel the beating of his heart in the pit of your belly, you feel the tremor of his spasms in your bones.

Gazing out across the Seine into the glittering night, we take in the moving gestures of the music. Tongues of fire play on black water, horns and woodwinds sparkle.

— It's like a Dalí painting, a man's orgasm. A woman's is more like Monet.

— Which Monet?

— The *Nymphéas,* of course!

— Of course. All 250 of them?

— Yes, when you're lucky enough to have a marathon of good love-making.

Is she crushed by scarlet, is passion spent, or is she still striving to lose herself in vermilion? Is she opening her legs to cool her loins, or busting her gut to come? Languorous elegance, violent frustration, the blue nude with head thrown back, black hair limp and damp, traces the contours of my confusion: Nicolas de Staël's *Nu couché bleu* testifies to the mystery of sex.

— This music's really lovely. You always choose well for us.

— Aravane's got a great jazz collection.

— Still, you have to know what to play.

The wind has blown white sugar into the mauve cup of midnight: In the saucers of your eyes, crystals scintillate.

— I was moved, Sprague, doing what I did. It was even better than the first time.

Wind, sand and ashes blow through the tray on the spotlit table between us: Is that the effect of the spirit you've drawn from my body, or of the textured colours and calligraphic lines the tray cannot confine?

— How's the tea?

I take a look.

— Just right, I'd say. Pour you a cup?

— Please.

The teapot's brilliant white illuminates the tray's interweaving of limitless line, a fine mesh that nevertheless fails to capture the emotion pouring out of me.

– I've never heard jazz like this before! These textures are ravishing.

Wind, sand and ashes polish the speckled egg of the world: Your eyes are glazed, they glisten: Unto themselves they are a universe.

– Hemphill's a great arranger.

Steaming water and oolong leaves: The two of us, thick as thieves.

– Have you ever felt ashamed, Sprague? About sex, I mean.

– No, never. Have you?

– Yes. I went through a really bad patch at thirteen-and-a-half, fourteen.

– After that incident with Dédé?

– Yes. I just couldn't cope with my body.

As the guitar threads its way through the texture of reeds, the flute devises traps for feeling.

– Your body escaped you, so to speak?

– Completely! It's effects were out of my control.

Is it the quiet fire of the torch ballad that's giving my tea this scintillation?

– It's strange, how the baggage you think you've jettisoned can suddenly resurface. I think I've touched all the extremes.

– In sex, you mean?

– Yes. And sometimes in a single night!

Vigil lights flicker, the city sleeps; in harmony with the elemental river, the elliptical music flows.

– What do you think? Can one ever really get rid of one's baggage?

– No, I'd say not.

– I'd like to get rid of mine. It's just too heavy sometimes!

Your hair in the light is pale blonde, the colour of a corn tassel; in the shadows the ambers of your eyes shine.

– You know, Marietta, a lot of women who seem so free with their bodies are simply caught up in a cycle of repetition. They've stopped growing, and instead of changing their lives, they wrap their sterility in a semblance of freedom. They forget their responsibility to themselves.

– What are you getting at?

– That even the lightest of travellers can bring heavy baggage to bed.

– It's not easy, is it?

– No.

You sip your tea.

– And yet, there was a time when it *was* easy.

Holding your cup, your fingers manifest the dignity of your hand.

– With Marco?

– No. Jürgen. He was a fantastic lover. Everything was happening for the first time, but somehow I knew exactly what to do—my instinct was infallible.

– You were... what? Sixteen, seventeen?

– Fifteen, almost sixteen.

– And then you met Marco?

– Yes. Suddenly there was love, and sex became complicated. After he died things changed drastically. Out of the blue, I found it difficult to accept being penetrated by a man. It's something you submit to, after all. It's a kind of responsibility. And then, to accept that a man sees you come, to accept that he *makes* you come, that's the highest degree of intimacy. To accept that is to accept everything. Well, at fifteen it was easy. At seventeen, it was impossible!

Mercurial, responsive, revelling in its capacity to experience changes of form, the river absorbs my emotion.

– We are what we remember, Marietta.

– But why at the most unexpected moments? Complicated, isn't it?

– Put things in perspective—think of the millipede.

– The millipede?

– Yes. On his wedding night, a millipede said to his bride, 'Darling, I know this night is special; it's the first time for both of us, and I want to do things right. But we've both had a long, tiring day, so why don't you just take off your stockings yourself and tell me which legs I should spread?'.

Your teacup rattles in its saucer; shakily, you set it on the table then slap your thigh, doubling over in laughter.

Air is the element of acquiescence, transparent and insubstantial: In the daring glass of the glazing, floating in luminous black, the white roses and Peruvian lilies affirm me in my resolution: For you I will redouble the energy of delusion, for you I will sacrifice drugs and sleep: You are inexhaustible, and everything is mine to learn.

Chapter 5

What are little girls made of? And little boys?

– Say, why do you squirm like a little worm? Anything wrong with your ding-dong?

The time and space of play are not teleological: Standing behind me, your left arm crossing my chest to the shoulder, you finger my tinkler over the toilet bowl.

– All's well, all's well! It's just that I'm starting to swell!

– Well open the tap, my good chap! Let yourself go!

Golden it comes, the ribbon of light; from porcelain impact to pool splash and back, you modulate the hissing jet.

– Put the wet stuff on the red stuff, the house is on fire! Put the wet stuff on the red stuff, the house is burning down!

– It's not me who started the fire, it's the kitchen maid! It's not me who started the fire, it's the pantry boy!

Around your wrist, a bracelet of talismanic stones: Is this the charm that protects the child from the adults' control?

– And that's it!

As the vortex drains the piss from the bowl, I spin out of your hold and position myself behind you. Slipping my left arm under yours, I cross your chest to the shoulder.

– Okay kitten, it's time for pussy to spill it!

– Sprague! There's no point gunning for my cat: Standing up, she won't rat.

– What? She won't tip her mitt? She won't sing, peach or spit? Well then, the third degree it will have to be! Spread your legs!

Legs apart, you lean forward and position your pussy.

– Okay doll, question number one: Alone, on your own, when did you first come?

– When did I first come?

– Yes, when did your body first blow your mind?

– It was in the Vaucluse. I was riding my bicycle along a dirt road, and the movement of my sex against the saddle...

– Now piss, baby!

– Sprague, I can't like this!

– Shall I relax you, sing you a song?

Tinkle, tinkle, little twat
Show me now what you got
Up above the bowl so high
Like a *con d'or* in the sky

You press your hand to your pussy.

– Sprague, don't make me laugh! It's going to splash all over the place!

– Tinkle, baby, tinkle!

– I can't control it like this!

I take your earlobe between my lips and suck it.

– Question number two: Alone, on your own, how did you do it as a girl?

– As a girl?

– Yeah, as a sweet little angel.

– On my back in the bathtub, the shower head between my legs.

I imagine the water pelleting your pussy, I imagine your pitched breath.

– Hey diddle ding, hear the bells ring? It's time to piss, baby!

– By and by, Sprague, by and by—though I might burst before!

I bring my fingers from your luscious to your loquacious lips: You lick them.

– Question number three: What first turned you on? Go way back in your memory and tell me what first got you going.

– Hmmm... Yes, I remember. I had a feather pillow with a little hole in it. I used to pull feathers out of the hole and hold them under water till they got soaking wet.

– Go on.

– That's it. I just wanted to see what wet feathers looked like.

– And?

– They were revolting! Yet they fascinated me. There was something obscene about them.

– And that turned you on?

– You bet! Had my *minou* meowing in no time.

Succulent is the strawberry in the tender moss; on the balcony the cantaloupes are ripe and lush.

– Oh Sprague, I'm going to die!

– Question number four: Your hottest fantasy, what is it?

– My hottest fantasy?

– Yeah, the one to which you make your moan.

– Getting fucked against a fence in a public— Sprague!

It comes, a quince yellow gonfalon, a streamer of tawny gold. Extending your arm to the wall, you fall forward. As you drive your butt against my crotch, you gain control of the stream; into the bowl you project it with precision, from porcelain impact to pool splash and back. Oh my biddable girl, what a master of the art you are! You spin out of my embrace.

— I guess we can drink out of the same bottle now, hey, my trigger man?

— All silk, my tomato!

— Close your head, baby!

And then, as if gowed up on giggle juice—lit, out on the roof!—we break into laughter, clad only in our mirth.

What an experience that was! Under the sign of the serpent we revisited our history. The serpent! No whitewash of sweetness could blanch his bright skin, the Shining One could be dulled by no sugar-coating: Frogs and snails and puppy-dogs' tails were wholly manifest: Sugar and spice and all things nice were but eye-wool. Marietta, these were our preconditions for loving, this was the challenge of the child's ingeniousness. Were we up to it?

Leaping and hopping

— Pass me the sponge.

— The sponge?

You reach behind you and turn a tap.

— Yeah, I'm going to give my pussy a little rubdown.

Exploring the possibilities of the bidet, you perform the ritual ablutions of the bordello. Meanwhile, I absorb the expansive spirit of the bathroom: Walls washed in primrose yellow, innocent and pale; floor tiled in black slate, warmed by subterranean wire. In a corner, by the sleek bars of brushed steel that dry the dark towels, a Louis XVI chair asserts its sophistication against the sobriety of the room. Directly above the chair, a domed skylight reveals the violet night. On the floor, in a corner by a cabinet, dry reeds in a jar of smoked ginger compose a still life. The shadow of the reeds on the wall leads to a garish Warhol: Marilyn. I imagine her in the cast-iron clawfoot bathtub, soaping a raised leg; I imagine her leaning against the sloping rear, its curves harmonizing with hers. Evoking meditation and repose, recessed downlights isolate, in the long niche to your left, milky beads in a boat-like vessel. Atop the vanity counter, 'Rouge andalou' and 'Violet Tattoo' lie on a bed of mother-of-pearl buttons. As you sit there astride the bidet, submitting your sex to the spume, I sit on the floor, my back to the wall, and feel your vitalizing heat. Look! Tinged in purple, the tiles brighten. You break into song:

— I'm being followed by a moon shadow, moon shadow, moon shadow.

Silvered clarity, lustrous white, a blessing of transparency through the skylight: A moonbeam slants into the room. Ay-yo! In a flash we're on our feet, dancing around the spindle of light, singing the childlike song. Oh love, do you feel it too? Do you feel the present alone is our happiness, and this stretch of time our immortality?

Norma Jeane Baker

– For me she's all about emotion, the emotion she arouses and that aura she gives off.

In your panties you lie before me as I sit in the Louis XVI chair, my foot a factor of friction in the hinge of your thighs.

– No matter what the role, she's always herself. She's pure, moving emotion.

So you say, as behind you Marilyn looks out at me through Warhol's manipulations: Her face is a milky pink with a mauve cast, her earrings a darker tint of the same hue; the blackened red of her lips sets off the blazing white of her teeth, while her hair is bright yellow and her eyeshadow, a guileless baby blue. You continue:

– She's the opposite of the femme fatale. She's fragile. And yet, despite herself, she's a bombshell. I think she can't help it. It's not an act, as it is for Rita Hayworth, for example.

A graphic border marks off the black towel you're lying on from the blackness of the floor; in the subdued light, the white of your body is luminous.

– I agree. She moves me too.

Opening your legs, you thrust toward me. In the ball of my foot I feel your heat, I feel it getting hotter.

– Tell me her story, Sprague.

With the heave of your haunches settling all my debts to time, my only desire is to fulfil my responsibility before you.

– She was nobody's daughter, undesired, an illegitimate child. All her life she was haunted by the question of love, endlessly repeating the same experience of abandonment.

Slung over the side of the tub, a bath rug the colours of a Munch sky emits a blood-red, blue-black scream.

– Either she sought an intensely close relationship in which she could be consumed, unreservedly offering herself to the man in an attempt to silence the demons inside her, or she felt rejected, worthless, in danger of falling into an abyss.

Hard you press against me, your butt rising off the floor; varying the flexure of my foot, I keep you in tension.

– What she was looking for was an enveloping love that could save her from the ravage inside her.

Marilyn in her frame of black—her hair the hottest, the most expansive, the most burning of colours—sears the blue in the background of her portrait.

– Didn't her movies bring her some peace? Didn't playing a role free her from herself?

Your amulet bracelet makes soft music as you throw your arms behind your head.

– In the beginning, maybe, but not towards the end. Her problem, from the point of view of the studio, was that she couldn't stop being herself—as you observed. She couldn't alienate herself in a role, the way an actress is supposed to do. For her, everything was real.

As you rub your sex against my sole, the little mole by the left corner of your lips echoes Marilyn's beauty spot. Now before my eyes the sugary pink of your nipples takes on a mauve cast.

– So no, movies didn't bring her any peace. But there was something that did—posing for photographers.

– Ah-ha!

The rose is the quintessence, the fifth element, the force that governs all others: Beneath the black, in the hothouse of your panties, I feel its power.

– Her identity was never well-defined. She often felt herself to be in a no-man's land, without references. All the ties most people take for granted, she couldn't.

Burnished by my heel, kneaded by my toes, your sex in my plantar cavern communicates with the stars of the depths.

– She was like a stray dog looking for a master, trying to keep herself together when the forces inside her were tearing her apart. At times she felt herself on the verge of madness.

Alone in an empty room, his arms wrapped around his knees, a boy rocks catatonically on the bare floor. Outside the window a banshee wails, her witch-blood a banner flying in her breath.

– Faster, Sprague!

Your sinews taut, to the ardour of my instep you submit your oyster, bucking as I polish the pearl.

– So, unlike in her acting, where even her perfectionism couldn't give her the illusion of control, in posing for a photographer she was a subject. The life force buried inside her could finally surface and express itself.

From a corner of the room lavender shadows come to quiet the bath rug's vermilion fire; ghostly upon a wash of light, the vanity floats.

– In front of the photographer's lens she existed at last; gone was the lack of confidence, the rejected and abandoned child.

Resolute, in the tense flexure of my foot you seek the edge over which to throw yourself.

- But of course the photo session had to come to an end, and when it did she was destitute again. So, to get herself through another night, she calmed her demons with barbiturates. And at thirty-six, she was dead.

Voraciously my foot caters to your craving; propped up on your forearms and the balls of your feet, you press your pussy into the sublime: We cannot abolish the abyss that separates human beings, but we can jointly feel its vertigo.

Marietta, if your eyes were jewels of chastity, then your lips were pigeon's-blood red: With the violence of your desire you fought your solitude: Did I fulfil my responsibility before you?

A promise of happiness

Shall I be a pristine blonde, forever young and innocent? Yes, a virgin under my father's roof, free from original sin, I could be a guide to the enchanted garden. With my girl-child body stopped in time—free from need, invulnerable—I'd inspire to spiritual heights all the men whose gaze I'd capture. And I'd never die, I'd just fade away: To the end I'd be winsome...

Lost in thought in a cone of incandescence, you sit in your panties on the vanity counter, picking at your split ends. The medicine cabinet, through the frosted glass of its diamond-grid door, emits a glow that sculpts the contour of your shoulder. Legs crossed, head lowered, in a hand-over-hand movement you isolate a sheaf of hair and twirl it around your finger; as the ends pop out of the twist, you lean back into the light and inspect them dreamily.

- It's tiring, Sprague, always being shadowed by your own image. That's why I like Warhol: He out-objectifies the object itself, draining it of any trace of sentimentality. I like the way he conveys the obscene: so ascetic, so ironic.
- Yes.
- As soon as I became a teenager I had to learn a foreign language, the language Marilyn had mastered.
- Femininity?
- Yes.

You look up from your hair.

- Pass me the scissors—they should be in the drawer of the cabinet you're sitting on.

Shall I be a perfect blonde, fuelling with my intellect the fire of my ambition? After a spell as an armpiece to affluence, cold-hearted and unkind, I could pursue my mastery of abstract systems. No child-bearing hips, no milk-on-tap tits, with my lean look I'm already kitted out for the role. Skiing in winter, riding in summer, swimming all year round: Tall, tanned and beautiful, it would cost me nothing to play the perfect partner, perfectly unattainable. No, they wouldn't smell sex on me, but nor would they have to sniff very hard to find it. I could even go as far as to have a relationship, if ever there were a good reason to do so. As for society, it would be from within, of course, that I'd climb to the top, but just because I'd buy into its tenets wouldn't mean I couldn't rise above it...

Snip, snip, snip: Into the trash bin the trimmed hairs drop.

— I feel completely out of step with how people see me. It has nothing to do with how I perceive myself.

Pale gold against pearl white, your tresses swing off your breasts to create a veil of modesty; left hand, right hand, left, you isolate a sheaf of hair, find a split end and rip it apart.

— It's alienating, being reduced to one dimension.

— I never realized—

— 'Cause you're not a woman! Even if you are beautiful.

Gentle it comes, your smile.

— Have you ever felt like a mannequin in a shop window, Sprague?

— No.

Left hand, right hand, left: You return to inspecting your hair.

— I have. That's why I love Warhol. He shows what it's like to feel like a mannequin—or a Christmas tree!—in a department store.

Behind the implacable symmetry of its diamond-grid door, the medicine cabinet calmly diffuses its frosted light. Cross-eyed, you zoom in on a split end: Your steely gaze turns rapturous as you rip the strand apart.

— I like that arid coolness he had, the coldness of his regard. He was the master of insignificance. He'd often say his ideal was to be a machine.

Over, under, over: Weaving your hair through the loom of your fingers, you shuttle down the sheaf, snipping off the split ends as they pop out.

— I like the honesty of that, his lack of faith in art. It's very refreshing.

Shall I be a bountiful blonde, full of abundance and goodness? Babies one two three I'd bear, plump little buggers. For their birthdays I'd bake a cake; when they're sick I'd make them soup. Patchwork quilt and pumpkin pie, a stint between the sheets: Husband, daughter, son I'd know how to satisfy. Yes, were I a bountiful blonde, I'd be the sun's accomplice, making flowers grow, colours bright, and hearts wholesome...

From the hollow of your clavicle you draw a golden curl. Search and destroy! Deft in their dirty work, your fingers rip the split end apart. On the vanity you float away, glazed eyes aglow.

– You know Sprague, after all these years, there's still moments when I'm at a loss.

– What do you mean?

– I don't know what to do when I'm stared at. I feel completely unarmed.

Gathering a sheaf of hair, you pick up the scissors and prepare another raid.

Shall I be a perverse blonde, a destroyer with a death wish? Cool and unencumbered, no emotions to entangle me, I'd draw to their doom all the men I'd meet. Yes, under starlit skies I'd promenade my perfection, a conquering erotic dream machine, loving but never lingering. My ashen hair upswept, my red lips set in a deadly smile, I'd slink through evenings of opium yet remain as lucid as a diamond (a black diamond, of course). My womb would be barren, my bearing composed, my face inscrutable. Dangerous, mysterious, a frigid femme fatale, I'd nevertheless be a woman of refinement, taking pride in her independence.

– So beauty's not a promise of happiness?

– A promise of happiness? It's a curse!

Incendiary fingers find a split end and rip it apart to the root.

Not for what I am, but for what I am not: So must I consent to be an object of desire. How to master the masquerade? How to outfox the fools? Playfulness and cunning, mockery and guile—that's what keeps me from becoming a gull.

Is that your stance, Marietta?

Chapter 6

In borrowed apartments we navigate the jungle of self-knowledge, in borrowed bedrooms we chart the topography of love: Magnolia pinks and muted blues, gradations of yellowish green: On pale oak parquet, on double herringbone diagonals, a black rug with floral motifs recalls Douanier Rousseau's *Dream.* On walls the colour of wet gypsum—a chalky, pink-tinged white—*Carnival Evening* and *The Sleeping Gypsy* confirm Baudelaire's theme: 'Genius is no more than childhood recaptured at will'. The moulded plaster ceiling with its intricate geometric lines mirrors the white embroidered bedcover now folded on a chair; the teardrop lamps on long cords echo the gleaming ebony of the headboard. Straight ahead, above a console table with cabriole legs, an oval mirror watches over an arresting triptych: In the middle, a black-and-white photograph in a bronze doré frame; on the left, an inkwell with epigraphic ornament; on the right, an incense burner of pierced bronze in the form of a lynx. Shamming a tunnel into the beyond, the mirror in its gold-black frame is a beguiling looking glass. Thus every object in Aravane's bedroom summoned and received my gaze: If not your mystery, then what did I see when they returned my gaze to me?

Aravane and the cat

— This is Aravane.

Dark the tapered arc of the eyebrow descends to the tip of the cat's ear; on each face—one eye deep in shadow, the other in a flare of light—the same unyielding stare.

— What presence!

Falling in a curtain to one side of her head, her hair crops the photo, bringing the faces forward and emphasizing the similarity of the eyes.

— And she's just like that in person—relaxed, yet very intense.

— Did you spend much time together?

— Two hours. They went by in a flash!

Sitting opposite each other, lotus-like on the bed, we contemplate the woman you're renting this apartment from.

— I can't get over this photo, Sprague. It's mesmerizing!

— Yes. There's definitely something about it. It's got rhythm, drama, tension.

— Yet a profound sense of peace. It's uncanny!

Nastassja Kinski.

— The cat is clearly tuned in to Aravane's vibes.

— Unless it's the other way around!

Simone Simon.

— Held back, yet penetrating—you're right, that look is more feline than human.

— But face-to-face she's no different!

Cat People.

— Do you like cats, Sprague?

— Yes, very much. And you?

Slung over her shoulders like a pelisse, the feline djinni inhabits Aravane's gaze.

— I'd like to like them, but they give me the creeps!

— All cats?

— Yes, just about.

Imp of darkness, emblem of sin, hide yourself away on my wedding day: What is it about cats that gets to you? I'd have thought you'd see in cats' eyes an image of your own independence; I'd have thought you'd see not an enemy of the sun or grimalkin but a cunning creature of forethought and ingenuity: One with whom you could identify.

— Pass it to me. I'll put it back.

Unfolding your legs, you slide off the bed and walk to the far wall. At the console, you place the photograph in its stand. Naked, seen from behind, your body is an hourglass that gives a stickiness to time: Suspended in the trickling sand, I hesitate between dream and reality. Was it just a moment ago you kissed my lips? Was it just a moment ago you straddled my hips, alternating wide circular movements with deep ones up and down? Through layered light you come back to me; dreamily your body affirms my sense of reality. Now plunge me into the heart of existence, stand up for contingence! Nine lives has the cat: Aravane demonstrates that.

The Sleeping Gypsy

— I don't like his drawing. Even if there's dignity in his effort, he's trying too hard.

So you say as, out of the burnous of my blanket, I stick my hand and take the glass you hold out to me: From a raid on Aravane's bar you've retrieved a bottle of cognac.

— Thank you.

— It's that combination of neatness and clumsiness that undermines it for me. It's just too stiff, too dry.

Sitting crossed-legged on the bed, you swing a cashmere throw over your shoulders.

– Sorry Sprague, I don't like Rousseau.

– Sorry? No need to be sorry. Cheers!

In the teardrop glow we clink glasses. Hot and velvety the cognac hits my palate.

– I wouldn't have thought you'd like him so much.

– I do.

– Maybe I'm missing something.

– Maybe.

– Then tell me what you see. What's it got going for it, *The Sleeping Gypsy?*

I could have spoken about the glow of the subtle colours, the rhyme of the precise lines or the immediacy that springs from the flattened perspective, but instead I simply said:

– The enigma of the encounter between the man and the woman.

– You mean the *lion* and the woman.

– No, the *man* and the woman.

And thus I came to explain that if the lion is Rousseau, it is because his unconscious reveals itself in a confession: In the dreamscape of his painting, interdiction and desire contend, creating a tension that makes the work magic.

– Aren't you reading his biography into the painting?

– No, his biography simply confirms what is already apparent.

– Explain.

– All right.

And so I came to share with you my experience of the painting: In an expanded present, in a vibrating space, a being confronts the mystery of what it means to encounter another: Condemned to failure, desire fills the canvas with foreboding. (That emotional charge, that feeling of doom, did it escape you so entirely? *The Sleeping Gypsy's* unfathomable simplicity, did it really leave you so indifferent?)

– Rousseau was a man who loved women, almost indiscriminately. He painted *The Sleeping Gypsy* at the time he was busy courting the woman who would become his second wife. One year before his death, he fell madly in love with another woman. She—it's clear from the letters—not only couldn't handle the violence of his emotions, but actually disdained them.

– I could never have imagined he was like that. His paintings are so childlike, so full of innocence.

– He's an artist. He turned his childhood fantasies into myths.

– And did he at least get that woman he wanted?

– No, he didn't. Instead, he painted *The Dream,* one of his greatest works. Dry apricot and honey greet my nostrils as I bring my glass to my lips; dense is the taste of being-with-you as I swallow a sip. Was I wrong to imagine, by the luminous amber of your eyes, that you tasted that taste too?

A Carnival Evening

Our backs to the headboard, we sit side by side on the bed, suspended in *A Carnival Evening.* Arm-in-arm Pierrot and Columbine, aglow in their lunar costumes, float in a ghostly landscape. I salute their celebration of dispossession, their disporting in strangerhood: In this souvenir from a dream I feel at home. As I watch the couple balance precariously on the cusp of their adventure—jauntily, as if just freed from the puppeteer's strings—I feel the grip of your hand in mine freeing me from the grip of my past.

Who's that hatted man with a moustache peeping out from the kiosk? Maybe it's not even a man, maybe it's just a mask? In delight you squeezed my hand when I pointed out to you that typical Rousseau touch, making me believe you're not totally immune to the Douanier's enigmatic art. Indeed, charmed by *A Carnival Evening,* you turned to reconsider the silence of *The Sleeping Gypsy*. What if the sleeper is dreaming the lion, what if the lion is simply afraid of his own violence? With these questions you plunged me into the enigma of your own desire. And thus we came to talk of animals as sexual ciphers, of paintings with satyrs and centaurs, bulls and serpents. When I mentioned *Leda and the Swan* your face lit up, and as your gaze held mine we knew that the divine bestiality of that bird moved us equally.

What do you see in me, Marietta, what do you want me to be? Shall I be an appalling Pierrot, the alter-ego of the alienated artist, isolated, disillusioned and doomed? In my silvery garments and chalky face, my boat-like hat and scarlet grin, I'd veil my innocence in pallor and dress my emotions in lunacy. Or, androgynous and demonic, I could appal as an unholy creature of corruption, hiding my pain behind a mask of bitterness. Marked for destruction, I could trade my white garments for the black of the dandy, cynical and misogynous. I'd finally make Columbine swoon, but should her fickleness become unbearable, I'd murder her and blame it on the moon.

Sole to dorsal surface, dorsal surface to sole, your feet, crossed at the ankles, caress one another. Dazzling me with whiteness, they twist and turn: So this is the mystery and holiness, this is the shining loveliness, of the spotless bird. You whisper:

— I'd like to be the swan, like in Michelangelo.

— And who'd be Leda?

— You, of course.

— Hmmm...

— Would you like that?

— Yes, if you're the swan.

— The swan dies singing.

— That's a good way to die.

What do you see in me, Marietta, what do you want me to be? Shall I be a perverse Pierrot, positing myself as the instrument of your overcoming? Indolent in my activity, skeptical in my credulity, I'd sport black pom-poms on my white costume and an impish grin on my painted face. An innocent waif courting Columbine, denying death and sexual difference, I'd enact a universe in which I'd survive any catastrophe: Never forced to choose one sex or the other, never forced to confront death's inevitability, I'd escape all the constraints of finitude. But in this lawless universe I'd neither crave belief nor claim coherence; I'd neither take my puppet-convulsions for a wielding of free will nor succumb to the illusion of culture. But don't get me wrong: My aim would be to establish the Law, not to undermine it: Columbine would be a dominatrix, a lawgiver whose orders I'd obey.

— That photo's still getting to me, Sprague. It's incredible!

Once more Aravane and the cat capture your gaze. You continue:

— It's a perfect fusion of secrecy and sexuality.

— Yes.

— You know, sometimes I think identity's just a set of ruses subject to revision. In other words, just a fiction.

What do you see in me, Marietta, what do you want me to be? Shall I be a pantomime Pierrot, a sad clown with a sensitive soul, pining for the love of Columbine? In my powdered face and black skullcap, my large-buttoned blouse and moondust pantaloons, I'd play the eternal dreamer, unvanquished by incomprehension. I'd knit my brow and pucker my lips, miming my sorrow; with a blink of an eye, a flick of the wrist, I'd banish my cares until tomorrow.

— I felt that very strongly, talking to Aravane.

— That notion of identity as fiction?

— Yes.

— You felt it about her or about yourself?

– Both of us. It was like we were making music, a two-part invention.

– And that invention, that's the set of ruses subject to revision?

– Exactly. That's the fiction of identity.

You're a tea rose on a trellised stem, you're sperm-and-pine resin; you're the rubbery powder on a tyre tube, you're mint-and-liquorice medicine: Your smell in my nostrils makes me want you again.

– Well, between you and Aravane, there certainly was something!

– Yes. And you know what? Even though we were strangers, it was as if we'd dreamed each other, and finally met in the flesh.

You're a bird taking a dust bath, you're a serpent uncoiling in the sun; you're a feline stretching deliciously, you're an impala leaping on its run: I love your alert luxury.

What do you see in me, Marietta, what do you want me to be? Shall I be a playground Pierrot, a crude buffoon in a knockabout world? Lovelorn, the butt of pranks, with my song-and-dance I'd dissolve all differences. Yes, in my conical hat and frilled collaret, madly I'd pursue Columbine, a punning jester to her impudent soubrette.

– And *have* you, in fact, dreamt of Aravane?

– How did you know?

– I don't. I'm asking.

– That's exactly what I wanted to tell you, Sprague. My dream of her.

– Tell me, then.

You're an English garden around a French castle, you're flesh-and-blood and courtly love; you're a book of hours in a pagan's hands, you're ice and fire when push comes to shove: Dream me the dream, Marietta!

– All right. I was out hang gliding with Aravane, and—

– Hang gliding?

– Yes. There's a photo in the study. She goes hang gliding off the Alborz mountains.

– Where's that?

– Outside Tehran. Anyway, we're in the air, maybe twenty meters apart. Below us, there's the slopes, brown and barren; ahead, the sprawling city. Then, before I know it, everything disappears. I'm alone in the void. No Aravane, no city, no dry plateau—nothing but blue. I don't panic, but I do feel anxious. Suddenly, out of this anxiety, comes a wonderful feeling of serenity. I couldn't see the world, I understood, because the world and I were one!

– Hmmm...

— I felt euphoric—until I realized there was nowhere to land! After an instant of panic, I felt strangely elated. Nothing could hurt me, nothing could touch me—I was invulnerable! And then, just as suddenly as they had vanished, the land was back, the city was back, but Aravane, she was nowhere to be seen. I picked myself a landing spot, started my descent, and just as I touched the ground I found myself beside Aravane—in bed!

— Are you sure it was just a dream?

— Quite sure!

— The dream's rather transparent, isn't it?

— Dreams are never as simple as they seem.

You're the sundial that tells moon-time, you're the warrior that fights for peace; you're the grass that grows in tarmac, you're the black sheep with the golden fleece: So what does the dream mean?

— It's like this, Sprague. Aravane's hair is jet black, like yours. Her eyes are emerald, like yours. Her skin is the same coffee colour, and it glows like yours. She looks me in the eye the way you do; she tilts her head like you do. And she wears the same watch you wear.

— And when did you have this dream?

— The night of our first kiss, after Le Muguet.

— Hmmm...

— So you see, identity's just a set of ruses subject to revision.

I'm a tinderbox of longing, I'm a jukebox of jive; I'm a failed suicide, I'm happy to be alive!

— Is it the moon, Sprague?

— The moon?

You point to *A Carnival Evening.*

— I'm bewitched! That mysterious face in the mirror!

— In the mirror? You mean in the kiosk?

— No. In the— Look! It's *my* face!

I lean over to see my face displace yours.

— Of course it's your face.

A boy slides open a shower curtain. Faeringa! His heart leaps as a stranger steps out of a mirror. The boy stares into the glass: His face configures a double of the stranger.

— But I didn't...

As you blush all my senses are seduced.

— It's only the mirror's way of dreaming, Marietta.

I take your hand and thread my fingers through yours.

— You didn't know what you were doing there, did you?

— No, I didn't. I'm sure that cat's put a spell on me!

— No, that's Rousseau's magic. Most of his best paintings, the ones with the greatest evocative force, are the ones with a figure in a landscape, and you don't know what they're doing there.

— Just like in a dream.

— Yes.

Your eyes shine and I see mine in them.

— Lick my palm, Marietta.

You do so. I pass my hand over my face.

— Sprague, have you become a cat?

— Didn't you say identity's just a fiction, a set of ruses subject to revision?

Laughing, you turn towards me and lick my cheek.

Does the hawk ask how the air holds it? Does the serpent wonder where its legs went? So why do I question this happiness? In the magic lantern of my mind I see a carnival of love; I see beguilement, I see transfiguration, I see all I've dreamed of. And then comes the unravelling, the wrenching, the doomed soul returning to the house of the dead. Marietta, between the idol of certainty and the harlequin of doubt, help me to find a useable figure of faith: I love you.

Chapter 7

When you surprised yourself in the mirror, when you became a stranger to yourself, who was the who you dreamt yourself to be?

– *Mirror, mirror, tell no lies, how do I look in Manet's eyes?*

– *In daubs of pure colour and blurred contours, in rough, painterly brushstrokes, you flaunt your wanton beauty in the face of all who would confront you. The shriek of the cat your* chatte *knows that but her hackled back is not your bent: Neither scorn nor adulation, neither odium nor idolization, can disturb your composure. Here there is no erotic mirage, nothing to trap desire; here there is only flesh and blood infused with ice and fire: The self-possessed cannot be possessed.*

Disembodied, then warm and husky, your voice returns from beyond the looking glass:

– It's always a reconstruction, isn't it?

– What is?

– Self-knowledge.

– Yeah, I'd say so. It's only in retrospect that we understand ourselves.

– Yes, but even then, the person we think we understand is no longer the person we are. We're just playing catch-up with the past.

– It's impossible to understand ourselves in the present?

– Impossible.

– So you and I, here and now—we don't know what we're doing in Aravane's bed?

– That's right. Close your eyes!

I close my eyes.

– I've got a little surprise for you.

A drawer slides out. Night table.

– Don't peek!

– I'm not.

The drawer slides in. The sheet flies off.

– Keep your eyes closed!

Feather soft, velvet flow; silken brush, breath blow: With exquisite touch you caress my cock.

– Open your eyes!

Big ears of silver grey, body an anthracite plush; black nose, black eyes, stubby arms outstretched: The puppet on your hand does a puppet dance; with you flopped down at my feet, in singsong it talks to my hard-on:

— My name is Kelly and I'm a koala, I eat eucalyptus and sleep all day long; I don't have much of a brain (and it's not because I'm blonde!) but I do know what to do with a ding-dong.

Surprised at the felicity of your rhyme, you break into a broad smile: My laughter is unrestrained. You stand up and toss me the hand puppet.

— Meet Kelly, courtesy of Sydney Airport.

Lifting the sheet, you slip into bed beside me. You ignore the Kodiak the koala's left behind.

— You know what, Marietta? I think Kelly's got the makings of a handjob queen.

— Bestiality! I once did have a dream.

Marian Engel.

— Of what?

— A great big grizzly!

Kicking off the sheet, you pounce upon my plenitude: A little too greedy, you gag. And then back into your mouth you ease the beast, find a rhythm, and before too long the torchlight of your twirling tongue has him growling in the cavern. Steely on his hind legs, straining for the stars, the silvertip in darkness begets asters in your eyes. You pause to admire your work, then bring your resisting mouth to his vehemence. As his head breaks through the barrier of your lips, you maintain the pressure until the wetness of your mouth overwhelms him: For the stars he strains. With indrawn cheeks you withdraw; with a flick of the tongue you finish. And then into your den you take him again, and with lips and tongue embed in his brain the possibility of a new beginning. Your ardour feeding his appetite, he receives every sensation you procure him as a gift from a dancing god: skunk cabbage and lily roots, mountain sheep and moose; elderberries and cutworm moths, marmots and molluscs: In your maw he feasts. Hail! It comes, the *ricorso,* silvering my nerves, it comes to preserve chaos from the closure of order. Egg white and almond, sea spawn and milk: Bringing your mouth to mine, you leave me a taste of your work.

Picking up the koala, you take your place beside me, your back to the headboard.

— I think I'll make her an outfit, something summery.

— How, in fact, do you know it's a her?

— Sometimes she's a her, sometimes she's a he. She can swing both ways.

— Make her a pair of Bermuda shorts. Stick some tits on her and let her go topless.

— She's not an exhibitionist!

— Run a pair of suspenders over her nipples. Like that, she'd be both stylish and modest.

— No, she's not a cabaret singer!

— I know: hot pants and a halter top!

— Too sluttish!

— Then make her a G-string and a man's shirt.

— And an umbrella!

— Yes!

— And polka-dot gumboots!

— Oh yes!

— And a hula hoop!

— Yes, yes!

— No. I think she'd prefer a grass skirt and a coconut bra.

— But she's from Australia!

— Yes. But her mother's from Polynesia.

— I see: She wants to appropriate her mother's powers of seduction! And what about her father?

— He's a master thief, born and bred in Coolangatta. Walked the plank at Snapper Rocks.

— Hmmm... I wonder if Kelly's still not a little in love with him?

— Oh she is, she is. That's why I'm going to make her a dinner jacket, so she can be a gentleman thief too.

— Excellent! Make it fall wide of her cleavage, so her breasts are half exposed—Hey, I heard a good one: Why do mermaids wear seashells?

— Why do mermaids wear seashells?

— Yeah, you know, on their breasts, as a bra.

— I don't know. Why?

— Because 'B' shells are too small.

You smile, then cup your breasts and say:

— Kiss them.

I turn and do so, one then the other.

— Lick them.

I do so, one then the other.

— Suck them.

I do so, one then the other.

– Now if you only knew what a pain in the ass they can be!

– Yeah?

– Yeah.

– Tell me about it.

And thus you came to speak of how, invaded by the changes budding girls undergo, you stopped denying your sexuality and surrendered your body—an external object, beyond your control—to the mystery of femininity. Colluding with the enemy, you'd wear tight panties: the better to stimulate your pussy. Put on a looser pair: sighing innocence and virginity. Yes, you already knew clothes would be critical in regaining control of your identity. But what about her, the other? Were you aware that becoming a woman would make you a rival to your mother? You sensed it in your nerves, you sensed it in your bones—and you trembled.

Chapter 8

When you surprised yourself in the mirror, when you became a stranger to yourself, who was the who you dreamt yourself to be?

– *Mirror, mirror, tell no lies, how do I look in Boucher's eyes?*

– *In brush strokes that caress the canvas, in paint sensually applied, you lie on your belly amid tumultuous sheets, naked and insouciant. Propped up on the arm of the divan, you have an air of sleepy alertness as you stare out of the picture frame. Tender, warm, desirable, a nubile child on the way to womanhood, you are oblivious to the effrontery of your wide open thighs blithely inviting penetration.*

Disembodied, then warm and husky, your voice returns from beyond the looking glass:

– I went to a Vivienne Westwood show in London.

– That's a hot ticket!

– Yeah.

– How'd you get it?

– Kassia Ibarra. She's a friend.

– Kassia Ibarra—'From Guernica to the Catwalk'?

– Yes. So you read her interview in *Libé?*

– I did.

– She received a lot of flak for that. But the fact is, both her parents are civil war babies. Her father from Spain and her mother from Greece. They met in Buenos Aires as refugees.

– So when she speaks of working as a war photographer—

– She's totally sincere. In fact, her photos from El Salvador are about to appear in *The Observer*. Remember her name, Sprague. I'm certain you'll be hearing about her.

– All right, I will.

I did remember. And when, a few years later, the Serbs' massacre of the Bosnians began, it was Kassia Ibarra's photos that made me understand the conflict was not a civil war, but the expulsion and murder of a people.

– Did you like the show?

– I did. Harris Tweed. In particular a bodice, cape and skirt on a ravishing redhead.

— I like Vivienne Westwood. I like her quirky originality.

— Yes, it's refreshing.

— She's got that in common with Sonia Rykiel. They're both self-taught, as it turns out. I'm sure that's no coincidence.

— Are you suggesting their style comes from their lack of schooling?

— Indirectly, yes. They abhor perfection. They're original.

— You do like that theme, don't you? Kahn, Manet, Satie...

— I do.

— One can be original and still be perfect, Sprague. Look at Saint Laurent.

— The imperfection in his life outweighs the perfection in his art. So long as the net result is imperfection, the art lives.

— Rather curious, your theory! And besides, you haven't defined perfection.

— It's the idea of closure, completeness. Nature can afford to be perfect, because it's constantly in a state of flux. There's always an opening for the new. Man cannot, because civilization seeks fixity and permanence. So if you add closure into the mix, it's a recipe for death. Perfection in art is deadly.

— A rather grandiose statement, don't you think?

— No. Just compare Cabanel and Manet. *The Birth of Venus* is perfection; *Olympia* is imperfection. Manet's painting is far more interesting.

— I defend perfection in the name of craft, not art. Being well-trained gives you the means to express your originality. And if you don't have any, at least what you make will be well-made.

— True.

What exactly have I got against perfection? That schooling and I never got along? That I prefer the wildflower to the cultivar? The stray cat to the lapdog?

— And you, Sprague, have you ever seen fashion up close?

— I have. With Muriel. And at Film School I worked on a documentary about fashion students at Saint Martins School of Art.

— That must have been fun.

— It was. The director was an amazing woman from Lebanon, Ariane. I was editor, transforming chance into destiny.

— I see. And did you work well together, you and Ariane?

I like the mischief in your eyes, the particular sparkle of yellow sapphire.

— Oh yes. We spent days and nights in the cutting room—we had tons of footage—and—miracle of miracles!—we had exactly the same vision of the story and how to tell it.

— And that's rare?

– Yes. Documentaries are really made in the editing room. With the same material you can go in very different directions.

– I see.

– Imagine the footage is a slab of marble—different sculptors will see different possibilities of what to do with it. When you're sitting at your Steenbeck—that's an editing table—and both of you see, for example, *David* in the stone, it's a fantastic feeling. You know that while you're chiselling away at an arm or a hand, the other understands that the foot and the leg have to echo them. You're working together to make one harmonious body. I can tell you teamwork doesn't always work out so well.

– So you and Ariane were both Michelangelo?

I like the devilment in your eyes, the distinctive glitter of golden beryl.

– You could say that. The film won the documentary prize at the School's twenty-fifth anniversary competition.

– Congratulations! Now tell me about Ariane and your long nights in the cutting room.

– Work, work, work. And she smoked like a chimney!

– Come on, Sprague, don't tell me her smoke didn't get in your eyes.

– Well, to tell the truth, it did.

– Go on then, tell me all about it.

I like the impishness in your eyes, the quirky glow of dravite tourmaline.

– What can I say? She knows how to walk in high heels, she can walk through fire and banana peels.

– I didn't say write me a lyric, I said tell me about your Lebanese lover!

– All right, all right—by and by.

In a flash you're astride me, grabbing my wrists and pinning me to the headboard. And then between my throat and clavicle you plant your lips and suck in my skin.

– Marietta! Stop!

You suck harder, then give me a final flourish of mouthwork before you withdraw.

– There, now you're going to have a nice little lovebite—signed Marietta Valero!

You release my wrists and take my head in your hands: Slow like honey and velvety as eau-de-vie is the *pelle* you *roules* me.

– Now let's take a look at my signature.

Between my legs your mouthwork is manifest, but a spot by my throat is what you inspect.

— It's nice and red now. In a little while it will be blue.

— Roses are red, violets are blue; I once knew a girl, God she could screw!

— Tell me about her!

— I'm talking about *you!*

You pivot back to your place beside me. Your back to the headboard, you draw up the sheet.

— Come on, Sprague. I want to hear all about the amazing Ariane.

— All right. Are you ready?

— Yes.

And thus I came to tell you of the transgressive thrill that accompanied the feeling of homecoming when I made love with Ariane: Our skin is the same colour, our hair of the same thread: She is Phoenician, Greek, Armenian and Arab—her blood, like mine, is mixed. Impure, outlaw, at home everywhere and nowhere, in her I recognized my kin: She was my sister, and that was incest.

And then I told you of *La chambre secrète,* Robbe-Grillet's *instantané* that, at Film School, Fernando had asked Ariane to read. She did. And when he asked her if she'd play the woman in it, she said she would. A few weeks later there she was, naked on her back on velvet cushions, chains stretched from her ankles and wrists and blood dripping from her breast: You could have heard a pin drop in the screening room. Fernando had brilliantly captured the mystery in Moreau's painting, the allure of Robbe-Grillet's narration. Out of the play between curling smoke plumes and shadowy colonnades, Oriental tapestries and a brilliant blood stain, Ariane's body distilled an intense eroticism: I knew that body, and I felt proud. But more than pride, I felt gratitude, for it was Ariane who'd shown me that sex in the bedroom need not be the shadow of sex in the head: It can be its enactment.

And then I told you of how, when Ariane was away, I'd stay in her apartment on Charlotte Street. By the bookshelf in her living room, Baal would salute me with a bolt of lightning. Standing there one day, I opened a book on Lebanon and my eyes fell on the epigram: 'Here I am, the wretched city, lying in ruins, my citizens dead. You who pass me by bewail my fate, and shed a tear in honour of Beirut that is no more'. That had been written by an unknown poet—in the sixth century. 'Lebanon is an illusion', I recalled Ariane telling me, 'family, village and religion are more important than being Lebanese. Society has been destroyed; we're going nowhere, playing in our own blood'. I flipped to a page further on, and learned that Armenians, Syrians, Kurds and Palestinians joined the citizens split into Sunni and Shiite, Orthodox and Maronite, and no end of other clans. And in this mosaic, I wondered, where did Ariane fit in? Maronite

Christian, Francophile Lebanese, in affirming the Arabic element of her identity she had become a traitor to her tribe. Both of us are of indeterminate affiliation, I reflected, at once citizen and stateless, but only she had her father, mother, and brothers blown up in a car bomb: Beirut, April 1975. It had been impossible to gather the fragments of the bodies and bury them: Ariane packed up and left for London.

And then I took you deeper into Ariane's past, telling you of how, in the early seventies, she had studied anthropology in Paris and—before the war interrupted her studies—architecture and graphic design at the American University of Beirut. In London she had a contact, and began a career in interior design. To keep going she needed a powerful painkiller, and found one in heroin. By a miracle of will she developed rituals to avoid addiction. Each time the drug in her blood crossed the barrier to her brain, she found herself in a heaven where nothing ever happens: safe at last in subtle euphoria, no need to fight or flee. After three years she traded in that heaven for a husband, and three years later, that husband for a psychoanalyst. That woman did her a world of good. And then she decided she wanted to make documentaries, and while continuing to work in interior design, winning ever-more prestigious projects, she became a film student.

And then I took you back into Ariane's apartment and told you of her Phoenician statuettes: Bes, half-demonic and half-divine, standing for protection; Taweret, goddess of motherhood, standing for life. In a wall, in an illuminated recess, stood a winged Sphinx with an enigmatic face. 'From the Sphinx there is no escape', Ariane would say, 'our fate is as mysterious as it is necessary'. I'd protest that freedom overrides fate. Ariane would reply, 'When you're my age, Sprague, you'll change your mind'. (She was right.)

Then I told you of the cruel irony of Ariane and maternity: She'd had two abortions by the time she was twenty; by the time she was thirty it was clear she could no longer conceive. At thirty-three, at Film School with me, there was nothing in the world she wanted more than to be a mother. A child of her own being impossible, she set out to adopt an orphan, an abandoned baby in Beirut: They wouldn't let her.

The ravage wrought by mother on daughter, the guilt when the mother is gone: Only the talking cure allowed her to free herself and bury her phantom babies, her little ones with no name.

I concluded by telling you what Ariane does today: She is a maker of documentaries, at once hard-hitting and fiercely intimate. You asked for an example. I mentioned *They Won't Get Me!,* a documentary on anorexic girls as moving as *The Glass Menagerie* and as funny as *Waiting for Godot*.

– I see what you mean, Sprague: Ariane *is* an amazing woman.

You kick off the sheet and spring off the bed.

– And so am I!

In a flash you're at my feet, pulling me by the ankles till I'm flat on my back.

– I too know how to walk in high heels, I too can walk through fire and banana peels. Raise your head!

You slip a pillow under it.

– Relax.

Your body heat in the pillow bears a promise—of what?

– Close your eyes.

I feel you on the bed, I feel you moving. Your body brushes against mine: A flock of starlings comes to roost on my nerve-strings. You're on your knees, you're crawling. Beneath my eyelids there's a shimmering of wings, on my skin a fluttering. You're moving up, you're approaching. Downy feathers are caressing my sides, I sense a flowering of plumage: Is a bird hovering above me? Yes, I feel the warm-blooded beating of its heart, I feel its vigilant presence.

– Hey, Sprague, you all right down there?

I open my mouth to speak: Your pussy comes to close it.

– Open your eyes!

On your knees astride me, you lean back, beaming. I place my hands on your hips; you lean forward and grip the headboard. My head in the hinge of your thighs, my lips on your lips, I move my mouth through the vowel chart of your valiance—hot joy sure view, she sit spread cat, jive up churn away—while my tongue articulates the consonants of your cunning.

– Welcome to your private lesson, lover! The subject of my talk today is 'What do high heels mean to a woman?'. Are you ready?

– Yum, yum.

– What?

– I am, I am.

In a swaggering rhythm you raise and lower your torso, brushing your lips upon my lips, pressing them upon me.

– Okay, let's go! In high heels a woman feels sexy and self-assured, feminine and conquering.

You lean back and offer yourself more openly to my delectation.

– A woman needs as many pairs as her moods. I, for example, have satin pumps in purple and blue, stilettos in pewter and python, and split T-bar sling-backs, to name just a few.

Over my nose you sweep your folds, back and forth you trace a swath.

— And now that I've learned you like Marilyn, I could get myself a pair of marabou-trimmed mules.

You rise on your knees and make teasing descents to my tongue, swooping out of reach friskily.

— Now let's consider high heels from an engineering perspective.

Around the perimeter of my mouth you take your pussy for a ride, my hands on your ass playing backseat driver.

— By raising the heel, stilettos shift the body's centre of gravity, throwing it into a state of tension.

You rise onto your knees; I spiral my hands around your thighs.

— The ass sticks out—like this—while the tits thrust forward—thus.

I bring my hands to the first hemispheres, I heave and squeeze as I mould the mounds. Bringing your *minou* to my mouth, you take my hands and place them on your breasts.

— The instep deepens, the legs become longer, the calves more shapely. The woman is elevated, her body is balancing differently. She feels both powerful and vulnerable. And all of that while she's standing still.

Between my forefingers and thumbs your nipples harden; as I work your breasts, you grind your ardour against my appetite.

— Is my exposition clear, Sprague?

— Mmm-hmmm!

Of all the ways to be tongue-tied, is there any more intoxicating?

— Now let's take a look at what happens when she walks.

To and fro, grinding against me, you continue.

— Her hips sway, her ass swings; she moves to a different tempo. And all the while, between her legs, there's a subliminal buzz of pleasure!

Hopping to my tripping tongue, your clit dances a rigadoon; a steady basso at your back door, my finger continuo gives the tempo.

— Now you see, Sprague... Ooo-hooooo!

Rising on your knees, you pause to regain your composure, and then once again, teasingly to my tongue you make descents, swooping out of reach friskily.

— ...the danger of high heels is that it's easy to look awkward in them. All the art, then, is aimed at appearing elegant.

Top to bottom, front to back, in a flowing caress I run my hands around your body.

— Does my presentation please you, Sprague?

You thrust your loveliness upon my lips.

— Mmm-hmmm!

Of all the ways to be gagged, is there any more glorious?

– Now ponder this, for it shows the power of high heels: For me, in the beginning, I felt more naked in high heels than I did in a décolleté.

Luscious and slow, long and delectable, the strokes of my tongue can do no wrong: Your pleasure is my pleasure.

– I'd never dare wear heels with a skirt—or even a dress—but with jeans there was no problem, I felt fine.

You lower your head and toss back your hair; gazing into your eyes, I sign my signature.

– So, my lover, you see high heels don't dress you, they undress you!

Your skin gleams; your hair falls forward, swaying.

– They change your mood, your perception of yourself.

Rising on your knees, you rotate your hips through my hunger.

– You can play a role, be someone else. Now tell me, Sprague...

Spiralling your pelvis, your present your pussy to my mouth.

– ...has my demonstration convinced you?

– Mmm-hmmm!

Of all the ways to be muzzled, is there any more magnificent?

– And now you know what high heels mean to a woman!

You withdraw your pussy that my mouth may speak, but it is my eyes that say, 'We belong together'. Gilding my fingers in the gold of your hair, I sweep up the light-shivered locks: Releasing them, I scatter glittering dust. Once more your lips shape my lips, once more your *moule* shapes my mouth. In my blood I feel your fervour, in my heart your holiness. Come, let us conclude the sacrament—let us go to the Garden.

Look! Rhododendrons, larkspurs, columbines and auriculas, poppies, roses and box: Tell me, Marietta, are you in their sway? Aye-aye: Credit your boldness to the columbines, your hilarity to the larkspurs. Thank the box for your stoicism, the auriculas for your devotion. And the rhododendrons? To them credit your gravitas: They know that no flower, tree, shrub or weed, no grass, fern or fungus—nothing in the Garden can offer an antidote to the poison of love. Yet the beauty of the roses cannot be denied: Blood-red atop their daggered stems, they uphold love's violence against the poppy's oblivion. So what will it be? Attar, or opium? Let us go deeper into the Garden.

On the damp earth I lie between your legs, my head at your hunger, my eyes everywhere. Look! Slugs are gliding up your instep, they're insinuating themselves between your toes. Against my lips you press your longing; eagerly my mouth intensifies it. Look! Butterflies have burst through their silk-fastened tents, they're streaming from your throat; ladybirds are crawling out of your nostrils, they've shed their steely coats. Slurping your succulence, I free your spirit from its veil of flesh. Look! Salmon-pink blooms are lighting up the rhododendrons, clematis is threading lilac through the trees; laburnum is cascading bright yellow flowers, violet is spiralling through camassia leaves. Enigmatic, immediate, your sex in my mouth affirms me in my strangerhood; vitalizing my being, your elixir brings me to presence. Look! Garden-pool carp are writhing on your belly, your pelvis is cinctured in snails; your sugary-pink nipples are crawling with ants, badgers are licking your fingertips. To a final flourish of my tongue your body gives up the ghost: Through earth, through air, through fire and water, the butterflies transport your soul; crossing the threshold of the creaturely, they deliver you to the quintessence.

Attar, or opium? In the quintessence they are indistinguishable.

Intermezzo 2: Vika

I've been walking the empty beach, Marietta, I've been walking the empty streets, threading my heart through the ghost of you. Yes, here in this city on the Baltic Sea, I've been walking in beauty and squalor, haunted by memories of you. The sun-and-rain mirror my eyes, the seagulls' cry echoes the crows', but resplendent is my dereliction because I did indeed speak true.

You are that oil stain on the asphalt
I am the sunshine that celebrates it
You are that dress hung out to dry
I am the breeze that undulates it

I am that bread loaf on a baker's shelf
You are the yeast that raised it
I am that bouquet in a tin bucket
You are the water that sustains it

Now where do dogs go to die
When the crawl space is crowded?
Where do wild horses roam
When the prairie is burning?

You are that bridge spanning the river
I am the initiation at the end of it
You are that red pine reaching for the sky
I am the sun that acclaims it

Now where do tigers go to drink
When all the rivers have run dry?
Where do swallows herald spring
When winter's pall is never-ending?

And thus it goes, a coffee in a café, a lyric a day, and your absence spreading like a bloodstain.

Braised duck with cranberry jam; carrot cake with quince ice-cream: How could I not think of you? Afterwards, the waitress insisted I try the local drink: black balsam and akvavit. I said I would if she'd join me. She did.

The firewater kick was welcome, but talking to Vika was the real attraction. A bedhead blonde with kohl-rimmed eyes, she had a punky edge to her Nordic pallor. When I asked her how long she's been working here, she said she doesn't, she's just visiting her parents who own the place. She's a student in computer science at Riga Technical University. I asked her what it's been like, saying goodbye to Communism. 'It's like coming up for air after having been submerged all your life'. She asked me what I'm doing here. 'I'm writing a lyric suite about surviving suffocation'. She said: 'You must speak to my mother'.

And so I listened to her mother speak of gestures of resistance: cheering for opposition sports teams when they were playing the Russians; the 'accidental' use of crimson and white, the national colours, in everything from a cake decoration to a flower arrangement; creating a counter-calendar to government-sponsored celebrations (marking the Molotov-Ribbentrop pact instead of the inclusion of the Baltic republics into the USSR). When her mother asked me why I was interested in such things, I sidestepped her question, but when I was alone again with Vika I explained that, somehow, I know what it's like to live in a culture of lies, to suffocate in hypocrisy, and consequently, I feel a sense of belonging when I'm with people who've lived through that. Vika couldn't understand; she thought I was talking politics. (Imagine my pleasure, then, at receiving an email from her when *Breathing Under Water* came out: She said she'd finally understood what I'd been talking about.) I fell silent and stared into her steel-blue eyes. And then, scratching the back of her head, she cast an oblique glance across the room, mostly empty tables by now. I don't know if it was the spider of black spinel that gleamed in her sternal notch, the lock of hair that fell over her eye or the way her top slid off her shoulder, but a longing for you suddenly pierced my heart. 'If you're free tomorrow', she said, 'I can show you around'. 'I'd love that', I replied.

Sitting beyond the shadow of her destiny, Vika sips her Krāslavas beer. From gunmetal to clear blue her eyes veer as she celebrates her freedom: Once I'd have been condemned to die here. The grinding of a streetcar rounding a curve leads to a conversation about Frida Kahlo; a palimpsest of graffiti under peeling paint leads to an exchange about John Lennon: Vika says her father once got arrested for writing 'Beatles' on a wall. Tar and rust and gasoline, oily brine and dust: Vika rubs her eyes and slips on her sunglasses. She smiles as I stare through her grey-green disguise; holding her gaze, I caress her cheek.

I don't think of you
When she straightens my collar.
I don't think of you

When she knots my scarf.
When she walks beside me and takes my arm,
I don't think of you.
But when the wind takes her hair
My heart sinks:
I'm trying very hard, Marietta,
But there is always and only you.

I don't think of you
When she talks to me.
I don't think of you
When she rolls a cigarette.
When she brews me tea and dries my hair,
I don't think of you.
But when the sun dies in her eyes
My heart sinks:
I'm trying very hard, Marietta,
But there is always and only you.

I don't think of you
When we go to the cinema.
I don't think of you
When she whispers in my ear.
When she talks of Stalin and Tarkovsky,
I don't think of you.
But when she licks a raindrop from her lips
My heart sinks:
I'm trying very hard, Marietta,
But there is always and only you.

The night is transparent as I walk the street, the sky is vast and clear. I've kissed Vika goodbye, I've brightened the gunmetal in the blue of her eyes. Blue, blue, blue—Marietta, hear me now, that I may honour you!

Chapter 9

— To think that all that beauty, that purity, that angelic innocence, was drawn from a two-bit café and a garbage dump!

In a restaurant on rue de la Roquette, across the glow of an indigo candle, we talk about *Je t'aime, moi non plus.*

— Now do you understand my silence?

— I do, Marietta.

— I was simply overwhelmed.

I am moved by the way this mythical tale of love in a no-man's land moves you, I am moved by the way you are touched by this tragicomedy of innocence lost.

— What a film!

I sip my Gewürztraminer: The fineness of the wine complements your fervour.

> Loosely framing your face, from your updo wisps of hair
> tumble down. Is it because they know, however elegant
> your array, your indwelling soul will always be wild?

— What's happening with *The Dustman's Daughter,* Sprague? Is it ever going to get off the ground?

— No. I think we can pronounce the last rites and bury it.

— Why not turn it into a play?

— No. It only works as cinema. It's kinetic, you have to feel all the movement, the flow, as one and the same movement, and only the camera can accomplish that.

— What movement?

— The movement from daughter to father, daughter to brother, daughter to lover.

— Funny, because it's really about son to mother.

Stunned, I hold your gaze.

— You understood a lot more than you let on, that night at Le Muguet!

You smile enigmatically.

— Why don't you just tell it straight?

— Impossible. Only the Greeks had the structures to tell such a story. Today it would just get stuck in a goo of psychologizing.

As you pinch a strip of wax pepper to a morsel of curried fish, the dexterity with which you handle your chopsticks impresses me. 'Hey Johnny Jane': As I hum the melody, the candle invents fire in the black of your pupil, the curried fish discovers the Indian spice kitchen, the wax pepper creates the hottest, the most expansive, the most burning of colours: Everything is happening for the first time.

> Pearly green sets off the amber of your eyes. Rusty orange darkens your lips. Is it because they know the lily needs no raiment that they are so discreet?

– You could have knocked me down with a feather when she said that!

– Said what?

– *'Je suis un garçon.'*

> Geometric swirls of river-green drop from your earlobes. Is it because their gentle tug maintains a subtle tension with your sex that they bear that nacreous glow?

– The homosexuality is entirely incidental.

So you say as you serve yourself from the prawn and pomelo salad.

– It's just a metaphor.

– For what?

– Love between a man and a woman.

Touched and disturbed by your lucidity, I lean back and sip my wine. I'm certain of the sincerity of your conviction, and wonder what it might mean for you and I. To what extent do we still believe, in the darkness of our being, that both sexes are within us, that we are omnipotent and immortal?

> On the black silk of your blouse, in a richly-printed rhythm, indigo, emerald and gold cluster into windswept leaves. Is it because your bra is offering them your breasts that the leaves tremble so?

– Sprague, ask that guy behind you for his pack of matches.

A mischievous gleam comes into your eyes.

– What for?

– You'll see.

He gives it to me and says 'Keep it'; I pass you the *pochette*. You break off a match and strike it, blow out the candle flame then into the smoke place the burning match. Whoosh! Down the trail of smoke the flame travels and relights the candle.

– Marietta! You're magic!

– I am, aren't I?

I blow out the candle: Down the trail of smoke my lips travel and alight on yours.

– You and Quentin, Sprague—there's something brotherly between you. You enjoyed seeing the film with my students, you enjoyed having a drink with us afterwards.

– Yeah, we're both bastards.

– And very good-looking ones at that!

With deft chopsticks you pinch up a morsel of chicken and chilli jam.

Algae bloom
In spring frost: A hint of green
In your fingernail gloss.

– Shall I tell you his story?

– You know it?

– Yes. He approached me last week, after *Paris, Texas*. I took him to Allard. We talked.

– Tell it to me, then!

In wisps of blonde
Earrings sway: From the treadmill of events
Time breaks away.

And thus I came to tell you the story of Quyen Thanh. It went like this. 1966. Vietnam. Mother met father at Phan Rang Air Base. He was in charge of logistics, she was a translator. He took her to restaurants, bought her gifts, played with her four-year old son. They fell in love and envisioned a future together. One day a warehouse accident leaves the American lying unconscious in a pool of blood; he wakes up three weeks later in a military hospital in Massachusetts. Seven months later his son is born. The father is discharged from the army and cannot get back to Vietnam; the mother cannot leave unless she abandons her first son. She chooses to stay.

Mother and baby, having stigmatized not only her immediate family, but also her extended family, future family members, and her ancestors, find themselves living in isolation, cut off from family ties. Quentin nevertheless grows up a happy child, despite the daily taunts about his difference. His mother can afford to have him cared for while she's at work; she also succeeds in getting him into school. He gets along well with his brother, who teaches him how to make spinning tops out of guava wood and kites from bamboo. One day at the beach at Nha Tran his brother disappears in the undertow; when the tide turns his body is washed ashore. Wracked by guilt, Quentin's mother is inconsolable; the kindness of Quentin's caregiver, a woman of seventy-two, helps pull them through.

Mother and father correspond, arrange a meeting in the Philippines that is thwarted at the last minute. Learning English from his mother, Quentin soon impresses her with his proficiency. He studies photos of his father, he studies images of the happy couple, and a certainty arises in his heart that one day they will be together. And then a new torment comes in the realization that the South is losing. Like all mothers of Amerasian children, Quentin's mother is terrified. Rumours are rife, panic spreads: The Communists will kill everyone who's ever been involved with the Americans.

The end comes faster than anyone had expected. While helicopters whirr overhead, letters and photos are thrown into a fire, souvenirs are destroyed. Mother and son run to a hiding place under a kindly neighbour's house. Four months later they find themselves in a desolate jungle near the Cambodian border: a New Economic Zone. Between forest clearing and farm labour, they undergo political indoctrination.

One day a former Viet Cong soldier, in charge of land reclamation, claims Quentin's mother as his wife. His first act as father is to tear up Quentin's school books and order him to scour the jungle for bamboo shoots they could steam and sell. In the evenings the man amuses himself by beating up Quentin and saying, 'I'm fighting America to help my country'! And then he beats his wife. When Quentin tries to intervene, the man drives him out of the house, refusing to let him ever sleep there again.

At the jungle's edge, in a deserted temple, the boy makes himself a bed of leaves. When soldiers occupying the temple force him to leave, he finds refuge in a wooden crate standing in a field of broken statues. Allowed to have lunch in the family hut, in the evening he either fries the fish he'd caught during the day or waits behind the chicken coop for his mother to bring him something. Her entreaties to the authorities are to no avail: She had worked for the enemy, and has no right to complain. Besides, what rights could a whore claim?

Encouraged by his mother to escape, the boy stows away on a truck and finds himself in Saigon. For some he is a victim of war, for others an image of the enemy: For all, he represents transgression. And thus his days of 'living dust' begin. Despite his beauty, hardly a day goes by without someone calling him 'half-breed pig-face'. What does he care? He has bathed in the love of his mother; his only concern is to free her from the impostor who calls himself her husband. Selling cigarettes, delivering ice, cleaning up after the market, he makes enough money to get himself to Phan Rang.

There he finds the old woman who'd looked after him in his early years; she finds him a place to stay with a couple who've lost three sons, all killed in combat with the Khmer Rouge. Quentin is ten but he understands that Vietnam is paradise compared to the killing fields of Cambodia. The couple's kindness towards him knows no bounds, but school is a series of humiliations. But what does he care if the children chant, 'Amerasians have assholes instead of eyes'? He's got a job to do: Figure out how to free his mother. Having memorized his father's address, he writes him a letter: 'Daddy, come and get us'. Using as a conduit the only orphanage in town that has not been closed down, he engages in a short exchange of letters with his father. Between the two countries diplomatic relations don't exist; the father petitions the Vietnamese authorities directly, to no avail. Quentin and his mother write to each other regularly, referring to his father in a code based on the availability of market produce.

Years go by. Nothing comes to unblock the impasse. And then one day Quentin's world collapses: His guardians receive a letter saying his mother has died of a fulgurating fever. The boy withdraws inside himself, beyond the sanctuary where his brother dwells, and floats away on a wave of white.

1982: Congress passes the Amerasian Immigration Act. Three months later Quentin is living with his father in Boston.

– What a story! How did he come to tell it to you?

– He recognized me as his brother.

– How?

– The same way the undead do: by the smell of impure blood.

Thai tea comes iced in a tall glass, with a sprig of mint and a straw. You get up and go to the washroom. I sip my tea: aniseed, orange blossom, tamarind. Suddenly at your empty chair an abyss opens; shuddering, I close my eyes and grip the table. And then I get a grip on myself. *Fort! Da! Fort! Da! Fort!*

– Hey!

– Hi.

As you settle into your seat, I feel blood returning to my cheeks. You stare into my eyes and begin to smile. And then you reveal your teeth: Bright red, your incisors glow. Taking on a dramatic voice, you say:

— I am your sister, my blood is impure. I am the monster breathing men cannot endure.

Winona Ryder. I remember the scene.

— In the shadow of death for all eternity, so am I.

— You are my love.

— You are my life.

— Always.

You pick up my glass and take the straw between your lips; holding my gaze, you suck up the tea. I take your glass and do the same.

— Shall we go? you ask.

Making a confessional grid of crossed fingers before my face, I whisper:

— I love you.

— What?

— I love you.

I lower my hands and position them in the flame of prayer.

— For your penance, drink ten Bloody Marys, kill three Our Fathers, and spend the night with twenty Holy Ghosts!

— Yes, Mother.

Out from the pit of my belly it breaks, a riot of laughter that overruns a wilderness of dreams. A waitress stops in her tracks, diners stare. I overtip our waitress and we leave in silence, hand in hand.

Chapter 10

In the Middle, Somewhat Elevated

With the applause my beating heart conspires to leave me breathless; I look into your eyes and see you are as stunned as I. What have we witnessed? Spiders in mating display? Matador and bull in the ceremonial kill? Karateka demonstrating combat stances? Aye, from our seats in the grand circle, we have seen the reinvention of ballet; we have seen the vestiges of academic virtuosity extended, accelerated and given a power that electrified the stage. Yes, in the Palais Garnier, two dancers in a pas de deux astounded us. Did they feel in their vertebrae, did they sense in their sinews, that this choreography is destined to endure? As the purity of their movements burned away all embellishments, did they know the erotic charge they were generating would lay bare our hearts? Unearthly angles and undulations, the steely majesty of wrenching turns: Who is the man with such a kinetic imagination? Helical motion and counter curvature, audacious extensions and volumetric form; off-kilter dynamics and casual contortions, high kicks and thrusting hips: Who is the master that conceived this miracle? Feline, vulpine, feminine, the sex and venom in a push-pull attack; virile, fluid, visceral, the violence and grace of a split kick snapped back: Who is the man who, in mingling the demonic and the divine, has resuscitated the corpse of classical dance? Forsythe. William Forsythe.

Was it his freedom that allowed him to turn the page on the past while preserving it in palimpsest? Was it his freedom that inspired the composer to write such unremittingly ecstatic music—telluric, architectonic, empyrean? Aye, was it his freedom that gave a spring to our step, a grace to our stride, as we stepped, hand-in-hand, into the night outside?

The walk

Silence burns along the edge of my breath, the gleam of metal in your eyes reflects it: Down the Avenue de l'Opéra, through folds of night stitched together by electric light, we walk as if we were meant to be. Marietta, in this relentless Haussmannian order, the quiet dissymmetry of your dress moves me; in this static Apollonian perfection, the flow of your silhouette inspires me. It's because of me, you said, this experiment with a Japanese dressmaker; it's because of me your wardrobe no longer reflects the person you feel yourself to be. Look! Swaying to your walk, the dynamic imbalance of black drapes its spartan elegance around your body. Slung over your shoulder, the flowing lines of your beggar's bag are a *mise en abîme* of your body. Who is the man who thus imbues form with emotion, shape with idea? Strawberry red are your lips, strawberry red your ankle boots; side-swept is your hair, sheer its flaxen fall. Are you happy with the self your new dress brings to the surface, are you happy with this possibility of who you can be? Your soft boots are silent on the tarmac, no click-clack measures your stride. Now, as we wait at the intersection, what is it that sets our interlocked hands swinging? Can ideas ever be as palpable as pirouettes, mental images as immediate as movement? May dance rescue us when ideas deplete the world, may we seek refuge in the erotics of knowledge! Onward! Look how your boots sculpt your movement, see how each step you take renews a moment of being! Behind you, your coat, your cloak, your cape—what is it?—catches the breeze. Paradox and contradiction, question answering question, the work only valid through the life it conveys: That is the message your movement relays. Who is the man who so artfully investigates your moving body, who is the man who so sensually envelopes your intimacy? Yamamoto. Yohji Yamamoto.

Was it his freedom that inspired you to supersede the dualisms of fashion—individuality and conformity, sex and success, man and woman—and refuse the game of the shifting erogenous zone? Was it his freedom that made you accept that black doesn't distract, that the face is the site of the soul, that in the serenity of your beauty you are free? Aye, was it his freedom that made you approve the red on my lips when you'd kissed me under the arcade?

Ambient luminescence, play of brilliants, the ellipsis of conjunctive loci: Walking through that architecture, did you, my love, like I, experience light as its fourth dimension? And just before we stepped into the square, did you catch a glimpse of the old theater's insignia? If you did, did you thrill, as I did, at reading the motto, *'simul et singulis'?* Who is the man who dreams of living like that with you, together and yet oneself? Who is the man who believes the quality of being together depends on the quality of being alone? As we step into the rue Saint-Honoré, I imagine Molière trading jokes over a beer with Shakespeare. And then Colette comes to join them, sparking the playwrights to a higher pitch with her ferocious vitality. Those are three who never let consciousness cannibalize the world! Who is the man who, inspired by Will and Sidonie-Gabrielle, vows before you to never let knowledge give things a less alien aspect?

Tuscan columns, empty medallions; denuded tympanum: The Revolution, or the Reformation? Walking by the Oratoire du Louvre, I reflect that our temple is wherever we are, wherever between consciousness and nature we build a bridge of metaphor. Who is the man who wants to worship in that temple with you? To take your hand and cross that threshold, to honour in equal measure naïve perception and conceptual elaboration, intuitive awareness and rigorous thought? Sprague. Sprague the harlequin. Holding your hand and opening his heart to all your presence brings him.

Duc des Lombards

Complexity in quietude, hushed sophistication; sublime understatement, emotion at midnight: So this is tenderness with a steely touch, this is chiselled grace; this is music for late-night lovers, a language not debased. Your body against mine in the plush booth expands my breath and pulse; while my lips delight in your earlobe, my hand pays homage to your heart. Who is the man combining formal beauty with lyrical virtuosity, inwardness with rhythmic propulsion? To your cool red lips you bring the grassy rye of your Manhattan.

— I was given to sudden outbursts, I couldn't clarify my feelings. I'd become full of suspicion, frustrated at my inability to communicate.

In the back of the bar, in the subdued light, you explain how your performing onstage counterbalances your vulnerability off it: In the spotlight, there you feel free.

— I would try to distance myself, and sometimes it worked.

Faithful to your inner promptings, true to your desires against the world's demands, you tried to solve the riddle of being without losing connection.

— I've never been able to conform to the requirements of social life.

Spartan left hand, free-form right; cool, meditative, other-worldly: Who is the man whose lush searching never loses sight of harmonic motion? Who is the man who dances through intricate structure, inventing in the fire?

— And then there's all the horrors of the world!

Maraschino cherry, bitters and sweet vermouth: I sip my Manhattan.

— The world will never work in harmony, Sprague. I'm certain of that. People simply can't pull it off.

Orange-pink and pale vermilion, your drink against black and white; ash-blonde and Venetian, your hair in shadow and light.

— That's why, in everything I do, I want a beginning and an end. It's my way of making sure I'll have nothing to reproach myself with, that I haven't been complacent.

— A beginning and an end—we don't always choose them, Marietta.

— That's exactly my point! I want to assume my responsibility, not just drift in and out of things.

— You demand a lot of yourself.

– If I didn't, I wouldn't go on. Why bother? Anyway, the world we've made is doomed.

You sip your drinking man's drink. The whisky seems to have gone to your head—why this sudden access of gloom?

– Music is one way I test myself, to see if I'm still in touch. And that's why, in performance, I come across as I do.

Your fingertips clear the mist on your glass; you take your cherry by the stem and swing it into your mouth. Who is the man whose sonorous fifths exude silence, who is the man who is running to stand still? Rubalcaba. Gonzalo Rubalcaba.

Was it his immersion in the moment that made you nostalgic for the stage? Was it his sensitivity that conducted you to yourself? What do you say, Marietta? Was it his quest for discovery that made you come out of hiding, was it his contained emotion that made you reveal yourself? And was it his taking himself perhaps a little too seriously that made you do the same? Did you realize it, and is that why you then did what you did? Remember? Sculpting my lips with your lower jaw, working your lips and tongue, you coaxed the cherry out of your mouth and into mine while your fingers, deft in touch, prepared my cock for the place the cherry had been expelled from. Aye, was it for that you did this?

Chapter 11

In the Jardins du Luxembourg

The model

The first step is to accept yourself. That's essential, it allows you to be at ease. The second step is to forget yourself—that's the key! Opening the lens to blur the background, I capture you in open sun as you embody these precepts of posing: In white jeans and tan jacket, navy sweater and canvas shoes, you crouch down among drifting leaves, your straw bag on the gravel. I love the way you inhabit your body, I love the way you assume your beauty: My Leica lets you know it. You hop onto a bench, step up onto the back and jump to the ground; you walk around and sit down.

– Take off your sunglasses.

You take them off.

– Tell me three things that annoy you.

– Three things... When the shop doesn't have my size in the shoes I want... When people park their car and don't straighten out the wheels... When the man beside me on a plane has a drink too many...

Every point has its pose; not missing a beat, I capture every nuance of your indignation. You spring to your feet and run off. In a quincunx of limes I catch up to you: Heart against heart at the centre, and a kiss for each corner of the world.

The football player

The ball rolls towards you, you jump out of your chair. Swiping it with the edge of your heel, you get it into the air then keep it there, juggling it with your feet. Aloft! Now you juggle it with your knees—left, right, left, right, left. Letting it fall, with your footwork you keep it from the ground. Stasis: In the crux between foot and shin you hold it, then flick it up and loop it before trapping it again. Aloft! Into the air you launch it and head it to the boy who'd come to retrieve it. He catches it and stands before you, wide-eyed and slack-jawed. Then, like all the onlookers catching the sun in their wrought iron chairs around us, he melts into delight.

Husband, house and baby

— We had a lot of fun, pushing Thomas and James along those wooden rails, towing Annie and Clarabel. I loved doing Sir Topham Hatt in German!

— The Fat Controller!

— *Bekommen Sie mehr Kohle, James! Jetzt!*

I laugh at your imitation of a supercilious German.

— Yes, for a while, babysitting was my favourite pastime.

I imagine the delight of the children in your charge. You continue:

— It's very refreshing, playing with children.

— Yes. Certainly preferable to exchanging platitudes with their parents.

— For sure!

Leaves rustle, the breeze picks up; the children sailing their boats in the pond let out delighted exclamations.

— You know, I once knew a girl who told me that just looking after a neighbour's dog gave her maternal stirrings.

— Maternal stirrings—from looking after a dog?

— Yes.

I shoo away a pigeon at my feet: In vain. It won't be diverted from what it's seeking.

— Did babysitting, perhaps, stir up your—?

— No, not at all. Husband, house and baby, that's never been my thing.

— But you have a house.

— Yes, but I don't live in it.

At the lip of the pond a boy salvages a boat, then sends it back out with a push of his bamboo stick.

— Who's living in it now?

— A Danish professor, her husband and two daughters.

— Was it difficult, deciding to let someone live in your house like that?

— No. One day I caught myself in a mirror, furiously vacuuming and crying hysterically. I knew it was time for a change.

— Why were you crying?

— Oh...

— Tell me.

— No. You'll figure it out, sooner or later.

Wooing a young hen, a puffing pigeon struts his iridescence in the dust.

— Let's just say that I don't believe one can have both stability and freedom.

— It's change that keeps you going?

— Yes. I never want to feel 'comfy'. For me that would mean stopping, no longer growing.

— Have you always felt that way?

— Ever since I was six. I decided right then I ought to earn my own living. I knew that was the basis of independence.

— At six?

— Yes. And when I was seven I began filling my piggy bank to buy my own house.

— And now you've done it!

— Yes. But not to be 'comfy'.

— For what, then?

— To be able to walk away. When you have your own house you can always walk away.

— From what?

— From whoever tries to trap you.

The gusting wind sends the sailboats crashing; the children work their bamboo sticks to set them right again.

Little Ronnie
Went to sea
In an open boat;
And while afloat
The little boat
Bended.
That's it,
My story's ended.

A cloud comes to block the sun.

— Shall we move on? you ask.

— Yes, let's.

Before I can rise you're sitting astride me, kissing me with the kisses of your mouth. Little Ronnie's boat is once again afloat.

Isn't sex always an experiment?

— I woke up this morning thinking it all a dream.

So I say as, through whimsical splashes of shadow and light, we walk around the Fontaine de Medicis.

— That's funny—I dreamt you were dreaming about it! And when did you realize it wasn't a dream?

– When I was having my coffee. It was only then I remembered we'd seen the film last night.

– That's a tribute to Robbe-Grillet. I'm sure he'd be pleased to hear that.

Bordering the pond, on pillars that punctuate the balustrade, classical urns of begonia and painted nettle prolong the autumn. I ask you:

– Do you agree there are at least three levels of reality in the film?

– Yes. But that's the easy part.

And thus we came to discuss *La Belle Captive,* a cinematic gem by Alain Robbe-Grillet; and thus, in so doing, we came to confront our visions of men and women at play. The ghost of our conversation still haunts the fountain; listen as I conjure it now.

On bright red stems amidst bronze-green leaves, orange flowers cascade from a concrete urn: I pluck one and stick it in your hair. Bending me over the balustrade, you take my head in your hands; soft on my throat your lips glide, hard on my skin your teeth bite.

– Aïe!

– Be careful, Sprague, lest a woman's enigmatic smile lead you to perdition.

You take my hand and lead me towards an urn of painted nettle.

– You'd have been a better Marie-Ange than Gabrielle Lazure!

– No, she was perfect. But the vampire dimension could have been done better. It needed a little more horror and fascination, don't you think?

– Yes. The eroticism lacked intensity.

Deep-purple is the heart of the nettle's brick-red leaves; yellow-bright their border. I continue:

– It's a shame, because had the sex been more powerful, Robbe-Grillet's game between 'real' and 'represented' would have worked even better.

– It's tricky for him, because he always wants distanciation.

– True. But cinema is an art of emotion. With just one close-up of Anna Karina, Godard could redeem his didacticism.

Bending me over the balustrade, you take my head in your hands; soft on my throat your lips glide, hard on my skin your teeth bite.

– Aïe!

– Beware, Sprague. A woman's enigmatic smile can lead you to perdition.

– Then I'll go for the sexual power of Sara Zeitgeist! How did you find her?

– Hot!

– Cyrielle Clair, she was great. The dark angel of death!

– Yes, she was radiant, luminous!

Floating leaves part in the pond, revealing our reflections in the water: We couldn't see ourselves joined in one breath, but we did feel the curtains drawing back.

– It's sex, isn't it? I ask. All those scenes of going through. The passage through the proscenium, the bite into the blood, the paintings you pass through.
– Yes, of course. But it's also the penetration into other worlds. The world of the dead, for example, coexisting with the world of the living.
– As in Walter and Henri de Corinth?
– Yes, but above all in Marie-Ange.
– What do you make of her, in fact?
– Well, she's Walter's fantasy, of course, and she's a vampire. And when it comes to crossing boundaries, you can't beat the vampire, can you?
– No, I suppose not.
– She exposes his limits, she reveals his anxieties about sex.
– Yes, I noticed how passive he is when Marie-Ange makes love to him. I saw that as an experiment on his part. He deliberately wanted to give up control.
– Isn't sex always an experiment?
– Yes, I guess it is.
– Marie-Ange confirms Walter's existence. That's why she has to be so aestheticized, so objectified.
– He both desires her and is afraid of her.
– That's the duality of the cliché: the virgin and the vampire. Every woman knows how it works.
– Is a man's desire really so transparent?

Looking at me askance, you give me your sly smile, then take my hand and lead me to an urn of bonfire begonia.

The nectar as sweet as the flower is fair

– The dreams within the dream, Sprague, that was brilliantly done!
– Yes.

The bonfire's stunning profusion of flowers lights up the dappled shade.

– That's the genius of cinema, isn't it? The ability to do that so seamlessly.
– Yes. Cinema's perfect for constructing the purely mental time and space of dreams.
– Because images are atemporal?

– More exactly, because they're always in the present tense. They don't report events, they express them. What's seen on the screen is seen as happening now.

– Yes, that's something that's always struck me about film, that immediacy.

The breeze picks up, the begonia I'd stuck in your hair falls out: I catch it.

– Sprague, you've deflowered me!

– Indeed I have.

– And so on the sly!

– The wind, the wind, Marietta. Hither and thither it blew, and naturally... your nether lips were what it led me to.

– And?

– The nectar as sweet as the flower is fair.

You cast a glance at the begonia in my hand.

– Eat it.

– What?

– Eat it!

I'd rather eat the tenor than the vehicle, but I obey. Citrus-sour is the taste: You sweeten it with a kiss. I swallow with a certain pleasure. You take my hand and lead me to an urn of painted nettle.

There are no absolutes

– Did you know painted nettles belong to the mint family?

As your eyes await my answer, their amber puts the nettle in the shade.

– No, I didn't. Can you eat them, then, like begonias?

Edged in green, bright yellow leaves speckled with rose-red stippling defy the glory of your eyes.

– You can eat the tubers. And you can get high on the leaves.

– Have you tried it?

– I discovered it by chance. Once, when I was mad at Pascale, I threw a temper tantrum and ate the painted nettle she'd just planted. That calmed me down.

– And what was the high like?

– Mildly psychedelic. Nothing like the real thing.

– LSD?

– Yes.

– That's my favourite drug!

Look at the painted nettle: What a clown of a coleus in its crazy colours, what a gladdening harlequin!

– It was mine too—for one holiday.

– With Nika?

– Yes. We dropped acid all summer long. The trips were wonderful, until I started bumming.

Your eyes shine and I see mine in them: What a larkish sprite in its robes of green, what a glorious sunset he swims in!

– It was the other way around for me. My first trips were bummers, and then the good ones came.

– It's slippery, isn't it, tripping?

– Yes, but real eye-opening!

– I'll say!

– I like the the fact that you know there's going to be some kind of story—a beginning, a middle and an end. You know it's going to come on slowly, then intensify and peak, before gradually coming down.

– Yes, there's that, but what I really loved is the way it makes everything become more fluid and provisional—there are no absolutes. The world really becomes relative, in Einstein's sense.

– Indeed. I remember one trip where somebody told the time—five o' clock or whatever—and I just burst out laughing, it was so irrelevant!

– Because you're moving *with* time, not *through* it. And it's the same for space—the way objects situate themselves in a field, isolating themselves in such original ways.

– Yes, I remember that very distinctly—the shifting focus, the clarity of textures, the way figure and ground reverse.

– And the colours!

You draw me to you and whisper in my ear:

– Only you make me see colours as I did then.

Oh batten on my blood, my beloved, don't wait for night to enfold us!

It's his own death they're staging

– And what did you think of Robbe-Grillet's use of Magritte?

You hesitate before replying, as if seeking a way to embody your response. And then you simply say:

– It's brilliant! You end up not knowing which world is real, the one behind the curtain, or the one in front. Exactly as in dreams.

– Yes. And did you notice how each successive vampire bite makes Walter weaker?

— I did. And the weaker he gets, the deeper he penetrates into the world beyond the curtain. But what he doesn't understand—poor guy—is that it's his own death they're staging.

— He doesn't understand, because the moment he comes across Marie-Ange lying bleeding on the road, he's continually distracted from the mission Sara Zeitgeist gave him. When Marie-Ange disappears, he gets caught up in the investigation—as detective and suspect. He never accomplishes his mission.

— He doesn't, and so he doesn't discover his own story. That, of course, was the point of the mission Sara gave him.

— Yes.

— And because he doesn't discover his own story, because he fails to grasp that digressions *are* the story, she condemns him to death.

— It's the story of Oedipus.

— It's the story of all abandoned sons.

— But what if he could have found—

Bending me over the balustrade, you take my head in your hands; soft on my throat your lips glide, hard on my skin your teeth bite.

— Aïe!

— Remember, Sprague, what Sophocles said: He who knows not his origins is damned.

— Yes, but—

— The child Oedipus, the lost little boy who knows nothing of his filiation, grows up to become an assassin.

Still the bright yellow leaves, edged in green, defy the glory of your eyes: Still your eyes put them in the shade.

— I do remember, Marietta. Didn't I write *The Dustman's Daughter?*

— You did. But you displaced the incest from mother-son to sister-brother.

It hits me, your observation, it hits me with the same impact as before.

— Yes.

You smile enigmatically, take my hand and lead me to an urn of bonfire begonia.

Fraught with stars

— And what about the use of Schubert?

Again you hesitate before replying, again you appear to be seeking a way to embody your response. And then, again, you simply say:

— It's brilliant!

There's something in your eyes that says you're elsewhere: I know it has to be a memory of the music.

– Do you know it well, the fifteenth?

– I do. It's my favourite Schubert quartet. Two years ago, we toured it up and down the West Coast. Vancouver to San Diego.

– Wow! How did that come about?

– I was in San Francisco, attending the SLAC summer school, and—

– SLAC?

– Stanford Linear Accelerator Centre.

– But you're a theorist.

– A theorist has to know about the physics of particle accelerators, Sprague. She has to understand just what can and cannot be done in the laboratory.

– Yes, of course.

– Anyway, I'd heard the tour of a local quartet was about to be cancelled—the first violinist had injured his hand. I contacted them, and offered to audition as a replacement. I got the gig.

Flaming, a profusion of orange-red flowers cascades into a fountain of foliage.

– I knew the programme—Schubert's 15th and *Death and the Maiden,* Hayden's *Sunrise* and *Emperor,* a number of Beethoven's late quartets. We'd play two or three per evening.

– Physics summer school in San Francisco, touring the West Coast, first violinist in a string quartet—what a great way to spend the summer!

– Hey, that's why I chose this job—for pleasure!

Once more I am faced with myself, my humble haiku, my imaginary movies. How can I be worthy of you?

– How *did* you decide to become a physicist, in fact?

– Through mathematics. You can discover things through mathematics. That's exciting. Imagine, the ultimate of matter, the particles and forces that make up the universe, expressed mathematically—that's a big turn-on.

– Yes, I can imagine.

– Imagine—that's exactly what you've got to do to create concepts in physics.

– You're recreating the world, Marietta, with your theory. Exciting!

Fraught with stars, my dream ceaselessly dreams me.

– Indeed!

Am I the man before you now, am I the man who wants you to awaken him from the big sleep?

– Come.

You take my hand and lead me to an urn of painted nettle.

A quick-fingered pickpocket

— And what was that jazz piece, at the beginning?

— That, Marietta, was 'The Mooch', a Duke Ellington tune played by Sidney Bechet.

Deep violet with a lacy green border, textured leaves shock with their hot pink centre.

— You call it a tune?

— A manner of speaking.

— With it's different movements, it's more like a concerto!

— That's the Duke, that's jazz's greatest composer.

— What does it mean, 'mooch'?

I take you in my arms and kiss you.

— That's what 'smooch' means: to kiss.

— I know. But what does 'mooch' mean?

— To mooch is to cadge, to borrow and not pay back. That's one meaning. Another is to loiter around, to walk aimlessly. And a third meaning is: to steal.

— I see.

— It's also a dance from the twenties, when the piece was composed.

— Very sexy, I imagine, very slinky.

You rub your body against mine.

— Yeah. 'Spades dance best, from the hip.'

— Now what does that mean?

— That's from Jim Morrison, *An American Prayer*.

— The Doors!

— Of course.

— But what does it mean, 'Spades dance best, from the hip'?

Very sexy, very slinky, you rub your body against mine.

— 'Spades' is the suit of cards.

— Black. I get it. And I've also got this!

You hold up my wallet in your hand.

— Hey, how'd you get that?

— Easy, I mooched it!

— Marietta, you're a master thief!

— No, just a quick-fingered pickpocket.

I take you in my arms again and kiss you. And then from my mouth it slips into your ear, three words in a whisper. Bending me over the balustrade, you take my head in your hands; soft on my throat your lips glide, hard on my skin your teeth bite.

— Aïe! What was that for?

— That, Sprague, that was... a love bite!

To your gaze your soul gives a softness; to your lips lust gives a gloss. Was it I who slipped my tongue between your lips and sailed the tip along their surface? Was it you who drew my lip into your mouth and sucked it? Or was it the other way around? I don't know, but I do know that when you took my hand and led me to an urn of bonfire begonia, it was I who was walking on air.

Pursuing phantoms

You relaunch our conversation:

— I like the way *The Execution of Maximilian* prefigures Walter's execution.

— The scene where he's going back upstairs to the bedroom?

— Yes.

— That whole sequence where Walter's finding his way in the flooded villa—the fluttering veils, the water in the passageways, the dark corridors—that's the sequence I like best in the whole film.

— It's lovely, yes. And it made the whole movie clear to me. The darkness, the water, the mysterious wind—Walter is walking through his own unconscious, pursuing a woman who's just a projection of his fantasy.

— But how else could he discover himself, Marietta?

— True. He is a man, after all.

— And doesn't he have to die, doesn't he have to submit to his own execution, before he can find himself?

— Of course. Just as Oedipus had to plunge Jocasta's pins into his eyes.

— Only the blind can see?

— Yes. The rest of us, when all is said and done, are just pursuing phantoms, mistaking one another for the one we want them to be.

You take my hand.

— Come.

The pact

In a secluded spot not far from the fountain, in a stretch of grass and towering trees, I sit on the ground with my back against a *platane* while you—back to me, head on my belly—recline between my legs. Your body against mine anchors me to myself; your body against mine renders words unnecessary. And yet, isn't it time we spoke about the two of us? Meshed in the light filtering through the leaves, caught in the snares of *La Belle Captive,* my courage vacillates. My hands on your shoulders, I bid the grass, the insects, the earth lend me their humility. You twirl a grass stalk between your fingertips; I run my hand through your hair. The plash of the fountain wafts from where we were; faintly into the pond the water flows.

– Let's talk, Marietta.

You stand up and turn around to face me; sitting down again, you fold your legs in front of you.

– All right, Sprague. If you stop being lyrical I'll stop being cynical. But I fear those are the only two ways to talk about love.

And thus we came to mark a milestone in our relationship. You spoke of the danger of thinking oneself free but not in fact wanting to be. Of the couple as a structure to relieve oneself of responsibility. Of monogamy, of infidelity and autonomy. Of how honesty and kindness need not be at odds with each other if we accept that exclusivity and freedom don't go together. Of the couple as a union of freedoms, not a series of compromises. What have you lived through, I wondered, that has obliged you to be so explicit? Your natural inclination would have been to trust in a tacit understanding.

As for me, what was my position? I concurred with everything you said. And then I shifted away from the tree trunk, took your hands and pulled you down upon me. As I wrapped my arms around you, the grass around us suddenly shot up: Sheafs linked branches to stems; sheathing the stems, narrow leaves rose rapidly and veered off into blades. As we kissed, they came—the spikelets, the flowers, the loose pyramidal panicles. Their scent was the scent of your skin; their texture was the touch of your hair. As we rolled in the grass, the florets of the spikelets fell off their rachillae, the glumes and bracts were laid bare. As my mouth made love to yours, autumn leaves became vernal grass. Sweet was the scent of the tender blades, sweet the dew that refreshed us. Florets then rose in green and purple; larks began to sing. And then, slipping your tongue through the seam of our lips, you spooled my breath into your body: I felt you receiving my soul. The word unsaid didn't need to be spoken: I was spoken for. I rolled off your body onto my back. You took my hand and held it. Staring into the wide expanse of blue, my body transfixed by telluric forces, I defied the earth and sky to match my pact with you.

As we walked through the park on our way out, you suddenly broke into a run. 'Catch me if you can!' you said. Hot on your heels as you zigzagged through the trees, bearing down on you as you kicked up dust, I pursued you with all the ardour of my emotion. You were swift, my love, you were nimble and sly, and yet with a feint I outfoxed you: Into my arms you ran. In a quincunx of limes I embraced you: Heart against heart at the centre, and a kiss for each corner of the world.

Intermezzo 3: Zora

Gone are the days when summer spilled from your whirling skirt, when you'd kick off your sandals and lay yourself down beside me. Only a ladybug climbing a grass stem could delay the moment your lips met mine; only a robin overturning a leaf could make you pause before taking the plunge. And when at last you'd surface for breath, my gaze in your eyes would exalt the subtleties of your tongue. Oh love, what halcyon days, when the curtain of your hair made a sanctuary for our kisses, a translucent realm of tenderness!

Now it's winter and I'm drinking Metaxa on a heated terrace. The night is soothing, but the heat lamp can't take the chill off my heart; the violet light obliterating the mountain is beautiful, but it can't erase my longing for you. What can I do? In the ocean of your absence my memories are but minnows; in the wake of your withdrawal I wander like a ghost.

Look at the austere beauty of the trees, stripped bare of their leaves! Look at the serene nobility of the citadel, aglow against the sky! Beauty, nobility—dump them in the depths of the ocean, bury them in the necropolis of dreams: There may they lie with the last of mine.

Marietta, didn't our hearts grow stronger when they left their safe-house? Didn't they wait humbly before the unpredictable, refusing to moralize love? Wildly you let yourself love me, then calmly engaged in a scrutiny of your commitments. And then you left me, and left me a phantom limb.

Now a woman is asking me for a light. Her dark locks tumble to her breasts as her cigarette crackles in my cupped flame.

– Look, she says, there's a wind whipping off the hills. It will rain hard tonight.

By the bend of the cypresses, by the whirling of the trash in the street, I know she's right.

– You must be the only tourist in the city. What are you doing here?

– Trying to forget a woman.

– I can help you.

– Why?

– Because I love your green eyes. Where did you get them?

– From an Irish sailor.

– Your hair's not red.

– From a Dutch trader.

– Your skin's not white.

– From the man who fell to Earth.

She takes my hand and holds it.

– Look, it's like mine. I'm Armenian.

– I'm not.

– Why did she leave you?

– Because she loves me.

– Well! She's an original!

I like the touch of her hand.

– What's your name?

– Zora. And yours?

– Hunter.

– Pleased to meet you, Hunter.

I finish my Metaxa, she her cigarette. Before the rain comes we go to my hotel.

In bed, after we'd made love, she sang me a folk song that resonated deep inside me. Then we took a bath together. In the wilderness in her eyes I found a certain freedom. I didn't write an ode to her instep, though I could have. I didn't memorialize her tits, with their nipples that turn from nut brown to plum after just a few tugs from my lips, though I could have.

– Shall I be your labyrinth, do you want to get lost in me?

– No, just sing to me again. I feel at home in your voice.

We ran some more hot water then she sang me another song. Her voice had a viola's timbre, and through its anguish and nostalgia I felt time surrendering to eternity.

– You move me, Zora. That's a heart-breaking song.

– It's a woman's lament. She's been spurned by her lover. It happens all the time, Hunter.

– Of course. I know I'm not the only one.

– But do you know that in the world there is one path that no-one but you can walk?

– I do. But I don't know where it leads.

– Do not ask. Walk it.

The rain drummed on the pavement, the wind howled through the trees. Zora stood up.

– Come, make love to me again.

Smooth as a conch's lips, the convolutions of her sex; her breasts, calabashes. We dried down and went back to bed.

I entered her body like a monk the mysteries; it took a while, but I finally got her natural scent to emerge through the perfumed soap. When she came she screamed my real name; how she knew it I'll never know. All I know is that in the morning I woke up alone, with your name on my lips.

Where do seagulls shelter in the driving rain, where do they find refuge? I don't know, Marietta, but I do know, on that clifftop, I spoke true: Hear me now, that I may honour you!

Chapter 12

– Cruelty sends me up the wall, Sprague. I loathe people who melt into the majority, I loathe humiliation and those who wallow in the humiliation of others.

Le Bonaparte is crowded on this autumn Sunday; a baptism party mills around on the parvis of Saint-Germain-des-Prés.

– It was thanks to Rüdiger that I finally found a meaningful form of political action.

I sip my Calvados. Through the silky bitter-sweet there comes an earthiness; through the elegance, a rusticity.

– Who's Rüdiger?

– My ex. After my fling with Niels.

Reticulated loops, undulating gold; crimson garnet, faceted stone: For a brief moment, the ring on your finger bears me away to some spirit realm, there from where Cupid hails.

– Haven't I mentioned him before?

– No.

– Are you sure?

My laughter is gentle as I hold your gaze.

– Quite sure. You only mentioned Niels. And Fabrizio.

– Fabrizio, or Tadzio?

– Fabrizio.

– Of course. Tadzio's not worth talking about. But Rüdiger is.

The pear is more pronounced in my Calvados now; a note of walnut has emerged too.

– Tell me about him.

– He's a very generous man, a surgeon who volunteers for *Médecins sans frontières*. He's worked in many conflict zones.

– Were you together long?

– Less than a year.

– And why—

– I had to leave him. He was just too possessive, too jealous. Paradoxical, isn't it, for someone so generous?

Half-up half-down, your messy chignon conveys both passion and calm.

– Yes, I suppose so.

I run a finger along the rim of my glass. You say:

— I don't know if jealousy is ever banal, but his was particularly intense.

— For example?

— No, Sprague.

— Fair enough. Just give me a snapshot of him, then.

— A snapshot?

— Yeah. Thirty seconds. Who is Rüdiger?

You swirl your Calvados. Taking a sip, you hold it, then swallow.

— He's a guy who can live thirty-six hours in a day of twenty-four. He tries to be discreet when he enters a room, but quickly he becomes the centre of attention. He spoils his mother. He never knew his father. His tennis partners say when his ball hits the band of the net, it always falls on their side of the court. He can play wrong notes on his guitar and make them sound right. He can put broken people together again, and you'll never believe they're the same people you saw before. In a war zone or a catastrophe, he's the one to be with—he's quick, he's resourceful, he's calm. What more can I say? He was a good lover, he was kind, but his jealousy nearly drove me out of my mind. I couldn't help him. I really tried, but I couldn't. I felt sorry for him, and you can't love someone you feel sorry for.

I sip my Calva.

Hatched, the egg of night;
Black thoughts, brooding monsters:
Fascination

— Niels seems to have been your favourite, of all your boyfriends.

— He wasn't my boyfriend. It was just a fling.

— But you speak of him with real affection.

— There was great complicity between us.

Keeping the base of the glass flat on the table, you set your Calva swirling.

— His clarity and purpose, steely concentration, ability to be in the moment—they perfectly matched mine. Then when our paper was published, we found we could switch gears completely and still be in synch.

— That's rare.

— Yes, especially amongst married men. Usually when they're having an affair they're full of euphoria, as if you've lifted a veil from their eyes.

The other woman, responsible to herself alone.

— The thrill of transgression?

– No doubt. But nervous excitement is their general state. They imagine they're on the verge of a new life, that their real self can finally emerge!

– And Niels wasn't like that?

– Not in the least. He could bring me roses and leave behind the sticky palms and palpitations. None of the flutter that comes from being caught up in a game you can't control.

– He had composure?

– Always. He could be light and airy, yet still engaging.

Niller was a killer, a real ladies' man.

– He remained himself?

– Completely. The opposite of Tadzio.

– What did Tadzio do?

– Oh, he was ridiculous! Felt himself possessed of a sudden power, just because he was cheating on his wife. The poor bugger bought himself a wardrobe more fitting for his son, thinking his new look would please me.

– And Niels just kept his old jeans?

The glint in your eye is as golden as your Calva.

– Sprague, are you jealous?

– I'm jealous of his composure, yeah.

– Don't be. You're a poet. You're in a whole other register.

– *Sturm und Drang?* I'd rather be cool and calm, like your Marlboro man.

– You're an artist. Much more interesting.

– True. The meanders of sublimation can be magnificent.

– Indeed.

– Do you know, Marietta, if Wagner hadn't had an affair with Mathilde Wesendonck, he'd never have written *Tristan und Isolde?*

– Yes, I'm aware that art owes a good deal to adultery.

> If erotic life makes a world,
> With you I have a world. But am I capable
> Of the pleasurable relationship?

– Was it in Copenhagen that you met, you and Niels?

– No, in Sicily. International School of Subnuclear Physics.

– Summer school?

– Uh-hm. I was the only woman among thirty physicists.

– I can imagine the electro-magnetic forces!

– Yeah. Poor me, all alone among the dorks looking for quarks.

– The strange particle!

– Yeah!

In your eyes the sparkle comes to a point: You fix me.

– Now listen to me, Sprague: *Your* desire is more important to me than your desire *for me.* I will do everything I can to sustain it. That's my way of loving.

You take my glass and raise it; I take yours and do the same.

– To our making up love.

– To our...?

– 'Making up love.'

I hesitate an instant, then understand. We clink glasses.

– To our making up love.

Liquorice, undergrowth and leather, the last of the Calva reveals a new aroma. Just how potent it was, you'd show me before the afternoon was over.

Chapter 13

Leaving Le Bonaparte, we cross the parvis of Saint-Germain-des-Près and turn into the boulevard, heading for the newly-opened Institut du monde arabe. You start talking about Simone de Beauvoir.

– A theory, a posture, lurking behind every page.

Tucking in the frayed trims of your plaid scarf, you zip up your jacket and buckle the belt.

– Something unpleasant in her personality. A coldness, a lack of spontaneity.

You slip your arm through mine, you press your body against me.

– Could anything unexpected, anything that exceeds us, ever happen in the world? Listening to her, you'd never think so.

You swing out your leopard-print bag of dark-brown leather: It's shadow catches your shadow as you walk tall in your straight-leg jeans.

– Honesty and humility before the unfathomable—she's simply incapable of that.

Les Deux Magots well behind us, but not the ghosts of its one-time denizens, we come to the statue of Danton.

– Camus is Danton. The humility of the man who loves life, the refusal of killing in the name of progress. Sartre is Robespierre. The hubris of the Cartesian mind, the *éloge* of violence.

I defended Beauvoir, I defended Sartre, despite the seductiveness of your intransigence. Finally in laughter we dissolved our differences.

In front of the Musée de Cluny we stop to study a poster. You read aloud:

– Now there dwelt in that same city of Paris a certain young girl named Héloïse.

Your belted jacket, gleaming in the sunlight, heightens the sensuality of your silhouette.

– Of no mean beauty, she stood out above all by reason of her abundant knowledge of letters.

A breeze comes to tease your hair; as your hand moves a lock back from your face, the sun conspires with your grace to burn that gesture into my memory.

– Utterly aflame with my passion for this maiden, I sought to discover means whereby I might have daily and familiar speech with her.

I step behind you and wrap my arms around your waist.

– Under the pretext of study we spent all our hours in the happiness of love, and learning held out to us the secret opportunities that our passion craved.

The nape of your neck offers the subtlest of seductions; as I graze in its gossamer, you reach back to touch me.

– Our speech was more of love than of the books which lay open before us; our kisses far outnumbered our reasoned words.

With one hand you hold the pennant aloft, with the other you caress the horn of the unicorn.

– No degree in love's progress was left untried by our passion, and if love itself could imagine any wonder as yet unknown, we discovered it.

Sweet are the notes of the organ you play.

– And our inexperience of such delights made us all the more ardent in our pursuit of them, so that our thirst for one another was still unquenched.

You turn around and beam the ardour of your eyes into the receptiveness of mine. Embracing you, I read aloud:

– In measure as this passionate rapture absorbed me more and more, I devoted ever less time to philosophy.

I nibble on the sweetmeat of your lips; you find delicacies in the storehouse of mine.

– Though I still wrote poems, they dealt with love, not with the secrets of philosophy.

You lean back against the fence; beaming your ardour into my eyes again, you say, softly but distinctly:

– Fuck me.

– What?

– Anywhere. Outside. Before it gets dark today. Fuck me.

From its bond with medieval Paris the high-gothic house frees itself, from the ruins of late antiquity the Roman baths release themselves: It will be done, before the afternoon is over, it will be done: From my reserve I free myself.

Chapter 14

Underfoot, overhead, left, right, behind, ahead: Omnipresent, metal and glass conspire to remove all our bearings; unmoored, we ascend in spidery space. In a riot of shadow and light the guts of the construction invade our vision; reaching for your hand I catch your gaze: In the depths of your eyes as our hands entwine, I see Winston and Julia about to commit sexcrime.

Daylight! We cross a footbridge and step onto the rooftop terrace. Look! Towering above the other buildings, the Ministry of Truth—or is it the Ministry of Love? Préfecture de Paris, Temple du Marais, Ile Saint-Louis, Notre-Dame. Look! In the strip of park between the Seine and the street, a long tractor-trailer: *Expo - Médecins sans frontières - Acteurs d'urgence.* You turn and walk away: I linger.

Jealousy, possessiveness, suffering love: What went on between you and Rüdiger? How could a man so fully alive, so given to compassion, be devoured by resentful bile? Jealousy blinds, they say, it transports and displaces; its bite must have been deep to have ravaged your surgeon so. Did you love another? Did you make Rüdiger feel he didn't exist any longer—excluded, rejected, nothing but the shadow of the other? Did he feel emptied, annihilated, invaded by hate; did he use devotion to allay your suspicion of his state? Aye, aye, Marietta, tell me: Was he a cat on a hot tin roof, biting back on his anger? Did he lavish you with gifts to disguise his wish for revenge? Of what was he capable, what forced you to flee? Perhaps he persecuted you with his suspicions, maintained when away you were with another? And when in bed together, did he suddenly ask you if your pleasure was greater in the arms of the other?

Look! Heading upriver, a bargeman pilots his flat-bottomed boat. Is he still number one in the eyes of the bargewoman? Is he still capable of steering a straight course? Or is he bearing a dull pain that, sharpening, makes him waver at the most unexpected moments? Yes, turned inside out like a glove, does he want to disappear into the bowels of his boat? At the helm of his own damnation, ferrying himself across the Styx, is that how he lives his jealousy?

And what about Bernard de Clairvaux? Between writing the *Book of Considerations* and fighting heresy, was this soldier of God ever overcome by the burlesque that ridicules love? In the eighteen years he spent studying the

Song of Songs, was he ever waylaid by that calamity? Yes, between the contemplation of Christ and the concupiscence of the flesh, between a tyrannical ideal and a voracious body, did he ever take a chance with love and find himself deranged by jealousy?

Anne de Courtenay, Rachel de Cochefilet, did they ever bid the Duc de Sully bide his time while death and suffering did their work? Did they share with him their wisdom? If so, then it's unlikely he ever experienced love as an affliction, a well of wretchedness and woe. No, he must have learned that he cannot refuse to be jealous, but he can refuse to let jealousy destroy him. Mastering what can be mastered, then, is that how he lived his jealousy?

And what of the architect of that iconic tower? He whose bridges bear the weight of steel wheels, was he ever emptied of himself when his beloved delighted in another? Did he ever feel his legs buckle as his love was rebuffed? Yea, when his body was no longer borne up by her desire, did he fall to the ground and just lie there, unable to move? If one can call that living, is that how he lived his jealousy?

And *le bon roi Henri, le Vert galant*, did his goodness preserve him from the suffering inherent in love? Did his sense of strategy allow him to avoid the worst of strategies: wanting to be loved, while making oneself unlovable? Every couple unique, never reproducible: From the terror of repeating childhood's destructions, did that insight save him? In his wisdom did he understand that smiling enemies do not derive from external contingency, but from a source within oneself? Accepting, then, that the hole left by the beloved's departure is a hole that was always already inside oneself, is that how he survived his jealousy?

— Sprague!

I take the hand you hold out to me; we cross the terrace and penetrate into the interior space.

Glass walls, polished floors; glowing columns, gleaming doors: Refracting, reflecting, surfaces shimmer with patterns of filtered light. And then it appears, a giant screen of geometric forms, a riot of proliferating motifs: Intensely-patterned panes unfold their symmetry. Look! Mirror-plates in meticulous rhythm, flashes of prudence and vanity; clockwork in crystal panels, wheels of time and fortune.

— Come!

You take my hand, and through filigreed light lead me.

Did your *acteur d'urgence* fail to come to terms with the hole inside himself? Did he become a stalker? What exactly was your role in his delirium? Veiling your secret in shadow and light, multiplying yourself in mirrors, you teach me that intimacy requires discretion: Preserving private space is what allows us to be so open. Back to the terrace you lead me.

On the rooftop, in the corridor between the empty restaurant and the Seine façade of the building, cubic modules of wicker furniture stack up in disorderly columns. Bearing witness to winter, Arabic urns of barren earth punctuate the passage. We slip in between two stacks of chairs and wend our way to the railing. Spinning around, you say:

— Take off your coat.

In the dark groves of your eyes sulphur butterflies swarm; ready to do what must be done, I shake my jacket from my shoulders and toss it onto a railing post. You slip off yours and sling it over mine. Turning your back to the *garde-fou,* you pull me towards you.

— Fuck me.

Bringing your hand to my crotch, you rub.

— Fuck me, Sprague!

The fire in your eyes shames the uncertain sun; the risk is calculated, let it be done: Bending you over the railing, I slip my hand between your legs. Your lush ripeness hardens me as I heave rhythmically.

— Go down and kiss it.

A sharp tug on your belt releases the pin; I fall to my knees, open your jeans and pull them down. Warm, wet and feral, at once lulling and unsettling, your sex beckons. I pull down your panties.

— Marietta!

— Pull it out.

Tugging on a wilted stalk, out of your body I pull a poppy. On the cotton sponge it glistens, your bright red blood, flaunting its power and virtue. Your maternal promise, your adolescent pain, your shame and pride, your pleasure and blame—all the perplexities and disappointments of your past, yea, the whole of your feminine history, I slip into a bottle: A letter you've written, but will never send.

You kick off your boots as soon as I've unzipped them; from your jeans you free yourself. I pull up your sweater: Your breasts flaunt their perfection. Unpinned, your hair flows over the abyss while your tits summon the invisible stars to bear witness: Empires have been drained for a taste of my beneficence, but where is the man who can win me with nothing but nakedness? Dropping my jeans, I rise to the challenge; into my embrace you spring and wrap your legs around me. Turning around, I step to the restaurant wall and press your body against the glazing. Within seconds my homing blood finds its home, bringing forth the spirit-breath that quickens your flesh.

The compatibility of our bodies makes the standing fuck easy; the higher you lift your thigh, the deeper you take me in. Now where does your satisfaction lie? In the hollow behind my knee you rhythmically rub your heel; by your pressure and pace I navigate your dream landscape. Grinding into you slowly, I suddenly switch to speedy thrusts; pumping deep, I abruptly shift to shallow probing. Verged in silver, the sulphur butterflies in your eyes swarm to violet. Hail! A flapping of wings sets your hair aflutter; your body shudders in my embrace. Look! It's not the liquid shine of languor that illuminates your gaze, but hunger's fiery sparks: You want more. Sifting darkness from light, seeking the shadow that gives shape, diligently I pursue the moving target of your mystery. In the byways of my blood I feel a force gathering; I feel your dream unfurling and flowing into mine. Hail! On the quick of your flesh the match of mine strikes a crackling flame: In the glory of your coming, I am at one again.

In the taxi, all the way home, your hand in mine affirmed that your flowers are for the living, your votive flame's for individuality; your holy book is your heart, your devotion's to singularity: Marietta, you are inexhaustible, and everything is mine to learn.

Intermezzo 4: Pina

Quiver, the discarded tail of a lizard.
Uninhabited here, as far as the eye can see.
Immemorial stones under endless sky—
Eerie.
Thewless vegetation.
Uncompassed fields.
Dark vessel:
Emptiness.

Pina's a freelance journalist. Writes on culture. She wanted to interview Seedy's 'mysterious lyricist', so she invited me here, to Malta. Back from the wilderness, we went to a bar in Valletta. Talked of the King James Bible and Hadewijch of Brabant, of Rimbaud in Abyssinia and *The Beggar's Opera*. Then she took me dancing. The ice and fire that composed her body were the same that made up mine; the pulse that freed her from the perishable was the same that purified me.

The next night, after a day of touring, we met in a laid-back lounge bar.

– Katie Quickfinger really moves me.

– Why?

– You really got inside her skin. I recognize myself in her.

In the orange-brown of her eyes I see the flames of Katie's fire. She continues:

– The music captures the orgasmic aspect of the stealing, while the lyrics convey the pleasure and the shame. And then, the fear of punishment! That's salvation, that's what procures the calm.

I like the way she inhabits her body, transforming otherness into intimacy; I like the way she looks at me, turning gravity into grace.

– How long were you a kleptomaniac?

– Three years. It was analysis that got me out of it.

– Did you steal the same things as Katie?

– Yes. I remember once, in the university amphitheatre, I felt a crisis coming on. I slipped on someone's leather jacket and calmly walked out. Like in a dream, past two hundred students who didn't notice a thing. Just like Katie! And of course I'd steal from department stores. Or pick a lover's pocket, steal something dear to a friend.

I like her double ram's head ring, its suggestion of penetrative power; I like the draping of her silk georgette, its sweep across her chest.

— And what about boyfriends?

— I was just like Katie. I'd choose them only for their looks. Three days, three weeks, that's about how long it would last. As soon as they'd start clinging, I'd break it off. I couldn't stand them loving me, I hated the idea of a couple.

I like her mindful insouciance, her lyrical violence; I like her wild serenity, her fidelity to herself.

— And girls?

— I'd have love affairs with girls, but we'd never go to bed. Or if we did, it was to dream.

— Were they intense, these affairs?

— Sometimes. I once went head-over-heels for a girl in school.

— What did you steal from her?

— Her boyfriend.

I like the fall of her hair, the frankness of her face.

— And what made you decide to see a psychoanalyst?

— My suicide. I blew it!

Edging her jubilant innocence, the sad glamour of her dark timbre moves me.

— You see, my mother died when I was fifteen. Cancer of the blood. Then my father went round the bend. Made a scene every time I went out. Got violent. That's when my depression started.

The terror of transgression, the anguish: How could I ever consent to his bending me to his purpose?

— I was torn between pity for him and wanting to get out of that damned house. Not only did he try to bed me—mind you, after wining and dining me first—but my uncle and brother-in-law started coming on to me too.

— Did they ever—

— In all but the act! I'd had enough. Decided to do myself in. Slit my wrists. Woke up in hospital.

Down the steps of the heart, descending into birth, you drag the future of the past: bright midnight in the orange of your eyes.

— Back with my father nothing had changed. He was either too tender or too violent. I wanted to leave but I couldn't bring myself to go. And that's when I picked a man's pocket, discovered he was a psychoanalyst, and gave him a call.

I don't believe in any god, but if I did I'd ask him to hold me tight until it hurt: Is that how you felt?

— And how did he interpret your kleptomania?

– He said it was like bulimia. The same orgasmic aspect.

– And?

– He said my stealing was an attempt to devour my father and destroy him. It took some time, but I finally understood.

Upholding your isolation, nurturing your solitude, you resolved to live out what is most strong and true in you: Is that what you did?

– And you, Sprague? How did you come to create Katie?

– Marietta held a mirror to me.

– And what did you see?

– I saw a man who couldn't commit parricide because he had only a ghost of a father. So conquering a woman, completing a work, would be the only way he could make a name for himself. You see, Pina, only a woman can kill her father through her mouth alone.

– Even one who eats nothing, like an anorexic?

– Yes. She eats nothing, but she's bulimic for a father—one without a name, without a body, without beginning or end.

– God?

– Yes. Just ask Catherine of Sienna. Or Simone Weil. Or any other of God's lovers.

After that conversation we went dancing again. I pursued my dialogue with gravity, feeling the resistance of the floor and the lightness of my body. Pina, on the kitten heels of her sling-backs, played with the malleability of space. Uprooting the insular, we danced ourselves into mystics.

In her car we kissed goodnight. I saluted her as she, waving goodbye, drove off. As I stepped into the darkness that gives light definition, I was happy with our time together. We didn't need to make love. You see, Marietta, we were otherwise intimate. We were brother and sister.

PART FOUR

Chapter 1

Softly they come, the seven names of love, spiralling black around a spindle of sulphur: rope, light, coal, fire, dew, living water and hell. From the siphonal canal to the tip of the coiled cone they wind, binding the egg of night to the snail's back. Dappled light plays upon white sand; in the retreating tide ribbons of seagrass sway.

– Whither goest thou, pretty bellyfoot?

– To pluck a corpse from the tree of the dead: I'll grind his bones to make my bread.

– May I pluck a name of love from your back?

– Take care, you who wish to deal with the names for love! Behind their sweetness and wrath, nothing endures, nothing but wounds and kisses!

Through the waters of regeneration the snail drags his refuge. Look! Upright on her tapered foot a conch stands, brandishing the flaming orange of her flesh. On her face no features, none but black pinprick eyespots at the base of stubby tentacles. Primed, her glandular skin tingles; to the burning point her senses rush as her eyespots pick up movement. Whoosh! Forward the mantle collar falls, backward footsole waves flow: Mad in pursuit, the conch harries the snail. As her labial palps bear down on him, he hurls himself up into the promise of the possible: Down he tumbles, twisting on the sand. Faeringa! Smothering the snail in her ventral folds, the conch ushers the creature into the unknown.

Seagrass sways in liquid light; sand rearranges its symmetry. Upright again, ragged strands of slime clinging to her ventral orifice, the conch stands. Look! Quest, love, knowledge, detachment, unity, amazement, annihilation: Lodged in the fat folds of the mollusc's mouth, the sucked-out shell displays its seven spirals. Crabs scuttle out of the seagrass; around the conch they scurry. Antennules rotate, mandibles move; around the giant the crabs jostle, pincers raised in battle. Oh brave cancrum! Up to the conch's mouth a crab scrambles, unhooks its legs from the columella of its shuck and stuffs them into the empty shell. Curling its legs around the spiral shaft, it frees its new-found abode from the conch's lobes, then back to swaying seagrass scuttles.

– Little crab, your journey's done; you've found a home, you belong. And I, when will I—

– Never. There is no sweetness and light in your birthright; honey and slumber you'll never know.

– Must it be so, forever and ever? Why can't I—

— It's too late.

— But my heart just won't give in!

— Be patient. Dying is an art. It isn't easy.

— But I want to live!

— Too late. The violated child is already entombed inside you. Only his soul still wanders.

— But—

— The tide! The tide! Goodbye, Wanderer.

— Goodbye, kind crab, goodbye.

The swash of a wave plashes up the beach; beneath my tread the tawny sand sings. I cup my hand over my ear: Sea-roar in my skull, wind-breath in my bones: Language languages, thought thinks itself. They say the value of a thought is measured by its distance from the familiar. But how does one pay for thoughts? With courage! And who is the most courageous person I know? Marietta! And I? All my courage goes into trying to become a human being. But what have I but words? Ciphers to make myself a subject! Still, I believe with these baubles of breath I can give Marietta an account of myself. Accent, tone, resonance, timbre—how is the audible intelligible, the sonorous logical? Mara sings, Marietta draws a bow over strings, I make patterns with breath: We all swear by air!

Seaward the ebb tide drags the swash line; on the strand-plain creatures stir. Look! Tubes, tunnels, tracks—trace and erasure, the saying ruptures the said. Hark! Circles whirl around a porcelain spike, seven circles of a lost tongue—seven vowels, seven wombs, seven mothers of silence.

— Pray tell, burrowing mollusc in your augur shell, will you accept a poem for a lesson in love?

— Aye aye, I shall: The transcendence of discourse is bound to love, and love goes beyond the beloved. That's your lesson.

— Thank you. I shall ponder that.

— Do.

— Already Mariatta lives inside me, but my love reaches beyond.

— You owe her everything. She loved you to the very depths of your idiocy.

— And that's why all my poems are in her honour. Here's the one I promised you:

> Summer's over,
> The beach deserted: Your hand in mine
> Knows no season.

— A bit sentimental, Wanderer. A bit on the soft side.

— Really? After all these years—

— You can't help it. You're condemned to weave yourself a shawl of tenderness. When you came into the world, no-one held one out to you.

— Let's not talk about that. My body remembers all too well. My skin still burns, on occasion.

— Of course. Touch can never be retroactive. The damage is indelible.

— Can nothing—?

— Nothing. Nothing and no-one. You are the cold, secret sign. Your destiny is the passage through the abyss. You can't fight it.

— But—

— You can't fight it!

— But there must be—

— There isn't!

— But—

— Goodbye, Wanderer! And thanks for the poem.

Backwards the augur burrows into the revealed sand.

— Wait! Here's another one for you.

He stops.

— Is it less sentimental?

— Yes.

— All right. Let's have it.

— Here it is:

> The night delivered
> New names for love,
> The word itself unspoken;
> Into the frenzy of desire,
> The infusion of devotion.

— Better, much better. Now when you understand that love names that which cannot be named, you'll really be a great poet.

— Love names—

— Until that day, these poems will make a fine addition to your file in the Archives.

— But poetry is for the living!

– A salutary desire! But what chance does poetry stand in the busy world? In the Archives your case will have pride of place—content yourself with that. Goodbye!

– Goodbye, kind mollusc, goodbye.

Callapa crab and sunset siliqua, razor shell and pelican's foot: Mara, we are only alive because we desire, and yet in our desiring we are obscure to ourselves. Let us continue to interweave our memories, that in the eyes of the other we may discover who we are.

Chapter 2

A boy slides open a shower curtain. Faeringa! His heart leaps as a stranger steps out of a mirror. The boy stares into the glass: His face configures a double of the stranger.

Was he insane? Every shower an ordeal, he fearing he'd become unreal should he fall under the spell of the pelting water and forget to think about himself. Unable to inhabit his body, he was incapable of inhabiting the world.

With reading it was the same: Persecuted by his own lucidity, obliged to be permanently aware of himself, he was unable to get beyond the first pages of a book: To lose himself in narrative, to leave himself behind—that was simply too much of a risk.

And his horror of drugs: When everyone was smoking dope and popping pills, he refused to, afraid that if he got out of his mind he'd never be able to get back in. When he finally took the leap—lipstick on a reefer was something he couldn't resist—drugs were an anti-climax: Nembutal couldn't match his own capacity for self-benumbment, nor could marijuana make animals laugh the way he could.

And, once more, his madness: That time with Phoebe in her basement. She took an atlas off the shelf so he could show her where he comes from. Opening it up, he felt he was opening up a world he might be able to slip into. *South Africa, here. East London, Cape Town, the SS Carinthia to Southampton. Stopped over in Madeira.* On the ship, an English girl with blue, blue eyes. They stood at the railing, staring at the horizon. She seemed to recognize him. He'd hardly said a word in weeks. He couldn't form a sentence. She wasn't afraid. She didn't walk away. Looking into his eyes, she said: 'I lingered round them, under that benign sky; watched the moths fluttering among the heath and harebells, listened to the soft wind breathing through the grass, and wondered how anyone could ever imagine unquiet slumbers for the sleepers in that quiet earth.' He felt himself drowning in the blue of her eyes. 'That's the ending of the book I've just read. Meet me here tomorrow at ten. I'll read something new to you.' The next morning, side-by-side in deck chairs, she read Angela Carter's *Heroes and Villains* to him. He began to speak. She took off her glasses and kissed him. He spoke the story. Pages and pages of it. Then she disappeared, the girl with blue, blue eyes, never to be seen again.

Had she ever been on the ship? Had he ever read *Heroes and Villains?* Had it all been a dream? Questions without answers. He was eleven years old. The girl was thirteen. 'I'll find her when I get to London', he told Phoebe, 'Maybe her mother and father would adopt me'. Why didn't Phoebe tell him he was mad? That *Wuthering Heights* and *Heroes and Villains* are fictions, that he's neither Heathcliff nor Marianne? Did she believe his fantasy could make him a meaningful world? Did she think the girl with blue, blue eyes was a wish fulfilled in a dream? Or did she believe it's better not to undeceive him because no girl, not even one with blue, blue eyes, could ever save him?

Swash lines and ripple marks, pinholes and sand domes: Still the retreating tide lays out the strand's topography. Rills drain swash back to the sea; the ebb dredges cusps.

— Mr. Lundel, I've got another one!
The boy drops an earthworm into a tin.

— Good work, Sprague. That's enough now, let's go.
In the coolness of the dawn they walk through silent streets, heading for the harbour. Under a streetlight, through a curl of smoke, the boy catches Mr. Lundel's blue-green eye: opalescent, like a marble: an accident. Still, his kindness shines through. Their shadows overtake them on the descending street; Mr. Christian coughs as the shadows retreat. He rubs his stubbled chin; the breeze catches a lock of his slicked-back hair.

— Sprague, we're counting on you to catch porgies for bait.

— Yes, Mr. Christian.
The tip of his cigarette crackles and glows; a whiff of whisky mingles with the scent of burning tobacco. Distant seagulls cry; between darkness and daylight the hour vacillates.

By sun-up Mr. Lundel's landed two yellowtail, Mr Christian a red steenbras, and five spot-tail porgies swim in the boy's bait basket. They break for tea. The men take the tackle boxes to the harbour side of the pier; on the ocean side the boy stares out at the untamed sea. Faint against the horizon, a ghostly ship... Bartolomeu Dias, Vasco da Gama... Scurvy and waiting for wind... India! Zamorin in Calicut.

— Sprague!
Mr. Lundel stabs open a can of condensed milk; Mr. Christian pours steaming tea from the flask. Seated on their tackle boxes, they watch the waters stir as the sea absorbs the river. From the bottom of the boy's mug the heavy milk mushrooms up and mingles with the tea; watching those mercurial forms, he

sees a hand falling, a face turning away. Tears well up in his eyes; the clench of his jaws furrows his face as he bites back on his pain.

In a forest of tree-like traces, water trickles seaward from the wrack line. Turritella and foliate tellin, acteon shell and festive volute: Creatures scurry to reclaim the lower realm as the tide retreats.

With deft fingertip on a red wax-cloth, a boy drags a black grain from the white.

— Sprague! How tall you are now man!

Auntie Janie steps into the kitchen.

— Say hello, Sprague.

— Hello Auntie Janie.

As the boy spreads out the rice, Auntie Janie begins shelling peas. Below, in the backyard, chickens cackle wildly, and then comes the scream of the captured one.

— I heard there's a good film at the Bioscope, Sprague. Have you seen it?

— Yes.

— Did you like it?

— No.

— Why not?

— Because the Indians lost. Again.

— But cowboys always beat Indians, don't they?

The boy, suddenly sullen, says nothing.

— Look, you missed one.

Auntie Janie stretches out a bangled arm, and with jewelled finger drags the runt into the rejects. The boy leans forward and casts a sidelong glance out the window: An axe glints above the neck of the cock.

— Sprague, bring your plate.

A silver-haired woman serves the boy.

— Thank you, Granny.

While the women chat the boy sorts rice, waiting for his apple fritters to cool. The smell of a chicken in hot water wafts up to his nostrils and takes away his appetite: And now Grace will lay the rooster across her lap and pluck it.

— You look hot, Sprague. Have a glass of milk.

Cushy cow, bonny, let down your milk: Granny's kind. The boy looks out the window and tastes the dust that James is sweeping over the blood of the dead bird. He turns away.

— Gus can't sell the shipwreck lot. The stuff's junk.

— Oh no!

The boy looks out the window and sees a pigeon trailing a stocking, smoke-black against a milk-white sky: undulating banner of coagulated blood, pervading the air with unforgetting.

Mara Marina, Mara Miranda, with delicate tongue I trace the outer rim of your ear, then nibble the earlobe. How shall we contemplate things in the face of despair? Why, as they would present themselves from the standpoint of redemption!

Chapter 3

Low ridges undulate toward an incipient dune; coarse sands accumulate along the crests. No ghost crab or moon snail venture here; here scavenging plover find nothing. Sorted and moved by water, transported and sifted by wind, skeletal remnants and calcitic oolites lie scattered in an impact splash. Look! Webbed feet limp on splayed legs, pink tongue stiff between chrome-yellow bill: Where is your airy grace now, seagull? Back in its cage of clay, its neck strangely twisted, the bird still shows a bright green eye. (Bright green—is that not the colour of my eyes?) Seagull, were you among the gulls that cried when we said goodbye? As we stood on that cliff, did your white splendour brighten the blue sky?

Mara, my ears have been cleansed by serpents, I understand the language of birds. Look! Body blanched in wrinkled skin, palms and soles blistered, your father lies on the beach, his eyes filled with empty sky. A fine foam, tinged with blood, oozes out of his mouth and nostrils. *The ligatures show the deceased himself tied his hands and feet.* Throttled utterance escapes your throat till all sound is choked off; vital heat leaves your face, your mouth remains agape. And then it comes, the scream, a piercing wail that rises in pitch until you black out.

Down the helix of your ear, up the antihelix, I glide the tip of my tongue: Within the womb of change, the stability of being.

– Mara, open the door!

In the blue of your eye the black deepens; between repulsion and fascination your eyes veer.

– Mara!

Persuaded your father has left you a letter in a locked secretaire drawer, you rip the unlocked drawers off their rails and reach into the unyielding one: Nothing. Your fingers find nothing.

– Mara, open the door!

The squeeze is tight as you try to extract your hand; you lose patience and pull it out through the pain. Oh blessed deliverance! As blood flows in diverging tracks down your forearm, you feel a rush of exhilaration.

– Mara!

You cast your gaze into the garden: Oh saturated hue, the bluest of blue, and the grass the summum of green! The veil of the world falls, and in that instant you know that this you who bleeds shall prevail. Look! The marigolds' petals are daggers of sunlight; the irises' leaves, spears. Yes, this you who bleeds shall prevail!

In the labyrinthine convolutions of your ear I contemplate the sublimity of tact: You close your eyes to the shine of the visible, but the ear has no lid: The voice that touches yields presence.

Corso Venezia, Raccordo Autostrada: Riding pillion with Bernardo, you're leaving Verona, heading for Ljubljana... The beam of the headlight bores through the night; you rest your head on Barnardo's back and let speed transport you... Bypassing Padova, you open your visor to feel the air on your skin; blood quickens in your cheeks, the night flows through your veins. You feel free, and yet in the vertigo of velocity something immovable remains: How can you fit yourself into your history, give meaning to your past, shape your future? In your innermost identity a strangeness endures... Marianne Faithfull, pale in her black frock, lingers in your mind: Rising from an abyss of loss, the gravel in her voice filters the pain in your soul... Flush against the footpeg you press your boot-heel, slide back your butt and lean into the curve: With one mouth boy, girl and machine devour the night... You watch the blackness absorb a red tail-light; your nostrils tell you the lagoon of Venice is not far... You've always enjoyed riding pillion, putting your life in the rider's hands: Into Bernardo's pockets you slip your thumbs and grip his jacket with your fingers; squeezing the saddle between your thighs, you turn your head and spit out the bug on your tongue... Looking over Bernardo's shoulder, you tip your weight into the bend; as soon as the curve gives him its camber, he opens the throttle again... Fast, fast, you're almost home: Tonight for the first time you'll make love with a boy.

Mara Marina, Mara Miranda, what do our memories aim at? Is it the enduring within mutation? Is it restoration? I stick my tongue in your ear: Flesh is the medium of touch, but the real organ is situated further inward.

In the shallows of the retreating tide, spotted digger and sundial shell, masked crab and sand gaper, move from the manifest to the latent world: There is something within us that exceeds the given world; let us continue to attend to it: It is driving us into what we will be. You take my hand and bring it to your cheek, you kiss my fingertips: If the past is buried but not abolished, knowledge has no light but that shed on the world by redemption. I press a finger into your navel and pinch your nipple: To be true, all meaning that discourse establishes of you requires recognition by me. You take my fingertip into your mouth and bite it: To be true, all meaning that discourse establishes of me requires recognition by you. You spittle your fingertips and run them over my lips: Speak to me! Is it your story you desire from my mouth? Yea, your story you entrust to my telling. And thus memory bids me board my boat: To recollect from oblivion I obey. I take up the oars, other shores to explore.

Chapter 4

Do you feel it, child? Through the reticulated veins of the leaves, through the xyloid channels of trunk and stem, the sap is flowing, soothing the pain that rises, unrelenting, from the heartroot. Hark! A steady susurration, a fall of fine powder, faint and unvarying: Between the bark and the cambium a beetle bores. Red runs in the labyrinth of her galleries; in the chambers of dead-end passageways, larvae are bursting with life. Look! Beneath the cuticular plate of the pronotum, the head drives the excavating mandibles: Onward she cuts her way, scarring the surface of the sapwood.

– Pray tell, busy beetle in darkness tunnelling, will you accept a lyric for a lesson in love?

– Aye aye, I shall: To love purely is to consent to distance. That's your lesson.

– Yes, my heart knows that now. My beloved has left me, but my love has grown, more pure than before.

– I can see that. You're glowing.

– You mean it shows?

– Yes, as it should: The heart is the wick to the lamp of the body, and love is its oil.

– That's a lovely metaphor!

– Second nature. I'm a creature of metamorphosis.

– Marietta is my Muse, she—

– She loved you to the very depths of your idiocy! She will always be your spiritual bride.

– That's why everything I do is aimed at honouring her. Here's the lyric I promised you.

Fragonard's Swing

Will he remember, when he's old and grey,
How his heart would flutter to the sway of her swing?
Will she remember, when she's past her day,
The kindling power of her petticoats?

Hearts like bells, celebrate the living
Mourn the dead, break the lightning

Toothless and dribbling, will he still recall
The arch of her instep, the sandal, the fall?
Her poise at the still-point between surrender and retreat,
Eyeless and infirm, will it still taste sweet?

Hearts like bells, celebrate the living
Mourn the dead, break the lightning

The thrill of expectation, the sudden glimpse—
Will they reminisce about their frivolity?
Will they be convinced by the instant's eloquence
That to transience the flower owes its beauty?

Hearts like bells, celebrate the living
Mourn the dead, break the lightning

– That's a good piece of work, Wanderer.

– Thank you.

– Come, let me kiss you, and consecrate you as a poet: We are brothers in the art.

I press my lips to the bark. The beetle pats them with his pedipalps. Ticklish at first, the sensation soon becomes a rather pleasurable buzz.

– In grace we meet, poet; in resolute endurance we go on. These are lean times for poetry. In the ambient noise, when language tries to make sensible the root of secrecy within itself, it can hardly be heard.

– I will fight to have it heard!

– I wish you well! Now, Wanderer, I must get back to work. Goodbye!

– Goodbye, kind beetle, goodbye.

Low over the bank of earth they ramble, fleshy, needle-like leaves, flashing clusters of tiny crimson buds on dark red bracts. Cracks and fissures run through fragments of fallen bark; from a patch of dry mud, lengths of filament stretch out. Faeringa! A shock of talons leaps out of the earth, black limbs articulate doom! From coxa to tarsus their movements mesh, until in the grapnel of the spider's embrace the cicada is clenched. Serrated claws press into the abdomen of the insect; fangs snap out of their groove. Hail! Into the head, between the eyes, fangs sink as venom flows: Into your skin, just below the elbow, you guide the razor blade. Down through dermis and epidermis, down past the capillaries to the dominion of pain, you press the bright steel flake. Around the burning edge a shimmering bead wells up; down the whiteness of your forearm you draw the mesmerizing red. Lifting open a secret trapdoor, the spider enters its burrow; as blood flows in rivulets across your skin, the predator descends with its prey. I stare into the tumult in your eyes; you bring your fingers to my lips. How do we measure the distance between God and man? Twenty-two finger-breadths make the universe: The cubit of your forearm bridges heaven and earth.

Draping the pomegranate bush in luminous colour, drowsy petals suck delicate hues from the sunset. Look! Across a filament a spider runs, trailing a strand of silk. She ties off her line, returns to the middle, drops another line then tightens it to a twig. To the junction of the two strands she returns, there to spin out radiating spokes. What shall the span of this life be? You tied your hands, Daddy, you tied your hands and feet. You wanted to be sure the instinct to live wouldn't overcome the will to die. Your body struggled anyway, retching out the seawater you'd swallowed. You sucked in your vomit, blocking your breath; your body howled for oxygen but seawater flooded its tissues instead. You started convulsing, the beat of your heart slowed—and then stopped: In Rovinj, on the Istrian peninsula, on the third day after the autumn equinox, 1976, your father drowned himself in the Adriatic Sea. You'd just turned thirteen. Faeringa! The capture spiral stretches and retracts: A creature sways in the spider's web. Sitting at the centre, her legs resting on the radial threads, the spider feels the tremors of her struggling prey. She pulls on the spokes, reading the signals: In the cockcrow hour of the orb, a flickering brightness of flame. The spider approaches the butterfly: Come, into the underworld I will conduct thee. From her spinnerets she pulls a silken shroud and wraps the wandering soul in sleep: Blood from your spleen bangs in your brain for answers that do not come; barren on your tongue, earth dulls your syllables. How can I get it into my head that you're dead? That your death is irreversible? How can I exist if you don't? I'd always slept on my stomach in freefall—now I sleep all curled up and fetal. Faeringa! The spider vomits digestive juices onto the body of the butterfly: You draw the blade through a wilderness of pain, cutting right to the heartroot. Lush and bright the blood comes, flowing down your forearm. Sharp and focused, the burn of the pain unburdens you of the weight of your feelings.

Behold the Plough, see how it wipes the intellect clean: Defined knowledge disappears, the shadowy world shimmers. More subtle than the rain, the dew on the grass is limpid with starlight. Milky sap rises in shrub stems; huddled in their umbels, flowers suck in the night. Mara, is it dark enough now for the unspeakable to be spoken, dark enough for me to inhabit the space your silence creates? Listen, I will tell you the story of your father's parents, the story from which all your stories come. I will tell you the story you told me.

Chapter 5

Friday May 11, 1945: Trudging up a dirt road, struggling up the ever-steeper slopes, your father's mother, heading for the Ljubelj Pass, carries her two-and-a-half-year old son in a home-made harness on her back. High in the Karavanke mountains they will cross from Slovenia into Austria. Her husband, your father's father, a battered suitcase strapped to his back, bears on his shoulders a roll of blankets. Between each other they carry, each holding a handle, a bag of sundry belongings. Five days earlier they crossed the threshold of their house for the last time. Neighbours showed no surprise. Partisans waited outside to seize what they could or to move straight in. Before joining the thousands of others on the road to Ljubelj, the fleeing parents stopped to pray in front of a barricaded church.

In an open field by the village of Viktring, near Klagenfurt, in a camp run by the 5th Corps of the British 8th Army, they spend nine days together before mother and child join other women and children in an abandoned factory nearby. Eight days later, on Tuesday May 29, the family, together with many other Slovene refugees, get into the trucks forming a convoy to take them, the British told them, to a better-equipped camp in Palmanova, west of Trieste. Instead of being taken to Italy, they are all unloaded at the train station and forced into the cattle cars and carriages of a train waiting to take them back to Slovenia. Once the British guardsmen, having closed and padlocked all the doors, draw back, the Partisans, who'd been hiding in the bushes and station buildings, take their places.

The train stops at Slovenj Gradec, just over the border. In a school that had served as a Gestapo interrogation centre and now serves as a Partisan detention camp, the couple watch as a priest among them continues to give absolution even after his hands have been hacked off. The Partisans separate your father's father from his wife and son, hurl him down the stairs and kick him black and blue. And the evening and the morning were the first day.

The next day he and other Catholics of the Home Guard are lined up on a gravel road, stripped of most of their clothes, and ordered to run. Partisans on horseback chase them, whipping them on the head and shoulders, jeering. That night they are marched across the countryside from Slovenj Gradec to Mislinje. And the evening and the morning were the second day.

In the morning they are forced to parade through the streets of the village, shouting: 'We are traitors, we killed women and children, we fought against our nation!'. That evening they reach the Teharje concentration camp. Parched throats beg for water. In vain. And the evening and the morning were the third day.

The next twenty-four hours at Teharje they all go without food. They are made to spend the whole day sitting on stones in the sun. In the evening the Partisans shout out a list of names. Those called are led out. They never come back. And the evening and the morning were the fourth day.

The next day they are given a thin soup made from pine needles. In the evening it starts to rain. The captives are ordered outside. Some can hardly move. The Partisans laugh and order those who have not yet been beaten to raise their hands. Nobody does. The Partisans shout out a list of names. While parading in front of a commander, a man who kept his rosary beads instead of throwing them—together with any remaining possessions—onto a cape on the floor as instructed, has his teeth smashed out with a truncheon. 'Pray with those', the Partisan commander tells him, pointing to the bloody teeth on the floor. That night the silence is repeatedly pierced by the howling of those who'd been beaten out of their minds. Some men begin praying and a Partisan shouts:

– Pray, you white dogs who listen to priests, soon Mathilda will come for you!

And the evening and the morning were the fifth day.

The following day they are told, 'The reactionaries have been poisoning the wells'. Everybody understands what is meant: Corpses thrown into ravines are contaminating the water. The captives are allowed to sip dew from grass and suck up puddles of water. They are given a thin slice of corn bread. Many of them have to spit it out because their throats are too inflamed to swallow. In the evening the Partisans shout out a list of names. One man swallows his crucifix and chain as he is being taken away. Those remaining are stiff with cold. They are made to stand up and lie down, again and again, in response to commands. Those who can't keep up are whipped. And the evening and the morning were the sixth day.

The next day they are given neither food nor water. The Partisans shout out a list of names. Your father's father's name is called. He knows his fate, and the Partisans know he knows. The guards tie him to another captive by a length of wire lashed around the upper arms. In bound pairs, the prisoners are forced to climb into trucks. The wire cuts into their flesh; their bleeding arms begin to turn blue. They are made to kneel face downwards, forty to a truck. In each corner of the truck a Partisan guard stands. Over the two-hour journey into the hills the guards beat them with truncheons; the captives fall over each other, the wire lacerating their flesh.

They are unloaded from the truck and marched into a valley. They hear shooting and screaming. Your father's father cannot feel his legs anymore. He notices a boy lying under a tree. His eyes have been gouged out and his skull is smashed. He is still conscious, sitting quietly; he is not moaning, just sighing. The captives are made to sing Communist songs. They are forced, again and again, to stand up and kneel down. Each time they do so, their wire lashes sever more flesh from the bone. They stumble a few meters, are made to turn and stagger back, then turn and stumble forward again. Finally they arrive at a huge pit.

The Partisans sing and shout. They beat their prisoners again, untie them, and order them to take off their rags. Hardly any are able to do so. A Partisan shouts at your father's father, gives him a shove and tells him to start running. His foot gashed, the remains of his pants soaked in blood, he hobbles forward, commends himself to the Virgin Mary, and breaks into a halting run. As he approaches the pit, bloody corpses come into view.

– Stop!

His spasmodic motion gives way to a sudden acceleration; he tumbles into the pit as shots ring out. Splayed across the corpses, he doesn't know whether he is dead or alive.

Gunshots fell more victims. Your father's father emits a gurgling groan as his mouth fills with blood. He calls for death: It will not come. He tries to crawl under the corpses and suffocate himself. Beneath the bodies he hears a constant trickle of blood. And then a wave of love for his wife and son washes over him. He feels guilty for having given up, he feels ashamed; he tells himself he will find a way to get out of the pit. A thrill runs through him; he thanks the Virgin Mary for his being alive. Extricating his body from amongst the corpses, he surveys the chasm walls for a way out. Faeringa! Flesh and bone fly in all directions; blood splatters everywhere: The Partisans spray the bodies with machine gun fire, then cast grenades into the pit. And the evening and the morning were the seventh day.

Chapter 6

— Crush the vermin! Dogs must die like dogs!

— Children are innocent!

The two-and-a-half year-old boy that is to become your father is taken from his mother. As he cries and screams, the mother pleads with every fibre of her being to keep him.

— Your father shouldn't have worn a German uniform, boy!

The soldier passes the child to a Partisan woman.

Crammed into a cattle truck, your father's mother is taken back to Slovenia through the Karavanke rail tunnel. At Kranje the train stops. While the men are being beaten the women are made to exchange their clothes for lice-riddled garments. Back on the train, pulling out of the station, they notice the joyful faces, the flowers and flags, of people cheering the end of the German occupation. Onward the train chugs, stopping once more at Sentvid, near Ljubljana, before unloading everyone at Kocevje. In a barracks that used to be a home for the blind, they are searched once again for any remaining watch, ring, or banknote. From there they are trucked to the killing fields of Kocevski Rog.

Bloodied uniforms of the Catholic Home Guard, supplied by the Germans, lie scattered on the ground. A man held down by a boot to his head screams as a Partisan's pliers pull a tooth from his jaw. Walking down the wooded hill to the pit in the valley, your father's mother, her husband and son at the burning point of her mind, makes a decision: I have fifty meters to refuse, to refuse to deliver myself: I will do it for you. With each decisive step the once-endless unfurling of time becomes a tether growing tauter. And tauter. And tauter.

— Stop! orders a Partisan. What's your name?

She knows that voice; she doesn't answer. Reloading his Luger, the Partisan shoves a magazine into the hollow handgrip of the pistol.

— Where are you from?

She doesn't answer. He racks the slide mechanism.

— I'm asking you: What's your name?

She looks him in the eye. He recognizes the girl he had courted before the war, courted so assiduously. She sees him at her garden gate, black grease from a bicycle chain stippling his ankle. His glazed eyes hold her gaze.

— Milena, when I say 'traitor', jump.

— I'm not a traitor, Janez.

— How dare you deny it? You are—

As the shot rings out she is already falling into the pit.

The daylight wanes. The last bodies descend, spraying blood as they land on the corpses. The buzzing of the black flies ceases; the moaning of the dying remains. Your father's mother is alive; she shivers, her teeth chatter. There's a knot in her stomach, a tightness in her throat. Her beating heart feels like a foreign body inside her. She hears the Partisans shouting to each other, and understands they are about to blast the pit with explosives. She crawls under the corpses. The reek of the abattoir suffuses her nostrils, the smell of the massacre makes her retch. Faeringa! In a rumbling cloud of dust the rocks come tumbling down. Four more explosions follow, making the darkness total. When the dust settles, the Partisans hurl spadefuls of lime powder into the pit. Your father's mother chokes and faints. The rumble of the departing trucks gives way to silence. Night falls fast.

In the frail light of dawn your father's mother, vomiting blood and dust, notices a beech tree that tumbling rocks have toppled into the pit. Crawling over the dead, she makes her way to it. She grabs a branch, pulls herself up, and clambers out of the pit. Scrambling clear of the edge, she heads into the forest.

Pain infiltrates her feet; she looks at her soles and sees they're bleeding. Faeringa! Her heart leaps as a man stares her down. Gazing out from a cocked head, his eyes are unyielding. She screams: His feet aren't touching the ground. She turns to walk away, then turns back. Using a flake of rock, she rips his trousers at the seams, tears off strips of cloth, then wraps them round her feet. She scuttles deeper into the forest.

Thirst sears her throat; her saliva won't flow. Across a clearing she spots a raspberry clump. Hurrying to it, she falls to her knees and ravishes the bush, her nervous fingers urging the berries into her mouth. Holding her hands, stained and dripping, before her face, she thinks of her husband and son, and then she thinks of God. *Yea, ye overwhelm the fatherless, and ye dig a pit for your friend. And I only am escaped alone to tell thee.*

She spots a church spire in the distance and makes her way toward it. From the edge of the forest she catches sight of a man and child walking beside a mule and wagon. She notices a water keg hanging from the back of the wagon. Slinking along behind, she breaks into a hobbling run, then stumbles and falls into a ditch.

It is dark when she regains consciousness. Was it all a dream, then, am I still among the dead? The biting of the lice brightens the stars; she crawls out of the gully. Walking parallel to a dirt road, she sees the light of a distant window and approaches it. She knocks on the door. A woman opens it and gasps in shock. Your father's mother begs for help. In the kitchen she is given milk and a raw egg. Weeping, the woman takes her by the hand and leads her up to the attic. On a mattress of horsehair your father's mother falls asleep.

Before daybreak the woman wakes her.

– You can't stay here. The Partisans would kill me if they found out. The village is full of spies; the OZNA are everywhere. You must go while it is still dark.

Your father's mother steps out into the darkness. She knows they want to make sure no survivor stays alive to speak of what they have seen. She thinks of her husband and son, and then she thinks of God. *They impose their belief, anyone who doubts they destroy. I serve thee, and yet it is they who enjoy the sun. Unlike I, they meet not with darkness in daytime, they grope not in noonday as in night. And I only am escaped alone to tell thee.*

At the foot of a hill she sits in grass, eating clover. Her forearm bears a bandage: Fleeing in a field, having slithered out from her hiding place in a hayloft, she owes her life to the drunkenness of the Partisan who fired the bullet. A woman washed her wounds with spirit and soothed them with ointment. She's lost her mind, the woman thought, when she heard her story. She believed it when she heard the Partisans had seized a man from his home, locked the rest of the family in the cellar, and set the house on fire. She believed it when she heard about her neighbour who hung herself because, hiding in the loft of her house, she had not come down when the Partisans were killing her mother, father, and brother below. But she couldn't believe your father's mother's story. Are not five sparrows sold for two farthings, and not one of them is forgotten by God? He wouldn't let it happen! The push of speech as your father's mother gives the facts confirms the woman in her verdict: This woman is mad. A pair of shoes, bread, apples, pears, nuts: These she gives her as your father's mother leaves the house before daybreak. Her stride is the stride of her husband, the pith of bread on her tongue is the morsel she feeds her son. And then she thinks of God. *I have eaten ashes like bread, and mingled my drink with weeping; by reason of the voice of my groaning, my bones cleave to my skin. Because I was not cut off before the darkness, neither hath He covered the darkness from my face. It is time to seal up the stars forever: And I only am escaped alone to tell thee.*

Slinking round a farm, she sees an old man carrying a bucket of water into the stable. She catches a shout in her throat. The man leaves the bucket on the ground. A horse approaches the bucket. The man walks towards a pitch fork leaning against a wall. Your father's mother rushes into the stable, falls upon the bucket and drinks. The man turns round, hesitates, then leaves the stable. He comes back with a woman and children. The woman grabs the pitch fork, sees your father's mother in the chicken coop, and shoos her out. The chickens cackle; the children call out:

– Thief!

– Traitor!

– Nazi!

She makes her way out of the barn and runs along a trail; she pauses to gob an egg. Partisans patrolling on horseback approach; she rushes into a field of rye. Crawling deeper into it, she falls to her face and cries. Crows squawk as they fly over the field. She thinks of her husband and son, and then she thinks of God. *When I looked for good, then evil came unto me, and when I waited for light, there came darkness. For now shall I sleep on the ground. Thou shalt seek me in the morning, but I shall not be. Bind the Pleiades, loose the bands of Orion—but I shall not be. My husband is murdered, my son plucked from me. The names in the Black Books are effaced from the world—beaten and starved, in the forests they fill the earth: And I only am escaped alone to tell thee.*

Her dress pulled up, her shoes hanging from her hand, she steps into the Sava Dolinka just before it surges round a bend and breaks into white water. Mountain ash and black alder push their dense mass to the verges of the river; at the water's edge, pale earth gives way to gravel. Her back to the high bank, she heads for the border: Austria! The cold water numbs her feet but cannot cool her fevered brain. Digging in against the current, her toes curl into the gravel as she steadies herself before each step. Behind her lie the ruins and rubble of Jesenice. She imagines the meadows that lie ahead, the meadows where once the scent of her husband's skin would fire her loins as they made love among the daffodils. In steps both tentative and deliberate, she wades through the water.

– Stop!

She swings round from the waist: Two soldiers, high on the bank, order her to come back. She notices the red stars on their caps, laughs, and swings back to keep going.

– Stop, or you're dead!

The water rises to her knees. One of the soldiers swings up the rifle slung at his side. He flicks the safety then lifts the bolt, letting its angled surface cam back the cocking piece.

— Traitor!

— Reactionary whore!

He flicks the safety again. Putting his right foot forward, he falls to his left knee. He raises the rifle and slips his index finger through the trigger loop. Caressing the trigger, he brings the butt of the rifle snug against his shoulder and rests his cheek against the comb. His partner calls out:

— Stop, Fascist!

The water comes up to her groin. The marksman levels the rifle. With his eye he places the post of the front sight in the V-notch of the rear. The eye equalizes the light bars, lines up the sights, and places your father's mother's head above the centre of the aligned irons.

— Stop, Fascist! German whore! Stop or you're dead!

She continues making her way toward the opposite bank. *Where are you, my son? How fast time goes by! One day I was a girl playing with dolls, the next a woman with a baby! Bruno, the laughter in your eyes, the delight in your smile when I'd rub the soles of your feet against my cheeks!* She swings around from the waist. Her mouth forms a word but her breath won't come. Lowering the rifle a touch, the marksman tightens his finger on the trigger: Firing pin strikes percussion cap, powder ignites as primer explodes. *Be a resonant glass that shatters while it is ringing.* The deflagration gases expel the bullet, sealing the cartridge case against the chamber wall. In the bore of the barrel the spiral grooves impart a spin to the projectile; out of the muzzle the bullet sizzles through the air. *Be a resonant glass that shatters while it is ringing.* In its copper jacket the lead slug continues its flight. *Be a resonant glass that shatters while it is ringing.* Scorching the skin, the bullet perforates the flesh and enters the body through the right shoulder. Tearing through the tissues, it passes through the scapula. *Be a resonant glass that shatters while it is ringing.* Above the clavicle it passes, through the apex of the right lung, perforating the pulmonary artery and penetrating the pericardium—deep in the heart it comes to rest. Before the blood spills inside it, the shocked body has already surrendered: Your father's mother is dead. As the white water buffets her body on the rocks, the marksman extracts the spent cartridge from the rifle chamber and loads another round. Into the forest, pursuing their patrol, the Partisans disappear.

Chapter 7

Sorrowful tears of sorrowful eyes
Thou breakest my heart in two

Thou sighest sore
Thy sorrow is more
Than my tongue can tell

Sorrowful tears of sorrowful eyes
Thou breakest my heart in two

Mara Marina, Mara Miranda, sirens sing while combing their tresses, Shiva weaves the universe from his hair, and I, running my hands through your hair, find a vertigo of flashbacks: In this epistemological striptease, shall we find the truths we are looking for?

Under a wide-open sky the plain expands, burnt orange meeting ethereal blue at the long horizon. Koppies and acacias break the horizontal; wildebeest and gazelle graze in scattered groups. Undisturbed by the breeze, the heat haze displaces distant hills and gives rise to phantom lakes. Faeringa! High into the air a gazelle leaps, the herd takes flight. Look! Hip and shoulder hurl the body forward, extended claws give traction: In a blur of dust a cheetah gives chase. To the rhythm of its long strides its spine undulates; set high in the head, its eyes focus on a single animal. Furiously through the body the heart drives the blood; rapidly into the lungs muscles pump oxygen. A twist, a turn, a straight-line stretch: Steering with its tail, the cheetah maintains its relentless pursuit. At last the dew claw of its front paw hooks the hind leg of the gazelle; losing its balance, the antelope tumbles down. The predator stretches across the shoulders of its prey, seizes its throat and twists its neck around: The gazelle succumbs as the cheetah's bite shuts its windpipe.

Drenched to your skin, your picnic blanket clinging, you stand in the cold wedge of a downdraft, haranguing the lightning.

— Have I not made myself hateful enough? Come on, hit me!

Lashed by rain in the windshear, you close your eyes and summon the executioner. Cleaving a cloud in a crack it comes, the bolt of lightning: Still you remain standing.

– God, why can't you destroy your creature? If it be not fire, then let it be flood!

Fulgurations take you to shining realms; you feel elation at the foreboding of ruin: In the fire of your vehemence you remain unconsumed.

– Why concentrate your ardour in a diamond, why store it in a star? Transfix me with fire, place a taboo on my body!

In a shock of thunder a flash of lightning rips open the sky: Still you stay standing.

– Why can't you hit me? Why can't you make me holy?

You peel off your blanket and bare your body to the sky.

– Come on, set your mark upon me, strike me down!

Hotter than the surface of the sun it comes, the bolt of lightning: Still you stay standing. Soaked to your bones and shivering, you break down and cry.

A curtain of rain obliterates the horizon; ghostly acacias howl through the gloom. In a flooded crater mud wells up, disgorging sludge into the savannah grass: The uneasy ooze of a watery inhumation, or the afterbirth of an abomination?

Against your skin the water glides, soft and silken; in its embrace your body moves, weightless: Giving yourself up to water, from jetty to jetty you make your way. Your muscles tense, your throat tightens; on your tongue the taste of ashes. Where is he, my only love? Where is he hiding? Underwater? In the forest? You feel the weight of your grief, your movements slow, and you wonder if you truly entrusted yourself to the water, could you let yourself go? Just remain still, and let the lake relieve you of your loss? You feel the drop in temperature, you feel the slime thickening the water. As your hand sinks into mud, your eyes open to blackness, the last bubble of air leaves your lungs. Despite your determination to stay down, your body rises.

Gasping for breath at the surface, you taste your devastation; staring into the empty sky, you feel at one with nothing. Total disbelief, utter bewilderment. In shock, dumbstruck, numb. Killed in a car crash nine months after you met, your only love is the lone fatality of the four people in the Fiat. Zoli was seventeen; you were fifteen-and-a-half. As soon as you saw him you knew he was the one. Doing street theatre on the waterfront in Maribor, you spent every spare moment together. In the hostel or on the island, on the banks of the river or in a café, like a starving child eating a stolen apple you opened your heart to his. It wasn't long before you were thick as thieves, your faith in each other absolute. His quiet courage, his ability to surprise, the tenderness and laughter in his eyes: Never again will you meet anyone who can move you the way he did! Down your temples your tears flow, the empty sky your only consolation. Drained of all vitality, you reach into your reserves and swim to the jetty.

Alenka sunbathing hardly stirs as you sit down beside her. You look at your picnic basket, and know your apple will not remove the taste of ashes in your mouth. You look at your bicycle leaning against a tree trunk, and know it can never return you to the one you love.

Stretching out, you lie face down and offer your body to the sun. Through a crack in the boards you peer at the water below. Lulled by its gentle lapping, you yield to the heaviness that comes upon you. Vaguely you hear Alenka speak; to whatever she is saying you sigh. Your last sensation before you sink into sleep is that of water rolling out of your ear.

Hand-in-hand with your father in a field bright with poppies, you walk down to a lake. Along the shore he points out the wild ducks and water hen, the lilies and the reeds, and shows you how damsels differ from dragonflies. Faeringa! Panicked wings scrape your skin, claws harrow your flesh: In a fever of determination a crow—trapped under your shirt—tries desperately to free itself. His black feathers turn crimson as your white shirt turns red; in a pandemonium of movement his talons lacerate your flesh. Between your flayed back and your blood-wet shirt, the bird grows bigger and bigger; when you feel the shroud of his blackness spreading around your body, you wake up screaming.

Holding your trembling body in her arms, Alenka assures you that your back is not bleeding. So why is it that wherever you look, you see a raven in a pool of blood?

Rain swells the river; along the banks, washed-up carcasses litter the rocks. The frenzy of the crossing is over; the survivors now graze in the virgin plain. Vultures tear into the flesh of wildebeest, long necks reach for inner organs: Drenched in blood, heads emerge, a dripping morsel of heart or lung, liver or intestine, in the heavy beak.

Birth, growth, death and transfiguration: In the savannah lands I continue my peregrination.

Chapter 8

In the short-grass plain, under a transparent blue sky, the vastness of the savannah is infinite. The river that when the rains come cuts across the plain is now a string of pools and swamps. Here there is no point of convergence, here the flux of phenomena find no resolution. How long must it rain before the separated waters become one?

In the Roncesvalles streetcar, a young man with green eyes and raven locks flips through André Kertész' *On Reading*. Suddenly a passenger cartwheels to a handstand; coins fall out of his pockets and roll down the aisle. The man who'd been flipping through the volume of photos shifts his gaze to the faces of the onlookers, framing them as photographs: beguiled, embarrassed, afraid. As the streetcar comes to a stop the handwalker drops his legs and springs to his feet. His eyes are bloodshot; on his face, a faraway grin. Giving him the coins he's picked up, the young man comes face-to-face with a young woman who'd come to do the same. At the Dundas West terminus they get out of the streetcar together.

— They say he just got out of 999 Queen Street, she says.

— Ah! Cancel my subscription to the resurrection!

— Send my credentials to the house of detention!

— I got some friends inside! they sing together.

Laughing, they rejoice in their shared love for Jim Morrison. Her stunning beauty—jet black hair, blue, blue eyes, milk-white skin—is spoiled by her teeth: Some of them are rotten.

— Except it's a loony bin, not a jail, he says.

— I've got friends in both! she laughs.

She's heading east, he west; they say goodbye. A few days later he sees her again at Dundas West station; she's got a baby, sleeping in a stroller.

— Hi.

— Hi. A girl or a boy?

— A boy.

An image of a baby falling from a window flashes through the man's mind. When the streetcar pulls into the station she unbuckles the baby and takes him out of the stroller.

— Could you hold him a sec?

Again an image of a baby falling from a window flashes through the man's mind.

– No, you hold him; I'll fold the stroller.

Following her instructions, he does so.

– I'm Inge, she says, as they get on the streetcar.

– I'm Sprague.

They sit down next to each other. The baby begins to cry.

– What's his name?

– Eric.

She rocks the infant in her arms, she gives him her little finger to grip. She turns to look at Sprague, her blue, blue eyes sparkling.

– As in 'God', she says.

– Eric Clapton?

– Yes.

Down Roncesvalles they ride, past the Repertory Cinema. Jean Eustache, *The Mother and the Whore.*

– That's a brilliant, brilliant movie. Would you like to go and see it with me? he asks her.

– Okay, but it had better be soon. My boyfriend's getting out of jail any day now.

– We can go tomorrow. Do you have a babysitter for Eric?

– No.

– I'll get my flatmate to look after him. He's a medical student.

– Ah, that could be useful.

He wonders what she means.

– Where do you get off? he asks her.

– Two stops. Marion Street. Would you like to come up for some tea?

– Okay, thank you.

In her second-floor flat the curtains are closed; she asks him to open them, then goes down the hall with the baby... Trestle table and slatted chairs; cushions, rugs and hand-made lamps... Patti Smith, Pink Floyd, Lou Reed... *Astrology, Karma and Transformation... Beelzebub's Tales to His Grandson... Thus Spoke Zarathustra: A Book for All and None...* Marijuana plants in tin cans, African violets in clay pots... An appointment card in a tarnished mirror: Methadone Maintenance Treatment - 33 Russell Street - 2 pm...

– Is Darjeeling okay, or do you prefer Earl Grey?

– Darjeeling's fine.

She comes into the room bearing a tray; they sip their tea at the table.

– Eric's okay now. He was born addicted to heroin.

Sprague's heart skips a beat.

– And you, are you okay?

– Getting there.

– It must have been very hard, both of you...

– Yes. I can't believe the things I used to do.

– Like what?

– Oh, when he'd cry I'd rub his gums with cocaine.

– Did he twitch a lot?

– Yes.

– I did too, they say, when I was a baby.

She looks him in the eye and holds his gaze.

– Are you a student?

– Yes. I'm studying photography.

– Would you take my picture?

– I'd love to!

The next day in the morning sunlight, soft through the sheers, he shoots her in black and white. Sitting on the hardwood floor, her hair pinned up with a silver spike, she looks over her shoulder into the lens: In the darkroom at Ryerson Polytechnic, as her features emerge under his fingers in the chemical bath, he makes a vow to be present to her. When he gives her the photo the next day she says:

– She's beautiful, isn't she?

– Yes. Very.

– But I can't keep it. My boyfriend would kill you–and me!–if he found out.

That evening they go to the Repertory Cinema to see *The Mother and the Whore*. Sitting beside him she smells milky, like a baby. He feels great tenderness toward her, but dares not touch her. He thinks of the guys in the line-up, all eyeing her. It must be hard to deal with, he thinks, the constant pull of sex that beautiful women elicit.

– Normally I only go to horror movies, she says. And any film with Marlon Brando! This will be only my second French movie.

– What was the first?

– *Last Tango in Paris.*

– I love that film!

– Yes, it's fantastic, isn't it?

– It's my favourite film of all time! After the one we're about to see, that is.

Her eyes catch the light in his.

– And you know what? The guy who play's Jeanne's boyfriend in *Tango* plays the lead in this film.

– Oh really?

– Uh-hm.

– Have you been there, to Paris?

– Yes.

– I'd love to go. Do you speak French?

– I do.

– Maybe you could teach me. I only speak German.

– I'd love to! And you can teach me German.

– It's a deal. But only when my boyfriend's in jail!

– Is he often in jail?

– Yes!

They look at each other and laugh. In the darkness, he steals a glance at her face, and is reassured: He knew she would either love or hate *The Mother and the Whore*, and by the glow on her face, he knows it's not hate.

He meets her again a few days later; they stroll Eric along the lakeshore, from Sunnyside to Marilyn Bell Park and back. She tells him her grandfather was a Nazi, her father an alcoholic, and her half-brother a rapist. 'Hope he rots in jail!', she adds.

Back outside her house she takes Eric out of the stroller and talks to him in baby talk. Sprague folds the stroller. Faeringa! Her head bangs against the door; she falls to the ground with Eric screaming in her arms.

– If you ever touch her I'll kill you!

A man with smoky eyes and matted hair pins Sprague against the wall; his breath reeks of alcohol, sweat rolls down his face.

– The child, pick up the child.

– My boy's none of your business!

– Go Sprague, get out of here! And don't ever come back!

Sprague reports what happened to a social worker at Saint Joseph's Hospital. She says they know her, they tried to help her, but she won't leave her boyfriend. Sprague insists they do something; she says they'll try once more.

Sprague saw Inge several times again, but nothing could bring her back to him. He gave her a camera, tried to teach her photography. She sold the camera to buy a fix. He went to the Addiction Research Foundation and began reading about drugs. He contacted a friend of a friend and learned to cook heroin, fix himself and shoot up. Nothing could bring her back to him. He contacted the social worker. She told him they'd lost trace of Inge, that she no longer lived on Marion Street.

Still today, wherever he is, Sprague keeps that photo of Inge—sitting on the hardwood floor, her hair pinned up with a silver spike, looking over her shoulder into the lens—on his wall. Her eyes—undying innocence shining through a wilderness of pain—remind him that the past is condemned to repeat itself, unless... Unless what? He thought the answer had something to do with sex, but it did not. He thought it had something to do with love, but it did not. He thought it had something to with knowledge, but it did not. It took him ages, but finally he understood that the past is irredeemable.

Mara Marina, Mara Miranda, in this vertigo of flashbacks, in this epistemological striptease, have we found the truths we are looking for? Now tell me: If truth requires both an infinite time and a time it will be able to seal, how much time is there for you and me? Nudity is not truth, but unquiet anticipation; it is not an unveiling, but secrecy: We have opened ourselves to secrecy, we have abandoned ourselves to grace. If the strands of your hair are prayer-sticks, I will climb a mountain to place them; if the strands of your hair are arrows, draw your bow and aim them.

Birth, growth, death and transfiguration: In the savannah lands I continue my peregrination.

Chapter 9

Tall trees and saplings curb the fluidity of forms; along the borders of the river, brown earth breaks into green. Between the phenomenal world and the unconditioned state, where lies the ford? I travel your body in search of non-attachment, but my senses I cannot extinguish. See the early morning mist blurring the horizon, see the flaming sky inaugurate the day! Naked as my thoughts in my arms you lie, your hair savannah grass, your back the open plain. Look! In the shade of an acacia, lions are making love; and there, a wildebeest licks the afterbirth from her newborn's fur.

– Say, lions, sorry to disturb.

Baring his fangs and growling, the male dismounts.

– Well, you must be the Wanderer. Good to see you!

– Indeed! says the lioness, standing up. We heard from the shrike that you're journeying in our lands. Big Daddy here just killed my cubs, now I'm in heat again. We've been at it since yesterday morning.

She yawns and lies down.

– You do look rather weary, both of you.

The lion stretches out beside his mate.

– It's a tiresome business, this fucking.

I seat myself, lotus-like, in the grass.

– Thank heaven it'll be over tomorrow! Can't wait to get my teeth into a juicy gazelle.

I feel the lioness' heat; I smell her estral odour.

– But why is sex such a burden for you?

She looks at me longingly.

– Well, unlike you, we're not kitted out for pleasure. Big Daddy's cock is no thicker than a pencil, and what's more, it's got barbs!

His yellow-green eyes appealing for sympathy, his tone pathetically earnest, the lion says:

– And she, she's always got the same come-on! All she does is approach me lackadaisical and flick up her tail a couple of times. Then she's flat on all fours while I do my thing, never the least opportunity for any variation. Boy, is it boring!

– So why do you do it so often?

– Statistics! Just a few weeks ago a PhD student from Iceland calculated that for every cub that manages to reach the age of one, we've had to fuck three thousand times.

– Well, I wouldn't be surprised if the statistic for humans is much the same. The difference, of course, is that for every three thousand of our fucks, only a very few are to make babies. The rest are purely for pleasure.

The lioness gets up.

– So I've heard, handsome, so I've heard.

She walks about a bit. Approaching the lion, she flicks up her tail a couple of times. The lion stands up. She lies flat on all fours. He mounts her and thrusts a dozen times. Growling and baring his fangs, he dismounts.

– Now maybe you can tell us, the lioness resumes, what it's all about, this pleasure thing.

– Yes, says the lion, it would be a good way to beguile the time. Just why are humans so obsessed with sex?

– That's a vast topic, lions! Let's just say it's because we're spiritual creatures, we have memory and imagination, we have language and play. Without that, sex would be just as boring for us as it is for you. With these things, worlds open up to us.

– What worlds?

– Our deepest selves, the whole of being.

The lion looks at me with puzzled eyes.

– What exactly is this 'spiritual' thing?

And the lioness adds:

– Yes, is it the same thing as religion?

Moved by their curiosity, I attempt an answer:

– Let's put it this way: Humans are impelled to reach beyond themselves, to find a reason for living. It's their spirit that demands it.

The lion looks mystified.

– So that's it, the spiritual thing?

– Yes. And in responding to the demand of their spirit, humans achieve their humanity. Each one of us is called upon to work on himself. It's a kind of quest. Every individual must undertake it, each in his own way.

– You mean you have to *work* to become human?

– Yes, it's not given. And that's what the 'spiritual thing' consists in. That work on oneself. It's very hard work, and just about everybody tries to avoid it.

The lioness gets up.

– And what's religion, then?

She walks about a bit. Approaching the lion, she flicks up her tail a couple of times. The lion stands up. She lies flat on all fours. He mounts her and thrusts a dozen times. Growling and baring his fangs, he dismounts.

– And how is it different from the spiritual thing? she adds.

Their keen interest inspires me to a pithy answer.

– It's the difference between the moon and the finger.

– As in Lao-Tzu?

Amazed that she's heard of Lao-Tzu, I conclude that her Asian cousins, long ago, must have passed on this knowledge to her ancestors.

– Yes, as in Lao-Tzu. The spiritual thing, the work on oneself, is the moon. Religion is the finger. Only fools look at the finger. The others, at the moon.

– I see, says the lioness. Very interesting.

– Indeed! says the lion.

Eyeing me up and down, with just a hint of desperation, the lioness asks:

– Would you like to fuck me, Pilgrim? I'd like to get a taste of the pleasure humans experience. See if I can feel spirituality!

The lion cuffs the lioness; she cuffs him back. Snarling and growling, they fight. Then she walks about a bit, determination in her stride. Approaching the lion, now resting but still tense and alert, she flicks up her tail three times. The lion springs to his paws. She lies flat on all fours. Roaring, he mounts her. She snarls, turns around and swats at him. He grabs the scruff of her neck between his teeth and thrusts two dozen times. Growling and baring his fangs, he drives in deep and holds it, then dismounts.

– Wow! That was the best one since we began yesterday morning! she says.

– Yeah! says the lion. Thank you, Wanderer. You've given our fucking one hell of a kick!

– The pleasure is mine, lions. Now I'll leave you to it. I've got to be on my way. Goodbye.

– See you, sexy Pilgrim. Love your long black mane!

The lion growls and cuffs the lioness. She cuffs him back.

– Goodbye, Wanderer, goodbye!

Birth, growth, death and transfiguration: I leave the savannah lands, other shores to explore.

Chapter 10

Sutures and ridges divide the hard capsule of the head; from the eardrum to the aedeagus the tubular abdomen stretches. The tegmina stir; a hyaline fan unfolds. Hark! Furious hindwings crepitate, infusing the air with anger: The grasshopper remains in place. Tibia and femur flex at the knee; from the thorax hindlegs rise colossal. Spur, tarsus, claw, arolium—a kick into oblivion! Piercing the mesothorax, rendering bootless his clamorous fury, a thorn pins the locust to the sky. A virescent fluid seeps from his mouth, darkening his articulations. In vain his filiform antennae flicker: He can capture the volatile compounds, but not the acacia leaves. Blankly into space his elliptical eyes stare. Spur, tarsus, claw, arolium! Again from the trochanter the hindlegs are hurled: again they encounter nothing. Between mandible and labrum vital fluid gathers into a globule.

– Transfixed locust, as the day stops dead at the place where you're pinned, do you remember when you were a nymph, squirming out of your seroso to take your first hop? Or, upon reaching your last instar, your first flight?

– The element of air and the element of earth, going into death is preparing for birth: I do remember.

– I too am alive with memory. The cavern of my heart is no longer a secret cell, walled against all creatures. Listen! Do you hear the breeze wafting through it?

– That is the stutter of the spirit instilling itself into matter. Only when you are one with your breath can you be reborn.

Spur, tarsus, claw, arolium: The blue of oblivion! The kick shakes loose the globule; from the maxilla vital fluid drips. In the eyes of the insect mirror walls dissipate the darkness of the apparent; on the rhabdoms the lenses focus light: Without predicate, preceding all positing, in the heart of the locust spirit discloses the real of the universe: a plenitude of epiphanies.

Under a wide open sky, clumps of cat's-tail dropseed and herringbone grass scatter across the veldt. Turn. A pair of koppies breaks the horizon. Turn. Velvet signalgrass invades a dry dolomitic eye. Turn. Purple aloes cluster around crumbling rock. Turn. Suspiration, syncope! Unopened eyes, bulging orbs, black hemispheres of a broken world: Beside the still locust, a naked bird sways from a thorn. Oh wretched hatchling! Bright red blood spills from his pierced throat; down the livid flesh it flows, down the awkward wing, a thinning thread trickling to a standstill. Hark! A sweet refrain! Tones run aloft, trail off in a trill, then float in the bright blue air. Look! Upright on the upmost branch, above the pinned locust and impaled nestling, a shrike sits, alert and serene. A burst of white is his breast, white scapulars break the black of his wings.

— Keen sentry, tell me, what is the nature of your work?

— I am a teacher of the heart.

— A teacher of the heart? So why this display of death?

— It is a lesson in love.

— My heart aches to learn. Won't you teach me?

Back from his bill a black mask stretches, through the eye to the ear coverts.

— Speak, handsome assassin! I thirst for your teaching.

On the hatchling's breast, among the feather tracts, curdled blood hardens.

— Wanderer, has there ever been a moment when it appeared to you without the shadow of a doubt that it is better to be alive than dead?

— Yes.

— When?

— Every moment of making love with Marietta.

— All right. Here's your lesson. I'll expect a poem in return.

— Of course.

— Love is a mark on identity. It is a trace which determines the self as never wholly itself. That's your lesson. Meditate it.

— Never wholly itself... Thank you. I will meditate that.

— Marietta enabled you to achieve a kind of existence. You owe her everything. She loved you to the very depths of your idiocy.

— And that's why all my poems are in her honour. Here's the one I promised you.

I bought you a guitar for your birthday,
A Spanish nylon string.
Why'd you do that? you asked me.
I replied, Cause you love 'Castro Marin'.

You began to strum and then you kissed me,
In the groove, you got a rhythm going.
In no time your fingers found a melody;
You called it 'The Cloud of Unknowing'.

The fall of your hair, the tap of your foot—
Why do you move me so?
I fall in love all over again—
And fix you an Irish Cream and Curaçao.

And then of a sudden you stop and say:
I've got it!
You pick up notepad and pencil,
You scribble and calculate.

And when the paper is published,
I read in the 'Thank you' line:
A special thanks to Sprague
For the Spanish guitar on my birthday.

— A bit sentimental, Wanderer. A bit on the soft side.

— Really? After all these years—

— You can't help it. On the borderline of being, you're condemned to tranform desolation into triumph.

How well he knows me, the shrike.

— Pilgrim, we'll meet again soon. See you.

— See you, kind shrike. And thank you.

Under a wide open sky, purple aloes cluster around crumbling rock. Turn. Velvet signalgrass invades a dry dolomitic eye. Turn. A pair of koppies breaks the horizon. Turn. Clumps of cat's-tail dropseed and herringbone grass scatter across the veldt. Turn. Suspiration, syncope! Through the throat the thorn thrusts; through the teeth the tongue extends: The heart is stopped. Translucent against the sun, blood fills the veins of bald feet; in the soft fur of the white underside, a crimson stain fans out. Look! White bars scintillating in black wings, on a branch above his display the shrike sits. A mantle of pearl slides down his back; light glints on the hook of his beak. From the tip of the mouse's tail, a globule of blood distends. The hatchling hangs limp, its mouth agape. Kick into oblivion! The grasshopper's death drags on: Fixed in their blank stare, gibbous compound eyes begin to turn dull. The shrike, bold in his black mask, begins a mournful song.

— Tell me, murderous troubadour, why this slaughter?

The shrike keeps singing.

— Strange teacher, do tell me: How can you sing amidst such carnage?

— I told you before, Wanderer: It is a lesson in love.

— It's a hard lesson!

— It's one you need to learn.

He resumes his mournful song.

— I want to learn! Teach me!

– Do you have a poem for me, a less sentimental one this time?

– I do, I do.

– All right, listen: The world is worth no more than a gnat's wing, words are mere beads in a rattle bladder, but love is the ineliminable residue of all articulation.

– I know that.

– Just as the beauty of the peacock's plumage springs from the poison of the serpents it swallows, so the beauty of the soul springs from the love in the heart.

– I know that.

– Memory is the past tense of desire, and the horizon of all desire is mourning.

– Mourning?

– Mourning. Now let's have that poem you promised me!

Kick into oblivion! Still the grasshopper's death drags on.

– All right. Here it is.

In Zürich, in your bedroom overlooking the lake,
I lay on your bed, barefoot and stripped to the waist,
And watched you pack away your winter clothes,
Unpack your summer things.

Mothballs for woollens, boots in boxes,
Coats in garment bags. And then the emergence
Of crepe-de-Chine tops and cropped trousers,
Bold-print dresses, sandals and skirts.

As the sun streamed through the window,
I watched you take off your jeans and T-shirt
And put on a tank top and billowing skirt.
I tossed you a straw hat from a box: You put it on.

And then I rose from the bed and approached you.
I took off your hat and in a zigzag of sunlight
Laid you down on the floorboards. In Sanskrit
I uttered a blessing, then crept up under your skirt.

Between your legs I performed the ritual of Spring,
It's called 'ploughing the first furrow'.
You'd worn the sacred headdress, I'd pronounced
The blessing. It was a wonderful summer.

– Better, Wanderer, much better. I think your scribbling just might ease your way.

– My way to where?

– Why, to your death, of course! Goodbye. And thanks for the poems! They'll make a fine addition to your file in the Archives.

– But poetry is for the living!

– A salutary desire! To highlight the obstinacy of the alien in the labyrinth of intimacy—but what chance does poetry stand in a world where debased language rules? In the Archives your case will have pride of place; content yourself with that. Goodbye!

– Goodbye, teacher of the heart, goodbye.

Chapter 11

Your breasts under my hands are smooth as moth's wings; on the heave of your breathing they rise and fall. Imperial apples, sovereign orbs, guide me into your kingdom! Across the millennia it comes, through water-gall and desert dust, the daemon that drives my craving: Into the soft receptiveness of my mouth my lips draw your nipple; with each successive suck the bonehouse of my body becomes more truly a temple. At last my lips relent. I raise my head: Welcome! Your proud nipple salutes me. Animal oracle, ardent eminence, they say to return to the root is to find rest. So why do I feel so restless?

Combs in jars of liquid blue duplicate themselves; clippers come in pairs on the counter top. A billowing sheet alights on a boy's body; at the nape of his neck the barber knots it. Calibrated for the cut by the comb, the boy's raven locks fall to the incessant snipping of silver scissors. Mr. Vassan's grip is tight; his dirty fingernails dig into the boy's scalp. Look! On the strop he hones a razor, then applies warm lather to the boy's skin: Touch, touch me! Behind his ears, along the nape of his neck, the barber's fingers apply the soothing balm. Again, touch me again!

Were you so desperate? Was your need so dire that even Mr. Vassan's dirty fingers were soothing? 'Again, touch me again': Child, were you a changeling? A black sheep, an ugly duckling? Motherless, fatherless, fed by a woodpecker and suckled by a she-wolf?

I breathe in and obliterate the world; I breathe out and bring it back anew.

— Mom, I'm hurting.

— It's not my fault!

A stitch comes undone in the fabric of time: The boy understands no connection will ever be possible: His experience will never be acknowledged.

— I never said it was your fault.

— Good. Because I'm not to blame!

Cradle me in your reverie, shelter me in your mind! It's too late. She never did, and never will. In the unbound surround the boy floats away. His mother's got a secret: What it is, he'll never know.

I breathe in and obliterate the world; I breathe out and bring it back anew.

What do I know about her? Not much. Her mother was a maid to a rich man. She doesn't remember her father, except for a single image: Handsome on horseback, he's coming to visit... Convent Farm. Sisters of the Holy Cross... Night distils the darkness, the dormitory fills with dreams. She stands by a window, sheers billowing behind her, and watches the flashing of the fireflies. 'How can we know the way? Whither I go ye know, and the way ye know. That where I am, there ye may be.'... She slips into bed, enfolds herself in her arms, and falls asleep. 'I saw by night and beheld a man riding upon a red horse'... When dawn puts the stars to sleep she awakes... Rosebud breasts, morning ablutions... Apples and apricots from a tin roof, dried sliced in the sun: Put them in porridge for breakfast!... On the way to school she stops in her tracks: Let the cows cross! Fearsome their long horns, their eyes thunder-black. To the dip to kill the ticks!... Reading, writing, and arithmetic; the lives of the saints... Sour milk from a calabash—the tang's delicious, I'll pour me some more!... And now it's time to check the fence and feed the chickens. Fatten them up, but not for foxes!... Swallows' wings usher in the evening; the setting sun brings out the orange in her eyes. Mother Superior intones a prayer: The novena of mourning for Sister Alphonsus begins... The mission nuns were Bavarian. She'd listen to them speaking German: the language of secrecy... Other than the priest at Mass, the only man she ever saw at the mission was the visiting vet, his arm deep in a cow's vagina... And then, too old to stay on at the convent, she moved to a town in Pondoland before going to high school on the coast. There she met a young man who courted her assiduously. They became sweethearts, and ten years later, got married and started a family...

Over the edge of the bed you throw your head, from the elbow your arms hang down. Your breasts rise abruptly to meet the heavens; at their base I begin my pilgrimage. With spittled tongue I climb in concentric circles, tracing contours of longing upon your flesh. Giddy at the summit, my begging bowl abrim, I render my devotion with all the kisses of my mouth. Mara Marina, Mara Miranda, why, at this very moment, does the aftershock of the broken shell send a tremor down my spine? Hush! In a whisper of eyelashes a thousand swallows take to the blue of your eye.

— Come! they call.

I flap my wings and fly.

Intermezzo 5: Vera

Vera's talking in her sleep. Little bursts of gibberish. Though it could be Russian or German, English or Italian, that's half-escaping the torpor of her sprawled body: A student of translation and conference interpretation at Astrakhan State University, she's fluent in all these languages. Met her in a café a stone's throw from the Volga. I was tapping out the rhythm as I reread a lyric I'd written; curious, she approached me and we began talking. Turns out she writes lyrics too: She's bass player and lyricist in a rock 'n roll band. She asked to see what I'd written. I showed her:

Black-winged kites block out the sky,
The Wall is down, the fence is high;
In the architect's vision intimidation is found
In the massed concrete, the treeless ground.

Forgotten, who cares, the children they roam;
A hole in the ground is what they call home.

Ghostly fog around the streetlights,
Ice on the wires, wind that bites;
Out of a car a man pushes a boy:
Life is dangerous in the division of joy.

Forgotten, who cares, the children they roam;
A hole in the ground is what they call home.

Fire pot, potatoes and lard,
Burnt-out buildings, mud in the backyard;
Shattered glass, in the mirror a girl,
Lipstick and heels to conquer the world.

Forgotten, who cares, the children they roam;
A hole in the ground is what they call home.

What is to be done with Lenin's legacy?
Will we ever get over the twentieth century?
Man against man and God against all,
The whore of ideology is always on call.

Forgotten, who cares, the children they roam;
A hole in the ground is what they call home.

— Wow! Where, exactly?

— Odessa. Read the next page.

She did, and read this:

> Down a manhole, in a cement chamber, on rag-covered ground strewn with trash, they live—orphaned, abandoned, on the run—beneath the contempt of the people above. Anton scratches his head and crushes a louse; under a leaking pipe he splashes his face. The yellowy glimmer of a bare light bulb can't warm the blue of his eyes; the bloodstain on the tarnished mirror can't weaken his will to get high.
>
> Into his lungs from a plastic bag Ivan draws acrid fumes of airplane glue; he stares at the light bulb and laughs as it pops in his mind.
>
> Trembling with fever, Vadim, sitting on his haunches, slaps invisible flies from his face.
>
> Dima bends to pick up a needle and sees a crown of thorns; dizziness overcomes him as the spiky mound spins round and round: In a splatter of vomit he tries to find what he's looking for.

— You spent time with them?

— Yes. Read the next page.

She did, and read this:

> Stripped to the waist, feet bare, Anton lies with drawn-up legs on a carpet of blackened purple. He offers his arm to Ivan. From the violet fabric red birds rise to beguile Ivan's eyes; idly in one hand he holds the syringe of *baltushka* while with the other he vaguely strokes Anton's arm.
>
> — Hey, come on.
>
> Out of the haze in Ivan's head an image takes shape, an icy blue image of Lake Baikal.

> — Hurry up!
>
> Glimpsed in the *Great Soviet Encyclopedia,* glimpsed in another lifetime, the Pearl of Siberia dissolves into the blue of Anton's eyes.
>
> — Stop wasting time!
>
> Hurrying to get the needle in, Ivan misses the vein: Anton screams in pain.
>
> How does one look into the eyes of a child who wants to be left alone to die? My status is abolished, my role too: Children, in the desolation of those with no hope of redemption, I am with you.

— Don't tell me you too...?

— Yes. Read the next page.

She did, and read this:

> 'I always knew Sprague would become either an addict or an artist': Do you remember, Marietta, that night in Arcachon, when Clara told you of her conviction? 'I once pulled him out of his vomit and held a mirror to his mouth. Barely alive.' As the boys sniff volatile vapours from a plastic bag, their slurred speech cannot stir them from their torpor: How, then, could they ever suspect that the man amongst them was once as outcast as they are? How could they guess that in a parallel city on an inland sea, as snow fell all around him, the boy who became that man retracted his lines of defence and withdrew, as each of them has done, into the citadel of himself?

— Sprague! Harlequin-McElhone!

Into the radiance of her eyes I cast my pride.

— I'd love to translate your lyric into Russian!

— All right. But first it goes to Gram.

— Of course.

Soon I was calling Vera 'Verochka'. We spent the next three days together.

In her beat-up Cinquecento she showed me Astrakhan. She showed me the *quartier chic,* built over the bodies of the thousands murdered in Stalin's purges. She showed me the endless patchwork of makeshift shelters, crooked houses in dustblown streets. Then we walked around... Aubergines and tomatoes the size of melons; goats grazing on sidewalk grass... Flies buzzing around a brace of fish; a caviar pusher flashing his black treasure (banned because the sturgeon are becoming extinct)... Still we have marriages: By the kremlin and cathedral, smiling brides display their virginal whiteness among the garbage and the flowers... Thus Vera showed me what had been the melting pot on the margin of empire, the crossroads, the gateway, the Silk Route station.

At night, in bed, Vera asks:

– Who's Marietta, Sprague?

– She's the woman who showed me how to make the shrivelling fire fecundating.

– What?

– She showed me how to rhyme love with creating.

– She's your Muse?

– Yes.

– She was your lover?

– Yes. I was an animal, I was a god. She made me human.

Her eyes twinkling, she fixes me.

– Well, I can undo that!

Four is the perfect square, there is something very solid about its symmetry: On all fours Vera offers herself to me. Our bodies one, the way of knowledge merges with the way of love: The cup dissolves, the cupful remains.

– Who are you, Sprague?

– I'm a letter in a bottle, looking for a beach.

– And how long have you been adrift?

– Not long enough to be so old that desiring me would be transgressive.

Her lips form a kiss. I kiss her foot.

Blue gloss
On toenails: Blue note
In my heart

– Maybe I'll find a clue in your notebook?

– Take a look.

She opens my notebook and reads:

> Stairs rise to empty skies, mirrors lose their logic; windows open to blank walls, shadows disdain the sun: Objects

swear they saw you, and when I look you're gone. But your ghost is everywhere: Freckles above a girl's breasts flood me with tenderness; an empty dress draws forth a tear, a broken sandal strap breaks my heart.

– Why did she leave you?
– To return me to my destiny.
– And what's your destiny?
– To be here, on a night like this, with you, Verochka.

Skin aglow,
The kingdom; eyes in the know:
Wisdom

– Where do you come from, Sprague?
– I don't know.
– Where were you born?
– I wasn't.
– What does it say on your passport?
– South Africa.
– Why don't you go back?
– I can't.
– Why not?
– Give me the notebook.

Sway of breasts,
Slope of shoulder: The flame,
The candle, the holder

– Here, read this.
She reads:

The country I come from has changed, but my ambivalence remains. What does it matter that I can't go back? That in another lifetime the beauty of the land might have dazzled your eyes as well as mine? And yet a searing anger washes over me when I compare what is with what could be. Why the gulf between the immensity of the resources and the meagreness of the benefits they bring? Why the millionaire ministers and the millions with

> nothing? Why all the handouts in the pockets of the party hacks? Why the systematic recourse to 'racist' to curse any who dare criticize? As for the continent at large, why the millions murdered at the behest of a megalomaniac? Why the lack of will to break the 'our turn to eat' cycle? Why the chronic incompetence in elementary skills, the preference for dash and flash over substance? Why the impetus to plunder instead of the desire to sustain? Why the inability to maintain when maintenance is called for, why the incapacity to foresee? Why? Why? Why?

– And you have no answers?

– None. Just anger.

– All right. You can't go back. But you don't have to wander forever. Why don't you settle down somewhere?

– Give me the notebook.

> Fall of hair, lake through leaves:
> Sifting what she knows
> From what she believes

– Here, read this.

She reads:

> What is the wound that drives me to wandering?
>
> A foreigner lives within me.
> He says I'm relative, not absolute.
> He says forever I shall remain aloof,
> Unable to take root.
> Incessantly he shapes and reshapes me,
> Leaving me no routine or rest.
>
> What is the wound that drives me to wandering?
>
> A stranger lives within me.
> He knows my loss is irredeemable.
> He knows my secrets, my particular alienation.
> He peels back my mask: Who are you, in the end?
> There is no end.

What is the wound that drives me to wandering?

An outsider lives within me.
He says my freedom is the freedom
To refuse, the freedom of solitude.
Over an empire of nothing
—experience passes, memory persists—
He leaves me to reign supreme.

What is the wound that drives me to wandering?

An alien lives within me.
He says however great my courage,
It can never overcome my humiliation.
He says whatever I undertake,
It is doomed to futility:
I am condemned to turn round and round
In the saga of myself.

What is the wound that drives me to wandering?

– Are you sure you're not in love with your loss, Sprague?

– What do you think, Verochka?

– I don't know. I don't know you well enough.

– Come here, then. Get to know me better.

She did. She came to me. She got to know me better. We found unsayable correlatives for the loss of consciousness.

– Now what do you think?

– About what?

– Am I in love with my loss?

– After what we just did, Sprague, it doesn't matter.

Sweat on skin, gleaming;
Hair a wheat field after a storm:
I want you again.

– Verochka, you're my Steppe wolf, my Siberian tiger!

– And what else?

– My taiga lynx, my tundra hare, my arctic fox, my hazel-grouse!

– Sprague, I'm only a girl trying to show you that you may be banished from humanity, but you're not barred from my love.

– Verochka, I—

With her liquid grace she traced the contours of my intensity; she stripped my tongue of syntax, she made me a babble of syllables. Paradoxical, isn't it, since in her bones Vera knows the only thing that remains close amid all losses is language.

Marietta, to create what is untranslatable even in its own tongue, that is what I am trying to do: Hear me now, that I may honour you!

PART FIVE

Chapter 1

Still I speculate, still I ponder: When you surprised yourself in the mirror, when you became a stranger to yourself, who was the who you dreamt yourself to be?

– *Mirror, mirror, tell no lies, how do I look in Egon Schiele's eyes?*

– *Gaunt, stark, raw in her nakedness, the girl you once were confronts you. Instantly you recognize her defiant vulnerability and self-subjugation, her vestigial femininity and proud isolation. A wave of tenderness overwhelms you, you feel a kind of homecoming: Never have you forgotten this girl who lives inside you, never has a day gone by without you paying her tribute.*

Burnt into your face, the embers of your eyes glow with contemptuous sadness. Your hair is falling out, your veins have collapsed; a layer of fine hairs covers your body like a fetus. The spindles of your legs end in swollen ankles; your fingernails are brittle and blue. A skeleton covered in skin, you are a walking corpse, a species of living dead. Jubilant in your decrepitude, you are an affront to the living.

Wearing layers and layers of clothes and cradling a cup of tea, you stand by the radiator but can't get rid of the cold: It lives inside you.

Looking at photos of yourself as a little girl, you break down and cry: Was I really like that once? You can't remember the last time you laughed, you can't even remember what laughter is like. You've lost the feeling of being young, you're convinced you'll never recover it: You feel you've already lived a lifetime.

A dinner party! For others you make a four-course meal; for yourself you ritually cut a slice of cucumber into sixteen pieces. For others the palate is to be delighted: For you it is to be denied. And so before ingesting any food, you strip it of its potential for reverie by counting every calorie and converting it to grams: Nothing over which you are not master will enter your body.

The scales are your touchstone of integrity, you've made others understand that, but how can you make your mother understand that you are killing yourself because you can live neither with nor without her?

It never lets up, the force that drives you, it never lets up for even a second: It pushes you to extremes, there's no in-between. One moment you're lying unconscious on the bathroom floor, a vein in your eye popped from the violence of vomiting, the next you're furiously peddling your bike along the lake. One moment you're crying yourself to sleep, the next you're devouring Wuthering Heights. *And then in the morning you amaze everybody with all you can still do. Up until you were hospitalized, you could do a month's school work in a week and still be tops in every subject.*

My God, why did I wear white? Your father at the wheel, his new wife beside him and you on the back seat, you make your way home from the Lucerne Festival where, from the turn of the opening trill to the wit of the adagio-presto coda, your performance of Beethoven's tenth violin sonata had been a triumph: A happiness that would soon belong to another lifetime. Between your legs the stain spreads, dissolving your dream of ambivalence. So red is the colour of reality, so red marks my limits. God, what a cataclysm! Thus you came to understand that the exterminating angel is female; yes, that even for you, the other sex is feminine.

Why can't my body be like a boy's, profiled for action? Why must it betray me with its loathsome blood and swelling flesh? My body is hollowing out, emptying out, unfolding; my body is scandalous! And all of it aimed at one thing: At making me—my God, never! Never! I don't want to be a woman: I want to be myself.

With this decision you begin your swim to the source, determined to be reborn in a body that belongs to you alone. And so you make yourself immune to others, you remove yourself from everything impure and begin to shed your flesh. Why should you eat? You lack nothing.

It's working! What a thrill when the scales testify to your will, what a thrill when your cross a threshold! Before long you're flirting with death like a matador, convinced that readiness to die allows you to live: In elation you realize that your ideal weight is not thirty-five, thirty or twenty-five kilos; no, your ideal weight is zero!

The joy of needing no-one and nothing, why didn't you think of it before? Accepting neither reasoning nor coercion, neither love nor interest, you declare yourself sole judge of who you are and recognize no link to anyone. You need starvation to live, you're in complete control—no one will take that away from you! What do they know, thinking you were trying too hard to please the opposite sex? The fools—if they only knew you were putting

> *an end to sex itself! Why can't they see that in your infinite nostalgia you are hungry for something else? No, it's all or nothing. You will make no concession, you will not be reduced to servitude! No!*

As your tears flow, you return from the looking glass.

> Drooling dogs roam empty streets,
> Seeking insects under ashes.
> Huff, huff, they whiff the dust:
> Tongueless mouths struggle to feed.
>
> Across fractured logs haggard dogs
> Stagger, their yellowy eyes oozing.
> Huff, huff, they whiff the dust:
> Toothless mouths struggle to feed.
>
> Skeletal dogs on a burning plain
> Drag their bones and dig;
> Deeper and deeper they dig,
> Until their graves are dug.

Marietta, how could you have done that to yourself? My head understands, but my heart rebels. Where I chose self-benumbment, a retreat into the citadel of myself, you chose self-violence, an attack against your very life.

> My love, I am an African daisy.
> My head is red and my heart is dark,
> But my leaves are felted and silvery-green:
> Touch me, that I may give you my tenderness.
>
> Dearest, I am a saxifrage, a rock-breaker.
> My stems are red and my leaves dark green,
> My flowers are soft plumes of salmon-pink:
> Touch me, that I may give you my tenderness.
>
> Precious one, I am an upright, bulbous perennial.
> My leaves are grass-like and ornamentally insignificant,
> But my flowers are starry, deep-blue spires:
> Touch me, that I may give you my tenderness.

Chapter 2

— I want to tell you about Inès, Sprague. A girl I knew.
Does the velvety feel of the cognac in your mouth, does its enigmatic aroma, assure you that no matter how much of yourself you reveal, your mystery will remain?

— But before I do, I'll tell you about Catherine and Pascale.
And thus you came to tell me about your double family: Pascale, the woman I met at the El Salvador concert, was your father's wife, but not your mother. Catherine, that was your mother's name, and she left you and Jean-Louis, your father, to go off to Poughkeepsie with Zoran, a man who has a daughter the same age you are: And the dish ran away with the spoon. But no: Over the following months the ceremony of unveiling confirmed all you'd said.

How shall I tell the tale, Marietta? By what measure shall I weigh my words? The mystery you are to yourself is not the mystery you are to me; the love that unites us divides us: The arrow that differentiates gives identity. My aim is not to pin down the fire but to propagate the flame: I will continue to weave Heraclitian signs into my carpet of memory. Until the next kiss I'll give voice to my lyre, forging my words in the heat of your fire.

Your family: A web of intersecting stories, an interlacing of desires across a minefield of mourning. And it was your mother that set the loom in motion. In 1956, on a Christmas vacation, Catherine met Jean-Louis on the slopes of Verbier. She was nineteen, a student in Art History at the University of Lausanne; he was twenty-five, designing electronics for jet fighters in Vélizy. You figured you were conceived in the earliest hours of the New Year (though it may have been a few days before). Six months later your parents got married and—your father having abandoned the prestigious Mirage programme and found the microtechnology research centre in Switzerland more to his liking—set up house in Neuchâtel. Years later, when you came to study their wedding photos, you found both bride and groom radiant: There was nothing to make you doubt that if you were conceived in lust, it was love into which you were born.

Your father flourished in his new job; your mother divided her day between raising you, studying part-time, and indulging her passion for pottery. By the time you started kindergarten she had built herself a studio and discovered her talent for sculpture.

Two years later she took part in a collective exhibition in Zürich. There she met Zoran, and before long they were madly in love. A Yugoslav exile, a renowned photographer and a widower with a six-year old daughter, he had just obtained a Green Card and bought a house in Poughkeepsie: He invited your mother to join him there. One year later she did, becoming Zoran's wife and step-mother to his daughter, Nika, leaving you and your father to live alone.

That was in 1964. You were seven years old. Six years later your father remarried: Pascale at twenty-two was seventeen years younger than Jean-Louis, and nine years older than you.

A ghost is the final character in this family play: Jelena, Zoran's first wife and Nika's mother, killed in an avalanche in the Alpes vaudoises on Saint Valentine's Day, 1962.

And thus from the age of seven, against this ground of mourning and desire, you set out to find a viable figure of yourself: You still had a father, you still had a name, but the guilt and pride mingling in your heart made you uncomfortable with this version of Marietta Valero.

After that fateful night when you surprised your parents' conversation (I'll evoke it later), both of them—separately and together—spent time talking to you: Your mother is your mother, but she is also a woman; your father and mother are your parents, but they are also lovers. Being a parent and being a lover are two different things: It is as lovers that we are separating, but as your parents nothing in our hearts has changed. If your mother now loves another man, the present does not change the past: Your birth was the most beautiful event in our lives; you were welcomed into the world by the full force of our love. Nothing can change that fact.

Nevertheless, I've lost my mother: And so you determined to never become dependent on anyone again. Your visits to your mother would not be demands for love, but opportunities to show your independence. And all the while meanwhile, you would have your father to yourself! A guilty victory that your father had the finesse to manage appropriately: He was fully with you as a father, but sacrificed nothing for you. Instead, he got on with living his life: enjoying his work, spending time with friends, travelling. And thus, even as you blossomed under your father's regard, even as you felt closer to him than ever before, you gained a real detachment from both him and your mother. Yes, if you thought of yourself as the living alliance of your parents, you nevertheless felt free to criticize them; if inside yourself you could always evoke their presence, it was in the world outside that you wanted to make your way: Violin, karate and horseback riding; mathematics, cooking and travelling, were passions you cultivated on your way to independence.

And thus it was with a big smile on your face and a 'Notice of Assistance for an Unaccompanied Minor' around your neck that you met your mother at JFK Airport in the summer of 1965. A brief pause to pee (where you were glad of the general din to drown out your crying), and then you were beside her in her convertible Thunderbird, tearing up the highway to Poughkeepsie.

Zoran was tall and dark, and the kindness in his weathered face as he welcomed you put you at ease. But it was Nika who made the stronger impression: She was as tall and thin as you, her hair was black and her eyes were blue, and her face bore a look of shame you immediately determined to erase. You said 'Hello', and with extended hand proffered a 'Pleased to meet you': You'd befriended an Irish girl at your school and had been taking English lessons from an *au pair* working in town. Nika sensed you understood her position, and had come with no animosity. She showed you to your room, and gave you a tour of the house: Everything was bright and airy, open and calm; the floors were of warm oak, the walls a cool white. At the back of the house, a big bathroom opened out onto a garden in full flower. Your mother's pottery found a place in every room; you noticed a new boldness and daring in her designs. The parent's bedroom (you were happy to discover), was downstairs and at the opposite end of the house to where, upstairs on the split level, your bedroom and Nika's were. While different in style to your house in Neuchâtel, this house nevertheless echoed the *feeling* of your home: You were amazed to discover the continuity.

That evening, as you sat in the living room after supper, you were suddenly overcome by a desire to be held in your mother's arms. She didn't seem to notice, and you held fast to your decision not to show your need. That night, as you lay in your restless sheets, the stars at once distant and intimate through your open window, you wondered: Am I not the child she dreamed I'd be when she carried me in her belly? Have I disappointed her? Why didn't she hold me? As your tears ran down your cheeks you felt the vastness of the night, and decided you had to stop asking yourself such questions: Tomorrow you would get to know Nika, and you would discover Poughkeepsie: What a funny name!

Blueberry pancakes for breakfast, then off to Wappingers Falls in the Thunderbird to buy a bicycle at the Firestone Tire store. You chose the coolest model—a Sears Spaceliner—and as soon as you got back you took it out for a spin, Nika ahead of you and Zoran behind. Look! Bizarre asymmetrical houses on big green grounds, one after another after another—and no two alike! Back at the house, grating carrots and slicing cucumber while your mother fried fish, you spoke of home.

After lunch you hung out with Nika in her room. 'Who's this?' you asked, looking at a photo of a skier posing at the bottom of a run. And thus you learned that Nika's mother had competed for Yugoslavia in the 1956 Winter Olympics, putting in an honourable performance in both slalom and downhill on the slopes of Cortina d'Ampezzo. Choking on the horror of death by avalanche—you knew it occurs by slow poisoning, the buried person's breath icing up the air cavity in which they breathe, making it harder and harder for oxygen to get in and carbon dioxide to get out—you took Nika in your arms and hugged her.

Later that afternoon your mother invited you into her studio. It was bigger and better equipped than the one in Neuchâtel: A rough marble figure on a rotating stand, a gantry against the wall; end cuts of alabaster in a corner, gritted paper in a cubby hole. On a workbench, mallets, hammers, and chisels; rifflers, files and rasps. A potter's wheel and bags of clay by the big window; at the back, two steel buckets and a cement sink. And in a perpendicular room, bare walls and an electric kiln. You climbed up onto a swivel bar stool; your mother flopped down into an old armchair. The filtered sunlight softened her angular features; her centre-parted hair, falling to her shoulders, gave her face a more oval aspect, different from how you had remembered her.

— You've got a lot of new tools!

— That's because I've got a new idea of what sculpture's all about.

— Oh yeah? What is it?

— Direct carving. I now believe that carving, rather than modelling, is the true road to sculpture.

What do you mean?

— When you make a mistake in carving, it's impossible to erase it and begin again. There's an absolute finality about every movement. With one hammer blow too many, you can ruin a year's work.

You feel a vague sense of foreboding, as if there were something momentous in that remark, but you can't bring your feeling to light. You remain silent.

— That pressure makes me a better artist. More alert, more aware.

You're intrigued, almost spellbound. Your mother adds:

— It's the challenge of working without a safety net!

Suddenly your dark feeling becomes resplendent: The idea of danger is appealing. You like what your mother has said, you like the idea of a tightrope walker. Vaguely, you sense that danger is linked to honesty, that to do things without danger is cheating. You feel your admiration for her growing, and then you feel her gaze on you.

— Turn your head a little, to your left.

Your admiration turns to anger.

— A little more.

You feel a flush of heat in your face.

— Yes, that's it. Would you pose for me, Marietta? Not now, but—

— No!

— Why not?

— Because I don't want to be turned into a statue!

— Of course not.

— I don't want—

You cut short your thought, and instantly forget what it was you'd wanted to say. Your mother stands up.

— Come, let me show you something.

She goes to an open-shelf closet and takes out a plaster cast; she puts it on a work table. You approach and stand beside her.

— What do you see?

You examine the stylized form.

— I don't know. A cat, maybe. Or a horse.

— What do you feel?

— Anger.

— Anger?

— I feel the animal's energy. It's moving. Something's about to happen.

— Yes. And that, as I see it, is the sculptor's job.

— What is?

— To make matter come alive, to give it a living quality.

— Why?

— To wake people up! Without art, they'd just sleepwalk through life.

Your mother lays a hand on your shoulder.

— You see, Marietta, what I want is not to turn you into—

— You couldn't if you tried!

— I don't want to—

— I don't sleepwalk through life!

— Of course you don't. And that's why I'd like to borrow your energy, to use it to make stone come alive. To make it sing!

— But I can sing myself. Do you want to hear me?

– I know you can sing! Why aren't you listening to me? Why are you confusing everything I say?

– What are you saying?

– I'm saying...

She pulls you toward her.

– I'm saying I just want to get close to you again.

You pull away. You want nothing more than her embrace, but you can't bring yourself to accept it.

– Why?

– Because you're my daughter. I love you.

– But you left me.

– Yes.

– You call that love?

– No.

– Will you come back?

– No.

– So why do you say you love me?

– Because I do—you know I do—but I can't live with your father and I need a new life.

– Without me?

– You chose to stay with your father.

– But not—

– What?

– Never mind.

– Marietta, you've got the best of both worlds. You can spend as much time as you like with each of us. To choose one doesn't mean you lose the other. Can't you see that?

– No.

– One day you will.

– Maybe.

– I'm sure you will.

– We'll see.

– So, will you sit for me?

– No.

– Why not?

– You'll understand. One day!

– Marietta, I'm sorry, but I had to do it.

— And I've got to do what I've got to do!
On that affirmation you run out to meet Nika, fired up for a game of badminton.

The landscaped grounds, bounded by a cedar hedge, extend some distance from the bungalow. The badminton net is strung in the largest open area. A brief warm up, then play to eleven, but at seven-all you no longer care to keep score and begin doing trick shots: Jumping high to return between your legs; letting the shuttlecock pass your body on one side then spinning round to return it on the other. And then cartwheel for cartwheel, handstand for handstand, you match each other on the freshly mown lawn. You then segue into a more fanciful goofing around: Nika, sporting a moustache of damp earth, uses the racquet as a cane and walks like Chaplin's Tramp; you, making of your racquet a mandolin, serenade a garden sculpture. Nika then grabs the shuttlecock and coyly fans herself; you bend a tea rose and present it to her.

— Hey-oh!
From the kitchen Zoran calls, offering cool drinks.

Drinks in hand, you walk through the house.

— Have you heard of Them? Nika asks.

— Who?
Enjoyable, the alternation of sensation of the rugs and floorboards beneath your feet.

— Them.

— Who's 'them'?

— Come, I'll show you.
She leads you to her room; you follow in excited expectation.

Nika, not finding Them, goes out and leaves you alone in her bedroom. What could 'them' be? you wonder. More so than yesterday, you feel at ease in her room; you like the white bed with its blue spread, the orange polka dots on the indigo pillow... One back, one forward; two back, two forward; three back, three forward: 'For every action, there is an equal and opposite reaction': You like the crisp clack of her Newton's cradle... Flying cranes and a school of fish: She said she'd teach me origami... Permanent mauve and rose madder, cerulean blue and cadmium red: the tubes of paint in her folding palette... You flop down into the corduroy beanbag as Nika re-enters the room.

— This is Them!
She hands you an LP album.

— Ah, 'Them' is a band!
'Them. Includes the original hit, Gloria'.

— Yes. A rhythm and blues band.

Nika opens her record player, a portable suitcase-type like your Dansette.

— You've got to hear this! she says.

As the tonearm lowers the stylus into the groove, it finds a groove in you that you never knew existed: A guitar figure, a ringing lick; an ostinato bass, a cookin' drum kit. Organ, harmonica, and then the glory of a singer at one with the song:

> Baby please don't go
> Baby please don't go
> Baby please don't go
> Down to New Orleans
> You know I love you so
> Baby please don't go

You feel your face flush as a nineteen-year-old Irishman from East Belfast shakes your bones and enters your blood. Yes! Fresh from the Seaman's Mission where his voice had set fire to the ballroom, Van Morrison infuses his sublime distillation of Black American music into your soul. You're lying on the floor now, you're lying on the rug of red-violet, rubbing your feet into it. Nika is sitting lotus-like beside the Dansette. From what she sees in your eyes, from the energy radiating from your body, she knows that she will trust you, trust you more than anyone since her mother died.

> Before I be your dog
> Before I be your dog
> Before I be your dog
> Get you way down here
> Make you walk the log
> Baby please don't go

You feel the passion in the voice, the fervour in the music. There's drive, excitement, commitment; there's a pushing to the limit with no safety net. Yes! This is the danger zone where honesty comes into its own, this is where grace alone can save one! But how could all this come through to a child not yet eight? How could the blues from the whorehouses and dance halls of Texas, the idiom of Lightnin' Hopkins and Lead Belly, speak to a girl from the squeaky-clean town of Neuchâtel? Yes, how was it possible that you, a little Swiss girl more familiar with Beethoven than the Beatles, could be blown away by Them, a Belfast garage band? The guitars pause to let the rhythm speak, content to punctuate it with sparks, until the undertow can no longer be contained and the wave breaks again. As it washes over you, you realize that your mother has left you, but not your mother tongue: Thanks to music, you will never sleepwalk through life!

And thus it was that in the two minutes and thirty-nine seconds of the song, you discovered that you are open to the world—no matter how removed it may appear from you—and that there is more in it than your mother.

That evening you had a guest for dinner: a neighbour, Hannah, a retired professor of history who'd just lost her husband. Your mother, this time, had refused your help in the kitchen (she's getting her revenge because I won't pose for her, you thought). Relaxing in the living room, you listened to Hannah talk about what's become of New York. She spoke about the city today, in the run-up to the mayoral elections, and the city in the early days, when she taught at Columbia. New Yorkers were proud then: Now they're demoralized. They're sick of burned-out slums and racial riots, brown tap water and filthy sidewalks; the police hand-in-hand with the criminals, telephone booths used as urinals. New York is worse than Naples; it's becoming as ungovernable as a Third World city. You listened in wide-eyed wonder, and when the conversation shifted to the antiwar protests and the civil rights movement, Hannah spoke in passionate support. You were fascinated by this forceful old woman, and sensed that it was her involvement in the world that kept her from collapsing now that she's alone: She's not a sleepwalker.

Chapter 3

The next day your mother took you and Nika up the Empire State Building (the rush of exhilaration, the inspiriting power!) and then on to the Museum of Modern Art: She hadn't giving up trying to persuade you to model for her. You and Nika were full of nervous energy, fooling around (and around) with the revolving doors in the lobby, competing to see who could make the best milk moustache in the cafeteria, trading T-shirts and sneakers in the washroom. And then your mother led you to the Brancusi exhibition. You were intrigued by the various versions of *Bird in Space,* their sleek form and soaring grace.

– He's not sculpting birds, your mother explained, he's expressing their essence.

They're lovely, you thought, contemplating the serene swell of the elongated bodies.

– A bird in flight leaves nothing but a memory of movement—Brancusi's sculptures leave nothing but their luminosity.

– Their light?

– Yes, that shine that comes from the perfection of the polishing.

Enlivened by a feeling of freedom, you thought: These sculptures would wake up any sleepwalker.

Warming to the art of sculptural observation, you found the different versions of *Mademoiselle Pogany* even more impressive than the *Bird in Space* group. 'When his mistress left Paris for Lausanne, Brancusi carved her likeness from memory': Does my mother want to make a sculpture of me because I'm not living with her anymore? But it is she who doesn't want to live with me: Despite what she says, I can feel it. Circling the figures, Catherine pointed out how each version is more abstract than the previous one. Nika preferred the white marble rendering; you the bronze with the black patina: It was more wild and mysterious. When Nika rested a cheek on the back of her hand and struck a pose like that of Mademoiselle Pogany, you thought, 'I'd rather be an artist than a model', and made with graceful hand an undulation in the air.

And then your mother led you to the Henry Moores: *Reclining Mother and Child* (1961), *Family Group* (1949), and another *Mother and Child* (1931).

– 'Henry Moore was obsessed with the theme of mother and child', you read aloud.

Nika is embarrassed, saddened, she wants to walk away: She stands firm and holds her ground because you are strong enough to stay.

– Why? you ask your mother.

– Because, from a compositional point of view, it's a very rich subject.

– Did he have a lot of children?

– Just one. A daughter, Mary.

– Like us! says Nika, aiming her complicit eyes at you.

– Yes, like us!

Nika throws her arms around you; your laughter harmonizes with hers. While Catherine speaks of the relationship between small and large forms, of position and balance, domination and tension, all you feel is emotion. As you circle the sculptures, something in you is stirred—despite your pride in your independence—by the tenderness in these depictions.

– Which one do you like best? Nika asks.

– This one, you say, pointing to the *Reclining Mother and Child*.

– Why? your mother asks.

– Because of the big hole in it.

As you sat with Nika on the backseat of the Thunderbird, returning to Poughkeepsie, you thought about your mother's mother and the novels she's written: She too is an artist. And what if, when mother was small, *grand-maman* left her? Didn't she move to Paris long ago, leaving *grand-papa* to run the hotel in Lausanne? What if Mum's just doing what her mother did? Tonight I'll phone Dad. I'll tell him about *Mademoiselle Pogany* and *Bird in Space*. I'll tell him about Hannah and Nika. But I won't say anything about Mum.

That evening, after supper, Zoran taught you some card tricks. You mastered them, but it only made you miss your father more. You said goodnight early to everybody, and as soon as you were in bed you fell into a sleep in which you soared in space like Brancusi's birds and walked through the streets of New York, hand-in-hand with Nika and Henry Moore.

Chapter 4

The remaining twenty-one days of your holiday followed the pattern of the first three. Gradually you got closer to Zoran, not fearing to betray your father: Hadn't your father shown you that however unshakeable, love needn't be possessive? He was getting on with his own life, as you had to get on with yours.

So, with Zoran at the wheel of his Ford Mustang, the four of you would set out to explore Duchess County or tour further afield. Having just published a book on the Hudson Valley, Zoran was an excellent guide, showing you buildings and places while feeding you tidbits of history, from the time of New Amsterdam to today.

Other days you'd cycle through the countryside, stopping to snap wild turkey crossings and thoroughbred farms, old homesteads and historic barns, on the Kodak Instamatic you father had given you. A picnic in the shade of a sycamore tree, a game of Frisbee, then back on the trail where you'd stop to photograph a Quaker house and a watermill, a clock tower and a country store.

Still other days you could be found spotting rainbow trout from the bank of a stream or an eagle's nest from a kayak, box turtles from the edge of wetlands or a woodpecker from a forest trail. And on days when Catherine was busy in her studio and Zoran working in New York, Hannah would invite you and Nika for ants-on-a-log and pigs-in-a-blanket, and a look at her collection of traditional Slavic dolls (the only thing that interested you about them were the costumes and how they were made).

And then, days before your return to Switzerland, the worst racial rioting since the War broke out in Los Angeles; President Johnson went on television to announce that Watts, the scene of the violence, would be named a disaster area. You recalled that a few days after your arrival, the President had announced on the news that another fifty thousand soldiers would be sent to Vietnam. And thus your first visit to Poughkeepsie would be bookended by Presidential addresses; and thus, still a child, you came to know that the world is burning and wanted to understand why: Hannah's explanations had piqued your curiosity.

On subsequent visits, year after year, you followed the theme with greater and greater comprehension. Of all the dramatic events of those times, there's one you cited as a turning point in your understanding: A photo from Vietnam, one man shooting another in the head with a handgun. That image would become an anti-war icon, and it would lead to the elaboration of a key aspect of your ethics: lucidity. As time went on, the context of the killing became clearer. Thousands of killings—of soldiers, civilians, and insurgents—occurred in those early days of the Tet Offensive, but none of those deaths impacted opinion the way the death of this man did. Why? you wondered. The wincing face as the bullet sizzles the brain, the hands tied behind the back, the executioner's outstretched arm: These three elements, you quickly decided, were what moved one. But must emotion cloud lucidity? Nguyen Ngoc Loan pulled the trigger. Nguyen Van Lem received the bullet. Thirty years later, upon the death of Nguyen Ngoc Loan, Eddie Adams, the photographer who took the picture, wrote a eulogy in which he said:

> Two people died in that photograph: the recipient of the bullet and General Nguyen Ngoc Loan. The general killed the Viet Cong; I killed the general with my camera. Still photographs are the most powerful weapon in the world. People believe them, but photographs do lie, even without manipulation. They are only half-truths.

You didn't wait for Eddie Adams' declaration to undeceive yourself. Already you had a horror of tepid thinking, already you knew that nothing is as simple as it seems. And so you left ready-made opinions to the lazy and—planting the seed of your ethics of responsibility—began cultivating your ability to resist. Bound, tortured and buried alive, the thousands of victims of the massacre at Hue had no photographer to take their picture. The massacre, concurrent with the execution of Nguyen Van Lem, was perpetrated by his comrades. Absolute truth does not exist, half-truths are unacceptable: Such a conviction made you immune to dogma, and unflinching in your readiness to think against the crowd.

And thus you found yourself, during your visits to Poughkeepsie, in the heart of a country at war. And then, in June of 1974, nine months after Elizaveta Voronyanskaya hanged herself after revealing to the KGB where the copy of *The Gulag Archipelago* that she had typed for Solzhenitsyn was hidden, you read Volume I as soon as the Paris publishers, working from smuggled-out copies, had made it available. It seemed to complete a certain phase of your education. From both the prosecutors of the war and the anti-war protesters, you freed yourself. From both Mammon and Marxism, you freed yourself. No longer in the margin of history but in the mainstream, you felt vindicated by your ethics of responsibility. And you were not yet seventeen.

Chapter 5

Between bewilderment and wonder your gleaming eyes vacillate, between immediacy and remoteness they waver. Is it what you've said, or what you're going to say, that's behind this turbulence? Is it that something's been amiss in my reception? Or is it simply that the enigma of the self deepens the more one talks? Ceasing to disdain its beauty, your face is effulgent; suspended in the instant, I feel a force gathering within me. Your parted lips quiver in anticipation, I close my eyes and seal our compact: In the moist warmth of our shared breath, my questions and your confusion dissolve in the immediacy of our flesh.

— Give me Kelly, Sprague. There, in the sheet.

I toss her to you.

— You're looking forward to your new clothes, aren't you, Kelly? I'm sure you dressed badly in the past.

— Why would she have dressed badly?

— Why? To punish herself. Or to punish her mother!

— Hmmm... And why is she always looking in the mirror? What's she hoping to find?

— A pleasing reflection, of course. An image that will finally be satisfying. Or maybe she just wants to retrieve that look she'd receive, long ago, when her mother found her extraordinary.

I sip my cognac.

— Marietta, you were going to tell me about a girl called Inès.

— I know. But first...

Schlack! You hurl the koala against the wall.

— ...I'm going to tell you about Pascale.

And thus you came to tell me of how a handsome couple—he, pushing forty, cool in a casual suit, open-neck shirt and canvas shoes; she, two years over twenty, radiant in a large white hat and tiered mini dress—exchanged their wedding vows (and in so doing, radically changed your life). Yes, on a late-summer day in 1970, your father remarried. At the precise moment when he kissed the bride, your nose began to bleed. It was a sign of things to come. And yet, as you watched them in the vaulted wedding room, their kiss seemed to hold out a promise of happiness for you too: It would put an end to Nanina after Martine, Elvezia after Jacqueline, in your father's bed. It would mean you'd be less alone. And it would mean you'd have, not a mother, but a woman you could call on when you wanted to (you were three weeks away from your thirteenth birthday). And so, between Lausanne and Montreux, in a village in the Lavaux, the signing of the register did not seem to be a sealing of your fate. Indeed, as the car taking you to the reception cruised along the route de la Grande Corniche, you felt full of goodwill. You seemed to see this familiar road as if for the first time, taking pleasure in the green and gold of the terraced vineyards, the blue and grey of lac Léman and the mineral peaks of the Mémises beyond.

You liked Alain, your father's open-hearted friend; you liked the cohabiting generations of his wine-growing family. So when you entered his house, the sight of the dining room all decked out for dinner and the salon become a ballroom gave you a thrill. After midnight, as the party approached fever pitch, the DJ played 'I Hear You Knocking'. Dave Edmunds' rhythm and blues celebration defied even the oldest to stand still. Passing off the bride to the best man, your father swept you off your feet and into the shuffling syncopation of the ragged and dirty beat. Through karate, you'd often been in close physical contact with your father, but now, with the slide guitar making love to the rhythm and the cocky vocals declaring 'I hear you knocking, but you can't come in', you suddenly felt ill-at-ease. Your body couldn't resist the seduction of the music, but in your complicity with your father your mind registered an interruption. 'I hear you knocking, go back where you been': For him, this night would mark a new beginning; for you, the end of Eden and a descent into hell.

On your last visit to Poughkeepsie Nika had been surprised by her first period, so you expected it would soon happen to you. But you never imagined everything would erupt at the same time: the blood, the breasts and the demon of sex, incarnated in Pascale. You were no longer a foal but she was still a filly: In the time between, step-mother became sister, as wicked the one as the other. Now you were the dark horse, and she was the nightmare. Marietta was no longer Mary, but a sea of bitterness: The whore was in the house. How naïve you were! Pascale was no maternal virgin, there to mother you! She was your victorious rival, and you were the outcast. In your father's bed she slept in your mother's place; in the fantasy you couldn't avow, she had prevailed. (And insofar as she was your sister, perforce the fantasy became more disturbing, even if still unavowed.) Now your mother became a good mother, for clearly Pascale was the bad. After all, when you'd hurl your rage at her, didn't you hear her say to your father afterwards, 'She's not my child'? But of course you weren't her child: So why did her remark so upset you? And so you took every opportunity to retort, 'You're not my mother!'. And thus you'd put her in her place, reminding her that she is the antithesis of your ideal, that she can never erase your father's relationship with your mother, of which you are the embodiment. Still, you felt guilty, and you wondered why: It was not you that was the whore, it was she: She'd taken the place of your mother.

You're in your party dress. You've slipped off your sandals, you've got your arms around your father's neck and your bare feet on his feet, shod in canvas shoes. They're playing a slow number; you're dancing under the dimmed lights, your body pressed against his. Effortlessly he bares the weight of your feeling as he circles you through the variations of his grace. Helpless in the half-light, you let yourself be led.

Is that a memory from that evening, or is it a souvenir from a dream? You've never been able to decide, and now you no longer want to: You've grown fond of that memory, a memory that recurs in waking as in sleep.

Now you remember how you would wonder: If I cannot be first in my father's life, will I ever occupy that place for another? If so, will that man consent to make me a mother?

And thus the first year of your new life passed in a rage of hate against your father's wife. Who could have imagined that, only a few years later—after you had done with trying to destroy yourself—you would come to love her more than you love just about anyone else?

Indeed, today, your devotion to Pascale knows no bounds. How on earth, you wonder, could she ever have forgiven you for the violence of your rejection? How could she have borne it? After all, she was but nine years older than you, as much a girl as a woman. Whenever she was mad at you, she'd bite back on her anger: Everybody knows step-mothers are wicked. And as long as you saw her only as the object of your father's desire, she was indeed the mean step-mother. How hard it must have been for her to stand in her own light when your mother's shadow was everywhere. Finally you came to understand, thanks to your conversations with Nika, that it was your own mourning that made your mother's shadow loom so large, leaving Pascale almost no place to fit into your family. 'You're not my mother': The sting of those words touches you, for you now realize that in her heart-of-hearts Pascale knew she was not in the right place: What girl dreams of growing up to be a step-mother? How could she have loved you immediately when you'd never dwelt in her womb, never given her occasion to dream of you? With all the rage and glory of your own history you came to her, ready-made: She'd had nothing to do with shaping you. You didn't choose her: But neither did you choose your mother.

You didn't choose her: But neither did she choose you. How deep must have been her solitude, and how great her love to have borne it with such grace.

Chapter 6

When you surprised yourself in the mirror, when you became a stranger to yourself, who was the who you dreamt yourself to be?

— *Mirror, mirror, tell no lies, how do I look in Courbet's eyes?*

— *The arabesques of your shirt rise to reveal the fullness of your breast; the lustre of your belly throws into relief the intoxicating cleft: Unspeakable, overabounding, your demonic majesty sends a shudder down the observer's spine: Trembling in blank wonder, he is blinded by the sun. And yet it is night that resides between your thighs, it is darkness that radiates this light. He is no longer master of his own eyes: It is you who strain toward him, it is you who compel his gaze.*

— *My demon twin, so intimate, so alien, your devastating presence takes my breath away. How you move me! There was a time when I disowned you, taking you for a foreign body. I couldn't accept your black magic, I couldn't bear how you shattered my self-image. In a frenzy of friction I tried to make you mine: the greater was my frustration. Then a day finally came when I could reclaim you, and on that day I bought a new dress: A dress to make whole the two halves of my body, a dress to integrate the top and the bottom. Alas, it was not the dress that would give a final certainty to my femininity! And so relentlessly I pursued the enigma of my desire, and so incessantly I renewed my second skin!*

Disembodied, then warm and husky, your voice returns from beyond the looking glass:

— You know what, Sprague? I think I'll make Kelly a Betty Boop dress.

— But she doesn't have Betty's waistline, she doesn't have Betty's legs!

— She doesn't have *any* legs!

— Make her a little black dress.

— What style?

— Keep it simple. Slip her into a shift.

— No, for that she would need a boyish body.

— Make her an off-the-shoulder outfit, then.

— She doesn't *have* any shoulders!

— Well then, make her a V-neck number out of a floaty fabric.

— V-necks are good for balancing curves: She doesn't have any.

— I told you: Stick some tits on her.

– Yes, I suppose I'll have to.

– How about making her a mini skirt? That will give the impression she has legs.

– No. She's got a big head, she has to use it.

– What's that got to do with a mini skirt?

– You can't think in a mini skirt.

– I see.

– No, this is what I'll do: I'll make her a really feminine dress, with a hem that hits the knee—if she had knees—and a chiffon overlay, with soft frills and lace.

– Sounds good. A Southern belle at her father's ball. Very feminine.

– Yes.

Schlack! You hurl the koala against the wall. Fireflies flickering in your eyes, you say:

– It started the day I cut my hair—the day I cut *off* my hair.

– What started?

– Everything Kelly's being saying.

– Explain.

– All right.

And thus you came to give me a key to your history: It only took me deeper into your mystery. What did you tell me? Put your ear to my heart and listen: I will tell you.

Once you were a little girl who believed you'd be your mother's pride and joy if you proved your independence. A toddler in your high chair, a two-and-a-half-year-old at table, already you could appreciate your mother's pleasure at your eating on your own. From kindergarten to the early grades you delighted in playing with boys; a high-spirited little girl, always on the go, they called you a tomboy. And yet, with your long flowing hair, you were also your mother's 'little sunshine'. Indeed, every evening, your mother's delight was to brush your hair. And then, out of the blue, they began: the asthma attacks, the migraines. On days of attacks it was out of the question you go to school: In a darkened room your mother sat by your side, brushing your pain away.

You experienced your body as both a tomboy, liking rough outdoor activities, and as a little girl who was her mother's treasure. Then, one night when you woke up to go and pee, you overheard your father say to your mother, 'He has a daughter the same age as Marietta—do you really want to bring her up instead of your own daughter?'. Quaking, you lingered, until the pounding of your heart drowned out their words: You were stunned, but you'd understood.

The next day you tried your best to believe it had been a bad dream, but as soon as you got home from school you wrote a note and left it on your father's pillow: 'Dad, is Mum going to leave us'? That night your mother and father, together, came into your bedroom to break the news: 'Yes, Mummy's leaving'.

Shocked, you didn't say a word. As you lay in the dark you couldn't believe your mother no longer needed you, no longer needed to be proud of her independent little girl. The following day, upon returning from school, you threw all your anger and despair into cutting off your hair: Wildly you cut it, close to the scalp, leaving nothing but a scattering of ragged tufts.

Secretly you believed that your mother was leaving because someone from school, out walking on the weekend, had told her she'd caught you 'fooling around' with a boy in the hills. Your guilt was compounded by the pain of being obliged to see yourself now as just another little girl in need of a mother, no longer independent.

Marietta, when you cut off your hair, did you understand you were sealing your heart? Did you believe that revenge would make you invulnerable? Or were you simply trying to salvage some pride after being reduced to a helpless little girl? Whatever the case may be, it is clear that you felt the only way to soothe your pain was to take total control of your body.

Your mother gone, you threw yourself into your twin passions, music and mathematics: Here you were immune to matter that might escape your control. You became a brilliant student, impressing your teachers year after year. You became a superb musician, studying under the finest teacher in Geneva. Fearless and carefree, that was the reputation you gained—a sign of your success, you believed, in disguising your suffering. Indeed, proving your ability to conceal your feelings, demonstrating your independence from your peers, became a source of great satisfaction to you.

O mes petites amoureuses,
Que je vous hais!
Plaquez de fouffes douloureuses
Vos tétons laids!

Rimbaud became your hero. On your wall you pinned *Rimbaud et son ombre,* the sketch by Cazals: Your resemblance to the poet in this pencil drawing—the carelessly-cropped hair, the finesse of the profile—confirmed your affinity with him.

Fade amas d'étoiles ratées,
Comblez les coins!
—Vous crèverez en Dieu, bâtées
D'ignobles soins!

Next to Cazal's sketch you pinned Verlaine's drawing, *Rimbaud à Paris:* Hand in pocket, hat on head, he stands in profile, smoking his pipe. For you a *Gitane* would do: Sitting on your bed, you'd blow smoke rings of love to the boy whose poetry so engaged your emotion.

Blancs de lunes particulières
Aux pialats ronds,
Entrechoquez vos genouillères,
Mes laiderons!

But if you were proud of your ability to conceal your feelings, if you took pleasure in your independence from your peers, did you realize that in cutting off your hair you had cut the link between yourself and your body? As that body ripened, your inability to connect to it gave rise to greater and greater anxiety. One morning you awoke with the wisp of a dream clinging to your consciousness: With a soft towel your violin teacher, a woman of Austrian origin, was drying you down. Before fading away, the dream-image evoked others: Your teacher had invited you home, washed your hair, given you a bath... As you jumped out of bed to splash cold water on your face, did you recognize your dependence and desire? And if so, did you realize, as you stared into the mirror, that unlike your dream, your dependence and desire could not be washed away? Open questions. What is certain, however, is that at that moment, you hated your body and wanted to put an end to your life.

Why didn't you? Was it because you couldn't resolve the paradox of wanting to kill yourself not in order to die, but rather to find a better way to live? Did your fantasy of death as a return to the womb, enabling you to be born again in a new skin, evaporate in the light of reason? Or did salvation come, when all is said and done, through your violin? Indeed, as your teacher reported, from Paganini's *Caprices* you extracted the *music* their role as virtuoso exercises had hidden: You brought out more musicality than she had heard in many a year. And then you immersed yourself in another masterwork for the unaccompanied instrument: Ysaÿe's *Six Sonatas for Solo Violin*. Alone in your room in Neuchâtel, savage in your solitude, you entered a forest of notes where nothing but the possibilities of the instrument itself, informed by the ghosts of its culture, spurred the virtuosity of the music. Confronting the composer, encountering yourself, from your fierce isolation you drew dark meditations, daring and disturbing. And thus into being you brought the music's power and beauty, and thus you expressed your passion and soothed your soul.

Marietta, it's all so clear now: In bringing the music into being, you were binding your broken self; in giving body to the notes, you were finding a use for your pain. Cradling the violin between shoulder and chin, swaying as you stroked the strings, you were rocking the girl who'd cut off her hair. Yes, cancellation of separation, reunion with what's been lost, through your violin you were restoring continuity to what had been interrupted. But did you know you were using your violin to distance yourself from the enigma of the unnerving other? Did you understand that all those solitary hours were the sign of your incapacity to be alone? And in the heart of midnight, in the meadows where you counted sheep, did you ever suspect you played so assiduously in order to forget that you couldn't forget?

Intermezzo 6: Giulia

Mad they call me, Marietta, for crossing blind the boulevard; mad, for singeing my raven locks, Lou Reed's 'Jesus' on my lips, in the flame of a votive candle; mad, for lying down with dogs at the foot of the Opera steps. Am I mad? No, I am not mad: I miss you.

It's cold and wet in this city on the Tyrrhenian Sea. The mountains are covered in mist. Enlivened by the rain, graffiti crawls on the walls of bombed-out buildings. Turning up the collar of my coat, I smell damp wool: My heart races as I see you in Zürich, knitting the sweater I'm wearing. Hark! The chiming of church bells: Still we have marriages.

Wednesday night, tired of wrestling with feverish sheets, I drew up the blinds, opened the window, and gazed at the shivering stars. As the world turned I remained still, letting the night unspool memories of you: Making gossipy conversation—the unearthly harmony of Maggie and Gavin's marriage, Saskia's repeated accidental pregnancies, the gayness of Huguette's husband—I pretend not to be touched while your toenails turn red under your lacquer brush... Restless in your sleep, you toss and turn. I slink beneath the sheets, place my head between your legs and take Princesse Tam-Tam for a dance. In the morning you tell me you had the most delicious dream: The cavalier of your clit remains still... As you bend forward in your panties and bra, your blow dryer following the brush, the fall of your hair moves me. The hiss of hot air drowns out my haiku, but your eyes when you look up shine with the epiphany...

Thursday, I ached for you all day.

Friday, when the endless rain began, I lingered in the Catacombe dei Cappuccini. Fascinated by the macabre grace of the mummified corpses, I was okay until the corpse of a girl rattled my bones: An abyss opened before me, into darkness I collapsed...

Saturday night I spent with a girl. Peachy white wine, sweet-and-sour aubergine with swordfish: In a corner nook, in the vaulted interior of a revamped osteria, I sat opposite Giulia, a girl with dark eyes and a tumble of black curls. My heart skipped a beat when she told me she's from Ticino. A student at the Accademia di architettura in Mendrisio, she'd just won a competition, of which the prize is a practicum here: converting a former tuna processing plant into two bars, a restaurant, a 400-seat performance space and a hotel. She told me about the Mafia, the siphoning off of EU funds destined for the renovation of the city. She asked me what I do for a living; I asked her if she liked Seedy Friedrich. 'They're my favourite band', she replied. She was hip to the *Twelfth Night* quotation of *An Apple Cleft in Twain,* she was hip to the pun on Caspar David. It turned out she also loves the mysterious landscapes of the great German Romantic, the radical subjectivity of his lonely wanderer that Gram so ravishingly turns into song. And thus, my love, a moment of grace between your wanderer and a sister of mercy allowed me to believe I was more than a ghost.

After dinner, the rain having let up, we went for a spin on her Vespa. The wailing of police sirens was never out of earshot as we rode through the glistening streets. We stopped at a jukebox dive where I played 'She's a River'; limber, her body found a rhythm that unlocked mine. Over a beer, she told me of her adventures working, in-between her studies, as a ski instructor in winter and a tennis coach in summer. When midnight came and the bar closed, we felt we'd known each other for ages; in bed there was whole-hearted tenderness, nothing needed to be said. So why, as a three-masted schooner ferried me to sleep, did I see a pin-up with Giulia's tits and your eyes tattooed on its mainsail? And why did I find myself stranded on the shore, with no prospect of a boat? I won't strew roses at your feet, Marietta, I won't rue and rue—just hear me now, that I may honour you!

Chapter 7

Intimate mirroring, disturbing estrangement: The piercing intensity of your gaze in mine.

– Marietta, you were going to tell me–

– I know. But I want to tell you about Valeria first.

I lay myself open to your devoration: Grace infuses gravity.

You met in Lucerne in 1972. You were not yet fifteen; she was twenty-one. Youth Orchestra rehearsal; Brahms, Piano Concerto N° 2. You were first violin; she was the pianist. Jet black, her hair fell straight to her shoulders. There was a pearly gloss to her pale skin; her eyes were dark and luminous. On her left wrist she wore a coral bracelet. The instant your eye caught hers, you felt a current pass between you. Blushing, you bent to fetch a block of rosin from your violin case. When you sat up again, she was talking to the conductor. For over an hour the orchestra worked through the *Allegro appassionato.* For once, you appreciated the man on the stand, feeling he understood the process the players must assimilate in order to sustain the architecture of the piece. Most of all, however, you were struck by the beauty of the pianist's playing. During the break she approached you. Strolling on the lawn in the late-summer sun, you learned that she is studying Comparative Literature and Anthropology at the University of Geneva. And you learned that this would be her last concert: She'd be giving up performing to devote herself to her studies. Your T-shirt, depicting a palomino clearing a barrier at *Les Hauts de Corsinge,* led her to tell you she's a rider too: Instantly you overcame your shyness, and invited her to come and ride with you in the hills above Neuchâtel.

Her name was Valeria. Your father took to her, and encouraged your friendship. She liked Neuchâtel, but she was a big-city girl: Soon you began meeting in Geneva, and over the next nine months you were thick as thieves. In the *quartier chic* of Champel, on the fourteenth floor of the Cité Universitaire, you'd meet her in her student digs, overlooking the Arve river and the Salève. In her room you discovered her world. Look! Jim Morrison, beaded necklace on bare chest, staring through the doors of perception. You were struck by his Samson mane and Cupid mouth, the power of his masculine beauty.

– And who are these people? you asked, examining some old black and white photos on the wall.

– That's my parents when they first arrived in France. They lived above a brothel.

And thus you learned that Valeria is of Romanian origin, though she's never been to Bucharest.

– And that's my father with other exiles, in 1955, occupying the Romanian mission in Berne.

Thus you found out that in the Swiss federal city Valeria's father, with other exiles, had taken hostage the Romanian diplomatic personnel, demanding in exchange the liberation of political prisoners being tortured in Communist jails. And then you cast a glance across Valeria's bookshelves: Tolstoy and Dostoevsky, Verlaine and Rimbaud, Lévi-Strauss and Marcel Mauss, Nietzsche and Michel Foucault. It wouldn't be long before Valeria got you off your schoolbook Descartes and on to Nietzsche, Greek tragedy and the Pre-Socratics: Cartesian doubt is but the shadow of sexual uncertainty, an infinity mirror signifying reason's flight from its debt to sex. Yes, the soul is something about the body: Philosophy will be carnal, or not at all! And thus Valeria honoured your intelligence, understanding that the amazing fifteen-year-old you were was ready for such an education. And then, stepping up to her desk, you flipped through her graduation thesis: 'epistemological and ethical issues in fieldwork... the prostitute as social versus sexual actor... self-representations and subjectivities... performing the prostitute: simulacre and self-respect'... And thus you learned that Valeria had spent nine months in Peru, doing an ethnographic study of the prostitutes in Lima.

– Do you think a woman could ever *choose* to be a prostitute? you asked.

– Yes, absolutely. Of course for a great many prostitutes it's not a choice, and in that case it's a scandal, an outrage.

– But how do you decide whether she's exercising her free will or whether she's forced?

– Well, in deciding between free will and determinism, abstract arguments count for nothing. It's only embodied words—language that comes from lived experience—that carry weight.

And thus you discovered that for Valeria, the mind and the body must work as one.

Soon you were spending all your weekends in Geneva, and for the first time really got to know the city—in style! Yes, Valeria got you into fashion: Strolling through the streets of old Carouge, sitting in a café off the Place de Sardaigne, you'd be wearing a printed tunic and trousers, a felt hat with floppy brim; Valeria, varying the theme, would be in thigh-high boots and a tunic dress. Or, walking along the lakeshore under the falling leaves, Valeria would be in a long patchwork skirt, a scarf tied gypsy-style around her head, while you'd be wearing jeans and a skinny-rib polo neck. Saturday evenings at the cinema—*The Bitter Tears of Petra von Kant*; *Aguirre, Wrath of God;* Rhomer's *L'Amour l'après-midi; Ludwig,* by Luchino Visconti—you'd be wearing a velvet coat, for example, with striped ribbed stockings, while Valeria would be in Victorian underwear and old couture clothes brought back from Portobello Road. And from London too she brought back music: Not the radio fare of 'Nights in White Satin' and 'A Whiter Shade of Pale', but 'John, I'm Only Dancing' and 'Virginia Plain'. One rainy day she played you The Doors, casting Chinese shadows on the wall to 'Riders on the Storm'; you quickly got the knack of it, and together to 'Hyacinth House' you improvised a shadow-play. Then she played you Sapho's fiery version of *'Le Dormeur du val'*; not to be outdone by Sapho's hairdo, you constructed a turban from twists of astrakhan and jersey, put it on your head and passionately declaimed *'Chanson de la plus haute tour'*. The afternoon ended with the two of you dancing to Bowie's 'Queen Bitch'—'She's so swishy in her satin and tat, in her frock coat and bipperty-bopperty hat'—taking each chorus as a cue to switch from Panama hat to pillbox, pork pie to Basque beret, raided from Valeria's pirate trunk.

And what of your father in your adventure? How did he play his paternal role to such an extraordinary fifteen-year-old? Did he believe your deathly jubilation at needing nothing, now that you'd renounced it and recovered so miraculously, meant you would find your way no matter where your inclinations led you? If you were disillusioned with him, did it mean at being a father he was deficient? Or in your heart of hearts did you understand—however much his bride reminded you of his treachery—that being a traitor to you is precisely what makes him a good father? At any rate, whatever your other feelings, you were grateful to him for letting you live out your relationship with Valeria.

And how you lived it out! Valeria had a nippy little Autobianchi, and in under three hours from Geneva you'd be visiting some city where you'd spend your weekend. Where? Milan, for example: Delighting in a *gelato* in the Parco Semione; ambling away the afternoon in Brera's cobblestone streets. Or Lyon: Traversing the old town, from Saint Georges to Saint Paul, marvelling at spiralling staircases and interior courtyards, then across the Saône to Place Sathonay, where two gallants from a century ago taught you how to put a spin on the ball in *boules*; finally, to inaugurate the night, *quenelles de brochet* and Pouilly-Fuissé, in a packed *bouchon* down a dark alleyway. Or Turin: You enchanting Valeria through the Egyptian museum, discoursing on the Goddess Sekhmet and the Altar of Isis; Valeria walking you through *Twilight of the Idols* and *The Case of Wagner,* Nietzsche's works begun in that magical spring of 1888 that he'd spent in Turin: That 'proud feeling of freedom' that made the philosopher fall in love with the city, you retrieved it as you walked through the streets. And thus began, after the earlier introduction, your intimate acquaintance with he who was to become your 'beloved Nietzsche', he who would strengthen your spirit of rebellion against all absolutes and ideologies, he who would articulate your aesthetics: 'What is good is light; everything divine runs on delicate feet'. As you gazed up at his top-floor room on Via Carlo Alberto, you imagined him playing four-handed piano with his landlord's daughter: 'Without music life would be a mistake'. For having said that alone you loved him! And as you reflected on his loneliness, isolation and poverty, his headaches, nervous exhaustion and fits of vomiting (you knew what it's like to be unable to do anything for days but lie in a darkened room), you were glad that girl, that landlord's daughter, was there for him. And always, in every city you visited, there was the thrill of returning to the hotel after an evening out, anticipating the pleasure your body against Valeria's would bring you.

Did your behaviour surprise you? Once shy, you now had, in Valeria's eyes, an edginess, an aura of danger about you. There was a plasticity in your personality, a certain unpredictability, and an inwardness, an intensity, and above all a bravery that encouraged Valeria and brought out the best in her. Breakfast in bed, a bath together, everything happened so naturally. Each of you, in the other's presence, felt a sense of belonging; there was a rightness to every word and gesture, there was nothing to be embarrassed by. The violence of the flesh that you once feared was not to be found here; no, between the two of you—lips and breasts, hands and sex—there was a delicacy, a transparency, a magical osmosis of love. A feeling of plenitude would overcome you as you lay in her arms; your body, your senses, would be fully alive, and with each new caress a bridge would be extended from your outward flesh to your interior world: You became more attentive, more caring, to what was going on in your heart. Yes, staring into Valeria's eyes, you soothed the stranger inside you. And thus occurred the initiation, the space of experimentation, wherein you could break the pact of ignorance that linked you to your mother.

You felt loved in the clothes you and Valeria chose; through Valeria you translated yourself into a variety of women. In touch with herself, in touch with all manner of other, she tried to teach you to flow in the world the way clothes flow on a woman. Loving your body, she made you feel that you could love it too; through a shared intelligence of the senses, she taught you its topography: From your earlobes (why do you think she gave you those Tuareg earrings?) to your toes, desire would flow; in her embrace you lost your fear that sex would make you lose control. The resilience of your body after the ravages of anorexia was astounding; from corpse-like emaciation you returned to a thinness that nevertheless had an appealing carnality. You looked within yourself, and invited

Valeria to fuse what had been fragmented, to free what had been confused. Out of the chaos inside you, you wanted her to make you a cosmos: Opting for alterity over identity, she did. Your pleasure knew no bounds.

It ended, your relationship with Valeria, as naturally as it had begun. She travelled to Australia to present a paper and returned with a handsome man: Her husband now, the father of her children, and the man with whom, in Sidney, she has made her home. For your part, you too were ready to move on.

– Oh Sprague, have you understood? Those days with Valeria were the happiest of my life!

Nothing perishes, parallels meet: In silence plenitude speaks.

– Won't you get Kelly for me again? I've got another idea for an outfit for her.

– Give me a kiss and I'll get her.

I melt into your embrace as you sit astride me; into the cast of your kiss I flow like bronze. Crossing the borderline where your lips meet mine, I lose myself: In the mutual attunement of our mouths you find me. The reciprocity of our lips, alternately yielding and seizing, combines with the findings of our venturing tongues to intensify the heat that is melting us into one: Do you feel it too? Do you feel that the solitariness of fucking can never provide the sweetness of unity that such a kiss procures?

– Now go and get Kelly.

I go. None the worse for wear, the little beast smiles as I pick her up.

– Catch!

You catch the koala. Hot on her heels, I dive onto the bed and position myself beside you, back to the headboard.

– Get this, Sprague—it's something I picked up during the dinner table talk at the Sydney conference: Male koalas have a bifurcated penis.

– So *that's* what physicists talk about at their get-togethers!

– Of course. They're almost all men. Now, here's my kit for Kelly: A fluid, drop-waisted dress, made in gold lamé, and a cloche hat and mousquetaire gloves.

– But she's got no hands!

– That's why I said mousquetaire gloves: They button at the wrist, and I could button them to her sleeve cuffs.

– Very clever. She'll be the most elegant koala in all Christendom!

– Yeah. And that will help her believe in herself.

– Believe in herself?

— Yes. And feel more like a woman.
Is it your visit with Valeria and her family that's got you so stirred up? Have you come back from Sydney with unfinished business in your baggage? Or is it simply your memory feeding your imagination? Schlack! You hurl the koala against the wall.

— Lie down, Sprague. Stretch out.
I do as you say. From shimmering copper to vibrant gold, cognac filters the light as you sip. Holding the eau-de-vie in your mouth, your swivel your body onto mine: I close my eyes, open my mouth and receive the water of life. As your hair caresses my skin, I swallow as if I'd always been given drink in this way; as you summon the emeralds of my eyes, I swallow as if making love had always been like children at play.

Chapter 8

When you surprised yourself in the mirror, when you became a stranger to yourself, who was the who you dreamt yourself to be?

— *Mirror, mirror, tell no lies, how do I look in Picasso's eyes?*

— *Aghast, you stand before me as my vibrating vision seeks a place of rest; in the wild confusion of coordinates, all I find is sex. Look! Within the constriction of the picture frame, you're exploded into five viragos, five Amazons of the archaic impulse, five avatars of Eros. Through your orgiastic iciness your black eyes pierce, giving me no escape from engulfment. Look! Figure and ground reverse, voids solidify; contiguity begets distance, depth surfaces: Everything about you testifies to the excess of sex.*

Disembodied, then warm and husky, your voice returns from beyond the looking glass:

— Excuse me a minute, Sprague.

Seven steps to your destination, seven modes of illumination: majesty-humility, will-obedience, infinity-asceticism, nothingness-compassion, love-unrest, remoteness-flight, strain-form: For you and me, Marietta, what's it going to be?

Trances, phantoms, hallucinations,
Death, sleep, dreams:
Between chaos and cosmos,
The natural and the revealed,
I seek neither the choice that justifies
Nor the road to salvation.

What then?

Nothing. I embrace all:
The land of spirits, the realm of shades,
The ethereal fire, the earthly flame.

Where do I stand?

I stand in this moment,
I lie on this bed;
Marietta is with me,

In nakedness and grace:
That is enough for me.

Enough?

Yes, enough. I am content
To survey the world
With her legs as my compass,
Her pussy the hinge.

I am content to find in her breasts
The vast abstract permanences
That underlie the flux of things.

In a word, I am content
To make of astonishment
A language for deciphering the world:
That is enough for me.

Back from the bathroom, you slip on a pyjama top, cross the right side over the left and knot it closed. You don't put on the bottom. Onto the bed you hop and seat yourself, lotus-like, opposite me.

— Marietta, you were going to tell me about a girl called Inès.

— I haven't forgotten. I will.

In the lavender of your covering, buds of green and burgundy pullulate: In the midst of the City you offer me the Garden, a garden of roses, cypresses, mandragora berries and jasmine.

— But first, I'm going to tell you about a guy called Jürgen.

And thus you came to tell me of a summer in Corfu, about a German family, about how they transformed you. And what a summer it was! How shall I tell the tale, Marietta, how shall I tell it true? Why, with memory and imagination, awake to the wonder of you!

CORFU, GREECE – SUMMER 1973 (1)

In an open-air cinema in Kerkyra, in a courtyard in Akadimias, you're laughing your head off to the foolery in Louis Malle's *Viva Maria!* You're sitting in a group with the whole troop of your summer household: your hosts at their house in Kalami, the Kluge family—Dieter, the father, and his wife Helga; the twins, Jürgen and Ulla, and their sister Veronika; Axel, Ulla's boyfriend, and Rudi, Veronika's—and your father and Pascale. It's three months since Valeria left for

Australia. And you too are reaching for distant shores: You're engaged in a quest to discover through sex the depths of yourself.

In a tavern in San Miguel, somewhere in Central America, a troupe of travelling entertainers performs their vaudeville show. A magician conjures a dove from a scarf; as it flies above the boisterous crowd, a drinker pulls out his pistol and shoots it down. You break into hysterics, just as you do at all the other gags in this motley adventure movie. No-one else laughs as hard as you, but no-one else (except Jürgen, of course) has made love all afternoon: You need to come down from your high. The gags give you the occasion, but release-through-laughter is not all you get from *Viva Maria!* No, you're also fascinated by the two Marias, delighting in their complicity while wondering about their different ways of being a woman: Jeanne Moreau holding out for the ideal of love, Brigitte Bardot seizing the day; one opting for wiliness and passivity, the other for forthrightness and risk. And then, too, the film offers you a space to reflect on political violence, so inconsequential in the movie and so bloody and incendiary outside. When the film is over, you don't ride back to Kalami with Jürgen as you'd come with him to Kerkyra: You are rigourous about keeping your nights separate from your days—that's part of what makes your experience in Corfu so exciting.

Kalami, The Kluge house

Dieter

You're sitting with Dieter on the terrace, looking out across the Ionian Sea to the mountains of Albania. From here, high in the hills above Kalami, the view is vast. You like this man and never tire of talking with him: about his job as curator of twentieth-century painting at the Neue Nationalgalerie in Berlin; about his experience at the end of the war as a 'Flakhelfer'; about his collection of Danish Modern furniture. Now you're talking about how he built this house in the mid-sixties, forming a company with his brother to buy the land, using his connections with a Minister in Athens to bring electricity and modern plumbing to the whole village. The talk then shifts to Greece under the Colonels, still in power six years after the coup. Dieter explains that their strongest support is in the villages, where the junta's anti-Communist discourse goes down best. When you ask why, he starts telling you about the Greek Civil War of 1946-49, explaining that Communist guerrillas were ruthless in the villages, killing anyone who criticized them and driving hundreds of thousands from their homes. You remark that today, in 1973, West Germany and Greece are both Cold War frontline states, and both host American military bases. That gives a particular intensity, you say, to the political battles in the two countries.

Dieter concurs, then asks you if you realize you are living through extraordinary times. You say you do, and that you're happy to be alive.

Helga

It's early morning and you're the first up. Except, of course, for Helga, who never needs more than five hours sleep: She's already got two hours of work behind her when you join her for breakfast. Everything is ready: yogurt in bowls of white porcelain, shallow cups of chopped apple and walnut; a bowl of sultana raisins, a jar of golden honey. From a steaming bronze briki she fills your cup with coffee. You enjoy talking with Helga even more than you do with Dieter: About life at the Free University of Berlin, where she is Professor of Modern History; about the Nazis in Greece, the subject of her last book; about marriage, and why couples only seem to find happiness once each has been divorced. You know, by her response to your question about whether it's by choice that she doesn't have children, that she was raped by Soviet soldiers when they arrived in Berlin in 1945. She has been unable to conceive ever since. Now you're talking about Erika and Klaus Mann, the subjects of the biography Helga had been working on before breakfast. She explains what exemplary Germans they were, tirelessly opposing Hitler at every turn; she talks about their twin-like, quasi-incestuous relationship, about Klaus' homosexuality and his suicide in Cannes. In the garden, after your morning swim, you read with ravishment the copies of Klaus Mann's letters Helga's given you.

Veronika

You're back from your Greek lesson with the tavern keeper's daughter; you're happy, for now you can hold a conversation. Veronika on the bench under the arbutus tree asks you to help her finish making her panama straw visor. In the cool of the house you show her how to backstitch the bias strip of fabric in place, how to fold in the excess and secure it to the tarlatan, and finally, how to complete the bind with a slip stitch. She marvels at your dexterity; you complement her on her quick learning. She's seventeen, about to enter her final year of high school. You ask her about her studies at the Evangelische Gymnasium zum Grauen Kloster, which you've heard is among the most prestigious schools not only in Berlin, but in all of Germany. She tells you about learning Greek and Latin and Protestant doctrine in addition to the usual subjects; she tells you about being on the rowing team and playing the flute in the orchestra. You ask her if she believes in God; she says she doesn't, but adds that Christianity as a religion of love is an antidote to egotism, and therefore is something she supports. She asks you if it's hard being an only child; you say yes, it is. She says she used to feel like an only child, what with her brother and sister being six years older, and twins to boot. She then tells you she's brought her planetary tables to Corfu, and asks you if you'd like her to do your birth chart. You say you would, and give her the exact time and place of your birth. 'I'll start working on it tomorrow', she says, 'when we get back from the boat trip'. A week later, when she presented it to you, you were amazed by its richness and complexity, and astounded by the accuracy of her interpretation. (Is that why, today, you are that rarity among scientists, a physicist who does not denigrate astrology?)

Axel

On a terrace, level on a side-of-the-house slope, you're playing ping-pong with Axel. He's got a killer backspin serve, but your forehand push is just as good; his topspin drives are wicked, but you hit winners off them. His style of play is all finesse; yours is crisp and aggressive. The games are very close. You've grown to like this man; you like his protective big-brother stance as much as you like his teasing. At the beach you're comfortable with his physicality, diving off his shoulders as you used to do with your dad. Is it only because he's doing a doctorate in anthropology that he reminds you of Valeria, or is there something else? What is it about some people that puts you so at ease? You like the way he relates to Ursula; you like the vigour of their debates as much as the tenderness in their affection. His wry humour strikes a chord in you, as does his defence of the liberal ideal in the face of compartmentalized culture (his thesis on Ernst Cassirer). The freshness of his opinions, his openness and finesse—that, you decide, is why you like him. That, and the fact that he's devilishly good-looking.

Ulla

You feel a slight uneasiness with Ulla as the two of you tend the herb garden, you sprinkling water on the raised beds of parsley, mint, coriander and thyme while she picks lemon verbena for tea. Is it because she's Jürgen's twin sister? No doubt. Where Veronika is more like you, angular and athletic, Ulla is all soft curves and *douceur*. She's as feminine as her brother is masculine. Yet her gentle appearance belies her fierce intelligence; a student with Axel at the Free University of Berlin, she's doing her thesis on Heidegger and the Pre-Socratics. You sense that she too feels slightly ill-at-ease with you. Is her awkward solicitude an attempt to protect you, or is her concern rather for her brother? Maybe, it crosses your mind, she's simply jealous. As she seats herself on a canvas cushion and leans back on the bench, she asks you how you like Corfu. What an innocuous question! You tell her you like it very much. And then she says:

– Last night I had a strange dream, about you and Gudrun Ensslin.

– Me and Gudrun Ensslin?

– Yes.

– Where were we, what were we doing?

– You were in a prison cell, both of you, and you were being force-fed. Because you were on a hunger strike, and they didn't want you to die.

You're shocked at the words, at the vivid images they evoke. Does Ulla know I was anorexic? you wonder.

– Let's go and make some tea, you say, then you can explain what I'm doing in your dream!

As you leave the herb garden, you don't know which is stronger, your sense of trepidation or your sense of elation.

Rudi

On the outside dining terrace, at the stone table, you're going through the equations for Rudi's engineering project: The Mathematics of Mobiles. He's understood the principles, you find, but his equations lack beauty: You show him how to make them more elegant. You'd watched him make the mobile, you'd admired his sense of craftsmanship as he cut and smoothed a concave curve in an aluminium element, used the round-nose pliers to bend the bail wire into the desired shape, or looped the connecting rods with precisely calculated twists. How far back does it go, your intuition that a manual task well-done has something to do with ethics? That the hand teaches the mind no less than the mind the hand, and that for the hand and the heart it's the same? You, who usually have no patience with teenage boys, find Veronika's boyfriend a worthy one. Rudi tells you he wants to work for BMW; when you discuss cars, he's impressed that your knowledge is as vast as his. When he asks you what you'd like to do for a living (he takes it for granted you'll never be a housewife), you say, 'I'd like to work in mathematics, or be a musician'. 'You really must come to Berlin', he says, 'I'm sure you'd love it there'. When you ask him what makes him so sure, he says he doesn't know, he just has a feeling its your kind of place. As you stare into his grey-blue eyes, you wonder what it is about you that defines your personality for others. It's not something you give much thought to, but you do wonder from time to time.

Jean-Louis

In the courtyard, under a pergola of jasmine and bougainvillea, you sit at a trestle table playing chess with your father. Deftly coordinating the knights and the bishops, the sly and the oblique, you attack relentlessly; sacrificing a knight to control the centre, you then force a rook to come out but suddenly find yourself on the defensive, struggling to reorganize in the face of your father's ingenious use of the queen not as a direct attacker, but as a support to buttress the other pieces. Finally you regain the initiative and force a queen exchange, thus beginning the endgame.

It's three years since your father remarried, three years that Pascale's been sharing his bed, and now you've got a man who can give you precisely that which he could not. You don't feel embarrassed before him, nor is he coy about what goes on between you and Jürgen. His faith in you is absolute. Still, sometimes, you wish he weren't so accepting. What if I really did something foolish, you reflect, just to test him? Would he care enough to intervene? You do understand that his devotion to Pascale has forced you to break with your family and become an individual; you do acknowledge that his refusal to be everything to you has freed you to find yourself in the world. But are you aware that it is on his attitude to Pascale that your faith in your capacity to be loved by a man depends? Are you aware that the way in which you will consider yourself as a woman depends on his attitude to all the women he has loved? As he checkmates you, instead of feeling defeated, you're glad that he's beaten you: It makes you feel less alone.

Pascale

In the library, Pascale sits at a rosewood desk, writing a letter. Legs flexed, you're sitting on the floor, your bare feet cool on a cotton dhurrie, your back to a bookcase. From the ceramic vase that sits on the desk, from its zinnias and pelargonium leaves picked from the garden, a gentle perfume wafts to your nostrils. It's thanks to Pascale that you're in Corfu, for Helga invited her and her family here. They've became good friends ever since they met at an Amnesty International meeting. As members of the commission on the problem of identifying the individuals and institutions responsible for torture, they've prepared a contribution for the first international conference on the abolition of this practice, to be held in Paris in December. You've grown to admire Pascale, and now, at last, your love has caught up with your admiration. She's twenty-five, she'll soon be called to the bar in Geneva, and she's told you explicitly not to expect any little half-brother or sister: She wants to devote herself to her career, she wants to specialize in human rights law. Now, as you sit in silence in the library, at ease in each other's presence, it strikes you as ironic that defending human rights should go hand-in-hand with foregoing having children. You know perfectly well that there's nothing in common between Pascale and Gudrun Ensslin, so you feel a flush of shame as you recall, following your conversation with Ursula, that Gudrun Ensslin gave up her child to save the world, just as Ulrike Meinhof gave up her children. As you feel Pascale's presence, as you realize how young she is, you feel yourself a child, even as you rush headlong into becoming a woman. You swing your torso around and run your fingers along the spines of the books (novels in German and English), and as you do so, you find it curious that Pascale, a hard-nosed lawyer, should so like reading love stories. Albert Cohen being from Corfu, she decided this was the time to finally read *Belle de Seigneur;* before that, she'd read *G.* by a guy called John Berger (a writer you'd grow to love) and *The French Lieutenant's Woman* by one called Fowles (who'd also become one of your favourites). Will I ever fall in love? you wonder. Here you're surrounded by lovers who never tire of showing each other their affection. I'd like to, you think, just to know what it's like. In the meantime I've got Jürgen. He's my school of sex. Slipping her letter into an envelope, Pascale asks you:

— Are you going to Kerkyra this afternoon?

— Yes. Would you like me to mail your letter?

— Please, if you would.

Like your father, she too dares not allude to what you do there. That's the way you want it, of course. Nevertheless, what you do there produces such strong sensations in you, with emotions that get heavy despite your intention to keep things light, that you do wish you had someone to confide in, someone to talk to. You stand up and take the letter Pascale holds out to you.

— You're not ill, are you? you ask as you read the address on the envelope.

— No, not at all. The doctor I'm writing to is helping to set up an international team of physicians pledged to travel anywhere to investigate charges of torture. I'm just giving him some legal guidelines. Come, let's go and get some sun—what do you say?

On the terrace, as you lie in your lounge chair, you undo your bikini top and let Pascale spread sun screen on your back. When you do the same for her, you no longer have any doubt: This new-found intimacy between you is the seal on your reconciliation.

Jürgen

Sweeping across the living room floor, striations of periwinkle blue unfurl their variations in the cool carpet; freestanding lamps diffuse soft pockets of light, the night outside deepens the intimacy within. Everyone is here: you, Jürgen, Dieter, Helga, Rudi, Veronika, Axel, Ursula, Pascale and your father. Some of you are drinking kumquat-and-pomegranate punch; others are sipping Metaxa or Tentura. Current events dominate the conversation, from the revelation of the secret bombing of Cambodia to the Black September massacre at Athens airport, from the plebiscite on the abolition of the Greek monarchy to the goings-on of the Baader-Meinhof gang. Everyone participates, everyone except you and Jürgen: After your afternoon of lovemaking, you've no desire to talk. In company, at home here in Kalami, you're cool and distant with each other; when forced into contact, you're courteous and formal. That's the way each of you wants it. You're both aware that this seeming indifference to one another, outside your House of Assignation, is an extension of your ritualistic lovemaking. Now—you isolated in your Danish Modern easy chair and he sitting alone on the Kaare Klint loveseat—you don't look at each other, but you, for your part, do hold him in your mind. What do you see? A dark, seductive beauty, menacing and intense; a simmering sexuality, with just a hint of cruelty. His sinewy body, angular and lean, shimmers with energy; his bearing, at once savage and princely, is that of a fallen angel. Long black hair frames his luminous face; his eyes are dark, his cheekbones high. Smouldering with ambiguity, his full lips could just as easily kiss as curse, and when he smiles, they kill. All in all, what in an ordinary person would be no more than an emaciated face and a gangly body, in him is incandescence. He is the antithesis of his twin sister's blonde, blue-eyed wholesomeness: In an earlier age, his birth would have been seen as the devil's work. What do you know about him? That he graduated from the Cordon Bleu school in Paris; that he works as a chef in West Berlin. That at school a time came when he could no longer bear to see a boy being bullied, so black and blue he beat the boy's tormentor, coming within a hair's breadth of permanently blinding him. That for this, not only was he expelled from school, but he had to spend weeks painting fences in the name of service to the community. You also know that once, in Paris, a woman who lived in splendour on the boulevard de Beauséjour offered him money to spend the night with her: He did not say no. What else? That he likes wearing Indian clothes, Nehru jackets and trousers. And that, despite his being twenty-three and you still in your teens, his power over you is no greater than your power over him.

The Twins' Birthday

In the indoor-outdoor kitchen, you're adding a garnish of mint leaves to the chilled tzatziki while Veronika keeps an eye on the souvlakia on the barbeque. The tomato salad has been made, the floured slices of courgette and aubergine have been fried, and the walnut cake that tastes even better on the second day was made yesterday. Normally, Jürgen does the cooking, but today is his birthday and despite your pact of indifference, you insisted you would cook and bake for the twins' party. Everyone is on the dining terrace, drinking Fix Hellas beer and dipping into bowls of olives and deep-fried anchovy balls. Here and there, candles burn in lanterns of sky-blue and pistachio-green; in ridged terracotta pots, fruiting lemon trees stand. 'Daniel', from *Don't Shoot Me I'm*

Only the Piano Player (your present to Ulla), is playing on the portable stereo. Jürgen, his wasted look given a focus by the choker you made him—a spiral pendant and bronze-dipped beads strung on a leather cord—is busy charming Pascale. With the cucumber-and-yogurt dip, the fried courgettes and aubergines are refreshing; with the grilled red onions and bell peppers, the skewered lamb is delicious. There's never a dull moment as jokes and pranks are traded; full of go, your father is in fine form. Later, Helga brings out the walnut cake you've baked, luscious and moist for having been soaked in a syrup of brandy, orange rind and cinnamon. Jürgen and Ursula, each with an arm around the shoulders of the other, blow out the candles in one concerted breath. His black hair as long as her blonde, he is all understated cool in his black T-shirt and linen jacket, while she is dazzling in a white spaghetti-strap dress. Suddenly you see them as yin and yang, coiled into each other like the left-hand right-hand complements they are. You know they can read each other's thoughts, you know they can feel each other's emotions, but as far as you're concerned, you'd never want to be born with your soul mate: You've learned too much from your isolation to trade it for what you see as complacency.

– *Zum Geburtstag viel Glück, zum Geburtstag viel Glück, zum Geburtstag alles Gute, zum Geburtstag viel Glück.*

Jürgen is not too cool to dance, but you do not dance with him; instead, as if for old times' sake, you show your father your sexual progress by moving your body in perfect syncopation to Stevie Wonder's 'Superstition'. The night ends in a festival of fucking in private bedrooms, but for you and Jürgen it is chaste.

Chapter 9

CORFU, GREECE – SUMMER 1973 (2)

1 - Kerkyra, The House of Assignation

The moment the decision is made you feel a buzz in your spine. The diffuse pulsation invades your pelvis and remains there all morning. When you mount the motorcycle to leave for Kerkyra it gains in intensity, and as you ride the coastal road, your arms around Jürgen's waist, your whole body vibrates with expectation. The ride on the R90S, BMW's new baby, is thrilling; you feel the throb of the reciprocating pistons, the grip of the ducktail seat, and as you lean into a curve you feel you're tracing the very contour of the world: You're certain when you return you will not be the same, and you're certain you've made the right decision.

In Kerkyra, on a street in the old district of Campiello, high above the harbour, stands the House of Assignation. It is in fact an apartment in a three-story mansion built by a Venetian merchant, an apartment which once served as an office for Dieter's brother's import-export business: When he died, he left it to Jürgen. You park the motorcycle and walk the warren of alleys behind the Liston to reach the apartment. The shops are closed, the grilles are down, the arcades almost empty: The siesta has begun, but it's not to take a nap that you're going to bed.

The moment Jürgen pushes open the street door, you enter a world of half-light, cool and calm. He offers you his hand: You take it. Side-by-side, you climb the six flights of stairs to the apartment.

Ornamental brackets and rosettes, spiral moulding with beads: Is it the gold trim glinting on the dark wood that makes you look up at the coffered ceiling as soon as you enter the front room? The ceiling is high, the room voluminous; the furniture evokes a past long gone. Jürgen leaves the room dim; you pass into the bedroom.

Black iron bedstead with brass trim, red cashmere blanket across cream spread: You kick off your shoes and take a running dive onto the bed. Was it the printed suede of the throw pillows that caught your fancy, or was it simply the inviting thickness of the mattress? You draw your body towards the headboard grille, you lean back against the pillows. At the opposite end of the room, Jürgen seats himself in a high-backed chair that sits low to the ground and takes off his boots. You like the innocent white of the bare walls, a white that is somehow warm; you like the ivory-coloured Persian rug, speckled with indigo and orange. You don't know if you'll get wild, but you have a feeling the amphora-like Majolica lamps, tall on their black night stands, might be put in danger if you do. You look at the wardrobe on its low plinth, you look at its doors of deep cream incised with gold diagonals, and you wonder, What will I find when I open them? What clothes has he found for me? To one side of the wardrobe stands a three-fold screen, its panels of ebonized wood outlined in silver-grey gesso; just beyond it a cheval glass stands, its mahogany frame elongated with silver-gilt mounts. Each time you come here you'll select something from the wardrobe, put it on behind the folding screen and check the effect in the mirror. Then you'll go out to Jürgen. You hope he's got your measurements right, that everything's in the right size. And what could be in that dower chest on the other side of the wardrobe? Could it be accessories for me? With its carved stars scintillating between chequerboard bands, it's a beautiful coffer. Jürgen, taking off his socks, explains that the chair he's sitting in, armless and spoon-backed, is for your use: It's low-slung and you can lean back, perfect for putting on stockings. Against the blue silk damask of the chair, you find him beautiful in his bare feet and black jeans, his dark eyes and long hair. He gets up and fetches two pairs of soft leather slippers from the wardrobe; slipping on the bigger pair, he leaves you the other and goes to the bathroom. You love the quality of this silence, you love the way it enrobes the rustling sheers, the soft ticking of the Lion of Venice clock, the occasional bird call. The light filtering through the louvres gives the room an air of mystery; you close your eyes and feel the pulsations in your pelvis: You're impatient to begin. Jürgen reappears, bare-chested, refreshed; you slide off the bed, slip your feet into your slippers and go to the bathroom.

White-and-blue wall tiles with powdered manganese-purple, washbasin and bath in black: You break into a smile as you enter this mix of contemporary and old-time. The shower glass presents you with a trident-wielding Poseidon; the little window, a view of closed shutters and open sky. As you look at yourself in the mirror, you accept that you're 'not bad looking'; as you wash your hands, you know they will know what to do: Thanks to Valeria, you have great confidence in your body. You've never made love with a man, but you feel hardly any apprehension. By the sureness of your gestures as you wash the road off your face, you feel your body is primed for what's about to happen; when you return to the bedroom, you head straight for the wardrobe. Minutes later, you emerge from behind the screen.

Loose, your hair flows from its centre part to your bare shoulders, the blonde aglow against the electric blue of your eye mask. Held up by a collar around your neck, your dress, cut away above your breasts, falls in a cascade of ruby-red ruffles to the flared skirt. For a lark with Veronika you'd painted your toenails red, and now you're happy you did for your feet are as bare as your legs. Jürgen watches you from the bed as you walk, the skirt of your dress swaying to your rolling gait. At the not-quite-closed shutters, you stop and rise onto your toes as you peer out past the New Fortress to the sea. You bring a hand to your behind and raise your dress just enough for Jürgen to note you're not wearing anything underneath. And then you stroll to a ladder-back chair of rosewood and leather, angle it to face Jürgen and sit down.

As carefree as a boy would be, you raise a leg, fold it in front of you and hold it parallel to the floor, your foot on the seat blocking the hinge of your thighs. You see a smouldering in Jürgen's eyes, you sense the slow-burn of his sensuality. Should you wait for him to make a move, or should you keep the initiative? Opting to stay in control, you rise from the chair and climb onto the bed. As he stretches out you straddle his body, running your ruby-red ruffles up and down his chest. Against his skin the silk is fluid, lush, living; against yours it is a soft caress. He tries in vain to free your breasts, in vain for the collar holds fast. Excited by his frustration, emboldened by your mask, you sit up, slide back, and draw down the zipper of his jeans. He is surprised by your authority, for you'd led him to believe you were a virgin. You yourself don't believe you are, for with Valeria you'd held nothing back. Still, here there is something more, and you know it is imperious. Jürgen in his laid-back intensity is willing to let you take the lead; nevertheless, you hesitate between continuing and letting him take over. Amber, white and electric blue frame the black of your pupil: Drawing up his arms and interlocking his hands behind his head, he dares you to confront the concentration of masculinity of which even he is not master. You unbutton his jeans, slide off the bed and pull them off, and then you pull off his underpants: Jack-in-the-box jolts you; a cavewoman on all fours, somewhere deep inside you, howls.

You don't pause to look or touch, but immediately straddle him again. And then you take it and touch it to your opening. He is amazed when you sit back and it slides smoothly in, amazed and blown away by the exquisite sensation: Your grip is glorious. Before your pleasure mounts, you already feel a sense of triumph; you feel vindicated, but for what you do not know. Seeing your assurance, he feels no pressure to perform; he lets you continue to dictate his role. Guided by nothing but the sensations between your legs, you lean back, place your hands on his knees, and rock back and forth. It comes, the self-overcoming, it comes before you've had time to prepare for it: Your whole body is a vibrancy of resonances, as if in some Buddhist temple a monk had gone haywire with the gong. And it doesn't stop, it only subsides to rise again as you rock. Jürgen strokes your thighs, he cups your butt, he kneads your breasts through your bodice. To him it feels like he's going in and out, but you know he's only moving in an arc, for doesn't this sensation recall your swinging at full extension, your father pushing you in the park? When the waves of pleasure overwhelm you, when they become too much to bear, you pull off your mask, collapse onto his body and break down in tears.

You don't remember how long you lay in his arms, you just remember that as the daylight dimmed he penetrated you, rolled you onto your side, straddled your hip with his thigh and then launched you into a conversation. The subject was the restaurant he dreamed of opening one day. His thrusts were very subtle as he answered your questions about the cuisine he planned on serving; soon he gave you to understand that you have to use your pelvic muscles to get the full flavour of the experience. And so, in-between telling you about the earth flavours—mushroom, eggplant, cumin, beet, potato and celery—he told you to alternately tighten your pelvic muscles (as if you were holding in your pee) and relax them, and as he explained the pairings for the creamy-fruity flavours—banana, melon, apricot, peach, coconut and mango—he broke off to have you imagine you were a Gopala-girl in India, milking a cow. The goal, he made clear—after telling you about a delicious drink made with milk, yogurt, melon and mint—is to get your pussy to act like the hand of the milkmaid. While he spoke of the marine flavours—shellfish, whitefish, oyster and caviar—you practiced contracting and relaxing your grip around him. 'That's delicious!', he said, and by the glint in his eye, you knew he was praising your skill as much as he was referring to the devilishly good contrast of prune-and-bacon with oyster. By the time he got to the spicy flavours—basil, cinnamon, cloves, nutmeg and parsnip—you'd really got the hang of the both the squeeze box and the milkmaid. And so you began varying the rhythm, tightening and relaxing now in rapid bursts, now in long, measured phrases, or spiralling the pressure from the depths to the surface, the surface to the depths. When he spoke of using nutmeg to perk up the pumpkin and ricotta filling for ravioli, you threw all your will into your love canal. He began grinding against you, his hands roving all over your body, but it was only when he spoke of the bitter spiciness of roasted parsnip and watercress, tossed with crumbled blue cheese and croutons, that Gopala Girl and Squeeze-Box Queen brought you both to a paroxysm of pleasure: In your bones you sensed his spasms triggering your contractions, in the pit of your belly you felt his heartbeat hastening yours.

You hugged him close on the ride back to Kalami; before you knew it you had already arrived: The R90S proved to be a machine that can not only cover distances quickly, but can also take lovers out of time.

2 - The Kluge house, Kalami

'Everything profound loves the mask': Like your beloved Nietzsche, you situate yourself beyond good and evil, making a mask indispensable. That your wore one when you first made love with a man is entirely fitting. The next day you felt in your bone-breath the gravity of what you'd done; you knew you'd adopted a metaphysics of ambivalence and that for you, sexuality would never be fixed. You were keen to recommence the celebration, keen to re-honour the god of masquerade. You wished Nika were in Kerkyra, you wanted to tell her what you'd done: You felt you'd realized a vision of yourself, and you wanted her confirmation. As for Veronika, she had told you her relief when she'd lost her virginity: 'I was glad to get it over with, glad to be out of the virgin club—at least I knew I wouldn't be the last one'. Being first separates you from others just as much as being last, you thought, but fitting in with your peers was never your concern: You'd known from an early age that your destiny was to be different.

The mask frees the imagination, the disguised face liberates: Who in the Kalami living room, as you sat amongst them in the evening, knew how impatient you were to get back to your experimentation?

3 - Kerkyra, the House of Assignation

On the motorcycle of silver and smoke, to the full-throated song of its fiery pipes, you ride the coastal road down to Kerkyra. You love the way the horizon tilts as you lean into a curve, you love the way the asphalt disappears as fast as it's unfurled. You've figured out how Jürgen applies the throttle through the cornering line, how for what comes next he's always in the right place in the road. Speed is in your blood, you've got a taste for danger; you believe in mastering all that can be mastered and leaving the rest to chance. As your hands meet around Jürgen's waist, you feel at one with him; as you approach Kerkyra, your cup fills to the brim.

Again, as soon as Jürgen pushes open the street door, you enter a world of half light, cool and calm; again, you walk up the six flights of stairs beside him, hand-in-hand. In the vestibule, you notice the coat rack is a rail of Venetian doorknobs with, in the middle, a bronze head of Dionysus (you can tell by the ancient map above the rail, you can tell by the vines). While Jürgen's in the bathroom, you run your hand across the buttoned-back silk damask of the boudoir chair, sit down on it and take off your boots. When he's done you take your turn, then head for the wardrobe while he waits on the bed. Minutes later, you emerge from behind the screen.

Tilted, your hat sits jauntily on your head; your skinny black tie is loosely knotted in the collar of your white shirt, your black lamb-leather pants hug your legs. Lingering before imaginary pictures on the wall, you stand tall in your ankle boots. For Jürgen you make real your gallery by your attitude before each picture. Contemplation: elbow on folded arm, knuckles under chin. Defiance: hands on hips, legs apart. Ambivalence: right-hand in front pocket, left hand behind ear. You're aware that Jürgen can see you only in profile or from the rear, and you're not unaware of how arousing that can be. Here, you move in close to study a detail, feeling very art historian; there, you crouch down to change perspective, feeling very masculine. As you lean forward you feel, under the soft cotton of your loose-cut shirt, the weight of your breasts; as you rise to your feet, your nipples register the cotton's caress. Did Jürgen notice the consequent inrush of breath? You don't look at him, but you know whatever your emotion, the magic between you keeps you attuned.

Crossing the room, you thrill to the soft, buttery rub of the leather between your legs; imbued with the power of your second skin, you feel your animal magnetism. As you demonstrate your mastery of the body language of looking, Jürgen believes you're fascinated by your phantasms on the wall: He's not wrong, but does he know they're produced by the sensations in your body? As the breeze through the louvres billows the shears, you turn around and look at him: Again, his dark beauty moves you; again, his laid-back intensity arouses you.

You take off your hat and shake loose your hair; taking aim, you toss the hat towards the mirror: It hangs itself on the mahogany frame. You pick up the ladder-back chair and place it beside the bed; you sit down and offer Jürgen your boot: He unzips it and pulls it off, then unzips the ankle of your pants and pulls off your sock. For the other foot he does the same, then says:

— Stand up, and take off your tie.

You do so, and wonder why that alone makes you feel naked.

He stands up and takes you in his arms. You feel the ripple of his muscles, you smell the scent of his skin, as he presses your breasts against his chest. As he begins to kiss you, you realize you've never really kissed him before. You find your mouths fit well; you find your tongues, working slow, know how to build pleasure. Pushing you up against the wall, he puts his hand between your legs.

You like it, you like how he varies the friction, you like how he looks into your eyes. Against your springy folds the supple leather produces new sensations, but suddenly you find yourself feeling inadequate, wanting. Sensing the change in you, Jürgen unbuttons your shirt, picks you up and carries you to the bed. On your back you feel at bay, forced into passivity: That feeling both excites and frustrates you. He unfastens your pants and pulls them off.

— You're a lovely piece of crumpet, Marietta.

He takes off his trousers.

— Yeah, you're a bit of all right.

You love it when he talks to you like that: It leaves you more free.

By what miracle are you so well matched? You've both come twice, and what's more, at the same time. Now, as you fan the flames of the latest flare up, you feel him fully inside you, you feel his hands gripping your buttocks and his groin against your clit. He's not moving in and out, but staying deep inside; he's grinding his pubis against your sex while his cock explores its depths. You love the full body contact, the sweat and the heat; you love the sensation of feeling filled and replete. And then your panting beckons him to light the wick, and your festival of friction gives way to fireworks.

You hugged him close on the ride back to Kalami; before you knew it you had already arrived: The R90S proved to be a machine that can not only cover distances quickly, but can also take lovers out of time.

4 - The Kluge house, Kalami

Is it possible that all women have a sex like mine and just pretend it doesn't astound them? How can they do what I have done and continue to wait in line at the supermarket, sleep eight hours a night and stop their car at a red light? And here, amongst everyone in this room, can't they see I'm not the same? Doesn't it show on my face? My shower did not disperse the life force my hat concentrated in my hair, it didn't wash away the bestiality my leather pants gave me. But why did I feel naked when Jürgen asked me to take off my tie? Suddenly you remember something you've never told anyone, something that happened in Neuchâtel when you were a child. Two events had brought it about. The first, your father had just got a new girlfriend, a girl with a pixie haircut; the second, all the boys, playing football, wanted you on their team because you could dribble circles round the best of them. Feeling proud, you went to a barber shop for boys to get yourself a pixie. As the barber was giving you a razor cut, his body rubbed against yours and you noticed he had an erection. You turned red with indignation, furious at being turned into an object but unable to protest, paralyzed by the gaze of the waiting males. As the bite of the blade, the crisp whisper of its cut, grated on your nerves, you felt trapped: Forced submission to this man's lust was a violation. (Marietta, was not your fury also fed by the man's erection projecting you into your future as a woman, passive and receptive? Was not your anger all the greater because you had expected your pixie to mark you out as a boy, not to degrade you to a mere object of men?) As you looked at yourself in the mirror you felt humiliated; and as you walked out of the barber shop you wondered how you would regain your pride. This memory casts a shadow on your happiness tonight: You can't wait to make love with Jürgen again, so you can efface it forever.

Chapter 10

CORFU, GREECE – SUMMER 1973 (3)

Contemplative ecstasy,
Humbly seeking enlightenment
In the sun:
Lizard, where do I come from?
Dream-work, night-times of dream-work.

Warden of the dark house,
Of what must I be aware? Speak, owl.
Milk binds
And restores, but not the milk of nightmares:
Nothing living is free of a shadow.

We are born of a mother, and we die alone: How to do so with dignity? Already, you are preparing your way.

1 - Kerkyra, the House of Assignation

If ever I fall in love with a boy, it will be one with a motorbike: On the motorcycle of silver and smoke, to the full-throated song of its fiery pipes, you ride the coastal road down to Kerkyra. You love the pitch and roll of the earth below, the land becoming the sea; you love the wind that blows your cares away, the connection that leaves you free. As your hands meet around Jürgen's waist, you feel at one with him; as you approach Kerkyra, your cup fills to the brim.

Again, as soon as Jürgen pushes open the street door, you enter a world of half light, cool and calm; again, you walk up the six flights of stairs beside him, hand-in-hand. In the dim front room you notice the panels of stencilled leather that line the lower third of the walls, the trompe l'oeil painting that tapestries the window wall. While Jürgen's in the bathroom, you run your hand across the buttoned-back silk damask of the boudoir chair, sit down on it and take off your boots. When he's done you take your turn, then head for the wardrobe while he waits on the bed. Minutes later, you emerge from behind the screen.

Tight, your spaghetti-strap top flaunts your breasts; crystal-studded strings draw the cups of the built-in bra together, making a glittering cage for your cleavage. A wide black waistband separates the red of the top from the black-and-white plaid of your schoolgirl skirt. Swept back and tied into a ponytail, your hair bobs as you toss your imaginary hacky sack into an imaginary hopscotch court and hop, skip and jump through the course. At every leap Jürgen expects your breasts to burst out, but somehow the strings restrain your liberality. Your skirt unfurls a fan of pleats as you spin around at the end of the course; on the way back, as you bend to pick up the hacky sack, it's bare where your panties would be. Your dexterity is such that were you blindfolded your feet would not miss a square. Jürgen, sitting in the lotus position on the bed, doesn't quite know how to respond to your girliness. To add to his confusion, you begin to mime the rhymes you've started reciting, rhymes learnt in Bournemouth when you were on a linguistic stay. Hacky sack on number three; hop, skip and jump:

> As I sat under the apple tree
> A birdie sent his love to me,
> And as I wiped it from my eye,
> I said, 'Thank goodness cows can't fly'.

The rhyme provokes a roar of laughter; the switch from German to English makes Jürgen rise to your game. Hacky sack on number five; hop, skip and jump:

> As I was going down the lane
> I thought I smelt some kippers.
> I asked a lady what it was,
> She said it was her knickers.

Again you've got him in stitches, as if he needed this relief. Hacky sack on number seven; hop, skip and jump:

> Mary had a little lamb,
> Her father shot it dead,
> And now it goes to school with her
> Between two chunks of bread.

As his peals of laughter resonate in the room, you hop, skip and jump back to the starting place. Spinning round, you pull up your top: Compressed from above, your breasts instantly shut Jürgen up. He bounds off the bed.

— *Hopp, hopp, hopp, Pferdchen lauf Galopp!*

With the dexterity of a circus rider, you leap onto his back and whip him round the room.

– *Über Stock und über Steine, aber brich dir nicht die Beine! Hopp, hopp, hopp, Pferdchen lauf Galopp!*

After that, he didn't feel perturbed when he made love to you as the schoolgirl you in fact were; nor did you, in giving yourself to him, have any sense of transgression. He came once, he came twice, but you couldn't come. Jürgen sensed something was wrong, but you didn't want to talk about it. And so, as you lay on your back, knees bent and apart, he knelt between your legs, slipped a pillow under your butt, and entered you at an upward angle. Cupping your breasts with his hands, he began to rock. You felt, just inside you, the rapid-fire friction of his shallow thrusts; with mounting pleasure, you felt the scintillation of his strokes. He had the feeling he could go on forever, and as the heat of pleasure spread through your body, you wanted him to stop just as much as you wanted him to continue. Still shallow-thrusting, he leaned back and surveyed your body, laid wide open to his view, and felt the contradictions flowing through you. And then, as your gaze seized his and held it, your body went into spasms as it became a meeting ground for underworld, earth and heaven.

You hugged him close on the ride back to Kalami; before you knew it you had already arrived: The R90S proved to be a machine that can not only cover distances quickly, but can also take lovers out of time.

2 - The Kluge house, Kalami

As Jürgen prepares supper—veal escalopes with sofrito and new potatoes—you sweep the terrace. Not because it needs sweeping, but because you need something to do. Your breasts are tender, you go lightly with the broom. Damn the pill that's made them bigger! You're feeling at sixes and sevens. You'd like to go for a run, but now even the best sports bra would be torture for your tits. Besides, it's too late now. What's troubling you? For one, the fact that you couldn't come. Or rather, that you *wouldn't* come: You'd stopped yourself from climaxing, until Jürgen's skill finally overcame your will. Why did you do that? For fear of falling in love. It won't happen again, you tell yourself, I will not fall in love: We like each other, and that's enough. And then there's the fact that your masquerade has confused you: You were a schoolgirl pretending to be a schoolgirl, you were pretending to be who you are. Impersonating yourself! So who am I? you ask. A woman pretending to be a girl, or a girl pretending to be a woman? Why did I choose that schoolgirl skirt when there were so many other clothes in the wardrobe? Am I moving forward or backward? Thank God Jürgen respects me, even if I am only a creature who craves penetration!

Suddenly you've had enough of sweeping up nothing. You step off the terrace and start raking the slope: the rust-and-cream peelings of eucalyptus bark, the copper-and-green exfoliations from the arbutus, the white petals of myrtle flowers. You pick up a sprig of juniper. As you twirl it between your fingers it bursts into flame: In its light you see yourself, bent over an ottoman in the dim front room of the House of Assignation. Jürgen is raping you while your father watches through a window. As the flame burns your fingers, you fling the sprig to the ground. Scandalized by your imagination, ashamed of the scene you've conjured, you run to Ursula who's lighting a lamp on the terrace.

— Have you seen my gold sandal? she asks you.

— I haven't.

— I don't know why, but I've only got one.

You spot it behind a juniper bush. You certainly didn't put it there, but as you retrieve it and give it to her, you feel guilty. Why? At supper you have no appetite, but when Ursula, trading places with Helga, comes to sit opposite you, your appetite revives. Why? It's been a strange evening. All you want to do is drink a glass of quince liqueur and go to bed: At quarter past ten you do. Sleep comes instantly.

In the morning you awoke early. You were tempted to go down and talk to Helga, but you stayed in bed. And then you began thinking.

A gentle breeze or a great storm?

Concord, submission, reverence and love:
His kisses are none of the above. What then?
Artfully, his kisses take me to where I know
Not who I am. He,
Graceful and savage, makes me
Ecstatic, in a space of pure letting-go.

Onward and onward,
Falcon on the wing, onward.

Perhaps
Everything
Repeats:
Sex constantly repeats the first time.
Perhaps
Everything, to be itself, must
Combine with its opposite:
The beginning with the consummation.

Impossible aspiration,
Vexing question: Am I only
Everything I am not?

Sex is not love: You know that. And yet, beyond the rawness and sensation, you feel a premonition of loss, abandonment and renunciation. In other words, love. Was it to ward it off that you resorted to philosophy, where sex reigns supreme?

3 - Kerkyra, the House of Assignation

On the motorcycle of silver and smoke, to the full-throated song of its fiery pipes, you ride the coastal road down to Kerkyra. As you recall your confusion of three days ago, you feel happy to be free of it—you're weightless, anonymous, invisible! As you reflect on your father's lunch-time foolery, you hear laughter ringing in your helmet—you're his daughter and that's all there is to it! Now you positively love the R90S, you'd love to learn to ride it. You'll never ask Jürgen to teach you, though, for you've decided your relationship must consist in sex alone. As your hands meet around his waist, you feel at one with him; as you approach Kerkyra, your cup fills to the brim.

Again, as soon as Jürgen pushes open the street door, you enter a world of half light, cool and calm; again, you walk up the six flights of stairs beside him, hand-in-hand. In the dim front room you notice the ottoman and its armchair; you notice Luca Giordano's oil study, *The Rape of Persephone*. While Jürgen's in the bathroom, you run your hand across the buttoned-back silk damask of the boudoir chair, sit down on it and take off your boots. When he's done you take your turn, then head for the wardrobe while he waits on the bed. Minutes later, you emerge from behind the screen.

Staggered, the stripes of your cropped black-and-white tank top echo the stripes of your open-ended tube socks; the rest of your body is bare. Your hair, pulled back into a ponytail and fastened in a loop with the ends sticking out, says you're ready for action. Half-naked on the bed, Jürgen stares wide-eyed; his pulse quickens, his lips part, his dark beauty becomes luminous. You step into the middle of the room and do a diver's stretch: Keeping your feet close together, you raise yourself up on your toes as high as you can and hold it. In the filtered light your body is a distillation of desire; in your tank top and tube socks you are nudity inspired. You ease yourself down then repeat the movement, your body a sigh of singularity as your quickened senses vie with your longing for annihilation.

Undoing your ponytail, you shake loose your hair then lie face down on the carpet. Jürgen moves closer to the foot of the bed. You raise your legs from the knees, reach back and hold both ankles; you breathe in deeply and, as you breathe out, raise your head and upper body at the same time as your thighs. You engage Jürgen's regard and don't let it go, the fiery amber of your eyes enflaming the smouldering coals of his. With every breath you pull your body into a tighter crescent; with every stretch you feel it preparing for what's to come. Letting go your hold, you roll over onto your back, stretch your legs out and rest your hands—palms up—at your sides. Eyes closed, you wait.

It comes, his touch; starting at your instep, it skips over your open-ended sock, glides along the curve of your calf, whispers up your thigh, floats along your abdomen and skims over your breasts.

– I'm going to blindfold you.

Between your legs you feel a twitch of anticipation.

– Okay.

From the silk cravat he's brought from the wardrobe he fashions a blindfold, winds it around your head and knots it at the side.

– Pull your legs up till your knees touch your shoulders.

Effortlessly, you do so. Kneeling astride you, he brings his right leg forward; entering your body, he drives in deep. His swivelling hips find a rhythm; feeling his power, he exploits his freedom: Up and down, from side to side or in a circular motion, he moves inside you, revelling in the flush of pleasure colouring your face. You've given him the keys to the city of your cunt; as he explores its attractions, you savour the sensations: the dreamy indolence of the old town, the Byzantine shimmer of the church mosaics; the lush calm of the Palazzo gardens, the exquisite refinement of the gargoyles. A kiss in the dreamhouse! You've been twitching in expectation of a surprise, and now at last, fulfilling the promise of your blindfold, it comes: No sooner has he withdrawn than his tongue is at your door, lapping up your lust. To the boom-boom of your heartbeat he performs his mouthwork; into a trance he drives you. As your muscles attain a peak of tension, you come in a resonant cry. Look! Moonlit, a sail billows in the marina. You glide away, past the breakwater, past the headland, into the open sea. The sky is a riot of stars, the sea an unfathomable rumour. At one with the heavens and the ocean, you are infinite.

And then it starts again, silvering your nerves, the ripple of desire that demands you drain your reserves: You want to feel him deep inside you, you want your senses to be consumed. Responding to your moans, he drives his ardour into you; deeper and deeper, he drives it in. You babble in a language all your own, your glossolalia starts to crescendo: Your banded eyes are transferring their power to your speech. Hail! A shuddering cry rocks your body as *The Rape of*

Persephone fills your mind's eye. And then into shining blackness you are absorbed. Silence.

You hugged him close on the ride back to Kalami; before you knew it you had already arrived: The R90S proved to be a machine that can not only cover distances quickly, but can also take lovers out of time.

4 - The Kluge house, Kalami

As Jürgen prepares the swordfish for the barbeque, brushing the steaks with a basting of garlic, olive oil and oregano, you lie alone in your room. You like the nuanced blues, corals and golds of your bedspread; you like the pale blue walls and the vase of flowers from the garden. In Neuchâtel, even in winter, your mother would always have flowers in the house. You miss her. What would she think, you wonder, if she knew about Jürgen and the House of Assignation? What would she think of what you do there? Your body is still glowing with pleasure; you're proud to have Jürgen as your lover. You feel like knitting something, but you have neither needles nor yarn. I'll knit my mother a sweater, you decide, for her birthday. Hope the pattern books have something good this season. Caressing your calf, you recall the delicate touch of the tube socks, the warm sensuality of the wool. How would Jürgen react, you wonder, if the next time you only wanted to lie in his arms? Too risky, you decide: He might think you love him. The curves of the wingback chair lose their edge; you flick on a light switch and bring a renewed beauty to the room: From atop its slim pedestal, a drum shade casts a soft glow on a group of ceramic bowls: How could you not think of your mother? Now that you do what she does, will she reject you a second time? Suddenly you are assaulted by an ancient image: You see your mother—head thrown back, lips parted and breasts swaying—and you experience a shock of recognition: For the first time you understand what she was doing, rocking like that over your father. Blood rushes to your face; you feel ashamed. Why? Because it's taken you so long to understand? Because days ago you did exactly what she was doing? Because you've proven to be the fool she must have taken you for? How you admired her, how you lavished your love on her before she left you! You'd hoped to grow up to be as beautiful as she, you'd hoped your body would be like hers, you'd hoped for so much—before she left you. Suddenly you long for Jürgen, you long to be back at the House of Assignation: You long to be filled with him.

Chapter 11

CORFU, GREECE – SUMMER 1973 (4)

A skeleton of leaf, scorched and charred.

Mystery, where the light nests.
Only, ever, always
Mourning, thickening the darkness.
Eclipse,
Negation;
The residue of a life.

Obliterated spoors, husks of needs:
Forgotten.

Serried rows of spectators,
The public burning of a heretic.
Incessant downfall,
Landslip, scree, stones—
Lapidary torture.
Nexus of scarecrows.
Exclusion,
Surcease: No
Spital-house bed, but deliverance.

Awaking in terror from this dream, you find yourself stunned by the contrast between your current vitality and the species of living dead you once were.

1 - Kerkyra, the House of Assignation

On the motorcycle of silver and smoke, to the full-throated song of its fiery pipes, you ride the coastal road down to Kerkyra. You're glad of the telescopic forks at the front of the bike and the twin shocks at the back, for you've secured to the rack a carefully-wrapped box. You haven't told Jürgen what's in it: It will be a surprise. As you lean into a curve, you rejoice in the fact that, even before you get to the House, this sweet sports machine obliges you to harmonize your body with Jürgen's. It also makes it impossible to hold a conversation, further intensifying your physical bond. As your hands meet around Jürgen's waist, you feel at one with him; as you approach Kerkyra, your cup fills to the brim.

Again, as soon as Jürgen pushes open the street door, you enter a world of half light, cool and calm; again, you walk up the six flights of stairs beside him, hand-in-hand. In the dim front room, as you pass the bookcase, you notice a leather-bound volume: *Die Geschichte der O*. What could that be about? you wonder. While Jürgen's in the bathroom, you unwrap the box you've brought, take out the Dansette, and set it up. You then run your hand across the buttoned-back silk damask of the boudoir chair, sit down on it and take off your boots. When he's done you take your turn, then head for the wardrobe while he waits on the bed. This time it takes you longer than usual, but before too long you're ready.

Mock-epic, melodramatic, glistening piano runs and arpeggios fill the room as you sashay out from behind the screen. Intrigued, Jürgen is struck by your bold look: Strong eye-liner, rich red lips and matt make-up give your face a sophisticated, sculptural elegance; slicked-back and pinned into a side bun, your hair—together with the rhinestone rosettes of your clip-on earrings—add a nostalgic, dreamy dimension. Cut from black silk, your dress is a fluid silhouette of gauzy layers, falling in delicate folds to a high-low hem. *She'll come, she'll go:* Over David Bowie's reedy timbre, you overlay the grain of your voice, giving 'Lady Grinning Soul' a double-tracked shimmer. Barefoot, you are a sylph in gossamer, light and supple, honouring in dance the element of air. Ever since April, when *Aladdin Sane* came out, the album has grown on you. 'Lady Grinning Soul', in particular, has entered your blood: You've transposed it to violin, and find it works beautifully on your instrument. Now you're singing it with utter naturalness and conviction. Jürgen is entranced. What is it about the song that moves you so? Is it the way it undercuts its arch-romance by its own excess, double looping the ideal and the real, dream and desire? Is it the way it juxtaposes irony and innocence, sincerity and suspicion? *And when the clothes are strewn, don't be afrai-ai-aid of the room:* Is it that which moves you? The virtue of masquerade, the active assuming of a role over and against the passive assumption of one? Identity is a delusion, authenticity a fiction, and the honour of the artist is to own up to that fact: Is it simply Bowie's example that appeals to you? Does he help you live your life artistically? As saxophone and Spanish guitar bring in new colours, your dancing, at once balletic and jazzy, becomes more expansive. Jürgen is subjugated, completely under your spell; your barefoot prancing has nothing of the passive princess, and everything of a woman assuming her becoming taking control. As you sing the last verse, your voice stirs him more than he realizes; it will only be much later, when he's a middle-aged man remembering his youth, that your voice will come to haunt him. You deliver the final chorus on the cusp of ambiguity, with neither coy parody nor naïve sincerity: *Touch the fullness of her breast, feel the love of her caress; she will be your living end.*

Lying on your side in your black silk dress, Jürgen deep inside you, you glow with satisfaction as you stare into his eyes. The pleasure you've given him pleases you as much as the pleasure you've received, and now as he embarks upon his pursuit of 'one for the road', you simply relax. Kneeling with his right leg over your left, your right leg crossing through the crook of his right arm and his left hand on your breast, he follows through each thrust with a forward push of the pelvis, maximizing penetration. Pulling your dress up, you deliver yourself wholeheartedly to his pleasure. Dark, his beauty hovers over you, a tropical moth over an orchid: Your reverie is scenic, not frankly sexual. All the more surprising, then, that when your orgasm comes it is convulsive.

You hugged him close on the ride back to Kalami; before you knew it you had already arrived: The R90S proved to be a machine that can not only cover distances quickly, but can also take lovers out of time.

2 - The Kluge house, Kalami

As Jürgen prepares the sauce for the sea bass he's about to bake, you water the flowers in the garden. Plumbago, agapanthus and allium; hibiscus, rose and gladiola: the marriage of fire and water, the infinite variety of the universe. As the roses climb their ladder of thorns in the mist of your spray, you recall that day in Poughkeepsie when Catherine said, 'You have beautiful legs. Like your mother'. Your face remembers the blood rush of embarrassment: Beautiful eyes, beautiful hair, a beautiful smile, okay—but beautiful legs? It must be a concern of grown-ups, you thought, it must, like all their secrets, have to do with sex. The taste of your dismay returns to your tongue; you relive your upset at your mother's remark. She had been the one who'd brush your hair to soothe your pain, look into your eyes to ease your apprehension: She had been the one you'd hoped would hold you in her arms again. Her remark had made you wonder whether you too would have to show your legs, lie with a man in bed, in order to enjoy your body. Is a woman's beauty, then, only made for a man's regard? Does it belong to him alone? As hibiscus sways in your spray, you recall your thought then: I loved her once, my mother, I loved her absolutely: I'll never love anyone that way again.

Inside a lupine rosette, a snowflake.
Saxifrage spreads a cloth of gold,
Orchids defy ice.

Look! Lichen-freckled boulders shelter fossils.
And now a new solitude overcomes you:
Trauma freezes time,
Irradiating absence with unknowing;
Only desire moves, refusing to concede
Never can two be one.

'There is no true love except in the aptitude of a subject to return to childhood': Only later would you learn this; now, struggling to leave childhood behind, you feel the weight of the grown-up world.

3 - Kerkyra, the House of Assignation

On the motorcycle of silver and smoke, to the full-throated song of its fiery pipes, you ride the coastal road down to Kerkyra. You love the way the cant of the road, the sharpness of the curve, the state of the traffic—everything, including the weather and the road surface—oblige the rider to be ever-alert; you love the care the machine requires and the rewards it gives in return. As your hands meet around Jürgen's waist, you feel at one with him; as you approach Kerkyra, your cup fills to the brim.

Again, as soon as Jürgen pushes open the street door, you enter a world of half light, cool and calm; again, you walk up the six flights of stairs beside him, hand-in-hand. As you pass through the dim front room, you admire the ingenuity of the basketweave parquet as it unfolds its geometry before you; you admire the beauty of the soft gold rug with its pale olive border. While Jürgen's in the bathroom, you run your hand across the buttoned-back silk damask of the boudoir chair, sit down on it and take off your boots. When he's done you take your turn, then head for the wardrobe while he waits on the bed. Minutes later, you emerge from behind the screen.

Radiant, in the luminous black of your cocktail dress, a camera dangling from your hand, you step forward. As you head for the sea-view window, the combination of slashed bodice and frou-frou skirt strikes a match in Jürgen. Every detail of the dress, from the frill on the capped sleeves to the satin ribbon that trims the tulle, speaks of a knowing craftsman; every movement of your body, from the swivel of your hips to the flicking back of a stray lock, speaks of an unspeakable girl. Carefree in your bare feet and ruffled hair, you inhabit the dress as a second skin, not a costume. Whence such naturalness? Jürgen wonders. How is it that the candour of your face belies any artifice even as your red lips dramatize your look? You throw open the shutters and frame the descent of the fortress to the sea. Opening the lens to blur the background, you focus on the leaves of a eucalyptus, hoping the peachy mauve of sky and mountain will make an effective ground for your green abstraction. You've borrowed Ulla's camera, and now you turn the lens of the sister on the brother. As the daylight moulds his cheekbones, you frame his beauty in your viewfinder. Click-click-click: Firing off one shot after another, you try to capture the aura of this man. What is it about him, you ask yourself, that touches you so deeply? Moving around the bed, changing angle and distance, from wherever you look you come up with the same answer: his aura of danger, his sexuality. Unable to resist any longer, you leave the camera on a night stand and leap onto the bed.

Does Jürgen feel responsible for you? That he is your deflowerer (for that, you decide, is how you see it), that he is so much more experienced than you, does that account for his willingness to let you use his body as you will? He's ravished you with his animality, he's ravished you the way you wanted him to, and now as you lie on your back, legs flexed and wide apart, you use your pelvic muscles to determine just how much of him you want to feel inside you, and where, as he kneels before you, leaning back. When you push your butt into the bed, his cock strokes your clit; when you thrust upward and pull yourself forward, you take him deeper inside you. All the while, he remains still: It is you who are in control. You don't know what you like more, using him or being used by him. Either way, you decide, you like it better than the simultaneous pursuit by each of their own orgasm. When yours comes, it amazes you: Over and over this afternoon your body has rewarded you, and now it finds still another way to do so. As you lie there on the floor, caressed by the sea breeze, you swear to yourself you'll never fall in love with Jürgen, even as he kisses you and laps up the tears that roll down your cheeks.

You hugged him close on the ride back to Kalami; before you knew it you had already arrived: The R90S proved to be a machine that can not only cover distances quickly, but can also take lovers out of time.

4 - The Kluge house, Kalami

As Jürgen prepares a dinner of hake and spinach with lemon-egg sauce, you sit in the lounge, listening to Rudi and Veronika talk about their four-day trip to Lefkada. You run your finger along the rosewood inlay of your caned mahogany chair; you find the texture pleasing. For a moment, in the House of Assignation, you felt eminently feminine; now, as you observe Helga, Veronika, Pascale and Ulla, you wonder why that feeling is so evanescent. Do they know better than you how to be a woman? Pascale, you find, pulls it off best. Your attention to the conversation picks up when you hear Rudi and Veronika speak of a windy beach in Lefkada and the brand new sport they tried there: kite surfing. 'I'd like to try that', you think, 'but I won't if I have to sacrifice a day with Jürgen'. You recall what he had told you: That he loves making love with you precisely because he knows the experience can never be repeated: You'll grow older, and then nothing of this can recur. With all the girls he's known, he said, sex quickly becomes repetitive, whereas with you, because you're so open and intelligent, it remains playful and creative. And then he added: 'You're a girl who won't be one much longer. Soon you'll be a woman, and then you'll become like all the others'. That very instant you vowed to yourself you wouldn't, convinced that in the feminine there is always something open-ended. (Hadn't you proven there is always a way out? Was that not a lesson of your miraculous emergence from anorexia?) Yes, you will remain free because in the feminine there is always something unformed. You told him that. He replied, 'That's a dream. That's a dream within a dream'. You didn't know what he meant, but you liked the formulation. Is that why, when he kissed you, you nipped his lip and tripped him onto the bed before letting him spank you?

Chapter 12

CORFU, GREECE – SUMMER 1973 (5)

Pathways of desire elude sextant,
Abacus, gnomon, and compass;
Unencumbered,
Skeins of nerves
Earth the aerial.

Will my body, you wonder, ever stop amazing me?

1 - Kerkyra, the House of Assignation

On the motorcycle of silver and smoke, to the full-throated song of its fiery pipes, you ride the coastal road down to Kerkyra. Jürgen gives the wave to an oncoming rider and receives one in return. You like this culture of camaraderie, you like this sense of individuals sharing a common fate. As your hands meet around Jürgen's waist, you feel at one with him; as you approach Kerkyra, your cup fills to the brim.

Again, as soon as Jürgen pushes open the street door, you enter a world of half light, cool and calm; again, you walk up the six flights of stairs beside him, hand-in-hand. As you pass through the dim front room, you admire the elegance of the easy chair and the finesse of the serpentine sideboard. While Jürgen's in the bathroom, you run your hand across the buttoned-back silk damask of the boudoir chair, sit down on it and take off your boots. When he's done you take your turn, then head for the wardrobe while he waits on the bed. Minutes later, you emerge from behind the screen.

Naked, you step forward, naked but for three adornments: a black-leather, open-cup bra with guinea-feather tassels covering your nipples; long, fingerless snakeskin gloves, and a cache-sexe of red fox fur. Soft, soft, under the thrust of your bare feet the rug becomes a forest floor; svelte, svelte, lithe and flowing, you walk like a panther. Facing Jürgen, sitting half-naked at the foot of the bed, you conjure a balloon from your hand. Long and blue it emerges from your mouth; with deft fingers you tie it off. A strip of plastic, insubstantial, appears in your palm; unfurled, it becomes a circular band. Flexing your knees, you pass the band between your thighs and draw it vigorously back and forth over the sleekness of your cache-sexe. That done, you start doing the same with the balloon, curving it to maximize friction with the fox fur. Silvering his nerves, wires trip up Jürgen's spine as he watches you rocking on the balls of your feet, your legs bent and wide apart, your instep an extravagant arch. Your movements are frankly obscene but your feline grace is classy; your posture is indecent but your expression, dignified. You stop rocking. Holding the balloon in one hand, with the other you take the plastic band and release it over the balloon: Caught in a sunbeam, a ring of light shimmers; guiding it with airy blue, you leave it to hover over your bed, a halo for your guardian angel.

When you made love, you found, as always, something new: As you stood facing each other, Jürgen ran his fingers through your fox fur and began rubbing rhythmically. Casting off your cache-sex, you jumped up and wrapped your legs around his waist. As he sought to penetrate you, the flicking of your teasing tongues mirrored the wriggling of your bottoms. At last you took him in. Tickling your nipples, suddenly more sensitive, the guinea feather tassels began to make you squirm. As Jürgen held your butt, you slowly fell into a handstand, your backwards motion coming to a halt when your palms reached the floor. Firmly in his hands, your ass was his to hold as he began to work his magic between your legs. Snake, fox and guinea fowl spiced the vigour of blood in your veins, and when you came, feather, fur and leather took your breath away: The bearer of the life-spark, luxuriously animal, bore you to ethereal realms.

You hugged him close on the ride back to Kalami; before you knew it you had already arrived: The R90S proved to be a machine that can not only cover distances quickly, but can also take lovers out of time.

2 - The Kluge house, Kalami

A sky of gauze makes rocks ghostly, cypresses blacken as they slope down to the sea: As Jürgen makes the sauce for the marinated chicken, mixing garlic and cucumber, coriander and mint, into the yogurt, you lie back in your lounger and watch the last rays of the sun make a mirage of the Albanian mountains. To your right, sitting in adjacent chairs, Axel and Ulla hold hands; to your left, Rudi and Veronika snuggle up together in one chaise longue. You like the fact that you don't go in for that; you're happy that you and Jürgen have elaborated your own way of being: You make love for pleasure, they to prove their love is real. You wouldn't change your state for theirs.

An early owl draws out its whistle; on the terrace a gecko crawls. Pelt, plumes, the serpent's skin; body and mind, adult and child, the double mediating: Was it the living vibrancy of your fox fur that showed you, all afternoon long, your animal other, clear in the mirror of Jürgen's eyes? Was it your snakeskin gloves that enabled you to find a balance between instinct and reason, nature and spirit? And was it your guinea-fowl feathers that freed you from gravity, giving you the lightness to do what you did? Look! The gecko's moving into the light, its throat's translucent. Snatch! Darting out its tongue, it catches a moth. And what if love is but a sedative, a way to tame desire? Looking at the lovers around you, you reproach yourself for feeling, not superior, but just a little smug.

That night you had a strange dream.

> Innocence, purity and secrecy,
> Nostalgia for the odour of chastity:
> The pearl coming to birth in the oyster
> Entangles the spirit in the flesh. Hark!
> Reverberation of the bell—
> Visitation of the plague,
> Awful, sublime, precious—
> Leeched, my blood becomes flowers and metals.

Losing something, something you cannot measure, you find yourself on the verge of grasping something not grasped before.

3 - Kerkyra, the House of Assignation

On the motorcycle of silver and smoke, to the full-throated song of its fiery pipes, you ride the coastal road down to Kerkyra. The adrenalin rush is just as strong as it was on the first day; you still delight in this intoxicating mix of individuality and anonymity. As your hands meet around Jürgen's waist, you feel at one with him; as you approach Kerkyra, your cup fills to the brim.

Again, as soon as Jürgen pushes open the street door, you enter a world of half light, cool and calm; again, you walk up the six flights of stairs beside him, hand-in-hand. As you pass through the dim front room, you smile at a Murano-glass harlequin in a recessed niche.

In the bedroom you ask Jürgen to carry the cheval glass to the middle of the room; you have him place it opposite the sea-view window. While he's in the bathroom you set up the Dansette. You then run your hand across the buttoned-back silk damask of the boudoir chair, sit down on it and take off your boots. When Jürgen's done in the bathroom you take your turn, then head for the wardrobe while he waits on the bed. Minutes later, you emerge from behind the screen.

The emerald spandex of your swimsuit gleaming, you step forward, a sleek machine of toned muscle. Your hair, slicked back and pinned into a bun, sports a glittery clasp; under your arm you're carrying a roll of blue. There's both candour and calculation in your smile as you unroll your roll of blue—an exercise mat—in front of the mirror.

– This is a swimming pool. I'm a synchronized swimmer. My partner (you indicate the glass) is Psyche.

You turn on the record player and drop the needle into the groove. As piano chords sound against a sax hush, you do your poolside deckwork, striking a different pose for each chord struck. At the entrance of drums and bass, you cartwheel into a handstand, diving into the pool. 'Still don't know what I was waiting for': In perfect synchronization with Psyche, over the next three and a half minutes you perform a water ballet to the shifting rhythms of David Bowie's 'Changes'. You cannot scull on your hands, but your legs transpose water-based movements to land with amazing fidelity. Barracuda, aurora, manta ray; flamingo, butterfly, porpoise: Vertical on your hands or horizontal on the floor, you find convincing equivalents to the figures and execute them with flair. Splits and arches, twists and extensions, flow smoothly one into another; front pike and back tuck, bent knee and straight thrust, compose an arresting choreography. 'Turn and face the strange ch-ch-changes'*:* Driving against the walking bass, you turn an eggbeater kick into an aquabob and somersault into a handstand; crossing the bridge of 'strange fascination', you tuck, pike and straddle into a dynamic V-up. Jürgen on the bed is blown away, as excited by your graceful ease as he is estranged by Psyche's intimacy: Your duet is perfect. While Bowie plays the saxophone coda, you peel off your bathing suit, stretch out and float in the blue of the pool.

On the exercise mat, facing the mirror, you made love for longer than ever before; watching yourself-as-another, you doubled your pleasure as the alienated other deepened the intensity of your self-return. To end, you lay on your stomach, facing the mirror, while Jürgen lay on top of you, his legs outside yours, his arms braced on the floor. You watched yourself watching yourself as his body heaved forward and drove straight down, expanding your selfhood. As he rocked back and forth, you fixed your eyes in the mirror and thought: More real than I alone is this union, and yet unbridgeable is the gulf between us. As that realization hit home, your blood and breath prepared you for annihilation. The oneness of destruction and creation, the totality of all archetypes: With a fascination equivalent to the contemplation of a tiger, you watched yourself coming until shining realms overwhelmed you.

You hugged him close on the ride back to Kalami; before you knew it you had already arrived: The R90S proved to be a machine that can not only cover distances quickly, but can also take lovers out of time.

4 - The Kluge house, Kalami

While you prepare the pie filling, Jürgen chops the scallions for the potato and feta salad; while you sauté the onions for the courgette rissoles, Jürgen shapes the meatballs in his hands: Knowing you will not return to the House of Assignation, you now delight in being with each other at every opportunity. Indeed, during your last three days in Corfu, you two were inseparable. When not in the kitchen you went on walks, Jürgen telling you about the mating habits of the blue-throated lizard or the lifestyle of the violet carpenter bee, creatures you'd spotted. Once, when your eyes were dazzled by a blanket of blue mist, he showed you it was sea holly, a whole colony whose thistle-like leaves had changed from green to blue. Another time, when you came across a field of chasteberry, he told you the legend that it cools the heat of lust, that women would use it as bedding during the festival for Demeter and Persephone. And thus began his giving you an education in Greek mythology, and thus began your passion for Persephone. You would go on to read Hesiod's *Theogony,* you would go on to read the 'Hymn to Demeter' in *The Homeric Hymns*. What was it about that homeless girl, fated to ferry between two worlds, that appealed to you so? Was it her being an abandoned child, ravished and left on the cusp of girlhood, forever ambivalent toward her mother? Was it her descent into a secret world, her encounters on the boundary crossing? Or was it simply her blending of sexuality and play? Whatever it was, she provided you with a mirror to reflect on yourself. Is that why you consider Persephone your sister?

***

Shortly after returning to West Berlin, Jürgen met the woman he would marry (a woman of Turkish origin, disowned by her family). He surprised everyone (but not you) by becoming a devoted husband and father. Three years ago he opened his own restaurant. He called it 'Kerkyra'. It's doing well. Once in a while you see each other. You talk about food, you exchange recipes. You talk about plants, you exchange bulbs. You never talk about Corfu. Never. You have strong feelings for him. You accept those feelings now. You recognize them as love. Whether you're with him or not, they're always in your heart, there, in the half-light, cool and calm.

Intermezzo 7: Ximena

Marietta, I'm sitting at a table in an all-night bar, soothed by the mint-green walls and cool Atlantic breeze. In a corner, two prostitutes are playing chess. The one with a sparkle in her eyes is losing to the one with a sultry languour. Opposite me sits Ximena. We're drinking a dark, brooding Oloroso. More than the nudity of her shoulders, I like her centre-parted hair that leaves her forehead bare; more than the ripeness of her lips, I like her full-throated laughter. She's studying Maritime Archeology and the History of Seafaring at the University of Cádiz. Wants to work in cultural heritage management. She's from Montevideo. Her grand-parents fled Italy in 1943, just before the Nazis raided the Jewish ghetto in Rome after the Italian capitulation. It was inevitable we'd meet: Not only did she recognize me, she'd just bought, at an all-night bookshop, a bilingual edition of *Holograms of Happenstance* (a collection of my haiku, with watercolours by Liselotte). I'd come here because sleep wouldn't come; it wasn't long before my mind became a magic lantern, turning up memories of you. I'd just finished writing up the third one when Ximena approached me.

After I'd signed *Holograms—To Ximena, from a man who still dreams of ocean voyages under the stars, of Pedro de Sintra, Bartolomeu Dias and Vasco de Gama*—she told me of her life in Montevideo (sitting on her patio reading Baudelaire, the scent of wisteria no match for the perfume of *Les Fleurs du mal).* I then asked her to read me something from the second book she'd bought, *El rosario de Eros* by Delmira Agustini. I remember only an image of a marble statue with a head of fire, and I remember the poet's story: Divorced one month after her wedding, she declared, 'Marriage is a vulgarity'. Then, shifting from wife to lover, she began seeing her husband in a bordello. Before killing himself, the bastard shot her dead. In the onyx of Ximena's eyes the murder still smouldered, their watery black took on a fiery glow.

Ximena then asked what I'd been writing; I passed her my notebook. She read the first entry:

> Sitting sideways in your reading chair, your legs slung over the armrest, you hold the phone to your cheek and explain to Pascale how to make that lasagna dish you served at dinner on Sunday. Stretched out on the sofa, I lay *To the Wedding* down and watch you, moved. Moved by this

> fleeting moment, moved by the innocence of your beauty in the light of the etched-glass lamp. Outside the living room, the streetlights conspire with the twilight to persuade me I'm dreaming. After all these years, Marietta, they've finally succeeded: Suspended in that moment now, I am a floating feather—one puff and you'd blow me away.

– I see, Sprague, that for you marriage is not a vulgarity.

– No, Ximena, it's not.

– May I read another one?

– Yes.

She then read the second entry:

> 'Puma' in glitter sparkling on your chest, your breasts flattened by a sports bra, you stand at the bar separating dining room from kitchen and drink from a bottle of Heineken. A thin film of sweat brings a glow to your skin and sticks a strand of hair to your cheek. Once again I am overcome by your virile femininity, once again my bowl brims over with your beauty. The sunlight conspires with the blinds to persuade me I'm just a pilgrim who's walked a mile too many. Was it just an hallucination, then, when I stepped up behind you and kissed the hollow behind your ear? Sunlight and blind proclaim their victory as I hover in that moment: A flick of your finger would suffice, Marietta, to knock me down now.

– Are you still together?

– No.

– May I read one more?

– Okay.

She then read the third entry:

> Under the skylight, as snow whirls outside, you stand in your bodysuit and stay-ups, ironing your shirt. A beep announces an email. You sip your coffee as you read it: Again the headhunter—he just won't stay away. In half an hour your taxi will be here. You finish ironing the shirt then

> slip it on; you step into your skirt and zip it closed. Your headband holding back your hair, before the mirror you put on your make-up. And then, giving your hair a final brushing, you decide to pin it up after all. Along the perimeter of the mirror, as you gather your hair in your hands, the tube of continuous light conspires with the amber of your eyes to persuade me I'm still a sleeper. When you twirled your hair and stuck in the stick, was that pang in my heart just my imagination? I succumb to the amber of your eyes, I surrender to the continuous light: A bat of your eyelids now, Marietta, would obliterate me.

– Such lightness! Did things get heavy, in the end?

– No. 'What is good is light; everything divine runs on delicate feet.' Marietta is divine.

Outside the café we walked some way together; then, there where her centre-parted hair leaves her forehead bare, I kissed Ximena goodbye.

Into sandstone walls as I walk the streets, daybreak mixes gold dust and magenta. At the market, a woman fetches buckets of roses from a van, men unload a fish truck. The day summons me to renew my senses, the day commands me to refresh my soul. I will go for a *café solo* and *ensaimada,* I will return to my hotel for a shower and a shave. Then I'll walk past the fortress, I'll walk past the beach, I'll walk along the shore to where the wild grass grows. There, before structuring my compulsion to recall, I'll lie down and give free rein to my reverie. If I become regretful, remind me you are not a bird that flew; if I get sentimental, give me another turn of the screw: Marietta, hear me now, that I may honour you!

Chapter 13

Old port and orange blossom, grilled almond and oak: On my tongue the cognac distills your personality.

– Do you believe in God?

– No.

– Good. I couldn't go out with a man who did. Ashes to ashes, that's about where I stand on it all.

Amaranth, tumbleweed, love-lies-bleeding, into whirling dust from out of his dream the startled dreamer steps; ragged and dirty are his raven locks, torn and frayed his cloak, yet look, look, look how he walks in splendour!

– What did you want to be when you were a boy?

– A *plaasjaapie*.

– What's that?

– A country bumpkin. Milking the cows and planting corn. Taking the turkeys to market in a wheelbarrow. And you?

– When I was a boy...

You give me your sly smile.

– ...I wanted to be a detective. A spy!

– Did you have a trench coat?

– Of course. And a telescope.

– A telescope?

– Yes. To see without being seen. It's very useful.

Bakery spices and crème brulée, gingerbread and cigar box: Does the cognac on your tongue distill my personality?

– If you were a detective, Sprague, what would you make of Aravane?

– What do you mean?

– What would you say she's got that's... special?

– How could I know, Marietta? I've never even met her.

– Yes, but you could guess.

– On what basis?

– Her record collection, her books, her apartment. And her photo, of course. Above all, her photo!

– I'd have to meet her.

— Come on, just for fun!

I sip my cognac.

— Well, I love her taste in jazz. Monk, Miles, Mingus. Julius Hemphill and Helen Merrill. That's already very special.

— That's not what I'm getting at!

— Then what are you getting at?

— Oh Sprague, can't you see?

You jump out of bed and fetch Aravane's photo.

— Look!

Draped in a negligée of darkness, Aravane and the cat emerge from out of the depths of their tenebrosity to confront the photographer's stare: Their mystery defies illumination.

— What do you see?

— Hmmm...

— Well?

— She's got a noble kind of beauty. Probably comes from a long line of handsome fathers. There's a sadness within her, but she's graceful in bearing it. Her humour is certainly black. She's courageous, she's lucid, but her dreams are boundless. I'm sure she reads Tarot cards with great finesse. She doesn't follow fashion; she evolves her own style. And—it's clear—the phrase 'carnal knowledge' retrieves all its depth and resonance in her.

— So you do see it! I was beginning to doubt your perspicacity.

— It's hard to miss. In another life she may have been a sacred prostitute.

— In the temple of Ishtar?

— Yes. The oneness of the living in the wholeness of being. She touches both extremes.

— Imagine you were an Assyrian then, how she'd send you!

— I don't need to. I've got you.

— There's nothing religious about me, Sprague.

— True. But you bind me, you send me back to the alphabet. That's religion. Your eyes shine, and I see mine in them. As you sip your cognac, dragons' heads free themselves from the abstract ornament circling the inkwell: The console shimmers with their breathing.

Earth, sky, underworld:
Through the realms she weaves me,
My plumed serpent

— Marietta, you were going to tell me about a girl called Inès.

— Yes. But first, I'm going to tell you about Marco.

And thus you came to tell me of a boy in Neuchâtel, about how you loved him, about his death on a motorcycle. How shall I tell the story, Marietta, how shall I tell the tale? Why, with simplicity and humility, in a voice quiet and steady.

Neuchâtel and Rome, 1973-74

You liked his dark, tousled hair, looking windswept no matter what the weather; you liked the squint that would betray his pleasure when he'd try to hide it by suppressing a smile. And you liked the hand between the open legs, pulling up the chair when he'd sit down. You were in your first year of *maturité gymnasiale* and your last year of schooling in Neuchâtel. He was a year ahead of you. He'd come from Rome. He didn't have to follow his father (who'd come to do a year of micro-technology research), but he chose to do so: He'd gotten heavily into drugs, and decided he needed to go somewhere quiet to get clean. Neuchâtel fit the bill.

It happened, the *coup de foudre,* soon after you'd left Corfu. You saw him outside the lycée, dismounting his motorcycle, taking off his helmet, shaking out his hair. The closer you got the clearer it became that he was the one, the one with whom you'd fall in love. When he didn't try to hide his vulnerability as you caught his eye, you felt a tenderness for him. When he shook your hand as you said hello, you felt a strange sensation: It's obvious, we are meant for each other. Everything felt right—that he'd spoken to you in Italian, that he'd given you a look of recognition, even that, before dropping it, he'd twirled in his fingers the stray leaf he'd plucked from your hair. As you listened to your rhyming steps while you strode upon the pavement, it seemed as if everything in your life had been leading up to that moment, and as you arranged to meet for lunch, choosing a tree to meet under, it seemed as if your very names confirmed you were destined for each other.

He told you about his addiction and his determination to free himself from it. Once, when he was really suffering, you took him to your doctor in Geneva (the one who'd put you on the pill). She referred him to a specialist. Thanks to your love, Marco pulled through and never relapsed.

Your relationship wasn't easy. There was a period when you preferred loving to being loved, while he—unable to reconcile love and sex—redoubled his love. You didn't like that. Nor did you like feeling obliged, sometimes, to fake sexual satisfaction. You hated feeling phony, but you told yourself you're doing it because it would lead to a solution. He also found you too independent for his liking. Once, when you fought, it came to blows, and you floored him with a karate kick. Still, you'd only have to look into his eyes to know you loved him. The one time you went away for the weekend without him, the moment you were on the train you missed him. He had a way of making every day unique. You also found it reassuring that he would always stand up to you in an argument (despite that karate kick).

It was in Rome that your pleasure in each other reached a new peak. You'd stay in the family house, among the cypresses and umbrella pines on Via Dandolo in the Trastevere district (since Marco had succeeded in getting clean, his family allowed him everything). In the evening, before going out, you'd be in the kitchen, learning how to cook *saltimbocca alla Romana* or make the most delicious *carbonara* sauce. (You were all the more welcome as you were seen as Marco's saviour.) You'd go busking—Marco had taught you to play guitar—and to avoid catcalls, you'd go disguised as a boy. You loved that! You also loved going skateboarding, competing to see who could do the most daring figures. And, Marco being an excellent coach and partner, you took up tennis with a passion.

When you returned to Neuchâtel your love-making suddenly got better. In that domain, as in the rest, you both felt you were growing. As if in consequence, your love deepened. In a sign of your growing complicity, Marco began calling you his *'fragolina'*, because you so loved strawberries, while you, in recognition of his insatiable appetite for sherbet, began calling him your *'sorbettino'*. You'd still fight, once in a while, and after you'd made up he would call you *'streghetta mia'*, his little witch, while you would call him *'tigrotto'*, little tiger. So it was with enthusiasm that you began thinking about how you could be together in Paris, where, starting in September, you'd be for your studies.

Then, one Sunday morning while Marco was riding towards Ballaigues on the Lignerolle road, a car came to a stop at the intersection near La Maladaire. As the car began turning left into the road, it cut off Marco's passage. The motorcycle struck the car, Marco was thrown off the bike and landed on the road. He died instantly. The car driver suffered shock but no injury. The police determined that both he and the motorcycle rider had obeyed all the rules of the road.

In the afternoon a taxi pulled up at your door. You opened the door to the ashen face of Marco's father. He embraced you and then said, 'Marco's dead'. You went numb. He explained how it happened, then embraced you again and said, 'Marco was never happier than when he was with you'. He then left to fly back to Rome.

You collapsed onto the sofa. Pascale and your father, each in turn, took you in their arms. You couldn't cry. You got up. You had to move. You went into the garden. You could no longer see clearly. You tried in vain to dry your eyes. You went up to your room. You couldn't enter it: Just hours ago Marco was inside. You sat on the stairs wanting to scream. You couldn't get a sound out of your throat. In the bathroom you drank directly from the tap: You feared what you might do with a glass, were you to hold one in your hand. You didn't dare look in the mirror. You decided to go for a walk. You put on your shoes. You no longer wanted to go for a walk. You asked for a glass of wine. Is this a nightmare? When will I wake up? The wine offered no answers. You went upstairs to your room. This time you entered it and locked the door behind you. You collapsed into your chair and stared at the bed. He appeared, sitting crossed-legged, stripped to the waist. On your tongue you could taste the salt of his skin, his dark skin whose scent of hot stone and wet linen, pine needles and green melon, moved you so. 'Hold me', you said to him. He just smiled at you, with that shy smile that would bring forth all your tenderness. 'Hold me', you said again. As he reached out, his stark beauty turned bleak; he floated, then faded away. 'Now that you found yourself losing your mind, are you here again?': Through your tears you saw his guitar, propped up against the wall. You heard the chords, the loping rhythm; you heard him singing 'I Believe in You'. He'd taught you that Neil Young song just before he left to go to Vallorbe station. You realized with a shudder that he'd never come back. Your breathing faltered; you fell to the floor and let your tears flow. And then your world turned white.

Chapter 14

When you surprised yourself in the mirror, when you became a stranger to yourself, who was the who you dreamt yourself to be?

– *Mirror, mirror, tell no lies, how do I look in Rodin's eyes?*

– *On cream-coloured drawing paper, in black lead and blending stump, you lie on your back with your legs apart. One hand is reaching up from under your buttocks, the other is rounding your raised thigh: Each is intent on satisfying your insatiable sex. Look! The line springs and swells as abandonment floods your body and your head fades away: Intimately feeling what the eye sees, the hand of the artist flows unconstrained…*

Disembodied, then warm and husky, your voice returns from beyond the looking glass:

– How do my teeth look?

Pulling a face, you show them to me.

– Ship-shape.

– You sure?

– Yes.

– Good. 'Cause in the mirror they looked like tombstones.

– There's nothing wrong with your teeth.

You cup your breasts in your hands.

– And these?

– Delectable.

– You know, when I first started taking the pill they suddenly became bigger. That was a pain in the ass! I had to adapt my whole personality around them.

You sip your cognac.

– Yesterday, Sprague, in the elevator at BHV, there was a man ogling me in the mirror. I sneezed, and these two huge balloons of snot came bubbling out of my nostrils. Not just one, but two! I gave him such a look, standing like that, you should have seen his face. That was sweet revenge!

Sly is your smile at you lower your head; I lick your vengeance off your lips. You finish your cognac and put the glass down.

– Now I'm going to tell you about Inès.

And thus you came to tell me of a time that glows in your memory, a time of love and labour, of exploration and intimacy. How can I give a sense of two personalities in their prime? Why, by opening myself to grace, and putting myself in your place.

1976-77

'No! Life has not disappointed me! On the contrary, I find it truer, more desirable and mysterious every year, ever since I was freed by the great liberator: The idea that life could be an experiment for the knowledge-seeker—and not a duty, not a calamity, not trickery': She approached you as you sat on the lawn in the Parc des Sceaux, reading *The Gay Science*.

– May I sit down?

– Yes, all right.

– You know my name?

– Of course. You're Inès.

– And you're Marietta.

– Yes.

– I just wanted to tell you that you thrill me to no end.

– Oh really? Why?

– Because you're the only person in class who speaks of Nietzsche in the spirit of Nietzsche.

You stared into her brown eyes, brightened less by the feeble sun than by a light within, and held her gaze before breaking into a smile.

– No, you're wrong. There's at least one other. You.

And thus it was, thanks to your beloved Nietzsche, that you met she who would become your lover for the next eighteen months. Ever since Marco's death you'd ceded to no suitor; you'd not only remained celibate, but had decided you'd never fall in love again. What was it about Inès that overcame your resistance? Was it the supple ease of her movements and the aristocratic poise of her bearing? Was it her exotic beauty, that felicitous blend of wandering Jew and troubadour, of Alsatian and Occitan? Or was it simply that you'd recognized, in the formatted world of Lycée Lakanal, a fellow free-thinker? Someone who, like you, could thrive under the rigours of this boot camp for the scientific élite yet still develop their individuality? Her body had a presence that spoke to you: You liked the open prairie of her eyes, the serenity of their wide horizons; you liked the hint of ferocity in her self-possession, the furtive wilderness in her sophistication. In her black hair the breeze brought out the russet, stirring your attraction to ambiguity; in her dangling earrings the daylight brought out the electricity, evoking the wonders of twilight. As she spoke of Genoa, where Nietzsche wrote *The Gay Science*, you knew you'd become lovers when you caught yourself watching the way she wrapped her lips around her vowels, and when you detected a slight lisp as she tongued her sibilants, you knew you would come to love her. While speaking of Salita delle Battistine, Nietzsche's favourite residence in the city, she lay her hand on your leg; when you got up to go back to class, it would already have seemed natural for you to hold hands as you crossed the park: That had to wait till the Toussaint holiday, when, in the city of Christopher Columbus, you kissed and held hands in the secluded gardens of Villa Durazzo-Pallavicini.

School was a grind, a force-fed regimen of sterile technicity—the game of competitive exams—rather than the kind of learning that stimulated you. But you'd never been one to let school stand in the way of your education, and since you could do in an hour or two what others would need four to accomplish, you had time to restore the conceptual richness and historical perspective that had been drained from the programme in order to facilitate cramming.

Inès had a studio in Sceaux, close to the lycée; you'd often stay over at her place, for your studio was across the park, in Châtenay-Malabry. Weekends you'd often spend in Paris. You'd stay at her mother's residence on rue de Varenne, a huge apartment overlooking the garden of the Musée Rodin. Her father, who'd left the apartment to Inès's mother when they divorced, had served as French Ambassador in Tokyo. When you would visit Tokyo that summer, Inès was the ideal guide. Her mother was curator of objets d'art at the Louvre; you enjoyed your conversations with her, especially since, besides objets d'art, she was an expert in Egyptian antiquities. Inès had one sibling, a much older brother who disapproved, as he said, of his sister's lifestyle. You'd never been confronted with such bigotry before; it simply left you cold. Fortunately, he only visited once when you were there.

You made the most of your leisure, for schoolwork consumed most of your time: The competitive-exam game focused not on absolute learning, but on relative ranking, and this on a national scale. Thus, you still recall with pleasure the clubs you went to where Inès donned the vestments of Garbo's Queen Christina while you, as Bowie's Thin White Duke, were the incarnation of cool. Or the two of you, in black capes and manly hats (a nod to Djuna Barnes and Thelma Wood), walking hand-in-hand down the boulevard. You even have fond memories of the beery clubs where bras and panties hung in garlands above the bar. You were faithful to each other, but enjoyed the theatricality of flirting; you thrived on ambiguity, on the play of possibilities. It was in the side room of one of these bars, the lounge across from the dance floor, that you met Riva, a girl who accused you of taking Inès from her. 'Ignore her', Inès said. 'It's not for nothing that we call this room the Lounge of Neon Lies.' Still, when Riva took you to the bottom of her story, you saw that Inès had not been kind to her: That, no doubt, was a versant of the ferocity you'd glimpsed in her self-possession. Yet you had no pity for Riva: Some people invite abuse.

Salle d'Armes du Cercle Militaire: Never prepared to sacrifice sport no matter how clamorous the call of work, you joined Inès's fencing club on Place St Augustin. Friday evening when others were cramming for the Saturday morning *devoir surveillé*, you would be developing your skills in the art of the foil while Inès would be honing hers at a higher level. Ever avid for a new challenge, you made rapid progress; by the second year you were able to compete with Inès. On-guard stance and mobility, thrust, lunge and recovery; engagement and change of engagement, feints, beats, parries and ripostes: Having mastered the fundamentals, you took increasing pleasure in the sport; it satisfied your desire to bring mind and body to a pitch of performance while making decisions for yourself. And thus your brought together in one adrenalin rush rigour, intuition and flair, patient observation and lightning response; and thus, with pride and humility, you discovered yourself in the mirror of the other, your opponent.

In your studio on the leafy rue Colbert, upon an evening, you'd continue to pursue the ghosts of Bach and Paganini in Ysaÿe's *Six Sonatas for Solo Violin.* Despite your familiarity with the pieces, you often found yourself having to pause and lie on your bed, overcome by the beauty of the music, its inexhaustible depth and boldness of invention. At such moments you'd feel yourself vast, as vast as the ocean that envelopes the earth, and as undifferentiated. And yet, at the same time, you'd feel with redoubled intensity that pulse in your blood that you know to be your individuality. And thus it was that your violin would simultaneously put you in touch with yourself and make you untouchable. Making love in such a state was magical: Supple, responsive, never making a wrong move, you, Inès found, were an inspired lover. For your part, you found thrilling her mix of sensitivity, skill and ability to surprise.

Should it rain, upon a Sunday afternoon, you'd cross the rue de Varenne to visit a gallery or two in the musée Rodin. You admired Rodin's genius, but his sculptures never really moved you: It was the drawings, the erotic drawings, that touched you. Picasso's were crude and illustrative in comparison to the evocative power of Rodin's. In the pressure of his pencil you felt the touch of the sculptor's hand; in the freedom of his line you felt the fascination of his desire.

And then there was she who worked in Rodin's shadow, Camille Claudel. You were struck by the tortured agony of her figures, by the emotional starvation they wore like a mask. Once, in a café on rue Cler, Inès told you what she knew of Camille's story. Offering an interpretation, she emphasized the artist's abandonment depression, seeing it as the key to her fate. The more you heard, the more you felt an uncanny fear. Before Inès had finished her version of the story, Camille had become your counter-model of how to be a woman: Never, you swore to yourself, would you let your history get such a hold on you; never would you allow yourself to become helpless and dependent.

Ai no corrida: Shortly after the film's release, shortly after your first night with Inès, you saw *In the Realm of the Senses.* It hit you hard. Walking at midnight in Saint-Germain, arm-in-arm under her umbrella, you paid no attention to the neon evanescent under your feet or the faces of the passers-by; no, all you could see as Inès led you to a bar were images of Eiko Matsuda making love to Tatsuya Fuji: Strumming the samisen as she sits astride him, she rocks him deeper into herself; with a languorous flutter of her eyes, she spills his sperm from her mouth; strangling him with the sash cord of her kimono, she sways as he twitches inside her. And the image of her, ecstatic upon her return to her dead lover, cutting off his cock with a butcher's knife. And then the writing in blood on his body: 'Sada, Kichi, the two of us together'.

In a bar on rue Mazarin you ordered a Fernet-Branca with Bourbon and Angostura bitters; Inès opted for a Lillet blanc with Cointreau. Though she had made love with men, she'd never known pleasures like those you'd experienced with Jürgen and Marco. She interpreted your post-film emotion as revulsion; little did she understand what was stirring you. But she did perceive your fascination, and so talked freely about the film. She'd lived in Tokyo for seven years, she'd read the notes from the police interrogation of Abe Sada (published as a book), so when she confirmed that every detail in the film is drawn directly from Sada's testimony, your stunned fascination gave way to elation, a buzz at once disquieting and liberating. Needing a moment of silence, you angled your chair away from Inès and picked up your drink. As you savoured the subtleties of the bitters flavouring the Bourbon, you caught her reflection in a mirror: Tapering down around her face, her bob with its black sheen and purple glow framed her full lips and high cheekbones: You'd have kissed her then and there had not her cateye glasses kept her beauty from being overbearing. As you turned to face her she was a little confused, a lover not yet used to the intensity of your inner life. You asked her, as she sipped her Lillet, to tell you more about Abe Sada. 'I want to know everything', you said, 'I love learning from you'.

It was with rapt attention, then, that you listened to the story of the woman who, thanks to the murder and mutilation she committed in her *corrida* of love, remains a compelling myth in Japan. What moved you most in her story was the way everything in her life—the years of prostitution, the gentleness with Professor Omiya, the intoxicating passion for Ishida Kichizo—seemed to derive from her parents' failure to recognize her feelings when, at age fifteen, she was raped by an acquaintance. Indelibly branded as 'damaged goods', irrevocably unmarriageable, she sought, if not redress, at least recognition of what had happened: Her parents offered only indifference or calculating indulgence. In response, her anger became contempt; she decided to assume her fate and take her life in hand. Geisha, she couldn't compete with the women who'd been training for that profession from childhood; whore, whether as licensed prostitute or freelance, she did fine; mistress, it all depended on the man. When she left the sex business she didn't get farther than being a maid; her middle-class childhood was now the mark not of some paradise lost, but the demonstration that nobody was worthy of trust. Sex, whether in the business or out, had become her greatest pleasure; her desire knew no bounds. Was that a factor of biology, or a means to assert her freedom in the face of her destiny? Was it a facile rebellion against a society that had cast her out, or a search for the love and recognition she'd never had? That was the strand in her life that intrigued you, that and her overwhelming passion for Ishida Kichizo. With him, not only was sex bliss, but love was strong and recognition absolute. But he was married, he had children, he had a business to run. When the days of uninterrupted sex in the teahouses could no longer be maintained, Sada was not prepared to be relegated from his be-all and end-all to his mistress: With his tacit consent she strangled him to death, and in a delirium of what she construed as love, cut off the organ that had given her so much pleasure. When she realized what she'd done, she decided to hang herself; she was arrested, however, before she could carry out the act. It was not a double suicide that didn't work out, it was one woman asserting her love over and against her lover and the world. Inès assured you that the transcripts show she was neither a deranged pervert nor insane, but had, in her own words, done 'insane things' in the name of love. Was it because you saw your experience of anorexia as similarly insane that you were sympathetic to Sada? Did your experience of maternal abandonment dispose you to understanding not only her anger, but also her inability to let go of the man who finally assuaged it? Or was it that her quest for recognition from her father was a quest whose frustration you also knew? As you finished your drinks, you decided that next weekend you'd go and see the film again: Its beauty, at once lush and austere, had moved you, but the mystery of love at its core had moved you even more: That is what you wanted to immerse yourself in.

– Come, Sprague, I've had enough of this mirror! Let's go and fuck in the living room.

I stand up. You throw your arms around my neck, you wrap your legs around me. As I carry you out of the bedroom, you stick your tongue in my ear.

— Let's do it in the rocking chair, you say.

The rippling energy of your body animates mine.

— Yes, let's.

Chapter 15

1

The beauty of a tone in decay, the grace of a sustained note dying: Cold, stark, spare and expansive, the brutal elegance of the music fills the room as you sit astride me on the rocking chair, your back to my chest, my wick in your wax. Impelled by the balls of my feet, spirit flows through my sinews to the point of balance between your legs. Thus, on a white circular rug, we rock in a chair of aluminum rings: two for seat and back, upholstered in reddish-brown leather, two for the sides, anchored in beechwood runners.

> Ride a cock-horse to Banbury Cross,
> To see a fine lady upon a white horse;
> Rings on her fingers and bells on her toes,
> She shall have music wherever she goes.

To and fro, high and low; the back roads, the straight and narrow: Between education and curiosity, passion and tranquillity, where—if there is to be love of life—must the line of gravity be grounded?

Its cushions of reddish-brown leather and frame of tubular steel echoing the rocking chair, the sofa unfolds its stillness in the glow of a torchère lamp. Except for de Staël's desperate nude, the muted blue walls of the room are bare. Illuminated by concealed lights, four Persian vases in a steel and glass column defy gravity.

> Margery Mutton-Pie and Johnny Bo-Peep,
> They met together in Gracechurch Street;
> In and out, in and out, all the way—
> No, said Johnny, it's not chop-a-nose day!

To and fro, high and low; swim upstream, go with the flow: Between the hiding place of normality and the self-exposure of excess, where—if there is to be love of life—must the line of gravity be grounded?

Evoking billowing sails and suspension bridges, two deck chairs unfurl their casual elegance in front of the floor-to-ceiling glazing. Between them, hanging from an arched stem, a lamp of concentric circles casts a moon-like glow. In that lunar light the turquoise canvas of the chairs, steel-rigged to cable-stayed frames, vibrates to the rhythm of its black-and-white stripes.

> See-saw, Margery Daw,
> Sold her bed and lay upon straw;
> Was not she a dirty slut
> To sell her bed and lie in the dirt?

To and fro, high and low; sharp sunlight, soft moonglow: Between knowing one's limits and fearing one's nature, where—if there is to be love of life—must the line of gravity be grounded?

Beyond the glazing, lit from below, a row of spiral topiary trees in terracotta planters lends stateliness to the balcony. Here, in the near wall, a rocaille cartouche centres the flowing lines of a sculpted marble fireplace. In front of it, black-and-red cushions top a beaten-up pirate trunk.

> If all the world were paper,
> And all the sea were ink,
> If all the trees were bread and cheese,
> What should we have to drink?

To and fro, high and low; battlements, a patio: Between self-sufficiency and vulnerability, between knowledge and discovery, where—if there is to be love of life—must the line of gravity be grounded?

2

Imbued with silence, stark tones trace a calligraphy of stillness; under the pianistic fingers of Paul Bley, tentativeness and doubt become crystalline.

'To cling is to immobilize and thus to miss the always-moving point of equilibrium': Sliding back your legs, you take my hands and bend forward till your torso is parallel to the floor. I stretch out my legs and lean back, then together we work the rocking chair into a steady rhythm.

> Titty cum tawtay,
> The ducks in the water;
> Titty cum tawtay,
> The geese follow after.

To and fro, high and low; open hearts, incommunicado: Between the protection of self-reliance and the risks of mutual belonging, where—if there is to be love of life—must the line of gravity be grounded?

Now the seeing, now the blind, my cock and your cunt explore the body's relation to mind. Our hands interlocked, we maintain a flexible tension in our arms, optimizing the angle of penetration. Each time the rocker reaches the limit of its downward motion, your nipples brush my knees; each time it begins its upward arc, your buttocks tighten: Arranged for pleasure, your body is an open invitation.

> Put your finger in Foxy's hole,
> Foxy's not at home;
> Foxy's at the back door
> Picking at a bone.

To and fro, high and low; free port, embargo: Between protecting ourselves from our desires and giving ourselves over to them, where—if there is to be love of life—must the line of gravity be grounded?

3

Stripping the harmonics from the melody, improvising upon a fragment, the pianist reverses the figure and ground of silence and sound. Taking my weight on my forearms, I slide my ass to the edge of the chair; as you slip me inside you, your eyes echo the eerie beauty of Aravane's. Bearing down, taking me in deep, you lay your head on my shoulder; into a relaxed rhythm you ease us. To the spirit of Aravane's cat you now submit your body: Your breathing becomes a tonal buzzing, an unmistakably feline purr; your hair, warm and velvety, becomes collapsingly soft.

> The hart he loves the high wood,
> The hare she loves the hill;
> The knight he loves his bright sword,
> The lady loves her will.

To and fro, high and low; bell above, island below: Between the disturbance of empathy and the calmness of isolation, where—if there is to be love of life—must the line of gravity be grounded?

Delicious is the languid rhythm; on the pivot of pleasure you maintain the tension. A gasping sigh escapes your throat as my *pattes d'araignée* brush your back; your teeth mark my shoulder as my fingers skim your furrow.

When I was a little boy,
I washed my mummy's dishes;
I put my finger in my eye
And pulled out little fishes.

To and fro, high and low; rules and regulations, tick-tack-toe: Between the experiment of relationship and the hankering for a contract, where—if there is to be love of life—must the line of gravity be grounded?

4

Out from the ambient silence Paul Bley draws a melody; in the stark beauty of his elegant searching, every note weighed before it is played, we rock on the beechwood rockers of our aluminum rings. You sit up and lean back, resting your forearms on my thighs. Again from the legs the force comes to generate a rhythm: Again our bodies collaborate to maintain a tension. Between your parted lips your breath flows, between your parted legs, my spirit.

Tightly pedalled chords and sparse right-hand figures stretch a tightrope between silence and sound: Constantly restoring his shifting balance, the pianist walks the rope. Not piano strings but aluminum rings make you an acrobat, Marietta: In your exquisite modulation of the rhythm, I feel your utter availability to pleasure.

As Tommy Snooks and Betty Brooks
Were walking out on Sunday,
Says Tommy Snooks to Betty Brooks,
Let's not go back till Monday.

To and fro, high and low; fire lake, rainbow: Between what is both impossible to satisfy and impossible to give up, where—if there is to be love of life—must the line of gravity be grounded?

5

'There is no sex without love or its refusal': On the generous ride of our aluminum rings, in the eternal recurrence where we embrace our fate, we sway between our smallness-under-the-stars and the immensity of our hearts. My shoulders against the backrest, my buttocks on the edge of the chair, I countervail your force: Legs flexed, feet with heel on the seat and ball on the backrest, you gorge yourself on me, pressing your pussy against my crotch while pulling my arms to full extension. Deeper now the penetration, making the pressure on your clit constant; you arch your back, pull harder on my arms, and coax my cock to your sweet spot.

> See-saw, sacradown,
> Which is the way to London town?
> One foot up, the other down,
> That is the way to London town.

To and fro, high and low; the consuming fire, vertigo: Between what we most wish for and what we are most careful of getting, where—if there is to be love of life—must the line of gravity be grounded?

Defining the arc of the oscillation, defying gravity, your wilful body in motion moves me: So this is the pleasure of the flying fuck, Newton's third law of motion; this is renovation of life at its root, the antidote to alienation. Look! Into the ellipsis of a turning rope a girl times her leap: Now! Her ponytail a blur of blonde, repeatedly off the ground she propels herself, letting gravity and lift contest her body. Faster now, faster, dual ropes are turned, a helix that makes a halo around the head of the skipping girl. Look! The halo shimmers, the child of light shines. Hail the unspeakable girl! Hail! As my flares join your fireworks, we surf convulsion waves; where they will, they wash us: To the Villa of Mysteries in Pompeii, where the walls are a dazzling red; to the slopes of Vesuvius, where lava stores sunlight; to Sevilla, where galleons back from Aztec lands unload gold, silver and cochineal; to Smyrna, Constantinople and Aleppo, where Spanish merchants lay out Guatemalan indigo; to Prussia, Alexandria and Persia, where in the purest of blues we plumb infinity...

> Lavender's blue, dilly, dilly,
> Lavender's green;
> When I am king, dilly, dilly,
> You'll be my queen.

Intermezzo 8: Zina

Dirt and nicotine turn the blue walls green in this derelict room where I lie. As the blown-glass lamp spills its yellowy light onto the worn floorboards, faded colours weave talismanic figures into the tattered carpet. From a vodka bottle, poppies drop their petals onto the tabletop. The urn by the washbasin, its red stars and vortices dancing in flowers and foliate green, reminds me there once was a curtain here.

Zina is asleep. Without the fire of her orange-brown eyes, it's her lips that come to the fore: Parted in a sullen pout, they speak of satin sheets on a bed of nightshade, moonlit lovers trysting on a forest floor.

Zina's in love with Chekhov. We met at the museum where she works: Anton Pavlovich's house. The White Dacha has been going to the dogs ever since the Soviet collapse found it caught in the cultural crossfire between Russia and Ukraine. Three stories high, with its seven entrances and mix of round and rectangular windows, it's a charming whimsy of a building. Zina was an excellent guide, situating Anton's domesticity in the context of a life governed by kindness.

The elusiveness of happiness, the nostalgia for what cannot be: Over a supper of *varenyky* in a cosy restaurant, we spoke of 'The Lady with the Little Dog', the only story Chekhov set in this town. Zina kept coming back to Anna on the pier, lingering after all the passengers have left, sniffing her flowers of welcome for no-one. What was she hoping to find, who was she hoping to see? All Chekhov's genius, we agreed, lay in that lightness of touch.

Zina then spoke of her Tatar heritage. The Stalin-ordered deportation, the difficulty of restoring rights in a culture of lies. Her mother supporting the two of them after her father died. Teaching piano, sometimes surviving only thanks to the fruitful garden.

In my room, between making love and sleeping, we talked.

– So your writing helps you get over her?

– No Zina. There's no question of 'getting over her'. It's rather a question of overcoming myself.

In the live coals of Zina's eyes I burnt the dust of her own doubt. She then read another extract from my notebook:

> Firelight in the living room, a blanket of snow on the boats below: Between mastering the art of fucking with no hands—stretched out, seated, or standing—we take turns reading aloud *Alice in Wonderland*... Midnight: fresh-squeezed lemon in iced Magellan gin, grilled shrimp-and-strawberry salad... The serene insistence of your energetic indolence, pulling me down into your arms. Roving hands caress my back, coaxing me to fuck you out of your *idée fixe:* You want to break your habit of impermanence, but you don't want to lose your stranger's eye; you want to live where you belong, but you don't want to feel you can't move on. And so you command my cock to break down your ambivalence, and so you confer on our fucking the power to clarify.

– Just who is she, Sprague?

– She's a surfer.

– A surfer?

– Yes. She surfs the cusp where homeless and unhoused divide.

– What?

– She's a new being, she's twice-born.

In the live coals of Zina's eyes I burnt the dust of her own doubt. She then read another extract from my notebook:

> On the Isle of Skye, at the foot of the Black Cuillin, you swim in your wetsuit through the peaty waters of Loch Coruisk. What a weekend that was! Gram had come up with a ravishing melody for 'You Can't Commit Suicide with a Safety Blade'; Seedy Friedrich had a hit, and I a stream of royalties: From London to Inverness we flew, then drove from there to Dunvegan. We arrived as the last shadows moved down the mountain, the gleaming road unwinding to reveal the lighted house where we'd stay.
>
> In the briny air we took a brisk walk, enchanted by moon and cloud inverting figure and ground in the island-dotted sea. As I pressed your body to mine, cashmere fleece and merino wool conspired to make you melt into me.

Inside, we savoured a supper of poached salmon and skirlie; we lingered over a whisky liqueur.

In our split-level room I lay on the bed, watching the black of the night brighten the glow on the wall. You stepped before the window and stared out; then, turning to face me, let fall your filmy gown: All night long, moonlight flooded through the doors of our perception, giving our creaturely pursuit of the absolute the blessing of the watery star.

The next day, after lunch on the terrace, we drove down to approach Loch Coruisk. On foot we covered the last few kilometers, then you donned your wetsuit and swam the length of the Loch—twice!

Slàinte. Here's tae ye! That night you were ravenous. We rounded off a scrumptious meal with hot marmalade pudding and Drambuie custard.

Reliving that weekend I wove a lyric; out of my lyric, Gram spun gold: Over staccato violins and brooding cellos, his melodic gift made a wonder of my words, producing another hit for Seedy Friedrich. Had you been with me, my love, we could have gone to other islands—the Coast of Blacks or Van Diemen's Land, the Island of Thieves or of the Naked Man—and spent my royalties in pursuit of our sainthood.

— Do you have any idea, Sprague, how far you still are from the end?
— I do, Zina. And it's only a girl like you, on a night like this, that allows me to go on.

We fell silent. And then the silence of her tongue gave way to the eloquence of her lips; in the light of present grace her doubt faded away: I'd whispered the words 'complicated' and 'difficult' in her ear, letting her know I'd caught her allusion to 'The Lady with the Little Dog'.

Chapter 16

Truth is with the axiom and the equation, but you cannot produce randomness mathematically: Waking to wonder I watch you, my heart filled with pride. As the projector lights up the side of your face, I bathe in the beauty of your reasoning; as you place a new transparency, a shadow falls on rationality.

– As you know, the quantization of non-Abelian gauge theories in the noncovariant Coulomb gauge, where the divergence of the vector potential is zero, has perplexed theorists for decades.

In your skinny black jeans and houndstooth jacket, you stand hands on hips, speaking fast and fluent.

– I'd like to propose a new procedure for computing Feynman integrals in the noncovariant Coulomb gauge, apply the new technique to the one-loop Yang-Mills self-energy, and then check the appropriate Ward/BRS identity, and thus the value of pi a b mu nu.

Calm and confident, you are wholly in the moment, invulnerable in your familiar world. And yet the way you look at the audience askance, just as you did at the El Salvador concert, tells them you will deliver what they want, but there is a line you won't let them cross. Why do you impose such a barrier? Why would a scientist need to take such a stance?

– The scalar ghost propagator reads i times delta a b over 2 pi to the power of 4 times q squared.

Your silver bangle taps on the glass of the projector as you write on the transparency; stepping back, you continue your demonstration. It's not for nothing you're a high-energy physicist: Left hand on hip, right hand twirling, you outline a chain of events; half-rotating your upheld hand, you ease the audience into your logic. With diagonal chops you punctuate a point; hand behind head, you ponder an explanation. Dynamic yet dignified, in one and the same movement of being you radiate intelligence and sexuality. Is that it, then? Is that what your withholding signifies? The restraint of a woman subjecting herself to the gaze of men? You who find poetry in a table of logarithms, you to whom rigour is a form of morality, Göttingen evokes not Riemann, but the

Brothers Grimm: Is that why you so clearly let your audience know you have a reserve of selfhood they will never access? Sex is an equation without remainder, that nevertheless remains unresolved.

– By a Coulomb-gauge integral we mean any Feynman integral containing one or more three-dimensional factors such as one over q squared, one over q plus p squared, etc.

Theorems establish stability, abstraction eclipses the chaos of desire and transcends the vagaries of opinion. And yet, even as you celebrate the triumph of instrumental reason, you regard nature with respect and contemplation: You know too much to dominate and exploit.

– We analytically extend this result to four-dimensional space by taking 'omega tends to three halfs' and 'sigma tends to one half', in either order.

As you change a transparency a question comes. With grace you engage in a short exchange then, smiling, you cross your hands at the waist and sweep them apart again, ruling out any further interruption: It is you who are in command. I know, my love, that between completeness and incompleteness, certainty and conjecture, it is the singular becoming, the living particular, that you favour. But in a world of abstraction, it is the absolute and the universal, the general and the formal, that count. So is that it, then? Is your withholding a means of compartmentalizing what you cannot make coexist in one moment? Is it your private freedom that requires your public reserve? Is it only in private that you can express, in one and the same movement, your love for Hilbert *and* Shakespeare, Euclid *and* Aeschylus, Gauss *and* Goethe? When the poets are forgotten the mathematicians will still be remembered: True, no doubt. But if mathematics is the means by which you honour the world, poetry is how you honour yourself.

– The results are encouraging, but clearly more calculations are needed before split dimensional regularization can be placed on a firm mathematical footing. Thank you very much.

As the applause breaks out you are all modesty: It is I who am beaming with pride.

So this is how, in an act of self-transcendence, you step outside yourself, this is how you testify to the dignity of the human mind. And yet, Marietta, throughout your presentation, throughout your mastery of abstract discourse,

I felt your singular vulnerability, your living particularity. Is that why you've left me not only in wonder, but awash with love?

Chapter 17

Letter from Cartagena

Dearest, outside my window the night is steamy. Inside, it's cool. Still, I can't sleep. Yes, beast of my heart, your silly Marietta is missing you.

It's been quite a week, immersing myself in the seediness and charm of this tropical city, but it's not so much Cartagena itself as the time spent in the house with Rolena and Molly that's been, shall I say... stimulating?

Maria Frederica von Keyserling is an American who calls herself Molly. Yes, truth is stranger than fiction. She traces her family back to the Baltic nobility. Her manners are not aristocratic, however, for she's rather bitter, having just gone through an acrimonious divorce. That's why Rolena invited her here, to her beautiful house in the Old Town, to prepare their new course. Molly teaches Women's Studies at Berkeley, Rolena Art History. They're preparing a new course together, an interdisciplinary affair on women and surrealism.

Have you seen Leonor Fini's illustrations for *Historie d'O?* 'Illustrations' is hardly the word—they're more like a visual echo of the text, dark-coloured washes over lithographed pen-and-ink drawings. Very evocative, but far removed from my own fantasy when reading Réage's love letter. I do like Fini's eroticism, though. Anyway, once you know that Molly is as American as apple pie, you won't be surprised to learn that when I told her how much I love *O,* she showered me with pearls of PC, such as 'Dominique Aury is an agent of patriarchy, reinforcing the myth of woman-as-victim, wallowing in woman's degradation'! When she'd finished ranting against this 'unspeakable image of women', I simply said, 'Imagine how bland sex would be if we had no fantasies of power and surrender'. Can you guess what she did next? She said, 'You're perverse, Marietta'. And then she came over and sat on the arm of my chair and tried to kiss me! I pushed her away—graciously—for how could she have known that it was only you I wanted?

I like this room, my bedroom. It's Antonio's studio. He's an architect, away on a job in California (designing a mansion for some millionaire). He's Rolena's husband. Second husband. 'The first is the phantom, the bearer of ghosts', Rolena says, 'the second is a man, not a screen for your projections'. Molly wondered at that. She's still blaming her husband for their failed marriage.

Rolena's right, of course, even if she believes serial monogamy is better than sleeping around. As for me, I'm neither sleeping around nor sleepy. And I know it's not because of the coffee granita (delicious, topped with condensed milk).

Sweet darling you, what will you appear as tonight? A plumed serpent, mingling with the beasts on my bedhead? Now put this letter under your pillow and dream of me!

Your Marietta

***

Postcard from Stockholm

Dearest, my presentation went well. There were lots of questions, and that's always a good sign. Stockholm's a beautiful city, all islands and bridges and sea. The hotel's lovely, a long row of rooms that used to house the Swedish Royal Marines. Outside my window the night is a silvery mosaic. That's my bicycle there, by the lamp post. Boats are docked nearby. O beast of my heart, be my *bateau ivre* tonight!

Your Marietta

***

Letter from Dunedin

Dearest, your clapped out Marietta is all alone in her big bed, a glass of Cloudy Bay on the night table and sushi on her tray. I'm listening to Elly Ameling singing Fauré's *Mélodies*. I'll have finished my meal when the music's over, and then I'm going to write you a big fat letter. Back in a while, crocodile!

It's later now, alligator, and I've got a little quiz for you.

MCQ 1

'Refinement and simplicity; subtle nuances and delicate detail. Tender, yet virile, never sentimental. Spiritual as well as physical; serene, yet passionate.' What does that description apply to?

(A) The sushi Marietta just ate.
(B) Elly Ameling singing Fauré.

(C) Sprague and Marietta's kisses.
(D) All of the above.

And the answer is... too easy! Oh Sprague, why am I awash with sheer, instrumental lust whenever I find myself in a hotel room, missing you? It blows my mind to think you're mine, and then I tell myself only separateness assures intimacy, only returning to myself allows me to respect your mystery. Sometimes I'm tempted by the allure of living together, the prospect of immediate fullness, but when I think with my brain and not my pussy I know I must not fall into that trap.

OPEN QUESTION 1: It's not a Flight de Ville. What is it?

Vroom, vroom! Did you hear that? I've got a bright yellow sports car, bright as the one in *Written on the Wind*. Can you guess what it is? I'll give you a clue: It's Japanese. Another clue: It's a throwback to the British and Italian sports cars of the sixties.

Well, did you guess? I've got a Mazda MX-5, and what joy it is driving it around Otago! The little beast handles brilliantly, changes direction like a go-kart. Her touch is divine—just a nudge on the stick and she shifts. And what a looker! Lean and petite and sexy as hell. Vroom, vroom! You can't catch me!

OPEN QUESTION 2: 'Weightless, yet powerful. Motionless, yet moving. Silence, yet roaring sound.' What was Marietta doing that fits that description?

You want a clue? All right, here's one: Toes on the nose!

And the answer is... Being reborn like Aphrodite! Yes, I've been surfing! And what a joy it's been, rediscovering the magical sensations. Lining up a wave, the last look over the shoulder, the miracle of walking on water!

MCQ 2

'Whitebait fritters, a bite of bacon butty; fennel slaw with mint dressing; berry and ricotta pudding.' Where did Marietta eat that lunch?

(A) In a harbourside pub.
(B) At the Farmers Market.
(C) In a restaurant at the end of an alley.
(D) In a trendy café.

And the answer is... At the historic railway station! Yes, Sprague, at the Farmers Market. Oh the loveliness of this little city! Dunedin is a dream town, laid-back but not sleepy (just like me, though I haven't been laid—back or front—since I left your bed). It faces the ocean, it faces the bay, it rambles across the valleys and climbs the hills. I love the gingerbread houses, white and blue in lush green; I love the gold-rush architecture, Scotland washed up in the South Sea. The people are proud without pretension, approachable in the best New World way. Then again, living in such a stunningly beautiful place, how could they could ever be blasé?

MCQ 3

'How wet do you want to get?' Marietta was asked that question when:

(A) She had to choose between Marlon Brando and Maria Schneider, on one hand, and Debbie Reynolds and Gene Kelly on the other.
(B) She was getting her ankles strapped.
(C) She asked her travel agent for tips about the South Island.
(D) She inquired about Kiwi cooking, about what would stimulate her taste buds.

And the answer is... when she was about to throw herself off the Kawarau Bridge! Yes, Sprague, while getting my ankles strapped I chose to be dunked into the river below. Turquoise and fast-flowing, that's where I'm heading. Goodbye, cruel world! Ah, falling, the void, heaven! And then the stress-strain curve kicks in and plunges me into the water—only to haul me up immediately and bounce me around like a victim in a mock sacrifice. Thrilling!

MCQ 4

'You are the girl of the golden mean, you are the girl who turns heads: You make me realize what I lack.' Who said that to whom?

(A) The spider to the fly.
(B) Experience to the parade of impressions.
(C) Little girl lost to frigid bitch.
(D) Caroline to Marietta.

And the answer is... You guessed it, Sprague. No sooner the flattery than the attack. 'Why are you still unattached? You can't be selfish and sacrifice everything to your career! Imagine when you're old, if you had to die alone.'

Backbiting I'm used to, but when your guard is down and it's in your face—fuck it, what can I do? Caroline can take a walk. I'm with you!

MCQ 5

In a pub on a rainy afternoon, what did Marietta, Sally and Paola talk about?

(A) John Major's mysterious moustache?
(B) Scientific research and women academics.
(C) Is Paolo Conte as sexy as his voice?
(D) Where did all the junkies go now that Needle Park is closed?
(E) The time they played as a trio in Milan—piano, violin and cello.

And the answer is... Sally's working on a side project, a vast international investigation of 'Women in Science'. So, after lunch, she had us reminiscing about how our passion for mathematics started. It was funny to see how much we had in common. I told them how, when I was learning to count, it suddenly occurred to me that the whole numbers go on *for ever,* and how that realization blew my little mind. And then, a little older, how appealing it became that in mathematics things have a definite answer, and this answer can be reached logically. And then, much older, how men would get competitive—even aggressive—when they'd find out I was a theoretical physicist.

OPEN QUESTION 3: 'Flowers a field, swallows the sunset, fire a forest'. And what goes with Marietta?

And the answer is... Sweet beast of my heart, you!

Your Marietta

Intermezzo 9: Siri

Marietta, I'm sitting in a café off Järntorget, the cranes along the Göta River joining with the bleak streets of Långgatorna to echo my mood. I'm happy! Yes, my love, since you've been gone I'm only happy when it rains, and while now there's but a louring sky, last night, what a downpour! Stripped the trees of their autumn leaves, painted the brownstones black. Just like the night before: As the wind drove the rain down the avenue, the chill invigorated me; I hailed a taxi in the storm and rode to a place called Pustervik, a converted cinema where I caught a rock concert. After the show, Siri, the singer, recognized me; we made a date to meet for brunch the next day. Now as I sit in this empty café on the day after, I'll tell you about our meeting.

Dziga Vertov impressed me with their playing—melodic bass, whiplash drums, spectral synth and spare, angular guitar—overlaid with Siri's richly-textured voice. Nothing girly in her upper register, just a shimmering loveliness, and in the rest a delicate play of shadow and light. In her cropped black top, red jeans and kohl-rimmed eyes she was beguiling, dancing spastically in the fast numbers and sensually in the slow.

We brunched on club sandwiches and coffee. Despite the two cups Siri drank, she was totally calm. Indeed, there was a placidity to her that at first I found disturbing. After a while, though, her freckled face and hazel eyes looking at me through oversize vintage glasses had me quite subjugated: She was positively beautiful, calmly aglow with drive and intelligence.

We spoke of Gram and our songwriting partnership; we spoke of how she mines her notebooks for lyrics while I begin with a rhythm of words, seemingly random phrases. We then spoke of Ingmar Bergman and Olaf Palme, the Columbine massacre and *The Matrix*. Gripping the cuffs of her shirtsleeves, she stretched her arms round her body in a self-embrace. 'Do you have a girlfriend?' she asked me. I told her I didn't, and summoned her to come and sit next to me. 'Why don't we just go straight to your hotel?' she suggested. So we did.

Siri wore her nudity as unselfconsciously as she wore her clothes. She'd taken off her cinched-in waistcoat, her pirate trousers and workman's boots; she'd taken off her shirt, socks, panties and bra, but she left it to me to undo her ponytail and take off her glasses. Doe-eyed and willowy, her hair down, she suddenly appeared much younger than before. When I saw, in the wavering gold and green of her eyes, that she had the kindness not to mask her vulnerability, I instantly found an attitude that allowed us to open the doors of pleasure. 'God I was gagging for that', she said when she'd come, 'ever since I saw you last night'.

It now felt as if we'd known each other for ages. Letting our pleasure blossom of its own volition, we spoke of her life while leisurely making love.

Her mother worked her way up from the shop floor to become a manager at the ball-bearing factory; her father was an alcoholic who, when Siri was thirteen, drank himself into a stupor from which he never recovered.

– He put my mum through hell. She never stopped loving him, and that only made things worse.

– And you?

– I had no trouble hating him. Things were clear between us. Though I did lose a screw when he died. If it wasn't for singing, I'd be dead too, no doubt.

– Singing saved you?

– Yes. Before Dziga Vertov I was in a punk band. Allowed me to flush out all my feelings. Then I read *L'Étranger* and decided there's no future in being a punk.

We both laugh. She bites my earlobe and does the Gopala-girl.

– Did you like Lady Di, Sprague?

– Billie Holiday?

– No. Not Lady *Day*. Lady *Di!*

– Princess Diana?

– Who else?

– Yes. I liked the way she fought, I liked her imperfections. Did you?

– Well, it wouldn't be very hip if I did, would it? But now that she's dead, I have to say I did like her. To have the world at your feet and still be unhappy—it's fascinating, isn't it?

– Yes. Makes you think.

In the innocence of her face there are no signs of experience; it's from her voice—that grain of Lady Day—that the intimation of chaos comes.

– Tell me, Sprague, what's your biggest fear?

– Oh, maybe that you're going to make me come before I've satisfied you.

– Don't worry about that.

— And what's yours?

— My biggest fear?

— Yes.

— To be abandoned. I'm afraid of being dumped.

Delicate are her kisses; soft, the caress of her hair.

— How old are you?

— Nineteen.

— Have you had many boyfriends?

— Just three. And it was always me who said goodbye!

— Better to be the leaver than the left?

— Of course.

Steadfast, the boat of her body plies the waves rippling through mine, its rolling motion not limited by any horizon.

— Have you had many girlfriends?

— No. You're my first, Siri.

— Sprague!

She grinds her groin against me, taking me in deeper.

— Be serious!

— All right. I had one, one above all the others.

— What's her name?

— Marietta.

— And why did you leave her?

— I didn't. She left me.

— You mean—?

— Yes. I'm a left.

— Poor Sprague.

> Stretch the tightrope tight: I will walk it.
> And if I fall, may I fall in grace;
> And if I hurt her, haunt my heart.

— What's she do, this Marietta?

— She studies dark matter. She made a great breakthrough in axion detection.

— Stop pulling my leg!

— I'm not. I'm pulling your tits.

She pushed me onto my back and straddled me; to Bedlam and part-way back she rode me.

— Why are you crying, Sprague?
— I'm not crying.
— You are. There's tears streaming down your cheeks.
— Sorry.
— Are you thinking of Marietta?

> Miracle night, miraculous woman,
> You turn my destiny into freedom!
> Play on: I am ready to face the music!

— You are. I know you are.
— No Siri. I'm happy here with you.
She kisses me with the kisses of her mouth.
— Speak to me of her, Sprague.
— No.
— I can help you.
— No.
She puts on her glasses.
— Look, I'm wise as an owl.
— Siri, you're so beautiful I could eat you!
— You already have. Now come on, tell me about her!
— No.
— Well read me something from your notebook then.
— No.
— Please!
— All right, fetch it. It's in my jacket pocket. But you can read for yourself!

Notebook in hand, Siri sat beside me on the bed, our backs to the headboard. Opening the book at random, she read out loud:

> Marietta, between the razor blade and the wrist, between the window and the sidewalk, there is time enough for memory. I remember: The beauty of your face in the dying light of a summer day, along the Zürichsee... I remember: Laying a cool hand on your fevered brow, spooning tamarind-and-tomato soup into your mouth; the flush of

> your face as the chillies and ginger, the garlic and cumin, brought you back to life. And then your laughter, prolonging the relief, as I danced my rag-doll dance... I remember: The fall of your hair over *The Unforgettable Fire,* your black jeans, your bare feet; then, minutes later, you the quintessence of chic in your concert gown... I remember: Your pubic hair, figuring a heart on a postcard, sent in an envelope from Oslo: 'You'd better be hungry when I get home. I've made my oyster more edible'. On your back, on the parquet, you were insatiable: I was a rapt gourmet... I remember: Your tears when your father died, your sudden desire to have a child. 'Sweet savage', you'd whisper as you pulled me down into your arms. And then, when we couldn't undo the damage from the time you had tried to die, I remember the wasteland of longing that wouldn't leave your eyes... I remember: The sun on your skin, your long eyelashes, your delight in the mountain grass; the gentian in your hair, the butterfly on your nose, your calm as you gave it welcome. And then, as your breath bade it goodbye, I remember the prayer in my heart: Go, silver-blue flutter, and tell the gods on high—those who made you crawl as well as those who made you fly—that she who lies beside me honours their creation. Tell them her grace becomes them, and convey my request that they, in their vigilance, safeguard her happiness. Go, tell them this, and if they demand my very life in return, tell them in loving her I have truly lived: Willingly, then, I will lay my life in their hands.

— Boy, you really loved her!

As I stare into Siri's eyes, my love multiplies.

— Why'd she leave you?

— I don't know. Maybe I was too slow.

— Too slow?

— To break free from my chains.

— And now, have you broken free?

I shake my head.

— I'm still trying.

She closed the notebook then randomly opened it and began reading out loud:

> Touch me. That's all I want. We don't need words. Your hand in mine, your weight on my body, your hair brushing my cheek. That's all I want. Smoked char with pickled quince and blue cheese: I'd have liked to have shared it with you. Toasting the devil while downing an akvavit: I'd have liked to have done that with you. But I don't mind that we didn't: Touch me. That's all I want. Your smile makes my history a fairy tale; your eyes put me in touch with my truth. Still, for a touch, I'd forgo your smile and your gaze. I bought a pair of boots. I'd have liked to have bought them with you. I explored this city of fjord, lake and mountain. I'd have liked to have explored it with you. But I don't mind that we didn't: Touch me. That's all I want. You levitate my body. You elevate my soul. And on the ground all the while you keep my feet. Still, for a touch, I'd forgo your magic. While I was out walking the whirling wind intensified; it hurled prickles of ice into my face. I closed my eyes and banished signs. I ended up in the Terminus Kafe. At the bar a man welcomed me to the North Sea. He asked me how I liked his city. 'Too many blondes', I replied, 'too many ghosts of the girl who's gone'. 'Cruelty is part of being a woman', he said, 'just as inhumanity is part of being human'. I replied, 'My friend, thank you, but I don't want your philosophy'. And I didn't. I don't want any of that anymore: Your touch, that's all I want. Last night, across a cold waste of white sheet, I reached for you. In the morning, clutching at emptiness, I awoke with a blizzard in my heart. I don't want you in my dreams again. I don't want to hallucinate you anymore. Touch me. That's all I want. Your hand in mine, your weight on my body, your hair brushing my cheek.

– God Sprague, you're a goner!

– Am I?

– Have you ever banged your head against a wall? Banged it again and again and again?

– Yes.

– Then it's just as I thought. You're the baby chimp in the experiment, kept in a cage with a wire model for a mother. Went mad. Couldn't stop banging his head against the wall. Only thing to calm him was—

– A rag. A bit of fluff. Anything approaching a living touch.

— That's right. 'Touch me. That's all I want. Touch me.' Things are pretty clear, aren't they?

— Yes, Siri. I am that chimpanzee.

She closed the notebook then randomly opened it and began reading out loud:

> I don't know what to do. I thought I could get myself together. I thought I'd pull through. I thought I could lay to rest the ghost I'd set loose. What a fool! I sip my soup. I wipe my mouth. I drop my serviette. I don't know what to do. I can't believe a wandering phantom is all I am. Where is my will to struggle? Do I not have inner resources, do I not have any reserves? Once a café like this, in a city like this, would be enough to rouse my spirits. Once a high-backed banquette, with lovers sitting like that, would make me raise my glass in homage. Now they make me cry... I don't know what to do. I had a beer in a neighbourhood bar. I felt out of place. I took a walk by the lake. I was so lonely I felt inhuman. At the Abaton-Kino I saw Bertolucci's *Besieged*. In the tenderness of its silence I let my tears flow. Leaving the cinema, I tried to talk to a woman. I asked her if she'd liked the film. She just walked away. I invited another for a drink; she said she's waiting for her boyfriend. I don't know what to do. There's no more Beatles on the Reeperbahn. I don't know what to do...

— God Sprague, it's frightening!
Visibly shaken, Siri shudders.

— I'll *never* fall for *anyone* like you have!
The intimation of chaos, the grain of Lady Day.

— How long's it been?

— I've lost count.

— Then there's only one way out!

— What is it?

— It only works for a little while.

— What is it?

— Watch!
She slipped down under the sheet and slid up between my legs. I didn't watch. I kept the sheet over her head. Surrendering my body to her power, I felt fine

for a while. And then a tear rolled down my cheek. A minute later, determined to honour her ardour, I threw back the sheet and watched her bring a river of stars into being, a river that stitched the land of the dead to the luminous serene.

That evening, at her place, we improvised an *eintopf* and ate it while watching *The Man Who Fell to Earth*. Afterwards, on the sofa, as she lay on her back with her head in my lap, we listened to *Low,* from 'Warszawa' to 'Subterraneans'. In bed, naked under her eiderdown, we slept like children. In the morning, milky coffee and marmalade toast. 'Blue, blue, electric blue—That's the colour of my room where I will live': We sung along to 'Sound and Vision', Siri a better Bowie than I. And then I took off her oversize vintage glasses and kissed her goodbye.

PART SIX

Chapter 1

Cold, cold, the current flows, surging clear over cobble and pebble, rushing white around resistant stone. Starbright! Sheathed in a robe of light, a dipper hurls the torpedo of his body through the rolling surface of the water. Rapid beat of rounded wings, grip of claw on stone: On the riverbed he treads, struggling. Drawn in by fire, enfolded in flesh, into the body the soul: Stitched together by breaths, our lips interlock. Your fingers glide across my cheek as I press my mouth to yours; you nip my lower lip and draw it in, sucking: From a palpitation of being to the fount of memory you ferry me. Air! Relenting claws leave stone, tarsi in tandem kick: To the surface the dipper rises, onto a mid-stream rock.

– Brekeke-kex, ko-ax, ko-ax, ko-ax, ko-ax, ko-ax!

Gusts of wind drive rain-pocked ripples across the surface of a pond; in the darkening sky ragged clouds hang low.

– Brekeke-kex, ko-ax, ko-ax, ko-ax, ko-ax, ko-ax!

Through the nostrils into the mouth the air is drawn then into the lungs is driven; back and forth across vocal cords it shuttles between lung and sac.

– Brekeke-kex, ko-ax, ko-ax, ko-ax, ko-ax, ko-ax!

Tympana vibrate, senses quicken; to the edge of the pond the females come. Amplexus! He clasps his body to her back. Skin on skin, slime on subtle slime, the couple delect in their lust. Amplexus, amplexus, amplexus! The orgy gathers pace: One pair after another, spiny pads digging into glandular skin, the frogs find each other. Willow reeds rim the pond; long roots bind the glutinous mud. Look! This way and that, blasts of wind sweep sheets of rain across the surface of the water: Through the eye of the earth a watch is kept on the world.

– Brekeke-kex, ko-ax, ko-ax, ko-ax, ko-ax, ko-ax!

– Frogs, do you remember? 9 September 1941, Butrimonys: 67 men, 370 women, 303 children, shot by a firing squad of neighbours and friends?

– We don't remember.

– 9 September 1941, Alytus: 1,279 shot through head and heart by volunteers happy to recover their victims' coats?

– We don't remember.

– 10 September 1941, Merkine: 854; Varena: 831. Men at the edge of the pit, women and children in front of them. Do you remember?

– We don't remember.

— Warthegau? You must remember Warthegau? Men were hauled from their houses and hung from lamp posts. Others, stones weighting them down, were hung from gallows. To slow their death, they lowered them inch by inch until faces turned blue and tongues lolled. And all the while, to drown the screams of their wives and children, the brass band played. Do you remember?

— Brekeke-kex, ko-ax, ko-ax, ko-ax, ko-ax, ko-ax! Never again! Never again! Never again!

Swift, swift, making chaos of the mirror of creation, melt-water tumbles over rock, leaving silica to sparkle in the sun. Starbright! Rapid beat of rounded wings, grip of claw on stone: Struggling against the current, at the bottom of the river the dipper overturns a pebble: In a field bordering a forest, Harun, gaunt and dazed, is pulled from a truck. Three blows from an iron bar buckle his body; he crumples to the ground.

— Stand up, filthy Turk! Get in line!

He struggles to rise. A boot to the groin caves his body in again; he blacks out in pain.

— Don't kill us! a man calls out. Our families in Germany will send you money.

— Those who have Deutsch marks will be saved! says the squad commander.

The militiamen laugh. Wielding their iron bars, they march the men over Harun's body.

— Don't kill us!

— Shut up, dogs!

They line up the hobbling men in front of a row of corpses stretching out to an oak grove. An excavator, spitting black fumes, carves out a pit in the middle of the field. A red kite hovers overhead, the white patches of its wings bright against the blue sky. Blood seeps into the flesh covering Harun's fractured collar bone. Before he blacked out, he pictured his wife, her face contorted, writhing under a soldier. Piss in his face brings him back to the world; screaming, he is dragged by the arm and kicked into line. The man beside him addresses a militiaman:

— Dragan, we grew up together! How can you do this to me?

— Shut up! Not a word from anyone!

— Dragan, I helped you build your house!

— Shut up, dirty Turk!

— Dragan, you married my cousin Camila, your children—

Blood spurts from his throat as a knife slices his windpipe. On brown earth stained red his body goes into convulsions.

— Anyone else want to talk?

As the murdered man gurgles, blood bubbling in his mouth, a bullet to the brain stops his convulsions.

— Now pray, you filthy sons of a bitch! Pray to your merciful God!

As the men bow down the bullets burst forth. The kite twists its tail and flees the killing field of Srebrenica.

There is no voice for the disappearance of voice, no light but a bearing witness to the light. Shall Harun's wife, Nadia, live a posthumous life, besieged by an irreparable past? Exiled in the world, forever outside time, the survivors of hell speak from the shores of death. Who will hear them? Who will even recognize them?

Mara Marina, Mara Miranda, they say to bear witness is to place oneself in one's own language in the position of those who have lost theirs. Teach me to narrow the gap between the saying and the said; teach me to cultivate the care of the soul. I take your head in my hands: Through the shadow of the haunting your eyes shine; through the portal of what is still possible our lips meet. I enfold you in my arms as you press your mouth to mine. Air! Relenting claws leave stone, tarsi in tandem kick: To the surface the dipper rises, onto a mid-stream rock. Shivering, he shakes the water from his feathers and flies off.

— Brekeke-kex, ko-ax, ko-ax, ko-ax, ko-ax, ko-ax!

Carp fry and flat worm, water beetle and dragonfly nymph: In the mud of the reed bed, in the water of the rim, the frogs feast.

— Brekeke-kex, ko-ax, ko-ax, ko-ax, ko-ax, ko-ax!

— Frogs, should you not interrupt your everyday affairs while others founder in a sea of cares?

— Life is short, we seize the day; every man his cross, every dog his day!

— They hurl the women into an abyss of humiliation, to the vilest of cruelty they subject the men. How can you stay a bystander in the face of such abomination?

— Cry now or cry when you open the archives, to stop them *we* will not lay down *our* lives! Brekeke-kex, ko-ax, ko-ax, ko-ax, ko-ax, ko-ax!

Watch out! Hit by heat, blinded by light, your body recoils; swerving and swaying, your jeep skids. Ahead, suspended in the fireball, the shattered vehicle floats. White noise blanks your mind; in the pit of your stomach a stone. In slow motion fragments of the vehicle fall before your eyes; you come to a stop then back into time your screaming drops you. Second in the convoy your vehicle is unscathed; burnt and bloody, the British soldiers in front of you lie in contorted stillness, the driver's insides spilling out.

Mara Marina, Mara Miranda, the driver was Steven: Lance-Corporal in Company C, First Battalion, deployed in Bosnia. Steven was a man whose heart touched yours; Steven was a man whose body, whose face—now fixed in an otherworldly rictus—you knew intimately.

A year and a day: A year and a day you'd spent interpreting for the blue-helmeted battalion, interpreting their daily exchanges with the killers from a lost country and the citizens they destroy. Through blood and fire you lived, until that explosion blew you here.

They say the past only exists because we have a future: You press your mouth to mine and slip your tongue inside: Absolute intimacy of the limitless secret.

Chapter 2

Bending the straight line of momentum into arabesques of grace, you speed down Mount Kanin. On a white planet where people don't belong, there you feel free! You're amazed you're capable of such feeling again (you're thirteen and a half years old, it's five months since your father killed himself). Faster, faster, faster! You thrill to the throbbing in the soles of your feet and to the touch of snow on your tongue; in command of your body, you push to the limit of losing control. Catching the air after a bump you catch a glimpse of the Adriatic; adjusting your edge angle you round a mogul then once more face the fall line. Schluss! Over ice, down an extreme steep, tucked down low you glide. Under your body you feel the mountain; fascinated by its secrets, you court the danger of short-changing friction for gravity. What is it you are looking for? Falling weightless into the turn, you hover between bliss and foreboding. You drop your hips, bringing your body farther inside the arc of the curve; to a higher edge angle the stance ski rises: In movement the smallness of your body embraces the immensity of the mountain. The side-cut and camber of your skis give a brisk bite to your edging; searching for the position that knifes the blood, in the place where desire confronts fear you carve a crisp, clean arc. Rushing on your run, zigzagging down the mountain, into the time that forms your history you insert yourself. Schluss! You're certain now that your future depends on how you interpret the past. At the bottom of the piste you perform the phantom move and parallel turn to finish. Lifting up your goggles, you raise your eyes to the mountain. Your racing heart grows heavy: You know that even as you change, something immovable inside you will remain.

Snowflakes fall in lamplight, tomorrow there'll be powder: In Bovec, below Mount Kanin, you lie on your bed in your hotel room, your head propped up on your hand. It's black outside, black but for circles of lamplight, just as on your pyjamas the domain of darkness is brightened by owls and stars. On her bed, facing you, your mother lies on her side, her angled bob glossy in the light of a concealed lamp. Softly the snow falls, soft in the unreal serene, deepening the silence, threading the air with breathing.

– Tell me, Mama, how did you and Daddy meet?

Her blue eyes sparkle as she recalls the scene.

– It was in the Südbahnhof. I was on the down escalator when a man came running up it. I had my cello on my back; he couldn't get around me. He raised his head and his eyes met mine, and in that instant I knew my life would never be the same again.

— Were you frightened?

— It was scary, yes. But thrilling, too!

— How did he look?

— Magnetic!

Your mother's eyes grow misty.

— Dark, intense eyes. Sensitive face. An aura of danger. I couldn't look away, as if I'd been hypnotized. We didn't say anything. Just stood like that, in silence, as the escalator took us down.

— Then what happened?

— He said, 'Ashes to ashes, dust to dust'. I said, 'What?' He said, 'Let's make something of the time in-between, you and me.'

— He said that?

— Yes.

— And what did you say?

— I said, 'All right'.

— Mama, he could have been a madman!

— He could have, yes. But I'd just had a big blow-up with my cello teacher. I didn't know what to do with my life anymore. It was as if Bruno had come out of a dream to tell me.

— And then what happened?

— We went to a café, had a coffee. And that's when I fell in love with the light in his eyes.

— And then?

— We spent three days and nights in Vienna.

— That was fast!

— Everything felt right, there was never a false note. We made love for seventy-two hours.

— Mama!

— And then we took the train back to Ljubljana. In a week we were living together...

Red roses bloom on white pyjamas as your mother rolls onto her back: It's a stunning tale, you think, but I alone know about Laura.

— And what was he like?

— Unlike any man I'd ever met before!

Rolling back onto her side and propping up her head with her forearm, Katja faces you.

— A world opened up when I met him: Italy, cinema, kayaking.

— And jazz!

— Jazz, of course. I soaked it all up like a sponge...

Do not swallow the pomegranate seed: On your pyjamas an owl stares out from her domain of darkness.

— The orphanage—when did he get out of it?

— When he turned sixteen. 1958. He was already an exceptional athlete; they saw his promise. Rome was 1960, Tokyo 1964.

— And when exactly did you find out about...

— All those horrible things?

— Yes.

— Just before we got married. One night, after we'd made love—

— Mama!

— How do you think you were conceived?

— All right, all right.

— One night, after we'd made love, he just started crying. Crying and crying and crying. And then it all came out...

Too late, too late, the owl has seen me swallow: Never shall I escape for long now into the light of day! Warm, warm, your tears flow, across the icy surface of history, trying to find a river to take you to the sea.

Mara Marina, Mara Miranda, let us continue to lend each other our eyes, for memory claims to have seen by itself what was revealed only through the gaze of the other. You bring your mouth to mine, and along the inside edge of ambiguity, between what is no longer and what is not yet, you trace my lips with your tongue.

Abeyance, the fall of a snowflake;
New-minted world, virgin.

A face in a mirror,
The slither of a serpent,
The flow of sand in an hourglass.
Erasure, interstice, absence.
Moth's wing, soft smoothness;
Petals falling from a dry stem,
The floating of a feather.

Alabaster, an egg in moonlight;
Talcum under a wedding dress.

Shrouded furniture,
Islands from the air;
Lovemaking while children wakeful.
Ellipsis, interval, caesura.
Night summoning nakedness,
Communion wafer;
Eternity, stars.

Intermezzo 10: Bettina

Filigreed silhouettes stir against the calm of the grey-blue sea; wisps of pink float in the transparent sky, a wash of orange and yellow marks the horizon: Dawn over St Brelade's Bay. Breathing softly in her sleep, Bettina lies sprawled on the bed. Parisian, she's at Ulm, preparing the *agrégation* in English literature. Seeking a change of scene, she'd come to Jersey on a whim. I met her in a cinema in St Helier; *Don't Come Knocking,* we discovered, had struck a chord in both of us. In the hubbub of a pub we created a bubble of privacy, an intimacy made intense by the timbre of her French. Wenders' tale of Earl and his angel sister, siblings ignorant of each other brought together by the return of a lost father, had us discussing filiation and belonging, home and identity. When the bar closed we didn't want to part. Outside, under a streetlight, we broke into laughter and embraced: Turned out we were staying at the same hotel.

In her room overlooking the sea, she sitting on the bed and I in an armchair, we continued talking cinema.

— Say, she asked me, have you seen *Kill Bill?*

— Yes. One and two.

— Did you like it?

— Very much.

— That film threw me right back into my childhood!

— You were a ruthless killer, a girl hellbent on vengeance?

— Yes! I went to Lycée Saint-Louis de Gonzague. I was a débutante in a couturier dress and strapless bra. Went skiing in Gstaad. Hung out with a horde of cousins in Biarritz and Deauville.

— I see. You were a deprived child?

— Exactly!

The camber of her cheekbones, the arch of her eyebrows, the curve of her nostrils, the cut of her lips—a face of chiselled purity, serene and luminous.

— And how does *Kill Bill* come into it?

— Fantasy, Sprague. When I asked myself why I found this film so much fun—I, twenty-one years old!—I realized the Bride is everything I was in my adolescent imagination. To transgress freely, to be relieved of morality—that's jubilation to a girl!

Subtlety and excess, intimacy and aloofness—beguiling, her beauty. She continues:

– And her determination! That really moved me. That implacable will, drawn from her deepest self. The dignity and grace of her isolation.

– Her control of emotion?

– Yes. The pitiless killing of Vernita Green. Her faithfulness to herself. Her vigilance—never letting her traumas defeat her. That's what makes her touching.

I don't want a somnambulist, she doesn't want a supplicant: Is that why I feel her blood in my heartbeat? I say:

– Amazing, isn't it? How a film with no obligations to reality can reflect reality so well.

– Yes. It's pure cinema. It struck a chord in me, as a girl.

– And as a boy?

– I'm not Rimbaud!

– Did you never rebel openly?

– I did. By the time I finished high school I was already free of my parents.

– That's an achievement!

– Yes, I suppose.

I love the inflections in her English; I love the way she lingers just behind the beat.

– Now my only goal is to be happy.

– Happiness can't be a goal, Bettina.

– Why not?

– Because happiness occurs by magic. You can't *earn* it.

– Why not?

– Because it has to come by enchantment!

On delicate wrist her hand twists and tucks her hair behind her ear; as she gives me a sideways glance, in the glow of the lamp her lips glisten. I make a lap of my legs; she comes and sits astride me. Leafing through the book of her lips, my tongue discovers a fierce poetry; as I linger over a haiku, the epiphany becomes blinding.

Afterwards, in bed, Bettina spoke of her experience.

– At five, I would reproach my parents for their fruitless 'cuddling'. They tried and tried to have a second child, never succeeded. Every morning I'd ask my mum, 'So, are you pregnant?'.

The enigmatic tension of desire, the incessant renewal of my second skin: Do they not flow from the same source?

— At the same age I had an obsession with roses. Spent my time drawing them. My father said, 'Rosebud, that's what I call a woman's sex'.

Questions apparently serious, and yet how playful was my experimentation with appearance.

— My parents, in effect, wanted to do away with boundaries.

— Like the one that divides the generations?

— Yes.

— Dangerous illusion.

— Indeed. For a while I fell for it, but when puberty came, I began fighting for my independence.

And how far I'd go! When people would become predictable, when the possibility of surprise would seem buried, I'd discreetly take off my panties and watch the world around me begin to glow.

— At sixteen, right after my Bac, I fell in love with a weirdo. Got out just in time.

I'd feel a lightness, an exhilaration: I'd feel lush!

— He made me hate sex. Gave me an image of it I couldn't stand. But making love was so important to me that I couldn't break it off. Finally, my parents gave me an ultimatum: Leave him or leave home. I left home. I couldn't accept them deciding my private life, even if this boy was making me suffer. A few weeks later, when I was ready, I left him for good.

By this little trick, I felt my desire no longer deadened: I'd reclaimed my right to see women as rivals, my right to be a woman amongst men.

— And you, Sprague, what were you like at my age?

— I was like Terence Stamp in *Teorema*.

— I love that film!

It was at once strange and seductive, as if in taking off my panties I had unveiled reality.

— So you were the stranger, the saint, the guest? she asks.

— Yes.

— Did you make love with men?

— No. But if their desire, unbeknownst to them, was homosexual, I was the one who'd reveal it.

— Did you make love with the mother, the maid, the daughter?

— Yes. But I myself didn't know my secret. I was simply silent and available. The girl always gave the signal.

Mystery returned to the world: Naked, I assumed my desire and felt free to play with identity.

– Did you read Rimbaud in the garden, like Terence Stamp?

– I did.

– And did you always wear white?

– No. But I wore the equivalent: black.

– And did you become an actor in others' erotic scenarios?

– Yes. I let them use me. I was simply there, passive until it was time to perform.

– Mysteriously present in their intimacy?

– Yes.

– And afterwards, after making love, were they transformed?

– They were. They couldn't go on living as they'd lived before.

And thus, Marietta, Bettina understood that the real cannot coincide with the truth, and so must resort to fiction. And now, as she sleeps amid the night's tumultuous sheets, I observe the awakening day: Milky in the transparent sky, pink floats; orange and yellow mark the horizon, silhouettes blacken the grey-blue sea: Like the details of the dawn you are inexhaustible, and everything is mine to learn.

PART SEVEN

Chapter 1

Nellie was not her name, nor was she anchored in an estuary. Nightfall was not the time, nor autumn the season. No, our vessel was the 205 GTI that you'd bought when you sold your Mini, and as we sped along the highway, hemmed in by the Forêt d'Ermenonville, the winter morning was luminous with our night's afterglow. Still, as we headed from Paris to Amsterdam, there was a bit of Marlowe in me, and something dark and African. Oh love, what tender days we had that December! Serene days of separation, wild nights of celebration, days of communion distilled in night's incorruptible core! How shall I take up our story, how shall I resume? Let's stay in that sprightly car, let's regard the horizon from its intimate atmosphere. Are you ready? Clutch up, throttle open: Let's go!

Yesterday, upon your return from Neuchâtel, there was a friskiness in our stride as we jogged along the Front de Seine. In the evening we ate with gusto the omelette you'd concocted. Then, last night, with ever-renewed pleasure we drew spirit from flesh. And in the morning, the surprise of your black hot-hatch: So, my little petrolhead, this is the body that aroused your lust? The defiant Peugeot looked raring to go. Vroom-vroom! That was barely an hour ago, and now already you are driving its virility past the royal city of Senlis, telling me of your time in Neuchâtel.

— So you see, for an only child with no children, Christmas isn't easy. I know I have to stand my ground, but I keep walking away... sideways, like Katie!

— That also comes from being an only child.

— You think so?

— Yes. And Katie's attitude—

— Do you still like her?

— Katie? I love her!

At the *marché de Noël* in Neuchâtel you'd bought me a sculptural assemblage, a little beast with personality to spare: a crab we christened Katie. Supple and spry, perched on a bronze spring, she sprouted aluminum legs and exorbitant eyes from a body of polished mahogany. Slightly sinister was her sloping mouth, crafty and mischievous her demeanour. Yes, that was the gift you gave me, a sideways-scuttling creature with fierce claws, a demiurge to fetch me up a world from under the sea.

— Zürich was more fun. And Florence was fantastic!

– What did you do in Zürich?

– Ate Geschnetzeltes with Rösti, Bratwurst with Büürli. Gave a party in my house. Revisited my old haunts.

And, one evening when you were out walking, twilight conspired with electricity to make magic of the hour: Catching sight of the Märli Tram on the Bahnhofbrücker, you felt yourself a five-year old entranced by angels. And then, walking on, you caught sight of the brightly-lit big top of Conelli's Circus and recalled how, as a little girl, you would lean back wide-eyed on the painted bench, amazed by the aerial acrobatics of the trapeze artists. Already then you sensed that life is all about risk, and now it's the risks you've taken that define your life. As you turned back to the river, you realized with pleasure that it's the future that opens up the past, and frees you to be fully in the present.

Clutch up, throttle open: Instantly the gears engage as you ride the lever through the ratios, leaving the *péage* behind. A smile lights up your face as the highway opens out.

– You like your new car, don't you?

The silence resounds in affirmation as you cast your glow upon me.

– Can't you just feel it, Sprague—how creamy the engine is? And so torquey!

– Torquey?

– Yeah, high torque at low RPM. That's why she's so nippy coming out of the gate!

– I see.

Forest trail, blanket of snow; bare trees, druid stone: Forests are sweet when the world does not enter them; there the saint may find his rest. Soft, soft, the back of my fingers along your cheek; subtle, subtle, your lips on my fingertips.

– I like your new baby.

– Well, if you like this one, you'd love Matteo's.

– What does he have?

– An Alfa Romeo Spider!

– Did you drive it?

– Of course.

– And what's it like?

– Pure pleasure!

And thus you came to tell me of how, driving that classic Italian droptop through the twisting roads of the Tuscan countryside, you felt imbued with its power, your double-clutch shifting making its twin-cams purr, your body and its chassis in ecstatic communion. And when you'd had enough of riding through the gently rolling landscape, you'd return winter to its quiescence and enter Matteo's family hearth. Yes, in a little village just south of the Arno, in a house not far from where Galileo was confined, you made a place for yourself among the refined Balestieri family. In the house, woollen rugs washed terracotta tiles in pale gold and green while chestnut wood lent its warmth to farmhouse furniture. Hunting motifs graced tapestried cushions on a gobelin-and-tent-stitched sofa; braided onions and bunched herbs hung from the kitchen beams. At table, you enjoyed black truffle on mascarpone, spinach and ricotta ravioli in sage-and-butter sauce; almond biscuits, wild honey, and baked pear. In town, between ignoring the *pappagalli* in the Piazza della Repubblica and dodging the hash dealers in Santo Spirito, you visited Botticelli and Michelangelo, Titian and Fra Angelico, the Bargello's *cortile* and Santa Maria Novelle, the Palazzo Vecchio and San Miniato al Monte. And yet, in this cradle of Humanism and the Renaissance, in that house of civilized tradition, you continued to pretend you were Matteo's girlfriend for to his family he couldn't come out.

Why, I wondered? Wherein lies the *disgrazia?* Are we not in the late twentieth century? *Terra prava, nido di malizia;* unspeakable practice, abominable sin: The most evil and dangerous of carnal vices, act *contra naturam*—surely the *ufficiali di notte*'s legacy has run out?

– 'Gay dignity', Sprague, 'coming out', are not Italian terms. *'Ambiguo',* that's the word for 'homosexual' in Italy.

– *Ambiguo?*

– Yes. It's not rare for Italian gays to pretend to have a girlfriend, for the sake of family peace.

– And how long have you agreed to the game?

– Exactly a year. We just celebrated our first anniversary!

– And did you sleep in his bed?

– Of course. The only difference with sharing anyone else's bed is that we didn't fuck, obviously.

– Yes, of course.

– Though every night I would jump on the bed a bit, just to get the springs going.

– Keeping up appearances!

– Exactly. That's Italian homosexuality. It's neither open nor clandestine, but tacit. Even when you go to a *club ambiguo,* it's only the transvestites who stand out.

– Marietta, you're one hell of a girl!

You bring your fingertips to your lips and blow me a kiss.

So these are the cultural limits of candour, but what lies on the other side of silence? Henry James and John Singer Sargent, the aesthete's Italy; repressed Fascists and Balkan rent boys, cinema's stereotypes. And then, cleansing my mind of these clichés, you spoke of Matteo's turpitude.

— Matteo's in mourning.

— For who?

— The man he loved. He died two weeks before I arrived.

— How did he die?

— Wretchedly. 'A severe bronchial infection'. 'A mysterious illness'. AIDS, in other words.

In silence I watch the trees go by, in silence I hear them sigh: the scourging angel, the black death.

— Water?

— Please.

I hand you the bottle. Looking out the window, I hear your double-jointed drinking and see Matteo in a mirror studying his imminent death. And then you enlighten me:

— Matteo's in mourning, but he's never been more alive.

— What do you mean?

— Well, for example, he investigated the burning of *extracommunitari* caravans and got his report into the press.

— *Extracommunitari?*

— Migrants, foreign workers, living in caravans on the outskirts of Florence. There's been a wave of night raids on their camps, a series of beatings and burnings.

— How can he have the courage to do that, and not have the courage to come out?

— Homosexuality's an aspect of one's subjectivity, Sprague, it's not just something you do.

— Yes, of course, but—

— Transparency's deceptive. It's masking that's more stimulating. I learned that a long time ago, ever since that summer in Corfu. Playing at being Matteo's girlfriend has only confirmed it.

— How, exactly?

— When you refuse to define, when you accept uncertainty, you're forced to constantly interpret what's going on. That keeps you on your toes.

— That's a definition of an artistic sensibility.

— It is, yes.

You glide into the fast lane and overtake an Audi.

– So you've learned a lot from Matteo?

– I have. Sex is not a fatality for him, he lives by no formula. To assume a gender doesn't exhaust who you are. I've known that for some time. His example simply confirms it.

Is that another grain of gravel in your sandal, then? Is that the source of your gangling grace, the signature way you walk? Does it explain your affinity with paradox, your taste for subterfuge? And does it account for the irony with which you wear a designer dress, the chic you confer on a T-shirt? And perhaps, too, your feeling of luxury when clad only in the atmosphere?

– You're an artist, Marietta.

Your eyes shine and I see mine in them.

Chapter 2

Bienvenue au Pays Compiégnois. Le Château de Pierrefonds, l'Abbaye-Forteresse de Saint-Jean-aux-Bois. Ushering its antlers to the edge of the wood, a roebuck stops to stare: These mechanized hounds are harmless.

– Sprague, look in my purse. You'll find a cassette and a blue notebook.

Soft folds of leather, gathered and cinctured with a narrow belt; a handcuff ring, a bolt-snap hook.

– Open it.

Gunmetal gives off a purple gleam; the clasp holds fast.

– No, Sprague, that's only ornament! Just pull it open from the top.

– Ah!

Lined in dark plumb, the bag presents its contents to my gaze.

– Here's the notebook. Now where's the cassette?

– It's in there. Look.

An Air France boarding pass marks your page in *The Unbearable Lightness of Being.* A mesh of silver sequins glitters at the end of a Moleskine pouch. Beneath your twistlock wallet, a wet-wipe envelope from Swissair. Under the folded blue plastic of a pop-up brush, rows of numbers pencilled on the back of a Doublemint wrapper.

– I don't see it.

– It's in there. Keep looking.

A flashlight embossed with the Peugeot lion, a tiny bar of soap from Four Seasons Sydney. An emery board, a fountain—

– Don't touch that!

– Why not?

– It's pepper spray.

– Disguised as a fountain pen? Clever. I hope you've never had to use it?

– Once, in Chicago. Zapped a guy on the Magnificent Mile.

– Wouldn't take no for an answer?

– Exactly. Look in the side pockets.

– At night, I suppose?

Rouge Dior.

– Yes.

Touche Éclat.

– Dumb of me to have been out at that hour.

Le Crayon Khôl.

— Fooled by the bright lights?

— Yeah.

— Hey!

I hold up a wedding ring.

— You hiding a husband, Marietta?

— That's my secret weapon, Sprague. Anti-flirt.

Smooth, bright, warm: 'I look at you and see the passion eyes of May'.

— And if that doesn't do it, I've got a heart-shaped pendant with interlocking 'M's.

— Marietta and Matteo?

— Yeah. Try the drop pocket.

— The drop pocket... Yes!

— Put it in the player.

I take the cassette out of its case and slip it into the slot.

— It lasts exactly thirteen minutes.

— What is it?

— We'll talk about it afterwards.

You press 'play'.

— Don't say another word!

Silence. And then it comes, the sense beyond signification, the singular voice threading its mystery through me. How, Marietta, could I ever convey the ravishment I experienced in those thirteen minutes? The voluptuous fusion of language and body, the festive return to a primordial state—how? Music alone can fetch a world from beyond meaning; only song itself can communicate the incommunicable. In those thirteen minutes, the ecstatic performance by an unaccompanied soprano of four electrifying songs shivered my spine and shook my bones.

Listen! Intricate melismas, awkward intervals; sublime tone, perfect pitch: Along the full range of her tessitura, the soprano places the syllables of her idiomatic song. Subtlety of nuance vies with intensity of expression, full-throated glory with elusive transparency. Expressing a dark and passionate vehemence, she varies the pressure as she moulds the vowels; evoking an other-worldly dreaminess, she drains her voice of all vibrato: I hear the scream of the butterfly.

Listen! Floating a pure, ringing tone, she soars to a radiant high; in brilliant dark timbre, she marks the subterranean movement of a line. Speech-song or cantabile, vocalise or outcry, beyond vocal effects, the colouristic expression of pitches gives sense to the sound. Between attack and extinction, what artistry in sustaining tension!

Listen! The sober gravity of incisive articulation, the compelling beauty of a long-breathed line; the beguiling movement across a span of pitches, the furtive emergence of muted vowels. Operatic in its breadth of register, dramatic in its large intervallic leaps—What is this masterpiece?

Listen! Glissando connections and glottal attacks, a shimmer of rich overtones; the exhilaration of continuous vocalization, the sadness of decay between notes. Essence of music, purest of instruments, the voice as miracle: What immediacy, what intimacy, what bodily presence! When the final tone dies it is I who am breathless.

– My God, Marietta! What was that?

– That, Sprague, was written by Matteo. Four songs for solo soprano, sung by a singer called Mara Zizek.

– Blow me away! It's brilliant!

– Yeah.

– Matteo's done it! This work will make his name! And who is Mara Zizek?

– She's from Yugoslavia. Lives in Vienna.

Opening the window, I gulp the cold air.

– That was amazing! I'm stunned by the beauty of it!

– So am I. I was so moved during the recording I cried.

– You were there?

– Yes. In Matteo's home studio. Just two days ago.

– Tell me about it!

And thus you came to conjure a woman who could have been your twin, standing before a microphone in a converted carriage house. I imagined the compressors, equalizers and mixers, the monitors and the reel-to-reel; I imagined the acoustic panels and bass traps, the condenser mic and subdued lights. But clearest in my mind was the image of a Slavic blonde in a Stones T-shirt, singing through a nylon stocking into the microphone.

– She's from Ljubljana.

– Slovenia?

– Yes. She also plays the saxophone.

– That explains her long breath!

— It does. And her ear—that incredible ear!—she attributes to her years of playing the violin.

— The mastery of specific and indeterminate pitches?

You nod your head in assent.

— She moved me, Sprague. From the roots of my hair to the tips of my toes, she moved me!

Astounded by the persistence of sound, we remain silent: The evanescent has decided to stay.

— And what are the words?

— You'll never guess!

— Rilke, Ingeborg Bachmann?

— No, it's Giacomo Leopardi, translated into German!

— What?

— Yes, believe it or not, it's Leopardi. Take a look, in the blue notebook.

> *Seit ich dich erblickte,*
> *welche ernsthafte Sorge hatte nicht dich*
> *zum Gegenstande?*
>
> Since I first saw you,
> Of what care close to my heart have you not been
> The ultimate object?

— Why in German, why didn't Matteo keep the Italian?

— Can you imagine these songs in Italian?

— No, I can't. Italian is *bel canto*.

— Exactly. Ironic distance, that's what Matteo was after, and only by setting Leopardi in German was he was able to obtain it.

— It works beautifully. It's unmistakably contemporary.

— Yes, but it still has a subliminal link to the *lieder* tradition. That's what he wanted.

— Well, he's succeeded brilliantly!

> Flesh made grace, at once
> Body and spirit; air made intimate,
> At once ethereal and real:
> Mara, how you move me!

– Yes, and it's all the more impressive because writing instrumentally for the voice is notoriously difficult. Mara says many composers make you hoarse after half an hour.

– Really? That's unforgivable. You can't replace a vocal cord like a violin string.

– Indeed. No danger of that with Matteo, though. His mother's a singing teacher. He grew up with song.

– I remember him telling me that.

– And because he's also an accompanist, no matter how far he pushes the envelope as a composer, he never loses that wonderfully supple sense of song.

– Yes, that's what's so impressive.

Jagged stalks, dusted with snow, recede to a row of bare trees marking the horizon: On both sides of the highway, stubble fields stretch out.

– Do you know Leopardi, Sprague?

– Yes. Do you?

– No.

– He's the brother I never had. I feel very close to him.

– Really? Tell me about him.

And thus I came to speak of my beloved Giacomo, of his early understanding that life is nothing but a process of losing: 'The only people who truly live until their death are those who remain children all their lives.' I spoke of his pitiless mother, haunted by a sense of sin, incapable of touching her children. I spoke of the boy bent over his books, freezing in his father's library. Homer and Virgil, Dante and Tasso, Seneca and Cicero: These were Giacomo's intimates. I spoke of his overwhelming longing for the tenderness of a woman, a tenderness he would never know. Intelligent enough to appreciate his genius, vulnerable enough to be kind: He never met such a woman. His scoliosis, the hump on his back, was but the visible sign, I asserted, that he'd been marked out for sorrow. And thus he was hurt into poetry. As you warmed to my portrait, I spoke of Leopardi's ethics of lucidity, his refusal of abstraction, his recognition of the individual as an absolute. His poetry, I explained, in restoring presence to things, creates a silence in which memory can speak. Suffering, mourning and solitude—yes, but in a graceful moon on a quiet night there is the promise of a woman and a shared life: Leopardi is the poet of tenderness.

– The brother you never had, hey?

Your eyes shine and I see mine in them: I want to wrap my arms around you, I want to press your body to mine. Or just fall down at your feet.

Chapter 3

Crossarms and ground stays, towers and foundations: Across the highway, across the trees, across the field into infinity, they carry vast spans of high-tension wire, living electricity. As you pass a tanker, a gleam brings a glow to your hair and deepens the intarsia in the knit Matteo gave you.

You've just told me that, this summer, you're going to be recording Kurtág's *Kafka-Fragmente* with Mara. What of Kafka has Kurtág captured? His single-minded pursuit of purity? The double-edged sword of his obsessions? His fusion of strict form and intimacy? Whatever it may be, I know that both you and Mara, through Kurtág, will honour Franz.

— What's she like, this Mara? She intrigues me.

— Me too!

I like the glint in your eye. And I like what it signals.

— Did you spend much time together?

— We did. From the time I arrived until she returned to Vienna. We spent the last evening playing pool!

— Yeah?

— Yeah. Matteo's got a friend—Riccardo—whose family owns a firm that makes pool tables and cue sticks. They run a club in Sesto Fiorentino, a suburb of Florence.

— Real pros, then. And how good's your game?

— Pretty good. I was in the billiards club at Engineering School. I could beat the house man at Clichy-Montmartre.

— That was your club?

— Yeah.

— Marietta, you're one hell of a girl!

You bring your fingertips to your lips and blow me a kiss.

— And Mara, what's her level?

— Excellent. She wasn't easy to beat!

— That's a match I'd liked to have seen! Tell me about it!

And thus you came to speak of your evening in a suburban Florence pool room, a rose and lilac sky silhouetting umbrella pines through the glazing. For months afterwards, my imagination would stage scenarios of your encounter.

Here's one: Nine-ball, race to seven. Let no one enter here who is ignorant of geometry! Right off the opening break Mara makes three balls, then with cool efficiency runs the table to take the first frame. A poor safety in your visit allows her to take the second as well, and before you know it you're down 0-3.

She moves me, but I mustn't show my vulnerability. Come on, give her a good match!

You make two balls on your break, but the pocket for the one is blocked by the six, obliging you to play a safety again. Mara lines up her shot, shoots and overcuts: The one misses the pocket, the cue-ball freezes in your favour.

She intrigues me, with her knowing silence. Disjointed attachment, connected autonomy—does she understand that's my style?

You sink the one, the two, the three, and then you catch fire: Angle of incidence, ball speed and spin—everything comes together and you're on the board at last: 1-3.

Velvet and internal is my feeling—oh let me not make a faux pas!

Mara fails to make a ball on her break. You pocket the one, sending it smooth along the length of the table. Killing the cue, you spin the two in, and now you've got yourself an easier table. With stellar position play you finish your run, winning the frame to make it 2-3.

What fun, trading T-shirts and belts, going along with Riccardo's presumption that we were sisters!

A powerful break gives you a good shot on the one; you make the shot, then play the two into the opposite corner. Already you're thinking of what to do with the five—the seven is blocking the pocket. You dispatch the three into a side pocket, then consider how to optimize the leave on the four. Imparting top spin, you sink the four and leave the cue perfectly positioned for the five. Rapidly finishing your run, you even the score at 3-3.

She undid my bracelet, I pinned up her hair. Easy reciprocity, exquisite intimacy—but oh those subterranean currents quickening my senses!

A jump shot leads to a foul against you, giving Mara ball-in-hand. She makes her placement, sinks the ball, then runs out the frame to go up 4-3.

The flesh sucked off an eighth of orange, the peel snug against the gums: What merriment, communicating with sealed mouths!

Three balls on the break give you a wide open table. You walk round to examine the triangle formed by the two-ball, the seven and the nine; you line up your shot and shoot: After impacting the two and sending it into the corner pocket, the cue ball takes a tangent to the nine and sends it into another pocket: You win the game in two shots, tying the race at 4-4.

Understanding without words, the mystery of her vibration. 'Steal not in, sweetbitter unmanageable creature'!

Putting backspin on the cue ball to bring the one around, Mara draws it too much and the one ends up hanging on the lip of the opposite corner. Still, with the eight-ball blocking the one, it looks like a safety. You go rail-first, get around the eight-ball and sink the one on the ricochet, then go on to run out the frame with perfect cue-ball control: You're leading 5-4.

To you from me it moves, this feeling, then ricochets back to hollow me out: I must not get light-headed!

It's your break and you use it brilliantly, pocketing three balls and parking the cue. In an impressive display of shotmaking you pocket one ball after the other, and then—your whole torso stretched out on the table—you pocket the nine to take yourself to the hill: 6-4.

She loves my KL. Said it sings on my skin. I said the same of her Opium.

Mara makes an excellent break, then runs the table with seemingly effortless shotmaking, narrowing your lead to 6-5.

Your stance for the break says you're not to be denied; you make three balls and the rest scatter into an easy configuration. One, three, four, six, seven, nine: With submission to the trigonometry of desire, victory comes!

Now tell me, Marietta, might it have happened like that?

Chapter 4

Leaving a blanket of lace upon the sleeping land, the quickening sky unseams itself from the plain and restores the horizon to us... Saint-Quentin, a blood-stained bird... Cambrai, a cambric shirt...

Fellini's Casanova: The 205 purrs as we discuss the film you'd seen in the Palazzo dello Strazzino with Matteo and Mara.

> The idiot boy
> In a witch's box
> On the island of Murano;
> Speaking to no-one,
> Never spoken to,
> Blood from the nose pouring:
> Casanova
>
> Withholding nothing,
> Hoarding nothing,
> Giving without calculation;
> The scandal of pleasure,
> The impudence of daring,
> Guilt and shame refused:
> Casanova
>
> Stealer of fire,
> Protector of darkness,
> The generosity of the poor;
> Lover of women,
> Abhorrer of suffering,
> The honesty of the outlaw:
> Casanova

You laugh when I tell you that between the two of us, it is you who are more fully the Venetian.

> We both know that having a roof
> Is no assurance of shelter;
> We're both convinced the biggest fool

Is the one who believes he can't be foolish.

Not for us the familiar mirror,
But the uncanny looking glass;
Not for us the fixity of closure,
But the flux of openness.

Too demanding not to desire the truth,
Too modest to reduce the world to it:
We both know that humility—
Not intelligence—
Is the opposite of stupidity.

So why do I say you are more fully the Venetian? Because the insolence of pleasure becomes you more than it does I.

– He's the brother *I* never had, Sprague.
– He is!
– I love his *réplique* to Voltaire: 'When you've done away with superstition, what will you replace it with?'
– Yes, that insight is extraordinary. It's a shame Fellini failed to understand him.
– Nevertheless, the film is still ravishing.
– Yes, but if he had understood Casanova, his film would have been—
– A different film! You have to accept it for what it is.
– Yes, of course. But still. Fellini's hysterical vengeance against I don't know what phantasm has nothing to do with the real Casanova.
– I agree. But don't forget that Fellini began as a cartoonist. He's drawn to caricature.
– Right.
– And think of the music! Without that *clown triste* dimension, that ridiculousness, you'd never have that ravishing score.
– True. And what a loss that would be!

Listen, my love, to *marilenghe,* listen to the words in the Friulian tongue:

Pin penin, valentin, pan e vin;
Pin penin, valentin, fureghin.
Le xe le voje i caprissi de chéa,
Che jeri la jera, la jera putéa;

Le xe le voje i caprissi de chéa,
Che jeri la jera, la jera putéa.

Now listen to the music: Wistful, ethereal, otherworldly, through a filigree of plucked guitar the glass harmonica bears the plaintive melody. Punctuated by electric bass, the sonorities are nocturnal. And now the glockenspiel comes to articulate the second motif—'These are the wishes, the whims of the girl, who yesterday was a child, a child at play'—before the acoustic guitar, against a wash of strings, plays the first motif again. How can a nursery song be so heart-wrenching? Is it because, in its very essence, it is an evocation of transience? Listen! In bewitching permutations, in ingenious alternations, the instruments transpose the figure and ground of Casanova as grown-up and child. Marietta, did you ever imagine, as you stared into the aqueous blue of Casanova's eyes—that pallor abrim with moonlight and spermatozoa—that loving you would turn my green eyes blue and bestow upon my tongue, too, the syntax that turns memory into music?

— *Miss Charpillon est plus putain que sa mère! Miss Charpillon est plus putain que sa mère! Miss Charpillon est plus putain que sa mère!*

Conjuring Casanova's parrot of revenge, you mockingly convey the spurned lover's venom. Retrieving your voice, you cut off my laughter.

— A brilliant gesture, but much too light to balance the humiliation.

— Yes.

— Especially when you think he was minutes away from killing himself.

And thus we recalled the facts of the saddest episode in Casanova's career, when a sweet-faced slut dared him to resist her: She would make him fall in love, she would reduce him to a dog at her feet. She did. Stripped of his dignity, his pockets filled with stones, he crossed Westminster Bridge to drown himself in the Thames.

— Could you ever do that to a man, Marietta?

— I've known men who've wanted nothing more than to be a dog at my feet. I've never been interested.

— Why not?

— I don't like power.

— Don't tell me you've never been tempted! Power demands you test it, see how far you can go.

— True. But once you've made a man cry just because you can, you move on.

Crystalline, the snow glistens.

These are the wishes
The whims of a girl

Who yesterday was a child
A child at play

Unbroken, the plain unfolds its flatness to infinity: The enigma of femininity feeds the vertigo of desire, infinitely.

Chapter 5

Crossing into Belgium we began a game of guessing the Flemish equivalent of French words—anatomy, animals, emotions. When we got to Ghent you asked me about the party I'd been to while you were away. And thus began our discussion of my African origins.

– How did it go? You seemed a bit cagey about it last night.

– Did I?

– Yes.

– I had a good time. Marcelina's got a fantastic apartment, rue Georges Braque.

– Marcelina's your student?

– No, Isata's my student. Marcelina works at UNESCO.

– And where's she from?

– Angola. She's a biologist, plant biology. Isata's from Sierra Leone.

– And who were the others?

– There were quite a few. Jean-Baptiste, Isata's boyfriend. He's a musician, from Zaire. Stella, from Nigeria. She's an economist—development economics—also at UNESCO. Dzingai. He works at Alliance Française in Zimbabwe. And Solange, of course, the friend from Uganda that I met in Tanzania. She's professor of history at Cambridge, but this year she's at the Sorbonne. And then there was Sprague. He's from South Africa. I don't know exactly what he does. Something to do with cinema, I think. Or is it poetry? Anyway, all I remember is that he's crazy about some girl from Zürich.

– Is he black?

– No.

– Is he white?

– No.

– Is he brown?

– No.

– So how does he fit in?

– Well, that's just it: He doesn't.

– Is he some kind of monster, then?

– No. In fact, he's very good looking—at least that's the impression I got, because first Stella, then Marcelina—then both of them together—tried to get him into their bed. But, as I told you, the guy's got it bad for some chick from Zürich, and he simply insisted on sleeping alone in his sleeping bag.

– That chick from Zürich, I heard she did the same thing, sleeping all alone.

– Well, let's hope in Amsterdam—

– They'll have a nice big bed!

The soughing of the ventilator stops: In the silence my heart expands.

Gand-Gent, Anvers-Antwerpen, Liège-Luik: The game goes on. You're better at it than I am.

– What's this one, Marietta: *Net vir Blankes.*

– Whites Only.

– Europeans Only. That's how it's rendered.

– Do you really feel you don't fit in anywhere, Sprague?

– Uh-hm. For the blacks I'm mixed masala, for the browns I'm a tomato bredie, and for the whites I'm just a leftover.

You laugh.

– And because I'm neither fish nor fowl, of course I'm not kosher.

Your laughter intensifies.

– You got a sweet tooth, baby?

– Yeah.

– Well I'm your man: I'm the jam between the bread.

– Sprague! I'm driving!

I remove my hand from between your legs.

– Moreover, I have terrible morals. I'm illegitimate, sexually promiscuous, and totally untrustworthy. Even the dogs are ashamed of me—I'm just a mongrel.

– A bastard!

– A Bushman!

– A degenerate!

– Don't ever bet on me: I've already drawn the wrong card. I'm just a bit-player in a sideshow.

– A coon in a carnival!

– A black-face minstrel!

– A freak-show mulatto!

– Yeah, I'm original sin, baby, one of God's stepchildren. I'm what you get when the devil imitates the Creator.

– Sprague, you're beautiful! You're the most beautiful man I've ever met!

– So what? Everybody knows Coloured people don't know where they come from.

De provincie Oost-Vlaanderen – heet u welkom.

– *Dank u wel,* you salute the road sign.

And then we practice some Flemish from the phrase book. I say:

– *Hallo, vriend. Ik he je gemist.*

(Hello, friend. I missed you so much.)

– *Kom met mij mee. Vanavind.*

(Come with me. Tonight.)

– *Hoeveel is het?*

(How much is it?)

– *Enkele reis of heen-en-terug?*

(One-way or return?)

– *Heen-en-terug.*

(Return.)

– *Honderd gulden.*

(One hundred guilders.)

– *Is er een specialiteit van het huis?*

(Is there a house specialty?)

– *Natuurlijk. Worst en boter.*

(Of course. Sausage and butter.)

And then we stop to pee at the Total station.

Back in the 205, we continue: *Antwerpen 35... BIJ MIST 2 TEKENS...*

– In foggy weather...

– ...two chevrons...

We look at each other and hesitate, then decide not to seek a joke in that. Instead, you ask me:

– How did Isata end up in Paris? Sierra Leone wasn't a French colony, was it?

– No. But Guinea-Conakry was. That's where her mother's from. She fled the country to go to Sierra Leone after the Sékou Touré terror in the early sixties. Wrong tribe. So Isata's perfectly at ease in both English and French.

– And why Paris, instead of London or somewhere else?

– She did live in London, in fact, before moving to Paris. Her mother's a lawyer, she studied intellectual property law at the University of Strasbourg. Got hired by an English firm in London, and then was posted back to France.

– It's a shame talent like that can't work in their own country.

– Yes. Either the country is totally dysfunctional, or else you're not from the tribe whose turn it is to feed at the State trough. Or both. So you look for opportunities elsewhere.

– And what does Isata want to do?

– Law, like her mother.

– And her boyfriend, what's he like?

– Jean-Baptiste? Wicked sense of humour. Dresses like a dandy. He was the DJ.

– What did he play?

– Highlife, jit-jive, Afrobeat. Great stuff! I'm hooked on Fela Kuti.

– I'd loved to have been a fly on the wall.

– Hey, you were already a bee in my bonnet.

– The ants in your pants!

– The birds in my bush!

– The bats in your belfry!

– Yeah, baby, I'm crazy—about you!

– I'm your eager beaver!

– I'm your alley cat!

– I'm your dark horse!

– No, *I'm* the *dark* horse!

Laughing, you blow me a kiss, a big wet smacker.

Through the bleak fields we ride, an occasional windmill lending a painterly touch to the landscape. You say:

– I imagine Stella and Marcelina are from the élite in their countries, to be working at UNESCO.

– Yes. Stella's a diplomat's daughter, and Marcelina's the daughter of a Communist millionaire, Minister of something or other in the government.

– And they're not just free-riding in Paris?

– No, far from it. Stella's a Commonwealth Scholar, very bright and hard-working. So much so that she gets flack from the slackers at UNESCO.

– I see.

– And Marcelina has nothing to do with her family anymore. Showed me a photo of her father—Rolex, Saville Row suit, gold chains galore. Staying in a luxury suite in London's most expensive hotel while ninety-five percent of the population live on a dollar a day.

– And Angola's Communist?

— Yes. The same families that monopolized business in the past set up a Communist system to guarantee their exclusive control today.

— What a country!

Alvo Supermarkten, Schraven B.V., Euro Leasing: Trucks turning off to the industrial parks around the interchange.

— And what about the history professor at the Sorbonne? Solange, right?

— Yeah.

— What's she like?

— She's amazing.

— As amazing as Ariane?

To the flicker in your eyes the fireflies in mine flash back.

— In her own way.

— And you first met in Uganda?

— No. Tanzania. Dar es Salaam. Shared a hotel room for a week.

— Really? How did that come about?

— Do you want the short version or the long?

— The long!

To the fireflies in your eyes the flicker in mine flash back.

— Okay. I went to Dar es Salaam to see if I could get involved with the South African freedom fighters there. Well, it didn't take me long to see that I was really looking for myself, that for me the liberation struggle was just a pretext to work out my own problems.

— Admirable lucidity!

— In the nick of time.

— And what problems did you have, exactly?

— Hey, we're going to Amsterdam, not Vladivostok!

— All right. Just tell me your main problem when you were in Dar es Salaam.

— I was in a free-floating state. Nothing mattered, nothing was real. I was looking for a situation where actions have consequences, where you have to pay for your decisions.

— Sounds like you never had a father.

— You could say that.

Indifference is the hardest thing. It's worse than absence. You'd have been better off killing yourself or going mad.

— Go on.

— Where was I?

— You were looking to take responsibility for yourself, for your choices.

– Yes.

– And so you wanted to become—what? An activist, a freedom fighter, a terrorist?

– All three!

– And what made you pull back?

– I never lost touch with the flame inside me.

– The flame inside you?

– Yes. My beacon, my touchstone, my truth and bone. The maimed refugee from soul murder.

You caress my cheek; I kiss your fingers.

– Go on, Sprague. Solange...

– Solange, yes... So, I'm in Dar es Salaam, staying at a hostel, sharing a room with an engineer from India. I remember us sitting on our beds, facing each other, spooning up ravioli from a tin can while discussing Hinduism.

– I can just picture it!

– I still remember his face, his sense of peace and self-possession. So different from my state.

– East meets West?

– More like quietude meets dazed-and-confused. By the way, do you know, on that song, Jimmy Page uses a violin bow on his Les Paul?

– Solange, Sprague, Solange!

– Okay! So, my next roommate was a Swedish student, studying Islam in Africa. When he left, I got stuck with a Tanzanian guy from the interior, a real *folle*. He was after my ass, so I bought him a paisley shirt and a Russian watch and asked him to leave. He wouldn't. And that's when I met Solange.

– How?

– I was having dinner at her hotel. I was sick of competing with flies for my food in the local restaurants. We shared a table, and when I told her about my importunate *folle,* she invited me to come and stay with her. I did.

– And did you sleep in her bed?

– Day and night. We couldn't get enough of each other. And then her husband suddenly showed up.

– Did you go back to the hostel?

– No. I went to the library. Shacked up with the assistant librarian then flew back to London.

To the flicker in your eyes the fireflies in mine flash back.

– And what was Solange doing in Dar es Salaam?

– Research. For her PhD. Something about political community—citizenship and belonging—in East Africa. Her family's from Rwanda. They had fled to Uganda.

– Wrong tribe?

– In fact, they had been the *right* tribe for a long time. They're Tutsis, and they had it good under the Belgians. But after independence the Hutu majority came to power, and that's when they became the wrong tribe. Solange's family fled to Uganda. They became stateless.

– So how on earth did she get such a good education?

– Thanks to Idi Amin! He murdered the Vice-Chancellor of Makerere University, where Solange had been studying, and the foreign academic staff quit. One of them was a British professor, and he arranged for Solange to come to London. That's how she ended up getting a PhD from the School of African and Oriental Studies.

And thus, Marietta, I told you about the people I'd met at Marcelina's party while you were in Switzerland. In that big apartment where rhythmic tapestries subtly rhymed their colour gradations, I experienced at once a kind of kinship and a feeling that I'd never belong. My caginess in responding to your question, the night before, had come from that ambivalence. When, once we'd crossed into the Netherlands, you asked me about the dose of Dutch I may have in my blood, I found myself feeling strangely nostalgic: I wanted to believe my mother's father had indeed been Dutch.

I was glad you'd understood my ambivalence toward both the country and the continent I might have called home. I can't go back, but I do feel a kinship with those who've fled the killer with a toothbrush moustache and the clown in a leopard-skin costume, fled the drugged-up child soldier and the machete-wielding murderer, fled the Big Man with a diamond on each finger and the Communist in gold-studded shoes. Like me, they have fled, they can make a new life, while the armies of the dead march through oblivion.

The forest hemming in the highway gives way to open plain; a wash of magenta seeps into the milky sky. I want to say 'I love you', I want to ask by what miracle have you come into my life, but I simply take your hand and bring it to my lips. Breda, Utrecht, Amsterdam, in no time we reached our destination.

Intermezzo 11: Pavlina

Marietta, I'm writing this letter in the arcade of a cloister, sitting at a table of a hotel that once was a convent. I like the spartan tranquillity of this place, the dignity of its Romanesque solidity. I like Alghero, the charm of the medieval city. Two hours ago I was in Olbia, seeing Pavlina off at the airport. She'd written to me when *Self-Portrait with Sphinx* came out. Czech, she's doing an MA in European Culture at the University of Konstanz. Wrote a very fine essay inspired by Jan Patočka's conception of Europe ('care of the soul is the central theme around which the life plan of Europe crystallized'). It happened to be her birthday when we met; I asked her what present would please her. 'Some sun', she said. 'Well then', I replied, 'let's go to Sardinia!'. And so we did, and spent three days together on the island.

She got her sun, she got the white sand and transparent water of Spiaggia della Pelosa; cycling the road between Alghero and Bosa, she got green mountain and blue sea. The second evening, as we savoured fruit-and-almond Vermentino on the lantern-lit terrace of a café, we pursued our conversation begun earlier. I said:

– What I liked about heroin is that it allowed me to sit still and do one thing at a time. For the first time I could read a book in an orderly way.

– How did you use? Alone or with others?

– Alone. Never with junkies. And never on more than two consecutive days.

– I learned that trick too. And kept up my friendships! Hung out only with innocents.

The immediacy of her sensuality, her embrace of pleasure: The shine of her rapture abides, making her eyes sapphires.

– You liked sex too much to let addiction dull your senses?

– Exactly!

Ambergris and iris root, lemon gardenia and cedarwood: Her scent adds a new savour to her taste on my tongue.

– I gave up drugs when I met Marietta. Redoubled the energy of delusion!

– The energy of delusion?

– Tolstoy. When he was preparing *Anna Karenina,* he wrote in a letter to his editor: 'Everything seems to be ready for the writing, for fulfilling my earthly duty. What's missing is the urge to believe in myself, the belief in the importance of my task. I'm lacking the energy of delusion'.

– Courage?

– Yes. To submit to madness, to submit and resolutely endure.

– Well, I don't know how mad you were when you wrote *Self-Portrait with Sphinx...*

The fervour of her mouth, the lushness of her lips: *Bocca basciata non perde ventura, anzi rinnuova come fa la luna*.

– ...all I know is that I love it!

Along a diagonal
The light divides. In the sun
A girl shields her eyes.
In the shadow children's faces
Stare wide-eyed: A boy,
Barely a toddler, stands balancing his future
In the palm of a man.

– Especially the Winged Fiend! Where does it come from, your view of the Sphinx?

– The Greeks. The Egyptian Sphinx is masculine. He's a figure of the sun god, an emblem of royal power. The Greek Sphinx is far more interesting, simply because she's feminine.

From the point of impact
The cracks radiate; out of the desert
A cypress flares: In a shattered mirror,
Darkness presses the dwindling sky
Into a premonition of poison rain.

– In Hesiod's *Theogany* she's the child of a woman-serpent and her son, a dog with two heads.

– Charming!

– On ancient Greek vases she's an incubus—lion's body, woman's head, eagle's wings and serpent's tail.

– Like on the cover of the album?

– Yes. And what do you see in it?

– In Moreau's painting?

– Yes.

– Well, it's very erotic. You feel the attraction.

The syncopation of her speech, the accent of her English: Is it only because we've just made love that I find her voice hovers between music and language?

– Yes. And that's far more interesting than the fight between hero and monster.

– Because of the enigma?

– Yes. The enigma substitutes for the fight. And the fight, of course, is already a substitute for fucking.

> Two-by-two, four to a page,
> Faces contorted in death—mutilated,
> Bloody, bruised—evoke a cruel agony:
> Young men all.

– And the second enigma?

– Who are the two sisters who bring each other into being?

– The night and the day! Where does that come from?

– It's not in Sophocles. It's a later addition.

– You use it brilliantly, that sun and moon motif.

– Masculine-feminine. Everything derives from that.

> Around the table numbed faces,
> Fixed in mute despair,
> Convey a quiet dignity:
> Women, young and old, all.

– And the song about the legs—reminded me of Shakespeare's beast with two backs.

– Yes. The mystery of where children come from.

– How does it go again?

– Four legs in a bed, two, a fifth that mysteriously disappears.

> Against the wall a woman in a white dress,
> Her hand over her mouth,
> Stands aghast.
>
> Between compassion and revulsion
> A boy, his arms folded across his chest,
> Stands fascinated.
>
> Beside him a girl, her hands folded in prayer,
> A lock of hair over an eye,
> Stands curious.

His torso bare, his head hooded,
From the back of a military truck a man hangs,
Suspended by his bound ankles from a steel pole.

— I love how Oedipus and Antigone end the album!

— Incest and the double. He's both her father and her brother.

— I think it's the best thing you've done, Sprague.

— Thanks to Gram. Truth be told, I don't really understand our relation.

— Does anybody understand magic?

We hold each other close as we walk back to our hotel. At the crossroads she takes me in her arms and kisses me.

— For weeks I had nightmares of my mother in my bed. Felt like a fight to the death!

So says Pavlina as we continue our conversation, she on the sofa and I in an armchair.

— Imagine, Sprague, my mother sleeping with my boyfriend!

In her eyes the Sphinx is all aflutter.

— When I discovered that I simply fell apart. Don't know how I'd have survived without heroin.

— And your father? How did he—

— He's dead. Died when I was a child.

A place in one's genealogy—I too have fought for that.

— And what did your mother have to say for herself?

— Said what she'd done was unforgivable. Then asked me to forgive her.

— Did you?

— No. And I never will.

A tremor flickers in the corner of her lips, her eyes shut but seal no certainty—I know that state.

— And you, Sprague? Ever experienced anything like that?

— No. But I knew a girl whose boyfriend was sleeping with her sister. Same thing. Sent her round the bend. Shattered her identity.

— So I'm not crazy?

— No. It doesn't have to be blood-incest to be incest. I once knew a family where the man was more father to his wife than husband. That's incest.

Completely perverted the relations between parents and children. One of them even went mad.

– I hardly knew my father.

– How old were you when he died?

– Seven.

– Do you remember much?

– I remember this: Once he sat me on his knee and said, 'Now tell me, Pavlina, how could I produce a child so ugly and stupid?'.

– My God!

– Yeah. Now come, let's forget all that!

So saying, she undid her dress. I undid the rest and laid her across the bed. In a circle of unbroken prayer we found the arc of pleasue. Yes, by the stigma of Saint Francis we danced with the Sphinx; within the convent walls we celebrated the enigma.

PART EIGHT

Chapter 1

Hush, my heart! Do you hear? Rainwater is percolating through the earth, dissolving what fire purged; leach is descending to embalm below, leaving alumina to form crystals of clay. That which glows without flame hurries through the gut of the earthworm, then into humus resolves itself. Can you feel the humus and clay binding the grains of sand? Can you feel, between the peds, the plant-roots opening pores? Hark! Heavy footfalls, drawing nigh, driving the mole hither. Listen! Earth crumbles as clawed toes gouge the tunnel wall.

– Insect nymph or spectre, nematode or lumbricus—What morsel there, mole?

– Just another—Hush!

Filtering through the soil, ceremonial words sound:

– Open up, earth! Do not crush him, but wrap him up as a mother wraps her child in the edge of her skirt.

I hear the coffin being lowered into the ground, I hear the soul of the infant, wailing sore, wandering in limbo.

– Toll the bell, sound the knell; in the twilight abode he is doomed to dwell.

As the dull sonance of the death knell reaches my ears, I sense the mole beside me.

– Oh mole, in this labyrinth of humus and clay you know your way—can you help me?

– What is it you seek?

– A way to disentangle love and death.

– You seek the impossible.

– But I can't go on like this!

– Just get yourself to the bridge. It will soon be over.

– No! Help me! Share your wisdom!

The mole's odour redoubles in my nostrils; his whiskers tickle my fingertips.

– Please mole! I'll give you—

– Scribbling, I suppose?

– Yes. A little prose piece, a meditation on a ring.

– Well, well, what do you know? That's exactly what I was looking for!

– Really? Why?

– I work in the Archives. Promises, Promises.

– Promises, Promises?

– The department where rings belong.

– Indeed.

– So, my wisdom for your meditation?

– Yes.

– All right. Come closer. What I have to say must be said softly.

Dull, the trickle of rainwater sounds in the earthen tunnel. I crawl up close to the mole's mouth. After a moment of silence, he whispers in my ear:

– Death lives a human life. Only love can overcome it. For each, you must grasp in one grip both the actual and the possible, and know both while keeping the difference visible.

– Oh mole, that is so difficult to do!

– You are one with the water lily, one with the willow: You must trust your intuition.

Faeringa! The mole snatches an earthworm. Pulling it through its paws, it empties its gut and eats it.

– I will do my best, mole. I will try to reconcile union and separation.

– Good. But it won't get you anywhere.

– What? You mean there's no—

– None. You birth was botched. You should never have survived being buried alive. All you can hope for now is not to make a mess of your death.

Faeringa! The mole snatches another earthworm, nips its aortic arches, and lets it go: as good as dead, yet alive.

– You're looking sad, Wanderer. Perhaps this will console you: Your scribbling is your epitaph. That's an accomplishment of sorts. Now give me the piece you promised me!

– All right mole. Here it is.

> In Zürich, in her house overlooking the lake, I stepped into the kitchen and caught sight of Marietta slicing onions, a pair of goggles over her eyes. The beam of my smile glinted off her lenses as the floodgates of my heart gave way to a gush of love.

– Wanderer, in the Archives—I'm opening a little window on our work—there's a lively debate about the nature of your emotion. Some have argued there's a touch of mawkishness to it, a maudlin edge, a soppy side. There's even an extreme view that detects a fawning bordering on perversion. Other researchers, however—the stork, the orangutan, the bandicoot—see in your emotion an all-consuming tenderness. My view is that your emotion is indeed the sign of a perversion, but a salutary one.

– Really?
– Uh-hm. My paper—'A Basset Hound in the Pursuit of Being: Masochism and Dignity in the Search for Love'—will be presented at our next conference.
– I see.
– But do you see what I'm saying?
– Well, love and dignity don't—
– I don't need any more evidence! Just get on with it. No gushing!
– All right. I'll try.

> In Saint-Jean-de-Luz, in a Basque house not far from the beach, I stood in the bathroom of aromatic teak and trimmed Marietta's hair. A kiss of thanks and a clean-up, then out to Boutique Margot to buy some buttons. She who is peerless at pick-up-sticks, at home in all handicrafts, bought some chestnut buttons which she would inlay with petrol-blue resin to make a chunky necklace; bright acid-drop buttons which she would thread with thong to make a multi-strand cuff; Victorian shank buttons which she would string into a vintage charm bracelet.

– Wanderer, I know that in love, all takes place between, or there is nothing. Is that what you're getting at, with these buttons?
– No, I'm just—
– Well then, is it that love arrives in secret, transported across the boundaries of the self while leaving the boundary in place, is that the meaning of the buttons?
– No, the buttons have no—
– Then drop the bloody buttons! Get on with the meditation on a ring!
– All right, all right. I'll make a fresh start.
– Good!
– So...

> The knitted mesh of her sneakers married her feet as she laced them up; up the Zürichberg I followed their imprint. As she climbed, the green of the larches matched the green of her shoes—

– And now it's the foot fetish! Wanderer, there's an even livelier debate about that in the Archives! Some say the twitch in your trousers provoked by a woman's feet, the strong erotic charge you derive— No, we haven't got time. It's a rainy day as well as a day of burial—I'm going to be very busy. Your meditation on a ring—just give it to me straight.

– I can't. I'm a poet. Poets don't do things straight.

Faeringa! The mole snatches an earthworm. Pulling it through its paws, it empties its gut and eats it.

– It's a feast day! Sorry, Wanderer. I do respect poets. After all, aren't they all blind, like me? Homer the bard, the clairvoyant Tiresias. And that Argentine, the blind librarian from Buenos Aires—what's his name again?

– Borges. Jorge Luis Borges.

– Borges! A very fine poet!

– One of the greatest.

– Indeed. All right, then, give it to me, your meditation on a ring. Give it to me as a poet! I won't interrupt you again.

– Thank you, mole. Here it is.

> I fetched the sheets from the dryer; we set to folding them. You admired the quality of the crisp white percale, you liked the charcoal thread that embroidered spring through primrose yellow and gradations of lime green. And indeed, that very day spring had come. (To celebrate the sun, we'd bought ice cream cones from a van on Keats Grove; you'd licked yours slowly and made it last till we got home.) As we pulled a sheet between us—smoothing the creases, sharpening the folds—I spun round and wrapped myself in half its length. Not missing a beat, you spun in the opposite direction and wound yourself to me: Geisha comes to guest in matching kimono! The game continued with the second sheet: nawab and tawaif in dhoti and sari! Finally, folded and refolded, the sheets were ready. You put them in the linen closet, then went to work at your desk. I lay on the bed and watched you, and lost myself in reverie... Will we ever bind ourselves to each other, the way married couples do? Bind ourselves in something other than bed sheets? How does our love, faithful and freely given, measure up to marriage vows? A ring is a promise, it binds and isolates; it makes lover and beloved each other's master and slave: With all of that you'd have no problem. Why then does my mind overrule

my heart and stop me giving you a ring? There's something frightening, I do agree, about the closed circle. Even if nobody, nowadays, believes in the indissolubility of a bond. But can modern times erase the millennial symbol of a bond that cannot be broken? Marietta, were I to give you a ring, would you refuse it? If a ring is a line representing no return (something you could never accept), less charged adornments you accept with utter naturalness. As I watch you now, with your scratch pad and equations, I see the Celtic knot in your sternal notch. A circle of silver and moonstone, its blue-white sheen, misty and dream-like, is the perfect pendant to the amber lucidity in your eyes. And what about those demonic angels of black opal, flaunting their nudity between *plique-à-jour* bat wings? Those demons that dangled from your ears last night consecrated you as the wickedest woman in the room. Overall, hot rocks leave you cold: Sparkling gemstones are not your style. At Xenia's vernissage, your enamel and pressed-steel marcasite brooch, ornamented in ochre yellow and greyed cobalt, drew admiration from the artist herself. So I didn't cross the line. Earrings, brooch and pendant posed no problem. Still, I had to force myself to forsake that token of a common fate. Resign myself to standing apart from that endless cycle of unbroken continuity, that universal yearning represented by a ring... And then there's the theme of children. It was only when I met you that I wanted to become a father. In fact, until I met you, I was positively against having children. As nestlings, fledglings, until they learn to fly, don't children need a sacred circle, a refuge from profanity? I remember what you told me in the Jardin du Luxembourg: 'Husband, house and baby, that's never been my thing'. It's never been my thing either, wife, house, children. And yet, ever since I met you, a vision of eyes-wide-open-in-wonder moves me to imagine a daughter and son, and once-quaint notions like 'fruit of our love' now don't seem so absurd.

As I lay on the bed, watching you working, such was my reverie. On that spring day in London, you'll readily agree, I could never have imagined that in Iceland, the ring we'd

travel would bind you to me as no band of gold ever could:
for good, irrevocably.

– Thank you, Wanderer. This meditation will make a fine addition to your file in the Archives.

– But meditation is for the living!

– A salutary desire! But meditation requires silence. Where on earth today does the busy world not penetrate? In the Archives your case will have pride of place; content yourself with that. Goodbye, Wanderer!

The mole turns into a side tunnel.

– Goodbye, kind mole, goodbye!

Chapter 2

Pearly feldspar, pillow lava; obsidian speculum, pumice: Dark talus stones grind beneath my boots. Where am I? Shadows float in the gloaming; domal mounds emerge only to disappear. Is this my landscape of belonging? Is that me in the granite glass? Why are you weeping, child? You are not dead, just sleeping.

Gliding my hands over the hemispheres, I stir the slumberous rotundity of your buttocks to a semblance of vivacity: Who would have thought these bold curves, beyond spurring concupiscence, could incarnate consciousness? Forceful or floating, my fingers and palms fashion your flesh, vaguely seeking a fresh beginning in the timeless circles they trace.

Mara Marina, Mara Miranda, reality discloses truth oblique, the eye sees but the real of its belief: Let us continue to interweave our memories, that in the eyes of the other we may discover who we are.

Listen! The hair of the bow across the string sends a thrill up your spine: A motif on the cello, played by your mother, opens Shostakovich's 8th string quartet. Off-centre, front row, you sit between strangers in the Philharmonic Hall, sheltered in the penumbra of the stage lights. Unfolding the elegiac opening, violins and viola come in to join the cello. *That's his signature,* your mother had explained, *that four-note figure is Shostakovich signing his name.*

On a black cord, a black shimmer: *The choker Daddy bought you in Milan. You two were always so in love, ever since I can remember. Wedding photo: Two love-struck teenagers, holding hands. And the next year—at twenty!—you had me.*

Beneath a singing violin your mother insinuates a dark bass line. *Why did I scream when I saw you wearing his sweater last Sunday? Why did I throw your glass of wine against the wall? Oh Mama, what will become of us?* Against a shifting accompaniment, the cello descends in register and solemnly intones a fragment of melody. *When you had calmed me in your arms you told me that not once did you and Daddy go to sleep when you were angry with each other: You would always make it up in some way, even if only by a stolen touch.* With increasing urgency Katja's bow strokes the strings. *And now, Mama, when you're in your bed, you have only Zaspanec purring beside you.* The violins attempt a gesture of closure, but the melodic figure crescendos and remains incomplete.

A slow upbow of the second violin fills the hall with pent-up power, and then the ensemble feeds the ferocity of Shostakovich's rage: A percussive attack of monolithic chords underpins a frenzied melodic line. Onward it drives, inexorable, in a headlong rush to—nowhere. *I've felt it myself, that futile rage. The horrible, impossible news, that morning in Rovinj.* Reminisce, dizziness, loneliness! The relentless fortissimo of the dactylic rhythm drives you deeper into yourself. *Daddy, your memories drowned when you did, but look how mine have a hold on me: Over* The Garden of Earthly Delights *I glide my magnifying glass, delighting in the little creatures, making the monsters the heroes of the stories we'd invent.*

The punctuating chords transfer to the viola and cello, leaving the violins to breathlessly bear witness—to what? And now the signature phrase on the first violin begins what becomes a ghostly waltz. *Daddy, they say Shostakovich, on the eve of joining the Communist Party, wrote the 8th String Quartet as a suicide note. He'd been cornered in his cat-and-mouse game with Stalin. Oh Daddy, your parents were murdered by the Party to whose glory your gold medals are dedicated! And what suicide note did you leave for me?*

As the falling contours of the principal theme recur, you find a light in the darkness: In the kitchen late at night, her bare feet propped up on a chair, your mother sits in front of the open refrigerator. Its coolness is no match for the heat, its light is the only light in the room.

— Mum, I can't sleep.

— Neither can I.

She pulls out a chair. Before you sit down you pour yourself a raspberry and mint concoction your mother had made. You'd spent the morning together, sorting through your father's belongings. Invading his solitude or letting it be, lucidly choosing or blindly disposing—each alternative brought unease. And yet, as you drop an ice cube into your glass, you think you're going to make it, adjusting to your new-found state as a family of two.

The bright pluck of pizzicato on one violin answers the other's open strings; below the brutal lyricism, the cello sustains the bass notes. Mostec forest, Golovec hill—you picture yourself standing there, pissing like a boy. And now you bleed like a woman. And ever since that first time you've longed to be held in her arms, just like when you were a little girl. Yet when she reaches out to you, you withdraw, burying beneath your resistance the longing she evokes in you.

Look how close to the bridge her fingers press the strings! Ghostly timbre of high tessitura. *Mama, I can't go on with this! Let's go out.* Wanting to silence your thought in movement but still be with your mother, you went running together along the Trail of Remembrance (once the path of a barbed wire fence).

The dynamics reduce, the timbre mutes; turned in on itself, the movement ebbs into shadowy silence. Rat-a-tat-tat! Triplets of fortissimo chords irrupt into the repose. Violate! Apprehend! Interdict! Neither the red nor the brown, but lucidity and courage in the maelstrom: Shostakovich's invocation.

As the largo floats into an arioso, you watch your mother inscribe into the lyrical flow the subtleties she teases from the strings. *God, Mom, you're beautiful! 'My beauty is an accident. It's something I accommodate, like the weather'. Remember the guy who pedalled his bike straight into a pond, unable to take his eyes off you?*

And then the circle is complete: Your mother plays Shostakovich's signature motif, just as it was played at the beginning. The viola launches the finale; the final movement unfolds. Beauty and sorrow, and a sense of farewell, intermingle in your heart. What are you saying goodbye to? Your childhood? Your confidence? Your faith in the future?

The muted timbres of the music leave you in your reverie. Studying the lines of the second violinist's face, you wonder if he has a daughter. If so, what kind of a father is he? And what kind of husband? Has he ever betrayed his wife? You look at your mother, underpinning the violins with the dark timbre of her cello. *I love her so. And I alone know about Laura.*

Pianissimo, the music distils its subtleties. In your body you feel its vibration, a velvety buzz in your *bas-ventre:* Were it darker, you'd put your hand between your legs. *'J'aime l'horreur d'être vierge et je veux vivre parmi l'effroi que me font mes cheveux.'* Is that Mallarmé or Rimbaud? Before you can decide, you realize the music is dissolving into silence: The 8th Quartet is over. As the applause comes thundering down, you stand up and join in the ovation.

Chapter 3

Red tongues loll in open mouths, cupped ears dwarf pendant heads: Suspended from the cavern vault, a throng of pug-faced bats. In glossy folds black wings multiply, in the cavernous gloom the creatures hang. With the claws of one foot while hanging by the other, some comb their fur to a brighter gloss; with meticulous lips and tongue, others oil their wing membranes.

– Oh bats, you who navigate the night—can you help me?

– What is it you are seeking?

– A way to say 'I love you' without reducing my beloved to an object.

– So, you want to get your letter right?

Out of the millions, one speaks at a time.

– Yes. Can you help me? I'll give you—

– A poem?

– No. A little prose piece, an extract from my letter.

– Well, well, what do you know? That's exactly what we're looking for!

– Really? Why?

– We work in the Archives. *Creatio ex libidine.*

– *Creatio ex libidine?*

– The department where love letters belong.

– Indeed.

– So, in return for your meditation, how to get your letter right?

– Yes.

– All right. I'll come down and whisper in your ear. What I have to say—on behalf of myself and all the millions here—must be said softly.

The bat swoops down and lands on my shoulder. Gripping my collar, he speaks in my ear.

– Every human is a placeholder of nothingness. As such, each is that which he is not, and not that which he is. Your beloved, then, must be apprehended in the emptiness her movement produces. If not, you make her incapable of her own incapacity.

– The way Brancusi captures the essence of a bird in flight?

– Exactly. The sculptures of Brancusi leave nothing but their luminosity, as a bird in flight leaves nothing but a memory of its movement.

– I will try, bat, I will try for the capability of incapacity. I will try to get my letter right.

— Good. But it won't get you anywhere.

— What? You mean there's no—

— None. You will always be ambushed by the blind spot of language.

— But—

— You can try, Wanderer, you can try! After, all there is nothing that is not kept alive by change and polarity. Now give us the piece you promised!

— All right bat. Here it is.

For a week in Antibes we slept on the floor. Construction workers had burgled our villa and stolen the bed. And our bags. And our clothes. But they left my Leica, your laptop, and Gram's DAT tapes. 'Arabs!' cried the rental office. Their work done, they moved on. So we stayed: You had one more week of teaching at Sophia Antipolis.

We drove to Nice, where we bought air mattresses, sheets and clothes. And, as I couldn't get over the loss of your braided leather sandals, we had to go to Cannes to find anything nearly as sexy. Kitted out again, we resumed our routine in our seafront villa.

Mornings I'd make coffee, then serve you a breakfast of grapefruit juice and toast, yogurt and sliced nectarine. While you'd shower and dress I'd go for a swim, returning just in time to plant a salty kiss on your lips before you drove off to work.

And while you were manipulating equations to explain the modelling and simulation of complex systems, I'd listen to Gram's demo tapes on the DAT Walkman: Just song structures, rhythm tracks with no melody, for which I was to write the lyrics.

Seedy Friedrich's new music impressed me: Industrial, jungle, drum-and-bass; an intensely aggressive music with a distinct personality: that of Gram's self-scrutiny.

I began with an image of a girl in a boutique, trying on a pair of sandals. She doesn't buy them, but steals them right under the nose of the sales girl. And thus, as one thing led to another over the week, I ended up writing *Katie Quickfinger, Memoirs of a Kleptomaniac.*

Katie's got a fancy mind and a fetching smile, but it's her sticky fingers that drive the story. In the end, she outwits the Sisyphus inside her and steals her own death from the Angel of Doom.

And thus my Katie would become a cult heroine, a girl who—thanks to her lucidity in sadness—chooses the terms of her own death.

The lyrics matched the music's angst and jubilation. Images were easy to find: Katie in a boutique, slipping under her sweater a pair of Dim Stay-Ups; Katie in her walk-in closet, calming her nerves by staring ecstatically at her twenty-nine stolen dresses. Weaving in a bit of background was equally easy: Her troubled relationship with her father, her ambivalence about sex (she had a preference for masturbation, at which she was daring and inventive), and her childhood scrapbooks.

And thus our getting burgled in Antibes led to an album with Gram that brought me a certain glory. But the point of this story is not to underline the evident, but rather to affirm the deeper meaning of *Katie Q.* Marietta, the contract I made with myself has been fulfilled.

The terms of my death—what would it mean for me to choose them?

I don't remember my expulsion from the womb, I can't recall my first cry, but I do remember struggling for air underneath the ice. And how time stood still.

One day the ice began to crack; time started to flow. I struggled to insert myself into the turning world. Instinctively, the pain of breathing in the open air made me reach out for a lifeline: The only lifeline I could ever get a grip on was always a girl.

> Slowly I learned to walk on the open earth. I learned the language of animals, I shared the life of plants. But with humans I felt foreign: I had remained too long, too deep, underneath the ice. Something in me had been irreparably damaged: I'd always be a stranger.
>
> Still I reached out, still I tried to get a foothold in the world. With each successive girl I slipped less. But I kept slipping. And then I met you. You taught me to breathe. You taught me to walk. You gave me my body and you gave me yours. You loved me as I am and thus, before you left me, you fulfilled the terms of my death.
>
> Every word I've written is a celebration of your freedom. Every word I've written is an assumption of my death. But that is not all: Every word I've written is my epitaph. I will keep my rendezvous with the river. I have no desire to linger. I have lived enough.

The bats break out in resonant laughter, filling the cavern with their scornful mirth.

— Silence!

Immediately upon the command of the bat on my shoulder, his fellows fall silent.

— Sorry, Wanderer. It's just that you're so near the end and you still believe your letter will redeem your life. Really!

A tear rolls down my cheek.

— Boys don't cry!

Again, the bats break out in resonant laughter, filling the cavern with their scornful mirth.

— Silence!

Again, immediately upon the bat's command, his fellows fall silent.

— Listen, a word of consolation: Your testament is a bit long, but at least it's free of dessicated signs.

— You'd have preferred it shorter?

— Yes. It would have been enough to say, 'I am the pronunciation of my name'. Never mind.

Claws dig into my shoulder as the bat kicks off into the air. He flies around a bit then circles back.

— Since your death is fast approaching, let me give you a farewell kiss.

He lands on my shoulder. Not the one he'd been perched on, but the other: Kissing, like dying, is an art. I turn my lips to his lips. Rather toothy, his kiss, but his tongue is deft and sensual.

– No wonder women put out for you, he whispers. You're a good kisser.
Spicy, his breath is pungent in my nostrils.

– To the bridge, Wanderer!
His claws dig into my shoulder as he kicks off into the air.

– Goodbye!

– Goodbye, kind bat, goodbye.

Chapter 4

Taking my fingers to your fundament, in feather touches I trace the furrow. Smack-smack! As your cheeks blush you rise up onto all fours. Smack-smack-smack-smack-smack! You look over your shoulder, carnal knowledge in your gaze, chastity in your smile.

— Do it again!

Smack-smack! Smack-smack-smack-smack-smack! Displacing the hemispheres, my hands attack the facticity of your flesh. Change it up! Subtle fingers refine sensation; fingertips decline rotundity. Look! Beneath the shadowed furrow, suspended from the pudendum, a filament of light dangles.

— Again, Sprague, again!

— I can't. I'm waiting for you to tell my fortune.

— Tell your fortune?

— Yes. When this wisp of wetness falls from your pussy, I'll know my fate. Tinker, tailor, soldier, sailor, rich man, poor man, beggarman, thief.

As I repeat the rhyme, you shake your hips, arch your back, rotate your pelvis.

— Tin-ker, tai-lor, sol-dier, sai— Sailor! I'm to be a sailor! That's my destiny!

Smack-smack! Smack-smack-smack-smack-smack! You fall forward and roll onto your side, facing me.

— How long did you live by the sea?

— Eleven years. My first eleven years.

— Is that where you got your green eyes? They're really beautiful.

— I don't know, Mara. I don't know where they come from.

You roll over to face the wall.

— Look.

Your fingers flowing arabesques, you animate shadows on the wall.

— Here's a boat on the sea.

You conjure the figure from your fingers.

— Wow!

— Now what's this?

I am the eggman. They are the eggmen.

— A walrus.

— No, a blind man with a cane. And this?

Perpetual transfiguration, beguiling harlequin; labile shadows, whimsical play.

— It's never the same.

— Normal, it's Proteus.
Leaning over you, I bring my mouth to yours.

The tremble of lust,
Gold leaf on squirrel brush:
My lips on your lips

— Shadow-play this, Mara!

There was a cat
That climbed a tree
When she fell down
Then down fell she

Dexterous fingers evoke a broad-crowned tree. A cat pops out of it, then falls down.

— Wow!

— Is that your fantasy, Sprague—two pussies in the same bed?

— Yes. But it's not at the top of my list.

— And what *is* at the top of your list?

I whisper in your ear.

— I'll do it for you.

— I can't wait!

— You won't have to.

— Do we have what's necessary?

— Of course. I was a girl scout.

— Be prepared!

— Always.

— And what's at the top of *your* list?

You whisper in my ear.

— I'll do it for you.

— I can't wait!

— You won't have to.

In three dimensions your hands collaborate to make magic in two.

— What's this?

— A butterfly flapping its wings.

— No. Two rabbits fucking.

You got me rocking,

Leporida: You got me
Cooking, cottontail

– Do this one, Mara!

There were two sailors
Went to Spain
When they returned
They came again

Again, in three dimensions your hands collaborate to make magic in two.

– But that's still the rabbits fucking.

– No, look more closely.

I scrutinize the quivering shadows.

– It's still the rabbits!

– No. It's the sailors back from Spain—and they're about to come again! Whoooshhhhh!

The tremor of southern light, the smooth sea—Mara Marietta, instil your joyful science in me!

Chapter 5

The scriptorium

In a monastery, in the scriptorium, in the cool of an autumn afternoon, a monk in a mantle of black sits at his sloping desk. With practised fingers he picks up a divider and pierces a row of guide-holes in the blank vellum in front of him. Outside, in the sunlight of the cloister, water flows brightly into a dark pool. Down a corridor, through a drop-arch doorway, in an earthenware pot in a long workshop, oak-galls and gum arabic, red wine and vitriol, coalesce in steaming water. Cochineal, saffron, orpiment, porphyry, madder, lampblack and tannin: In oxhorn receptacles and vessels of shell, concoctions of pigment sparkle on a workbench. Pulverized under the pestle, cinnabar, malachite and lapis-lazuli, each in their own mortar, rest on a granite block. Ready to bind the powders, fish-glue and albumin, in leather sachets and earthenware phials, stand on a stone ledge. In a niche in the wall, acacia gum dissolves in glass bottles; in another, chopped roots and saffron stigmas macerate in murky jars.

The hotel room

In Vienna, in a sky room, in a hotel a thousand and one stories high, a woman lies blindfolded and bound upon a bed. Four turns of braided rope cuff her wrists in black; a bowline on a bight fixes them to brushed metal posts. A reef knot, its tails tucked under the turns, locks the ankle cuffs; fast to the bedposts a taut-line hitch holds them. Between her legs a man lies, his head in the hinge of her thighs. Through the floor-to-ceiling window moonlight floods into the room, dusting the keizerskroon tulips on the night table and cooling the water in their cut-glass vase. A spray of stars, cast by a lamp of sculpted aluminum, arcs across the ceiling; in the shadows below an aquarium glows. Look! In it's gently bubbling water, angelfish thread through ribbons of leaf while neon tetra illuminate a petrified forest.

Preparations for illumination

In the quiet of the scriptorium the monk reaches for his ruler and lines up the pinholes on the parchment. With lead point he traces guidelines for initial, text and margin, then from his desk he selects a goose feather quill and sharpens it with a pen knife.

The lover's prayer

Constant heart, stalwart and steadfast, between past and future you abide; in that gap where I could never insert myself, how long you have waited for me! And now into the present you usher me; up from where I was buried alive my being flows. Yea, out of darkness you call to me and bid me be born. Heart, infuse me with your grace while with my tongue I trace all that you utter; yea, with your voice out of silence speak through my mouth.

The scribe, the lover

In the monk's hand the trimmed quill, dipped into the oxhorn inkwell, bends to the pressure of expert fingers: As the nib traces the letters *y-a-n-a* on the parchment, the tip of my tongue traces them on your cunt. Come, I'll make you more come-at-able! Hoisting your hips, I slip a pillow under your buttocks. Hey hello! A kiss on your mouth I cousin on your breasts, then down to the middle of the world I descend. Sweetwater mingles with salt as my spittled lips ride the swell of your labia; tightly-angled, I drop in crouched and surf inside the perfect curl of your unfurling flesh. Into my mouth I suck a nympha and with the tip of my tongue inscribe *m-e-l-k-n* upon it. Into the inkwell the monk dips the quill then resumes writing. A ride up the perineal raphe beginning my run, a flick on the skittle ending it, one by one, in cursive script, I meticulously trace each letter he writes: *o-w-n-o*. You tug at your restraints, breath swooping into your body and emerging in a moan. I reach behind and run feather-tip fingers along your footsole: The taut-line hitch tightens. Back to the sanctum I bring the hunger of my soul. As the monk wipes his quill with a rag of linen, with the 'V' of my fingers I hold open the pearly gates. And then he gives the cue: Upon your vestibule my cupping glass kisses place the letters *t-h-o-w-t*. You bedew my nose with your squirms; I release the nymphae. Look! There in the scriptorium a demon goes with a sack of syllables on his back.

The alley accomplice

Deftly the tip of my tongue whirls around the crown of your clitoris. From its subterranean hideout it peeps out more pertly as I slip back its hood.

– Hello, you!

– Hello!

– What you been doing down there in your lair?

– Devising rhymes!

– Rhymes? Well then, rhyme me my love!

– All right, listen.

Ickle, ockle, blue bockle,
Fishes in the sea,
If you want a pretty maid,
Please choose me!

Star-burst on the perky bud—again and again and again—then slowly my pursed lips draw tight the knot of pleasure. Apply yourself now! One thick, one thin, rising and falling between the lines, from the split nib of the quill the letters run: Dashing off the straights, inscribing the curves, upon your voluted flesh my tensed tongue traces *o-t-e-l-l-t*. The spindle of your clit draws live wire from your sinews; you buck up your hips and push hard against my face: The ropes say, 'Stay, it is not time'. Withdrawing my mouth, I lay the heel of my hand on your mound and move Venus round and round: *Luxe, calme et volupté,* morning is restored to the evening star.

Phase one, in which Doris gets her oats (the end)

Hey hello! A kiss on your belly button rebounds on your breasts; in the pit of your arms I blow my breath. The monk dips his quill into the inkwell, starts to write—then stops. Deft fingers gather moist pith of bread. With breadball monk begins to erase errant syllable: Upon your pussy my lips play, nibbling and sucking, licking and lapping, until the monk brings my tongue to a point: Around the carina, in the vulval cleft, it inscribes *h-e-e-w*. Your muscles tense as you fight your restraints; breath swoops into your body and emerges in a tumble of Slovenian syllables. Hey hello! I shut you up with a kiss, then bestow upon your tits the homage of my lips. Back to your pussy I then repair, and at the junction of your little lips I meet my alley accomplice.

– Hello again, my little friend!

– Welcome back! I tremble every time you pass my door, and now at last you linger. Got no more kisses for little lasses?

– My lovely lass, how could you imagine that? Of course I've got kisses for you!

Into the inkwell the monk dips his quill, out flows the fluid script: In up-and-down flicks or from side-to-side, with the flat of my tongue or the tip, I garland your clitoris with the letters *h-o-l* then crown it with *a-m*. The monk has reached the end of the line; he wipes his quill and leaves his desk.

The tulip stem dipped in Curaçao blue

Figuring infinity, my hand loops round your breasts then flies down your midriff to the landing strip. Hey hello! Into your quim I slip a nimble finger. Another!

begs your obliging passageway. Demonstratorius joins impudicus. You arch your back and heave against my hand: The ropes say, 'Stay, it is not time'. Under my mouth your moans become a whimper, and then your teeth take my lips to the borders of pain: In three quick nips they ferry them over.

— Ouch!

I kiss your forehead above the blindfold, then from the vase on the night table I take a tulip. In a folded ticket to the Kunsthistorisches Museum (Adele Bloch-Bauer masquerading in the enjewelment of her flesh) I dry the supple stem, then into a bottle of Curaçao Blue I dip it.

— Mara, let's do a rhyme.

— All right.

— I'll tell you the first couplet, you tell me the second.

— Okay.

— Jeremiah, blow the fire—puff, puff, puff!

— Come, let me kiss you—huff, huff, huff!

— No. I want the original line.

— Oh Sprague, how could I know?

— I'll write it on your skin, letter by letter: You figure it out.

With tulip stem I trace liquid letters in Curaçao blue: On the inside of your thighs, on your breasts, your abdomen, the letters drip. One by one you call them out, sometimes right, sometimes wrong, and before too long you know the words, and then we've got the rhyme:

> Jeremiah, blow the fire;
> Puff, puff, puff!
> First you blow it gently,
> Then you blow it rough!

The whipping

Hey hello! The swoosh of your sandal strap singes the air; with a sharp lick it lashes your footsole. Extending your toes you tense your instep. Swoosh! Swoosh! Swoosh! Smart is the lick of the lash, keen the sting of the strap. You struggle and squirm; a flush of heat floods your foot and brings a blush to your pussy. Swoosh! Swoosh! Swoosh! Taut sinews heighten your sensations; billowing heat penetrates your body. Dash to mini bar, back in a flash. Hey hello! The violin strings of your nerves sing, your body trips the light fantastic: I speed an ice cube along your skin, then—Curaçao!—lick you clean of the blue liqueur.

The initial

In the scriptorium the monk has returned to his desk; in the square he'd ruled to lodge the big initial, he sketches with lead point. Then, with pen and ink, he outlines the contours of his sketch. Behold! In each loop of a 'B', a bird perches; flowers and leaves follow the curves, a strawberry and pear dangle from the upright. With Armenian bole on marten-hair brush, he primes the cloisons for gold; then, building a ground of gesso, with spoon of bone he spreads a mixture of plaster, glue, gypsum, and chalk. He takes a flat brush of squirrel underfur and rubs it against a hare's foot. Look! From a book of leaves a cutout of gold rises to meet the brush. With tooth of boar he smooths it into a cloison, then with an agate stone he rubs it. Overlapping edges he corrects with pointed brush, and then continues: Hands voyage along the length of your body; from the soles of your feet to the hinge of your thighs, from your bound wrists to your mound of Venus, they discover new worlds of sensation. I retrace the trip and upon my return the gold leaf is done.

Colour, thickened with ceruse and kaolin, the monk now proceeds to apply. Tone over tone, from pale to bright, in tiny dabs or broad strokes, the paint gives life to the letter: Light and quick or slow and deep, upon your pussy my tongue lavishes its touch. The ruby-red 'B', the blue-and-gold birds, the flowers, the leaves, the strawberry and pear—with articulate finger and tongue tip, with broad thumb and puckered lips, I imprint all on your pussy. You buck up your hips and push: Impudicus I slide inside. Papillary ridges find pressure points: evolution and involution, emanation and return.

Index, annularis, impudicus

Long and slow my tongue bestows its teaching; snug inside you, my finger speaks to your heart. With one hand massaging the mons, index and annularis of the other join impudicus inside: Tight in the engorged enclosure, expanding the breadth of your being, they beckon the hour of dispossession. Struggling against your restraints, you arch your back and bob; as my fingers inside you silver your spine, I summon the annihilating angel. Look out, here she comes! The sky, the sky! Clouds race across the sun, the day darkens, the air cools. Oak, alder, oak, alder, oak, alder, oak: Black loam flying off bare feet, you speed through primeval forest. The ocean! You're walking on water, your seven-league stride is swirling the sea. Look! In a mermaid's stare time drowns; in a nymph's bodice flowers bloom. Starbright! The mirror of your mind shatters, stripping the world of representation and yourself of identity. Unlimited by any horizon, you are vast as the void, everywhere and nowhere: The ropes that bind your body allow you to escape all bounds.

Slowly you regain possession of yourself. Tarrying with the negative in the reflux of restoration, your spirit abounds in your body. Look! Contracted fingers relax, the day's work is done: The monk has finished the illumination, all colours now bounded in black.

The sailor

Luminous night, immediate moon, a spray of distant stars: Nestling you in my arms, I gaze out the window wall.

– Radiant craters, dark seas—Imbrium, Crisium, Tranquillitatis—when will I find serenity?

– Why ask, when you know the answer?

– Stars, instruments of time, who shall I say I am?

– A child of the moon and spilt milk.

By a name I know not how to tell thee who I am.

I see the moon
And the moon sees me
God bless the sailors
On the sea

– He has no feet, no swift knees, no shaggy genitals; he is mind alone: That's what they said of me.

– Like Empedocles of God?

– Yes. They said I have no feelings. They said I'm the man who died of cold.

By a name I know not how to tell thee who I am.

Sailing, sailing,
Over the bounding main;
Many a storm shall blow
E'er Jack come home again.

– Neither alive nor dead: They said I am undead.

– Excommunicated, stillborn, a suicide?

– Yes. A mysterious stranger, crossing boundaries that shouldn't be crossed, polluting the blood of the pure.

By a name I know not how to tell thee who I am.

A sailor went to sea, sea, sea
To see what he could see, see, see
But all that he could see, see, see
Was the green of the sea, sea, sea

— Pulling me out of my vomit, holding a mirror to my mouth, they said: 'I told you, he's not an artist, he's an addict—he's a good for nothing'.

— You'd withdrawn into the citadel of yourself?

— Yes. My sheltering was shattered, the humming shell was mute. Not by deluge or inundation was I snuffed out, but by slow suffocation.

— The flame never died. That's the miracle.

— The miracle of the child in me.

By a name I know not how to tell thee who I am.

Amber oriental, sandalwood and cinnamon, mingle with the smell of sex in my mouth. On your wrist a ropemark: With spittled tongue I salve it.

— Hold me tighter.

I squeeze you in my arms.

— Sprague?

— Hmmm?

— I want to break you heart!

— What?

— And give you mine!

You roll out of my embrace and pin me spread-eagled to the bed.

Chapter 6

The woman in the mirror

From star to star, exhaling vapour into the vastness of the void, they hiss to a racing heartbeat: Through the night, from station to station, trains speed. Staked-out with bowline bonds, a man with raven locks lies naked on a bed, aloft in a room a thousand and one stories high. He turns his pillowed head from the window-wall to the glass-block corridor: In the bathroom, a woman in black bra and jeans stands before a mirror, her bare feet aglow in the kick-space under the counter. In successive sweeps her hands gather her hair into a ponytail; securing it, she draws it through an elastic band slipped from her fingers. A long-held din on an electric guitar takes over from the trains to stitch the stars together; ragged and dirty, it make its way through the man's body, creeping along the byways of his nerves. Two chords, ghostly through the fog of feedback, iterate from hammered strings; following suit, bass and drums come in. In the crease of her eyelid, from inner canthus to outer, the woman applies a pearly copper; from the crease to the brow bone, pale heliodor. She straightens up and looks at her reflection. At the smoothness of her image in the mirror she smiles sardonically. Bah! Putting a hand on her hip and pulling a face, she sticks her tongue out at herself. Clean and metallic, the rattle of maracas punctuates the bass and drum. And then the voice enters, detached and steely: 'The return of the thin white duke, throwing darts in lovers' eyes.'

Mara Marina, Mara Miranda, they say everything pertaining to play once related to the sacred: Between us in this pantomime, Bowie mediates. Yourself as another you examine in the mirror: As blue eyes pop in a radiant face, in the space between being and seeming your imagination comes alive.

From Kether to Malkuth: From the crown to the kingdom, the first cause to the sublunar chaos, the ten names of God. With us all names are metaphoric, but not with Him. They say the whole of the Book is nothing but the Name; they say the knowable and unknowable are one.

> Who will restore me to my name?
> I am fossil, I am sediment,
> I am compacted of altered remains;
> I am hard, I am stratified,
> I am metamorphosed but still the same:

Mara, consume me in your flame!

The union of body and soul is mediated by song; between deliverance and downfall the song is all: Riffing guitar and percussive piano let loose the daemon of rock. Through pierced flesh you thread the stem of a grape cluster, a silver and citrine glow you suspend from each earlobe. Lowering your head, you let a tiger-eye pendant fall between your breasts; the chain hooked at the nape of your neck, the tiger's eye now rests in your sternal notch. And then it comes, snaking below the rhythmic surface, the slow-burning lead guitar.

The dancer

Turning to face me, your whole body comes alive to the rhythm of the music: Snapping fingers loop-the-loop at your back and belly; five bands of fuchsia streak the travertine floor. Swinging out your arms you free your hips to sway; not missing a beat, you blow me a kiss. Your solar plexus funkifies the clockwork universe; your arms and legs climb the axis of the earth. And then, catching yourself in the mirror, you stop and tip into strangeness: Is it so, that horror can give way to happiness? From the invisible the visible streams as you stare at yourself. Who are you, Mara Zizek? I am... I am... I am a fever of being!

The juggler

Out from the bathroom you step into the room; striding past the aquarium, you're walking on air. From a fruit bowl on the console you pick up apples one two three. God and man and all the variety of the universe: In your juggling hands they revolve in an eccentric circle. Back in the bowl you place the apples: Nature is free, no proud masters needs she. Reaching behind your back, you unhook your bra: Let the ceremony begin!

The hand and the heartbeat

The subjective is the singular realization of each singularity: Kneeling astride me, your butt on my breastbone, you grip my sex. At every second beat of my heart you give a quick, smart stroke. Through my veins the blood flows, washing away all the dead determinations of the past. One-to-five, five-to-one! Lightning strokes inflame the remnants of profane life: Your hand races my heart. And then back to the measured pace you go, leaving me a moment between each movement to gather and stay my soul. Changing hands, you change your grip; between forefinger and thumb the lingam rises as you press down to the origin. So this is how you perform the work, the translation of love into knowledge; this is how you transform heat into light.

The signing of the name

One hand on the root-shaft, the other on my chest, you lie between my legs, clearing a path to the unspoken. My sex in your mouth, you swirl your tongue around the head, circling the parallel of the rim, pausing to climb the grooved meridian: Closing the circle of your lips around me, you open the possibility of a world. As you draw me in deeper your eyes hold mine as firmly as your hand grips me. Starbright! The blue of your eyes bursts into flame: With your gaze you sign your name. Look! Out of the night the tiger's eye draws the last remnants of light; chatoyant upon your throat, it scintillates as you suck.

A thousand butterflies

Far behind me now, the flitting from flower to flower in days of noisy dissipation; petal-soft, honey-slow, your tongue brings my soul to silent concentration: With long licks, from the root to the crown, you ravish my lingam. And then you take me into your mouth and with a slow, sucking motion, move me in and out. Holding me in the warm unction of your embouchure, you swirl your tongue around the crown. Unfigurable feeling! I strain at my restraints. With the blue of your eyes you fix me, and then you begin to hum: Encircled by your lips, the head of my hardness captures the vibrations of your bones. Unfigurable feeling! A riot of resonance, a thousand butterflies! What is it you are humming? What is this familiar melody? *Freude, schöner Götterfunken, Tochter aus Elysium.* Mara Marina, Mara Miranda, deaf he did it: Shall I die dumb? Bury me standing, but sing on!

The gaze and the name

Who speaks when I speak? To whom am I speaking when I speak? To submit to language is to forget: Poetry occurs where language gives way. Mara, your lips around my sex dissolve the outer circles of ourselves, leaving us unprofaned in the inmost. You look me in the eye and make me beautiful: The body is shaped by the desires addressed to it. Your gaze offers me a name: To name is intimacy itself. Your fingers handmaiden to your mouth, in pules of pleasure innocence sighs as you move me in and out. Over the head you close your hand, down the shaft you slide it: I rise through the ring to slip between your lips. Acrobatic, your tongue drives me along a tightrope over eternity.

The choice of a name

Before the tribunal of others, what name shall I assign myself? The gods call things by their true names: The language of men does not. Love. What is love? End this agony of dereliction, this endless pursuit! Music is the naming of naming: Mara, play me again! My sex hard in your hand, you tense your tongue and vibrate it against the crown, then up and down the frenulum you flick it. In the blue of your eyes my body floats, in unreal space you map it: This is your shoulder, this is your heart; these are your lips, your hands, your feet... Once more into your mouth you take me and whirl your dervish tongue: As I strain at my restraints, the borders of my body dissolve... What is the task of poetry? To push toward the origin of language. Memory and devotion, invocation and address: the spirit and the word... Before the tribunal of others, what name shall I assign myself? The rejection of flight and the will to return. To the house of love? No, to myself: Language is the only home I inhabit.

The tiger's eye

From knowledge I steal language, against knowledge I use it: In the cavern of my heart a firebrand flares; on the blood-red walls shadows play. Mara, I have fought a good fight, I have finished my course: Break my heart and give me yours! You slide my sex between your breasts. Evolution and involution, manifestation and return: The lesson is quickly learned. Feel it, child, feel it! The wick melts the wax, the wax feeds the flame: Yes, by flesh is spirit sustained! The tiger's eye changes in lustre as you lurch; as I strain at my restraints, my consciousness drowns in your chatoyant eye.

The swing raises the wind

Suspended on your earlobes, the grapes sway. Marietta, no matter how far out of reach, I never once said they were bitter: Now I long for your blessing. The swing of the grapes raises the wind, the wind brings rain. Love, in the flood anchor me; grace, grant me the lightness to sustain relation. Into your mouth you take me again. Along the shaft you whirl your hand, around the corona your tongue: Unfigurable feeling!

The attributes are no more

Breath through my body doubles the divisions of time; as your lips press their ripeness into my flesh, your hand brings the ambrosia into play. I strain at my restraints, and then you deliver me: From the tips of my toes it comes, rushing through my legs; from my fingertips it speeds straight to my heart: Light races along my nerves, making my mind a Möbius strip of heaven and underworld; surging, it hits your palate hot, leaving a shooting star to burst in the blue of your eye: Your gaze scintillates as convulsing muscle empties the wellspring of the world. 'I am I and the attributes are no more; I am I and the qualifications are no more. I am the pure subject of the verb.'

The rescue of the name

Holding the semen in your mouth you kiss me; in my mouth you leave a spicy warmth. You hoist yourself up, slide off the bed and walk to the aquarium. Plants sway in bright water; through petrified forest fish swim. Wavering, light plays on your breasts as you open the roof panel. You turn to catch my gaze: The blue of your eyes sparkles. You bring your fingers to your lips and blow me a kiss, then turn to the tank and surrender my temporal soul: Spilling from your lips, the sperm drops into the water. Milky cloud, swirling; evanescent smoke, curling: The fish feast in the dissolution of form. You pluck a recalcitrant strand from your glistening lips; drawing up the beaded thread, you stretch it taut between your hands: An abacus on which I count my blessings. Into your breasts you rub the sperm, then you lick your fingers: There is no pain, suffering or sighs; the righteous take their rest.

The giving of the heart

Out of the back pocket of your jeans you pull a slip of paper. You sit beside me and hold it before my face.

Respect secrets,
Mould movement to resistances.
Let be what you cannot grasp.
Trust, and accept distances.

You kiss my lips and release me from my restraints.

PART NINE

Chapter 1

Amsterdam deepened our way of loving, intensifying your mystery while making it manifest. Once more you made space for my heart to expand, once more you increased me in bewilderment of you. Yes, in the Jordaan district, in Ingrid and Klaas' loft on the Brouwersgracht, you confirmed you are inexhaustible, and everything is mine to learn.

The moment Ingrid opened the door you fell into each other's arms; as she leaned over your shoulder I was struck by the emotion in her eyes. By his firm handshake and frank gaze I knew I'd get along with Klaas; with Ingrid I sensed there might be friction. Then we met Lia, their five-year-old daughter on amphetamines, as she leaped into her father's arms, and Joost, her three-year-old brother, ready to defend his mother from me, the intruder.

The loft, on two levels, was a miracle of harmony. White walls and immense windows, black frames and hardwood floors, all configured themselves into a flowing continuity of rooms. Globes of ribbed paper suspended from the high ceiling lent a rhythm of light to the main room; our room, upstairs, had what we'd wanted—a big bed. Lia took my hand and led us to her room. You won her heart when you made Chinese shadows, imitating the flock of winged light bulbs in flight on her wall. As she jumped onto her father's back and made her arms wings, little Joost flew us to his room. On a wall, panels of stylized flowers cast a gentle glow. That's all I saw of the room: Joost wouldn't let me in. The salon, despite its spaciousness, radiated an inviting intimacy. A grand piano stood open in a corner, majestic in its silence. Lia then led the way to her daddy's workspace, a room that looked like an art installation, total chaos yet everything in its place: a zebra rug and a rainbow step ladder, alphabet mobiles in various fonts; a mannequin in a wheelchair, clothes pegs in bright colours; a model yacht and steam engine, a giant poster showing the genealogy of reptiles and birds. It was only when Lia began explaining how birds evolved from pterodactyls that I realized how natural and fluent her English was.

Streetlights and buildings glowed as we stepped out into the twilight. As the snow fell, the houseboats moored between the hump-backed bridges raised their gunnels of white. Lia, playing tour guide, pointed out the lifting beam and hoist in the gables of the buildings; her father chimed in with how their shape and shutters indicated their warehouse origin. You were happy to be back in

Amsterdam, a city where you'd done a lot of music-making; for me it was a first-time visit, and I was thrilled to be discovering it through your friends.

Back in the loft, Joost refused to eat his supper without his mother; you accompanied her to the kitchen while Klaas joined me in the main room. We talked about his current work—designing graphics for cultural institutions and signage systems for public buildings. I loved the passion with which he spoke of the lineage of the Roman alphabet, the flowing elegance of Liberty and the monogrammatic quality of Juliet. I liked the poetry in his rugged masculinity. He asked me about myself. I spoke of my passion for cinema; I told him of my love for Paul Verhoeven's *Spetters*. He asked me if I knew that Hans van Tongeren, the actor who played the male lead, had committed suicide, just like his character in the film. I told him I didn't, and must have been visibly moved because Klaas gave me a look of recognition. Then, having put Joost to bed upstairs, Ingrid came down to join me while you, having unpacked your bag, accompanied Klaas to the kitchen.

As Ingrid sat down beside me on the sofa, I saw her as if for the first time, and as she turned to face me I was struck by the quality of her presence: Framing her face, her stringy black hair hung limp, yet enhanced her beauty. Her blue eyes impressed with their pallor, yet were penetrating. She had an aura about her, something wasted and otherworldly, yet the physicality of her body took possession of the space. You'd told me she was three-months pregnant; you'd told me she'd just finished recording Prokofiev and Ravel. I asked her how the recording went.

– Good. But I don't like making records.
– Why not?
– It's so different from playing live. You've got to cultivate a different kind of interpretation.
– Because of the technology?
– Yes, and the whole process of recording. For me there's nothing more personal than making music, it's as personal as making love, but in a studio it's as if you're faking it.

A smoker's voice, but no ashtray anywhere.

– There's a push to standardization, like when you play in a competition and the most important thing is not to make any wrong notes. In a live performance I can make interesting rubatos or lingering pauses, for example, but on record the listener will just hear that as something affected or irritating.
– So the context changes everything?

– Yes. At a concert you hear a wrong note played out of élan differently from a wrong note played out of fear, but on record it's just a wrong note, period.

She's all of a piece; the quiet in her fire doesn't diminish its heat.

– I think I know what you mean. It's the difference between performing a play and making a movie.

– Exactly!

Her nightgown billowing, Lia runs into the room, wings of glittering cellophane strapped to her back. She's the kind of child who makes me want to have a child, I think as she flaps about in the open space. She responds to my delight with a radiant grin, then—like a fairy from *A Midsummer Night's Dream*—leaps into Ingrid's lap. Though she is the blondest of blondes, I can see exactly how she is her mother's daughter: that distinctive mix of tenderness and danger. She kisses me goodnight as if she's known me for years, then goes to the kitchen to say goodnight to you and her father.

– Why did you choose Prokofiev?

– I've always loved him.

– Marietta played me your recording of the third Piano Concerto. Blew me away! I'd never have imagined straining at the leash with such reckless abandon could produce such poetry!

– I like risk.

The current flows, her gaze lights up.

– I wanted to prove that percussive brilliance doesn't have to sacrfice substance. As long as I'm not losing colouristic range.

– You succeeded with flying colours. And why Ravel?

– I like challenges.

In her washed-out eyes I see an emerald fire.

– And how would you define the challenge of *Gaspard de la nuit?*

– To evoke, through the strictest rigour, atmosphere.

– So the polyrhythms, the complexity—it wasn't the technical difficulties that motivated you?

– No. The way I see it, Sprague, the most formidable musical task for a pianist is not the playing of a bravura piece, but rather to play a slow movement from Beethoven, Mozart or Schubert—to play it well, with perfect nervous and sound control…

You'd brought your violin to Amsterdam: I couldn't wait to hear the music you'd make with Ingrid! As we got up to set the table, I was struck again by her paradoxical beauty: ethereal, watery, pre-Raphaelite, and yet as immediate and raw as rock 'n roll.

Klaas was an artist in the kitchen as much as he was in his work; with relish you stowed away his recipes. That first night he served a simple starter of *platte kaas* with chopped chives and shallots on dark rye toast. Red gurnard with asparagus and celearic sauce made up the main dish; dessert was poached pears in spiced wine. After eating it we moved to the lounge area of the main room. Ingrid took the divan, stretching her legs out and leaning her back against the rounded rest, while Klaas and I sat on the sofa and you stretched out in a deck chair, your body flowing along its undulating lines.

– So how did you two meet? Ingrid asks, looking first at me and then at you.
You reply:

– At the lost luggage at Charles de Gaulle. I was coming back from South Carolina and Sprague from Tennessee. We were on the same flight from Atlanta and they had lost both our luggage; while they tried to trace it we had a coffee together. In the café, I fell in love with Sprague's green eyes. I just couldn't stop myself from staring into them.

I'm not yet clued in, but I do know there's a game going on.

– We were both very tired, but that didn't stop him from making me laugh. Add to that his looks, and you can see why I wasn't about to let him go.

I think I'm going to like this game! You pass the baton:

– And you, Klaas, how did you and Ingrid meet?

– We met in Berlin, at Checkpoint Charlie. I was about to cross into the East, to see the Bode Museum's coin collection, and Ingrid was crossing back into the West. As soon as I saw her I said to myself, 'That's the girl for my poster'. So I turned back and invited her for a drink. She said, 'Here, or in Amsterdam?'. 'However far you want to go', I said, pointing to the motorcycle I'd borrowed from a friend. 'Let's have it on the Ku'damm, then', she replied, and so we did.

Ingrid says:

– Klaas wins this one, wouldn't you say, Sprague? His story isn't quite as plausible as Marietta's.

In a flash I've figured out the game.

– Yes. I agree.

– All right. Klaas, a question for Sprague.

What's coming up?

– Sprague, describe something you've done that required great precision.

– Great precision?

— Yes.

— Okay... I was deep underground, in a labyrinth of tunnels. The oxygen was slowly running out. The tunnels were all very narrow, and in every one there was a girl, naked and breathing easily—the oxygen was only running out for me, it seems—and if I touched a girl trying to get out, the tunnel would get even narrower and I'd have to turn back. No matter how precisely I moved, I couldn't get by a girl without touching her. I woke up screaming, gasping for breath.

I pass the baton:

— Ingrid, describe something you did that required great precision.

— Okay. I was in the final of a pinball competition. The match was very close. My opponent had just come off a fantastic game, but I believed in my chances, I'd really learned the angles and my control was just about perfect. Still, to win, I would need greater precision than ever.

I love her voice, the darkness in the timbre, the quietude in the strength.

— My concentration was excellent, I was closing the gap in the score, when something flashed in my mind and I lost the ball. I never recovered. Game over.

I love her delivery, the lazy caress of the velvet, the gravel's slow roll.

— What'd happened is this: I'd noticed that the pin-up on the backglass—it was a scene from a Western, with a cowboy on a horse approaching the blonde—I'd noticed that the pin-up's gun was smoking. That disturbed me. I'd never noticed it before, and noticing it in that instant was how I lost the game.

Klaas says:

— Well, Marietta, what do you say?

— They've both told us their dreams. It has to be a draw.

— A draw it is, then.

The game continued for two more rounds. At the end, we toasted Ingrid by knocking back a shot of *jonge jenever:* She was the one who'd best stretched credibility while remaining plausible.

— Tell me, Sprague, how did you and Marietta *really* meet?

— I was just about to ask you and Klaas the same question!

Klaas says:

— I'll tell you. I was asked to do some design work for Ingrid's first album. I met her after a recording session, and the moment I saw her I knew we'd be together. I knew it with absolute certainty.

Love at first sight.

— And you, Ingrid?

— I knew something was happening, but I didn't know what. He just looked at me for I don't know how long. Then—this is what so surprised me—in a flash I saw myself in his eyes. I was touched.

— Why?

— Because I felt myself desired.

— But you'd felt that countless times before, certainly!

— Every time I walk down the street!

Entirely plausible. Does not stretch credibility.

— But you see, Sprague, I was madly in love with someone else at the time, a hopeless love that couldn't go anywhere. I was suffering. Horribly. It was as if it'd been raining endlessly, and when Klaas looked at me the sun had suddenly come out. Then, when he finally broke the silence, I felt he'd opened my fist and removed the obsession I'd had in my grip.

Fixing me, she holds my gaze. Before I drown in her watery eyes, she releases me.

— Now will you tell me, Sprague, how you and Marietta met?

— Yes, of course.

I told her of our encounter. She listened intently, lapping up every detail. By the glint in her eye and the way she tried to suppress a smile, I had the distinct impression she wasn't hearing about New Jersey for the first time. And then I realized she certainly knew more than I did about your experience of our first encounter. I suddenly felt a fool. But then when I saw how our meeting in Paris blew her away, how she found the conjunction of Ravel and Petrucciani magical, I stopped reproaching myself: Innocence would always haunt me, no matter how long I'd been in hell.

That night, in our big bed, we fell asleep spooned together. In the morning—did I ever tell you this?—when your kiss brought me to consciousness, I was dreaming a scene from *A Midsummer Night's Dream*.

Chapter 2

— She really fell for me, Sprague, she made my life hard. I refused to be drawn into her passion.

In a *bruin café* on the Prinsengracht, in the mild buzz of a mid-afternoon pub, we talk about Ingrid.

— So last night, when she said she was madly in love with someone else when she met Klaas, that someone else was you?

— Yes.

Outside the window, bicycles and bare trees, pale sunlight on fresh snow.

— It's incredible, that you've managed to remain such good friends.

— That we *became* such good friends. Yes, it is incredible. Only for a brief moment did her love turn to hate.

— When?

— When she understood I'd never be what she wanted me to be.

— But you did love her?

— Yes.

You sip your Christoffel, I mine. Pleasantly tart, the piney hops prickle my palate; I find a lemony freshness in the grassy bitterness.

— And today?

— A tender friendship.

— I see that, and I'm moved by it. But I sense a disquiet in Ingrid, in contrast to your serenity.

— Disquiet? She came through fire, Sprague. That's what passion is. No-one survives it unscathed.

You look away, wistful, then with resolute eyes turn toward me.

— Remember, I too was addicted once. Never again.

How could I ever forget? Drooling dogs roam empty streets, seeking insects under ashes. Huff, huff, they whiff the dust: Tongueless mouths struggle to feed.

— I've had my fill of the hunger artist.

So saying, you pick up your glass and drink.

Marietta, sellers of roses weave their way through crowded nights, not empty afternoons: I know that. Still, I wish one would pass by now: I'd choose a deep red bud on the verge of unfurling, moist with hot-house dew, and offer it to you. Then you would hear, as the firebird of its fragrance hovers before you, what I am silently saying: Intimate, without limit, you are inexhaustible, and everything is mine to learn.

I resume our conversation:

— I'm happy Ingrid's found Klaas. He seems perfect for her.

— I think so too. But she tells me that even if their bond is very strong, it makes her feel at odds with herself.

— You've been in the same situation.

Pensive, you assent with a tilt of the head. And now in daylight you reiterate what you told me in the dark:

— Yes. In New Jersey, with you.

Strolling along the beaches of Barnegat Peninsula, I tried not to be drawn to the figuration of your feet: I wasn't the only one bewitched by their sleek allure.

— Sexuality's always conflictual. 'Normal loving' doesn't exist. I accept that. Ingrid doesn't.

Up here there is no airglow, no shining envelope of the earth; up here it is cold, cold, cold.

— She's still hankering after identity?

— Yes—that set of ruses subject to revision! Trouble is, if sexuality makes identity necessary, it also makes it impossible.

You sip your Christoffel.

— Once I understood that, I stopped worrying about 'who I really am'. All Ingrid's talk of her 'true self' is simply naïve. She won't accept there's no such thing as 'the real thing', she won't accept there's no identity without suffering.

— What do you mean?

— Perfect satisfaction is impossible. To choose one thing is to refuse another. I mean, we're never just one thing or another, are we? We're always a mixed bag.

You lean forward, presenting your cheek to be kissed: I pirouette away. The engine warmth that penetrates my body is no substitute for the heat I seek from yours; still, it is soothing as I lean against the side wing of the Cabriolet, trying to make you linger.

— That's why Ingrid would make me laugh when she'd say, 'You're only bisexual from the tits up'. As if there's an essence, fixed for all eternity!

— It's the relationships you're in that make you what you are?

— Of course. If I hadn't kept myself open to surprise, I wouldn't be here with you now, would I?

Oh, would it were a crowded night and a seller of roses would come by! This time I'd choose, not a Damask rose with a heady scent, but a cool, pink Persian: A cunning flower, all silky whispers, that within its pale innocence would conceal a musky voluptuousness. Then you would hear, as the bud unfurls the fullness of its fragrance, what I am silently saying: In the compass of your embrace my life unfolds in amplitude.

– Ingrid was tyrannical. She became obsessed with defining things, and someone who's obsessed with defining things is someone who wants to be controlled.

– Definitely not your department.

– No.

– All the same, sex is at the heart of love. You couldn't blame her for—

– I didn't. It's the tyranny of her passion I couldn't accept. That simply wasn't the air I wanted to breathe.

– She wanted to tie you down?

– Yes, even wanted to exchange rings. When I refused, she could do no better than to scream, 'You never loved me!'.

– Hmmm...

I think of the Vermeers we've seen this morning, I think of their silence and serenity: A woman pouring milk from a pitcher into a bowl, another reading a letter at an open window. What a world away from the agitation of my dream of a *Midsummer Night's Dream,* from Helena, Hermia and the Amazon queen! Yes, but what about the lacemaker? Absorbed in her own thoughts, she is removed from the world, suspended in a timeless moment. What could the blood-red thread that leaks out of her sewing cushion, spills onto the table and accumulates in a stain on the tapestry, what could it possibly have to do with her? Totally calm on the exterior, might she be ravaged by interior pain? Ingrid, your shift from passion to domesticity intrigues me: In the lunar light of your eyes, I see prayer wheels spinning.

– You know, Marietta, already I feel very close to Ingrid.

– I knew you would. I think you've got a lot in common.

– What? She's far more accomplished than I—there's no comparison!

– Your time will come. I'm sure of it.

Now where is that seller of roses? This time I'd choose a white rose, a flower of pure luminescence. Perfectly still atop its daggered stem, it would vaunt its spiral motion: The staircase I'd climb in my quest for transfiguration. Then you would hear, as you knelt in the flame of its perfume, what I am silently saying:

Your faith will allow me to be instrumental, to leave a trace in the world. I kiss your fingertips and taste immortality: You are inexhaustible, and everything is mine to learn.

– Let's go, Sprague.
You take my glass and finish my Christoffel. I take yours and do the same.

Chapter 3

Dramatic is the introduction; agitated, syncopated, the figure that holds the forms together: Seated in the intimacy of the salon, Klaas in an armchair beside me, I watch you and Ingrid playing Schumann's second violin sonata. Ingrid, you'd told me, feels a particular sympathy with Schumann's music; when it is sombre and unsettled, as here, when it stands still and become a mere murmur, leaving you with nothing to hold onto anymore, that's when she comes into her own: Her perceptiveness is served by a touch of the highest sensitivity. As one both passionate and introspective, dreamily inward and expressive, she responds to both strands of the composer's character. You hadn't been a fan of Schumann's violin music, you'd found his tendency to stay in the lower register unattractive and his writing somehow lacking. And then Ingrid played you on the piano the violin part of his violin concerto, and you found it marvellous. As you worked on the sonatas during your previous visit, you found her depth of understanding, her affinity with the music's psychological underpinning, so impressive that you had no choice but to raise your game. And so, challenging your preconceptions, you found the fingerings and bowings that rendered the right nuance for every note, the right inflexion for every bar, and thereby revealed the astounding expressiveness of the music. Now as I listen to you I cannot separate melody from accompaniment, and so I cue my heart to the rhythmic pattern and consider the duo constituted by the two of you.

Clearly, your friendship is creative, vitalized by the tension between connection and separateness; clearly, there's an easy reciprocity between you. And yet as Ingrid moulds this mercurial composition, never letting a note slip from her control, I don't find it difficult to imagine her as shaky, weepy, out of control. There's an extraordinary intimacy to your performance, you are playing for yourselves alone. Still, I can imagine Ingrid as a nine-year old, playing on stage for the first time; I can imagine how she felt herself the focus of attention, at last recognized. Did she decide there and then that this was her destiny? That this was the way to win back her mother, her mother permanently in mourning for her first daughter, killed in a car accident? Yes, her mother devoted herself to the dead sister (as you told me last night) and used whatever energy she had left to dote on the brother. And yet, I imagine however great the acclaim, the only regard that ever counted never came. Is it that disjunction between the applause received and her inner need that gives her beauty an intimation of the tragic?

When she fell for you, opening herself to intimacy, was she rebelling against the personality she had built? And you, when you met her, were you craving distance? Was your sense of self no longer feminine and affiliative, were you now in a masculine mode, emphasizing difference? Was that where you were at when Ingrid fell in love with you?

Restless, life pours forth from your violin; always on the edge of passion or introspection, it sings. With it, Ingrid's piano sustains a fluent conversation. The blended texture of the music does not give opportunity for solo display: It is as one that the two of you play. Again I am struck by Ingrid's face, her aura of vulnerability, of disinterested sovereignty.

Sometimes, Ingrid, your smile
Is as fragile as the moon in a morning sky;
Sometimes your regard
Is as hard as tempered steel.

Sometimes you're the hunter,
The hawk at one with the wind,
Suspending the world on a wingbeat
In pursuit of the hare.

Sometimes you're the hunted,
The hare—nostrils flared, heart racing—
Standing petrified
In the shadow of the hawk's wing.

But hunter or hunted, hawk or hare,
When you gaze into my eyes
All the world folds into a corner of your smile,
And I recognize my incestuous sister.

The music, sombre and unsettled, comes to an end. Ingrid stands up, you put your violin down; approaching one another, you fall into each other's arms. I am moved, moved by Ingrid's emotion as the hounds of love assail her heart.

Chapter 4

Janneke and Ruud, Veerle and Kees, would join us for dinner on our second evening. While you and Ingrid were busy in the kitchen, Klaas and I played with the children. With Joost I made a lion mask, cutting the eye holes from the paper plate he'd fearsomely daubed in yellow and orange: the better to repel me from his mother. As I cut slits around the edge of the plate and curled them around a pencil, making the mane, Klaas helped Lia make an eye mask, a lilac fairy affair with beads, feathers and flowers. I had to run when Joost began to roar, but when I made him an airplane that actually flew he feared me less as a rival. This time he accepted his supper from Klaas; later, the report from the bathroom was that the boats I'd made him from paper cups had all been sunk with glee. When the guests arrived, Lia jumped on my back as I went to greet them.

The dinner you'd prepared with Ingrid began with cream of watercress soup—onion, leek and potato blended in with the peppery plant. Duck breast with turnips served with a braise of apples and red cabbage followed; the wine that flowed with it was brought by Kees from the Côtes de nuits, a Vosne-Romanée rouge. The meal ended with a dessert of cheesecake with sour cherries, spiked with Kriek lambic. The conversation was animated, governed by Lia's good fairy that distilled, in equal measure among the eight of us, substance with laughter and wit.

When I was asked about myself I realized, as always, that people simply couldn't place me. I didn't romanticize my hybridity and peregrinations, I didn't identify myself with a role. I tried neither to hide the fact that I have no accomplishments nor to disguise my love for you. I realized, once again, that despite people's goodwill, they find it hard to understand that one cannot belong anywhere. It was as if I'd been asked for my papers and could produce neither birth certificate nor home address, let alone an identity card or kin who could vouch for me. Opportunely, Lia came to rescue me with a quick game of peek-a-boo.

Later, as we sat in the in the lounge area of the main room, Kees raved about Neil Young's concert at the Musiektheater. Veerle expressed regret that, Bono having lost his voice, U2's Amsterdam shows had been cancelled. And then, breaking the lull in the conversation, Ingrid said:

— I had a strange dream last night.

Around her wrist, braided silver glimmered in the coils of her black leather bracelet.

— Tell it to us, Veerle said.

Ingrid began:

— The dykes had broken in Amsterdam, the pumps and sluices couldn't stop the flood.

— Everybody's nightmare! Ruud remarked.

— No, it was a sweet dream. You see, our loft had become an island, surrounded by arcades, and in the middle there was a garden. Beautiful flowers and exotic fruit grew in it. When you walked in the galleries you'd here Mozart. From the outside, however, there seemed to be nothing special inside. It was an Amsterdam building like any other.

— That's a pregnancy dream, Janneke said.

She stood up and took off her cardigan.

— When I was expecting Stientje I had them quite often.

Pulling her tee-shirt out of her pants, she reseated herself in the deck chair.

— Can you explain it? Ingrid asked.

— I can try. The cloister—the arcades—that's your seclusion, your withdrawal into yourself. The island is your self-absorption.

Veerle, looking very rock n' roll in her black jeans and studded jacket, jumped in:

— Yes, and the flood outside is simply the world all around you—it's not your concern. It's what's inside you now that's special.

— And what's the garden? Ruud asked.

— That's the baby.

— But it's also Ingrid, Janneke said. It's a garden of discovery.

— Discovery of what? Ingrid asked.

— Of yourself. New aspects of who you are. Like the flowers, blossoming inside but hidden to the outside world.

I was impressed by the way Ingrid inspires openness: There was none of the glib wit and dumbing down that typifies social conversation, none of that drive to up the ante in irony. And so the conversation turned to pregnancy and babies, each of the mothers sharing some aspect of their experience while the rest of us listened with varying degrees of fascination.

Ingrid spoke about maternity as having the courage to begin again. She was happy that this time, unlike for her first two pregnancies, she did not feel pulled back into her relationship with her mother.

Veerle talked about how, pregnant with her first child, she had misgivings—doubts, regrets, anxieties—yet even to herself couldn't voice her feelings, afraid that the baby inside her would be harmed by her ambivalence. And then, during the later months of pregnancy, when the butterflies and twitches in her belly turned into jabs and kicks, she was overcome with love and impatient for the baby to be born.

Janneke spoke of being frightened to have a second baby because she was her mother's only child. She was afraid of 'doing better' than her mother, and felt guilty about that. Even succeeding in her job or being happy in her marriage made her feel she was betraying her mother. Finally, the pure presence of the children before her, their ability to delight and surprise her, allowed her to overcome those feelings.

And thus, for the first time, I understood that pregnancy is a state of heightened sensitivity, one which brings to the surface what is normally hidden within. The woman is forced to confront herself, to engage with what comes up from the deep, and then construct a new identity. Is there anything equivalent for a man?

That night, in bed, when I asked you the question, you said of course there is, it's being an artist. And then you moved your body onto mine, kissed me and said, 'I'm going to make you a baby'.

Chapter 5

Making wandering figurations in the upper register, two oboes invite us into the fairytale. From the rear of the stage, from behind the shutters before the backcloth garden, two parti-coloured cats make their way to a fireplace. Before the flickering flames they lay their feline sensuality. Suspended in the ethereal music, Lia leans forward between us as we sit front and centre in the Musiektheater: *L'Enfant et les sortilèges,* Ravel's opera-ballet performed by Jiri Kylian's Nederlands Dans Theater, is now underway.

Oversized and askew, the fireplace and the furniture—grandfather clock, chair, armchair, table—configure the space into a room where all of a sudden the Child who'd been standing behind the table, his head face down in his hands, breaks into dance and mime while a mezzo-soprano, offstage with the orchestra, voices his thoughts of rebellion. Teapot and cup in hand, to the accompaniment of a clarinet phrase Mother enters the room; towering over the Child, she examines his exercise book while an off-stage singer asks, 'Has Baby been good, has he done his lesson?' No, the Child has not done his lesson; moreover, he neither regrets his laziness nor promises to work, nor will he beg Mother's pardon. Instead, he sticks his tongue out at Mother, who retaliates by giving him dry bread and sugarless tea, and confining him to his room with the injunction, 'Think of your bad behaviour, think of your schoolwork, and think, above all, of Mother's sorrow'. Failing to keep him under her skirts, Mother leaves the room.

As the orchestra bursts into brassy agitation the Child, joined by the Cats, expresses his abounding spirit in acrobatics. Spurred on by unruly piano runs, he proceeds to wreak havoc in his room: Teapot and cup, and his books to boot, he hurls against the wall; to crashing percussion he overturns the table, throws the caged squirrel into the garden, rips the wallpaper and sends the hands of the clock spinning: In a feast of destruction he celebrates his freedom. And then the magic spells begin: A growling bassoon brings Armchair to life; Chair and Armchair, mezzo-soprano and bass, refuse the Child rest. Dancing a minuet to piano and woodwinds, they denounce the Child while blithely ignoring him.

A gentle flame, abiding and steadfast, the memory of that afternoon still glows in my heart. In our plush seats before the thrust stage, you, Lia and I, moved by the naked art of dance, were, for a while, a family. Yes, with Ingrid and Klaas visiting friends and Joost with his grandmother, we were parents to a fairytale daughter, and she was with us in flesh-and-blood. I was your husband, you were my wife; we lived happily ever after, for an afternoon.

We both loved Ravel's music, and we both detested Colette's libretto. How could she, such a master in mining ambiguity, produce a tale so devoid of contradiction? So linear, so flat, so singularly lacking in multi-layered meaning? Lia herself found the Child silly and the Mother 'much too heavy'. And yet, thanks to the transformative power of dance and the magic of the music, my senses were heightened, Lia was held spellbound, and you radiated a beauty that left all possibilities open.

Ding, ding, ding: Trumpet triads in driving rhythms set loose Grandfather Clock's cymbal-crashing dancer; curves counter angles in striking kinetic images while the rich baritone of Clock's counterpart laments the days when he 'told the hours, each like the other, in this changeless house'.

'Each like the other in this changeless house': What a wretched thought! And this deathly desire posited as a virtue by a writer who celebrates life! No matter: The raw physicality of the dancer and the beauty of the balletic line negate that death wish. Lia beside me is wide-eyed with delight, her animistic thinking accords with mine. And you, my love, you who in your intimacy with the Queen of Sciences formalize space-time, are you too delighting in the destruction of the Clock?

As Clock returns to his grandfather casing, trombone and contrabassoon bring on Cup and Teapot to dance a foxtrot. In vain the Child, braving Teapot's threats, tries to interrupt the duet. Cheese grater and whip introduce a touch of ragtime, then, as mezzo-soprano and tenor sing trilingual nonsense, the Chinese Teacup dances a chinoiserie. When she leaves the stage with Teapot, the Child now regrets the loss of his beautlful teacup.

Things cannot feel and act: Lia knows better! She is a child attuned to the deeper stirrings of the world, she is a child uncorrupted by rationality: Enlightenment cannot override enchantment, no accumulation of facts can compete with her personalized concepts! To raise a child like that, would we be up to the task? We would, I'm certain of it! Instinctively, we'd validate the fantasy that allows her to bear feelings of anger, jealousy or frustration. 'Now I am light, now I fly, now a god dances through me': Are we not children of Nietzsche? Of course we'd be up to the task of raising a child like Lia!

In defiance of his emotion the Child throws into the fire Teacup's dancing shoes: A shrill coloratura yells 'Get back!' as Fire and Cinders leap out of the fireplace and proceed to dance a balletic duet. 'I warm the good but I burn the bad', warns the coloratura as Fire and Cinders pursue the Child. Woodwinds and pizzicato strings then come in to reinforce the fiery attack: 'Watch out for the dancing flame, Child! You'll melt like a snowflake on its scarlet tongue.' The unremitting menace of the music's rhythmic pulse drives the Child to seek shelter, but Fire once again confronts him with his wrongdoing. As the full orchestra drives home the message, the Child confesses he is afraid.

And thus, relentlessly, morality pursues the lion in the desert, determined to transform it into a cud-chewing camel. No, that is not how we'd raise our children, not by threats and coercion, for we know that a child deprived of dreaming cannot manage reality. How, then, to help her recognize the song of the other in herself? We'd start simply by not estranging her from her inner life; we'd tell her fairytales that she may tackle her contradictions. We'd put schoolwork in its rightful place and let her imagination be, for play is the foundation of reality. What do you say, Marietta? Is that how we'd raise our daughter?

As the side drum beats out an ostinato rhythm the chorus sings; Shepherd and Shepherdess, torn apart when the Child ripped their pastoral wallpaper, come on to dance a duet in remembrance of their lost partnering. It was to them the child gave his first smile, the chorus recalls; it was their sheepdog that watched over his sleep. Now, separated forever by the Child's maliciousness, nothing can console them in their grief.

Again, propulsive force and intimate partnering, raw power and balletic precision, endow the dance with an infectious sense of freedom: This is the seriousness of child's play, these are adults free of adulthood. There are no moral lessons here: The liberating sensation of energetic motion nullifies the anti-life lyric.

Above harp arpeggios a solo flute hovers, conjuring a Princess in a flowing gown; her supple fluidity and graceful lines marry the lyricism of her counterpart's aria. She remembers how she inhabited the Child's dreams and reveries; she remembers how, in the heart of the rose, he would look for her.

Rising, Lia twirls on her toes and pirouettes into my lap. In rapt attention she watches the Child compete with the masked Enchanter for the Princess' hand. Look! Sculpting her body in space, the dancer's dress flows as she traces rhapsodic lines. I wonder: If Lia believes the dress—organza and taffeta, a glittering bodice—makes the Princess, is that all there is to her idea of beauty? If so, it won't be long before others will let her know there's more to it than that. And when that day comes and she finds herself before a mirror, languorously combing her long golden hair, will she come to disdain her beauty, the way you did yours? Will she see the desire it arouses to be at the origin of all her troubles? Or will she, without any ambivalence, slip her foot into the glass slipper she'd lost at the ball? As I slip her back into her seat, I imagine the challenge of being a good father to a daughter.

Unmasked, it is as Night that the Enchanter comes to reclaim the Princess. The Child, having ripped up his book of fairytales, is powerless to defend her. Left with nothing but a thread of her golden hair, a wisp of a moonbeam, he hangs onto the fragments of a dream. Clarinet, oboe, horn and bassoon, in alternation, double the violins that trace the contours of his desolation.

Harsh dissonance heralds the arrival of Mr. Arithmetic, a giant hand with a pointing finger on his mechanical arm. Sung by tenor and chorus, his fast-paced litany of problems soon becomes a load of stuttering nonsense. Pursuing the bewildered Child around a giant blackboard, the acrobatic professor attempts to drill his erudition into the boy's head. To the virtuosic declamation of multiplication tables, he robotically puts him through his mechanical paces. Imitating the tapping of a T-square on a table, crisp wood-block claps intensify the orchestral terror. Multi-coloured hands pop through the blackboard to scribble crazy circles; the Child takes refuge amongst them, then the dizzying music comes to a climax and dies out.

Would our child be as hopeless at mathematics as me, or would she be like you, plain brilliant? Could she explain why a spider that starts its crawl along the floor of a double Möbius strip, upon returning to its starting point finds itself on the ceiling and, what's more, to get back to the floor would have to go round again? Or would she be so enthralled by the spider's crawling that such a question would leave her indifferent? Aye, my love, what of you and I would we pass on to our children?

Bowed bass and celli awaken the cats; to woodwinds in the moonlight they rise. Sinuous, sensual, slinky, they begin a mating dance. Naively the Child tries to join in; the Cats spit and hiss him away. Voluptuous miaows, baritone and mezzo, punctuate their nocturnal duet; when the orchestra sounds *tutti,* they accomplish the act. Humbled, the Child follows them into the garden.

Now how would having a child change our lovemaking? Would we still be able to escape ourselves through each other, defamiliarize the familiar, unhouse ourselves in our home? Having a child, would we continue our reciprocal unveiling through fucking? Would we still conceive of sex as the truth of our couple, and not merely as one element among others in our relationship? Would sex, in short, remain both the reality and the enigma of the bond between us?

Owl hoots and birdsong, a trio of bats; frisky tree frogs, a dragonfly: Pulsating with life, the garden comes alive as the Child wanders through it. But life has been mutilated: The Child has knifed a tree and killed a bat and a dragonfly. Tree groans and Bat and Dragonfly, upbraiding the Child for his violence, each lament the loss of their mate. In the ceaseless choreographic flow of the phantasmagoria, the boy begins to realize his claims to life are not exclusive. As Big Mother, towering atop her apron-skirt, appears as an apparition, the harp's subtle harmonics combine with the wind-machine's rustlings to stir the Child's conscience.

I wonder how Lia sees this story, this vision of French schooling that is the very antithesis of her Montessori. No inner-directed action, no culture of responsibility—nothing but tradition and compulsion. Lia is a flower that could never thrive in a French garden, a garden ruled by geometric alignments of topiary trees. Where then would we school our children? You had the best of both worlds: Swiss schooling as a child; as an adult, a French education in science. I couldn't be schooled: beyond the walls, I explored the wild garden.

The hoop of Mother's skirt becomes Squirrel's cage; as Bats and Frogs dance, Squirrel stands imprisoned. Squirrel warns Frog of the Child's violence; Frog need not fear, for the Child is now humbled in his isolation. Languorously he regrets being so alone; innocently, he cries out, 'Mama'. Apologizing to Squirrel, he explains, 'The cage, it was so I could better see your agility, your four little paws, your pretty eyes'. Mocking him, Squirrel replies that his beautiful eyes, now glistening with tears, once reflected freedom.

And you, Marietta, your mother left you when you were seven; with the help of your father you raised yourself. Does that have anything to do with why you don't want children? I've never wanted a child in the abstract—but concretely, with you, I do. You see, I don't believe in a blissful paradise of maternal love. Without ambivalence on the mother's part, how could the child constitute himself as a subject? Every life is the story of one's failure to be the centre of the world for someone else. Yet to be the centre of the world for someone else would be to live a smothered life. So, if ever you change your mind about having children, Marietta, would not ambivalence make you a very good mother?

Vengeful, the animals rise up against the Child, each outdoing the other in threats of violence. Their polyphonic battle cry cuts right through the orchestra, but in their frenzy it is not the Child but each other that they injure. Trapped in the cage with wounded Squirrel, the Child binds the animal's paw with the veil he'd kept in his pocket, the veil of the Princess. Impressed, the animals dance in trios, moved by a sudden tenderness for the Child. They notice that he too is wounded; pizzicato violas and bassoons accompany their confession that they don't know what to do. Remembering that earlier he had cried out 'Mama', they turn the cage into a cradle and rock him to a lullaby. As the music rises in splendour, they sing the Child's praises. And then once more the cage becomes the hoop for Big Mother's skirt; seeking his mother's embrace, the Child climbs up the skirt as the animals retreat. Against a backcloth of moon, as the chorus of animals sings a fugue sealing their reconciliation, the Child throws his arms around Mother's waist and exclaims, 'Mama!'. The lights fade out: The opera-ballet is over.

What a wretched vision of childhood, what an abominable view of being a mother! No matter: Ingrid is the antithesis of Big Mother, and Lia is already affirmed in her individuality: She has enough chaos inside her, untainted by dime-store morality, to give birth to a dancing star.

Waterlooplein to Westermarkt: Outside in the street we found the Number 14 tram. Seated in the streetcar with Lia between us, I was full of desire as we passed the Blue Bridge over the Amstel, the drunks and dopeheads in Rembrandt Square, the bacon-strip brickwork of the Mint Tower, the book market on the Spui, the Royal Palace in the Dam. When we got off at Westermarkt, Lia took your left hand and my right, and we walked home to the loft and lived happily ever after.

Intermezzo 12: Lucia

Windblown, her hair gives her a wistful air. That, and the scarf bunched around her neck, its emerald and indigo echoing her eyes. We'd met at a movie. *Taxi to Portugal.* Came to this café afterwards. She's back in Bucharest for the holiday—just finished her first year of Film School in Paris. Wants to be a director. We spoke of Jean-Jacques Beineix and Luc Besson, Lars von Trier and Béla Tarr, but we kept coming back to *Taxi to Portugal*. This film of deathbed truth and adoption, of accidental brother-sister incest, had touched us both deeply.

– My father had no love to give me. We never got along. What he really wanted was a son. Looking back, I see I became a tomboy just because I was trying to get closer to him.

Her kohl-rimmed eyes intensify her boundless trust in me. I'm not wearing white, but I feel like Terence Stamp in *Teorema*.

– Not once did he ever hug me. When I would put my arms around him, he would pull a face and tremble in horror.

Neither broad cheek bones and wide-set eyes nor a dark Latin scintillation, she's a Saxon beauty: Bucharest is a melting pot.

– One evening, at dinner—I had spent all day revising for the Bac—I expressed my anxiety to my mother. My father went into a rage and spoke to me with a hate that really shocked me. He said it was I who had caused my mother's depression, I who had obliged her to go out and work, I who had made her so tired.

Viennese, Parisian, Turkish, Italian: Is cruelty the same in all cultures?

– That really hit me. It was poison. I realized he simply wasn't worth the effort I'd been making. I could no longer love him. Or even pretend to love him.

Cold, lonely, sidereal: The feeling of freedom.

– I go a job, moved out. Burnt my bridges. Never saw him again. A year and a half later he was dead. Crashed his car. Accident or suicide, nobody could decide. Whatever it was, for me it was hell.

She's hugging herself. I'd like to hug her.

– There's a rhyme, Lucia, that may have some relevance to you. It goes like this:

As I was going up the stair

I met a man who wasn't there
He wasn't there again today
O how I wish he'd go away

– What? Say it again.

I repeat the rhyme. Lucia understands. I continue:

– A daughter is always ready to believe her father loves her. Despite all evidence to the contrary.

– Yes. That's what's hell.

She sips her cocktail of rye, rum, bitters and port.

– I remember, every Sunday after lunch, he would listen to Leonard Cohen. Always the same album, *Songs from a Room*. I hated this habit of his. And yet I was intrigued by Cohen because, for once, my father had showed an interest in art. Every Sunday, without fail, he'd play *Songs from a Room*. It was like a need, he never got tired of it. I, of course, rejected Cohen, because if my father liked him, he couldn't be good.

There's a misty shine to her eyes, a glow to the emerald and indigo.

– In fact, I was jealous. Couldn't understand why a stranger was more important to him than someone living under his own roof.

– Did your father understand English?

– He couldn't speak it, but maybe he understood. What's certain is that he found listening to the album soothing. Just that voice and a guitar, yet so powerful it filled the room.

Seems so long ago, Nancy.

– And today, do you like Leonard Cohen?

Her smile is radiant, yet her eyes are soft with sorrow.

– Yes.

She sips her drink. By the way she savours it, I know she is alive to the way the rum mellows the tang of the rye, the port the distillates: I know she's going to be all right. Yet the bitters have not lost their edge:

– He lived only for my mother. It was a *folie à deux*. Only with her would he talk normally. For him I was just a foul-mouthed liar, not worth talking to.

– You didn't put up with it. You had the courage to leave. There's nothing else you could have done.

– I know. But still...

I give her my hand: She takes it. I think of the architecture of Bucharest. Venetian palazzi with French mansards, Turkish balconies and Scottish turrets: No matter how you mix it up, suffering is the same.

Outside the café we embraced and bid each other goodbye. Walking the streets, I imagined Lucia looking for her father through a viewfinder.

Marietta, Lucia did better than I did. I believed I'd be looked on as a child: She knew the fatted calf would never be killed for her. Did I so much want a family with you in order to start anew?

Chapter 6

Though there be many in this bar tonight, I am alone here with you. Listen! As loud as the drums at the worship of the snake, your beauty bangs in my blood. The coral hibiscus of your lips, the silky oak of your eye; the Arabian jasmine of your cheeks, the balsam pear of your hair: In the equatorial calm of your face flicker the frenetic ceremonies of the convulsive. I want you, I want you, I want you! Is that plain enough? Still I embroider the screen of the baroque, making something of my desire before it devours me. How else to beguile the time before your are mine tonight? I am the guinea fowl, the tamarind tree, the fair-skinned mulatto with sea-green eyes; I am the black goat, the calabash, the man in rags in a subterranean place: I am your lover. The kestrel wing of your candle-lit hand, the flamingo when you move your mouth; the sulphur crest of your cockatoo hair, the crimson topaz of your eyes: You are my lover. The supremacy of the senses, the body over the mind, let us enter into contact with the divine: Kiss me, kiss me, kiss me! And thus I pursue the seduction of the Muse, and thus I refuse the Cross: I am and must remain a sorcerer. Now wrap your wrists in cowry shells, put bells on your ankles and bones in your hair, then rattle me with your love! Marietta, Marietta, Marietta! You are Egyptian cotton and agave cactus, you are fireweed and bat flower; I am midnight lily and sacred lotus, I am cassava and sugarcane: Let us share our gifts, pursue fate's logic, and return to the source. Come, let us seek the hidden face of the universe!

– Looks lovely, smells great, but how do you drink it? you ask me.

– First you admire it, preferably with some backlight—see how beautifully it's built?—then you knock it back in one go, like this.

I tip the B-52 into my mouth and savour the complex bouquet of Kahlua, Baileys and Grand Marnier.

– All right, here I go.

Orange essence, eau de vie; Irish cream, aged whisky; rum, vanilla, roasted coffee.

– It' delicious!

The fire opals of your eyes confirm the pitch of your pleasure.

Rainbows, haloes and auroras, the flap of butterfly wings; the calm in the eye of a hurricane, a total eclipse of the sun: No matter what the weather, the body's initiation is the birth cry! High-flying mare's tails, an encroaching mackerel sky; hail's violence and snow's silence, the vagaries of the wind: No matter what the weather, the infant's affirmation is the scream! Life! Spring to the bound of the tiger, venom to the bite of the snake; jungle fever to the adventurer, ecstasy to the saint! And I, no sooner born then begun to die: Why? A tale of trans-generational trauma, a tale no-one can tell. No-one. And so I take myself in hand, and so I take my stand: I love you, I love you, I love you! Feel me! I am the metallic brocade in your petrol-blue skirt, the wool in your merino leggings; I am the suede in your ankle boots, the silk in your crepe-de-Chine top. See me! I am the powderfinger on your trigger, the switch-blade in your swagger; I am the jewel that chastens your breasts, the ardour that parts your lips. Marietta! Marietta! Marietta! You are the pulsation in my bloodstream, the arrowhead in my heart; you are the whore that haunts my dreams, the earthquake in my art. Yes! You woke me from the big sleep, you brought me to presence; the fable superseding science, you gave me an education. I want you, I want you, I want you! You are the electricity in my articulations, the fire in my loins; you are the spark in my imagination, the heroin in my veins. Whoosh! Down from the sky in the dead of night, down comes the herald of doom: What care I for the tireless predator? What, indeed, for death's messenger? I love you. All the rest is but worry beads in a rattle bladder, worth no more than a gnat's wing. I love you. With your kick I come alive, with your breath I breathe again. Whoosh! Across the candle flame it comes, the kiss that melts us into one. I love you!

– How about a Baileys, Sprague?

– Sure.

– Tell me about Claire. I'm intrigued about her link to Palestine.

– All right. Do you want the short version or the long?

– The long!

– Okay.

And thus I came to tell you the story of a girl I knew, a Montreal girl who made my world anew. Or rather, the story of her genealogy. It went like this: One day, rummaging in the attic, Claire's father came across a box of letters. The stamps intrigued him: Overprinted in black ink on desert sand, 'Palestine', with Arabic script above the English and Hebrew below. Postmark: 25 June 1926. Address: Hannah Kaminskaya, Nizhnenovskaya Street 14, Apartment 1, Minsk U.S.S.R. Translated, it became clear the letter was from a Zionist pioneer in Palestine: 'We are draining a mire by digging huge ditches; before the ground dries we use long-handled mattocks to dig out the tree roots. Malaria is a big danger; even though the nausea it gives me is sometimes unbearable, we take quinine every morning before starting work.' The salutation read, 'My dearest Annushka'; the sign-off, 'Your ever-loving brother, Kuba'. Soon Claire's father learned that 'Annushka' is 'Hannah', 'Hannah' is 'Anaïs': Anaïs is his mother. Furthermore, he discovered that 'Kuba' is 'Jacob', and 'Jacob' is 'Jacques': Her father's mother had named her son after her beloved twin-brother who had died at twenty in Palestine.

Anaïs: Who was she? A girl from Minsk, the 'Jerusalem of White Russia', the city of unspeakable slaughter. No, she did not sit in the street in winter with a pot of burning coals at her feet, selling pretzels to school boys: Her father was a lawyer. Between the impunity of autocratic lawmakers and arbitrary administrators, a democratic judiciary defended individual rights: Thus did her father seek redress for the survivors of the pogroms, for the victims of the myriad forms of persecution. Ancestral memory, moral inheritance, code of ethical conduct: Far from the messianic, his religious vision expressed itself in the struggle to end discrimination and bring on the rule of law. In the cauldron of civil war and assassination, terror and tyranny, what chance did he have? And then he read the writing on the wall, and while there was still time left Byelorussia with his wife and daughter.

Odessa, Istanbul, Athens, Messina and finally Marseille and on to Paris: Within two weeks Hannah's world had changed completely. While her father—pursuing his mission of protecting the most universal of all interests, the interests of the human individual—quickly established himself as an activist in the field of international law (stateless persons, refugees, rights of minorities), she frequented cap confectioners and cabinet-makers, artists and intellectuals: Working for various self-help organizations in Place Saint Paul and le Marais, around la Bastille and in the *beaux quartiers,* she got to know her co-exiles. And then she turned herself to mastering French and qualified as a translator and interpreter. At a meeting of the League of Nations she met a young French diplomat. To marry him she converted to Catholicism, and two years later, in 1933, she is in Shanghai with her husband on his first posting.

'Mort aux Juifs!' Pregnant, in Paris for the funeral of her father—dead from a heart attack during a demonstration—she receives, together with their terrible news, the homage of the German Jews he had helped. She promises her mother she'll be back before long. Visions of her father harassed by fanatics, nightmares of her brother dying in a malarial fever in Palestine, haunt her on the voyage back to Shanghai. *Thank God the life stirring in my belly will never know what it means to be a Jew!* In the maternity ward of the Hôpital Sainte Marie she gives birth to a dark-haired son: Jacques. The phantom limb of her twin finally fades away: *My son will be invulnerable!*

And thus Claire's father was born in the French zone of the International Settlement to a Jewish woman in Shanghai. Soon there would be the unspeakable atrocities committed by the Japanese in Nanking, the heroic work to defend the Chinese conducted by John Rabe, Nazi and good German, and on and on with bloody history until Jacques becomes a writer and gives birth to a daughter, Claire, in the Basses-Pyrénées, today Atlantiques.

– And when you were with Claire, she had no idea of her grandmother's story?

– None whatsoever.

– And you, have you looked for a box of letters in *your* attic?

– There is no attic, there is no house. When I went back to South Africa, everything had been destroyed.

– Well then, you'll just have to live without knowing where you come from.

I don't care where I come from, so long as you're with me. God, you're delicious in your ribbed leggings, lovely in your miniskirt! You're my cheerleader when the chips are down, my bitch in a chastity belt. Now I'll be your butterfly and you'll be my flower; I'll be your bush viper and you'll be my burrow. Oh my succulent oyster, I give you my thought in motion: You give me the semantics of metaphor. Now cockle me baby in your mussel, slurp me into your mouth. Blow, blew, blown! Passerine, passerine, you're my bird of paradise; you're the lyrebird feasting on the food of love. Fly, flew, flown! My wagtail, my pipit, my flycatching robin, I can't wait to bring my lips to your chikadee and tits. Know, knew, known! I'll be your snow leopard when the lights are low, your black panther between the sheets; I'll be your dolphin, leaping and water-slapping, I'll be your fire-breathing amphibian: Now deep in your jungle, baby, give me fever!

– Sprague, there's a taxi. Quick!

In the cab home I kissed your hand; in bed I kissed your whole body: The night lived up to its promise. Leopards and panthers and vipers and dolphins, cockles and mussels and wagtails and tits—all the animals I could muster proclaimed my love for you.

Chapter 7

The transformation of awkwardness into grace, the paradox of impetuosity and patience: Waiting in the salon, I study a framed poster of Nicolas de Staël's *Portrait d'Anne*. As I configure the colours—ultramarine and crimson, lead white and yellow—into the form of a girl, her decided step, her gangling gait, evoke you. Ingrid is downstairs, on the phone with her agent, while Joost is at his grandparents and you, Klaas and Lia are out skating. As scarlet bleeds into grey-blue, I wonder: Does Ingrid know that as de Staël transcended the opposition between figuration and abstraction, he was in the throes of a love affair that would kill him? Does she know, when she contemplates the violence of his palette-knife, that this violence was his means of penetrating to the tenderness underlying his heartbreak? And when she listens to the silence that resonates in his colours, does she have any idea of the vehemence of his feelings that would drive him to his death? Hopelessly in love with another man's wife, he wrote a letter to Anne, his thirteen-year old daughter, before he threw himself from the tower in Antibes. In vain he'd left his family and implored his beloved to live with him; in vain he'd tried to reconcile wife and mistress. A fury of work—nearly a hundred canvases in a few weeks—brought no salvation. Shortly after he'd left a letter to Anne on a table in his studio, a streetlight picked out his shattered body on the pavement.

Sitting on the sofa, I think of you, Ingrid and I. Her watery eyes, the pale blue clarity of her regard, are so different from the amber intensity of yours: The flash of your fireflies would not survive in her aqueous blue. Her jet-black hair is the opposite of your blonde; the sidereal glow of her skin contrasts with the solar sheen of yours: You radiate vitality while she evokes the vampire. Yet both of you rose above your problems, had the stamina for intense competition, and the scientist in you, the artist in her, was every inch a soldier: Beyond the shining potential of your talent, you knew how to fight in the world to bring that talent to fruition. While I, what have I accomplished?

— Sorry, Sprague. My agent and accountant are having their annual end-of-the-year fight! I had to arbitrate.

Ingrid, taking a seat beside me, folds one leg in front of her and turns her body to face me.

— Was it difficult? I ask.

Placing a cushion behind my back, I match her position.

— No, I've got enough experience now to resolve these disputes quickly.
She reaches for her bottle of water and takes a sip. Closing the bottle, she licks a drop from her lips: Instantly, I have a poem.

— Tell me five things about yourself, Sprague.

— You like games like this, don't you?

— I do. But I always play fair, so you have nothing to fear.

— Will it do if I tell you five things I like?

— Okay. On condition you also tell me five things you don't like.

— All right. But in any order.

— Fine. Go.

I look into her eyes and the words come easily.

— I like Dutch swear words. I don't like girls who wear half-stockings. Stockings should go from the foot to the thigh, not stop in-between. I like winter nights when the sky's so clear you can see a million stars and your breath comes out in clouds. I like the natural grace of Indian women. I don't like airplanes. I love live performance, whether a Hamlet soliloquy or a ventriloquist. I like neither cynics nor sentimentalists. I love lucidity. I like dipping a thick slice of bread and butter into a mug of tea with condensed milk. I love the English language. I don't like people who burn a candle to their inner idols and assume their gods are universal. I hate groups and clubs and crowds. I like women with jet-black hair, milk-white skin and pale blue eyes. I hate moralizers. I love Marietta. Does that make ten?

— That will do. Now you can ask me anything you want to.

How far can this game go?

— First I'll turn on the light. It's getting dark.

— Turn on the one behind you.

I flick the switch and the silver shade gives moonshine. Not much, just enough for me to draw two haiku from Ingrid's eyes:

If she were to bite
I'd join the undead: The life
Of all flesh is blood

But I am already
Bitten: Returned in body
She is you again

The thought gives me a twitch in the trousers. All the more so as she's still in her T-shirt and stretch pants.

— Wouldn't you be more comfortable without your sneakers?

— Is that your question?

— Yes.

She undoes her shoelaces and takes off her shoes: The life of the unselfconscious body, conscious of its appeal, moulds her white socks—streamlined, tensile, taut—to the curve of an awakening cat: The arch of her instep, the velocity and repose in her feet—

— Is it my turn, Sprague, or do you want to ask another question?

— 'Do you believe in love at first sight?'

— 'Yes, I'm certain that it happens all the time.'

— 'What do you see when you turn out the light?'

— 'I can't tell you but I know it's mine.'

— Tell me true: Do you believe in love at first sight?

— No. Lightning never strikes out of a blue sky. It's when you want to change your life that you fall in love.

— So when you fell in love with Klaas—

— I was obsessed with Marietta. I wanted to change my life.

— Do you still love her?

— Yes. And I always will.

Looking me in the eye, she gives me a wistful smile. She is my sister, my incestuous sister: There's no doubt about it now.

— I can see why Marietta fell in love with your eyes, Sprague. They're beautiful.

— I wouldn't know. I can't see them. In fact, there were times when I felt I was going mad because of that.

— Because you can't see your own face?

— Yes. I felt something horrible had happened to it, and I was the only one who didn't know. But that wasn't the worst of it.

— What was, then?

— The sensation that I didn't exist, that the whole world was an illusion. The panic was unbearable. I'd lie face-down on the floor and pray for a girl to come and walk barefoot on my back, to convince me I exist.

— Well, the next time that happens, come and see me. I'll walk barefoot on your back.

In the aqueous blue of her eyes, I drown.

— Do you realize what you're saying?

— I do.

She takes off her socks.

— You do mean it.

— I do.

Tenderness and defiance illuminate her face, or is it just mine in reflection? Along her foot my undulating mind flows upwards from a fixed point of desire—enough!

— Ingrid, do you know Albeniz's *Iberia?*

— Of course. It was thanks to 'Corpus en Sevilla' that I won my first piano competition.

— Would you play me 'Evocación'?

— With pleasure!

As she slips her foot into her shoe the fall of her hair frees my emotion: I feel how we are bonded through you. She takes her place at the piano; I seat myself on the rug.

It comes, the melody; within the narrow compass of an octave it circles, encircling me in its delicate nostalgia. This is the sound of souls touching, this is silence speaking. I lie back on the rug and listen. What does the music say? It says that in loving you, Ingrid has touched me; it says that in loving you, I have moved her: The touch of her fingers on the keys is your touch reaching the core of us. Listen, she still loves you: That syncopation is your sly smile; that offbeat quality, your gangling gait... Words fall away, the music washes over me... Silence.

I sit up.

— Ingrid, I love your playing!

— Thank you.

— Those hesitations and half-tones, the way you make the musical line emerge, that sombre dreaminess—you render it beautifully!

— Thank you. But thank Albeniz more. He wrote it.

— Are you sure it's not you who composed the piece?

— That's what interpretation's all about, Sprague—to convey the impression of inevitability. When you do that, you know you've got it right. Now lie back and listen to this.

I lie back and close my eyes.

Slow, quiet, contemplative, the chords come, unfolding a percussive melody veiled in an infinity of vibrations. So this is the place she is taking me to, the overtones at the edge of awareness; the place where, unbeknownst to us, we were destined to meet. What is she telling me? That friendship between a man and a woman is characterized by sublimation, and therefore is necessarily an ethical relation? That the feminine horizon where she and Marietta lie will always be ever-receding to me? That even in marriage, fluidity cannot be confined? Conjuring subtle sonorities, she explores the resonance of dying sounds. What is she telling me? That the appropriation and exclusion that characterize a sexual relation need not deprive the friend of intimacy? That friendship between lover, ex and beloved can be full of subtle harmonics that promise a new music? Listen how they come, as if from a distance, the resonances that give birth to melody; listen to the beauty of the sound. Gathering the silence into a slow arabesque, a rhythmless motion where love resides, Ingrid gathers in my thoughts. Not stating harmonic resolution but letting the overtone imply it, with meticulous control of touch and pedal she sounds a note—soft, softer, dying...

— Ingrid, you're amazing! What depth in so few notes!
She smiles. We rise and return to the sofa.

— What was it?
— Debussy. 'Canope'. From the second book of *Preludes.*
— It's very moving, that immobility.
— The kind of paradox I like! Yes. It's masterfully written. All harmonics and voicing.
— Have you recorded the *Preludes?*
— I haven't. I enjoy playing them, I've got them firmly in my fingers, but I feel no need to record them.

The porcelain glow of her skin brightens in the lamplight; from pale blue to ash grey her eyes veer as she turns to face me more fully: I'd never have imagined otherworldly pallor could be so beautiful.

> Touch me, fatal sister.
> Come, possess and destroy me:
> Infect me with love.

— You're really immersed in Schumann these days, Marietta tells me.
— Yes. Chopin is perfection, Schumann is flawed. But I engage more with Schumann, I can bring out more. I love the tensions in his music, the emotional extremes.

> Torture me, my twin.
> Exhaust me in your lust for life:
> You're no blushing bride.

— And you, Sprague, what exactly do you do?

— Not much. I write haiku.

> Bite me, pollute me,
> Mingle your blood with mine:
> Take the stone from my mouth.

— I sort of teach cinema, but it's more a pretext to talk about life than cinema as such. Do you see many films?

— Yes. *Scooby-Doo Meets the Boo Brothers, Basil the Mouse Detective, The Adventures of Pippi Longstocking.*

— I see! Your children are really lovely, Ingrid. That Lia is Alice in Wonderland!

— Yes, she's quite something.

— And little Joost—boy is he in love with you!

She pats her belly and says:

— Hope he won't be too jealous.

— That could be tricky.

— We'll see.

— Lia, I find, is amazingly self-contained. She can amuse herself with anything.

— Yes, but she's very sociable too. At her age I was already a loner.

— So was I.

Voices sound downstairs. Klaas announces:

— We're back!

— Yoo-hoo! Ingrid calls.

She looks me in the eye.

— Remember, if ever a day comes when you doubt you exist, call me: I'll come and walk barefoot on your back.

I take her hand and kiss it.

— I hope such a day never comes. Never comes again.

We stand up. I say:

— Maybe I'll keep a mirror in my pocket, in case of a panic attack.

She captures my gaze.

— I'll be your mirror.

— Ingrid!

I feel like throwing my arms around her, I feel like enfolding her into myself. I don't: I will simply embrace her when we say goodbye.

Chapter 8

How shall I convey the shadow and light of our last evening in Amsterdam? The shadow was within me, the light came from you. In the salon, Klaas, Lia, Joost and I watched you and Ingrid playing Mozart's Violin Sonata in B-flat major, K. 454. As I listened to you render Mozart's humanity through your capacity to listen to each other, I thought of Lia's evolutionary tree—the birds from the reptiles—and wondered: What am I? Marietta, when your gaze met mine on that patio in Princeton, I felt the crack of the egg; I felt my serpent's tooth making me an opening: I slithered out, I learned to crawl, but I still haven't learned to fly. When will I? Listen! Your violin effortlessly takes over a theme in the middle of a phrase and then hands it back to Ingrid's piano, leaving a thrill to run through me. Once again I am blown away by your virtuosity; once again I am moved by your virile femininity: In your flats, T-shirt and jeans, in your black and white and gold and green, you send me as you soar. Listen! You and Ingrid are so entwined that I can't tell when she takes the cantabile out of your bow and when she puts it back: I simply let the ravishing lyricism of the *Andante* course through my veins. And now once again I am overcome with love, once again I give thanks for the light: And then the shadow falls. I can't forget the abortive search, the darkness of asylum; I can't forget the silent screams, the air grabbed in gasps. Yes, I remember the dread of impending madness, the head-banger banging at my door; I remember the days when I couldn't be still, fearing I'd lose myself, forget to think about myself, slip out of reality. I'd watch the clock, keep busy, for if I didn't I'd no longer know who I am. I tried to read, but reading had become a game of infinite regression, an exercise in stealth: Persecuted by my own lucidity, obliged to be constantly aware of myself, I couldn't accept the coin of signifiers lest it depredate my soul. No girl's touch came to remind me that the most immediate, the most trustworthy, the most integral source of knowledge is the body. Then again, I didn't have a body. I was weightless, a wisp of smoke escaping from the citadel of myself, a faint signal of a murdered soul: I was an idiot. Look! Walking across a field of white, a boy feels a tremor running up his spine: He's just realized the bare feet trudging through the snow are commanded by his mind. Look! The girl in the school bus, the terror in her eyes as the boy stares into them: 'Know me. I want you to know me'. Look! The creeping rootstalks, the tender grass—look at the boy watching them grow; the mangy dog, the stray cat—see them licking his face. I can't forget, I can't forget, I can't forget! And then once again I am overcome with love, once again I give thanks for the light: You're tirelessly improvising, creating music in the moment: In the reprise the theme is never the same.

Marrying inventive brilliance with intimacy and simplicity, virtuosity and gallantry with purity of soul, you honour the artist whose impeccable taste compelled the chaos at the heart of man to become a cosmos. And I, what am I? Crawling on the ground yet aspiring to fly, what am I?

The sonata over, it was time for Joost to take his bath. Knowing this, he crawled under the piano and undid the laces of Ingrid's sneakers. Then he began pulling on the drawstring of her pants. When she promised to come and tell him a bedtime story, he consented to leave with Klaas. Lia decided to join them: I'd made some new boats.

Spontaneously Ingrid began playing 'Of Foreign Lands and People', the first of Schumann's *Scenes from Childhood*. You stretched out on the sofa and lay your head in my lap. As the limpid tenderness of the melody drew me back into my interiority, I knew that if anyone can meet me there, it is you. In the fire of your soul you forged yourself when your world fell apart; to a beat away from your last breath you starved yourself to be free. And when your lover, your one and only, was thrown to his death from a motorcycle, you faced down the Furies and wailed yourself well. When the structures of competition offered you a way into the world, with pencil and paper, with violin and bow, you played to win and won. And I, born into emptiness, had but a flame in my heart, a gentle flame in the last redoubt. And with me, always, the chill chafing of a hand, the hand of madness awaiting me should the flame go out. Listen! Nostalgia makes distance intimate: Ingrid is conjuring grace from sadness. Resonant interiority, a slow cadence of chords: Silence, and a deeper silence.

Ingrid stands up and steps onto the rug; you leap up and embrace her. I'd like to embrace her too, but I dare not: I'll do it when we say goodbye.

– I promised Joost a bedtime story. Light the fire downstairs; I'll join you as soon as I can.

As I lit the fire, I felt the flame within me burning steadily, and as I sipped my wine, I swore I would blaze a path of poetry, if not through the annals of art, at least along the length of your body.

Klaas served up a supper of grilled chicken salad with chorizo-stuffed olives, dressed in a citrus-kiwifruit vinaigrette. Dessert was pears simmered in port, with grapes, walnuts and blue cheese. The wine was full-bodied, the conversation intimate, and the night outside, deep. And thus ended our stay in Amsterdam.

Chapter 9

Utrecht, Antwerp, Ghent: It seemed like only a moment ago we'd said goodbye to Ingrid and Klaas, Lia and Joost, and, on a lark, turned off and headed for the Flemish coast. (At last I'd taken Ingrid in my arms, at last I'd pressed her body to mine—thanks to you, who'd turned Klaas around—and what a flutter she sent down my spine when she pressed her lips to mine!) Yes, instead of continuing down to Paris, we drove up to the North Sea hamlet of Sint-Idesbald. After visiting the Paul Delvaux Museum with its sleepwalking nudes in spectral landscapes, its piazzas and ruins populated by ghosts, we set out for a walk along the beach.

I was pre-disposed to like Delvaux, and disappointed that I didn't. I liked his universe, I felt at home in it, and so felt frustrated, even guilty, that it left me cold. Venting my frustration in physicality, I ran straight ahead then turned around to face you.

— Pom-pom pull away!

— Where are the boundaries?

— The sea and the dune. But you must pass as close to me as possible!

— Like the matador to the bull?

— Exactly!

Nimble in my retreat I speed backwards at your approach; heading straight to me, you head-fake but I'm not fooled: I lunge to the right: you pass me on the left.

— How'd you do that?

— Magic! Do you want to defend again?

— Yes.

I run straight ahead then turn around to face you.

— Pom-pom pull away!

Approaching me in an easy stride, you try to wrong-foot me as you stutter-step; watching your hips, I stay with you as you swerve: You spin around and pass me on the other side.

— You'd make a good matador, Marietta!

— And blind you with my suit of light?

— No, I'd be a bull with Ray-Bans. Now you defend.

You run straight ahead then turn around to face me.

— Pom-pom pull away!

I set the tom-toms beating in my blood and feel the rhythm in my body; I head straight toward you, head-fake, side-step and pass you cleanly.

– Did you really try, Marietta?

– Of course I did. I thought you'd do a double fake but you didn't. Again! You run straight ahead then turn around to face me.

– Pom-pom pull away!

I run wide, heading for the dune; fleet-footed, you stay with me. Stopping on a dime, I make to cut back inside: You're bouncing like a boxer, ready to tag me. How to break free? My stutter-steps you mirror, my head-fakes can't wrong-foot you. Hey-ho! I spin around, run, and dive into the dune. The moment I'm on my back you're on top of me, pinning me down in the soft sand.

– You're a very clever bull.

– Yes, now give me the coup de grâce!

Bringing your mouth to mine, you slip your *estoque* between my lips and still my trembling heart.

The wide strand becomes even wider as the tide recedes; under a grey-blue sky the North Sea unfolds its flatness to infinity. We are alone here on this winter beach, even the seagulls have gone elsewhere. Look! A sunburst shatters the glass sea, splinters of light make a scintillating mosaic: The press of your hand in mine tells me it's delighted you too. As I fill my lungs with iodine air, I feel my heart expanding; as you slip away and fetch a stick from the sand, I take out my Leica and capture you in its lens:

> Bending a piece of driftwood,
> You bend destiny to your desire:
> Isn't that what vast horizons are for?

Twirling the stick like a baton, you toss it up, spin around and catch it.

– You're a right royal majorette, Marietta! Where'd you learn that?

– With Nika, in Poughkeepsie. I'm celebrating, Sprague.

– Celebrating what?

– Remember those data sets I suspected may contain indirect signatures of decaying dark matter?

– Yes.

– Well, last night, while you were sleeping, I found the final analytic formula to reconstruct the electron/positron source spectrum from the observed flux. In other words, I've shown that the inverse problem can be solved analytically!

— Fantastic! Give that baton another twirl and toss it: I'll catch it in my camera.

As I look through the lens you get into the rhythm; you wind up and toss the stick. I click:

Heavenward, you launch
Your thanks and praise: Joy overcomes
Creatureliness

You catch the stick, twirl it, and toss it up again. I click:

Land, sea and sky,
One unbounded plain: As boundless
As my love for you

— The light is lovely, Marietta. Let's do some more!

Mannish in your moss-green parka, feminine in your woollen cap, street-style in your high-top sneakers, sexy in your skinny black jeans: You offer my lens many possibilities.

— Shall I take off my cap?

— Yes, and shake out your hair.

I look at you through my Leica:

Blowing your hair, the wind
Hides your face: Into the open
My ardour is driven

Parted, poised to spread,
Your lips pause: The eternal
In the instant

Tilted head, tight frame;
Fortuity: Whole is your beauty
In half a face

Shock of recognition:
Through the lens I see it is you
Who are looking at me

Offering what it withholds,
Furtive yet forthright: Your face
In its inner light

— Sprague, let's do a topless!

— All right.

You shed your parka, blouse and bra; you fall to your knees and spread your legs. As you put your hands to your heels and lean back, your breasts thrust out; turning your head to the side, you flick your hair to veil your profile. I crouch down and capture you against a sullen sky. Moving seaward, I mould your breasts with shadow; heading toward the dune, I sculpt your torso with light.

— Swing your head to the other side.

Standing tall, I consecrate your submission; lying low, I recognize your domination.

— Fantastic! Do another pose.

You rise on your knees and turn your torso toward me; you place one hand on your inner thigh and the other on your ass. Lowering your hips, you turn your head counter to the rotation of your torso and let your hair fall over your profile.

— Lower your butt a little more, maintain that tension... Perfect!

Moving around your body, I arrange the lines to glorify your contours, I distribute the tones to highlight your splendour.

— Lovely, Marietta, lovely!

Two weeks later, examining the contacts, we chose two images for poster-size blow-ups:

> You refuse the eye the possibility
> Of appropriating any one part of your body:
> Tying desire up in knots, you intensify it
>
> In a harmony of forces and counter-forces
> You affirm your subjectivity:
> Acceding to submission, you assert your sovereignty

On my black wall your brooding eroticism made a stylish diptych.

Shimmering water, shallow expanse, a caress unravelling a skein of ripples: The wind picks up. Look! A scattering of sanderlings, pale in their winter plumage, busily pecking their way about. Paradoxical birds: Swift and direct of purpose, yet looking random and lost.

— If not Delvaux, then who do you like, Sprague, in surrealist painting?

— Dorothea Tanning. *Eine Kleine Nachtmusik*. Do you know it?

— No.

— It's magnificent!

— Where can I see it?

— In the Tate. And there's also *Self-Portrait on 30th Birthday.*

— In the Tate too?

— No. It's in a private collection. Look! Sanderlings and...

— Oystercatchers!

While the black-and-white birds with red beaks poke about, the sanderlings skip along the foamline, fleeing the wash of the waves only to pursue the backwash seaward, sticking their beaks into the bubbling sand.

— Ingrid reads a lot when she's pregnant. For Lia it was Tolstoy, and for Joost, Dostoevsky.

— Maybe I could send her a book?

— Of course.

— But what?

— Whatever you think she'd enjoy.

The Book of Laugher and Forgetting? Nights at the Circus? Letty Fox: Her Luck?

— I know: *Ada, or Ardor.*

— Nabokov? She's read all his novels.

The Hearing Trumpet? The Transit of Venus? Hunt the Slipper?

— How about *Two Serious Ladies?*

— What's that?

— Jane Bowles. 'I dreamed I climbed upon a cliff, my sister's hand in mine'.

— Don't know it.

— Perhaps *A Maggot?*

— Rebecca Lee the Puritan? I think Ingrid would find her strategy of dissent tedious.

— *Mantissa,* then. It's Fowles at his most Nabokovian.

— Yes! She'd love it!

The air was crisp as we headed back to the car; the light, soft and silvery. I had two frames left on the roll. One I shot as you leapt across a pool of water:

> Body in flight,
> Silhouette afloat: Grace
> Makes gravity luminous

The other I shot in the dune:

In tall grass we crouch.
Three, two, one, click! A portrait
Of Cathy and Heathcliff

I'd been thinking about Emily, about her ravaging love story, ever since Ingrid had told us she'd been commissioned to write the music for a dance version of *Wuthering Heights* that a Dutch troupe was developing.

– I can't wait to hear what music she'll come up with!

– Whatever it is, it'll be powerful. She loves *Wuthering Heights* as much as I do.

A gust of wind rattles the brittle grass; softly, the soughing of the breeze resumes.

– Marietta, I am Emily.

– Like a million other readers!

– You think so?

– I'm sure of it.

– Yes, I suppose so. It's amazing, isn't it, how she bewitches us?

– It is. When I was seventeen I was quite in love with her. And that feeling has never really diminished. It's very subtle, the sexual power she exerts, but no less strong for that.

– How do you explain it?

– The book doesn't flatter the reader, it guards its secrets. And that, as every woman knows, is an aphrodisiac.

– And yet she died a virgin. Unknown.

– But not unknowing. She may or may not have loved someone at Law Hill School, but what's certain is that she loved herself. That's enough to know the essential.

– You think so?

– Yes.

– I don't.

– My view, Sprague, is this: All the mirroring in the book, the mixing of names and genders, suggests a lesbian consciousness. When you understand the role of Heathcliff, it all becomes clear.

In the car, the doors open, we were both pensive as we sat sideways in our seats, shaking the sand from our shoes. My boots back on, your sneakers laced, we pulled the doors closed and in the same instant turned toward each other and made our breaths one.

— So you believe Emily was lesbian?

— I'm sure of it.

We cross the border into France.

— What makes you so sure?

— *Wuthering Heights* is a book shot through with ambivalence, and driving it all is Emily's sexuality. She was your age, Sprague—twenty-seven—when she wrote it. And at that age...

Her demonic masterpiece, and my humble haiku.

— ...all she knew was that she was an oddity. The language didn't have the resources for her to conceive of herself any other way. 'Invert', maybe.

— So the tension in the book—it derives from her response to her sexuality?

— Yes. It's an expression of her ambivalence. And all the violence is a sign of her frustration.

— At what?

— At not being able to affirm herself frankly.

The traffic's light; you're pushing one sixty.

— 'I am Heathcliff': How do you interpret it?

— Heathcliff is the cipher of Emily's homosexuality. The outsider, the alien, the odd one out. He's Catherine's double, not her complement.

— He embodies her sexuality?

— Yes. That strategy of doubling is very lesbian. Catherine and Heathcliff are one and the same.

— So when she has to choose between Heathcliff and Edgar Linton...

— She has to choose to affirm or deny her homosexuality. She chooses Linton and her world falls apart. The pain of abandoning such a fundamental part of herself kills her.

Staring at the stubbled fields, I suddenly imagine them as golden wheat.

— Yes, I see that now. It all makes sense!

I open the Evian.

— How could I have missed it before?

I pass you the bottle. When you give it back, I drink a mouthful and find myself savouring it: So this is the taste of transparency.

— Did you really see that scene as Catherine confessing to Nelly her dilemma in choosing marriage partners?

— Yes, I suppose I did.

— You *are* sentimental, Sprague.

— I told you, when I give up haiku, I'm going to write a Harlequin Romance.

In your sly smile I see my future: I don't have Emily's genius, I cannot write a novel as vicious as hers. Instead, I will write one that walks the knife-edge of tenderness, and when I'm done something more will remain than the sheen of my blood on the blade.

– For every lesbian, that scene with Nelly is perfectly transparent. Catherine is confessing that she's going to deny her homosexuality, and she's aware that it's a fatal mistake. Remember, she says, 'If all else remained and he were annihilated, the universe would turn to a mighty stranger'.

– And in rejecting the stranger, she becomes a stranger to herself.

– Yes. Without Heathcliff, she loses all sense of who she is. She didn't die after giving birth to Cathy, she died when she turned her back on Heathcliff.

You're pushing one-seventy. I caress your cheek with the back of my fingers; you kiss my fingertips.

Teach me to walk the high-wire,
Till I vanquish my need to fall;
Teach me to turn my back,
On the irreversible.

May I always meet you
In the place you cannot master;
May I always complete you
Without making you whole.

I feed on your hunger,
You feed on my greed:
You are inexhaustible
And everything is mine to learn.

Two-and-a-half hours later we were back in Aravane's flat. You put on your sleep mask and took a nap while I had a leisurely shower and shave. In the mirror I practiced looking mysterious and grave, but the indestructible innocence of my reflection kept mocking me. Later, while you were getting ready, I flipped through Aravane's photos from Iran while grooving to Al Green and Otis Redding. Speculating on the proposition that the Sufi mystics and these soul musicians were animated by the same impulse—to realize the immanence of the temporal in the eternal—I said to myself if I could sing like Al Green or dance like a dervish I'd happily abandon the solitary labour of fiction. Yes, the sly smile you'd given me in the car, the one in which I saw my future, had made me realize that I was but three years away from the age at which Emily died but light years away from even approaching the shadow of her achievement. I felt the hounds of time yapping at my heels and didn't know which way to run. All the more so because ever since you'd declared your faith in me, that afternoon in the *bruin café* on the Prinsengracht, I had begun to feel not unworthy, but impatient to be more of a man for you. Creating a work that lives outside of me would allow you to love me more savagely: That's what I wanted. Those were my thoughts, Marietta, when you walked into the room and blew me away with your beauty. Stunned, I didn't say anything: It was you who complimented me on how good I looked. It was thus with a spring in my stride that I matched your gangling grace as we walked to Muriel and Adelaide's loft, ready to rock out the old year and roll in the new.

Intermezzo 13: Tasha

Marietta, I'm sitting in a sidewalk café in Laiki Geitonia, a stone's throw from the Venetian wall. The morning is sleepy but I'm wide-awake. Spent the night with Tasha. Russian, she teaches contemporary dance at the University of Nicosia. Gram wrote the music for a fifteen-minute piece she choreographed last year *(A Passion Stronger than Truth).* It was he who put us in touch. Natasha had been a dancer with the Stuttgart Ballet and 'went round the bend' after the collapse of a love affair. Came here to get herself together. Liked the island so much she decided to stay. From the day of her arrival she began writing, a flood of logorrhea that evacuated her hate. Empty of anger, she burned what she'd written and began writing anew. Soon she discovered she had a fiction on her hands. In the silence of the night she shaped it into a novel that a passing Russian publisher would read. And thus she found her new vocation.

We met in a lounge-bar on Adamantiou Korai.

— It was in a park in Saint Petersburg. I was five. My father took me to the puppet show. *Beauty and the Beast.* At the end of the show I couldn't stop crying. The puppeteer himself came to console me. He said, 'Look, the ugly beast is dead, now the handsome prince will marry the pretty girl'. I was furious! I screamed, 'No! The prince is ugly! The prince is stupid! It's the beast who's beautiful, the beast who's strong! I didn't want him to die!'.

She's wearing a silver death's-head ring—silver is open-heartedness and fair dealing.

— So you see, Sprague, when I had that disastrous love affair, I'd forgotten what I already knew at five.

— What? That you prefer the beast to the prince?

— Yes. Only sex is real. Love is an illusion.

The day you gave a talk at Paris-Dauphine you saw a trailer in the Bois de Boulogne, a whore at the door. What was that tingling between your thighs, that flutter down your spine?

— I don't go for princesses either, Tasha.

Arrows of indifference fly from your loopholes, silence pours from your assommoirs: You've barricaded yourself inside a fortress, you've built a moat around your heart. How can I get around your towering spurs and curtain walls, your barbican and drawbridge?

— No, but you fell for love.

Woof, woof! Is this your dog you've sent to fetch me, is this your messenger? Into the depths of his eyes I spill my despair; in the meniscus of the overflow I see my reflection: I am a rag-and-bone man with a wheelbarrow.

– Listen, Sprague. You've got to choose between Don Juan and Casanova. Don Juan was never a dupe. Casanova was always a fool.

Your nostalgia for stability, Sprague, is a nostalgia for something you never had. You dream of it, but like me, you don't really want it. You're always shocked when you meet people who live in the same city they were born in.

– Don Juan is a myth.

– Precisely! And what keeps the myth going? Hunger for the mirage of love! *Love! Have you tried drugs to cure yourself of it?* I have. No cure. *Have you tried colourful remedies, like Mercurochrome or Brilliant Green?* I have. No cure. *And have you tried howling, a bright red scream?* I have. No cure. *Then I guess you'll just have to live with your illusion.*

– I can't wait to read your book, Tasha, to see what flesh you put on these bones.

– My agent's just sold the translation rights. Maybe this time next year you'll have it in your hands.

– I hope so.

– And you, what are you working on?

– A rock opera about a Russian novelist on a Mediterranean island who falls madly in love with a wandering poet.

– Not a chance! But there's a great club I know. Would you like to go dancing?

We went dancing. The resplendence of the music effected the transfusion of our senses; her bodily presence, her kinetic intelligence, blew me away. Yes, with the sway of her hips she sowed my desire, with the tilt of her head she tended it. That night, the gift of her vulnerability fused with the assertion of her sovereignty to blur her distinction between love and sex. At breakfast, the stark nobility of her face was enlivened by the sparkle in her eyes.

– And what about your novel, Sprague? Gram said—

– It's a letter. A long love letter.

– A *love* letter? Haven't I cured you of that?

– I'm afraid you haven't.

– Well, next time you're in town, look me up. I'll give it another go.

Just before I left she gave me a translation of her first novel, *The Dream Grows Cool*. I opened it on the epigram: 'Neither fever nor languour, in a meadow or a bed. A friend neither ardent nor weak. A friend. The air and the world, unsought. A life'. Rimbaud, 'Vigils' I. I put the book in my bag. Taking her in my arms, I pressed her body to mine. Then, without a word on our breath, we said goodbye.

Chapter 10

The moment Adelaide opened the door I knew the night would be magical. Her grey eyes glowed as she kissed you; embracing me, she signed her name with her scent.

— Love your threads, Sprague!

Her feathered mini skirt swirled as she led us into the cloakroom (that is to say, the office where she writes her articles, now rigged up with clothes racks from Muriel's boutique).

— When did you get back?

— Around five.

Pyramid studs on black leather, dark crystals on scarlet twill.

— We stopped off on the coast.

As she hands me a hanger, the bracelets around her wrist bind our wills into one: to seek in the closing of the circle an opening to community.

— One last kick of oxygen?

— Yeah.

— So you're all gassed up and ready to go?

— You bet!

Her top of shimmering brocade glistens as she turns to hang up my coat; you take your sling-backs from your bag and slip them on. Fallen angels, death wish: On her wall, Brian Jones, Jim Morrison, Janis Joplin and Jimi Hendrix line up large in fine gradations of black and white. Look! From her blonde updo to her black ankle boots, Adelaide is luminous in the Psyche mirror. Ash-grey, the feathers on her satin skirt tickle my fetish spirit; in her eyes I see the same ardour as when I first met her: Simple Minds, The Barrowland Ballroom: 'Tonight, under the crystal light, surrender everything to me.' Hush! In a whisper of silk-chiffon you bring your body before the mirror. The softly-structured silhouette of your mint-green dress brings your femininity into relief; a tug on the olive waistband augments it in the pleated bodice.

— Marietta, forgive me for saying so, but you are stunning!

Crossing your eyes, you hold the tip of your tongue behind your teeth and say:

— Shlankew.

Winning, your smile forgives Adelaide. Just then, one of the couple's cats—Matty, the blue mitted ragdoll—shines your rose-gold shoes as it slithers between your legs.

— Hello! you say.

Bending down to stroke it, you stare into the unreal blue of its eyes; as you rise you give me a wink, your eyes sparkling with Aravane's spirit.

– Come, says Adelaide, let's go in.

Layered washes and pools of light articulate the huge volume of the room, two floors tall under its glass roof, bringing an excitement to the space that the hubbub of the guests intensifies. From the railings edging the galleries, serpentine streamers in bright metallic colours, interspersed with silvered balloons, fall to varying depths. Floating above the ferment in a texture of silver and brass, Herbie Hancock's piano weaves a dreamy web. I feel your presence beside me, I feel your head held high, as we walk into the room.

– Sprague! Marietta!

Sleek in her navy silk jumpsuit, her gunmetal pumps gleaming, Muriel steps forth. As she lays a hand on your shoulder and kisses you, the blackened spikes of her caged ring remind me she's come through fire.

– How was Amsterdam?

– Lovely!

– Where did you stay?

– With friends, on the Brouwersgracht.

– Come, I'll introduce you to the twins, Joaquín and Gabrielle. They're our bartenders.

'A Kiss in the Dreamhouse': Tall in black jeans and a Siouxsie and the Banshees T-shirt, Joaquín steps up to shake your hand. Bravado and shyness, swagger and finesse, mingle in his attitude. To my bygone handshake Gabrielle, a girl on the cusp of womanhood, accedes with charm. In her silk camisole and georgette blazer, her hair in an easy updo, she looks in a hurry to grow up: Her mischievous eyes say she isn't. We learn they are the children of Isabelle and Diego, Muriel and Ada's next-door neighbours. Gazing into my eyes, Gabrielle gives me a smile as impish as 'The Loop', the tune unfolding under Chick Corea's fingers. There's a hint of disquiet in her admiration, something adolescent: It's you she's attracted to. Shuffling to the spirited waltz, she shimmers in her Capri pants to her place behind the bar.

– What will you have, Marietta?

– Something different. Any recommendation?

– Yeah. How about a Casablanca? It's not Rick's Café, but it is Morocco.

– What's in it?

– Gin and soda with lemon-ginger cordial, mint and cinnamon.

– I'll have it!

While the twins prepare our drinks (Joaquín's making me a Negroni), I turn around and survey the scene: Ahead, a bevy of women around a tall bar table, its polished chrome contrasting with the braided trunk of the Malabar chestnut beside it. Drinks in hand or eating from plates, the women convey an animated complicity. To my left, above the sleek curves of a steel and glass table, a lemon tree displays its winter blossoms; around the table, two men and a woman break into laughter as a punch line is delivered. To my right, two couples stand in the silvery glow of fairy lights, talking, it seems, in English. We take up our drinks.

— Here's looking at you, kid!

In the sparkle of your eyes I re-invent myself: If you're Bogie, I must be Ingrid Bergman.

— Florence is a researcher, and Xavier is the American correspondent for your favourite French paper!

Adelaide leaves us.

— So, Xavier, how do you like the man who married the female lead of *All That Heaven Allows?*

— Long live the Reagan Revolution!

— Long live Jane Wyman!

We raise our glasses.

— Now he's married to Maggie.

To Florence's remark, you retort:

— The one who said, 'Poor dear, there's nothing between his ears'?

— The very one!

The sparkle in your eyes is reflected in Florence's. Addressing Xavier, I say:

— Did you know Reagan was considered to play the role of Rick in *Casablanca* before Humphrey Bogart got the part?

— Really? So just reading the script was enough to fire him up?

— Fire him up? For what?

— Keep us rocking in the Free World.

— Yeah, must have been!

Rock 'n roll and cinema: I like this man.

And then Florence turns to you.

— Ada tells me you're in physics, Marietta.

— Yes, I'm a theoretical physicist. And you, what's your field?

— Philosophy. I'm trying to do justice to the death of God.

— I like it! Tell me more.

– I'm trying to think from a post-theological perspective, free from the shadow of religion.

– So you reject both theism and atheism?

– Yes, in favour of philosophy.

– And what's your position in relation to Nietzsche?

– He wasn't radical enough.

– That's a bold position! But who said, 'We godless anti-metaphysicians still take our fire from the flame of a faith thousands of years old'?

– Yes, I know Nietzsche was aware of accommodating religion's terms of engagement.

– So when he asked, 'What if God should prove to be our most enduring lie?', he didn't go far enough?

– No. What I'm trying to do is to think *after* God.

– Without being complicit with theology?

– Exactly.

– A courageous project. Good luck!

She's beautiful, with her ghostly hair and high cheek bones. I like the black of her jump suit against her pallor, I like the halter neck that leaves her shoulders bare. Smoky, her ombré earrings dangle before my desire, my desire to put Providence back in its place.

And now she speaks to me:

– And you, Sprague? Ada said you're at the American University.

– Yeah. I'm learning from my students. In the name of cinema.

– What do you mean?

– Well, take the parting scene in *Casablanca*—'We'll always have Paris'. When Bogie says, 'The problems of three little people don't amount to a hill of beans in this crazy world', that's a great line to launch a debate about the pursuit of happiness in a world of horrors.

– I can see how it would be. But practically speaking—

– I've got students from Sierra Leone, Iran, Vietnam. They've seen more horrors than I ever have. And, until I met Marietta, more happiness too!

Turning to me, you raise your glass and say:

– Here's looking at you, kid.

Decidedly, I must be Ingrid Bergman.

– Hey, Bill Evans!

Florence snaps her fingers to the beat and gives the name of the piece:

– 'You and the Night and the Music'.

Onyx and jade circle her wrist in brilliant cubes of black and green: the power of Cleopatra. As the piano's melodic line transports us to the buffet, the bent of Flo's mind makes me wonder: Will she go home with Xavier tonight? If so, when they make love, how deep will she take him into her godless universe? And will he be man enough to find the divine in it?

Chapter 11

Singing to my senses, the buffet is a smorgasbord whose beauty invites me to eat with my eyes: On a table scattered with sparkling confetti and origami objects—spike-heeled boots and feather boas, hand bags and head gear—a spread unfolds that defies me to resist it. As presented by Gabrielle, the cold buffet includes filo cones of crab-and-mango salad, canapés of salmon mousse and dill cucumber, smoked trout and avocado blinis, bites of chestnut and prosciutto, and chicken, bacon and walnut terrine. We make our selection and head for the lemon tree.

In the fragrance of the blossoms we stand at the bar table with Callum and Frieda. He's English, she's South African. They have two children and live in London.

– Where in South Africa are you from? I ask Frieda.

– Bloemfontein. And you?

– East London. Do you miss Bloemfontein?

– Of course. It's impossible not to miss where you come from.

What an abrasive gem! Horseradish, mustard, sun-dried tomato: In my mouth the chestnut and prosciutto comes alive. Frieda sips her Tom Collins. She's pretty, in her red chenille dress. I could sit next to her now, but in South Africa we'd be forbidden to sit on the same bench. I ask her:

– Zola Budd's from Bloemfontein, isn't she?

– She is, yes.

– I went to see her at Crystal Palace. I was one of those who didn't boo her.

– You don't run with the pack?

– I don't. Making life hell for a naive eighteen-year-old will not make life better for the oppressed. The ethics of sport should be inviolable.

– I agree.

– And besides, I could never boo a girl who runs in bare feet.

Frieda smiles knowingly: So Callum too has a crush on Gradiva. Listen! The lush chromaticism and gritty swing of Keith Jarrett, Gary Peacock and Jack DeJohnette: 'Too Young to Go Steady'.

– You know, Frieda, talking to you now, I have the strangest feeling of getting in touch with something deep inside me. And I've just met you.

– It's funny how these things work, isn't it?

I feel the crunch of the crab-and-mango salad; I feel the kick of the chicory and red chilli. Listen! There's ecstasy in the trio's playing, there's exultant rhapsody: 'Too Young to Go Steady'.

— I try to understand what makes things tick.
That's your answer to Callum's question.

— What things?

— The fundamentals of matter. In the extreme scales, from the subatomic to the cosmic.

— You're a physicist?

— Yes. Theoretical physics.

— And you like the extremes?

— I like excitement. And you, what do you do?

— I travel for a living. I'm a writer.

— Exciting!
My ears prick up: I know this man.

— Are you Callum Walcott? I ask him.

— I am.

— *The Blues of Red: A Burmese Journey?*

— Yes, that's it.

— I've read your book! And so has Marietta.

— Really?
You come back in:

— Yes. Ada lent it to us. It's excellent!

— Thank you. But why do you think so?

— Because you're a fabulous writer! And you leave me free.
And I, will I also be a fabulous writer who leaves you free?

— Please explain!

— You look over someone's shoulder, yet you filter it through your own individuality. That's invaluable. You're not moralistic. That's refreshing. You don't indulge in pathos or irony, yet you're not complacent. That's stimulating. Shall I go on?

— Please do!
You pause, suspended in the first chords of 'Golden Earrings': You're acquiring a taste for harmonic imagination on the spur of the moment, the figuration of melody in unforeseen modes. You let Jarrett's Standards Trio play, and then you continue:

— You convey an exciting sense of confusion in the most sober language. You don't try to lull my critical sense to sleep with exoticism. And when I get to the last page of a chapter, I see that the story has emerged organically, with no striving for effect. I look back, and no matter what the emotion, no matter how complex the situation, I feel a sense of freedom. You've respected my intelligence, you've trusted my sensitivity.

Callum is visibly stunned by what you've said. So is Frieda. As for me, I long to attain a transcendent objectivity, that you may love me beyond my contingent self: I long to embody my soul in a work that lives outside of me.

– You're the kind of reader I've dreamt of, Marietta, but never imagined could actually exist!

– A reader can only be as good as the writer invites her to be.

– Yes, definitely, Frieda says.

She removes a strip of lemon rind from her blini and eats the trout-and-avocado. Callum follows his salmon canapé with a stick of celery. Listen! Modal-hued and waltz-tempoed, bearing Chick Corea's touch, 'Summer Night' sweeps into the room to assuage Frieda's jealousy.

Chapter 12

Is it the glow of the tea lights under the table-top warmers that gives rise to the frisson of delight at the sight of the hot buffet? Muriel's origami emblems have been replaced with talismans of Adelaide: Ingeniously folded, paper scorpions and peacocks, geckos and iguanas, pop up from the scintillating confetti. Look! Grilled herbed oysters, balls of sea bass; curried lamb samosas, tiger prawn kebabs; lamb and courgette koftas, cheese and tomato tarts; carrot matchsticks tied with chive stems, green beans with a prosciutto strip; wild mushrooms in potato baskets, grilled vegetables in Parmesan creels: Spoilt for choice, we choose.

At the bar, Joaquín warms to you. Seduced by the simple grace of a Martini glass, you go for a dry Martini. I choose a concoction of gin, elderflower cordial, pink grapefruit juice and crème de mûre.

Under the glass-and-metal staircase, cantilever chairs of woven cane gather around a table of black fibre glass. We seat ourselves. 'Summer Night' had segued into 'Night and Day', and now the mood is Ellingtonian: The Duke himself is playing a rich chord progression. As he thickens the chromatic descent with suspended harmonies, 'Prelude to a Kiss' sounds more like post-coitum blues: Tenderness and nostalgia, sadness and loss, emerge to colour the melodic motifs. Keeping the melody moving, the tone combinations envelop me in the sensuality of their sound.

— These are delicious, Sprague. Can you taste the Fontina cheese, the sultanas macerated in masala?

— Uh-hm.

All I can taste is you: the intelligence of your body, the beauty of your mind.

— Be discreet: See that woman in a pant suit, the one with long black hair?

I see a velvet shimmer of plush burgundy, I see a woman who evokes Italy.

— Yes.

— That's Riva.

— Riva? From when—?

— Uh-hm. To judge by the look she gave me, I'd say she still believes I took Inès from her, all those years ago.

— That's a long time to bear a grudge. Is she Sicilian?

— No. She's from Rome.

— How did she end up in Paris?

— Her mother's French. Got divorced, then moved back here with Riva.

— And who's that blonde beside her? Got a certain something, wouldn't you say?

— That's Simona. Jewellery designer. The cuff I'm wearing is hers.

Intricate lace in rose gold wraps its grace around your wrist.

— And what does Riva do?

— Don't know. It's years since we last spoke. Hmmm!

Eating a samosa, you mime your delight. You feed me the other half.

— I love the subtle apricot.

— Yeah, it's the chutney in the curry.

The chutney in the curry
The attar in the rose
The silk in the mulberry
The dots on the dominoes

It's you, my love, you who are delicious!

The tongue in the bell
The fuse in the dynamite
The bucket in the well
The venom in the snakebite

It's you, my love, you who are delicious!

The doubt in the definite
The horn on the unicorn
The who in the whodunnit
The oak in the acorn

It's you, my love, you who are delicious!

Your body sways as Ellington plays the lilting riff of a twelve-bar blues: 'Things Ain't What They Used to Be'. Like a river current the rhythm gathers us in its forward motion; in our blood we feel the underlying pulse. Floating on this luxurious surge, our bodies move still closer together: With his distinctive touch the Duke finds the supple rhythm of slow love-making, the elusive groove of a leisurely fuck. Now he lets the tone linger, now he strikes it staccato; now he plays it in a whisper, now he bangs it out: No matter what the touch, the message is the same: Titi-boom, spang-a-lang, you're my baby!

Chapter 13

Here she comes, a pleated silk blouse over a black bustier, a man in an open-necked shirt and a three-day beard beside her. We invite them to sit down. He's Raphaël, she's Maya. Revelling in the oyster she's sucked from the shell, she swallows it then says:

– I like this music.

I like her green-grey eyes, her shaggy black bob.

– Me too, I say.

At a sprightly clip, Ellington gives his signature buoyancy to 'B Sharp Blues'. Infectiously communicative, between relentless movement and supreme relaxation the swing suspends us all in its contradiction.

– I'm a lighting designer.

Dipping his lamb kofta in a jar of herbed yogurt, Raphaël raises his head and looks you in the eye.

– I can light anything you don't want to do in the dark. And you?

– I'm a physicist.

– A physicist? You guys do such cool things!

About to slurp another oyster, Maya asks:

– Like what?

Raphaël answers:

– Photonic crystals, like the iridescence in your opal ring. Lasers, like the harp at Jean-Michel Jarre's concerts. Movies, like making things invisible.

You sip your Martini.

– We can do even cooler things than that.

– Like what?

– Shoot laser beams through holographic gratings, and so twist the light ray. The twisted light's got orbital angular momentum, like a moon orbiting a planet. Project that over a star, and you block out the star's light, allowing you to see any planets they may be orbiting it.

– Cool! says Raphaël.

– I don't get it, says Maya.

Taking a tiger prawn by the tail, you explain:

– It works like this: In the centre of a ray of twisted light you have a circle of perfect darkness, because the light interferes with itself and cancels itself out. That creates a coronagraph, sunglasses that filter out the glare. Fit that onto a telescope, and you can find planets outside the solar system.

Picking up her Bronx, Maya says:

— That *is* cool!

As she sips her sweet and dry vermouth, her gin and orange juice, Thelonius Monk comes in to give his version of 'It Don't Mean a Thing if it Ain't Got That Swing'. The catchy phrase has you hooked, the syncopation sets you swinging.

— And you, Sprague, what do you do? Maya asks.

— I'm trying to turn a haiku into a novel.

— That's very ambitious.

— Yes.

— Do you have enough material—how many syllables are there?

We all laugh.

— Seventeen. But it's not the poem, it's the image that inspired it.

— And what's the image?

— It's a woman observing herself in a mirror while sperm slowly spills from her mouth.

— I see!

She slurps another oyster.

— And what's it going to be? A porno novel, a summer bestseller, a literary masterpiece?

— All three!

Decidedly, I do like her green-grey eyes, her shaggy black bob.

— Recite me the haiku.

— All right.

> The blue of your eye
> Scintillates: You surrender
> My temporal soul

— It's very subtle.

— There's another version. An image of her dripping the sperm into her bath. It goes like this:

> Milky cloud, swirling;
> Evanescent smoke, curling:
> Who am I? she asks.

— I like that one! Put the two together and you've got a perfect poem. It makes a sequence, it gives it closure.

– Closure's against the Zen aesthetic. Anyway, those are the seventeen syllables I'm trying to turn into a novel.

– And what's the story?

Danger comes to edge her eyes, mischievousness to wet her lips.

– The book begins when the story's over.

– Then it won't be a bestseller. People want stories. That's why they read novels.

– I know. But for me, everything interesting happens when the story's over. That's when you can cut to the bone, that's when there's nothing left to distract you from your soul.

– Then it won't be a porno novel. Readers of porno don't want introspection.

– I know. But pornography's only interesting when it's combined with philosophy.

– Then it won't be literature. Readers of serious books don't want pornography.

– I know. So what do you suggest I do, Maya?

– I don't know.

She slurps her last oyster.

– But whatever you try, here's to you!

She raises her glass. You and Raphaël join in the cheer.

– To your literary-porno bestseller!

In the lambent silver-blue light, in the daring-glass of my dreams, I see an artist who can accomplish anything, because you are part of his schemes.

'You'd Be So Nice to Come Home To': Easy and elegant, Art Pepper blows his pinched and jittery tone through the changes of Cole Porter's urbanity. The alto sax brings a brooding quality to the bouncy melody, telling us insouciance is not all it's cut out to be. I think of *Straight Life,* Art's brutally honest autobiography; I think of the abortion his mother wanted him to be: Something in his tone remembers—his lyricism is all the more moving for being naked and raw.

– When you're really in the moment, you can do no wrong.

So says Maya as she twirls a sautéed mushroom on a cellophane-frilled cocktail pick. She's an actress.

– You're in a space where you're no longer yourself, and the buzz is like a drug.

She eats the mushroom.

– You're extraordinary when you're acting. So when you're not acting, you miss the forces that flow through you. And that's a downer!

— Because you feel ordinary? I ask.

— Yes. And because you're frightened of just being yourself.

She begins cutting her potato basket into bite-size pieces. As you sip your Martini, I think of you on stage. It's extraordinary, how you refuse acclaim.

— At the end of the day, it's the writer that saves me.

I like how she eats. At one with her body.

— The writer? I ask.

— Yes. Maybe I do have some advice for you, Sprague.

— I'm listening.

— It's what I learned from plays. Create characters who are a riddle. Put them in situations where nothing is black or white. That's the foundation on which great works are built.

— That's excellent advice.

— It's what works on stage, anyway. When a writer gives you a character who is a riddle, and I'm able to convince an audience that I embody that riddle, that's quite a kick. I'm extraordinary, and the audience, too, goes beyond their ordinary selves.

Around her wrist, stacked between bands of woven silver, a serpent flashes its emerald eyes.

— Thank you, Maya. I'll remember that.

She sips her drink. Suddenly you break into song:

— 'On a sidewalk, one Sunday morning, lies a body just bleeding life.'

Maya joins you:

— 'And someone's sneaking round a corner, could that someone be Mack the Knife?'

Relaxed and poised, Sonny Rollins, the Saxophone Colossus, does justice to the sardonic menace of Brecht and Weill's vision. Listen! Brilliantly inventive, with swirling runs and staccato moans he invites us to syncopate the possible. Accepting the invitation, your body sways with Maya's: You're ready for anything.

— 'Bet you Mackie's back in town', you sing together.

Maya lights a cigarette.

— Viola. *Twelfth Night*. That's my favourite role. The one I learned the most from.

Blurring the green and grey in her eyes, the smoke blurs the bounds of her sexuality. She gives me a cocky look, as if she's Viola again. The blouse that drapes her bustier, however, is no disguise for her curves. Look! Her cigarette crackles and glows as she takes a drag: Now she is eminently the actress, in the masquerade.

– It's a very liberating role. And a lot of fun!

What's with Raphaël, head down, making a grid of his carrot matchsticks?

– A woman disguised as a man—it frees you to act out all you are.

With a stylish tap she flicks her ash into the ashtray.

– Androgyny's a state of mind. It goes beyond sexual orientation.

Her smoke's getting in my eyes: Why does feminine masquerade move me so?

– Gender can be a prison. Take Olivia and Orsino. She with her foolish mourning, dropping out of sexual circulation. He with his silly conception of how a man should love a woman. It's Viola, the androgyne, who liberates them.

Her hand as graceful as the glass, Maya sips her drink. Resting the glass on the table, with subtle daring she strokes it.

– Ever since I played Viola, I'm more able to play with these things.

Indeed. Raphaël, having eaten all his carrot matchsticks, is now unwrapping his prosciutto-bundled green beans and arranging them in a lattice on his plate.

– What things? he asks.

– Gender. Sex roles. Sex.

– And what's the point?

– Fun!

She flicks back her hair: The way it falls into place fills me with a sudden tenderness.

– But isn't androgyny just a fancy word for unisex?

– No, Raphaël. It's the opposite. Androgyny—how shall I put? Androgyny embraces difference. Unisex refuses it.

– I don't get it.

Twirling a ring of orange rind around her index finger, Maya looks at me knowingly and says:

– Can you explain, Sprague?

– I'll try.

A little slow to disenthral myself from her cunning fingers (now subtly sliding the orange rind along her distal phalanx), I finally say:

– Androgyny's the bent teaspoon, half in air, half in water. It's unstable and dynamic, there's tension. It's an invitation to play.

Now it's along the proximal phalanx that she's fingering the orange peel.

– Unisex is the straight teaspoon in an empty glass, static and stable. No tension, no play.

– I'm not convinced, Raphaël responds. Refraction doesn't explain why unisex and androgyny should be opposite.

Training her ambiguous eyes upon you, Maya asks:

— Marietta, can you explain?

— I'll give it a go.

You sip your Martini, then address yourself to Raphaël.

— Have you ever lighted a fashion show?

— I have. Yves Saint-Laurent.

— Perfect! Now would you agree that the masculinization of women's clothes, like in Yves Saint-Laurent, intensifies a woman's femininity?

— Intensifies her femininity? Yes. Makes her more sexy—but that's a paradox!

— Exactly. That's androgyny. It's paradoxical.

— Okay.

— Now a man dressed in feminized clothes—is he more masculine?

— No. Definitely not!

— There you have it. The feminization of men's clothes does not intensify a man's masculinity. On the contrary, it diminishes it. There's no paradox. That's unisex.

— So androgyny is paradoxical and unisex is not?

— You've got it!

He finishes his drink.

— Very clever, your demonstration!

Maya, beaming, blows a series of smoke rings. You pick up the strip of orange rind she's let fall from her finger and give it to me. Turning to Maya, you say:

— Now tell me, Maya, did you ever guess, before you played Viola, that disguise could be so fruitful?

— I had an idea it would.

She takes a drag on her cigarette.

— But it went beyond my wildest dreams!

Milky cloud, swirling; evanescent smoke, curling: Who am I?

— Your dreams weren't very wild then, were they?

I toss the orange peel back to her.

— No, I guess they weren't.

As one, the three of us finish our drinks.

Intermezzo 14: Izolda

Marietta, making love with Izolda I didn't fantasize about you, but now that she's gone I do.

The bold demeanour of your breasts,
The rose-petal lips of your pussy;
The arch of your instep,
The refinement of your fingers,
The dimples in the small of your back:
They are pavane and bolero,
Madrigal and canticle,
Sonata, concerto and symphony to me.
Yes, your breasts are Ravel, your ass Purcell,
And your pussy, pure Wagner!

Izolda's a girl I met on the train, coming to Szczecin from Berlin. She's a student at the university here, studying geosciences (coastal morphodynamics, the sedimentary continuum from river systems to continental margins). The sculptural lines of her face contrasted with the easy fall of her hair; her feminine earrings with the masculine cut of her clothes. We talked about Gombrowizc and Żuławski, Stanisław Lem and Grotowski, and all through the conversation we knew we'd end up in bed: When I opened the taxi door she got in without a word being said. I wasn't wearing white, but that's how it happened.

Afterwards, I taught her some English:

– Knock knock!
– Who's there?
– Boo.
– Boo who?
– Don't cry. It's only a knock-knock joke.

– Knock knock!
– Who's there?
– Little old lady?
– Little old lady who?

— Hey, you can really yodel!

Then she pulled out a copy of *Elle* from her bucket bag and read me her horoscope:

> Ready for a mental vacation? Your ruler Mercury, planet of the mind and communication, slips into your twelfth house of rest and the subconscious for two weeks. Take a break from all the heavy-duty thinking and analyzing. Record your dreams, write in a journal, meditate. It's time to declutter your psyche, rather than overload it with new information.

She said she didn't think she could keep a journal. I asked her to try, and wrote her a first entry in the notebook she'd pulled from her bag:

> Spending the weekend with Sprague. He's given me a quiz: Of the following options, which one would you choose?
>
> (A) I would prefer my lover to make love with someone else and fantasize about me.
>
> (B) I would prefer my lover to make love with me and fantasize about someone else.

That hit a nerve with Izolda: She was in the aftermath of a difficult breakup with her boyfriend (a Polish-German love story, *Romeo and Juliet* along the Oder-Neisse line).

— I'd choose 'A', she said. And you?

— 'A' too.

— Surprising. For a man.

— Maybe.

There is no fixed personal fullness, only a plurality of subjectivities; we are not one, not two, but intricately multiple: It all depends on the relationship. I could have said that to Izolda, but I didn't.

— Do *you* keep a journal, Sprague?

— Yes.

— Can I see it?

— It's in my jacket pocket. Go and get it.

I watched her as she walked. Like your sway, hers is all the more sultry for its self-possession; like your blonde pallor, hers has an inner fire.

Notebook in hand, she sat opposite me on the bed. Opening a page at random, she read out loud:

> Marietta, I'm sitting in a café by a bridge across the Bosphorus, trying to keep the sadness at bay. I watch the shoe-shine boys, the dogs, the fortune-tellers; I drop a coin into a blind man's cup: I am no more a stranger here than anywhere; there is no country I call foreign, no country I call home. But when you desired me I had an address, when you wanted me I belonged somewhere.
>
> Over the water the sun is setting, the domes and minarets are silhouetted against the sky, but what is their beauty compared to the amber of your eyes? An orange haze hangs over the hills, there's a blue cast to the buildings below, but what care my eyes for these colours when they have seen your hair turn the breeze gold? Across the bridge cars go by, suspended lights link the shores: Can it really be easier to link Europe and Asia than to unite us once more?

Izolda closed the notebook.

– Well, well. So your lover left you too?
– Yes.
– And you still love her?
– Yes.
– What I've learned, Sprague, is that the past has no future.
– But it does, Izolda, it does. Memory is the future of the past.
– Memory! If there was no memory I'd still be with Geert! It's memory that tore us apart.
– Yes, I can imagine. The horrors of history.

Turning the page, she read out loud:

> Clarinet and long-necked lute, goblet drum and oud: I like this music, Marietta, it soothes my longing for you. The singer's got liquid eyes, expressive hands, and a voice of

> varied hue; she's got a jewelled bra, an ankle bracelet, and a skirt of electric blue: But she's not you... Silently the Bosphorus hauls its history to the sea, silently I tell the story of you and me: Marietta, can you hear me? In darkness I evoke these memories, in darkness I try to bring you back to me. To what good? Tomorrow like today, no woman in a crowd will turn around when I call your name, no 'Hi' in your voice will answer my 'Hello'. Tomorrow like today, I will not find you among the press of people at the dock; at the station, I will seek your face in vain.

Izolda closed the notebook and put if down.

– You're hanging on to a shadow, Sprague. She's gone.
– No Izolda. Marietta is the flame in me that casts the shadow you see.
– What?
– The wick that draws the wax is language drawing memory. As long as I'm alive, Marietta will live in me.
– The wick that draws the wax?
– Come, I'll show you.

Saying that, I took her in my arms and pronounced her name: Izolda! Leaping up from my solar plexus, the flame that carried the vocative slipped between her lips. Joyous in exhausting our bodies, joyous in feeling them to be inexhaustible, we drove each other deeper and deeper into exaltation: To there where the sediment of memory is washed into the sea.

Marietta, you who honour the self-astonishment of which your sex is the fountain, give me your blessing: That shadows may faithfully evoke what lies before the fire, that text may capture texture. Fie on cave dwellers! What if we be apart? It is the breath of life that sustains your flame: It is your flame that sustains my heart. In its light I know what to do: Hear me now, that I may honour you!

Chapter 14

Sending a funky vibe through our bodies, hip-hop jazz-funk fusion from the Brecker Brothers gives a bounce to our bearing as Muriel leads us to the bevy of women by the Malabar chestnut. The introductions made, she leaves.

– AIDS and Black Monday have put an end to the eighties. The nineties have already begun.

In the black plunge of her crêpe-de-Chine top, in the sparkling sheen of her iridescent jacket—electric blue, purple and lime green—Héloïse is striking.

– Or do you think this decade's not quite dead yet? she asks me.

Free-flowing, her reddish-brown hair, highlit in blonde, falls straight to just short of her shoulders.

– It's dead. But why go by the calendar? We can feel the vibes of the times in our bones.

– Yes, but the calendar puts them in perspective. Reminds you where you're coming from.

That abrasive gem again! Nicole jumps in:

– Are you afraid to look back, Sprague? Do you think you're going to lose your Eurydice like Orpheus did?

There's a steely edge to the blue of her eyes, echoed by the blue of the jacket and pants she's wearing. White T-shirt and tennis shoes: Cool.

– To tell the truth, I've never understood that mysterious moment when Orpheus looks back. All that effort to reach Eurydice in the Underworld, and then—just before reaching the light—he looks back and loses her. I confess, I just don't get it.

– It's about faith, Simona says.

– Faith?

– Yeah. Rumour has it that love can't survive without it.

The scalloped hem of her voile skirt falls to just above her knees: I won't fall that far. She continues:

– He didn't have the faith to believe she'd still be there. He didn't love her enough.

She loves me, she loves me not: White daisies pattern the navy skirt, white as the white of her sweater. Riva comes in:

– Then again, it could be the opposite. Maybe he loved her too much. Maybe it was excess of love that made him look back.

Beneath her plush burgundy blazer, the black of her silk-chiffon top is transparent. As transparent as she is?

— Either way, she continues, we all know what happened to him!

— Remind me, I say. I've forgotten.

I like her red lips and long hair. I like the light in her eyes.

— A lost soul, Sprague. That's what he became. Ended up getting ripped apart by the Maenads.

— Who were jealous of his love, Héloïse specifies.

— Legend has it only his head survived, Nicole adds. Fell into a river, drifted down to the sea. And do you know where it washed up?

— Where?

— In Lesbos. That's how Sappho got her gift of song.

I think of a Sappho fragment. I want to recite it, but the words won't come. Instead, I ask:

— Am I in the way, Riva?

— What are you talking about? We're happy to meet Marietta's lover.

She raises her glass:

— Here's to the two of you!

— And to your beautiful eyes! Héloïse says.

— Yes, Nicole adds, they go very well with Marietta's.

Vodka and gin, rum and Bourbon—is that the taste of ambiguity?

Riva caresses a Malabar leaf.

— It's been a long time, Riva. How are you?

— I'm fine, Marietta. It's good to see you.

— Is it?

— Yes. A little troubling at first, I confess. But it's definitely good to see you.

Silver, the spikes of Riva's heels glow.

— Have you tried the desserts? she asks us.

— Not yet, I reply.

— Help yourself, she says, sweeping her hand to the plate on the table.

— What are they? you ask.

— Wonton with strawberries and mascarpone. They're delicious.

I help myself to one.

— I'll have a bite of yours, Sprague.

You eat from my hand.

— Hmmm. This would go well with champagne.

As if on command, Joaquín brings you a glass.

'Stand to face me beloved
And open out the grace of your eyes':
It comes to me now, this fragment of Sappho;
It comes to me from the depths of my soul.

Sappho, I hear your voice in the hills of Mitylene,
I hear your lyre in the mixolydian mode:
With unabashed frankness you reveal yourself,
With undeceived insight you lay love bare.

I would like to pay you homage, however humbly;
I would like to pass on what you have given me:
The conviction that love needs no premeditation,
That in the being of another one's self expands.

And so I tune my lyre to your intonations,
From my lyric I expunge ornament and explanation:
It is enough that I open myself to grace.

– So, what are you up to these days? you ask Riva.
– Translation. I've just finished an anthology of erotic fiction. By women, of course.
– Of course. French to Italian, or the other way around?
– The other way around. Italian to French.
– And how long have you been working as a translator?
– You don't remember?
– No.
– I'd already started when I was going out with Inès.
– Is that so?
– Yes. Now I can afford to translate only what I like.
– You must be very good.
– I've worked hard...

So this is Riva, the woman who, before she met Inès, had never had an erotically satisfying relationship. Neither with a man nor a woman. Struggled against her homosexuality. On experiencing its power, she was shocked and desperate, appalled at her own response. Felt condemned, as if she'd just signed her own death sentence. This Inès told you in the Lounge of Neon Lies.

— You know, Marietta, there's a story in the anthology that makes me think of you.

Never experimental, never casual, never promiscuous: That, we would learn, was how Riva was in all her affairs: Serious. Always serious.

— Yeah, really?

— Yes. It's by Ippolita Avalli. It's called 'Simena'.

— I've read it. Ten times. That's how much I love it.

— But my translation's not out yet!

— Have you forgotten I'm perfectly at home in Italian? But if it would please you, I'll read your French translation.

— No, no, if you've already read the original...

Interlocked with the bass guitar, the snare drum sounds the backbeat while the kick funkifies it; vamping on a single chord, the piano thickens the mix, leaving the saxophone's rhythmic hits to accent it. Against this ground, a trumpet figures silver sound.

Simona approaches you.

— Marietta! Such loveliness! You've got the perfect look to show off my cuff.

— It's a beautiful piece, Simona.

— You're the perfect model for it! Could I tempt you into a contract?

Down into a deep frown you bring the corners of your mouth, purse your lips and stick out your tongue like a taco; drawing your tongue back into your mouth, you fold it into a four-leaf clover. Fascination and revulsion, delight and distaste, play on the faces around you.

— Good luck, Simona, but modelling's not for me.

— Just a few photos—and a lot of money!

You cross your eyes, then, keeping one crossed, glide the other to the outer corner—left eye, right eye, left. Once more you bring about the awe inspired by otherness, this time accompanied by whispers about your 'criminal beauty'.

— Whichever way I look at it, Simona, I always come up with the same answer: No thank you.

— My loss, Marietta, my loss. But I'll get over it! I'm working on a new project.

— Great. What is it?

— I've been commissioned to design a perfume bottle.

— Congratulations!

— It's for Leonora. They're launching a new scent, Demoiselle de la nuit.

— What's it like?

— Wonderfully perverse! A mixture of masculine and feminine, woody patchouli and white floral, with blackcurrant, lime, and a touch of liquorice. And—here's the real kicker—something overripe and perfectly louche!

— I like it! And the bottle, will it be louche too?

— Louche, no. Erotic, yes!

Your eyes sparkle.

— Tell me more!

— I first toyed with the idea of a bottle that goes against the scent. You know, something for prim girls in glasses.

— Who go wild at night?

— Exactly!

— Like Riva! Héloïse jumps in.

Riva whirls her head wildly, then pulls a prim, perfectly straight face. Everybody laughs.

— As it turned out, Marketing didn't like the idea. Then I took the opposite tack—baroque and humorous, in the spirit of *Ladies Almanack.*

Djuna Barnes—the slow narcotic of *Nightwood,* the anatomy of love: through a black diamond, lucidly.

— You know, tipping the velvet, tongue in cheek.

The joyful wit of her *Vanity Fair* portrait, white wine with Joyce at the Deux Magots.

— In a word, louche, but ironic.

Sticking her tongue in Nicole's ear, Héloïse flicks it languorously. Everybody laughs.

— No, Marketing didn't like that either. So finally I decided to combine the sober and the obscene, without irony. A naked woman kneeling, head thrown back.

That's exactly the photos we made at Sint-Idesbald! I say:

— The essence of power, the scent of submission!

— Yeah!

Héloïse pulls her belt out of her pants and wields it over her head like a whip.

— On your knees, Sprague! Lick my boots!

Everybody laughs.

— Yeah, that's what I'm going for. But not so straight! The key to my figurine-bottle will be ambiguity.

— Maybe Demoiselle will become the Kouros for girls, Riva says. Then they could smell us. I'm sick of being taken for straight.

Héloïse jumps in:

– Oh Riva, not that again! Every lesbian who's not butch simply has to accept that femme and hetero are indistinguishable.

– I don't like false advertising, Héloïse. It makes for frustration all round.

– Do you want to live in a ghetto?

– No. But I do want to be recognized for what I am.

– Oh come on, you're not exactly living in the well of loneliness!

– Of course not. But the fact remains, for the butch we don't belong, and for the straight we're one of them. Why do we have to walk down the street holding hands to be recognized for what we are?

– Is it really such a big deal?

– *You* can handle being come on to by guys. I can't.

I jump in:

– Why don't you wear a T-shirt, Riva, saying, 'This is what a lesbian looks like'?

– What do *you* know about it, Sprague?

– Well, I know a pigeon in a box can easily be recognized, but it can't fly like one who is free.

Héloïse says:

– Sprague's right. Besides, everybody's somebody else's outcast. Isn't that so, Marietta?

You smile enigmatically.

– Yeah.

I say:

– You know, Riva, I can see myself in you.

She stares into my eyes.

– Not literally, I hope?

In the general laughter we recognize each other. Or so, on the last night of the year, I choose to believe.

Chapter 15

– Ten minutes. That's the time you've got to get to know each other before I move you on.

So says Adelaide as she leads us across the room. Funky bass line, earthy feeling; sax, synth and drums: Threading its animality through our spinal marrow, Herbie Hancock's 'Chameleon' gives our stride an offbeat energy.

– Julie, Jean-Luc, I'd like you to meet Marietta and Sprague.

A Botticelli angel, plump of face; a candour in her regard. Ruby-red are her pumps, blonde her bedhead bob. Star-bright! Sequins scintillate in midnight blue. Julie is a puppet artist, Jean-Luc a paediatrician. When I quote him Hemingway's quip that an unhappy childhood is the best training for a writer, he says:

– Only if the child breaks the chain of transgenerational trauma. Otherwise, one is more likely to see psychosomatic illness, not art.

Then he explains how the Balint group of fellow clinicians he leads is on the lookout for this phenomenon. Julie, for her part, speaks of juju and djinn, masks, idols and automatons. *Ubu roi*, Avignon off. And then Adelaide returns to move us on.

– Diego, Isabelle, I'd like you to meet Marietta and Sprague.

There's wisdom in her eyes, the blue sparkles with intelligence; from her sensual mouth the words come, trippingly on the tongue: She's a psychoanalyst, she's written a book on love.

– I could use your services, I say, but I fear if I did, my hand would no longer fit the glove.

– What glove?

– The one I wear to tell my story in shadows on the wall.

She gives me an enigmatic smile. In her stretch-leather pants and fetish boots, she is Eros with a death wish.

– It seems I've made my bed, Isabelle, and I've simply got to lie in it.

In the ice blue of her eyes, something melts: Would she lie with me in my bed, or want me on her divan? You jump in with a question for Diego:

– Would you agree that Picasso's ceramics are the best things he did since *Guernica?*

Diego, a potter by day and a drummer by night, answers:

— I would. He lost the spark after that. Except for the erotic drawings!

— I find Rodin's more moving.

— So do I, says Isabelle.

Again, the enigmatic smile. And then Adelaide returns to move us on.

— Sean, Elena, I'd like you to meet Marietta and Sprague.

Sean is an Englishman. He's still young enough to feel the anger of bad days at boarding school but no longer young enough to believe he's indestructible. From self-gratification pursued every minute of the day he's switched to patient devotion to starving artists, artists he's decided will never starve again. With a skinny tie in the open collar of his retro shirt, he is impeccably cool. Now that he no longer believes a party is nothing but the institutionalization of intoxication, he's proud to display his eloquence. When you upbraid him for talking to your tits, he explains: 'No, I look down because I'm shy'. Elena, a model, is his wife. Their parents gave their consent to their marriage at seventeen. The laughter in her blue-grey eyes in no way undermines the dignity in her regard. Her beauty is more oblique than yours, it's less breathtaking. Still, she's a stunner (as Millais and Rossetti would say). Milling in the in-crowd, clearly, has refined her art of subterfuge; yours is just as polished, but not by the social grind. The complicity between the two of you is instant: I can tell by the way you meet the sparkle in her eyes with the flash of your fireflies. Adelaide returns to move us on.

— Loïc, Roxana, I'd like you to meet Marietta and Sprague.

Loïc is a literary theorist, teaching French literature at an American graduate school. He's got a way of stretching his final syllables that I find irritating; there's a subtle but distinct mannerism in his head and hand movements. Born in Toulon to Navy civil servants, this Breton knew while still a student that he wanted to leave his native land: The flourishing of French theory in American universities gave him an embarrassment of choices. Now it's Flaubert who's brought him back to France for a research visit. What's Roxana doing with him? She's an international correspondent for a French TV station, a woman whose restless eyes tell me she's like a fish out of water when away from a war zone. Is it only I to whom she's transparent, is it only I who see her soul? I know following other people's struggles allows her to walk away from her own; I know flying from country to country allows her to flee the hothouse of intimacy. Where is the man who can move her, stay with her when the road unwinds? I feel a pang of sadness, because clearly Loïc is not that man.

Get down! Handclaps, harmonica and drums extend an all-embracing invitation; the electric bass comes in to punctuate the groove, then Lester

Bowie's trumpet phrases the Sonny Boy Williams tune: 'Bye-Bye Bird'. The lights dim, anticipation heightens: It's forty-five minutes to midnight. Raphaël and Joaquín wheel in a drum kit on a platform, followed by Diego and Gabrielle, each with an amp. While the Art Ensemble of Chicago continues grooving its grits 'n gravy blues, everyone gathers before the space that evidently will serve as a stage. Defined by the music—gospel, roots and prayer meeting—the mood is one of approaching revelation. Like interior dogs sensing the opening door, bodies begin to move; like waves gathering far off shore, they're accumulating energy. Raphaël and Joaquín leave and return with mics and stands; Gabrielle brings on a bass amp while Diego sets up the keyboards. And so the to-and-fro continues, while under squealing trumpet and growling sax, the rhythm section keeps the groove going. And then, as the heady brew comes to a brim, Joaquín lowers a backcloth while Raphaël, from his console upstairs, turns on the backlight truss. The music fades out, the band steps on stage.

Chapter 16

– Ladies and gentlemen, please welcome the greatest band in the City of Light, taking you from now to midnight: Adelaide and the Oysters!

As Joaquín leaves the stage, Raphaël brings up the backlights and turns on the PAR-can spots. Simona plays a riff on her Rickenbacker bass, Héloïse doubles it on bass drum and toms: Applause gives way to bubbling delight as 'Time of the Season' begins. Cool and soulful, Ada's richly-textured vocal fills the space; Riva rounds off each line with a lick from her keys while Muriel punctuates the flow with Strat downstrokes. It's clear this band can play: There is no play-acting here, no kittenish coyness or bashful bluffing, no mannerisms to disguise inadequate means: The band is tight, and delivers the song with utter conviction. 'What's you name? Who's your daddy?' The call-and-response works like clockwork; the chorus sounds with powerful authority. The joy in the room becomes tangible as Muriel lays down snappy guitar licks beneath Riva's keyboard solo; what most impresses me, though, in the instrumental ending, is the majesty of Héloïse's drumming: From behind her five-piece kit, her articulation of the music is impeccably rhythmic. The audience, divided between those standing in groups and those seated on the sofas, is one in their enchantment.

Through the Zombies, the Stones, the Beatles, the band celebrates the spirit of rock 'n roll even as, fully in the moment, they incarnate it. Listen! Giving 'She's Not There' a spectral quality, Ada's vocal finds the ethereal pitches of absence, while on 'Tell Me', her dark swagger complements the band's sultry menace. Flaunting bravado in the face of vulnerability, the defiant chorus of 'Heart of Stone' belies the relaxed cadence of the verses.

Listen! The band's rendition of 'Old Brown Shoe' is ebullient; its shuffle beat and surging bass reaffirm our conviction: Only a god who can dance could move us to believe! 'You're Gonna Lose that Girl': The call-and-response alternation of lead and harmony brings a potent charm to the full-band vocals. Then, on 'Lady Madonna', pounding boogie-woogie piano, underpinned by rolling bass and syncopated drums, make the exuberance irresistible.

Listen! Muriel's chopped guitar chords strike a reggae-like accent while Simona's bass lays down a legato rhythm; over this blues backbeat, Ada's throaty vocal proclaims, 'She's a Woman'. Héloïse, in the chorus, punctuates the sibilant fricative of Nicole's maracas with blows to the bell of her ride cymbal. Riva takes the solo, bending the strings to create a jangle as warm as her Fireglo. But it is Muriel's brash downstrokes that rule this rocker, keeping us all bopping to the close.

Listen! Tight and dirty, Riva's wicked Rickenbacker rhythm combines with Simona's ostinato bass to quickly bring 'I Saw Her Standing There' to boiling point: The earthy rawness of the playing electrifies me. Ada's voice is the vital spark that sets the mix aflame, blending human and divine, fusing body and mind: Is that not why I am here tonight? To make of my body and senses the subject of my self, to honour the feminine in me? I feel your presence quickening my blood as the vocal harmonies fill the room; as you turn to face me, my heart goes boom!

Look! A countdown clock appears on the backdrop, infusing time into eternity. The band gives the coda a final flourish, then segues into the collective countdown. Zero hour! A mirror ball heralds midnight. With your lips you extinguish a thousand lights as I take you in my arms; with a slip of your tongue you bring them back on, this time as scintillating stars. I have seen the light! Now let the ceremony begin.

Chapter 17

'Etienne', Guesch Patti

Egyptian cobra, blue coral snake; Malaysian pit viper, tropical rattlesnake: Lithe, supple, slinky, you celebrate the serpent, making your body an abode for the great regenerator. With every sensual entwinement you extol corporeal intelligence, with every coil you embrace carnal living. And thus all your extensions, flexions and rotations expunge convention from your flesh, and thus you accommodate the shadow that safeguards ambivalence. Vibrant notes, dense and dirty, sizzle off the guitar. Look! Your body is a rose, unfurling its lushness, flaunting its mystery. As my heart beats out the shape of my desire, my body petitions yours: Receive me in your secret cell, that from your attar my ardour may distil the unforgettable!

'Bang a Gong (Get it On)', T. Rex

Kodkod, ocelot; desert lynx, margay: Mischievous djinni, imp of darkness, you beat the rhythm that fires my loins. Yeah! You can stalk and pounce or pursue with speed, you can mimic sunlight pouring through leaves; you've got retractable claws in velvet paws, you've got omnidirectional ears and night vision: All very fine—I must be just—but finest of all is your gift of lust! Delivering your body to the lascivious groove, yielding your spirit to the boogie, you distil to the quintessence this elixir of lewdness: I can smell it, I can taste it, in every one of your moves. Dancing, you hypnotize yourself, making whole the division within; dancing, you dream yourself, holding the flow from above. And thus, while you honour the self-astonishment of which your sex is the fountain, my body meets yours in the open, beyond all confines.

'Woolly Bully', Sam the Sham and the Pharaohs

Grey crowned crane, houbara bustard; purple swamp hen, common coot: If the birds' elaborate mating displays are impressive, they've got nothing on the pirouettes and head-bobbing, the bowing and jumping, to be found on the dance floor. While you dance with Joaquín (who's kissing you in his dreamhouse), I dance with Héloïse. The enticing curves under her camisole are moulded by a strapless bra; there's silver embroidery on her black leather cuff and a boar's tooth on her bracelet. She's lean yet round, she's modest yet proud; there's something sublime in her earthiness. See how she moves!

Buoyant, as if still on her drum stool. Is it the way she alternates between the pogo and the Charleston, her hair whipping across her face, that makes me say to myself, She so beautiful I could eat her?

'Let's Stick Together', Bryan Ferry

Yellow-throated marten, Siberian sable; black-footed ferret, American mink: Like Gabrielle (with whom I am now dancing while Joaquín won't let you go), these mustelids have a slim body, a flexible backbone and a bounding gait. Unlike her, however, they do not ovulate automatically; instead, they have to copulate for at least two hours at a stretch to stimulate ovulation. Go girl! I like the way she finds the flow, that harmony of movement and emotion; I like the way she responds to me, that echo and variation. And so she licks the honey from my hands, and so I drain the innocence from her eyes.

'Sex Crime (Nineteen Eighty-Four)', Eurythmics

Tasmanian devil, barred bandicoot; Virginia opossum, marsupial mole: The marsupial mole can tunnel down to two-and-a-half meters in desert sand. It swims through the quartz crystals, leaving no permanent tunnel: This way of living is shared by Muriel (with whom I am now dancing) but not by Adelaide (with whom you are now dancing). 'Sex crime': Muriel knows *Nineteen Eighty-Four* by heart. I guess its images serve as analogies: Her maniacal mother, her strait-laced father. She's never lost the reflex of playing possum. For a while, with she and I, it was the blind leading the blind. Faith preserved friendship. Now, discreet and oblique, the walking wounded play games with each other's crutches. It's a kind of loving, I suppose. 'The difference between us, Sprague', she'd say, 'is that you, with your scribbling, want to leave a trace of yourself, whereas I want to cover my tracks. That's why I'm in fashion: It's ephemeral'. 'Sex crime!' I think of our respective murders in suburbia and how we'll never be rid of the scars; I think of the friendship between us, the solidarity of survivors. Is that why, as the song comes to an end, there's such tenderness in our embrace?

'Same Old Scene', Roxy Music

Black-breasted snake eagle, hen harrier; Andean condor, red kite: The Andean condor can soar at altitudes of over five thousand meters, travelling great distances with only the occasional flap of its wings: There's something aloof about Nicole (with whom I'm dancing while you dance with Xavier), something of the long-distance runner. I love the sensual cadence of her swaying, her give-and-take with time. I move in close and learn that she's mad about horror movies. Body snatchers, aliens, ex-humans with crazed eyes. That gets her excited. 'And what excites you?' she asks me. 'Art', I answer. 'And Marietta, what excites her?' 'Risk!' She gives me a knowing look. Now as she and I strive to derive the immortal from mortality, I imagine her screaming in a late-night cinema. Is it horror's obsession with feminism that draws her to it? Does she have fantasies of being a final girl? Nicole, Nicole, to rip the veil from your world I'd have to lick the blood from your knife: Those days, thank heaven, are far behind me now.

'Golden Years', David Bowie

Spectacled bear, Asiatic black; Alaskan grizzly, polar bear: Compared with other carnivores, bears walk slowly and deliberately, with all five toes as well as their heels touching the ground: She hardly moves her feet, Julie, when she dances (I'm dancing with her while you're dancing with Jean-Luc). She compensates, though, with a sexy to-and-fro of her torso and a charming *je-ne-sais-quoi* in her arm movements. There's a fullness to her flesh, a real physical presence, yet as puppet artist she must have mastered the world as shadow play. Her modesty moves me. How many ways are there of being a woman? In the infinite variety of the universe, nothing touches me more than femininity. So many women, so little time! No, that's not it. For in every woman there are all women. No, that's not it either. What then? Shut up, just dance! I surrender to Bowie's impeccable taste. Look! The Botticelli smile on Julie's face has been replaced by the swoon of Bernini's Teresa! Oh Julie, Julie, I tell you truly, more than how you dress, I love how you undress me! Use me, use me, my puppeteer, use me to burst your body into flame: Have no regrets when the dance is over.

'Slave to Love', Bryan Ferry

Golden tree snake, black-headed python; African tiger snake, emerald boa: A serpent's tongue is never trapped in the interlacings of language, but for us, speaking is necessary to create the silence in which to approach: My hands resting on the small of your back, yours meeting at the nape of my neck, we silently choreograph the eros of redemption. Eyes met and matched, our bodies attuned, in contact, we sway to the voluptuous syncopations of Ferry's lush song. And thus, intoxicated by the courage that freedom requires, we create a space in which we are alone in each other's presence. Deep in the heart of the flowing music, in the twists and turns of its undercurrents, I find a stillness in which I can touch you in the light of your transcendence. It's quarter to two on the morning of New Year's Day. I love you. That's all I wanted to say.

'I've Seen that Face Before (Libertango)', Grace Jones

Ring-tailed lemur, slender loris; thick-tailed galago, ruffed lemur: Like you and I, lemurs store darkness in their eyes: They know that light never illuminates the whole without paralyzing becoming. Between shadow and light, therefore, they insist on a sharing, for discourse loses its relation to desire when it breaks with becoming. And if not desire, what else makes life worth living? Thus, threading our moves into a sequence that preserves connection, we come to transpose to tango our search for stillness in motion. That Saturday night not so long ago when we listened to Astor Piazzolla, we must have listened with our bodies—how else to explain our knowing what to do when Grace Jones set her words to the Argentine's tune? As we conduct our *corrida* of love, I feel in my bones the despair Grace Jones speaks of. And yet it doesn't silence the song in my blood, it doesn't diminish my pleasure in you. The mad pleasure of knowing you're mine even as you belong to yourself alone; the sad pleasure of all I want to give you compared to the little I can. Marietta, this reggae-tango is the very mark of my *métissage*, it's elegance and dignity is the signature of your style. And now as the boat of your body courts the river of time, I know I will love you till that river runs dry.

'Black Magic Woman', Santana

Jaguar, cheetah, lion, tiger: All cats have large forward-facing eyes that enable them to judge distances accurately. The pupils contract to a slit in sunlight and dilate widely at night, giving the cats excellent vision: Eroticism begins with the gaze, my love, it begins with fascination: As the Latin rhythms create a force field to which every sinew in your body responds, the guitar sears its sensuality into your flesh: Ecstatic—your whole body given over to pleasure, your beauty at fever pitch—you dance in a voodoo trance, fascinating me. What is the secret that preserves your mystery? Love hasn't brought you out of the wilderness; familiarity hasn't tempered your strangerhood: Your mystery remains as dark and enticing as ever. As your feet outline ellipses and your hands sign arabesques, I am suspended between the way you move your hips and the way you part your lips. Why does the poet of Genesis says Adam knew Eve, not Eve knew Adam? Why do we say a man knows a woman and not a woman knows a man? You know me better than I could ever know you, you know me better than I know myself. Dancing with you, I peel through the Biblical palimpsest and discover Lilith where there was Eve; I discover the simultaneous creation of man and woman in the place of Eve's derivative birth. Lilith's banishment did not abolish pleasure, Eve's expulsion did not cause the misery of man. Marietta, you are my black magic woman: You are inexhaustible, and everything is mine to learn.

Chapter 18

After the party we walked back to my place. Sleep was sweet, but sweeter still was the tenderness that preceded it. Midday, while running your bath, you came back to the bedroom and pulled a scroll of paper from between your breasts. You sat beside me on the bed and unfurled it.

I know it's New Year's
Not Valentine's Day
But it's today that my heart wants to say
I love you

Happy New Year, Sprague!
Marietta

Was it the kiss you blew me that made the *Black Prince* glow as I cast my gaze around the room? Was it the splendour of your smile—tossed over your shoulder just before you stepped into the corridor—that made the *Carpet of Memory* scintillate? Or was is simply my heart reaching out to yours that transfigured everything?

And on that meeting of hearts, Marietta, on the promise of that New Year's Day, I end this dream-time telling of us before Iceland.

Before we go to the island, however, answer me this: If you are Marina, I'm no governor of Mytilene; if you are Miranda, I'm no Prince of Naples. But if you are Mara, I must be Ariel. Now tell me, Marietta-Prospero, when our story's told, will I return to the tree or be set free?

Intermezzo 15: Iskra

The waiter took us for brother and sister, Iskra and I. Her hair's as black as mine, her eyes as green. Guess that allowed him to overlook my southern cast and her northern hue, her youth and my youthfulness. She's doing a PhD in plant science at Sofia University (mutant seedlings with aberrant circadian rhythms). Spent two years at Sheffield University. Speaks English with a Yorkshire accent! We met in the Botanic Garden. She was sitting on a bench, crying. I sat down beside her. Didn't say anything, just reached out my hand. She took it. (I wasn't wearing white, but that's how it happened.) When we parted five days later, it was a strange goodbye.

She was crying because it was the anniversary of the day her boyfriend had left her.

– I'd take it very badly when Kosta was upset with me. I'd fall into depression.

– You were afraid he might leave you?

– Terrified! I ended up accepting everything.

– Which made you even more depressed, I suppose?

– Yes. I was anxious all the time, had crying fits. I felt like destroying myself. I knew I was becoming somebody different, but I couldn't help it.

A caul of discretion, the fall of her hair frames her face.

– I was terrified of becoming like my mother. Finally Kosta left me.

I picture a man adrift, unmoored in an emotional sea. Dry land.

– Your mother, why do you say—

– She killed herself. Chronically depressed. Injected poison into her veins.

– She was a doctor?

– A veterinarian.

– How old were you?

– Five. I was told she was very tired and went away to rest. I only learned the truth when I turned sixteen.

– How?

– My father told me.

– You'd had no idea before?

– None. Or let's say, there were signs, but I didn't want to see them.

A shadow falls across her face. I take her hand and hold it.

– And how did you react?

– I was in shock. My world crumbled. I couldn't believe I'd been lied to so long, and that I'd believed the lie.

I imagine her anger, her shame. I squeeze her hand as she averts her gaze.

On the walls of the café, abstract paintings in bright colours, palimpsests of gouache and crayon, provided an apt image of secrets and lies, but not of suffering unspoken. The wax crayon of the absent mother, gouached over by the father, came through like a bloodstain. What could I offer Iskra? I, her twin brother? I suggested we go for a walk.

We ended up renting bicycles and riding through Borisova Gradina, a park where we didn't need to speak, content to feel the other's presence.

The next day, after lunch, Iskra gave me a tour of the Botanic Garden. She showed me John Fowles' favourite orchid, *Ophrys tenthredinifera*. Yes, she's a Fowles fan, with a particular affection for Rebecca Lee in *A Maggot*. (She was pleased to lean the English title: She'd read the book in French, where it's called *La Créature*.) In the evening we spoke for hours. She cried again and again, but I could tell she was becoming stronger. I told her to leave a note at my hotel if she wanted to see me. Two days later she did. I wasn't wearing white, but as soon as we met again she wanted to go up to my room. I didn't want to make love, but she wouldn't be refused. Drawn by the magnet of her emotion, I explored the continent of her body. Her movements my map, each clutch and clasp, each moan and gasp, moved the needle of my compass. When she came, it was I who had a feeling of homecoming.

In the morning we were woken by birdsong. In my arms she tried to hide her tears. I ran her a bath. When I made to leave the bathroom, she said, 'No. Stay'. I did. I soaped her down. I washed her front and back, top to toe. As the water flowed down her face, I didn't feel like John the Baptist. As I dried her feet, I didn't feel like Jesus. And yet, as soon as she had dressed, she said:

– I feel reborn, Sprague.

And then she kissed me. She kissed me as Rebecca Lee might have kissed before she became a Shaker.

I walked her to the university. We shook hands by way of goodbye. And then, as she entered the building, I don't know why but it was I who began to cry.

PART TEN

Chapter 1

Monday August 29, 1994

Icelandair Flight 451, London to Reykjavik. Eyes closed, feet on the footrest, you're leaning back, listening to Eno's ambient music on your headphones. Gently your hand in mine communicates the music's breathing pulse; through the silence you distil the seven tones: quietude, calm, tranquillity, peace, composure, stillness and serenity. Is this it, then? Have we crossed the sea of passions, have we reached the far shore? I turn from the clouds and bathe in your placidity, until the movement of your toes captures my attention: Animating your slipper socks, they draw forth my tenderness as they conjure you, ensconced in an armchair, knitting these whimsies for your feet. Yes, my love, after seven years of sharing your life, it's still moments like this that move me. And now we're going to spend two weeks together, circling the island of Iceland, where each of us has a friend.

Yours, Steinar, meets us at the airport: So this is the Professor of Environmental Science, this is the man who said he cracked his problem, his intractable inverse problem, only because he'd stepped outside his discipline—hydrogeology—and solicited your intervention. I've always found it easy to connect with the Nordics, and with Steinar it's no exception. His mischievous eyes repudiate his spectacles, his baritone voice belies his scraggy face: I immediately see it's his simultaneous touching of intimacy and distance that makes him so present to me.

Forty-five minutes later we're at his house, a bright red walk-up—three stories tall—with white door and window frames. Eygló, his wife, comes to greet us. There's a dreaminess about her—so different from her husband's air of rugged practicality—yet there's daring in her stare. And then we meet their sons—Tómas, a shy thirteen-year-old, and his bolder little brother, Jon. Steinar's excited about his latest conference; while you indulge his impatience to tell you about it, I speak to Eygló about Björk:

– She's certainly raised the profile of Iceland. You're going to see a boom in tourism!

– Interesting you should say that.

And then she tells me about her job with the Icelandic Tourism Board and the background paper she's presenting to the Strategic Discussion Group. I listen with relish as she talks about the 'touristification' of society. And then you and

Steinar join our chat, debating whether 'looseness of attachment' has indeed become the very principle of modern social relations. Listening to Eygló as she fills you in, it occurs to me that she talks the way Helen Merrill sings, just slightly behind the beat; she unfolds her thought swiftly, yet gives the impression of a slow pace. Is that the source of her dreamy seductiveness? Just then Jon interrupts the conversation to suggest we go for a ride. Minutes later we're all on bicycles, riding to the wide beach with the lonely lighthouse in the evening light.

Chapter 2

Tuesday, August 30

In the morning we swim lengths in the rain; in the afternoon the sun finds us biking around town then riding to Fossvogsdalur. Back in town, we pick up the car you'd reserved for our road trip. In the evening we go out to dinner with Steinar and Eylgó and their lawyer friends, Halldóra and Konrád, a couple who work for competing firms. Again I am moved by feminine masquerade: Halldóra's ankle-tied heels are worn with white lace socks over red tights; when she takes off her Little Red Riding Hood coat, I admire the zebra-stripe waistcoat over her white shirt, the fall of her black layered skirt. She works in litigation, arbitration and dispute resolution; Konrád in energy, natural resources and environmental law.

After the sushi we play word association; when 'law' comes up I say 'Kafka'. Konrád pulls out a pen and sketches a perfect replica of *Three Runners.* And thus we discover a common love for Franz. Everybody knows the story of Kafka and Milena, but nobody that of Franz and Dora Diamant: I tell it. The telling done, what moved them was not the air that cut like razor blades over Franz's vocal cords nor the alcohol injections into his laryngeal nerves; neither was it the sister of mercy who made it her mission to ease his way to death. No, what moved them was how Kafka's total absence of solemnity in his relationship with Dora contrasted with his tortured love for Felice and Milena. But what moved you and I was our notion of fragility, how it came about that the writer and insurance officer from Prague met the girl scaling fish in a Baltic kitchen; how that girl, having survived the Nazi fire and the Soviet frying pan, specified in her will that she be buried next to the man whose eyes saw everything.

In the bar we go to after the restaurant, Steinar mentions the velvet divorce between Prague and Bratislava, and suggests the world Dora knew is definitively gone. Halldóra agrees, citing the recent inauguration of Mandela. And then you remind us of the genocide in Rwanda, and mention Pascale's efforts to leverage the law to put an end to it.

— As always, Konrád suggests, everything comes down to Realpolitik.

Everyone seems to agree, against their inclination. Then Eygló mentions Leonard Cohen, his concert at Laugardalschöll, and tells how she was far more moved, politically, by his version of *The Partisan* than by the evening news. No-one picks up the challenge of her remark. Everyone seems to realize that pursuing happiness in a world of horrors is our common fate: How each of us does it is his own business. And then the conversation turns to music, to U2's *Zooropa* and Björk *Debut*. Halldóra mentions there's another Icelandic star, a soprano who's giving a concert on September 10. When she mentions there's Ligeti and Kurtág on the programme, my eyes light up.

— Are there still tickets? I ask.

— I wouldn't think so, she says.

And then Konrád volunteers:

— If there aren't any, I can probably get you a pair. I know some people.

Konrád did indeed get us the tickets, and we did indeed go to the concert, but I'll get to that in due time.

Chapter 3

Wednesday, August 31

Morning, pale sunshine, leaving Reykjavik. You're driving your dream car, a Saab 900 16S, a black three-door hatchback with a tan interior. Again, my little petrolhead, I delight in your pleasure behind the wheel; the car's traction may secure you to the earth, but the glow of your face says you're in heaven.

Graben pools and lava gorges, dwarf birch and pastel heath; mudpots and fumaroles, hot springs and geysers: By the drowning pool where the continents drift, on the plain of the first parliament, it is not immortality we seek, but rejuvenation.

Sandwiches and soup in a café; the impression of a desert but for the distinct horizon.

Through silence and nothingness we drive to the roaring tumble of a glacial river; confronted with the paradox of changeless impermanence and static dynamism, we lose our thoughts in the mist.

In a valley, in a church, in a tower lined with books, I see the light from a clerestory window sanctify you in your watchful ascension: Not for you, the crisis of redemption.

In a restaurant by a river we supper on smoked trout with pickled cucumber, fennel, rye bread, an apple and yogurt. And then we drive deeper into the valley.

Together we pitch our tunnel tent. The guylines taut, the tent trim, we align the air mattresses inside and roll out our sleeping bags. I adjust the ventilation vents, slip my water into a stowage pocket and stash my clothes; you attach the light diffuser to your headlamp and hang it from a hoop, then stretch out on your sleeping bag. Kneeling on mine, I say:

– Turn off your mind, relax and float downstream.

You close your eyes and cross your arms over your breasts. I lay my body on yours and—tracing the bow of your lips with the tip of my tongue—begin my work of resuscitation. You open your eyes and look into mine.

– Sprague, before we make love, I want you to know I'm going to leave you.

My heart crashes into my rib cage, I gasp; you draw my head down and seal your lips to mine. And then you release me and say:

– I love you.

My mind is as unhinged as my heart, no more can thought resolve itself than a desert pin down its sand in a storm. What? Still? You make my sex hard and take me inside you: Beyond here lies nothing! How is it that my body still knows what to do? Why does it still transcend itself under your touch? If something is wrong, why does it say everything is right? There's no dryness in your welcome, you're wet; you still work me like a Gopala-girl. So why are you leaving? You are a vibrancy of being, from your earlobes to your toes you thrill to my thrusts—how can that be if you no longer want me? Hail! Transmuting your lust, I drive my ardour into you until the void reclaims each of us.

Hanging from a hoop, your shaded headlamp diffuses its light: The glow of your face outshines it. You're leaving me: I know you mean it, but I can't bring myself to believe it. You're leaving.

– Why?

– I can't tell you why.

– Why not?

– Because I don't know myself.

– When did you decide?

– A few weeks ago.

– Then surely you must know why!

– I don't. I just know it's the right decision.

– Is it something I've said?

– No.

– Something I've done?

– No.

– Something I didn't do?

– No.

– Is it because I am the man I am?

– No. I'm leaving not because of anything you said or did or didn't do, and certainly not because you're the man you are.

– Why then?

– I told you: I can't tell you because I don't know myself. All I know is that it has to be this way.

At once intensely intimate and distant, the lamp in the black of your pupil is a solitary star.

– Do you feel that you're no longer free, when you're with me?

– No, not at all.

– Does it have to do with somebody else?

– No.

– Does it have to do with sex?

– Sprague! How can you ask me that? Don't you see how you send me?

– Do you want to live with a woman?

– No.

– There must be a reason.

– The reason is because I love you. There, now you have it.

– You're leaving me because you love me?

– Yes.

– I don't understand.

– Stop trying to.

– Stop trying to? How can you say that? Are you determined to deny me—

– I love you. That's all you need to know. I love you more than ever.

– I'll go mad.

– You can ask me anything, Sprague, I'll do anything for you. Just don't ask me to explain or change my mind. From the third day after the autumn equinox, I'll never see you again.

– So you've thought it all out?

– Yes.

– When's the autumn equinox?

– Friday, September twenty-third.

– So... from Monday the twenty-sixth, you'll never see me again?

– That's right.

– You'll never see me again?

– Never.

– What?

– I'll never see you again, from Monday the twenty-sixth of September.

– I'll go mad.

– It' up to you.

– I'll go mad.

– It' up to you.

– I'll go mad.

– It's up to you.

– But we'll spend your birthday together?

– Yes, of course.

— You can't leave me, Marietta. No matter where you go, you'll be in my heart.

— I know that, Sprague.

— I will love you all my life. Until my last breath, I will live in the joy of loving you.

— I know. That's why I can do what I'm doing.

— Kiss me.

It comes, the touch of your lips, it comes with the playful, probing pressure of your tongue: It comes to abolish the future and insert me into the present.

— Now tell me, we've got three weeks and a day to spend all out time together—what can I do for you?

— Anything?

— Anything. Except explain or change my mind.

— I want us to continue our trip, as planned.

— Of course. And what would give you the most pleasure, over this period?

— Dye your hair red. Then whip me with it.

— All right, I'll do it when we return to Reykjavik. What else?

— Walk barefoot on my back.

— I'd do it right now, it the tent were tall enough. Tomorrow.

— And every day after that.

— With pleasure. What else?

— Walk with me in the rain, until we're drenched.

— Okay. We'll do that in London. What else?

— Make me come without touching me.

— Easy. What else?

— Stare into my eyes for ten minutes non-stop.

— All right. What else?

— Go dancing with me in Reykjavik.

— I'd love to! What else?

— In Reykjavik, let me treat you to the best at Hotel Matthías.

— How could I say no? Anything else?

— Yes. Keep on loving me no matter who else you may love, and know that whatever happens, the happiest days of my life are the days I've spent with you.

— I will, I do.

You kiss me.

— Goodnight, Sprague.

It comes, my scream, a wild shriek from my primitive being, a wail to make a banshee proud: With a touch of theatre I attempt to distance my pain at the same time as I inhabit it. And then it gets the better of me, I can't resist it any longer. You roll your body onto mine, you take my hands and stretch out my arms. Fast and furious your kisses come; you're crying, your tears are mingling with mine. You sit up, reach back and take down the light. Click! The darkness intensifying your touch, you stretch your body out on mine and still my rattling bones.

Chapter 4

Thursday, September 1

Seljalandsfoss, Kvernufoss, Skogafoss

Waterfalls and rapids, cascades and plunge pools; slip-off slopes and wetlands, lakes and ponds: The descent of a stream down a vertical slope is a waterfall; a series of waterfalls is a cascade. When a stream in a tributary valley reaches the edge of a major valley that has been deepened by erosion, the fall is spectacular: So this is the descent of the spirit into the fields of cinnabar, this is the place of rebirth: Had I the courage, I'd dive in to meet my destiny.

Dyroholaey

Thunder holes, arches, wind and waves; blowholes, stacks, cliffs and caves: A headland, or promontory, is especially vulnerable to marine erosion because it is exposed on three sides. Narrow headlands are likely to be eroded right through, giving rise to an arch: Is this the task, then? To rise above the clogging flesh, the maternal sea; to triumph over material banality? I don't believe so. No, my love, not I. I'd rather have my feet on the ground than my head in the clouds; I'd rather hold your hand than dream of heaven. Yes, Marietta, I'd rather intoxicate my senses than forego my suffering.

Reynisfjara

Pillows of lava from an undersea vent, glistening columns of basalt; stacked flows of cooled lava, coils of pahoehoe: While still very hot, basaltic lava flows freely, and the rock formed from it has a smooth surface, a gleaming coat of volcanic glass: Upthrust of rock against overcast sky, white surf on black sand: On the beach we walk, hand-in-hand.

> You slip a violet
> Into the folds of my dream:
> Aflutter, I find it

Black, black, black: This is the chaos at the beginning of time, these are the lower waters: Only the rhyme of your footsteps with mine restrains the horses of death, only your hand in mine keeps me from nothingness.

Driving to Kirkjubæjarklaustur

In the soft embrace of my leather seat, afloat on the supple suspension, I feel at one with you as you drive. I hear the engine rise in pitch as the turbo kicks in; I surf on the wave of torque vrooming us through the valley. It's clear, Marietta, the distinctive individuality of this car matches your personality; far from rebelling against its quirks, you delight in them: Is that why it submits so willingly to your mastery? And I, have I been a passenger too long, have I failed to direct my life? Your quick reflexes and sense of responsibility, your self-control and adaptability: You were meant to be in the driver's seat—what good at the wheel would I be? 'I'm always crashing in the same car'. Yes, my love, all day long Bowie's *Low* has been on my mind: 'Please be mine, share my life, stay with me, be my wife'.

Night in a guest house near Skaftartunga

Around a rustic dining table in Pála and Brynjar's cottage, we revelled in the company of the guests as we relished the evening spread laid out before us. Alternating between utopian and dystopian visions, you entertained us with stories of how Tim Berners-Lee's software, once only for insiders like you, would revolutionize our lives now that it had been put in the public domain. Everyone was curious about Seedy Friedrich. I drew on my store of anecdotes. Ramona, contrasting Singapore's diversity with Iceland's homogeneity, spoke of her trip to that city-state: Her Barcelona studio was designing the interior of a hotel bar and restaurant there. Guillem, her journalist husband, was preparing a travel piece on Iceland and was eager to compare everyone's perceptions of the country with his own. Pála and Brynjar gave us their impressions of Paris and the French: Their daughter Nina was studying fashion at the École de la Chambre Syndicale. Jessica gave us her outlook on AIDS: She works in immunodiagnostics. Despite the recent announcement that the disease had become the leading cause of death for all Americans aged twenty-five to forty-four, she was relatively optimistic. Her husband, Derek, spoke of life in Vancouver; you'd been spending time at the TRIUMF lab there, and enjoyed talking about the city with him. Takashi, a ceramic artist, spoke of his conception of pottery as pure form: He uses neither colour nor decoration. Akiko didn't say much during the meal. Afterwards, however, in the cosiness of the living room, she became the centre of attention.

The glow of candlelight on the coffee table, the rich patina of the floorboards: The wood came from ships that ran aground in the shallows of the coast. And for the rough-hewn dining table too? No, that wood—most likely—drifted up on the Gulf Stream from Mexico... So this is the history that abides in objects, these are the stories honest things tell... Could we live in the country in a cottage like this? Could we—

Vertigo, recall—
Your prophetic dignity:
You are leaving me

Could I, then, find sanctuary in a place like this? I do like Pála and Brynjar's style: There's charm in the clutter, panache in the mismatch. Wouldn't that be good for me? No, I don't think so. I've always been leery of cosiness: I prefer empty rooms with bare walls. And yet, don't I seek a natural, unselfconscious existence? And isn't it in a place like this that I could find it?

Unselfconscious,
Natural: Freak, you'll never know
The natural!

Have you noticed Akiko's been eyeing you? Is she struck by your beauty, intrigued by your demeanour, as you sit on the sofa beside me, legs flexed, stockinged feet on the footrest? I like her allure, her high cheekbones and free-flowing hair. I like the contrast of her loose cardigan and stretch-knit top, the subtlety of black on black. I like her black ankle boots, her black skinny jeans, her black eyes and black hair. But I'm not in a black mood. In fact, I'm feeling as luminously white as Terence Stamp in *Teorema*. Is that why innocence and honesty, in the conversation that followed, dispensed with the armour of irony? Is that, indeed, why a girl, a guitar and a mangaka brought us such grace and good cheer?

Akiko works as a hostess in a high-class club in Tokyo. At twenty-three, she still falls into the most sought-after category of youthful beauty. The job pays extremely well, but it's only a pastime while she's taking a pause in her career: She's a mangaka, a star in her genre.

Jessica expressed shock that Akiko's work as a hostess could be worth so much to corporate Japan (when she quits at the end of the year, Akiko will have made $100,000 in six months). Takashi explained the rationale: Life in the day is strictly governed by social codes and work pressures; at night, in the water business, the guests at the clubs break rank and dispense with formal courtesies. The art of the hostess consists in balancing flattery with foolishness to make every member of the visiting party feel both good about himself and bonded more closely to the others in his group: That is what his company requires. While Takashi spoke, I reflected on what you'd told me of your 'anthropological research' with Inès in Tokyo: That a man can choose between 'hate health' for a rendezvous in a love hotel and 'company health' for office sex; he can select 'fashion health' to get girls in disguise and 'delivery health' for girls to come to his door. He can also find what he's looking for in the baths of soapland and the massage parlours. In hostess clubs, however, especially high class ones, sex is not sold. There being no lesbian scene in Tokyo, Inès had nothing to show you there. Instead, she complemented your Japanese experience with tales of her work in a hostess club. Yes, just like Akiko, she had lit the guests' cigarettes and poured their drinks, initiated conversation and kept it going. She'd been witty when the men inquired about the state of her tits; when asked what kind of man gets her wet, she'd give the profile of the most pathetic among them. Finally she would sing them a song, then take two or three to the microphone. If the singer was good his colleagues stopped up their ears; if he was bad, they all applauded. When they were sufficiently drunk, she would accord them a kiss on the cheek by way of goodbye. And thus she paid for her PhD from MIT. Listening to Takashi, I came to understand the value placed on Inès' and Akiko's idle flirting.

The conversation then turned to 'boy love', Akiko's specialty as a manga artist. Boy love, Pála and Brynjar told us, had been Nina's obsession (an obsession she'd shared with her French pen pal). Nina is 'sorting herself out sexually', and while they 'don't want to interfere', they do feel helpless when their daughter falls into depression. Could Akiko help them understand? Yes.

The questions came from all of us, the answers from Akiko:

– What are boy-love manga?
– They're graphic books. Written by women and read by girls. They deal with love between boys. The ambiguous love between ambivalent boys. Not pornographic, they're more suggestive than explicit. The emphasis is on romance—a longing look, a stolen kiss. Just enough to generate an erotic charge.
– When did you become a mangaka?
– At nineteen.
– Why boy-love?
– It's transgressive—you get around the 'strong man/weak woman' model. Impossible to do that when you show a straight love relationship.
– But why love between two guys?
– Because a male couple gives new possibilities. You can describe a more equal relationship. Create something richer, psychologically, than is possible with a heterosexual couple.

— Like what?

— A man who can't control his feelings. Who expresses his emotions. His hurt. Rare in Japan, to see a man's individuality. Boy-love allows you to break that taboo.

— But why take two guys who look like girls?

— Because then the reader—the girl—can identify with the characters without thinking about things like her appearance or starting a family.

— Is sex still taboo for girls in Japan?

— No. But a lot of girls still find it easier to approach sex through love between boys. They like boy-love because they can play any of the roles. There's no imposed model of a love relationship.

— What about the fantasy girls often have—that male homosexuality is a beautiful and pure form of romance?

— It's very naïve, of course, but just the fact that it exists is transgressive—and what's transgressive is good for girls.

— So boy-love can help a girl grow up?

— Yes. It can be a stepping stone, a transition, between girl and woman. It's a way for a girl to buy time.

— Time for what?

— To give up her bisexuality. To decide one way or the other.

— But what if she never decides?

I jump in to answer Brynjar's question:

— Then she'll be an artist, a dancer.

— A dancer?

— Yes. She'll run garlands from star to star and she'll dance.

— Sprague, what are you saying?

— I'm saying that in the house of the soapmaker, those who don't fall learn how to dance.

Suspended between delight and unease, Brynjar hestitates. I myself am surprised by my pirouette from the poem to the proverb. Why do I always associate Rimbaud with girls' becoming? Because of you, of course! Because of your evocation—way back when, in our conversation on the floor—of what this boy has meant to you.

— Maybe, Sprague. Maybe she'll become a dancer.

— I think she will. After all—as far as I can tell—there's more to being a woman than the coupling of opposites.

Why am I speaking like this? Is it because I believe that you, face-to-face with Nina, would offer her—simply by your presence—an image of a satisfying future? You come in:

— I think Sprague's right. I wouldn't worry about Nina. She'll work it out. Twenty's still very young, when you think in terms of adult sexuality. If such a thing exists!

Nervous laughter. You've spoken frankly, yet everyone seems struck by your aura of mystery, the touch of danger emanating from your unsettling of binaries.

— Well, Pála, Brynjar says, if Nina turns out half as well as Marietta, we've got nothing to worry about.

— Nothing at all! Pála says.

Crossing your eyes then whirling them, you say:

— I wouldn't be so sure!

Everybody laughs. Brynjar calls out:

— Guillem, the guitar's tuned—play us a song!

Everybody encourages Guillem. Pála hands him the house guitar.

— Let's see, what can I play?

— Something lively!

— Okay, I've got it.

Allegro, Guillem launches into the rhythmic *corrido*:

La cucaracha, la cucaracha
Ya no puede caminar
Porque no tiene, porque le falta
Una pata de atrás

As one, as if somehow Nina were everybody's daughter, we lose all inhibition and in a magic synthesis of emotions, get up and start dancing.

Ya la murió la cucaracha
Ya la lleven a enterrar
Entre cuatro zopilotes
Y un ratón de sacristán

With Ramona I whirl, with Jessica I jive; with Akiko I twirl, with you I'm glad-alive!

Chapter 5

Friday, September 2

Last night, against the powers of annihilation you gave me firmness of purpose: Into every pore you pressed your regenerating power as you walked barefoot on my back.

Driving to Skaftafell

In the cockpit of the Saab you are in command, the radiance of your face lighting up the landscape; forever renewed, your pleasure at the wheel amazes me: You were born to be in motion. Is that why you are leaving me?

I'd go anywhere with you:
In the Mini Cooper to Kyoto
In the RAV4 to Vladivostok
In the 205 to Odessa
In the Cabriolet to Guangzhou

Yes, I'd go anywhere with you:
In the Porsche 964 to Albuquerque
In the MX-5 to Brisbane
In the Saab 900 to Thessaloniki
In the Cinquecento to Chandannagar

Yes, anywhere to be at your side
I'd ride, ride, ride
But what I most want to do
Is go home to a house with you

Skaftafell

Ice moves in three modes: Internally deformed, it creeps; over soft sediment, it is displaced; over hard rock, it slides: Pole in hand, helmet on head, in our crampons we hike over the glacier. Look! Sand plains cut by glacial rivers, mountains carved by outlet ice; rhyolite thrown up by eruptions, lagoon formed in morane wake. Look! Meltwater mud, desiccation cracks; ridges of gravel, deep crevasses: So this is the site of concealment and revelation, this is the cavern of the heart; this is where the hidden yields to penetration, this is where emptiness offers a new start. Why, my love, does it come to me now? Out of the blue came the attack, on his doorstep he collapsed: Your father, on a summer's day in 1990, ceased to exist. Heart failure, dilated cardiomyopathy. He had just turned fifty-nine. I held you up when the ground gave way under your feet; I nursed you out of your numbness. Then, one Sunday evening, autumn leaves clinging wet to our boots, you said, 'I will be pregnant by spring; if not, I'll give up this crazy dream'. We made love repeatedly, but in the darkness where the miracle takes place the light never went on. When spring came, in the same flow in which you mothballed your woollen clothes, you nullified the dream.

To conceive, did you need to identify, but couldn't, with the mother who soothed your throbbing temples in a dark room? Did you need to recognize, but couldn't, that a baby would relegate your mother to grandmother and push you back a generation, closer to your death? Was your sudden desire to conceive a means to avoid mourning your father? Did you believe that by some magic he who begot you would beget your child? An incestuous desire, then, a last-ditch attempt to hold onto the dead and restore your immortality? Or was it something else all together, something of which I cannot conceive?

Jökulsárlón

Seaward margin of ice-cap outlet, underwater keel of iceberg; crackle of near-submerged growlers, low wallow of bergy bits: As icebergs melt, their centre of gravity shifts; former waterlines, arches and pinnacles, once underwater, become exposed to view: Through the calm of the glacial lake, through its ghostly stillness, we ride in our spirit boat. No, I am not bearing my own entrails in an urn, I have not lost the magic in my spinal column: But I do feel my bonds are loosened, I do feel this cradle may yet become a coffin. Oh love, can you blame me for feeling blue, can you admonish me for loving you? I'm trying hard not to brood on the past, I'm trying to live in the present, but my future is foreclosed: How can I go on without you? Look! The ice too is turning blue, the clear blue of purity: I'm not pure, I'm obscure, but my love for you is luminous. Where did I go wrong? Why don't you want me anymore? I am a phantom on a ship of fools, a mooncalf on a ghost-ship. I don't know anything anymore. Except that I love you.

Höfn

Apricot lingers in the lilac afterglow; black tinges the cobalt of the sea and darkens the mountains' mauve: Across a wooden table, in a restaurant overlooking the harbour, we dine with Rolf and Magda. Parsley, garlic and butter bring out the succulence of the langoustine; the fragrance of the Gewürztraminer complements the aroma of the crustacean. And yet, as we sit opposite this couple we've just met, I feel it's not me looking at the view, it's not me eating: I am elsewhere.

Rolf and Magda are from Zürich. They live in Basel now. She works in research for Ciba-Geigy; he's a robotics engineer for ABB. He's telling you about his efforts to make robots work more closely with human beings. I love it when you speak German; I love how you articulate the agglutinated syllables and attack the hard velar stops: Your thought becomes more sculptural, more three-dimensional; your femininity becomes more muscular: Flowers in a cut-glass vase. And then it hits me: I'll never see you in Zürich again! A flame in my heart flickers. Don't look back. Be here now. Breathe. The flame goes out. Oh love, what tender days we had in your house by the Zürisee, what airy days of ardour and nights of discovery! Never again—how can that be?

Now Magda's talking about Ciba-Geigy's acquisition of Chiron. She explains that the pharmaceutical and biotech companies are merging, that the idea is to improve the chances of drug discovery. You don't care anymore. Matteo's dead. Whatever they find won't resurrect him.

They're younger than us, these two. How long will their couple last? She's a sporty girl, Magda. I like the way her ponytail's pinned up. I like the way she looks at me, the hint that her good health doesn't mean her pleasures are wholesome. She must enjoy experiencing her body. I'd like to experience it with her. Now she's explaining how the Chiron takeover was structured, like options pricing, with payments upon reaching milestones. It's all Greek to me, but you follow perfectly.

— And what do you do, Sprague? she asks me.
— Nothing. I'm just a talented layabout.
— Talented at what?
— Oh, I can make a mean bed in the morning, after a long night of love.
— What?
— And I used to be good at popping zits, but now I'm out of practice.
— You're pulling my leg.
— Am I?

She looks to you for confirmation: You don't give it. Rolf smiles at me, then turns to you and says his ambition is to head up a team in the ABB Research Centre. He'd like to test his ideas for service robots. His father's a surgeon.

Medicine and surgery, that's where the applications are. You don't care. Your father developed a micro-robot that can swim in the human bloodstream. He's dead now. You don't want to talk about robots anymore.

He's got rugged good looks, this Rolf. I like his combination of he-man stubble and thinking-man glasses. Magda keeps looking at me. She's Rolf's belle. Michelle. They go together well. How long will their couple last?

— Stop kidding, Sprague, Rolf says. Tell us what you do.
— Yeah, tells us. I know you're somebody famous.
— Famous? Not at all.
— I'm sure I've seen your picture somewhere.
— I'm not famous, Marietta, am I?
— No, you're not. Just a little, perhaps.
— Do you write songs? Magda asks.
— In a way.
— Do you write songs with Gram McElhone?

I say:

> She's bleeding, but her insolent blood is unspent
> The copper's violence won't make Katie spill it

— I knew it!
— I write the lyrics, he writes the music.
— I adore Seedy Friedrich!
— Me too! Rolf says.
— *Apple Cleft in Twain, Katie Quickfinger*—I know every song by heart!

And thus another conversation turns around Gram and the band. I don't mind fielding their questions: They're the best of fans.

— I used to write poetry, Magda says, when I was a teenager. I tried to write some again not so long ago, but I'd lost the spark. How do you it, Sprague?
— I just lay about and listen to my heart.
— Have you written anything today?
— Yes.
— Can we hear it?
— All right.

> The mountain floats on the horizon

The waterfall goes into reverse
The stars shine, I see a sign in them
Everything aligns to confirm the curse

I've got a herringbone hangover
I've got the roadhouse blues
For a while I walked in clover
But I was always born to lose

– Can you say it again? Rolf asks.

As I repeat the verse and refrain, you take my hand and hold it.

– I like it! Magda says. Will it become a song?

– Only if it inspires Gram. He's the only one who can write music that works with my words. I'm not a good lyricist.

– What? You're fantastic! Rolf says.

I don't feel up to explaining. I just feel down, down, down.

In our room in the guesthouse, in the silence by the sea, we sat lotus-like on the bed, facing each other. You began staring into my eyes. After maybe a minute my tears began to flow. They were tears of sorrow, to begin with, but soon they became tears of joy. Unflinchingly, we held each other's gaze until the beep of my watch told us ten minutes were up. As we fell into each other's arms, an overwhelming love for you surged up in me. At once exhausted and exhilarated, I felt at one with you in a present that needed neither past nor future.

Chapter 6

Saturday, September 3

Driving to Borgarfjörður-Eystri

The ergonomics are perfect, everything falls easily to hand: Woman and machine are one as you marry the curves of the coast, threading the car through the mountains. Under your command the Saab is not a bull abiding the yoke, not a stallion sustaining the bit: No, it's a falcon obeying the falconer, in perfect intelligence: Along the unbarriered cliff it soars with confidence; upon a seaward vista it pauses to perch. And thus to the exercise of power and control you bring elegance and finesse. When you're gone, don't expect me to forget.

Borgarfjörður-Eystri

Valleys of trunk glaciers, black-sand beaches and mountains of rhyolite; rock knobs and drumlins, hanging valleys and waterfalls: Trunk glaciers that reach the sea deeply erode the lower reaches of their valleys to a depth well below sea level. These lower reaches, which become filled with ocean water as the ice melts and sea level rises, are fjords: So this is the drowned coast, this is the flood the mountains flee in their heavenward exaltation: But not I. No, I shall not seek to escape the deluge that awaits me; willingly I'll accept my dissolution: My faith in you is absolute. Last night, as you walked barefoot on my back, didn't your feet impress my freedom into my destiny?

In the guesthouse restaurant, on the shore of Lake Logurinn

Against the chalky off-white of the wall, the charcoal grey and aqua green of the chairs convey a muted intensity; glinting on our wine glasses, low-hanging lights give a gleam to the dark table. You blow on the lobster bisque in your spoon; before you swallow you savour its smoothness. Waxed black, a cord of leather around your wrist passes through beads of paua shell to make you a bracelet, one that echoes the iridescent dolphin in your sternal notch. In your storm-blue chambray jumpsuit you've got that androgyne edge that I adore; in your patchwork sneakers, the irony that augments your allure. Brightening the amber, kohl rims your eyes. Marietta, I know you didn't intend to make your beauty heartbreaking. But you have. Now how can I forget that in twenty-three days you'll be gone?

Our pan-fried halibut comes with parmigiano risotto and chanterelles. I'm glad our long hike—colourful hills and isolated coves, puffin nests on sea-cliff slopes—has given you such an appetite: The relish with which you eat delights me. So this is the loving break-up, this is how you leave me. But do you know you're only making me love you more? On the Rond-Point du Pont Mirabeau I swore I'd never let you go: When you're gone, don't expect me to forget.

I reach into my jacket pocket and take out my notebook.

— I've made a portrait of myself.

I rip out a page and hand it to you.

— Will you keep it for me?

Your peruse the page.

— All right, Sprague. I'll do that.

My Favourite Films

1. Possession, Andrzej Zulawski
2. Last Tango in Paris, Bernardo Bertolucci
3. La Maman et la putain, Jean Eustache
4. In the Realm of the Senses, Nagisa Oshima
5. Teorema, Pier Paolo Pasolini
6. Cul de Sac, Roman Polanski
7. The Passenger, Michelangelo Antonioni
8. Damnation, Béla Tarr
9. The Element of Crime, Lars von Trier
10. The American Soldier, Rainer Werner Fassbinder

My Favourite Albums

1. Even Serpents Shine, The Only Ones
2. Rock 'n Roll Animal, Lou Reed
3. Broken English, Marianne Faithfull
4. John Lennon-Plastic Ono Band, John Lennon
5. Closer, Joy Division
6. New York Tenderberry, Laura Nyro
7. Outside, David Bowie
8. Chelsea Girl, Nico
9. Strange Days, The Doors
10. Exile in Guyville, Liz Phair

11. Blue, Joni Mitchell
12. Sticky Fingers, The Rolling Stones
13. X-Dreams, Annette Peacock
14. Ancient Heart, Tanita Tikaram
15. New Skin for the Old Ceremony, Leonard Cohen

— These lists bring back a lot of memories.
You turn the page over and take a look at the back.

My Favourite Novels

1. Watt, Samuel Beckett
2. Ulysses, James Joyce
3. Nightwood, Djuna Barnes
4. Histoire de l'œil, Georges Bataille
5. L'Amant, Marguerite Duras
6. Histoire d'O, Pauline Réage
7. Notre-Dame-des-Fleurs, Jean Genet
8. The Bell Jar, Sylvia Plath
9. To the Wedding, John Berger
10. The Trial, Franz Kafka

My Favourite Biographies and Memoirs

1. Dog Heart, Breyten Breytenbach
2. The Café after the Pub after the Funeral, Hattie Gordon
3. La Bâtarde, Violette Leduc
4. Giacometti, James Lord
5. Diane Arbus, Patricia Bosworth
6. Lee Miller: On Both Sides of the Camera, Carolyn Burke
7. Lucia Joyce, Carol Loeb Schloss
8. At Home with the Marquis de Sade, Francine du Plessix Gray
9. The Beautiful Fall: Yves Saint Laurent and Karl Lagerfeld, Alicia Drake
10. Francis Bacon: Anatomy of an Enigma, Michael Peppiatt

— A good self-portrait. But you've left it unsigned.

— After coming so far for beauty?

Playful, imploring, pensive: your heart in the mirror of your eyes. You fold the paper and put it in your bag.

— I'll keep it. Always. But I don't need it: I know who you are.

For dessert, we do half-and-half: raspberry pudding, sorbet and pistachio sponge; skyr panna cotta and birch ice cream. As the sorbet melts in your mouth, you give a sigh of pleasure, then say:

– I can't wait.

– For what?

– To be back in our room. Tonight I'm going to make you come without touching you.

Chapter 7

Sunday, September 4

Driving to Dettifoss

The radiance of the morning can't eclipse the brilliance of the night, the prowess of the swans can't transcend the finesse of your loving: With exquisite subtlety you made me come without touching me. How did you do it? As the swans fly in formation, as the sun gives a glow to the air, let me linger in the ravishment you staged in our room.

You were no cliché of a Salomé, no decadent daughter of Herodias; you did no dance of the seven veils, you asked for no head on a platter: With your eyes alone you did it. Naked, my hands tied above my head to a post of the bed, I stood before you as you sat on a swivel chair, dévoré flowers tumbling down the folds of your kimono. While your feet slowly wheeled you closer and closer to me, you sat in calm concentration and alternately stared into my eyes and fixed your gaze on my cock, building tension as you varied the time between the two. Ecstatic as Saint Sebastian, I received the arrows from your eyes. When your gaze held mine, I felt myself in freefall; when you stared at my sex, the Cyclops stared back. The parting of your lips sufficed to race my heart, the tilting of your head to halt my breath. Your gaze made my cock the core of my being: I *became* that ravenous throb of vitalized flesh. Desperate for your touch, unable to reach you, I felt the chafing of the rope on my wrists. Finally, purified in the fire of your eyes, I felt my tendons tightening. Cupping your hands before my craving, with wide-open eyes you stared into mine: In the intensity of your regard I delivered my elixir, in the rapture of your look I filled your cup.

Has the splendour of the morning given the Saab wings? No, we're just one with the world greeting us through the windscreen.

— Sprague?

— Hm?

— I love you.

I feel the divine in me, I feel myself soaring. Where are those swans? I will fly in their slipstream.

— Now is that any reason to cry?

I kiss your fingers as you wipe a tear from my cheek.

— You're amazing, Marietta. You overwhelm me.

— I love you. When I'm gone, never forget it.

— Let's not talk about that. Let's sing a song.

— All right. Which one?

— 'Andalucia'.

— Okay. One, two, three—

We sing together:

— 'Andalucia, when can I see you, when it is snowing out again?'

In the loveliness of the melody, in the resonance of your voice, I lose my sorrowing love.

Dettifoss

Blood in the wind, a flutter in my mouth, flaming the air I breathe: I don't care about the order of angels, I don't care if they don't hear my cry: It is to you that I address my scream. But you don't hear me: The wingbeats of thunderbirds, the banging of blacksmiths, overwhelm my wail. What awaits me here? Annihilation? Revelation? Or simply the understanding that ending a relationship can be an act of love?

From the still centre the water falls, displaying its infinite potentiality. And my potential, what is to become of me? The dream language of cinema, the *mysterium tremendum* of music—how can I distil from the ferment in my soul an arrangement of words to rival that? How can I do it if you're not with me? One thing is clear: I will not survive if I do not create: Between the fecundating fire and the shrivelling, I must choose.

Ásbyrgi

'She lives on Love Street, lingers long on Love Street': It's not Laurel Canyon, but it is a canyon: As we walk along the edge of the cliff, overlooking the river that runs through the forest of larch, pine, and birch, The Doors' sprightly ballad is on my mind. 'She has a house and garden': Why does it haunt me so, this crazy dream of domesticity with you? Whenever we lived together, whether in London, Paris or Zürich, we always made a home for ourselves, if not as nest builders then as cuckoo birds. But it is you, my love, you who are the master of the intermezzo: I never claimed to have a body without organs. Still, I fancy myself a nomad, and now my longing for a fixed abode, a house and garden with you, makes a mockery of that. And it's all your fault: Didn't you sit by the fireside, the yarn slipping off your fingers as you lined it up in loops on your needles? As the repetitive motion of your hands dissolved the day's tensions, didn't I safeguard your meditation? I am wearing the socks you made me, the ones you striped in the Fibonacci series, so don't expect me to forget. And didn't you flip through your recipe books and cook me something new whenever you had the occasion? Didn't you find that it relaxes your mind to sip a glass of Riesling while preparing the fish for the stir-fry? I did the cleaning up, I brought a gleam to your utensils, so don't expect me to forget. And what about the garden? Didn't you find the solution to an equation while pruning the climbing roses, discover where to look for a particle while planting a bare-root tree, unearth the truth about a Simenon character while hoeing the ground on a sunny day? I have photographic proof—straw hat on your head, Dutch hoe in your hands—so don't expect me to forget. Yes, Marietta, I used to consider every destination not a stop but a way station; I used to delight in going to a place for the pleasure of leaving it: Now I'd like to stay put with you. All right, forget about the house, forget about the garden: Just keep me in your heart when you go.

Húsavík

'I thought I would sail about a little and see the watery part of the world. It is a way I have of driving off the spleen': Sailing just below the Arctic Circle in a converted fishing boat, I think of Melville's allegory of reading and wonder what I will write. All I can say is that it will be an attempt at redemption, a love letter to you. Keeping my eye on the water as we go in search of the whale, I see nothing but the shape of manifestation. Look! Already the waters have no shores, already they've wiped out what has gone before: This is the mirror of creation, the watery abyss from which all creatures come. There she blows! Look! The bearer of the cosmos, looking to cast ashore the pilgrim in her belly: Upon what shore will I be cast, in what strange land will I wander, ceaselessly asking myself why?

On the eastern shore of Skjálfandi Bay, in the wild

By what miracle are you still with me? Of what mettle are you made that you lie with me even as you leave me? In our zippered-together sleeping bags, in our tunnel tent, as surely as the mountains rising out of the sea—there, across the bay—you prove that you are still with me. It's not supposed to be this way. Usually, 'I'm leaving you' proclaims what has already taken place: 'I've left you—only you haven't noticed yet'. But that is not true of us: You are closer to me now than my jugular vein, your body and mine interpenetrate. And yet, though my limbs melt as I lie in your arms, I know the boundaries between us can never dissolve. Still, no greater parting gift than this could you give me, this intensity of your presence to me. Even if I have forebodings of what's to come.

– Sprague, you must be braver than you've ever been. In twenty-two days I'll be gone.

– But why?

– I love you, but I have to leave.

– You'll never see me again?

– Never.

– Can I write to you?

– I won't read it.

– Can I call you?

– I won't answer.

– Why?

– It's been a beautiful seven years. I gave you everything I had to give. Everything you gave me, I received fully. And it will be the same for the next three weeks and a day. Then it's over.

– But why?

– It has to be.

– Why?

– Don't ask me why. Just know that I love you. And that I always will.

I am a child in your arms. You are miles above me. I am stupid and ignorant; I know nothing anymore. Except that you have to go. And that I'd give anything to go with you.

– Come now, Sprague, stop crying.

You kiss my eyes, you wipe my nose. You say:

– MLS45V5R1A4.

– What's that?

– That's the root of my password at CERN.

– You want me to memorize it in case you forget?

– No. I want you to know what it means.

– And what does it mean?

– Marietta loves Sprague for ever and a day.

Delicate and subtle they come, your kisses, until you become ravenous; long and slow they deepen, until your lips from below pivot to receive my blessing. Meshed in your indomitable desire, I am not yet just a man among men: I am still the chosen instrument of your pleasure, happy to be alive again.

If this is the coda to our song, I'm going to be okay; if this is how you close the book on us, I'll live to see another day. In the downy warmth of our mating bags, in the cool, crisp air, we fall asleep, sated.

Chapter 8

Monday, September 5

Lake Mývatn

Breathing craters of milk-blue water, smouldering fields of tranquil fire; scalloped wetlands of green marshes, windswept plains of orange-brown earth: Strapped into our soft leather seats, we fly above the landscape around Lake Mývatn in a Cessna 206. Hurled through the heavens by a whirling propeller, you're in your element—what is it about risk that makes your beauty so otherworldly? Through you the thrill happens for me, through you the experience becomes a pleasure: Otherwise, I'd much rather be in an ocean liner, sailing the open sea. But there are advantages to being up high: From the air it becomes apparent that the lake is an oasis fringed by a desert, the land an evisceration of the Mid-Atlantic Ridge.

Our pilot is happy that we're happy; you ask him about the airplane. No, he can't do a fast climb into higher altitudes, he can't take us sky-diving: This is a sightseeing trip. You pull a hangdog face; he accelerates and goes into a 45-degree up-line before levelling out and descending to normal altitude: Even you are surprised by the effect of your childish charm.

Look! The russet and gold of late-summer trees, the multi-coloured clay of mud pits: I prefer the dramatic blacks and whites that give visual coherence to this country. I haven't been using my Leica. Why? People move me, not landscapes. And why haven't I been photographing you? I stare out the window and toss my question into the steaming vents. The earth coughs back the answer: Because if I'm going to fall, I prefer to fall with no safety net. And besides, when you're gone, photos would only make me miss you more.

— Look, Sprague, how contorted they are, those volcanic pillars!

— Yes, I like this landscape. Takes me back to the beginning of time.
You take my hand and kiss it.

— When the earth looked like this, time was already nine billion years old. Nine billion years. And I've got less than three weeks left with you.

— Are you a scientist? the pilot asks you.

— No, I'm a chef. I run a restaurant. But my husband is a scientist. Tell the pilot what you do, dear.

— I'm an entomologist. I study insects.

— Well, you've come to the right place! This is the only location in Iceland where we have insects.

— Yes, I know. They're very important to the ecosystem here, to the birds and the fish. In fact, I've come to calculate the quantity of larvae an arctic char must eat to make a fish steak on your plate.

— I see. Is that for you PhD?

— No, no. For my PhD, I calculated who has a longer life expectancy after making love—a male praying mantis, or a male scorpion. Adjusted for their respective life spans, of course.

— The things you scientists do!

— It's a living, like any other. Look at that crater! It's enormous!

— Yes, that's Hverfell. If you're feeling fit, you can climb up to the rim.

And thus, my love, you got me out of my brooding, and set the tone for a perfect day.

After our aerial tour we picnicked on the promontory of Höfdi (you were as wild about Stóri Dímon as you were on the day we first discovered that creamy blue cheese). We lingered among the flower-covered lava outcrops, then went for a walk in the birch forest before going bathing in the geothermal pool.

Akureyri (1)

— Welcome!

I'm taken aback by the twins, I can't find my coordinates. Is this a déjà-vu, an hallucination of you? These sisters, are they avatars of the Sphinx? We spent two weeks together just a year ago, and now how they've grown!

— Come in, please. Mum and dad will be back in an hour or so.

Anna's eyes hesitate between brown and green, then settle into hazel; her hair blends white and gold as she flicks it back from her face. You step across the threshold; I hold Gudrun's gaze: Ambiguity hovers in the blue of her eyes; in the black of her hair, vanity renounces the renunciation of itself. No, Anna-Gudrun, you are not the devouring Sphinx: You are simply incomplete creatures, suspended between girl and woman.

I step inside and let Gudrun lead me down a hallway of muted flagstones to a living room with glowing floorboards. In the softness of the aubergine sofa you and I seat ourselves; Anna slinks into the bucket seat of an armchair while Gudrun takes up the lotus position on a love seat.

– It's good to see you again, I say. How are things going?

– Good, Anna replies. Today in German we sung 'Neunundneunzig Luftballons'. Do you know it?

– Yes, it was a big hit. It's a great song!

You ask:

– Are the two of you in the same class?

– Yes, Gudrun replies. We wanted to be together one last time. I'm moving to Reykjavik next year.

– Really?

– Yes. And it's because of you two.

– Sprague and I?

– Yes.

– How's that?

– Remember when you took us to see the Frankfurt Ballet at the Zürich Opera House?

– Yes. William Forsythe.

– Right. Well, I liked it so much that now I want to do dance, contemporary dance. I'm going to Reykjavik because there's a good preparatory programme there.

I say:

– That's great! I didn't realize the performance had moved you so much.

– It did. *In the Middle, Somewhat Elevated*—I've never forgotten it.

There's a sculptural quality to her face, a finely chiselled look that goes well with her tall body. She says:

– Marietta, would you like to do a workout with me?

– What kind of workout?

– Just a Pilates warm up, then the floor barre.

– Sure. When, where?

– Now, before supper. In the recreation room. We've got more than enough time before Kári and Begga come back.

– All right, let's go! Can you lend me something to wear?

– Of course! Come.

I remain with Anna as you and Gudrun leave the room.

– Enjoy your workout! I call out.

Anna's legs are restless; in the bucket seat she doesn't seem to know what to do with them. I like what she's wearing: a loose minidress in a Jackson Pollock print, black drip on cream ground; plain tights and black flats, a beige cardigan and a gauzy cream scarf, its knotted ends standing in for her breasts: She is an Artist. Looking at the assemblages of sticks on the wall, I say:

— I love those fish, Anna. Did Berglind make them?

— Yes. From driftwood.

— Brought here by the Gulf Stream?

— No. Gulf Stream drift only reaches the south coast. Here the wood comes on currents from Siberia.

— That's a long journey!

— Yes.

Strung together in shades of grey, white and brown, the creatures, each brought to life by an all-seeing eye, evoke tribal talismans.

— And you, I ask her, have you been keeping up your photography?

— I have. Would you like to see what I've done?

— I'd love to!

She stands up.

— Come, let's go to my room.

— No, show me here.

— It's too much trouble. I want you to see the ones pinned on the walls.

— All right.

Through the literary forest of the corridor I follow Anna to her bedroom. As I cross the threshold I feel the presence of the Sphinx: Once again I am struck by childhood's end, by the infinite incompletion of the end: So this is your teddy bear, admirably Arctic in white despite its yellow spots; this is your jar of marbles, your collection of bumblebees and pearls, tiger-eyes and turtles; these are your marionettes, pinned in jaunty postures to your burlapped wall. Look! On the bed, stretched out on the pale blue spread, a cat in its ash-grey coat. Anna sits down beside it and takes it in her lap.

— This is Snúlli.

As she strokes the cat, its ashen coat takes on a blue-grey sheen; screwing up its orange eyes, it begins to purr.

— I need more light, Anna.

She leans back and flicks a bedside switch: I sweep my gaze across the walls and quickly it becomes clear that Anna is not playing at being an artist: She is well on her way to becoming one. Black-and-white, blurred motion; a naked body in a bare room. Never the full figure, never a frontal view, everything always oblique and partial. And yet, despite the mood of mystery, the evocation of a secret event, there is a directness that dares one to be indifferent, an implicating intimacy.

— Anna, these are excellent!

— Really?

— Yes. The framing and the staging are brilliant; it's just the printing that could be improved. You can optimize the effects in the dark room; you need a dark room teacher.

— Yes, I know. I have a good book, but—

— You need someone who can show you how to trick the light under the enlarger, how to play with the chemical baths. But you've got what no-one can teach you, and that's far more important.

— And what's that?

— A personal vision. An eye that knows what to leave out.

— Thank you, Sprague. You know if it wasn't for the Hasselblad you gave Begga, I probably would never have become interested in photography.

— I'm glad I gave her the camera, then. Can I see some of your other work?

— Yes, look behind you. Third drawer from the top.

— Third drawer from the top...

I pull it open and take out an album.

— This?

— No, that's not a portfolio, that's my diary. Bring it to me please.

I step over and hand her the spiral notebook.

— Look again. It's a presentation box. Black.

— Got it.

I seat myself at the worktable.

— I love this surface! The lime green goes very well with these pin-strip boards.

The cat jumps off the bed; under the table, it rubs itself on my legs. Anna, her back against the headboard, draws up her legs and hugs her knees.

— Snúlli likes you, Sprague. It's rare she's affectionate with anyone but me.

She smiles into my eyes: Her gaze is disquieting, there's an aware sexuality in her charm. I open the box: In one photo after another, in subdued Kodachrome colours, Anna and Gudrun take turns to play the drowned Ophelia: Now submerged in a stream, flower-strewn hair and long white dress flowing in the grassy current, now floating in reedy water, eyes and hands open to heaven, they perform variations on the Pre-Raphaelite ideal of femininity. As I study the images, Anna studies her face in a hand mirror.

— They're really lovely, Anna.

— Do you like them?

She takes off her cardigan.

— Yes, very much.

With consummate skill she's captured all the tropes of the romantic myth: still water as a call from the deep, reality yielding to dream, death as sleep.

— You've mastered light on water, Anna.

— You mean I know how to use a polarizing filter.

— And the flowers are very well arranged.

— Flowers! Snúlli, come!

The cat jumps onto the bed; Anna stretches out her legs and places the animal in her lap. So this is how you manage the ambiguities of adolescence, this is how you cope with its contradictions: Stroking the cat in your lap while Ophelia preserves your innocence, her death arresting you in childhood. Yes, you've staged things beautifully; you've realized your fantasy of a pure sexuality, a sexuality without the sex: The dead Ophelia, your second twin, never having become a woman, saves you from the violence of becoming one. But your photos are out of date, they don't fool me: I know that though you be fifteen, you are impatient for deflowering—I can tell by how you blossom in my presence.

— Can I make a photo with you, Sprague?

— Sure.

She lifts Snúlli from her lap and places her on the bed. The cat jumps off and runs out of the room.

— It's for my diary. Let's go next door.

Before the backdrop in the bare room I stand. Anna turns on the lights, looks through the lens, then adjusts the reflectors.

— It's perfect you're in black. You're going to play Hamlet.

— Oh, really?

— Yes. Here, hold Ophelia.

She hands me a blow-up of herself, half-submerged among floating flowers.

— Hold it level at your waist.

I do so. She looks through the lens.

— No. With your black top we can't see how long your hair is. Hamlet has to have long hair. Take off your shirt, please.

— I say we will have no more marriages.

— What?

I pull my Polo over my head and toss it onto a chair.

— Those that are married already—all but one—shall live; the rest shall keep as they are. To a nunnery, go.

— I'm not going anywhere. Tilt Ophelia up a touch.

— Do you have a filter to get rid of the reflection?

— Of course. That's good. Keep that 'to a nunnery' expression. Good.

She takes the shot, and another, and another.

— Take off your socks.

I take off my socks. She studies me.

— Your green eyes are beautiful, Sprague, but they might be deceiving. Hold Ophelia like a mask to your face.

I do so.

— Your belt's perfect. I like the buckle.

She takes the shot, and another, and another.

— Thank you.

She turns off the lights.

— Now let's go and see what Gudrun and Marietta are getting up to!

Fondu devant, fondu à la seconde; rond de jambe à terre, rond de jambe en l'air: Beyond the cowhide rug that gives a focus to the white walls and black floor of the recreation room, you and Gudrun lie on exercise mats, doing a floor barre routine. You're looking good in plum-coloured hot pants and a black camisole top; Gudrun's your baby sister in black bike-style shorts and a magenta T-shirt. Anna and I plop down onto the sofa and watch Gudrun demonstrate the moves before the two of you do them together: *Adagio left leg, adagio right... Grand battement left, grand battement right... Full port de bras, full port de bras in reverse...*

— And that's it! Gudrun says.

The two of you relax, eyes closed, on the mats. And then, standing up, Anna says:

— Hey, I wanted to do some with you!

She takes off her scarf.

— Oh Anna! her sister moans.

— Plea-ea-ea-se!

— All right, five minutes.

— Come Sprague, Anna says.

I follow her to the middle of the floor.

— On your hands and knees! Gudrun calls.

We fall to the floor.

— We'll do a cat and reverse cat, five times to stretch your spine. Do as I do.

You get on all fours and join in.

— Now curl your back like a cat, push your spine upwards... Now relax your neck and let your head drop.

On all fours in her minidress, Anna is one hell of a flirt. Is she a playful kitten or a cat in heat? Both, it would seem.

— And now we'll do a sphinx into a rollup, then roll back down to starting position. I'll demonstrate once, and then we'll do it five times.

Gudrun is fully at home in her body; grace abounds in her physicality. Her hair, like yours, is tied back in a ponytail. Is she aware that her hair concentrates her qualities? Is she aware that her modesty is moving? Sitting on my heels I extend my hands, sphinx-like, until my forehead is touching the floor. Breathing in and drawing my navel to my spine, I slowly roll up one vertebra at a time until I come to a kneeling position. Bottom on heels, arms at sides, I pause, then breathe out and roll down to the starting position: I am the Sphinx, standing on the brink of a fate which is both necessity and mystery.

When Berglind and Kári returned from work, the twins had already got the supper going. We soon sat down to a dinner of roast cod with avocado purée, chorizo and artichokes. We gave our impressions of Iceland, then Begga and I entertained the table—especially the twins—with anecdotes from our Film School days in London. I was happy to note that time had not diminished our complicity. She too had abandoned filmmaking, having fulfilled her desire to make a documentary on Icelandic fishermen. In addition to teaching, arts and crafts—making design objects and selling them through Reykjavik boutiques—was her work now. Listening to Berglind, I was reminded of what had drawn me to her in London: The philosophical sadness in her eyes and her uncorrupted femininity. Now, as then, there is no violence in her beauty, no cynicism in her speech; she'd rather be than have, rather do than talk. She could kill and skin an animal, but never to satisfy a ritual; she could climb a mountain, but never to plant a flag. Fresh in her preference for the particular, she is provocative in her refusal of the general. Between silence and the radio, she'd choose silence; between faith and proof, she'd choose faith. Is that why, when missing you began killing me, I would seek shelter in her wisdom?

You asked Kári how he likes his new job: From refrigeration engineer, he'd moved on to become supply chain manager. He likes it, he said, but wished he had more math so that he could manipulate the software instead of being manipulated by it.

— What do you need? you asked him. Queuing theory, statistical process control, simulation under uncertainty?

— All of that, he replied. I've been teaching myself, but I'll register for some courses, somewhere. But in the meantime, the fish can't wait!

— Well, you'll just have to squeeze in your courses around the catch, then!

— Yes, that's just what I intend to do.

Anna asked you if you enjoy being an engineer. You explained that where you were educated, 'engineer' means someone who can solve complex problems mathematically, someone who can travel easily between theory and reality.

– And, you added, because 'reality' is usually not 'real' the moment you get into the very big and the very small, that makes the work a lot of fun!

Dessert was berry pie with skyr, followed by coffee. We talked about the end of the world: Gudrun had asked you about the comet that, in July, had crashed into Jupiter. You said:

– Thank goodness for Jupiter! If it wasn't for its gravity, we'd certainly have a lot more asteroids crashing into Earth. Who knows, we might never have evolved to where we are now, or we may already have become extinct.

At that Anna got up, ran into the living room and began rolling on the rug. Gudrun ran to the nearest wall and pressed her back against it, squirming.

– They're Sagittarians, Kári says, they're ruled by Jupiter.

– More seriously, says Begga, they can't bear the thought of the world coming to an end.

– Is that right? you ask. Gudrun? Anna?

The twins drag themselves back to the table.

– Yes, Anna says.

– It's bad now, Gudrun explains, but it was worse before. It used to really drive us up the wall.

– How will it happen, Marietta? Anna asks. How will it end?

They know the story, but want to hear it again. This time you tell it this way:

– One day the sun will get hungry and get a craving for toast. The Earth will be near at hand. But for now the sun's got enough breakfast to last some billions of years. When the time is finally up, the greatest of our great grandchildren will already have become creatures in the dreams of intelligent beings somewhere else in the universe. In other words, life on Earth will die out, but it won't matter: We'll have become supernatural, just like the elves in Iceland.

Your story works like magic: As Anna sings an old Icelandic song, Gudrun takes to the floor and starts dancing. Watching her, I feel like rolling on the floor or pressing against a wall, I feel like defying the fate that deprived us of a baby: I want to make love with you. Yes, into the same world whose certain end once brought me jubilation, I want, with you, to bring a child. And then I remember that though the sun may take a billion years to die, in just twenty-one days you'll be gone.

Chapter 9

Tuesday, September 6

Akureyri (2)

In the morning we went horseback riding on Eyjafjördur's eastern shore; in the afternoon, Anna and Gudrun brought some friends back from school to meet me. We talked about *Memoirs of a Kleptomaniac.* They were intimately familiar with Katie Quickfinger; they taught me things about my heroine I did not know. Then the conversation focused on *An Apple Cleft in Twain:* Is the doubling real or imaginary? How can one be both oneself and another? Is the man in black really the brother or just a figment of the Wanderer's imagination? Who is the lady in the mirror, who the shadow on the wall? And what if all the characters are simply the Wanderer reflected through a prism? I answered their questions with questions; I explained that the role of the double is to negate unicity and thereby undermine mimesis, I explained to them what that means. Why, then, after having undermined mimesis, I asked them, would I want to prop it up by closing off possibilities? That seemed to please them, even as it set them debating among themselves.

When the friends leave, Anna and Gudrun, you and I, linger in the living room. Then Anna stands up and asks:

– Marietta, will you come to my room? I want to show you something.

– Sure.

You get up and follow her. I remain with Gudrun.

– I like your friends, I say. They're sharp.

– You think so?

– Yes.

– And what about me?

– What about you?

– Do you think I'm sharp?

– Yes, you're sharp. And you're cut on the bias, as they say in fashion, like a 1930s gown.

– Cut on the bias? What does that mean?

– It means you're not obvious.

– Not obvious? Sometimes I think I'm too obvious! I wish I could wear a hat and veil.

– That would go well with a 1930s gown.

– Sprague, you're teasing me!

She gets up and fetches what appears to be a wastepaper basket from a corner of the room. Placing it on the floor about a body length from me, she sits on it and starts to rock.

– What's that?

– It's a rocking stool. Look, I can rock in all directions.

– Cool!

On this ingenious tribal drum, with its seat connected to the base by a criss-cross of chromed-steel rods, Gudrun holds my gaze as she sways. She's very schoolgirl in her black-and-white skirt, red shirt and black tights; she's such a girl angling her legs like that.

– So, why do you say I'm not obvious?

– Well, when you're riding your... machine like that, maybe you are a little obvious.

– It's not a machine, it's a rocking stool, and it's me that's working it.

– Yes, I can see that. Well, if you are obvious, keep on rocking like that till you disorder your senses. Then you'll become a seer. Like Rimbaud. And you won't be obvious anymore.

– Who's Rimbaud? And what's a seer?

– A seer is someone who can see into the unknown. Rimbaud was a poet, a boy like you.

– I'm not a boy.

– How do you know?

She stops rocking and pulls up her shirt to reveal her breasts in her bra. She starts rocking again.

– He was French, I suppose, this boy Rimbaud?

– Yes. Do you speak French?

– I do: *grand plié, relevé, tendu derrière.*

– You speak ballet. Why not learn French?

– Why should I?

– So you can read Rimbaud.

– All right. If you want me to, I will.

– Good. I'll send you some books and CDs. Now stop rocking! You're making me dizzy.

– Didn't you say I had to do it till I lose my senses?

– I did, yes. *Disorder* your senses. Consume the poisons in you and keep only their quintessence.

– What's 'quintessence'?

– It's what's left when you burn away everything in you that doesn't correspond to your own desire.

– Then I'll be able to see into the unknown?

– Yes.

– I'll tell you a secret, Sprague. Since we got this rocking stool last year, I've already become a seer. Three times.

– Only by rocking?

– Yes.

– That's wonderful, Gudrun. It proves you've already been burning your poisons. Now listen, I'm going to recite you a poem by Rimbaud. It's called *'Sensation'.*

– In French?

– Yes.

– Recite it, then, while I try to become a seer again.

Squeezing her thighs together, she further angles out her legs, squirming as she rotates on the rocking stool. I recite the poem:

Par les soirs bleus d'été, j'irai dans les sentiers,
Picoté par les blés, fouler l'herbe menue:
Rêveur, j'en sentirai la fraîcheur à mes pieds.
Je laisserai le vent baigner ma tête nue.

Je ne parlerai pas, je ne penserai rien:
Mais l'amour infini me montera dans l'âme,
Et j'irai loin, bien loin, comme un bohémien,
Par la Nature, heureux comme avec une femme.

The rocking comes to a standstill as Gudrun squeezes her thighs tighter; her head thrown back, through blind eyes she sees into the unknown.

– What's the poem about, Sprague?

– It's about a blue summer night, a night like this, when you set out along the byways in search of tenderness, a tenderness you never had. Rimbaud's mother was very severe.

– Was he very young when he wrote it?

– He was exactly your age. Fifteen and a half.

— Really?

— Uh-hm.

— And does he find the tenderness he's searching for?

— He does. He experiences the sensations of tingling skin as he walks through wheat, the dreamy coolness of grass under his feet, the wind blowing through his hair.

— But only in his imagination?

— Yes. Though he would go on to walk for miles and miles and miles. He's given up trying to find tenderness in a woman, so he looks for it in Nature instead.

— Nature is feminine. But is it enough?

— No. Rimbaud died very lonely and bitter.

— So why do you want me to read him?

— It's just a hunch I have, an intuition. I think you'd get along very well together.

— On a blue summer night?

— On a night like this.

— You could be right. I did see into the unknown as you recited his poem. Even if I didn't understand anything.

— The music of his words was enough.

— The sound of your voice, more like. And the look in your eyes.

— The look in my eyes?

— Yes. I don't know how to describe it. I just feel you admire me. And I like how that feels.

— Like Rimbaud, walking in the wind?

— Yes. But I'm not a vagabond looking for love!

— And I hope you never will be.

She stands up and picks up the rocking stool.

— Look, it's got a convex base. That's why it rocks.

— Very clever.

— I've got a bit of homework to do, Sprague.

— Go and do it, then.

Carrying the stool back to its corner, she turns to look at me over her shoulder.

— Will you try some stinky shark and Black Death after supper?

— I sure will.

— I can't wait to see that!

— You think I'll survive the experience?

— I hope you do. But I don't guarantee it!

— We'll see.

— Come to my room while I work. You can keep me company.

— That would be a pleasure, but I think it's better if I stay here. I'll watch the news.

— But you don't understand Icelandic.

— I'll figure things out, so long as it's not just talking heads. It starts on the hour, I suppose?

— Yes, in twenty minutes. I'll come watch it with you. I don't have much homework.

— Okay. See you in twenty minutes, then.

— See you.

Grand plié, relevé, tendu derrière: Gudrun runs out of the room in ballet steps, her flouncy skirt—beautifully cut on the bias—floating.

The news found all four of us in front of the television. Gudrun and Anna gave us a running commentary in lieu of a translation, impressing us with their perspicacity.

Liquorice beets with caramelized oats and goat cheese; smoked haddock with mussel sauce, roasted cauliflower and barley: Dinner, made by you and Berglind, is delicious. Kári's in fine form, excited about the possibilities of making the most of his new responsibilities at work.

— What you spoke about last night, Marietta—how in particle physics you build statistical models to determine the probability of an event in the detector being signal or background—that gave me some ideas of how we can better exploit our database.

— Great!

— I've got a couple of questions I'd like to ask you later.

— Sure.

— And don't forget, tonight I get my revenge at chess!

Anna interjects:

— Daddy, you haven't got a chance!

— But I do, Anna, I do. Don't forget my secret weapon: Marietta and Sprague are leaving in the morning, so tonight's their last chance to have hákarl and brennivín!

— Oh yes!

You say:

— Well Sprague, we'll hold hands and say our prayers—we either survive or die together.

— Yes, if we want to make it, we'll have to be on our mettle!

We ask Berglind about her teaching, about how her lecture went.

— Good, she says. It was on William Morris and the Arts and Crafts Movement. The work is so beautiful, the students always take to it.

This leads to a discussion on the Pre-Raphaelites. Anna and Gudrun had been devouring Begga's books on the subject, so I speak not about the paintings but about the artists and models. The twins lap up the anecdotes, and are particularly moved by the story of Lizzie Siddal, the drowned Ophelia in Millais' painting: Insufficiently educated to become a governess or teacher, too talented and intelligent to settle for factory work or shop assistant, she built a career as a model for the Pre-Raphaelites. Rossetti fell in love with her, but the marriage that would give her a social existence was repeatedly put off. To make her less lower class, to give her the opportunity to cultivate herself, Rossetti wanted her to give up modelling, or rather to pose only for him; the sole alternative to marriage would then become impoverished spinsterhood. Lizzie did give up modelling, seeking to elevate herself in society, but not before posing for Millais: Stretched out in a bathtub with oil lamps underneath to heat the water, she posed as the drowned Ophelia. The last session lasted five hours, the oil ran out in the lamps; Lizzie was chilled to the bone, but did not complain: Her capacity to give herself up completely is what makes the painting so convincing. Finally married to Rossetti, she became pregnant; the child, however, died in her womb. Lizzie then took an overdose of opium and alcohol and killed herself.

— It's horrible, how hard it was for women to be independent in those days, Gudrun says.

— Yes, her father concurs, thank God things have changed.

Then Begga says:

— I didn't know that story, Sprague; thanks for telling it.

— Such stories sustain me. I'm not sure why.

— Interesting. Would you know why, Marietta? Begga asks.

You look into my eyes: I give you my blessing.

— Sprague does read a great deal of biography. I think it simply takes him out of his isolation, gives him a feeling of connection. An artist is always an outsider. It can get very lonely, no matter how much you are loved.

Gudrun interjects:

— Don't be lonely, Sprague! I love you.

— Me too! Anna says.

— Well, thank you. Such love calls for a celebration: Will you help me write a song after supper?

— A song for Seedy Friedrich?

— Yes, if it's good enough.

— We will, we will! the twins exclaim together.

I look at their parents, each in turn, as if to apologize—for what, I don't really know.

Dessert was mousse of skyr with crispy oats-and-hazelnut crumble, red currants and cinnamon-rhubarb sauce. In order not to spoil the lingering pleasure of that scrumptious closer, the stinky shark and Black Death were put off till later in the evening. The twins and I cleaned up, fooling around to 'Friday I'm in Love'. While you and Kári played chess—he, having upped his game, giving you a good run for your money—the twins and I came up with a lyric that, though conceived to a poppy beat, was much darker than what I'd imagined we'd write: The news had affected us all. I wrote the chorus and middle eight, Anna and Gudrun the verses. We called the song 'Any Right to Be'.

'Don't move' said the curfew man
'Infidel', the Ayatollah
'Buy buy buy' said the TV ad
'Five minutes to go', the prison guard

Yes, I was feeling bad
Had many reasons to be sad
Then out of the blue she said 'I love you'
Now I'm happier
Than I have any right to be
Any right to be

'Suffocate him' said the torturer
'Burn his groves', the colonist
'The whole village' said the general
'Every house', the militiaman

Yes, I was feeling bad
Had many reasons to be sad
Then out of the blue she said 'I love you'
Now I'm happier
Than I have any right to be
Any right to be

Now the day is done, night's come along

There's love in her eyes and fear in my soul
You see, it's not the world of horrors
That's worrying me, it's something
Long-standing deep inside of me
That makes me say when she says 'I love you'
That I'm happier
Than I have any right to be
Any right to be

'Burn the book' said the preacher
'War is peace', the politician
'Close the border' said the voter
'Loose the dogs', the policeman

Yes, I was feeling bad
Had many reasons to be sad
Then out of the blue she said 'I love you'
Now I'm happier
Than I have any right to be
Any right to be

Gram came up with a nippy tune and, as always, a superb arrangement; within six months Anna and Gudrun were co-songwriters with a hit on their hands and money in the bank.

The lyric written, the chess games played, there was no escaping now the rotten shark and aquavit. The twins' excitement was infectious; we stuck our toothpicks into the putrid flesh, brought the cubes to our mouths and affected to faint. Egged on by everyone's laughter, we began to chew the ammoniacal offence to our senses, each movement of mastication intensifying the savour redolent of the urinal. Quick, quick, the aquavit! With watery eyes we knocked back the firewater, purging ourselves of the piss.

— Could we have some more, please? you asked.

Initiated into the ritual, we each ate a second cube and knocked back a second shot, pleased that Kári's pale blue eyes were glowing with approval.

'The first time I saw lightning strike, I saw it underground': Glad I've got my Cure albums on me, I put on 'Hot Hot Hot!' and join in the dance that instantly breaks out. So this is how it ends, our stay in Akureyri; this is how Berglind and Kári, Anna and Gudrun, will remember us: dancing joyfully. When you're gone, don't expect me to forget.

Chapter 10

Wednesday, September 7

Driving to Austari-Jökulsá

I find myself feeling sad at leaving Akureyri. How can I be missing Anna and Gudrun so soon after having left them? I think of Prospero and Miranda, Pericles and Marina; I think of the father I might have been to the daughter we'll never have. Why do Anna and Gudrun move me so? Is it that their signature as subjects makes no concession to propriety? Is it that they confirm my intuition that the paradigm of creativity is a girl becoming a woman? That all creativity is an erotic act? No doubt. And no doubt I will accept their invitation to renewal: Their self-creation as subjects stimulates me. Is one ever finished with adolescence, then? I don't think so. Alone in her room with you, Anna went through her wardrobe, searching for a model of femininity. Alone in her room with me, I thought she'd already found it: Innocent yet knowing, vulnerable yet unafraid, she charmed me with her nonchalance. Yes, she lifted the veil on the rites of adolescence, she straddled the contradictions between exhibitionism and inwardness, play-acting and sincerity. Now, as I recall her casual sophistication, she's got me feeling dreamy. And what about Gudrun's ingenious transcription of this dangerous passage? Neither Narcissus bedazzled by her new-found sex nor a nymph bent on seduction, she did not recoil before her discoveries nor rush into deploying her powers; no, her rocking before me demanded nothing but recognition. Thus I offered her Rimbaud, an interpretation for her sensations, a fellow adolescent about to walk the world.

— You're looking dreamy, Sprague.

— Am I?

— Uh-hm.

— I'm missing Anna and Gudrun.

There's a wistfulness in the smile you give me: Do you see yourself in them?

— They're quite mad about you.

— And I them!

— It's lovely to see how well you get along. And you know what? I detected just a hint of jealousy in Kári.

— Really?

— Yes. He's crazy about his daughters.

– I'd noticed that before, but not so much this time.

– It's still there, that overflowing love, but maybe he's trying to keep more distance now.

Aglow in your loveliness, I feel a pinch of bitterness: How I'd love to have had a child with you. Why this obsession? I take your hand and kiss it.

– Thank you for last night.

– My pleasure. Didn't I say I would do it?

Last night, like every night since Skaftartunga, you walked barefoot on my back, pressing me deeper into existence, instilling your buoyancy into my spine: So why do I feel so sad now?

Austari-Jökulsá

A seven-man raft where chance supersedes control and group individual is not your idea of how to run white water. Still, you were game for a go down the East Glacial River. So, in wetsuit and dry top, life jacket, helmet, booties and gloves, we placed ourselves under the authority of a guide, made up a crew with a German couple and two Japanese men, and ran the turbulent river. For you, white water meant *wearing* a kayak, sitting low in the river with your hips, butt, knees and feet in direct contact with the boat, assuring maximum control: The raft was an altogether different experience, more funfair ride than test of skill. The guide and crew were good, though, and so we followed a tongue into a rapid, punched effectively through hydraulics, used the upstream current of an eddy to regain control, and generally made the most of our paddle power. We completed the run with no wraps, flips or pins, though the German woman did go for a swim. And thus, by antithesis, I gained some sense of what you experience when you go kayaking: immersion in the power of moving water while managing the risks alone. I didn't get to see you do a combat roll or midstream turn, a flat spin or kick flip, but nevertheless I did delight in the way you blossom when risk is present.

All in all, then, we did not return to the undifferentiated state, we did not flow down to the sea. Nor did we return to the divine source by rafting against the current. Instead, we made of the river a river of grace, one more place where you tried to teach me that separation is a constitutive aspect of love—not its negation—and that faithfulness to the flux of life is the supreme fidelity.

Sauðárkrókur

White foam on charcoal, sky overcast, air crisp and cool. Black, your sneakers rhyme with my boots; blue, your sweater matches my mood. Look! An old wreck of a herring boat: my ribcage with my heart ripped out. Enough! Your eyes don't say you're far away, they say you're immediate to me; your hand in mine doesn't speak of the past, it celebrates the present: Would that I could forget the future is foreclosed.

Weaving and unweaving their watery motifs, the waves roll in to reproach me: I have not fought hard enough, I have been too acquiescent. Fight? For the Kingdom of Love? If she is Lear, am I Cordelia; if I am Lear, she is the Fool. I cannot keep her: She keeps her word.

> If tragedy is ruled out by free love,
> The rites of separation withstand;
> If undoing our ties undoes me,
> What of the telling of a story that ends?
>
> What remains?
> Your blue sweater, your black cap,
> Your long hair loose;
> Your smile, your walk,
> The touch of your hand.
>
> Must it end, my love?
> I still have so much to learn.
> You are the sea,
> Refusing no river yet never filled,
> Washing every shore yet never emptied:
> You are inexhaustible
> And everything is mine to learn
>
> Must it end?

— Look, Sprague, driftwood. I wonder if it's from Siberia.
You hand me the stick you've picked up.
— Could be.
Would that it were a hazel-wand: I'd wave it to make you stay.
— It's very hard, it's saturated with salt.
— Yes.
In a flash your sneakers are off your feet; you pull off your socks and roll up your jeans. I bend to slip out of my boots.
— Catch me if you can!
Doing anew what I adore, once more you're ahead of me: Through the swash, the icy backwash, through the freezing slack-water and uprush, you take me to

the realm of the senses, there where sensation regenerates. Marietta! I love the spiral matrix of your moves, I love your puckish mobility; you are the blue wolf that takes away my blues, you are the red fox that enlightens me: I love you from your eyelashes to your fundamental eye, I love you from the ends of your hair to the tips of your toes.

I like bearing the weight of your body, I like your legs wrapped around me: Across the beach I carry you to an incline of grass. Be still, and still, and know: I seat you on the slope. Into my hands I take your foot. Incarnation of creatureliness, equilibrium in chaos; conductor of the numinous, stopper of the mind's stuff: Raising your leg with one hand, with the other I sweep the sand from your foot: May it come, the fullness of denudation, the living in depth; may it come, the transfiguration. A thousand grains of black grit speckle the white of your skin: It is too late to set your womb alight, but there is time enough to eat the earth through every pore. At the ceremony there are no witnesses, it's just you and me here. Here in this empty space where the wind blows; here, between fire and water, where I worship your feet. I whip them with my hair. I bring heat and colour to their cold wet whiteness. My palm I marry to the instep, my fingers to the toes. With my nails I trace the lumbricals, with the heel of my hand the soles. Yes, I brush the silt of existence from your feet until they glow with the serenity of essence. In that light I hunger for the absolute, for a naked encounter with our truth. The waterside is a holy place. Marriages are solemnized here. So why not separations? In my hands your foot is a vital force, a reverberation of correspondences between my origin and my end. I fooled myself, Marietta. In my heart of hearts I always knew I was not made for happiness. Which is why, during this ceremony, I am filled with gratitude. Yes, I thank you for the joy you've given me, the inexpungible joy of the life we shared. I love you, and it's killing me...

– Sprague, I'm here, with you.

Ashes to ashes, dust to dust, and salt water to the sea...

Chapter 11

Thursday, September 8

Snæfellsnes

In the austere glory of the landscape you lie on a jut of rock, your hair golden on its moss-green cushion, your body clothed in black. Confronted with the tumultuous sea, blue sky and white mountain remain imperturbable: like you confronted with me? No, it's not as clear-cut as that. Last night it was you that cried and I who upheld your resolve. Isn't that strange? Yes, if I felt less outlawed by my own desire, if your tears made me feel more human, I nevertheless have too much respect for you to press you under duress: free you must love me, free you must leave me.

You could yearn for your virginity
When we make love;
You could hold back and be evasive
When we talk.
You do not.

Instead, you look me in the eye,
You beat your wings and burn me.

You could play hide-and-seek,
You could leave me in the lurch.
You could be present
Without being present to me.
You could say,
Wrapping cruelty in generosity,
'Let us remain friends'.
You do not.

Instead, you fold a lesson in ethics
Into your lesson in love,
You give me the lushness of your presence
In this barren landscape.

Is that why,

In this phantasmagoric geology,
In this distillation of the elements
To their essence,
I feel such humility?

Driving to Reykjavik

It's not a band of gold, but it is a ring: Late afternoon, less than an hour to Reykjavik, we're about to close the circle on our Icelandic escapade. We've spent eleven days circling our love, eleven days giving it a circumference: Once its centre was everywhere and its circumference nowhere. I'm looking forward to the evening, I'm looking forward to our three nights in Hotel Matthías, to dinner, dancing, the concert. Come Sunday we'll be on a plane back to London. One more fortnight together then I'll be on my own, alone, without you forever: I shudder at the thought.

– I'm looking forward to Reykjavik, Sprague.
– Me too! But won't you miss driving the Saab?
– No. I love my MX-5. But I'll probably miss the Saab's backwards-sliding bonnet, the key in the floor, the crazy sweep of the windshield-wipers.
– You're a funny woman, Marietta.
– Am I? I've grown fond of all that. Not to mention how everything behind us gets small very quickly when I shift into high gear!

The smile you give me melts my heart; I hang on to my dignity lest I fall down at your feet.

Reykjavik

Hotel Matthías: The restaurant

Violet, the tea light flickers between us: Love's fulfilment, purification by fire? No: Light may reveal, but it is shadow that defines and gives form. So what will the shadow make visible, what will the buried seed bring forth? May it be roses! Aye, but of what quality? The bright expansiveness of the yellow, the impulsive passion of the red, the innocence and secrecy of the white? Or perhaps the impossible of the blue? I don't know, but I do know what's on the menu: For you, it's sautéed langoustines with wine-shallot remoulade on mini rösti; smoked lamb with rose pepper, dates and cashews; sorbet of skyr with lemon and liquorice sponge. And for me, mussels with chilli, ginger and einstök beer; salmon with lobster sauce and marinated shrimps, carrot pureé and scallops; mascarpone ice cream with chocolate, raspberries, dill and skyr.

– Imagine her jet-black hair and ruby-red nails, her glowing skin and dark eyes; imagine the flash of the dagger as time and again she stabs it between her fingers. Picasso wanted to change his life, he was ready to fall in love. That afternoon on the terrace of the Deux-Magots was when Dora Maar seduced him.

Over the meal, we spoke of the master and his mistress: In your purse you'd discovered a bookmark from the Picasso Museum in Barcelona.

– What I don't get, Sprague, is why as soon as his women got close to him, he turned them into doormats.

– They weren't all like Dora Maar. Françoise Gilot never let him wipe his shoes on her. And Jacqueline Roque always had the upper hand. She appealed to the worst in him, and it worked. She didn't commit suicide until thirteen years after he died.

– And what about Marie-Thérèse Walter?

– She hanged herself four years after Picasso's death.

– But Dora—

– She said, 'After Picasso, there is only God'. She sought refuge in religion.

– What a man! But why did he go in for this goddess-to-doormat thing? Why would he need to abuse and humiliate?

– He had a genius for manipulation. Never allowed himself to be vulnerable, always insisted on complete control. What's behind that, we'll never know.

Hotel Matthías: The bar

On a long, low-lying sofa, in a pocket of light from a paper lantern, you sit opposite me, one leg folded under you, your Mata Hari in your hand. How is it that your black stretch blazer, so perfectly fitted to your body, takes nothing away from your air of languid abandonment? Just as the thought crosses my mind, you stand up, take it off, and resume your position. Your grey suede boot on the olive-green leather, your black camisole and Burgundy pants, the way you sip your drink—is it that that has turned your languid abandonment into a positively exuberant lassitude?

The bar is surprisingly full for a Thursday; the local crowd is mingled in with the foreign guests. Look! In the night sky the lanterns glow: a Magritte effect of the glass. You ask me about Mata Hari. (You take it for granted now that I'm a walking dictionary of biography.) So I tell you the story of Margaretha Zeller, the Dutch woman who mastered the art of femininity and was murdered for it. I tell you of her attraction to men who could fascinate her the way her father did; I tell you that it was in the Dutch East Indies that she became the 'eye of the day'. Sipping my blend of spirits, spices and juices, I tell you that in the context of the war, a woman who travels widely and sleeps with whoever she wants to simply couldn't be tolerated. The French convicted her on no evidence whatsoever. She had the effrontery to be shameless, and she paid for it with her life. And then I segue into the story of another Dutch woman, one I really admire: Xaviera Hollander. I tell you that she too had an adored, dashing father; that she too spent time in Indonesia and in a transit camp before becoming the free woman who was the Happy Hooker. 'Let's try to visit her the next time we're in Amsterdam', I'm just about to say, and then I remember that we'll never be in Amsterdam together again.

Marietta, how can I live in the world knowing you're in it but having to pretend you're not? How can I think of you in the past when you will always be present to me? Don't you see you're asking the impossible of me?

Love is not a pact, but complicity; only thus can we find what is profound in pleasure: In bed, once again, you proved it to me.

Chapter 12

Friday, September 9

Reykjavik

Hotel Matthías: Our suite

'What bitter's love but yurning, what sour lovemutch but a bref burning till shee that drawes dothe smoake retourne?' Lying on the sofa in our suite while you're out shopping, I hone my wit on the stone of *Finnegans Wake*. On cue, you return just when I get to Issy's interrogation: 'Of I be leib in the immoralities? O, you mean the strangle for love and the sowiveall of the prettiest?' You're used to my laughing out loud at the *Wake*, so you simply say:

– Hi.

– Hi.

Glossing 'It's Dracula's nightout. For creepsake don't make a flush!', I call out:

– Did you find what you were looking for?

– I did, my darling.

On cat's paws you've come to me; I turn around and I'm transfixed: In red hair you stand before me, inhabiting your glory with utter conviction. I am moved to silence.

– So, what do you say?

– You take my breath away, Marietta. You're amazing!

You flick back your side-swept bangs. Sleek and straight, your long hair spills its vibrant copper to just below one breast, leaving the rest to tumble down your back from the side part.

– Do you like it?

– I love it!

– Long and straight makes a better whip than wavy. Do you like the colour?

– It's perfect!

It's not just your hair, it's your whole presence that's metamorphosed: Your body is speaking a new language, one I'm eager to learn.

– I've bought some new colours to go with it.

– Colours?

– Make-up. And that pair of shoes I couldn't forget.

– From the store where you bought your crazy-coloured sneakers?

— Yes.

— And what's in the big bag?

— You'll see tonight.

— I can't wait!

Your striking look inspires me to renew myself: Already I feel invigorated.

The miracle of you
Wings my heart
The miracle of you
Sings me

The miracle of you
Iridesces my soul
The miracle of you
Dreams me

The miracle of you
Intimate, without limit
The miracle of you
Heals me

Gathering up your bags, you say:

— How about room service tonight? This suite's so lovely.

— Yes! I'll get the menu.

— And the wine list!

Your eyes sparkling, you turn and take your bags to the bedroom.

Pale blue and chocolate brown, sage green and cream: Is it the coppery glory of your hair that makes the room's colour scheme sing? And as you lie there on the sofa, leafing through *The Observer,* is it the majesty of your mane that accounts for your laid-back solemnity?

— Hey, Isabelle Huppert's got a new film coming out.

— Oh yeah? What is it?

— *Amateur*. An American film. Hal Hartley.

— Never heard of him.

— And also...

— What?

— Boy, somebody up there likes you!

— What is it? Tell me!

— Adjani's got a new film out too!

– Really?

– Yes. *La Reine Margot.* Patrice Chéreau.

– Wow!

Over dinner (lamb meatballs and spiced rice, a bottle of Rioja Alavesa) we spoke of the two actresses who move us both so. Adjani: Animal, instinctive, passionate. The voice classy, the diction perfect. Her eyes, blue wells of emotion; sparkling, sublime. Her body? Always in movement... Huppert: Interiority. Ice. Under the ice, not fire, but emotion contained, intense. Body impassive. Lips thin and nervous. A low-pitched voice, urgent and commanding. Eyes? Green as standing water, ambiguous, complex...

– If you had to choose, Sprague, which one would it be?

– You know.

– Adjani?

– Yes.

– Why?

– The searing beauty of breaking down! Her generosity. Stripping down to a truth, rather than trying to build it up. And you?

– I'd choose Adjani too. It's her physicality that really moves me. The way she acts with her whole body. The urgency in her playing, the way she courts risk.

– She's exciting, yes, she makes a scene come alive.

– I just wish she were offered more scripts that are worthy of her.

– Indeed. She's not meant to play Ophelia, but Hamlet.

– Adjani as Hamlet? I'd love to see that!

As you thrill to the possibilities, I thrill to your beauty: It's not bright, it's not dazzling; it's not ardour and vitality, free and victorious: No, the red of your hair is the red of the wine-dark sea—female, nocturnal, secret: It suits you perfectly. Yes, there's a new edge to your beauty, a deepening of your mystery. No perfume of hysteria wafts from your body, no monstrous aura of unfeeling beast: Only a smouldering sensuality, an intelligence of the dark.

Watching you walk to the bedroom as you leave to get ready, I notice a change in your carriage: No longer with the decided step of your wilful self nor the gangling gait of your nonchalance, you move with a sensual poise, at once laid-back and alert. I attune myself to the silence of the room.

the gleam of the floorboards
                the flow of the curtain wall
the zen of the solitary flower

the uprightness of the lamp
the rhyming of the cushion colours
the softness of the rugs
the elegance of the tableware
the quiet of the walls—

A day will come, Marietta,
When I'll whirl these images like dice in a cup
And tumble them into a poem

There'll be nothing random in the result
For everything will testify
That on a Friday in Reykjavik in 1994
I loved you with a love
That was purer for your leaving

Buttoning my shirt, I step into the living room and stop in my tracks: Wow! In a black mini-dress you stand by the sofa, looking for something in your purse. Slashed into stripes, laced up at the back, black suede peep-toes echo your cut-away shoulders and racer back. Turning your head you swivel your torso; over your shoulder you toss me a smile. I say:

– Come here, my love.

Softly swaying as you walk to me, the skirt of your dress highlights the tight-fitting top. I place my hands on your hips as you stand before me, I contemplate your face.

Blue shadow, metallic sheen;
Edged in brown, a hard outline:
In your eyes I am the fire.

Redefined, darkened,
Arched and tapered out:
In your brows I am the arrow.

Cupid's bow, mahogany;
The light that lives in darkness:
In your breath I am the spark.

– Marietta, you'd bring eyesight to the blind!

– And legs to the lame?

– Yeah!

You flick my lips with the tip of your tongue.

— I can't go out with these sandals though. It's too cold.

You step away.

— You're really hot in them!

— Not enough to warm my feet! I'll wear my ankle boots.

Does a man's body holds less mystery for a woman than a woman's body for a man? As you sit on the sofa, changing your shoes, I am moved by the grace of your movements. Such a simple act, sitting. Yet a woman has to master the art of crossing her legs without drawing attention to herself; she has to guard against revealing her tits: A man can plonk himself down any old how.

Bióbarinn

In the bar I played the Seedy Friedrich card, the perfect ice breaker. In with a group of lively locals, we sipped our highballs of Tanqueray and tonic and spoke of islands, music, and the ambivalence of Pisces. Your surfed the dark edge of your redhead personality, playing to perfection the role of rock 'n roll girlfriend. Then someone came in to announce that in the screening room upstairs two short films—Maya Deren's *Meshes of the Afternoon* and Buñuel's *Un Chien andalou*—would soon be starting. I knew them well and thought you'd like them; we decided to go and see them.

We stepped upstairs into the little cinema and stepped into Maya Deren's dream; fifteen minutes later, Buñuel's call to murder came across as a decidedly dated scream.

Minja frá draumi

You say:

— They're both about sex. Buñuel plays up repression; Deren focuses on the woman's ambivalence. I find her film much more interesting.

Inspirited by mojitos, we talk through the din in Souvenir from a Dream.

— Why?

— There's no political posturing, no silly fetishism. She expresses a woman's point of view. She doesn't need Church and Police to show that sex is transgressive.

— I agree. Her film is poetic—it doesn't impose, it resonates.

— It's a feminine film.

— Yes. But I find *Chien andalou* holds up better than you suggest.

— I liked the vaudeville!

— And what about the razor slicing open the eye?

— A vicious metaphor! Gave me a jolt, but when I saw the jelly falling out I quickly recovered.

You take my glass and finish my mojito.

— Let's go dancing!

As I suck up the last of your highball through your lipstick straw, you lower your head and look at me through your locks: Amber through copper turns desire into seduction.

— Let's go!

Kaleidoscope Klub

Shaking your body free from the bonds of the perishable, you regenerate time in the instant consumption of energy. Feel it! To a riffing synth you sculpt the air while backbeat clap and bass drum, open hat and snare, pulse your blood with syncopation. Look! White light pierces the blue, the void opens to infinity: Your hair pinned up, your long legs bare, you take me there. Marietta, this is how I love to love you, this is how you'll remain in my memory: dancing to a drum in a circle of fire, your rapture restoring my animality.

Now there's an acid bounce to the synth wash, an offbeat to the kick pattern. Feel it! Your arms become a shining glory of omni-dimensional moves, your pelvis a pivot for your legs and torso. Look! Red light pierces the green, the serpent enters Eden: Your hair concealing your eyes, your racerback revealing your flesh, you bite the apple and give me knowledge. Marietta, this is the pattern of repetition, this is the eternal return: This is our asylum.

Now the backbeat syncopation gives way to a steady four-on-the-floor; with exquisite sensuality you lock into the groove. Feel it! Your undulating body alternates profiles; in the pause from one to the other, you toss back your head and recover it in a caress. Look! Yellow light pierces the black, differentiating chaos into a cosmos: Your hair, flying loose as you go wild, bodies forth power. Marietta, I love your courage, I love your pride; I love the way you refuse to conform to what you are ascribed: Always you escape their ascriptions.

Now varying loops are making polyrhythms, a fabric of synths punctuated by bass and drums. As soon as you find a point of orientation, your body becomes a dynamo. Feel it! Dissolving the temporal in the eternal, you expand your being in a choreography of grace. Look! Orange light pierces the blue, the emblem of lust enters the absolute: Your hair—generous, dark, mysterious—is loose and impulsive. Marietta, as you cradle your flame, I safeguard your obscurity: You are inexhaustible, and everything is mine to learn.

Hotel Matthías: Our bedroom

The bare walls' cream is orange-tinged, echoing the coral accents on the rug's khaki ground. Diffusing its opaline glow through a blown-glass dome, a lamp stands low on each nightstand. Parrots and budgerigars brighten the black percale bedskirt; a contour light under the frame floats the bed off the floor. Like the walls, the cream sheets radiate an orangey warmth. Naked, a man lies on his back, his head thrown over the foot of the bed. Standing with her legs open above his face, a woman bends forward and whips him with her hair.

Is it thus, my love, that I pay my debt to time? Is it thus that I find redemption? In this blossoming of pleasure, in this carnal complicity with you? With every swish of the lash, the whip of your hair declares your love; with every smart stroke you remind me of the miracle of our encounter. Now as the nudity of your sex holds my gaze captive, its glistening involutions open. To the unending rose I bring my lips; to its dewy petals, my tongue. As your attar feeds my ardour, you redouble your lashings. Marietta, you are the phoenix, I am the dove; consumed in your fire, I am resurrected: 'Love hath reason, reason none, if what parts can so remain.' And thus, even as we separate, we are one in flame. Swish, swish, swish! With the silk of your hair you whip me till I see with my pineal eye; with your fiery locks you lash me till I am I and need no reason why.

'One is always wrong, but with two, truth begins': Watching you as you lie sleeping, I find, for the first time, Nietzsche's aphorism limpid. Is it because happiness simplifies life that I finally understand the saying? It must be, because suddenly sadness comes upon me and I no longer know what it means.

Chapter 13

Saturday, September 10

Reykjavik

Baltamákur Tónleikasalur

I've always enjoyed the pre-show buzz, those few minutes before the curtain goes up on a performance. The hall is packed and (thanks to Konrád) we're sitting in the best seats. We'd had brunch at eleven-thirty, then lazed into a stay-at-home afternoon, stirring ourselves only to take a walk along the shoreline at Álftanes. Later, at Vegamót, we met Steinar and Eygló for a dinner of tagliatelle and lobster tails. And now you're sitting beside me, your red hair loose over your black T-shirt, a spider of black spinel sitting Gothic in the V-neck.

'Lamento III: Friede', for soprano and piano

Andreas Gryphius / Karl Amadeus Hartmann

Down the keyboard a chromatic descent makes it clear that art is my home and exile my state: Love is but the madness that impels me from one to the other. Over the driving turbulence of the piano, over the staccato dissonance and the crashing chords, the voice of a survivor in a field of corpses comes to offer thanks. Now into silence the piano trills, breaking the singer into prayer. From the hollows within her body, a voice comes to plead for the living after the massacre. So this is the song you first heard at the Kluge's house in Corfu, the song by a composer who moved you in that summer of '73. Perpetrator, victim, bystander? Mastering the art of inner emigration, from within Nazi Germany he bore witness, making a music of protest and mourning while living a life of resistance. And thus, in your discussions with Jürgen's family, Hartmann offered an illustration of how resistance can surpass the human, all too human, trilogy.

Look at the singer: Her hair is exactly the same red as yours, the red of copper in the evening sun, the copper by which gods enter the ear drum. Does she remind you of Mara? She does me. Listen! Now fiercely tender, now declamatory, there's depth and immediacy in her every phrase. How does she manage to combine such authority with vulnerability? Look at the pianist: The curl of his fingers, the relaxation of his wrist, as spider-like he spins out a soft, fluid legato—only to execute a violent, flat-fingered attack right after. I look at you and I am moved: The moist glow of your eyes tells me you're thinking of Matteo. And thus, into this juxtaposition of the Third Reich and the Thirty Years War, into this song of suffering and remembrance, comes the death of a friend. Dark-hued, entreating, the singer's voice captures your emotion.

From *Four Poems from 'Atemwende' by Paul Celan,* for voice and piano

Wolfgang Rihm

'In the Rivers'

Tossing off three arpeggios, the pianist tosses me into expectation: I am a fisherman, casting out the net which you have weighted with stones. Hesitating, you wondered whether one more stone would be one too many, one less one too few: You have found the right tension, for in the clear water my net is suspended (the shadows of the stones tell me so). There is nothing to do now but wait. Listen: The music makes no claim to grasp meaning, the voice pursues its own phantoms. Before it's over, Marietta, tell me: Why are you leaving me? Haven't we been good at managing the distance that makes intimacy possible? Haven't we found the right tension, the tension that allows us—time and time again—to sparkle in our self-becoming? Oh set your stones again, my love, the river has not yet reached the sea; let me cast the net again, beyond what you and I can see: Do you no longer have faith in me?

From *Nocturnes and Arias,* for soprano and orchestra

Aria I: 'In the Storm of Roses', Ingeborg Bachmann / Hans Werner Henze

Over harp-plucked arpeggios, woodwinds and strings, the full-blooded soprano soars; dark and dramatic, she sweeps me up into this evocation of a relationship gone wrong. I lose my bearings, lost in the myriad modulations: So this is the architecture of breakdown, this is the fog that enfolds when rhythm becomes unfixed and tone has no home. I cling to the words of the poem, the poem that Ingeborg Bachmann slipped into a letter to her ex-lover, Paul Celan. For all its dissonance, the music is ravishingly lyrical, alternating vehement strings with the understated violence of woodwinds.

Do you know, my love, the story that gave rise to this anguished song? It goes like this: At the crossroads of the twin plagues, in 1942, a young man from a

German-speaking Jewish family tries in vain to persuade his parents to escape while there is still time. The parents stubbornly insist on staying; in a fit of anger the son leaves the house. That very night, the Masters of Death come to arrest his parents. In a forced labour camp the father dies of disease; worked to exhaustion, the mother is shot in the head. Wracked by guilt, the son is overcome, traumatized by the consequences of what he did and failed to do. He survives the war, and three years after its end moves to Paris. There, writing in German, he pursues the practice of poetry.

In Austria, in 1938, a twelve-year-old girl finds her father jubilant after the incorporation of her country into the Third Reich. A full-fledged Nazi from the earliest hour, he is finally free to openly devote himself to the Masters of Death. She grows up to become a famous poet, known for her visceral opposition to Fascism. Torn between her passion for truth and her need to deny, she will never be frank about her father.

In Germany, in 1935, a nine-year-old boy is enrolled in the Hitler Youth. In 1942 he begins his musical studies. In 1944 he is conscripted and promptly captured; he waits out the war in a British prisoner-of-war camp. After the war, he resumes his studies and becomes a composer. In 1953, elated as if rescued from a disaster—from the beginning he had hated the Masters of Death—he crosses the Alps into Italy, the country in which he will make his home.

In Vienna, in January 1948, the Austrian poet meets the poet from the crossroads; they strike up a friendship, and later a love affair. In Paris, in 1950, they live together for two months. The relationship is turbulent; the couple never manage to set it on a stable footing. In 1952 the poet from the crossroads marries a French woman. That same year, the Austrian poet meets the German composer; a year later, she visits him in Italy and they end up living and working together (he is homosexual). She writes 'In the Storm of Roses'. A few years later, she adds a second stanza and sends it to the poet in Paris. The new stanza speaks of a leaf he had given her; she says in her letter that though the leaf is no longer in her medallion, it is not lost: She still thinks of him. The composer sets the poem to music. In 1970, in Paris, the poet from the crossroads jumps off the Pont Mirabeau and drowns himself in the Seine. In 1973, in Rome, the Austrian poet—no longer living with the German composer—suffers serious burns when an unextinguished cigarette sets her bedroom ablaze. Hospitalized, she is deprived of the barbiturates she is addicted to and suffers seizures as a result. She dies a few weeks later. The German composer is devastated by her death; his music takes a darker turn. When they would write to each other, they would often write in Italian, and occasionally English and French: Where the poet from the crossroads cultivated an ever-greater intimacy with the German language, the two friends who felt ashamed of their parents and homeland needed to distance themselves from it. Listen! The singer ends the song, speaking of a leaf floating towards the mouth of a river.

Did you hear, my love, in the maelstrom of this music, the nexus of relations in which the song arose? Did you hear the anguish at the intersection of history, family, and vocation? In sum, did you hear how happiness is overcome by horror?

'Mysteries of the Macabre', concert aria for coloratura soprano

Gyorgy Ligeti (arrangement by Elgar Howarth)

Bongos, maracas and castanets, glockenspiel, police whistle and tom-tom: Together with brass, strings and woodwinds, the percussion weaves a texture of hysteria that the soprano pierces with coloratura cries. Going from raucous gibberish to biting interjections, soaring flights to bird-like calls, she is desperately trying to make conductor and instrumentalists understand the urgency of what she's reporting. The conductor doesn't give a damn, the musicians rise in defiance. *'Ja! Nein! Nein! Ja! Nein! Nein! Ja! Ja! Nein':* Is she a whore on heels, a chorus girl seeking a cancan? Is she Cassandra in an ecstatic trance or Oedipus back from the Oracle? *'Kakakakakakastrophe! Er kommt! Er kommt! Er kommt!'* Of what is she so afraid? In a tizzy of trepidation she reaches a paroxysm of panic; her hair flies out as her fear mounts: *'Er ist schon da! Er ist schon da! Er ist schon da!'* Perhaps she's an escapee from Pitié-Salpêtrière or a visionary of divine vengeance? Maybe she's being ravished by an incubus, reliving the trauma of Red Riding Hood? No. She is Gepopo, chief of the secret police of Brueghelland and *de facto* angel of death: She has come to warn the Prince that the end of the world is at hand. And thus we relive Ligeti's ironic take on the Requiem: The alienation induced by the grotesque, a means to overcome the fear of death.

And we, Marietta, how do we accommodate the exterminating angel? Last night after we made love, when I said I would die for you, you said nobody can die in the place of another; when I said it's an enormous responsibility, the irreplaceability of one's death, you said that's precisely why you feel guilty: You could never be responsible enough. *Er! Er! Er! Er ist schon da! Schon da! Da! Da! Da! Da! Da!* The Secret Police Chief finally ceases her hysteria; in a bubble of calm, the redhead recomposes herself as the applause thunders down.

Intermission

Outside, the night is infinite, the air crisp and cool.

– Does it make you feel like being on stage yourself, Marietta, a performance like that?

– No, I'm happy to be in the audience. It's nice to be able to relax and just enjoy it.

Lights glitter on dark water; for a fleeting moment, my hand in yours finds eternity in the instant.

Your red hair, your royal blue jacket;
Your white sneakers, ghostly in the night:
How you move me!
Suddenly the wind rises, I feel a chill in my teeth:
I'm thirty-four, but I feel old.

– Look Sprague, how bright the stars are!

Are the stars twinkling, or is it me that's trembling? You throw your arm around my waist; as we walk, you press your body to mine.

Do not show me stars:
I don't want to conceive of distances.
Do not hold me too closely:
I may never let you go.

– We'll go to the boats then turn back, okay?

– Okay.

The lapping of the water,
The sailors' lullaby;
The lapping of the water—
Boys don't cry.

– Look!

You run to a bollard and leap up onto it; you do a little tap dance.

– You're radiant, my love!

– All the better to light you up!

Dancing, you dance me out of time.

You are all the moments
We have lived together;
You are all the lightness
I'm about to lose.

Jumping off the bollard, you say:

– Race you back!

Neither one of us can outdistance the other; breathless, at the entrance to the hall we embrace.

Kafka Fragments, for soprano and violin – Part 3

Franz Kafka, *Diaries, Notebooks, Letters* / György Kurtág

In the spotlight on an all but empty stage they stand, the violinist and the singer. He is dressed in black. She's draped in a white tunic. Fluid, the silk flows in a loose silhouette to the knees of her black leggings. Her high collar isolates her face; her red hair is pulled back into a ponytail. Listen! There's anxiety in the violin's elegy, restlessness in the soprano's lyricism: the fecund tension of ambiguity.

You and Mara scored a triumph with your Munich recording, a triumph only outdone by your subsequent recitals. Is there enough variation now for you to make a comparison between your interpretations? Given the brevity of the pieces and the detail of the score, can one even speak of interpretation? The answer comes when I recall that every high-wire walker apprehends their fall in their own way, that every acrobat walks a tightrope differently. I think of my bedsit on Palmerston, the dark wood panelling, the damask wallpaper; I think of my lonely bed and late nights reading Franz: In becoming animal I became an artist.

Listen! The voice takes on an oboe-like drone while a tuning-peg glissando gives the violin a flute-like shimmer: In this music as in Kafka, there's no place for complacency. I think of my bay window and the foreclosure of my future; I think of Franz's answer to Felice when she asked him about his prospects: 'Needless to say I have no plans, no prospects; I cannot step into the future'.

Listen! The violin's left-hand pizzicati; the voice, resonant and staccato. With Felice, Franz was insufferable in his suffering. How could he ever have imagined he could be happy as her husband? And yet he was always lucid: 'On the pretext of wanting to free you of me, I force myself upon you'. The better match was Milena: Franz just couldn't overcome his fear.

Listen! The paring away of the inessential, the sculptural purity of concentrated sound: Fragment after fragment confirms the depth of the music, the depth of the darkness the spotlight lays bare. Kafka at Goethe's house, flirting for days with the keeper's daughter: Is there a link between his success with Greta and his failure with Milena? Might not his ease with girls be the other side of the coin of his difficulty with women? Could it be that girls, simply by accepting him as he was, gave him a sense of unconditional love that sexuality precluded women from giving? However great his lucidity about the world, it was not as great as his yearning for intimacy, a lasting intimacy with just one woman who—as he wrote to Milena—would enfold him. I think of you, I think of how you enfold me, and I feel the world falling away beneath my feet at the thought that you're leaving.

Listen! Slow, full of rubato, the violin plays a shivery undertow to the singer's soft parlando; as she ends the vocal fragment—a diary entry about hiding places and paths to salvation—the violin simultaneously plays a trill and a glissando: Marietta, ever since you told me you are leaving, you have refused all hiding places. Instead, you have been with me continually, in unending loving-kindness. I accept that you are leaving. I accept there'll be no explanation. I even accept that you'll never speak to me again. And yet, if there is to be salvation for me, you will have been my path to it: I will honour you in language because that's all I'll have left.

Listen! Now fleeting as from afar, now full and familiar, the singer sings of two violinists making music in a tram speeding through the streets; now slow and sentimental, now fiery and free, the violinist plays, first on one violin, then on another: Capturing the charm of Kafka's 'Scene on a Streetcar', the musicians remind us that all his life, Franz was moved by the most simple things. And I, Marietta, what moves me? I am moved by the child struggling to hold back his tears, not by the child who cries; I am moved by the dog on his last legs, his dignity when he steals away to die; I am moved by the wallflower who dances alone, not by the one who fades away. When you're gone, I will try to be worthy of the child, the dog and the wallflower.

Ollea, four poems by Heinrich Heine for unaccompanied soprano

Aribert Reimann

Naked, the voice lays bare the soul as the naked body cannot. Listen! The poem conveys a feeling of life ebbing from the body, but the voice refuses the facility of illustration. Instead, as the singer moulds the air in her mouth, she gives it a cold, silvery shimmer. Taking the vampire by the hand, she adopts a stance of distance: Love is colder than death, and it's not effusion of feeling that can capture that.

Listen! From her diaphragm, through the modulating chamber of her mouth, comes a perfection of pitch, a purity of tone, that derive from the indifferent stars. And yet, despite that starry distance, the singer is bodily and spiritually present. In her voice I feel her singularity: Its overtones are echoes from her past; its relief, the terrain of her experience. Penetrating her receptivity, I am an arabesque of breath; caressing the hollows of her body, I am the air she spins and expels. Her voice is not a promise, her voice is not a lure: It is the pure presence of her being.

Listen! Now she's repeatedly attacking the same syllables, she's undermining naïveté. And thus once again she takes a detour to gain access: Her voice is a diamond that doesn't blind with its sparkle, but shines with an inner light: The more I lay myself open to that light, the more present I am to myself; the more present I am to myself, the more I admire you. Silence. We rise to our feet together with all in the concert hall. In bestowing this lavish applause, to whom am I really giving thanks and praise?

'Naturtränen'

Nina Hagen (arrangement for string quartet and soprano by Diljá Dögg Pálsdóttir)

What a delicious surprise! Transposed to string quartet, 'Naturtränen' is magical. Listen! Holding irony and innocence in tension, the soprano embodies the spirit of the song. Look! She takes me back to London, 1979. I was working on a screenplay on a gloomy Sunday when Jane came by with two tickets to see a German band. 'I heard Nina Hagen sings Schubert to Johnny Rotten', she said, 'let's go and see her, she's playing at the Lyceum'. A few hours later we were floored by the virtuosity that came from Nina's malleable mouth; the songs were excellent and the band kick-ass. 'She's an original', Jane said, 'she's the real thing'. Yes, 'punk from East Berlin' was a pigeon-hole that couldn't confine her: Possessed of the sacred fire, she could fly. Now here she is being sung by a red-haired soprano in Reykjavik, a metempsychosis that testifies to the shamanic power of art. Is it not here where I belong, rather than in the throes of love? Marietta, go, if you must, but know that when you're gone, I'll love you through my powers as a shaman!

Listen! The singer now begins the ravishing vocalise. The beauty of her voice against the strings is overwhelming: If you've got to go, Marietta, go now, before the music's over: Enfolded in this voice, I can bear your leaving.

Listen! The exclamation that interrupts the coloratura blows me away just like it did in London; the guttural snarl that reclaims rock from opera moves me now just as it did then: If music renews itself in each performance, have I renewed myself? The viola drones under the violin harmony; the cello plays a heavy bass line. Well, have I renewed myself?

Listen! The singer is in the flow of her vocalise; she is at once aware and unselfconscious, focused and at ease. If she is your parting gift to me, my love, then go, go now: When the music's over, she will be with me.

Chapter 14

Under the streetlights the red of your hair goes through a thousand hues, a thousand facets of what you mean to me, a thousand blessings I'm about to lose. The rhyme of your steps with mine is the rhythm that runs through my language; your hand in mine is the touch that redeems my vagabondage. On your biker jacket the epaulettes are the insignia of your independence; the zipper aslant your breasts is the mark of you singularity. Lamb-soft, the leather is my tenderness for you; royal-blue, the colour is the dignity I'm trying not to lose. Now let me put my love in your pockets, there where you can find it at will; let me slip it under your collar, where it may warm you when the wind turns chill. Marietta, I love you in your sneakers, I love you in your jeans, but when you're gone I'll only be able to love you in my dreams. So tonight I'll slip off your bra and taste your strawberry creams, I'll roll you over and ream you till nothing is what it seems. As if reading my mind, you throw your arm around my waist and draw me closer to you. Under a streetlight we pause: Delicate and dark the kiss comes, a smooth, supple melter with a long, persistent finish.

– Everything she did onstage—even the simplest gesture—she did with utter conviction.

So saying, I resume our conversation.

– Yes. Which is not to say there isn't also calculation. You're naked up there as a soloist. You've got to generate energy and make the audience work. Never give them exactly what they want. Otherwise, you're just a whore.

I think of the man with the muted trumpet, I think of his style and grace.

You remind me of Miles, Marietta. You've got the same defiant dignity onstage.

– You think so?

– It's certain! Your refusal to be a whore makes you his soul sister.

– Brother Miles and sister Marietta!

– Yeah!

Pulling you closer to me, I align my stride with your swagger. I must have been mad, a moment ago, to think, 'If you've got to go, go now'. I will make the most of every remaining minute: To the end I will be open to grace. Under a streetlight we pause: This time the kiss comes with a powerful, bursting individuality, beginning with the impression we were made for each other and ending with the certainty. Am I wrong to believe that even as your day of leaving is fast approaching, the sensation you experienced was not too different from mine?

Chapter 15

Sunday, September 11

Looking out into space over the north Atlantic, I feel your presence beside me. I, who usually rejoice at leaving a place behind, find myself sad to be leaving Iceland. Why? I know of no-one whose lover left them as tenderly as you're leaving me. Nor of anyone who denied their ex as definitively as you'll be denying me. Turning towards you I take your hand and hold it in mine on the armrest. At the sight of your feet in their domino-square socks, resting on the footrest—

> Wrap a baby in plastic,
> Keep him at one remove from the world.
> Never look into his eyes,
> Never touch him.
> Give him nothing
> But a wall to bang his head against.
> Then see if he doesn't drown
> In the least tenderness.

—I am touched: In your living room overlooking the southern edge of Hampstead Heath, I sat opposite you as you knitted them. We were listening to the second of Beethoven's late quartets, and I vividly remember, when the cavatina emerged from the danza tedesca, looking at you and saying to myself, 'I have no right to this happiness'. I was not wrong.

I let go of your hand and turn to look out the window. I must overcome this sadness, I must make the most of the next two weeks: I feel it's already over. What will we do in London? You'll be resuming your research, doing some teaching. I don't know what I'll be doing. Creative work is out of the question: I want to live out this loss, no matter how painful, not in my imagination but in reality. I might ask Gram if I can move in with him. Just for a while. Yes, I think I'll do that: His place is big enough for me to be alone. And should I need him, he'll be there.

– Marietta, how do you see the next two weeks?
– Exactly as I said: You stay with me. We live our normal lives. I've arranged my schedule so as not to be too busy.

– What I'd like is this: I stay with you for the first week, then I move in with Gram for the second. We still see each other every day, we still spend the nights together—if you'd like to—

– I'd love to! But be forewarned: I've got the decorators in on Wednesday and Thursday. You can always take the tradesman's entrance—if you'd like to—

– I'd love to!

– Good. All our nights together. And we see each when we can during the day. You can come to lunch at the Faculty Café. The rice pudding's delicious!

– All right. But I'd also like us to spend some time in my room at Gram's.

– With pleasure, Sprague. I think that's a very good idea.

– Yes, it would comfort me, when you're gone, to feel your presence there. Blood in the wind, a flutter in my mouth, flaming the air I breathe: I struggle to suppress a scream.

> Who do you think you are?
> Do you really believe there can be a transition?
> Are you so naïve to assume her ghost will comfort you?
> I tell you, there'll be no subtleties in the sunset:
> Upon a wasteland swept by an icy wind
> Darkness will descend, unvarying.
> Nothing will change that.
> Nothing and no-one.
> Face it.
> Didn't you say you want to live out this loss in reality?

– And do you think Gram will respect my way of doing things?

– Because I do, he will. Besides, you know he's got nothing but admiration for you.

– He loves you. That's more important. And Georgina and the children do too. You'll be in good hands.

– And you?

– I'll continue my life alone. I think I'm onto something big.

– Very big but very small?

– Yes.

– Quarks?

– Three quarks for Muster Mark! I'll be very busy.

– What you need, Marietta, to get to grips with your quark, is not *Finnegans Wake,* but *The Hunting of the Snark*.

– What's that?

– It's *An Agony in Eight Fits,* by Lewis Carroll.

– Oh, I'd love it, Sprague! Do get it for me!

– I will. And with Ralph Steadman's illustrations to boot.

Immediately nutty, the kiss comes, big and bold and punchy; backnotes of chocolate linger, with highlights of coffee and a hint of bitterness.

Chapter 16

Our first week in London was as glorious as our finest days in Iceland. Every day you delighted me with something you cooked, something your wore, something you said and something you did in bed.

The second week was even better. Gram was lovely with both of us, perfect in his timing of silence and speech. Georgina, expecting twins, was a benevolent goddess, as light in her touch as her body was heavy. The children—Aileen, Kirstie and Grace—all had a poise that spoke of a rich inner life even as they burned up their energy in action. Your ability to attune yourself to their individualities amazed me, and made me regret our failure even more.

Thursday you came home to find my birthday presents on your bed: an excess of Anglomania. Unable to decide what jacket to choose, I'd bought you three Vivienne Westwoods. I hoped you'd interpret it not as a sign of my insecurity but as a token of my knowing what would suit you: In charcoal and white, a pinstriped twill with an asymmetric hem and peaked lapels; in navy denim, a military jacket with a double-breasted placket and gold-striped cuffs; in black leather, a biker jacket with variable fastenings. You had the grace to interpret as haste my panicky indecision.

In the evening, at The Flask, we reminisced in laughter with Ariane and her Nicaraguan lover, moving on to share present news with equal good humour. In your new biker jacket, your white jeans and striped top, you were the coolest incarnation of chic: Was the black-and-white look your way of teaching me not to go over the top? At any rate, with your red hair flowing straight from your centre part, you looked ravishing. You and Ariane got on like a house on fire, as you always do, and when the talk turned to real houses on fire—occupied Palestine, Nicaragua—humour, black humour, prevailed.

Friday you wore the charcoal-and-white pinstripe to work, and in the evening, at your surprise party at Gram's, you were a hit in your military jacket and zip-pocket pants, your hair slicked back, braided ponytail wrapped into a bun: Was it you way of teaching me that one can pull anything off, provided the inner and the outer work in harmony? The party was joyous and easy-going, inspiring me with laughter and forgetting (I didn't forget it was the autumn equinox, but it didn't matter).

And then it was your turn to surprise me.

Chapter 17

And what a surprise! Saturday morning we set out in your MX-5 for a weekend on the Welsh Coast. Tearing down the motorway, I felt we were leaving on our honeymoon, and indeed the tenderness and pleasure we'd been experiencing with each other, far from waning, was waxing. I felt I was more worthy of you now, that at last I'd risen to the challenge of your leaving. So, as soon as we crossed the Severn Bridge, I took the initiative to announce that we would say goodbye on the coast, that I would not return with you to London but would stay on in Wales. Immediately you understood the sense of my decision. On the way through Carmarthen, then, we stopped at Avis and I chose a car. Thus it was in a Ford Fiesta, with *The Psychedelic Furs* for company, that I drove the last twenty-five miles to our destination, following your MX-5.

Arrival! We pull into the driveway of the place you've booked, a ranch-like bed and breakfast beautifully set along a river in the green isolation of Pembrokeshire. Our suite is magnificent. The lounge gives onto our private patio overlooking the river, the walk-in shower onto our own garden. I sweep you off your feet and carry you to the bed, I lay you down and cover your face in kisses. Marietta, it's not just a feeling—this really is our honeymoon. Yes, I am the shoreline, you are the sea; I am yours, as you belong to me. We've only got twenty-four hours left, twenty-four hours before you'll never see me again. It doesn't matter: As certain as all things must pass, I will love you till the last grain of sand in my hourglass.

Poppit Sands to Cemaes Head, Cemeas Head to Ceibwr Bay: Our three-and-a-half-hour hike along the Pembrokeshire Coast National Trail was an exhilarating encounter with sheer cliffs and expansive sea, sheltered coves and wide-open beach. Ascents and descents were steep; a brisk breeze blew intermittently. We came face-to-face with rock samphire in crevices and sea aster on ledges, lichen-covered boulders and moss-covered stone. And then, unfurling a carpet of colour, late-flowering gorse and red fescue, crested-hair grass and wild carrot, freshened the trails we walked through. As I climbed one steep slope after another, I wasn't Sisyphus shouldering my desire; as I contemplated the calm sea, I was not seeking enlightenment. No, I had my two feet firmly on the ground. I was happy. I didn't long for initiation, I didn't seek to penetrate the mysteries: You and I, walking the earth, that was enough for me.

In the evening, after dinner at the Black Lion Hotel and Bar in Cardigan, we lingered in the bar. I ordered a cherry brandy; you, a sloe gin.

– Don't you think you should settle down, Sprague, get yourself a home base?

– Why?

I was hoping you'd say, 'So I'd know where to find for you', but instead you said:

– Because you're an artist. And you haven't done anything yet.

– Nothing?

– Nothing approaching your potential.

– The lyrics don't count?

– No.

– And the poems?

– Neither. You've got to write a book. You've got it in you to write something of real breadth. If you continue rambling around, I think you're making it harder for yourself to get beyond road movies.

– I like road movies.

– But you've been trying for years to turn your fragments into a coherent fiction. You've gotten nowhere. I think you should try something different.

– What?

– You're an idiot, and you have to write your book as the idiot you are.

– Full of sound and fury, signifying nothing?

– No. More like your beloved Terence Stamp in *Teorema*.

– I see.

– It's who you are, Sprague. You're one of a kind.

You sip your sloe gin. Then, fixing me in the eye, you say:

– Do it. Do it for me.

I feel wings sprouting from my shoulder blades, I feel I'm about to fly.

– I'll do it, Marietta. I'll do it for you.

You take my cherry brandy and finish it; I finish your sloe gin.

Back in the MX-5, we head up the High Street. I am overwhelmed, uncomfortable in my wings; I try to hide my emotion by being flippant.

– I'll stay on at our riverside ranch. I'll get me a horse to replace you, and I'll become a Marlboro man.

– I saw a lovely sorrel mare on the way to Moylegrove. And if you miss the old Marietta, just outside St Dogmaels there's a beautiful palomino.

– I won't have to choose. I'll ride both. Hey, aren't we going the wrong way?

– Yes. But it's the right way. We're aren't going back to our big bed till midnight. I've got a little surprise for you first.

– Hmmm...

Twenty minutes later you were leading me through a wood, blanket in backpack and flashlight in hand. As your light swept through the leaves, I felt it was restoring flux to fixity, sweeping through our past in order to find us a future. The hoot of an owl raised the pitch of my excitement; bats roosting in branches turned my world upside down. 'Adventure', Marietta, is your middle name: I'd follow you anywhere. Listen! Hard upon the crash of breaking waves, the plash of spreading surf: The path opens up to a beach, a wide expanse of sand. Look! Beyond the reach of your flashlight, it stretches out on either side; shadowy presences loom in the darkness, then configure themselves into cliffs.

– This is Penbryn Beach. Isn't it lovely?

– It's magnificent!

– We'll walk a little way, and then we'll spread our blanket. We're going to lie down and look at the stars.

In the soft sand my bare feet bathe in a storehouse of the day's heat; in the torchlight spill your toes play hide-and-seek with themselves. After some distance we stop. You take out the lantern from Iceland and set it on the sand; together we spread our blanket. The whiteness of the lantern light gives an alabaster glow to your skin; your lavender scarf sets off your red hair, making you a Viking.

Oh conquer me, my beloved,
Claim me as your own;
Take me as your husband,
I will build you a home.

We'll live on fish and berries,
We'll live on knowledge and love;
We'll have a clutch of kids,
And books undreamed of.

Silence alone can honour the sublime; only the cosmic breath can open the bud: Lying beside you on the blanket, a plaid over our bodies, I am overcome by the numinous presence of a million stars. And I, what am I? I am flesh and bone animated by breath; I am saliva, blood and sperm. A thousand lights silver my nerves, through the pinholes of my pupils enters the universe.

– It's breathtaking, Marietta.

– It is. Would you like me to point out the constellations?

– Yes.

We sit up. You take a star chart from your backpack, along with a pair of binoculars.

– You see that long, fuzzy blob there?

– Yes.

– Look at it through the binoculars.

I lean back and look.

– Amazing!

– That's the Andromeda Galaxy. What you're seeing is only the bright, central region. It's got more than twice as many stars at the Milky Way.

– And how many does that make?

– Close to a trillion. They're so far away, their light takes over two million years to reach us.

– Don't forget, Marietta, once I get past my fingers and toes, I can't count any further.

– All right. It's unimaginably far away. Now look at the chart. This is the great square of Pegasus. Look in the same direction and link those four stars together.

It takes me a while, but I do so.

– Okay, I see the square.

– Good. Now count how many stars you can see inside it.

Silently I count the stars.

– Fifteen.

– Fifteen is excellent. That means there's very little light pollution here. The sky is very dark. Now look at the chart.

I do so.

– This is Cassiopeia. Can you find it in the sky?

– I think so. It's the only constellation I know well.

Scanning the inexhaustible hierophany that seems to be absorbing me, I find where to look and bring the binoculars to my eyes.

– Yes, I see it.

– You do know it well, Sprague. And how did that come about?

I lay down the binoculars.

– 'His shadow lay over the rocks as he bent, ending. Why not endless till the farthest star? Darkly they are there behind this light, darkness shining in the brightness, delta of Cassiopeia, worlds.'

– James Joyce?

– Yes. That's what kicked my love for the English language into overdrive. That was when I understood that with sound and rhythm, you can create a world. I'd wanted to do it in music, but I knew I didn't have the talent. So I chose the next best thing—words.

You look at me, gravely, your eyes suffused with tenderness.

— Creating a world to redeem my life, that's what I've been trying to do ever since I understood I've never been born into this one.

— And yet you still haven't done it, Sprague.

I gaze into the sky and curse the guardian of fate. Yet my fate is no secret to me. Is that what you are doing, in leaving me? Forcing me to act on what I know?

— And do you know why I haven't done it yet?

— I do. You know I do.

— Tell me.

— Because you've been like a dog chasing its tail, believing you could make happen what never happened, undo what's been done, go back to the womb to be reborn.

Staring into the scintillating dark, I think of Jagrati, I think of 'Night Sky', I think of the invisible orders of being in which I am but a phenomenal accident.

— It's impossible, Sprague. Nothing and no-one can change that. You could have a thousand women but not one of them could give you what the one who should have given you never did. And the sooner you accept that, the sooner you'll be on your way with your work.

Look! A shooting star! No, it's only stars through my tears.

— You've kept your word, Marietta.

You remain silent.

— I have nothing left but my eyes to cry with.

Silently, calm and steady, you hold my gaze.

— But why do you have to banish me? What's my crime?

— None.

— But if you love me—

— Never doubt it! I love you more than ever. Haven't I proven it? Do you want to tattoo your name on my tits?

— No.

— Go ahead!

You reach for a fragment of shell and toss it to me.

— Use that!

You pull up your sweater and expose your breasts.

— Do it!

Your eyes are glistening.

— Come on!

You seize the fragment of shell and sweep it across your hand—

— Marietta!

Bright, an arrow of blood arcs from your index to your wrist.

— It's sharp enough—what are you waiting for?

My heart heaves, I take you hand: skin-deep, no more; mercy. Careful to avoid the cut, with the tip of my tongue I lick up a trickle of blood; feeling a thrilling confusion of feelings, I tap the wound dry with a tissue. Withdrawing your hand, you say:

— It's nothing.

And then you scream:

— Now come on and cut me!

Baring your breasts, you fall back and draw your sweater up over your face. The relief I've been feeling now turns to shame: I have been selfish, I have not tried hard enough to put myself in your place.

— Marietta, I'm sorry. Forgive me.

I say the words with a certain bitterness, which only makes me feel more ashamed.

— Forgive you? Cut me!

Suddenly I see that if I apologize again, you'll begin to hate me.

— Do it!

On each breast the lantern casts a long shadow: Your nipples are erect. Straddling your body, I grab hold of your wrists and pin you to the blanket. My body is ready to do what you want me to do.

— Come on!

You want me to rape you. At last I understand. Letting you feel the heat of my loins, I tighten my grip on your wrists. And then I rise onto my haunches.

— Listen to me, Marietta. You have given me love enough to last a lifetime, more than enough to sustain me for the rest of my days.

I pull down your sweater and gaze into your eyes.

— You are free to go without any guilt.

The amber of your iris glows; love wells up, and overflows...

Never in a million years
Will I forget your resplendence
Forever and a day
I will admire your intransigence

You spring to your feet and take my hand to pull me up: I resist.

— Come Sprague. Let's go back to our bed. I've got another surprise for you!

I pull you back down, down on to me.

— Let's lie here a little longer. There are still so many stars to see. Squeezing you tight, I press your body to mine. They come, your kisses, they come like roses strewn at my feet.

Never in a million years
Will I forget your loving-kindness
Forever and a day
I will draw visions from blindness

On the blanket, under the plaid, we stare into the night sky, your hand in mine reminding me that I'm luckiest man alive. The stars, at once distant and intimate, take me beyond my tiny self: I thank you, stars, for teaching me to reach beyond my self-regard. I love the woman beside me more than my own life, but I have not loved her well enough: Teach me now, in the hours that remain—the hours!—teach me to love her as well as she loves me.

In our walk-in shower we walked in the rain, untamed and innocent; in our big bed we made love for the last time. Marietta, your surprise drew sperm from my spinal marrow, you melted my nerves and illuminated my mind: In your embrace I was one with the divine.

Venus is red in the pale light of dawn
Red is the colour of your hair
Venus heralds rebirth and homecoming
Rebirth is your answer to my prayer

In my mind I see your face
In my heart I hold you
In my soul we are wedded in grace
With my body I enfold you

The Pole Star is the nail of heaven
Nail is your role in my life
The Pole Star is the hole in the sky
Hole is your place as my wife

In my mind I see your face
In my heart I hold you
In my soul we are wedded in grace
With my body I enfold you

Night is potential and indeterminacy

Potential is the being you give me
Night is germination and gestation
Germination is your dream of me

In my mind I see your face
In my heart I hold you
In my soul we are wedded in grace
With my body I enfold you

Sleepy spoons, your back to my chest, we fall asleep in full body contact, two children trying very hard not to think of tomorrow.

Chapter 18

Sunday morning I surface from a dream to find a woman gazing at me: Propped up on her elbow, her hair falling red to one side, she looks at me with tearful eyes. Is she real? Is she a messenger come to tell me there's been some mistake? That I mustn't awake, that sleep is a safer state?

— Good morning, my love.

A tear falls onto my cheek as she bends to kiss me; her skin is soft and warm. I breathe in her scent, I slip back into my dream: In a parking lot in Princeton, a woman puts her hand on my shoulder and presents her cheek to be kissed—one, then the other—while kissing the air beside mine. I reciprocate these curious kisses of seeming intimacy. I dare not yield to my longing for her lips, but I do throw my arms around her and press her body to mine. Face to face, we speak:

— Were you not a redhead, once?

— No, I've always been blonde.

— And your eyes? Have they always been the colour of the morning sun?

— Yes, my eyes have always been amber.

— I once knew a girl. Her eyes were brown and her hair was black. She was killed in a plane crash.

— I once knew...

— What?

— No. Let's go for a walk. Or take a drive. But let's not talk about that.

— I know you, I know your name. It's Marietta.

— Yes. And what's yours?

— I don't have a name. Will you give me one?

— Yes. I'll call you Sprague.

I feel her lips on my lips, I feel her overwhelming tenderness.

— Wake up, sleepyhead! We're going to Llangrannog!

In the Ford Fiesta I followed you in your MX-5; a half-hour drive took us to our destination: A lovely village in a narrow valley, right on Cardigan Bay. We frolicked on the beach as the tide retreated; we clambered up the cliff slopes and scrambled around the rocks. Then, as the breeze picked up, we went to the pub of the Pentre Arms Hotel for our Sunday lunch: braised shin of veal with roast potatoes, carrots and mixed greens; a tart of pear and walnut with brandy custard. Our imminent parting stretched our souls like the wind a sail; on a sea of loving-kindness our words rode the waves. When coffee came you left your seat to come and sit beside me, and as you pressed your body against mine your voice trembled as you said, 'We'll go for a walk, at Penbryn on the coastal path, and then I'll go'. Who first broke into tears? Who first buried their face in the other's hair? Me? No. It must have been you. For I distinctly remember bursting into tears only when I heard you say, 'I love you'.

The sea is a good place to say goodbye. The iodine air is bracing. The sun that gilds the sand and renders lush the greenery is carefree and defiant. Infinitely receding, the blue horizon is an old hand at vanishing, just like the clouds that annihilate themselves in the limitless ether. Look! The watery patterns of the waves testify to constancy in change. And there, halfway to heaven, there where the gulls protect the daylight from the raven's stealth, the cliff-top heights extol elevation. The gorse declares kissing will never be out of season, while the trees speak of birth, death and transfiguration. All in all, the sea is a good place to say goodbye.

Marietta, what is there left to tell? Just this: That in our last hour we walked in silence. That with each step we took your love became more palpable, until I knew that if I hurled myself off the cliff you'd be there to catch me. That with each passing minute my love grew, but your loveliness outgrew it. That a butterfly closing its wings on its colours couldn't match the delicacy with which you closed the book on us. That with each tender kiss, the knitting of our breaths bound our spirits as it could never bind our flesh. That vulnerability took the terror from your beauty and transferred it to your will. And finally, that last night's stars were still in the sky, invisible witnesses to your vow that you would always be my woman.

– Well, this is it. Goodbye Sprague.

We fall into each other's arms. We press our bodies together and hold each other tight. The circling seagulls cry.

– Goodbye Marietta. I love you, and I will always love you.

I watch you walk to your car. It comes, the smile tossed over your shoulder. It tears my heart in two. I know if I approach you now, I'll never let you go. I wave. You wave back. I watch you drive away.

I go down to the beach. I lie face down in the sand. I hear the waves. I hear children at play. Hammering in my breast, my heart beats louder and louder. And then a light from inside me illuminates the darkness. Softly, but distinctly, I hear myself say, 'I'll do it, Marietta. I'll do it for you'. Hammering in my breast, my heart drives me deeper and deeper into myself. The darkness shimmers, then overwhelms the light. Silence.

EPILOGUE

In Paris, in a bistro called Le Muguet, two women sit side by side, facing the Pont Mirabeau. Are they twins? One is drinking Fernet-Branca with Bourbon and Angostura bitters; the other, a Lillet blanc with Cointreau. His back to them, an old man crossing the bridge turns up his collar, blows on his hands and slips them into his pockets. The chill song in his jawbone, the wind that sings in his teeth, invigorates him. Suddenly daylight conspires with electricity to remind him that dream is woven into reality. He feels a sudden desire for music: modal jazz or a violin concerto, an Indian raga or rock 'n roll. Lovers holding hands overtake him; under his breath he utters a blessing. And then it comes, the music, in the depths of his soul it sounds: footfalls in a forest, the silent dark; a pool of water, a clearing.

Free! The music has set him free. Of what? The fear that his dream of redemption is but a miasma of nostalgia for what might have been? That his thirst for love is like the river that runs through Heraclitus' parable? That between himself and his name will always fall the shadow of he who has no name? Again the wind sings in his teeth, again the chill song in his jawbone exhilarates him. His face! It is not the lamplight, it is a light from within, that glow on his skin. He steps up to the railing and leans over: Deep-swirling, the rain-swollen waters of the Seine flow swiftly. Look! Along the river his laughter ripples, from his servitude to his freedom his smile stretches. He hoists himself onto the railing, composes himself and says a prayer: Receive me now, watery womb; silence forever the murmur of my mind. Faeringa! A hand grips his arm, another his shoulder.

— Old man, don't be foolish.

Anger vies with elation, tears of sorrow with tears of joy. The old man shakes off the hands of the man who holds him and continues on his way. Look! Suddenly there's firelight; on the boats below, a blanket of snow. A taste comes to the old man's tongue: fresh-squeezed lemon in iced Magellan gin, grilled-shrimp-and-strawberry salad. The man resolves to throw away his last possessions, keep only his hat, his coat, his boots; he resolves to seek the fire that makes the firelight, the ever-living fire of Heraclitus: That is how he will honour her, she who, in another lifetime, opened his lips and gave him language to speak the loss. Crossing the bridge with a sense of purpose, he picks up his pace. A young man with raven locks approaches from the other side. The old man stops him.

— Got a pen?

— A pen? Yes I do.

He reaches inside his jacket pocket.

— Here you are.

— Some paper?

He takes out his notebook, rips out a page and gives it to the old man.

— Thank you.

The old man goes to the railing and with slow deliberation, traces the seven letters of his name. He gives the pen back.

— Something you don't want to forget?

— You could say that. Something given me, in a room by a river, in another lifetime. Or was it only in a dream?

The young man smiles as he looks into the old man's eyes; a current of tenderness passes between them. The old man continues:

— Her hair was red, I seem to recall. Her eyes were the colour of the morning sun.

The young man takes his notebook and pen back out of his pocket.

— Here. Take this.

— What for?

— To write your story. Memory is the past tense of desire, and that's all you've got left.

— Hold on—she was blonde. Yes, I remember now, her hair was blonde and her skin the colour of milk and honey.

— Write it down, take my notebook and pen.

— Young man, I don't need them. You see, my story's already written.

— It is, is it?

The young man stares into the old man's eyes.

— Indeed, you look like a memory come alive. Now tell me, why did you try to jump? I saw you.

The old man doesn't answer. The young man says:

— As long as I'm alive, I will never let you do that.

He holds out his hand. The old man takes it. Again, a current of tenderness passes between them.

— Fare thee well, old man. Goodbye.

— Goodbye, kind fellow, goodbye.

Each continues on his way, the young man to meet the women at Le Muguet, the old man to warm his bones by the fire under the bridge.

Toronto-London-Paris-Toulouse
2007-2016

maramarietta.com

A website – The World of Mara Marietta – provides a wealth of resources to complement your reading of the novel. You will find, for example, images of paintings, playlists of music, carousels of film stills, as well as essays and translations. The site is regularly enriched.

A 'References and Bibliography' document in pdf can also be found on the World of Mara Marietta.

Oronce Fine, *Mappemonde en forme de cœur,* 1534-36
BnF, Paris

maramarietta.com/mara-marietta-culture-blog/

The Mara Marietta Culture Blog offers a series of reflections on the arts in contemporary culture, with occasional forays into other domains. To seek the calm in the eye of the hurricane, to oppose the silence of music to the whirlwind of noise, that is its aim.

RICHARD JONATHAN

Printed by CreateSpace | Cover design by Jérôme Fabre
Agoralys Creative Studios, Toulouse

A 'References and Bibliography' document in pdf can be found on the World of Mara Marietta.

maramarietta.com

Should you care to make any comments on the book
you are welcome to contact me via the site.

R.J.

maramarietta.com

'Mara Marina, Mara Miranda, reality discloses truth oblique, the eye sees but the real of its belief: Let us continue to interweave our memories, that in the eyes of the other we may discover who we are.'

Richard Jonathan, *Mara, Marietta,* p. 489

Made in the USA
Las Vegas, NV
28 January 2024

85023698R00393